BONE SILENCE

The third book of Revenger

Alastair Reynolds

This one's also for my Mum

This edition first published in Great Britain in 2020 by Gollancz
First published in Great Britain in 2020 by Gollancz
an imprint of The Orion Publishing Group Ltd
Carmelite House, 50 Victoria Embankment
London EC4Y 0DZ

An Hachette UK Company

10 9 8 7 6 5 4 3 2 1

Copyright © Dendrocopos Ltd 2020

A CIP catalogue record for this book is
available from the British Library.

ISBN 978 0 575 09069 9

Typeset by Input Data Services Ltd, Somerset

Printed in Great Britain by Clays Ltd, Elcograf S.p.A.

www.alastairreynolds.com
www.gollancz.co.uk

1

It had begun as a distant glimmering dot; now it was unmistakably a world.

At the front of the rocket launch, from her control position behind the forward windows, Fura Ness tried to fly exactly like any other prospective visitor. Too confident in her approach, and she would draw attention to herself. Too cautious, and she would look as if she had something to hide.

Which – of course – she did.

The sweep was bouncing range-location pings against the outer shell of Mulgracen. A dial showed their closing speed, now down to just six thousand spans per second.

'That will do nicely,' Lagganvor said, as he leant over her shoulder to study the instrument board.

Fura took her time answering. She flipped a switch or two, worked a lever, tapped her nail against a sticky gauge.

'This ain't my first approach, Lag.'

Lagganvor's reflection smiled back from the burnished metal of the console.

'Nor mine.'

Fura applied a little more counterthrust, dropping them to five thousand five hundred spans per second. They were threading through the orbits of other ships gathered around Mulgracen that ranged from little runabouts like their own to fully-rigged sailing vessels, albeit all close-hauled so near to the gravity well of a swallower.

'All this way for a pile of bones,' Prozor said, in a familiar complaining tone.

'Bones we happen to need,' Fura answered.

Prozor rubbed the dent in her head where a metal plate had been put in. '*You* need 'em, girlie. The rest of us is quite satisfied never goin' near those horse-faced horrors.'

'I share your reservations,' Lagganvor said, directing a confiding smile at Prozor. 'But I also appreciate the need for up-to-date intelligence. Without a viable skull, we're operating blind.'

'And this intelligence,' Prozor said. 'It wouldn't have anything to do with gov'm'nt men turnin' over every rock in the Congregation to look for us, would it? Gov'm'nt coves with ships and guns and undercover agents and plenty of intelligence of their own?'

Lagganvor scratched at his chin. 'It might.'

'Then why in all the worlds is we . . . goin' anywhere near a world?'

'We've been over this,' Adrana Ness said, turning to face Prozor from the seat immediately behind her sister's control position. 'It's all very well keeping to the margins, picking off other ships for essential supplies – that's served us well enough since The Miser. But it's not sustainable. We've only adopted piracy as a temporary measure, not a business for life.'

Prozor nodded at the forward windows, where Mulgracen was now large enough for surface details to be visible. 'And offerin' our necks on the choppin' board by voluntarily going to a world – that's meant to be an improvement?'

'It has to be done,' Fura said, sighing hard. 'None of the skulls we've found on other ships were worth a spit by the time we got our hands on them. So we've no choice but to shop. But I ain't taking silly risks. Mulgracen's a long way out and there's no likelihood that anyone will be expecting us. It won't be like Wheel Strizzardy . . .'

'The risk was supposed to be contained there as well,' Prozor said.

'It was,' Fura answered through gritted teeth. 'Just not contained enough.'

*

Mulgracen was a laceworld, orbiting the Old Sun in the Thirty-Fourth Processional. It was neither entirely hollow, like a shellworld, nor entirely solid, like a sphereworld. It was, instead, a sort of sugary confection, made up of many thin and brittle layers, each nested delicately within each other and inter-penetrated by voids, shafts and vaults through which a ship could move nearly as freely as in open space. The outer surface – from which the launch was bouncing its range-finding pulses – was only loosely spherical. There were gaps in it, some of which were whole leagues across. Between these absences were irregular plates of uninterrupted surface, some of them joined by thick necks of connecting material and some by only the narrowest, most perilous-looking of isthmuses. Nowhere was this surface layer more than a tenth of a league thick, and in places it was considerably thinner. Little domed communities, never more than a quarter of a league across, spangled against the firmer-looking bits of surface. Now and then a tiny train moved between them; a luminous worm hurrying through a glassed-over tube.

With their speed reduced to just five hundred spans per second, Fura dropped the launch down through one of the larger gaps. The thickness of the surface plate swept up past them, and then they were into what was technically the interior of Mulgracen. There was little sense of confinement. In many directions it was still possible to see stars, as well as a dozen or so nearer worlds and the purple-ruby glimmer of the greater Congregation. Beneath them, about a league below, was a smaller broken surface, ornamented with domes and the fine, glistening threads of railway lines. There were domes and lines above them as well, for there were communities attached to the underside of the outer shell, as well as to its outer surface. Only

3

the thinnest of connecting structures bridged the two layers, and it seemed quite impossible that these feeble-looking columns and walls could support anything, let alone many square leagues of habitable ground.

But they did, and they had, and they would. Mulgracen was already millions of years old, and it been claimed and lost and re-claimed many times during the long cycles of civilisational collapse and rebirth that made up the recorded history of the Congregation.

Fura dropped their speed further still. Traffic was thick all the way into Mulgracen. Rocket launches were coming and going in all directions, with little regard for any sort of organised flow. Cargo scows and rocket tugs growled by on their slow, ponderous business. For every ship about the size of their own launch, though, there must have been ten or twenty smaller craft that were only used for shuttling within and around the world, and these seemed even more cavalier about navigational etiquette. They were nosey about it, too, swerving close to the launch and only breaking off at the last second. The anti-collision alarm was going off so frequently that in the end Fura cuffed it into silence.

They went down another level. Only now was it getting hard to see any clear part of space, and the communities at these depths had to rely on artificial lights at all times of day. There were more of them, packed more closely together, and in places the towns had merged so thoroughly that they were now merely the districts of city-sized settlements, easily the rival of anything on the Ness sisters' homeworld. The domed-over buildings were huge, multi-storied affairs, and their windows so numerous that they seemed to emanate a soothing golden glow of comfort and prosperity. Carved animals reared up from roof-lines, picked out by spotlights; neon advertisements flickered on the buildings' sides, traffic lights threw red and green hues across pavements and intersections. People were still too small to see except as moving dots – even the trams and buses were like tiny gaming pieces – but it was not hard to imagine being down there, dressed for the season and strolling along lovely marbled boulevards lined with grand shop windows and no shortage of enticing places to dine and dance.

Fura looked at her sister, wondering if Adrana felt any pangs of homesickness at this spectacle of bustling civilisation.

'I'd forgotten—' Adrana began.

'—how pretty things could be,' Fura finished darkly, and her sister met her eyes and gave the merest nod of mutual understanding. 'How nice decent society looks, from the outside. How pleasant and inviting. How ready to accommodate our every wish. How devious and deceitful! It's a trap, sister, and we ain't falling for it.'

'I didn't say I was about to.'

Fura slowed them again. They descended through the gap between two domes, then continued on down through the thickness of another layer, until they emerged beneath its underside. There was one more layer below, totally enveloped in a single glowing mass of buildings. That was the closest settlement to the swallower, which was somewhere deep inside that final sphere. They didn't need to go quite that deep, though, which pleased Fura as it meant a little less expenditure of fuel.

'There,' Lagganvor said, jabbing a finger at the windows. 'The landing wheel.'

Fura had been forewarned about the arrangements, but that did not make her any less apprehensive as she brought them in for the final approach. The landing structure was a very odd sort of amenity. It was like a carnival wheel, jutting down from a slot in the ceiling, so that only the lower two thirds of it was visible, turning sedately. There were platforms on the rim of this wheel, each large enough to hold a ship, and some cogs or counterweights kept them level even as the wheel rotated, lifting the ships up into the slot and the hidden part of their rotational cycle.

A third of the platforms were empty. Fura selected one and brought them in belly-first, toggling down the launch's undercarriage and cutting the jets at the last moment. She'd chosen the rising part of the wheel, and it did not take long for its rotation to take them into the slot and up to the apex, where ships moved through an enclosed reception area on their smoothly rising and descending platforms. Fura and her crew were not yet ready to leave the ship, and they were already descending by the time they had completed their suit preparations and gathered in the main lock.

'Names and back-stories?' Fura asked.

'Drilled into us so hard I might be in danger of forgettin' my actual name,' Prozor answered. 'Come to mention it . . . what is my actual name?'

'Doesn't matter, so long as you don't slip up,' Fura said.

Prozor knelt to squeeze some oil into a knee-joint.

'Anyone would think you wasn't overly sympathetic, girlie.'

'I'm not.' Fura knuckled the chin-piece of her brass-coloured helmet. 'I'm sympathetic to my neck, and to keeping it attached to something. And that means sticking to our roles.'

'I think we are tolerably prepared,' Lagganvor said. 'Now, may we discuss the division of chores? I think I would be most effective, and speedy, if I were permitted to operate independently. Obviously I can't help with the procurement of a new set of bones, but the other items on our shopping list . . .'

'The sisters can take care of the shivery stuff,' Prozor said. 'You can stick tight by me, Lag, seeing as you know the terrain.'

'I have been here once, dear Proz; that hardly makes me qualified to write a tourist brochure.'

They made a last-minute inspection of each other's suits. By then the platform was just coming back round to the apex. Fura opened the lock and they tramped down the access ramp with their luggage, onto the platform's gridded metal surface. At the edge they waited for the platform to come into line with the fixed surface of the reception chamber, and then stepped briskly from one to the other. It was a nimble operation, but no crew who had just come in from a string of bauble expeditions would be fazed by such a test. From there it was a short walk into a reception lock, after which it was possible to remove their helmets.

They found themselves at the back of a shuffling line of crews being questioned by immigration clerks and revenue men. The room was full of low murmuring, bored questioning, the occasional stamp of a document. Once or twice a clerk stuffed some papers into a pneumatic tube that took them further up the administrative hierarchy.

The line moved sluggishly. Fura and the others put down their luggage and nudged it along with their boots as another crew joined the line behind them, and then another.

It was brazen, just being here. They had avoided any contact with civilisation for months. Nor was Mulgracen some outlaw world, where a blind eye might be turned. It was prosperous, long-established, well-connected: unusually so, given its orbit within the Frost Margins. It did a lot of trade, and that was the crux of Fura's gamble: she had been relieved, not disheartened, when she saw how many other ships were coming and going, and it pleased her now to be at the back of a grumbling, slow-moving queue.

From behind them a gruff voice raised a complaint as one of the clerks abandoned their desk and left a 'closed' sign, forcing two lines to converge into one.

'You did well,' Fura whispered to Adrana.

Adrana dipped her nose, looking at Fura over the bridge of her spectacles. 'High praise.'

'For once I wasn't the one making the choices. It's good for you to show a little . . . initiative . . . now and then.'

'Don't think too highly of me. All I did was pick a world we could reach that wasn't too far in and had a halfway decent selection of bone shops.' She glanced back at the crew behind them, who were grumbling about the closed desk. 'Any other benefits are . . . incidental.'

'Incidental or otherwise, they'll serve us nicely.' Fura dropped her voice. 'I'd say "well done, sister", but perhaps it's about time we slipped into character.'

'Whatever you say, Captain.'

The line moved in fits and starts, and after about thirty

minutes it was their turn to be questioned. Fura put their papers onto the table and stood with a hand on her hip, affecting a look of mild but compliant impatience. She was still wearing her vacuum suit, and for once she had a full sleeve and glove over her artificial hand, instead of the pressure-tight cuff she normally wore.

'Captain . . . Tessily . . . Marance,' said the clerk, a heavy-jowled man with a persistent low cough. 'Captain Tessily Marance. Tessily Marance.'

'Don't wear it out,' Fura said.

He held one of her papers, squinting as he compared the photograph with her face.

'In from the Empty, are you?'

'No law against it.'

He licked his fingertips, turning pages quickly.

'Where was your ship registered?'

'Indragol.'

'Describe it.'

'It's about four hundred spans long, with rooms inside and lots of sails and rigging.'

He looked at her with a stone-faced absence of humour.

'The world, not the ship.'

'Why, are you planning a holiday? All right, Indragol. It's a cesspit down in the Twenty-Eighth. Tubeworld. Besides the *Grey Lady*, the only other good thing to come out of it was my father . . .'

'His name?'

'Darjan. Darjan Marance.'

He shifted his gaze onto Adrana. 'Who is she?'

'She can speak for herself,' Fura said.

Adrana looked down her nose at him. 'Tragen Imbery.'

'Occupation?'

'Sympathetic.' Adrana leaned in and added, in a near-whisper: 'That's a Bone Reader, you know.'

He held up a different page. 'Take off your spectacles.'

Adrana complied, staring at him with a fierce, level gaze. He continued holding up the page, frowning slightly, and beckoned one of his colleagues over. The first clerk handed the papers to the second, murmuring something in regard to Adrana. The second clerk sat down and began going through their papers with a heightened attentiveness, taking out a pocket magnifier and consulting a reference document, presumably looking for tiny flaws in their forged credentials. Meanwhile, the first clerk began asking Prozor and Lagganvor questions.

Off to one side of the desk, a small flickerbox was showing successive grainy images of the faces of various felons and persons of interest.

Fura started to sweat. She had thought that being combative and surly might help her case, because it was the last thing anyone would expect if the actual Ness sisters were trying to sneak their way through immigration. Now she was starting to wonder if she had taken the wrong tack.

The second clerk leaned into the first and cupped a hand to his mouth. The first clerk scratched at a roll of jowl and reached for an empty pneumatic tube canister. He was beginning to curl some of Fura's papers up, preparing to stuff them into the tube.

'Did you say Darjan Marance?' asked the gruff voice from behind them.

Fura turned around with an imperious lack of haste. 'What if I did, cove?'

'Darjan Marance took two hundred leagues of triple-filament yardage from us, down in Graubund. An' he never came back with payment.' The speaker – a tall, scar-cheeked, rough-voiced woman with a stiff brush of green hair – shook her head in mocking disbelief. 'I never believed this day would come. Been keeping eyes and ears out for Marance's crew these last ten years in case we crossed paths, but I never thought you'd be so stupid as to use your own name, right in front of me.' She pushed forward, interposing herself between Prozor and Lagganvor, and pointed at the clerks. 'She's a thief. I don't care if it was her father stole that yardage, she inherits the crime – she and her whole scummy crew.' She waggled her finger. 'You don't go letting 'em into Mulgracen. They'll be out and away before I see them again. You get 'em locked up *now*, and I'll fill out any papers you need me to, laying out what she owes us.'

Lagganvor raised his hands, smiling hard. 'My dear . . . Captain? Perhaps we might come to an . . . amicable settlement? If there has been some . . . entirely innocent confusion? I'm not reliably acquainted with the current rate for triple-filament yardage, but I should think six hundred bars might be not unfair recompense, for any grievous . . . misunderstanding?'

The green-haired woman gave a derisive snort. 'Six hundred bars, cove? Is that some sort of joke? Have you any idea what six hundred bars'll get you, nowadays?'

Lagganvor grinned desperately. 'Presumably . . . not *quite* enough to settle this matter?'

'Arrest them, all of them,' the green-haired captain said. 'I'll do whatever it takes. It's not about the money, it's the principle. I don't mind if I have to take two hours or six setting down our side of the story . . .'

Behind her, her crew began to groan. Clearly they had other plans for the day.

The first clerk looked from the green-haired captain to Adrana, then back to Fura. He leaned over and confided something to his colleague. The second clerk shook his head ruefully, pinched at the corners of his eyes, then pushed himself up from the desk. The jowly clerk still had the semi-bundled papers, nearly ready to go into the canister. He hesitated for a second, then flattened them out again, before reaching for his stamping tool and punching his way through each of their sets of personal documents. 'You're lucky, Captain Marance,' he said, eyeing Fura. 'Normally we take a very dim view of such allegations.'

Fura looked at the clock above the clerk's position. It was only twenty minutes off noon, and more than likely that was the end of the clerk's shift. Perhaps his colleague's, as well. The last thing either of them wanted was to activate a process that involved additional checks, more paperwork, superiors, interview rooms and so on, all on the doubtful say-so of a crew whose past might be equally blemished.

'She's got the wrong Marance,' Fura said, but with a touch more politeness than before. 'I'm . . . grateful not to be delayed, all the same.'

'Spend your quoins while you can,' the clerk said, handing back their papers.

*

'That was a good try, earlier on,' Adrana said to Lagganvor, as they ascended to street level. They were alone in a cramped elevator car, squeezed in with their luggage around their legs, while Fura and Prozor took the next car along.

'A good try?'

'About it making sense to go off on your own.'

Lagganvor's living eye gleamed with vain amusement. The other – the duller, glassier eye – stared through her with a supercilious indifference.

'I was only thinking of making the best use of our time.'

She placed a hand on his shoulder, almost affectionately, and allowed her fingers to wander to his collar. They were not wearing vacuum suits now. They had taken them off, leaving them at an office on the same level as the immigration department, and changed into the ordinary clothes they had brought for their time in Mulgracen. Adrana's knuckles brushed against the stubbled side of his cheek and Lagganvor smiled, but not without a certain wariness. Then she pushed her hand behind his neck, seized a thick clump of his shoulder-length hair, and twisted it hard.

'Bringing you here was a risk,' she said, as Lagganvor squirmed and grimaced. 'But less of a risk than leaving you on the ship, where you could easily signal your masters.'

'Signalling my masters,' he said through gritted teeth, 'is a thing I do for your benefit, not my own. While they know I am alive and monitoring you, they are content and not attempting a long-range kill.'

'That logic works while we're out in space,' Adrana said, still clutching his hair, and still twisting it. 'But now we're on a world, I thought you might start having other ideas. Like calling in the reinforcements to take us alive, while we're preoccupied with shopping.'

'I wouldn't dream of it.'

'Be sure you don't. We'll be sticking together like glue, Lag. Just you and me. And if you so much as raise an eyebrow in the wrong direction, never mind anything to do with that eye of yours, I'll tell Fura exactly what you are.'

'That . . . might not go down very well for either of us.'

'She'll understand why I had to shelter you.'

'I'm glad you have such faith in your sister's continued capacity for reasonableness,' Lagganvor said, reaching up to dislodge her hand. 'Me, I might need a little more persuading.' He sighed and looked her hard in the eyes. 'You can trust me not to go against my word. I signalled them twenty days ago, feeding them an erroneous position and heading; they won't be expecting another update until we're long clear of Mulgracen. They have no knowledge of your whereabouts here, nor your plans beyond it.' He caught his reflection in the elevator's side and began to fuss with his fringe. 'Incidentally . . . what *are* those plans?'

'I think it would be for the best,' Adrana said, 'if those plans stayed between Fura and I. Just for now. Oh, and *Brysca*?'

He blinked, discomfited by the use of his real name.

'Yes?'

'You're quite right; I wouldn't take a chance with Fura. It'd be far less trouble to kill you myself.'

*

They met at the top of the elevator shafts, at the five-fold intersection of Virmiry Square, which was itself near the centre of Strenzager City, one of the larger conurbations at this level of Mulgracen. Fura craned her neck back, taking her first proper breath since she left *Revenger*. A city's flavours filled her lungs. Brake dust, pavement dirt, animal grease, monkey sweat, hot oil, electric fumes, kitchen smells, sewerage stink, the vinegar-tang of a drunk stumbling out of a nearby bar, the steam of an all-night laundry. It was a sort of poison, taken in extremis, but after months in space breathing nothing that had not been reprocessed through the vegetable membranes of lightvine, nothing that did not taste subtly, pervasively green and slightly stale, it was as fine and thrilling to her senses as a perfumery or chocolatier. She had missed the smell of cities. She had missed the smell of worlds, of life.

She had better not start getting used to it.

'One drink,' she declared, 'then we split up. Adrana and I will cover different bone shops, since it's far too risky to be seen together while being open about our talents. We'll stay in touch by squawk and meet when we've got something to discuss. But I *do* need a drink, and—'

'Something's happening,' Adrana said, nodding beyond the nearby bar.

A group of people were gathering at the corner of one of the intersections where the five main boulevards met Virmiry Square. They were pressing together, almost like a throng of theatre-goers waiting for the doors to open. Above them rose a grand edifice with complicated ornamental stonework and numerous floors. It might have been a huge department store, or perhaps the head offices of an insurance firm. At the back of the gathering a small child was hopping up and down to get a better look at whatever was going on.

Adrana stepped between trams and joined the rear of the gathering, Fura, Lagganvor and Prozor close behind. Adrana was craning to look up at something. There was a slow-rising scream, like some kind of siren starting up.

Fura looked up as well, tipping back the brim of her hat. She could see all the way up past the tops of the buildings, beyond the neon signs and the scissoring search-lights, out through the fine-fretted glass of the pressure dome over this part of the city, up and up through a league of vacuum, criss-crossed by the fast-moving motes of ships, all the way to the next interior layer of Mulgracen, where a pattern of inverted cities – whose buildings hung like pendants – lay strung across that broken surface like an imaginary constellation, made up of smeared and twinkling stars of every hue.

The scream – which was coming from a throat, not a machine – had its origin only twenty or so stories up. There was an open window, a tall sash-window that faced out onto a preposterously narrow balcony, and a tiny pale form was trembling as it gripped the lower pane and stared down to the pavement and the gathering crowd, of which the Ness sisters were now on the periphery, clotting around whatever it was that had last come through that window.

A hand settled on Fura's shoulder. Something cold and sharp touched the skin of her neck.

'One good turn could be said to deserve another. Wouldn't you agree, Captain Marance?'

Fura turned around slowly with the cold point still pressing against her skin.

Adrana, Prozor and Lagganvor were standing back with expressions of abashed helplessness. They had been caught off-guard. Lagganvor was the only one of them who had a weapon, but to reveal it – even without the actual use of violence – would have drawn exactly the sort of attention they were trying to avoid.

'You never knew my father,' Fura said.

The woman – the green-haired captain – gave a half laugh. 'I'm not sure you did, either.' She was out of her suit now, her hands ungloved. She scraped a black nail down one of her own scarred cheeks, leathery and wrinkled as an old book's spine, cocking her head thoughtfully, but with some small amusement at Fura's expense. 'Was any part of that true?'

Fura thought for a second. 'In fairness, Indragol is a cess-pit.'

'On that, at least, we can agree.'

Fura nodded back to the crowd, which had swollen by a third

since their arrival. The people were so engrossed that a tense stand-off between two newly-arrived crews went totally unnoticed. Up above, the screaming person was still screaming. It seemed quite impossible that a single pair of lungs could produce such a continuous, harrowing exclamation.

'Do you know what that's all about?'

'A squelcher,' the green-haired captain said. 'It's the new thing – an employment initiative. All the rage across the Congregation. Or have you not been paying attention to the news?'

'As I said, in from the Emptyside.'

The point moved away a little. 'Then I'll bring you up to date, a little. About six months ago, every quoin, everywhere in the Congregation – in every pocket, every purse, every safe and vault, every bank, every investment house, every chamber of commerce – *every single quoin* underwent a randomised re-setting of its intrinsic value.'

'I heard something along those lines.'

'Would've been hard not to. It's the single biggest financial upset to hit the Congregation since the start of the present Occupation. Makes every other slump or crash seem like a pleasant dream. The banks are calling it the Readjustment. Makes it seem distant, abstract – not something that affects real people, real lives.' The woman's tone became wistful. 'But then, I suppose they had to call it *something*.'

'I suppose they did.'

'The thing is – the curious thing . . .' The woman shook her head. 'Well, it's silly. But there's a rumour doing the rounds that two sisters had something to do with it.'

'Two sisters?'

'Two prim-and-proper little madams from Mazarile who ran away, got a ship – a very fast, dark ship – and poked their noses into something they oughtn't have. Something that made *this* happen.'

'I wouldn't know about that,' Fura said.

'No,' the woman said, appraising her. 'I don't suppose you would.'

There was a silence. Fura reached up and very gently deflected the tip of the blade.

'If you knew about these sisters, would you turn 'em in?'

'That'd depend. There's many that would. That Readjustment has hit people hard, and not just those who could stand to lose a little money. It might be months since it happened, but the banks are still going through their accounts, telling their clients what they now have in their savings. It'd be bad enough if it was just a case of the quoins changing value; then it would just be a simple accounting exercise. But the truth is, no one's sure what a single bar means now. Is a ten-bar quoin worth more now than a ten-bar quoin six months ago? Or less?' She nodded out over the heads of the gathering. 'You can be sure *that* fellow got some unwanted news.'

'People lose fortunes all the time,' Fura said.

'Well, that's true. Harsh, but undeniably true. And the fact is – even though the banks have put up a small fortune for the Ness sisters – not everyone thinks too fondly of those institutions to begin with. You know how it is when you desperately need a loan to keep your ship operating, and the institutions don't oblige.'

Fura nodded tentatively. 'I can't say my family was treated too well by 'em.'

'May I . . . intercede?' Lagganvor asked gently. Very slowly he opened his coat, and with equal caution he dipped into an inner pocket and drew out a plump purse, jangling with quoins.

'What're you proposing, cove?'

'A gesture for your kindness in digging us out of that hole at the immigration desk.'

'Someone had to. Your captain's mouth certainly wasn't doing you any favours.'

Lagganvor bounced the purse on his palm, then offered it to the other captain. 'That figure I mentioned earlier, relating to the non-payment of the yardage? There's about the same in here, maybe a little more. Does that suffice, as a token of our gratitude?'

She snatched the purse from him, stuffing it into a pocket of her own without once glancing at the contents.

'Let's say it does.'

'Then we're square,' Fura said, dry-mouthed.

The woman's blade retracted with a snap. It had vanished back into a tiny bird-like brooch, far smaller than the blade it contained, which she pinned back onto her collar.

'We're square. But two things before we part. The first is that not every crew feels as ambivalent about that reward as we do, so the Ness sisters would do well to watch their backs. The second thing . . . there's a message you might pass on to them, if your paths ever cross.'

Fura nodded earnestly. 'And . . . what would that message be?'

'Tell them they'd better be damn sure they know what they're doing.'

*

The white-whiskered man in the bone shop looked up from his bench, peering at Adrana over a pair of complicated spectacles set with many interchangeable lenses. She was taking her time, moving around his shelves, picking up and examining his wares. It was tourist tat for the most part: nothing that was of any practical use to a genuine Bone Reader. There were fist-sized skulls made out of bits of old rat, cat and dog, sutured together until they looked passably alien, and then stuffed with a few glinting threads of something that might, in a cooperative light, just about fool someone into thinking it was active twinkly. There were fragments of larger skulls that had, possibly, been alien at some point, but were now useless except as ballast.

'I see you have an eye for the good pieces, my dear,' the man said, as Adrana examined one of the larger faked-up skulls.

'I have an eye for a con,' Adrana answered levelly, before placing the skull back on its shelf. 'To your credit, Mr . . .' She picked up one of the neat little tags attached to one of the skulls, moving her lips as she read it: *Darkly's Bone Emporium, 62 Boskle Lane,*

Virmiry West, Strenzager City, Pellis Level, Mulgracen. 'Mr Darkly . . . that *is* you, Mr Darkly? To your credit – your very minor credit – there's nothing here's actually labelled as being authentic; you are merely content to let the unwary make the assumption for themselves. Do you get many takers?'

Mr Darkly set down his tools. There was a skull on the bench before him, positioned on a padded cradle, and it was three times as large as any of the counterfeit pieces. If it was fake, it could only have come from a camel or a carthorse. If it was real – real and alien and ancient – then it was at the smaller end of the typical range of specimens. But she had seen smaller, in other emporia.

'There's no harm in servicing a demand for souvenirs. If tourists want a little skull to take back Sunwards with them, something to put over a fireplace and remind them of a nice holiday in Mulgracen, why should I deny them that harmless little pleasure?'

'It's tricked-up junk,' Adrana said, studying him through her own glasses. 'Worthless scraps. I wonder where you get the bones from. Do you have a little deal going with the local veterinarian? Do you set traps in the back alleys, then boil the animals down?'

Darkly pulled his complicated spectacles off his large, red-veined nose and set them down on a half-folded newspaper next to the skull. He brushed crumbs from his bib. 'Ask yourself a different question: the tourists will have their souvenirs, and they'll pay for them. Deep pockets, even now – anyone who can *afford* to get here isn't down to their last quoin. Would you rather they were sold a harmless replica, a perfectly nice and harmless trinket, or that a real, functioning skull went out of circulation, ending up locked away where no crew could ever benefit from it?'

Adrana sniffed, disliking his logic even as she was persuaded by it.

'I suppose that would depend on whether you actually have any real skulls to offer me.'

'I might,' Darkly said, with a faintly salacious half-smile. He was a scrawny, liver-spotted man of advanced age, with two eruptions of white hair either side of a perfectly bald pate, the two flanking tufts lovingly combed into up-sweeping swan's wings, their effect carefully augmented by nimbus-like growths of hair sprouting from his ears. 'The question is, my dear, would you recognise them if I did? You don't have the look of a sympathetic—'

'There's a look to us?' Adrana asked with sharp surprise.

'I would've said you're past the age . . . or near the limit.' He stopped himself, shaking his head once. 'But you know your bones, it seems. There are . . . other wares in the back room. Some that I think may be a bit more attractive to you.'

'Excellent, Mr Darkly. I should like to test one or two samples.'

A tram rumbled past the shop, and the smaller bones rattled on their glass shelves.

'You are welcome to test any of our wares. I should warn you that we have a swallower near us, as well as all the disturbances of the city, so you mustn't judge the skulls too harshly. They'll all work much more reliably in open space. But . . . I imagine you knew that.'

Adrana reached into her jacket and took out a small pouch. 'I brought my own neural crown. I trust that won't be a problem? It eliminates a number of variables.'

'You do what you must, my dear.'

Darkly was moving to the door to flip the 'open' sign while he was engaged with Adrana in the back room when another customer came in, the bell over the door tinkling. It was a black-haired man, tall, broad-shouldered, and dressed very finely. He looked around the shelves and cabinets, hands in his pockets, swivelling on his heels, grinning like a boy who had found the secret door to a sweet shop.

'Are these all real?'

Darkly nodded gravely. 'They are indeed real bones, sir.'

The man flicked back his dark fringe. He had slightly mis-matched eyes: one livelier and gleaming more than the other. 'And these skulls . . . they're old?'

'The atoms in them, sir, are as old as the stars.'

'And . . . aliens used these?'

'These bones have seen a great deal of employment, sir.' Darkly turned the sign around and shut the door from inside, leaving the key in the lock. 'May I . . . direct your attention to that shelf to your left? The topmost selection? Some of our finer wares. They are not for everyone, but I see you are a man of taste and discernment . . . please, take your time, while I attend to another customer. We shan't be too long.'

Adrana left Lagganvor front of shop while she went through a beaded curtain, along an unpromising corridor and into the rear of the premises. Although she kept her wits about her there was nothing too sinister about this arrangement. Most bone shops did their business in squalid, windowless back rooms, with customers who rightly disdained the trinkets in the window display. This was where the serious, profitable stuff was kept, and if her manner had been a little brusque, it had earned her the right to be treated with respect.

'This way, please,' Darkly said, opening a heavy metal door that led into a low-ceilinged room with many dusty cabinets, teetering piles of cardboard boxes and great wads of packing paper on the floor. He closed the door behind her, and all remaining sounds of the city were abruptly silenced. The room was acoustically sealed, and probably electrically isolated as well: not up to the level of insulation around a ship's bone room, but as good as one could reasonably hope for on a world.

It was half testing chamber, half storeroom. A partly finished meal sat mouldering on a tray. A bucket of something unspeakable stood in one corner. In the middle of the space was an inclined chair with a padded head support, and next to it was a trolley stacked high with metal boxes. The boxes were electrical devices, connected together by cables and with glowing dials and screens on them. The ensemble gave off a faint, anticipatory hum. Somewhere else in the room some old plumbing gurgled to itself.

'We don't need to run an aptitude test on you, do we?'

'You can if you wish,' Adrana said, settling herself into the chair. 'Or we could get on and test some bones.' She took her neural crown out of its pouch and began to unfold the delicate, skeletal device.

Darkly slurped down whatever was left in a mug, then wheeled over another trolley. Instead of metal boxes, this one had a flat platform on top. He took down one of the larger cardboard boxes, only just managing it on his own, and set it on the trolley. He folded back the box's flaps, partially exposing a medium-sized skull with a very strong mottled brown colouration. It had been extensively repaired, with zip-like suture marks and many metal staples driven into the weaker parts. One eye-socket was intact, the other partially collapsed, and the front part of the upper mandible was missing completely. Input sockets in various stages of corrosion knobbed the skull like metal warts. A damp, soil-like odour drifted out of the box. It was an ugly specimen, to be sure: not the sort of thing to tempt a magpie-eyed tourist into opening their purse. But almost certainly *real*, Adrana thought, unless she had greatly underestimated her own gullibility. Whether it would oblige, whether it would mesh with her talent, was a different question.

'Would you suggest an input point?' she asked, drawing out the contact line from her neural crown, now settled down over her freshly-trimmed hair.

'Try that one there, on the cranial mid-line. I'll dim the room and . . . give you some privacy. Try a few inputs. You'll know before long if there's anything to be had. Are you quite comfortable?'

Adrana wriggled in the chair. 'Well enough.'

'Good. I shan't rush you – that other customer may have need of my attention – but there are two or three more I think you might try, if you don't take to the first.'

'I'll try as many as I'm able before making a decision,' Adrana said, not adding that any really promising skulls would need to be tested by Fura as well, before any money changed hands:

there was no point acquiring a skull that only suited one of them. She watched as Darkly turned off the main lights, leaving only dim red secondary illumination as he shut her into the testing room. She did not hear a lock being turned, but the heavy metal door was the only way in or out, so there was no chance of her stealing a skull, nor of making her escape if she damaged the wares. She had no intention of doing either thing: her identity might be subject to concealment, but she was here on honest business, and she believed she could afford any skull on sale.

This one was viable, at least. The twinkly glimmered out of its sockets, like a play of faint, reflected carnival lights. That *might* be faked, but these emporia tended to draw a sharp line between the dubious goods front of house, and the real items in the back. Fleecing a few tourists was all right, but making enemies of crews was very bad for the long-term viability of a business.

She collected herself, took a few deep breaths, decided that her mind was as clear as it was going to get, and plugged in on the mid-line socket.

There was nothing.

It was as comprehensively, resoundingly dead as an un-plugged telephone. She tried the next socket along and there was something, just possibly, at the absolute limit of her de-tection faculty. Though it might have been a carrier signal, or some stray noise coming through the circuits. She unplugged and tried again, in a site bored into the thin bone behind the damaged eyehole. There it was, a shade stronger than before. A faint, faint hint of a conversation going on, some interchange between two distant ships, somewhere out in the vast spaces of the Congregation and the Empty that surrounded it, but it was as if she had her ear pressed to a thick dividing wall between two houses, able to sense the presence of dialogue without once detecting a coherent word or phrase. It could have been in any language around the Old Sun. It might, ultimately, have been all in her imagination. But she was not too discouraged: if a skull worked at all this close to a swallower, it stood a good chance of working much better in the bone room of a ship. Adrana unplugged. There were still plenty of sockets she had yet to try, but she had an intuition about these things and felt it was worth testing a couple more skulls before she spent too much time on one candidate. She began to leave the chair; she could open a few boxes herself until the proprietor returned. He had not exactly forbidden it.

Darkly returned. Lagganvor was with him.

'Turn on the lights,' Lagganvor said.

Darkly did as he was instructed. He had little choice in that particular matter: Lagganvor was pinning his arm back firmly, while using his other hand to hold a small, sharp tool against the man's neck.

'Oh, must we,' Adrana said, sighing as she took off the neural crown. It had been a calculation, having Lagganvor remain front of shop while she went back, but on this evidence she had been right to chance it. 'He seemed almost helpful.'

'I'm sure he was,' Lagganvor said, grunting as he restrained the man. 'So helpful that as soon as he was front of shop he was onto his telephone. There was a newspaper on his bench, next to that skull he was digging into. Turned to a snappy if sensationalist little column-filler about the on-going search for the Ness sisters, and with two admittedly not very clear images of said sisters.'

Adrana extricated herself from the chair and dipped her neural crown back into its padded pouch. 'Did he make his telephone call, Lag?'

'Mercifully not.'

'That's lucky for us. I should have cut straight to the chase, I suppose, but it seemed rude not to show a little interest in his wares.'

'Very rude,' Lagganvor agreed. 'Would you like to squawk our friends?'

'Not just yet: I think we've got the matter agreeably in hand, for now. Put Mr Darkly in the chair, if you wouldn't mind. There must be some string or rope in here somewhere.'

'String will suffice,' Lagganvor said, shoving Darkly into the chair she had just vacated.

'Don't hurt me,' the whiskered man pleaded.

'I'm not going to,' Adrana said. 'At least, not while you cooperate, which you can start doing right away.'

'Take a skull. Take any skull. Take *two* skulls.'

'I'll be honest, Mr Darkly: this was never really about the bones. My sister's out shopping, and she can take care of that bit of procurement well enough on her own.'

His jaw wobbled. 'I was hoping . . . I was hoping you'd deny it. I only thought you *might* be one of the sisters.'

'And now that I've admitted it, now you've seen my face . . . you know there's no hope for you?' She shook her head at him, pityingly. 'I don't know what they printed about us in that rag, but I doubt even a tenth of it's true. You help me, and no harm'll come to you.'

'She means it,' Lagganvor added, rummaging through boxes while Darkly stayed in the chair.

Adrana took off her glasses, polishing them against her sleeve. 'I have a minor confession . . . I didn't just stumble into *Darkly's Bone Emporium, 62 Boskle Lane*. I was after a well-connected man that might have useful connections, and my . . . information . . . suggested you were a very, very promising candidate. About three years ago – closer to four now, I suppose – Bosa Sennen sent a man to speak to you.'

Darkly swallowed hard.

'Did she?'

'Oh, don't pretend you've forgotten. His name was . . . well, it's complicated and confusing enough for me, so I won't trouble you with that. But you'd remember him well enough. A very persuasive fellow, and if you saw him next to my companion here, in a dark alley, you might mistake one for the other.'

Darkly looked stricken and perplexed.

'The point,' Adrana continued cheerfully, 'is that this man was sent to ask you about another individual, a gentleman called the Clacker. Now it seems – and I admit I can't be too sure about this – but it *seems* Bosa's man never quite got as far as meeting the Clacker; that there was some snag or interruption that prevented him from making the desired rendezvous. And what I'd like from you – no, strike that – what I'm going to *get* from you, is an introduction to this gentleman.'

'I've never met the Clacker.'

Lagganvor was busy securing Darkly to the chair with some string he'd found. He glanced up from his work. 'But you know of him?'

'No . . . not until she mentioned the name.'

'Mm.' Lagganvor made a regretful grimace. 'That's not what our research tells us, Mr Darkly. The Clacker is one of your favoured bone brokers. An intermediary between you and the other aliens . . . a black-market go-between. And you must have his telephone number.'

'You've got the wrong man. I don't know this . . . Clacker. I don't deal with aliens. Clackers, Crawlies . . . they've got their business, I've got mine.'

'It's come to this, hasn't it?' Lagganvor said.

'I fear so,' Adrana said.

Lagganvor popped out his eye and bounced it off his palm in slowly increasing parabolas, smiling like a street huckster until the eye's apex took it level with Darkly's face and it stopped, suspended with an iron stillness. Lagganvor stood back and the eye began to pulse with a soft pink glow. The glow intensified, the pulse quickening, the orb drifting nearer to Darkly, concentrating its cycling light on his own two eyes. Darkly made a small clicking sound in the back of his throat. Lagganvor's eye clearly had some powerful paralysing influence on him: he could not blink, avert his vision, or twist his face away.

The clicking continued and a tremble spread down from his neck, his limbs quivering against their restraints. The chair creaked on its pedestal.

'Enough,' Adrana whispered.

'Oh, just when we were starting to have fun.'

'Enough!'

Lagganvor lifted a finger and the eye backed off, the light dimming very slightly.

'That can get worse, Mr Darkly,' Lagganvor said. 'Very much worse.'

Darkly was drooling. Adrana dabbed it away with the edge of his collar.

'Give us the Clacker's number, or better still his address. Once we've verified that the information's accurate, we'll return to set you free. Better still, persuade him to come here directly. That will end our involvement the soonest.'

'I don't ...' Darkly cleared his throat with a hacking wet cough, and Adrana dabbed at his mouth again. 'I don't need to persuade him to come to me.'

'I think for your sake you do,' Lagganvor said, flicking a curtain of hair down over his enucleated eye-socket.

'You misunderstand me,' Darkly answered. 'There's no need to call or summon the Clacker. He's already here.'

2

A few blocks away, a stop or two down the Green and Purple Peripheral Interurban Lines, yet still within the Virmiry West district of Strenzager City, the younger Ness sister was also doing back-room business.

'I'm startin' to think,' Prozor was saying, as they ascended a flight of stairs, 'that this was never about bones to begin with.'

'It was always about bones,' Fura retorted sternly, glancing back over her shoulder. 'We've need of a skull, and that need ain't evaporated. But I reckon we can depend on Adrana to sort us out a skull that meets our requirements. When she's found one, which won't take her long, I'll examine the relevant item and decided for myself whether it's a suitable purchase. But there ain't any sense in the both of us doing donkey-work. I have . . .'

'Loftier concerns?'

'Not the exact phrase I'd have chosen, but . . . not far off the mark, either.'

At the top of the stairs was a short corridor, floored in red carpet worn through to a beige stripe down the middle. At the end of the corridor was a sturdy wooden door, flanked by a pair of potted plants. Fura pulled her metal fist out of her pocket, raised it in readiness to knock, and then looked into Prozor's eyes for some confirmatory sign, some reassurance that she was on safe ground.

'Whatever's behind that door, girlie, it's between you and your conscience. You've been spooked ever since that green-haired captain had your mark, ain't you? Rarely seen you so twitchy. No wonder you couldn't get a peep out of any of those bones, the state you've been in.'

'I don't like being recognised.'

'Nor me. I know you were applyin' some reverse psychology at that immigration desk, playin' difficult, 'cause that's exactly how Fura Ness wouldn't behave, if she was tryin' to sneak her way into a world . . . but next time, if there is a next time, maybe try a bit of forward psychology as well. Never know, girlie – it might help.' Prozor pushed her sharp features into half a smile. 'I wouldn't worry about that captain – I think she meant what she said: that there's some against us and some for us, and she wanted to let the Ness sisters know that they can count on some support . . . unless you really make a mess of things.'

'That's meant to help?'

'All I've got, girlie.'

Fura rapped on the door, her gloved hand sounding like a series of hammer blows. She dipped her fist back into her pocket and stood back. There was nothing to be gained in knocking again; their arrival could not fail to have been noticed.

'It wasn't just the captain,' she said quietly.

'The thought of that cove, splattered all over the pavement?'

'You could put it a *touch* more delicately.'

Prozor touched the dent in her head where the metal plate had been put in. 'They knocked the delicacy out of me when they screwed this into my noggin. Not that there was much to be knocked out even then.'

'You astonish me.'

'I know you're thinkin' what happened to that cove had somethin' to do with what you did to all those quoins . . .'

Fura touched a finger to her lip. 'Proz . . .'

'It ain't a secret between us, girlie, and if anyone's thinkin' of listenin' in, it's 'cause they already know who and what you is, and most of what you done. You shouldn't dwell on that cove, though. I ain't here to be your conscience, or your voice of reason, but I am here to let you know that not everythin' that happens – or will happen – has to be your fault.'

'They must've lost something in the crash, Readjustment, whatever they want to call it.'

'And maybe their troubles were brewin' long before the Ness sisters went off to space. The point is, girlie, you weren't to know what'd happen when you brought those quoins together. True, you might've given it a little more consideration before you started pokin' your nose into somebody else's onions, but it wasn't you made things the way they are. There was somethin' rotten goin' on long before you drew a breath.'

'Just tell me I haven't made it worse,' Fura said.

'Sometimes things have to get worse before they get better. And that ain't always bad.'

A latch sounded and the door opened. A strange, dead-eyed girl stood on the other side, with a continuation of the corridor beyond her. She was nearly as tall as Fura, thin to the point of cadaverousness, with a slumping, lop-sided posture that made it seem as if she were hanging by invisible puppet strings. She had ribbons in her hair and was dressed in the sort of pretty, pink-and-blue striped dress a girl might wear for her tenth birthday party, yet Fura felt certain that she was at least sixteen, and perhaps older still. Her mouth was a toothless slash, smeared around with black lipstick.

'Who?' she asked, in a rasp of a voice.

'Captain Tessily Marance,' Fura said.

'Hirtshal,' Prozor added.

The girl had a notebook. She flipped its pages and dragged a black-nailed finger down a column.

'The Pharmacist will see you.'

They followed her. She had ballet shoes on and moved on tiptoes, hardly in contact with the floor. The carpet in the corridor beyond the door had been replaced more recently and there were photographs and paintings on the wood-panelled walls. At the end was a door constructed mostly of pebbled glass, through which penetrated a trembling green light. The girl opened the door and beckoned them into the room beyond, which was as cool and damp as a crypt.

It was an aquarium, or rather a room filled with many individual aquarium tanks. They covered the walls and quite a lot of the floor. Each tank was lit from within, and each was full of countless luminous fish of many sizes and varieties. They moved in restless shoals, swimming around coral formations and diving in and out of miniature caves and fabulous sunken cities made of jewelled stone.

Fura gawped for a few seconds, half saddened and half delighted. She had forgotten how much she used to enjoy the aquarium house at the Zoological Gardens in Hadramaw. Just being in this room, with its smells and noises – the dampness, the low illumination, the quiet gurgle of pumps – made her think of ice-creams and souvenirs and fine days away from indoor chores.

'Captain Marance and her associate for you,' said the girl.

'Very good, Pasidy – wait a moment, will you? Excuse me, Captain – my little darlings must be attended to.'

The speaker – the Pharmacist – had his back to them. He was propping himself up on a stick while he sprinkled feed into the open top of the one of the central tanks. Behind him was an old-fashioned wheelchair made mostly of wood and wicker. The fish – little blue darts with fiery slashes down their sides – pushed their mouths up to the surface as the Pharmacist shook loose the last few granules from his bag. 'Please come over, Captain Marance – I am very eager to make your acquaintance.'

Fura and Prozor walked up to the man. He settled the lid back on the tank very carefully, then eased back down into the waiting wheelchair. The girl – Pasidy – lingered slump-shouldered and sullen at the door for a few moments, biting at a strand of hair.

'Thank you for agreeing to see me at such short notice,' Fura said.

'I should congratulate you on your industry in finding me as easily as you did. For reasons that I need not dwell on, I maintain a deliberately low profile.' The man flicked a patterned blanket across his knees. He was very nearly as cadaverous as the girl, with stick-thin wrists jutting out of the sleeves of a white surgical smock, buttoned at the sides and over one shoulder. A tide of damp green licked around his rolled-up cuffs where he had immersed them in the water. He had a permanent grin, one that was so fixed that its effect was maniacal rather than reassuring. His eyes were heavy-lidded and copiously bagged, drooping away from either side of a long, steep-sloping nose. His ash-coloured hair was combed sharply from one side of his scalp to the other, forming an asymmetric wave that dipped down over half his face. Fura could not begin to estimate his age: he was either a young man gone to precociously early seed, or a geriatric who had smuggled a few faint traces of youth into advancing years. 'You have the necessary list?'

Fura passed a piece of twice-folded paper to the Pharmacist. He took it in his fingers, pressed it against his nose, smelled it carefully, then opened it out and read down the column of items Eddralder had prepared for her.

'You have a physician in your service, I see. Would it not have been quicker and easier for him to come to me directly?'

'He prefers to stay on the ship. Anyway, he said there wasn't much here that would be difficult to find.'

He ticked his finger down the list, mouthing softly. 'Tranzerome, ten standard measures at the usual dilution. Twenty ampules of Theramol. Six units of oral Axanox . . .' He lifted his eyes to her. 'A dangerous game, bauble-hunting?'

'I never said I was in that line of work.'

'Whatever other work is there, for an honest captain? These are the medical supplies of a crew expecting injury, above and beyond the common ailments of space travel.'

Fura shrugged. 'There are risks.'

'Can you supply the girlie with what she needs, is the question,' Prozor said.

'Yes . . . yes.' He looked at her with a faint flash of irritation. 'For the most part.'

'For the most part?' Fura asked.

'The bulk of this is straightforward enough . . . you'll be paying black market prices, you understand, but I guarantee the product and you won't have the trouble of going through any official channels. For a reasonable surcharge, I'll supply enough export documentation to grease any wheels on your departure.'

'We can pay,' Fura said.

'The only difficulty is . . . your man has requested twenty vials of Mephrozine?'

'If it's on the list then we need it.'

'Mephrozine is *very* difficult to come by. Very difficult, and very expensive. I can't supply twenty vials, not at short notice. Ten is the best I can do, and I guarantee you won't have any more success elsewhere in Mulgracen.'

Prozor jammed her hands on her hips, giving him her best sceptical look. 'Got the market sewn up, have you?'

'Let's just say that the little Mephrozine that circulates through Mulgracen tends to pass through my hands. Might I . . .' He was looking sharply at Fura.

'What?' she asked.

'Mephrozine has several uses . . . but one of the principal ones is to counter the advance of *acute progressive parasitic lightvine syndrome*, or the glowy.' He frowned, studying her with a deeper interest. 'You have it, don't you? The skin patterning may be concealed, to a degree, but less so the presence of it in your eyes, and I see the glints. The spores reach the eyes via the optic nerve; so it is already in your brain, beginning to affect your cognitive processes.'

There was no denying it, so Fura stiffened her jaw and shrugged. 'Do you have the Mephrozine or not?'

'Ten vials.'

'I'll take them all.'

The Pharmacist examined the list again. 'Six thousand bars will cover this. Six-thousand-three-hundred for the goods and the export papers. For that, I'll throw in a box as well – it'll save you stuffing your pockets.'

Fura looked at Prozor, who dug into her coat for the bag of quoins she was carrying. Six-thousand-three-hundred bars was extortionate, but she wanted the medicines now and without too many other questions asked. Prozor sorted through the bag, squinting at the bar patterns on the quoins until she had something close to the desired figure. When she was done, she handed over twelve of the medallion-sized objects.

'We're twenty short, but you ain't going to quibble about that, are you?'

'I don't suppose I am.' The Pharmacist took the quoins and sifted through them with a quick and attentive eye. He held a quoin up to the wavering green light, peering into the inter-locking pattern of bars on its face – criss-crossing threads suspended over an impression of depth much greater than the thickness of the quoin. 'Pasidy – take this list and fill out a trav-elling box. Captain Marance may have all ten of our remaining vials of Mephrozine. Her need is not in doubt.'

The girl took the paper and left through a back door between two rows of tanks. 'She won't be long,' said the Pharmacist. 'Pasidy is *very* efficient, bless her.' He stuffed the quoins into his tunic pocket, wheeled his chair along a pace or two, then pushed himself back up so he could feed the fish in the next tank along. 'These must be trying times for someone in your line of work. The Readjustment has caused all sorts of diffi-culties. When credit can't flow, neither can commerce. Local economies like Mulgracen can just about function, but things are much worse between the worlds. Luxury goods continue to move, but the less glamorous items, where the margins were always . . . *marginal* – things like foodstuffs, medicines, or the chemicals need to make them – they're hardly moving at all.'

'Bad times for honest captains and their crews,' Fura

said. 'Bad for legitimate wholesalers. Not quite so bad for black-marketeers.'

He leaned further over the tank, sprinkling the food. 'One must make hay while the Old Sun shines, Captain. Would you rather I wasn't in business?' He strained, leaning further, and some quoins tipped out of his tunic pocket and into the water.

Fura watched with only faint interest as they submerged, descending edge-down.

'You're careless with your money,' she said.

'No harm shall come to them, and Pasidy can fish them out later. She has the reach for it.'

Fura folded her arms and angled a heel against the floor, willing Pasidy back with the medicines. Idly she watched the quoins sink, descending with their faces pointed back out of the tank's side. The last of them was coming into its final alignment; it ceased its axial rotation as neatly as if it had come into contact with an end-stop. Then it continued descending, until – along with the others – it sank its rim into the silt at the bottom of the tank.

Fura's curiosity prickled like an itch behind her forehead. 'Is there something magnetic in the frame of that tank?'

'Why do you ask?'

'No reason,' she answered, realising that he had seen nothing unusual in the way the quoins descended; nothing in their curious alignment.

The door opened again and the girl entered with a heavy wooden box swinging against her hip. The Pharmacist had settled back in his wheelchair, shaking the last few crumbs of fish food from his fingers. He pointed at Fura, and Pasidy gave her the box, leaning forward at the waist like a crudely-jointed puppet, then jerking back up as the tension was released. Her arms waggled by her side and her head lolled as if her neck was broken.

'You may examine the goods,' the Pharmacist said.

The box was the sort of portable chest that hinged open down the middle, with four layers of separate drawered compartments, each of which was stuffed with drugs. On top was a sheath of plausible-looking paperwork. Fura took out a set of vials, holding them up to the ceiling and squinting at their labels.

'They're either real or they're not,' she said, directing her words at Prozor. 'Either way, only Eddralder's going to be able to tell.'

'Is the Meph in there?'

Fura nodded. She had already identified the black wallet containing the Mephrozine doses. 'It'd better be genuine,' she to the Pharmacist. 'We'll find out if it isn't, and Mulgracen's not exactly off the beaten track. You wouldn't be a hard man to find a second time.'

'Which is why I'd never countenance selling anything I didn't have confidence in. You may depend on the articles. Use them cautiously, of course ... some of them are *very* potent. Especially the Mephrozine.'

Fura returned the items to the chest and latched it closed. 'Pity you couldn't sell me more of it.'

'Hopefully that will tide you over – if you haven't left it *too* late, of course.' His grin unwavering, he regarded her with tissue-thin sympathy. 'I do hope you haven't.'

3

The four of them met again on the tram back to the docking wheel. Lagganvor had called through to Prozor on the portable squawk, saying that he and Adrana were on their way back to the launch, that their shopping had gone well, and that it might not be a terrible idea if Fura and Prozor were to join them. He said no more than that, and kept to their false names, but Fura could not help but pick up on an undercurrent of urgency.

Fura and Prozor came aboard via the rear door. It was a squeeze, standing room only, but they pressed their way through the other passengers until they were within muttering distance of Adrana and Lagganvor. Fura had sworn she would limit contact with her sister while they were in Mulgracen, but they had got on at different stops and would only be sharing the tram for a short distance. In the squeeze of all the other passengers, she thought they would be safe. Everyone was too close to everyone else anyway, and many of the passengers were already arguing or complaining to themselves. Fura had not exactly endeared herself to anyone, coming aboard with the hefty, square-edged medical chest, but she was far from the only passenger with luggage. 'I paid my ticket, cove,' she said in reply to one muttered complaint. 'Ain't no law says I can't bring my belongings with me.'

Adrana was not making herself much more popular. She had

a huge and unfamiliar item of luggage at her feet: a rectangular case with metalled edges. Fura noticed it with a measure of relief, thinking that a container of that size could only be used for one purpose.

Over the hubbub she mouthed: 'I hope it's a good specimen. You must've had a great deal of confidence in it, to buy it without my say-so.'

'I have a great deal of confidence in it,' Adrana replied, while Lagganvor observed their exchange with a look of quiet if strained amusement. 'But it isn't the item you think.' She dipped the direction of her gaze down to the box Fura had brought aboard. 'Yours, on the other hand . . . I presume you had equal confidence in that? It's an odd sort of container; smaller than I was expecting. I do hope you spent wisely.'

'I spent very wisely indeed,' Fura said.

'She ain't got the thing you're thinkin' she has,' Prozor said to Adrana. 'And if I'm not too mistaken, you ain't, either.'

Adrana lowered her nose, looking down at Fura over the tops of her spectacles. There was something scolding and older-sisterly in her expression. 'We had one objective. One reason alone for coming to Mulgracen.'

'We did,' Fura agreed. 'Which I was counting on your fulfilling.'

'And I was counting on you. You are . . . the more adept one.' Adrana winced, as if this one admission had cost her physical pain. 'I thought I could depend on you.'

Fura kept her voice level, but there was an edge to it. 'I thought I could depend on *you.*'

'Voices, down,' Lagganvor said, in a friendly but emphatic tone, smiling doggedly. Their tense exchange had begun to draw glances, with travellers lowering their newspapers or breaking off from their own arguments to watch this far more interesting interaction. 'Might I ask, dear Captain Marance, about the contents of that very handsomely made chest?'

'Medicines.'

Lagganvor turned to Adrana, shrugging good-humouredly. 'You cannot deny that we needed medicine, dear Tragen.

Perhaps not as urgently as we might have needed another item, but it's not a frivolous purchase.'

'And your box?' Fura asked. 'Something nice in that as well? I'll give you this – whatever it is, it looks big and heavy.'

'Pals,' Prozor said, in a sudden and urgent manner.

The tram had stopped and two dark-hooded figures had boarded via the same rear door Fura and Prozor had used. Fura understood why Prozor had clocked them immediately: there was something instantly wrong about these newcomers; something alarming in the casual manner in which they were shouldering their way forward, utterly unconcerned about the other passengers.

'We have to get out,' Adrana said, squeezing her way to the forward part of the tram. The 'stop' light above the front windows was already illuminated, but Adrana rang the bell twice more, yanking her own box along despite the ankles of the increasingly irate passengers who were standing between her and the door.

'Would you like me to stop them?' Lagganvor asked mildly, beginning to lift up his fringe.

'No!' Fura said.

The two figures were halfway down the tram now. They had ash-grey coats on, with oil-cloth extensions over the shoulders and their hoods drooping low so their faces lay mostly in shadow. Fura caught a pale flash of a pocked and stubbled jaw from one; a half-crescent gleam of yellowing teeth from the other. Someone took exception to being barged aside and delivered a swipe with their umbrella. The stubble-jawed one seized the umbrella without glancing aside, then tossed it through the open ventilator above one of the side windows. Another man had his broadsheet raised too highly, and too far into the aisle: the yellow-toothed man ripped a fist through it and tossed it to the floor, grinding it into a greasy mess under his heels. Both men continued their advance, and the tram was carrying on, crossing junctions but showing no signs of approaching its next stop.

Adrana was ahead; Fura and Prozor had now slipped past Lagganvor. He was still regarding the men, holding his ground and fingering the skin around his eye.

'Don't do this, Lag,' Fura said. 'You'll make more trouble than we need.'

'I rather think the trouble has already arrived.'

'Who are they?'

'Men who would rather we didn't leave with Adrana's box.'

'It *was* paid for, wasn't it?'

'Payment,' said Lagganvor, with a faint sidelong smirk, 'is not *entirely* the issue here.'

'What the chaff is in it?'

The tram slowed hard as its brakes went on. Passengers jostled into each other, and for a moment the stubbled man looked on the point of tripping. He reached up to support himself on the back of one of the seats, then used his free hand to dig into his ash-grey coat. Fura had just enough time to glimpse something small and bone-white between his fingers, like a skeleton key or some elaborate toothpick.

The tram had braked at some lights, but it was not a scheduled stop and when Adrana tried to push open the door the driver barked something at her and raised a warning finger from his enclosed control booth. Adrana turned around and pressed her face to the window separating her from the driver, shouting something. Ahead, the lights changed to green, though the driver waited for some pedestrians to clear the crossing in front of the tram before ringing his bell. Prozor squeezed in next to Adrana and started shouting through the glass. Lagganvor pressed himself against the side of the tram and let the stubbled man approach his level.

Fura glanced around and realised that this unwanted attention was nothing to do with their being the Ness sisters, at least not directly. The men had never given her a glance, and if they hadn't recognised her, then their apparent interest in Adrana might be solely connected to the item in her possession.

She breathed in, collected herself.

'Do nothing,' she mouthed to Lagganvor.

The tram started moving again, nosing its way across a busy intersection, and following close behind another tram on the same line. The stubbled man passed Lagganvor, never giving him a second glance. His companion, behind him, mouthed something into a grilled box tucked under his collar.

Fura waited for her moment. The stubbled man was nearly level with her, and the space before her had opened up a bit. Trusting that its contents were snugly secured, she swung the medicine chest as hard and high as her surroundings permitted, and with the entire force of her being.

She caught the stubbled man on the chin and dislodged his hood, which slipped back away from his face to reveal . . .

She would never forget what it revealed.

The man was not a man. The upper two thirds of his face, from the point where his nose might have begun, was a jumble of insect parts stitched together like the pieces of a rag doll. Instead of skin he had plates of glossy integument; instead of a nose he had a proboscis from which projected a cluster of twitching sensory feelers; his eyes were huge and faceted, and there were two mis-matched sets of them, jammed into the jigsaw of his face with no thought for symmetry. His eyes' facets glittered with shades of ultramarine and lapis lazuli.

She saw all this in an instant. She was still following through with the swing of the medicine chest, and it knocked away the man's glove, as well as the white thing he had been holding. His hand was . . . not quite a hand, she saw, but a sort of whiskered pincer.

Lagganvor saw his chance and grabbed for the white thing before it hit the floor. He appraised it for a bare instant, then drove the sharper end of it into the creature's neck. The would-be attacker twitched and slumped as screams and startled cries spread down the length of the tram. Some brave soul flicked down the hood of the other pursuer, and the head that was revealed was no less grotesque than the first.

'Muddleheads,' Lagganvor said with an odd finality, as if that utterance resolved every question she might have had.

Fura gathered her breath. The second one was still advancing. He was put together differently from the first, as if assembled from a different box of scraps, yet with the same disregard for form and harmony.

What were these creatures?

Ahead, Adrana was using her own hefty box as a bludgeon, swinging it repeatedly against the forward doors. The driver was yelling at her, and Prozor was yelling at the driver. They were so engrossed in this exchange that the business with the muddlehead had gone entirely unnoticed. Lagganvor still had the white thing between his fingers, and seemed to be evaluating its usefulness to him, versus the proven efficacy of his eye. The muddlehead on the ground was twitching, and perhaps regaining strength. Fura pressed her boot heel onto the creature's chest, pressing down through the ash-grey coat and whatever layers of clothing were underneath. Something gave way with a sudden soggy collapse, like a piece of rotten floorboard, and a horrible moaning gasp came out of the twitching muddlehead.

The tram stopped with a lurch. The driver's fist came down on a pneumatic control and the front doors wheezed open. Adrana almost fell out, the box tumbling ahead of her. Prozor was next, then Fura, her boot heel nastily sticky under her, and then Lagganvor. Decamping from the tram, he raised a hand to the driver, a sort of apologetic half-wave. A commotion was still going on inside, as the second muddlehead progressed toward the front door. Alarmed passengers were already spilling out at the rear.

Lagganvor helped Adrana regain her footing, then grabbed the larger box. They were in the middle of an intersection. Fura still had the medicine chest, clutched so hard to herself that it hurt her ribs. Prozor pointed away from the tram and the immediate focus of the commotion; Lagganvor nodded and they all moved as one. The streets were still busy and it was surprising how quickly they lost themselves in the anonymity of the crowd. Fura looked back over the heads of street-goers.

She could still see the tram, and it was still stopped, but no one would have given it a second glance now.

Prozor's intuition had taken them down a secondary street: a little less busy than the main thoroughfare that the tram had been on, but not so quiet that four newcomers stood out. It was lined with neon-lit saloons and dining parlours that were a step below from those on the main drag; just a little seedier and more run-down looking. Above the narrow channel formed by the opposed rows of buildings was the fretwork of the dome, and far above that the lights of the next layer. They seemed as distant as the fixed stars, and Fura began to wonder whether she would ever see the space beyond this world.

'They were going to kill us,' she said, realising that she was out of breath. 'Weren't they?'

'Our welfare was certainly not uppermost in what passed for their minds,' Lagganvor said. 'They had one objective, and that was the recovery of the box now in our possession.'

'What . . . in the worlds . . . were they?'

'Muddleheads,' he said. Then, because some clarification was evidently in order: 'Sometimes called motleys. Temporary agents, operating for the benefit of aliens. They knit them together out of body parts – monkey or alien; anything that will do, anything that can be made to shuffle around for a few hours – and give them just enough volition and free-will to accomplish a job. Is that not right, Proz?'

'Heard of 'em, Lag, but never got myself into such deep water that I had to discover they was real.'

'Well, they are real – *very* real. I confess I had some dealings with muddleheads during my time in Wheel Strizzardy. It was never agreeable. I had rather hoped not to run into the likes of them again . . .' Lagganvor tensed and slowed.

'What?' Fura asked.

'That's what,' Prozor said.

Two more muddleheads – for that was surely what they were – had stepped out into the street ahead of them. Like the first two, they were garbed in heavy coats and face-concealing hoods. Fura might have passed a hundred such men in the course of the evening and not given them a second glance, but now she was attuned to their nature and she thought she would recognise a muddlehead anywhere.

There was no traffic coming up and down this secondary street, and as if by decree, all the other pedestrians and by-standers had melted back into shops and shadowed alleys. It was just the four of them, standing in line, facing the two muddleheads. One of the pair was muttering something into his collar, just like the one on the tram.

'Let us by,' Adrana said. 'Let us by, and there'll be no trouble.'

The other muddlehead pushed back his hood a fraction. A wash of yellow neon caught the angle of his jaw, which was too sharp and pale to be anything but raw bone. A buzzing electrical voice came from him, while his mouth stayed completely still.

'Give us the box. We only want the box. Then you may leave.'

Adrana shook her head. 'No. He's mine now.'

Fura looked at her sister. There were many things she would have liked to ask Adrana, starting with the question of who 'he' was, and what 'he' had to do with the box she was carrying.

'He has committed wrong acts,' the buzzing voice said. 'He has betrayed confidences and risked the integrity of respectable institutions. These crimes of his are not your concern. If you shelter him, they become your concern. Then you become our concern.'

'Who?' Fura hissed.

'A Clacker,' Lagganvor said quietly. '*The Clacker*. Apparently.'

'A Clacker?' She gasped out her fury. 'Why in the worlds are we troubling ourselves over a filthy alien? They want him, they can have him.'

'No,' Adrana said. 'He's with us. I gave him our protection.'

'I wasn't consulted.'

Adrana gave a tiny shrug. 'I wasn't consulted about whatever's in that medicine chest. The alien's our responsibility now. He's made enemies of his own kind, and others. Do you know what that makes him to us?'

'A nuisance.'

'No, it makes him useful to us. He knows things. Things that you'd like to know as well. That's why he's running, why they want him dead, and why he's coming back with us. That's why this *isn't* a negotiation.'

'Give us the box,' the muddlehead stated again. 'Then you may leave.'

'How much does the cove know, exactly?' Prozor asked.

'Enough,' Adrana said.

Lagganvor reached up to his eye, making it seem like a thoughtless mannerism, a nervous reaction. 'It's not like we had a chance to become intimately acquainted, Proz. As soon as we met the gentleman, it became imperative to move him. Now we must get him as far and as quickly away from Mulgracen as we may.' With one quick twitch of his fingers he had the eye out, and had tossed it in the direction of the muddleheads. A whip-crack sounded and the entire street flashed pink-white. Fura reeled: half blinded, half deafened. The muddleheads were black paper silhouettes; one stooping, one reaching into the folds of his coat. A pure white beam lanced out, slicing an arc toward them. Lagganvor shouted and Fura started running. His eye flashed again. One of the muddleheads fell into two pieces, littering the road like garbage. The other was still coming after them.

Adrana stumbled her way into a narrow alley between two of the saloons. Lagganvor and Prozor followed her. Fura collected her breath and came up behind them. Adrana propped the box against the side-wall of the alley, while Lagganvor pressed himself against the corner. The alley was dark, and the street they had just escaped was still being lit by the pink-white flashes of his eye and the purer white of the muddlehead's weapon. It was as if they were in the darkened stalls of a theatre, watching some inscrutable performance up on the stage.

It was impossible to tell what was happening.

'They got him,' Adrana said.

Fura looked down. 'What?'

'His box is damaged. They got a shot at him.'

Grey smoke was seeping from a corner of Adrana's box, where it had been caught by the energy beam. From somewhere inside it came ruby sparks and a powerful acrid gas.

'Well, he's useless to us now,' Fura said. 'Whatever we got mixed up in here, it doesn't have to continue.'

'I said the box is damaged, not that he's dead,' Adrana countered. Even in the alley's gloom, her scolding look was obvious. 'He comes with us. He knows about quoins, sister. He knows what we've started and what it means. That's enough for you, isn't it?'

Prozor laid a hand on Fura's shoulder. 'If she's done a deal with him, he has to come with us.'

'We've got papers for the medicines,' Fura said, grinding her teeth. 'How are we supposed to take an alien with us when he's already got half of Mulgracen trying to find him?'

The pink-white flashing was at last abating. Lagganvor stiffened and raised a hand, and the sphere of his eye whisked around the corner and into his palm. He rolled it in his fingers as if it were either very hot or very cold.

'I suggest,' he said, 'that we do not delay our departure. There will be others, I'm sure.'

A muddlehead staggered into view. His gait was lop-sided and foot-dragging. He stepped over the bisected remains of his colleague, one half of which was still twitching, still attempting some parody of animation. Lagganvor stepped back, the eye still in his palm.

'Do something,' Fura said.

He looked back, flashed a guarded smile.

'I have.'

The muddlehead came apart, collapsing like a tower of laundry that had been piled too high. His scissored edges sparkled with pink embers. Lagganvor waited a moment, then walked over to what had been the head and upper torso of the muddlehead.

'You ought to have let us leave,' he said, with a surprising reasonableness as if, despite all that had passed between them, he bore the muddlehead no ill-will. 'Then we wouldn't have had to go through with this.'

'Is it dead?' Fura asked, joining him.

'Deader.'

She inspected the head where the hood had fallen away. It was assembled from a different selection of monkey and alien parts, with the eyes resembling clusters of chimneys rather than faceted orbs. There were grasping, feeler-like things jutting from gaps in the cheekbones, and a glassy, green-filled transparency over what ought to have been the brain-case.

'Would they have killed us, Lag?' she asked.

'Most certainly. Not because they have any interest in our exploits – I do not think they even realised who we are – but because we stood between them and their quarry. They wanted the Clacker very badly.'

Fura went back into the alley, where Adrana had the box horizontally against the ground and its lidded side hinged up. She laughed: a hollow, disappointed laugh.

The box was empty.

'Whatever that trouble was about, sister, someone obviously saw you coming. If there was an alien in the box when you saw it, they must have—'

'He's still here.'

Adrana beckoned her sister closer, indicating she should kneel next to her and extend a hand into the apparent emptiness of the box. Fura did, as much to please her sister as to satisfy any curiosity of her own, and felt a cold tingle slither up her metal fingers.

She withdrew the hand, unsettled, but at a loss to explain the cause of her disquiet.

Lagganvor was standing over her. 'Effector-displacement systems. Either Clacker-indigenous or fifth or sixth Occupation Occultist technology.'

'I don't—' Fura began.

'The alien is still in there,' Adrana said. 'But he's concealed, along with his life-support apparatus. There's a field, to make him invisible, and a device that moves the atoms of your hand somewhere else, temporarily, so that you feel as if you're reaching into an empty space.'

Fura pushed her hand back into the box, detected that cold, then pulled it out, flexing her fingers and warming them in the palm of her other hand. 'It's like Ghostie technology.'

'Perhaps not unrelated,' Lagganvor said.

'Feels just as wrong.'

'But very *right* if it helps us spirit this fellow away, which it will.' The box flickered, and just for an instant there had been *something* in it; a box-within-the-box, a sort of mechanical container with windows, and something pressed into that, something folded and alien and breathing. 'We should not delay,' he added. 'The damage done to the box is affecting the effector-displacement systems. If they fail, there'll be no hiding the fact that there's a Clacker in our luggage.'

Fura rubbed her metal fingers. The cold had bitten them thoroughly. 'What would've happened . . . what would've happened if I'd had my hand in there when it failed?'

'Nothing advisable,' Lagganvor said.

*

Two hours later they were in the launch, slipping free of Mulgracen. To Fura's relief and surprise they had not been detained on their way out: the papers in the medicine chest had satisfied the customs officers, and the curiously empty box in which the alien resided had drawn only a few quizzical looks. No one had even bothered reaching into the seemingly-empty space. The effector-displacement mechanism had kept working precisely as long as was needed, and the Clacker's presence had not been disclosed. They had gone through without a second question, and even their suits had still been where they left them in storage.

'I thought there might be a block on anyone leaving,' Fura said, as Adrana worked the launch's controls and navigated them through the congestion of local traffic, threading between runabouts and taxis out into the clear space where their main ship floated. 'After all that bother we got into . . .'

'Those muddleheads were not acting in any sort of official capacity,' Lagganvor said, absently picking dirt from his finger-nails. 'The forces behind them depend on anonymity for free movement, and they won't get that by blabbing to customs officials and asking for some innocent crew to be detained at their pleasure. There'll be something about a disturbance in the morning papers, but I very much doubt that the customs men had any idea of the trouble that happened tonight. I was entirely confident we'd sail through.'

'So why were you sweating like the rest of us?' Fura asked.

'That, dear Captain, was a necessary part of the act. Any half-way honest crew would be sweating a bit on the way out.' He paused and dug into a pocket of the inner layer of his vacuum suit. 'I smuggled this about my person, just in case we *were* questioned. It always helps if you give them something to find, so they can go home feeling terribly clever.' He took out a small stoppered bottle, unscrewed it, sniffed at the aroma, took a sip, gasped theatrically, then passed it to Prozor. They were under gravity from the thrust of the launch's rocket, so it was entirely possible to sip from a bottle, and she did, generously, before wiping the top with her sleeve and returning it to Lagganvor.

'Very tasty, Lag.'

'You are more than welcome, dear Proz.'

'But you *was* sweatin', all the same.'

Lagganvor put on a pained expression. 'Of course I had *some* concerns for the welfare of our new companion. Especially after the poor fellow was shot. But the damage seems to be confined to the outer box, not his principle hibernation casket.' He patted the sturdy container, which was wedged into the space next to his feet. 'He will be quite safe in here, and he won't eat into our supplies on the ship. The casket supplies all that he needs.'

'I thought you said he'd be useful to us,' Fura said.

Adrana twisted around from the console. 'He will.'

'Not much use if he's dozin'. What if I want to get some answers out of him, like you said?'

'All in good time,' Lagganvor said. He rubbed his hand along the edge of the box. It had metal edges, inlaid with black. 'We communicated with him very briefly – just enough to establish the terms of our cooperation. He needed to get away from Mulgracen, and we had the means. But that casket of his has a fixed minimum sleep interval. Now that he's gone into it at the deepest setting, he won't be roused for at least two or three months, perhaps longer.'

'We'll see,' Fura said.

'He's our guest,' Adrana said. 'Not our prisoner, not our pet, not our plaything to be interrogated.'

'Who is he, anyway?'

'A fugitive, renegade, whistle-blower, whatever you wish to call it. Bosa Sennen was seeking him because of the information he holds, and if he was of interest to her, then I think it safe to say that he is of interest to us.' Adrana's look was pointed. 'Do you disagree, sister?'

'Depends what he knows. Depends what he wants.'

'Passage,' Lagganvor said grandly. 'Free passage to Trevenza Reach, where he has allies. And he has promised us that in delivering him to Trevenza Reach, we will find answers to some of the questions that have troubled us.'

'Some?'

'And perhaps answers to one or two you haven't even thought of.'

Fura moved the fingers of her metal hand. They still carried some memory of the chill she had picked up from the Clacker's box. 'How long ago was this all planned?'

'It wasn't "planned",' Adrana said. 'I had a lead from Bosa's journals, which you could just as easily have found for yourself. I meant to find us a skull – that was always the intention – but I saw no harm in asking about the Clacker while I was about it.'

'We visited a bone merchant called Darkly,' Lagganvor said. 'It seemed likely he'd know of the Clacker's whereabouts, since the Clacker was part of his supply chain. Adrana only wanted to be put in touch. What we didn't realise was that Darkly was already sheltering him. He'd got the Clacker in the same room where he lets his customers test the bones, since the shielding stopped the Clacker's enemies locating him with their trackers.'

'He could've stayed there.'

'No, he could not. The muddleheads were getting nearer, and it was only a matter of time. Darkly woke the Clacker up temporarily and explained the situation. He agreed to throw in his lot with us, accepting a heightened risk of capture if there was a way off Mulgracen.'

'So we've inherited a trackable alien that some other people want dead.' Fura dropped her eyes to the metal-edged box. 'As far as I'm concerned, there's only one question. Front lock, or belly door. Which do you think?'

'We've given our word to look after him,' Prozor said.

'Queer how I don't remember being consulted about that.'

'And I don't remember being consulted about the purchase of those expensive medicines,' Adrana said. 'They had better be worth it.'

'Take it up with Eddralder – he gave me the shopping list.'

'And the rest of it,' Prozor said.

'The rest of what?' Adrana asked.

'You may as well come clean about the special medicines,' Prozor said to Fura. 'Then both of you'll have clear consciences, won't you?'

Fura growled, angry at her friend, and yet angrier still with herself, for she knew that Prozor was right, and she had no moral advantage over her sister. 'I purchased some Mephrozine. Eddralder said it was the only thing that stood a chance of arresting my glowy.'

Adrana nodded slowly. 'How much did you get?'

'About half what I was hoping for. And it's no miracle cure; Eddralder never promised me that. But it's better than nothing, and if it stops it getting as far as it did with Glimmery, or slows it . . .'

'You should have told me,' Adrana said.

'Because you'd have argued me out of it?'

'Because I would have agreed and told you to use every quoin in our possession, if it would make a difference.'

The two sisters were silent for a few moments. Lagganvor offered Prozor another sip from his bottle, the two of them watching with the nervous air of spectators in a bare-knuckle boxing den.

'I s'pose I ought to have told you.'

'And I ought to have mentioned the Clacker. But I didn't want to build up your expectations until I was sure we had him.'

Fura felt some easing within her. There had been differences between them these last few months, and there were days when she was certain Adrana was hiding secrets, uncomfortable secrets, so she much preferred it when they were of one mind, and such times had come to feel finite and precious to her, like the last dwindling days of some long holiday.

'I think we can agree that a skull would still come in handy.'

'No dissent from me. The Revenue ships haven't had any easy time finding us while we could be anywhere in or around the Congregation. But Lag says they're concentrating their efforts within a month or so's sail of Trevenza.'

Fura regarded Lagganvor. 'Had your ear close to the ground, have you?'

'While the opportunity was there. I'm not saying we go back on our word to the Clacker. Quite the contrary: we should deliver him with the utmost urgency. But those ships will be out there, and on high alert for us.'

'We'll dodge 'em,' Fura said. 'Done it before, we can keep doing it. Of course, a skull would still be very nice to have. Very nice indeed.'

'Pity the poor crew you have to steal it from,' Lagganvor said.

4

In the control room of *Revenger*, ninety days out from Mulgra-cen, the only sound was the dependable ticking of an antique stopwatch. Fura had started the timepiece when the first coil-gun went off, and now she was counting the seconds until the sail-shot began to arrive at its target. Based on Paladin's ranging estimates, the relative speeds of the two craft, and the muzzle velocity of the sail-shot, she expected to see impact signs after thirty-two seconds.

'Twenty-five,' Fura said. 'Keep 'em peeled, Lag.'

'Nothing yet,' came Lagganvor's hollow-sounding voice, drift-ing down via speaking-tube. He was inside the sighting room: a pressurised observation bubble pushed out from the hull on a hydraulic ram.

'Thirty,' Fura said.

'Nothing.'

'Thirty-two.'

'Still nothing.'

Fura paused before replying, the stopwatch's ticking filling the room like an amplified heartbeat.

'Verify your aim.'

'Nothing wrong with my aim,' Lagganvor answered. 'Wait a moment. I think I see . . . yes. Sail-flash.' Now his tone shifted from mild affront to one of clinical reportage. 'Multiple speckles, spatial spread, increasing.'

Fura snapped the button on the stopwatch, freezing the ticking and recording the delay between the first salvo and the first instance of sail-flash.

'She's slipped a little further from us,' Adrana said, twisting Fura's stopwatch around to see the face for herself.

'Tryin' to run,' Prozor said, with a no-good-will-come-of-it shake of her head. 'Poor saps. Better off bowin' to the inevitable.'

'They are,' Fura said, with a predatory delight. 'They just don't know it yet.' Then, raising her voice: 'Paladin, recompute and prepare for a second volley.'

Paladin's mechanical mind might have been ensconced in the captain's quarters, but he had eyes and ears and mouthpieces throughout the ship.

'Do you wish to gauge the damage done by the first?' he asked in his deep, tutorly voice, one that the sisters had known throughout childhood and adolescence. 'It may already be sufficient, judging by Mister Lagganvor's report.'

'No,' Fura said. 'We'll offer 'em a little bit more encouragement, just so they don't get any silly ideas.'

'As you wish, Captain.'

Lagganvor spoke from the speaking grille. 'Sail-flash is heavy and widely distributed.'

'Good,' Fura said. 'Dish 'em another helping.'

Paladin let off the coil-guns for a second time, the middle of the three volleys that were possible without breech-reloading.

Clang, clang, clang.

Fura initialised the stopwatch and restarted it with a firm depression of her metal thumb.

Tick, tick, tick . . .

Sail-flash meant that their sail-shot was ripping into the other ship's rigging and sails, disrupting them badly. Square leagues of sail were being torn away or shredded, free to flap and twist beyond the captain's discretion, and therefore maximising the chances of casting sunlight in an adverse direction.

Thirty seconds passed, then five more, and Lagganvor reported a second wave of sail-flash superimposing itself on the tail-end of the first.

'Multiple heavy flashes, maybe some hull incidence . . .'

No one doubted his observations. With his artificial eye, Lagganvor had the keenest acuity of any of the breathing crew.

'Hold the third wave,' Fura said, stopping the timer and holding up her flesh fist by way of emphasis.

She had not intended to score direct hits against the hull, but it was a known risk given the uncertain ranging, and she would not compound matters by sending more sail-shot.

'Open squawk, short-range only,' Fura continued. 'Be ready for return fire. Lag, you can come back in; tell Merrix she's up next.'

'Squawk is open and ready,' Paladin answered.

Fura pocketed the stopwatch and snatched one of the squawk handsets from its wall-mounting. 'Do you want to do the honours, dear heart? Has to be said you've got a sweeter way with it than me.'

Adrana took the handset from her sister, raising it to her lips, the coiled line stretching out from the wall.

'Unidentified craft: this is Captain Ness. We've crippled you and are about to board. If you abide by our conditions, there'll be no need for any trouble. We'll take what we want, but no more, and we'll leave you alive and capable of making port. Our physician will be with us, and if you have injured parties he'll see to your needs. All of that, though, is contingent upon your total cooperation. Our guns stay on you the whole while. If we see so much as one warm coiller, you'll be destroyed outright. There'll be no clemency, no mercy, no taking-of-prisoners, no kindly treatment for your wounded.' She breathed in, fingers caressing the switch on the squawk handset. 'This is my last word on the matter. Prepare to submit, or prepare to die: the choice is yours.'

She closed the transmission.

'How was that?'

'Commendably done. If you weren't my own blood, I think I might be a little afraid of you as well.' Fura returned to the speaker grille and selected a different channel. 'Surt, Tindouf. Ready the launch.'

*

Fura brought the launch to a crawl when it was a league from the other ship. With another control she brought up the flood-lamps, brushing fingers of light across the rigging, sails and hull of the injured craft.

'Oh dear,' she said, with a false sympathy. 'What have we done to 'em.'

It was a spectacle of chaos, a dark, visceral conundrum of knots and tangles, and the phantom-like forms of limp or collapsed shrouds and gallants, some parts of them still moving. There was a time when the damage would have been inscrutable to her, but now she gauged the success of her action with a keen and confident eye. A few parts of the sail-shot had struck the hull – there were bright, clean wounds to prove it, where paint or cladding had been ripped back to bare alloy – but so far as she could gauge there had been no puncturing. The inner-most elements of sail and rigging had not been badly touched; it looked worse than it was because the outermost areas had been drawn back in under the tension of sail-control gear, once they had lost the counter-balance of photon pressure to hold the torque-lines and stay-preventers under load.

Fura reached into a pouch on her left hip and took out a little purse-like affair made of cushioned material. With the tips of her metal fingers she extracted a rough-edged rectangle of smoky glass, then slipped it into her other hand, where she was not yet wearing a gauntlet.

Raising the stone to her eyes, she squeezed very gently. The lookstone responded, becoming dark instead of smoky, and she pivoted her gaze very slowly, stars oozing across that letterbox of darkness until the other ship came into view. She squeezed a little more and the ship's outer cladding melted away, disclosing a ghostly, wobbly impression of its interior compartments and mechanisms.

'Anything?' Prozor asked in a whisper.

'Five, maybe six individuals.' Fura was concentrating intently, trying to make out the dense knots of bone and muscle that were the ship's crew. 'Four of 'em cooped up in one place, which I think might be the galley, and another two back near the stern, very close together.'

'Do you see coil-guns, anything like that?' Lagganvor asked, holding his helmet in his hands.

'Maybe a small piece or two, aft and stern, but no broadside batteries.' She passed the lookstone to Prozor, who – like Lagganvor – was pressing in behind her pilot's position. 'See if you can spot any hideaways. I don't want to go into the ship thinking there's just six of 'em, and have another dozen spring out of hatches. That box the Clacker came in has got me worried about things that might be hidden away.'

'Effector-displacer systems are very rare,' Lagganvor said, in a low confiding tone. 'And valuable. Any crew that was lucky enough to have such a thing wouldn't need to be scrabbling around in this neck.'

'We are,' she said.

'But we have ulterior motives.'

'Let's hope *they* don't.'

'I'm only seein' six so far,' Prozor said, making a curious spectacle of herself as she held the lookstone up to her own face, for there now seemed to be a rectangular tunnel stretching all the way through her, out beyond the launch and into open space.

Fura opened the short-range squawk back to *Revenger* and reported on their findings so far, informing her sister that she did not believe the crew capable of putting up any significant resistance.

Cautiously, she edged the launch deeper into the carnage, closer and closer to the hard form of the hull. Loose rigging scratched along the smooth lines of their hull, making a dry rustling sound. A fragment of sail snagged on one of the fins, then a corner of it fluttered against the flame of the exhaust and the entire scrap vanished in a soundless white deflagration.

'Do you see a name?' Lagganvor asked.

'Not yet.'

Prozor handed back the lookstone. 'I still ain't seen more than six. I also ain't seen much in their holds, either.'

'If they have a skull, I'm happy.' Fura slipped the lookstone back into her purse, and the purse back into her pouch. 'Doctor Eddralder: are you ready?'

'Tolerably so,' Doctor Eddralder said. The tall physician with the tombstone face was making a final inspection of his medical chest: the same one that Fura had brought him from Mulgracen, although now stocked only with the drugs and instruments that were likely to be useful in the immediate aftermath of a boarding operation.

'I see something,' Lagganvor said, jabbing a finger at the windows as the launch came around to the other ship's mouth-like prow. 'Red letters, nearly faded away.' He tapped a finger against his temple, sending an acoustic signal to his eye. 'The *Merry Mare*, I think. Is this a ship known to anyone?'

'Not me,' Prozor said.

'They'll be just like we were,' Fura said. 'Just some happy, hapless saps out of their depth. If they ain't from Mazarile, they'll be from somewhere just as dirt-poor and hopeless, betting everything on one big score.' She set her jaw. 'Well, I'm sorry to bring their dreams crashing down.'

'I just saw a face flash against one of those large windows,' Doctor Eddralder said.

'Good,' Fura said. 'Always nicer to have a welcome. I expect they're putting the tea on for us already.'

*

They docked. The two craft made a solid, resonant contact, and a moment later Fura activated the capture latches so that the launch could not be shaken loose.

She unbuckled and worked her way back from the console position. There was a lightweight hatch in the treaded walkway that ran between the launch's two rows of seats. Fura flipped it up, exposing a heavier door beneath, with a spoked locking wheel set into its face. She bent down to spin this wheel, which in turn unlatched the inner pressure door of the belly lock. She lowered herself down into this cramped space, then set about loosening a second wheel set into the outer pressure door. Lagganvor and Prozor leaned in above her, directing crossbows over her shoulders as she worked. It was a two-handed job and Fura could not bring a weapon to bear until she was done with it.

'Brace yourselves,' Lagganvor said, his voice emerging through his visor, but also communicated to the others via suit-to-suit squawk, so that it had a double-edge to it, one muffled, the other buzzy and sharp.

With the boarding party all suited, it would not have mattered if the door led to vacuum, but when Fura had opened the outer door – with the inner one still open – there was no drop of pressure.

Facing them was another door, but painted brown this time. It belonged to the *Merry Mare*.

'The sooner some clever cove comes up with a substitute for breathin', Prozor was saying, 'the happier I'll be. Spent half my life going in and out of ships.'

'And the other half complaining about it,' Fura said, twisting around to take Prozor's crossbow and using the haft to hammer firmly against the brown door, before passing it back again. There were a few seconds of silence, then a faint metallic scuffling from beyond the door. Fura reached beneath her chest-pack and closed her artificial hand around the hilt of a long-bladed Ghostie knife. She detached the knife, and brought it into her line of sight. Though she ought to have been able to see it plainly, the Ghostie weapon resisted her attention, weaselling out of focus unless she averted her gaze.

The brown door began to hinge open in their direction. Fura eased back to allow it room to swing, ready with the blade should she need to hack or stab.

Prozor and Lagganvor covered her with the crossbows.

A round, helmetless face bobbed out of darkness, like a pale balloon unmoored from its string.

'I know you're going to kill us,' the man said, defiant and cocksure in the same breath. 'But if you've one shred of decency left in you, Bosa Sennen, you'll make it quick.'

They faced each other across the threshold of the lock, Fura behind her visor with its grillework and surrounding ornamentation of spikes and bone-parts, the man's head protruding from a tall, wide neck-ring marked with badges and emblems of service.

'I ain't Bosa Sennen, cove.'

'We heard your threats,' the man said, fighting – or so it now seemed to Fura – to keep a tremble out of his voice. He had a freckled face, eyes set wide beneath a prominent, sweating brow, a dusting of red hair on the scalp. His gaze slipped to the Ghostie knife then just as easily slipped off it. 'I heard what you said you'd do to us.'

'That was just a little bit of . . . patter. A bit of persuasion to get you agreeing to our terms and conditions,' Fura said.

'We know what you've done. What you've always done. We'll keep to your terms and still you'll slice us up. That's what you do.' He spat at her, and his spit formed a drunken cobweb across the grille of her visor.

'Kill me. Torture me. Whatever you will. But show the others some mercy, if you still know the word.'

Slowly and deliberately, Fura pulled back the Ghostie blade and fixed it back under her chest-pack. It clacked into place by means of a magnetic latch.

'What's your name?'

'Cap'n Werranwell, as you must already know.' His face wobbled beyond the glistening strands covering her visor. He set his jaw, trying – it was obvious to Fura – to look and sound more assured than he felt. 'Werranwell, of the expeditionary-privateer *Merry Mare*.'

She reached out her metal hand, as if they might shake on terms there and then.

'Much obliged to make your acquaintance. That's a fine ship you have ... had, I mean. I'm Captain Ness, as was already explained.'

He spat at her again. This time it formed a slimy membrane between her fingers.

'Ness, Sennen, whatever you choose to call yourself. To hell with you and your crew.'

She shook her hand, trying to dislodge the spit. 'We're getting off on the wrong footing here, Werrie. Why'd you not shoot us while you had the chance, by the way? You had chasing pieces. They'd have been worth a go, wouldn't they?'

He sighed, rubbed at his forehead. 'Lasling would have had me risk a positioning sweep, and maybe a volley or two. But it wouldn't have been guaranteed to stop you, and all we'd have done is give you a juicier target to aim for. We're a bauble-skipper, not a plunderer – just an honest ship trying to make an honest living. Still, I wish I'd listened to Lasling ...'

'Well, you're right – it wouldn't have helped. But it's not all doom and gloom, Werrie.' She put her finger under his chin. 'Be sweet with us, don't try anything silly, and we'll be out of your hair in two shakes. Then you can be back about your business...'

He managed a mordant laugh.

'Business? My ship is finished. Or did you not notice that, as you were destroying our sails and rigging and throwing a few shots at the hull for good measure?'

'Necessary damage,' Fura said.

Prozor and Lagganvor jabbed the crossbows past her shoulders for emphasis. Captain Werranwell retreated back to clear the lock and allow Fura to pass through onto the *Merry Mare*. She remained alert and ready for action as she did so, trusting nothing, especially not the captain's apparent capitulation.

It was no ruse, though. She was convinced of as much as she

drifted into the *Merry Mare*'s galley and took in the collective mood of the gathered crew, assembled in the chaos left after the engagement. Game pieces, cooking utensils and cutlery drifted free, knocked loose from magnetic tables and latches. A chair had shattered into wooden splinters. Blobs of water had become quivery, mirror-like forms, drifting around like strange alien pets. Lightvine, ripped free from the walls, formed loose, writhing tendrils of glowing colour.

There were three besides Werranwell: two men and a woman. The four figures she had seen through the lookstone. They were beaten, dejected, thoroughly surrendered to their fates. They all wore suits or parts of suits, but none of them had helmets and only one, the woman, had got as far as fitting her gloves on. There were no weapons or defensive items to be seen, not even a little dagger or energy pistol.

'Don't think we wouldn't have put up a fight if we thought it would get us anywhere,' the woman said in a low, measured voice shot through with bitter acceptance. 'A trip or two ago, we'd have given you something to remember us by. But we've been short-handed since we lost Ives and Mauncer at His Foulness, back in ninety-nine. Then we traded our last good piercing piece for a better skull, thinking intelligence would serve us better than armament, in the long run.'

'And did it?' Fura asked, with what almost sounded like genuine curiosity.

The woman affected a pitying, sarcastic look. 'Oh, it's worked out handsomely, wouldn't you say?'

'You were at His Foulness?' Prozor asked, following Fura into the galley and sweeping her crossbow into the room's cluttered corners with a quick, confident manner, as if it was something she hardly needed to think about.

'Does that mean something?' Fura asked.

'It means they're either lyin', or they deserve our respect.'

'Is this the lot of you?' Lagganvor asked, looking around. Clever, Fura thought: testing the captain's veracity, rather than reveal that they already knew about the other pair.

'This is my crew,' said Werranwell, lifting his chin. 'Save Meggery, who was injured in your action, and Ruther who's with her. They're in the sick-bay.'

'What's up with Meggery?' Fura asked.

'What's it matter?' asked the woman, raking a hand over her dark red hair, which she wore combed to the right of her head, the left side completely shorn, and the hair braided into an elaborately stranded tail that was long enough to reach the small of her back. She was exceedingly skinny, sharp-cheekboned, small-chinned, with a jangle of earrings on the shaved side of her head. 'We'll all be going Meggery's way soon enough.'

'Let me clarify something,' Fura said. 'I mean what I said – what we promised you on the squawk.'

Werranwell cut across her. 'You sounded different when you were laying out your terms.'

'Does it matter how I sounded?' Fura turned to call back in the direction of the lock. 'Doctor Eddralder! Shift your sticks! Got some employment for you here.' She refocused on the crew before her. 'What are your names, besides your captain here?'

'Why d'you care?' asked the woman, fingering the tip of her hair-braid. Some lingering pride apparently caused her to collect herself, glance at her colleagues, and say: 'I'm Cossel: Assessor/Opener on the *Mare*, and a damned fine one when I had the chance.'

'Vouga,' said the compact-looking man to her left, who was completely bald, with curiously small ears, two deep grooves between his long-curved nose and his small, nearly feminine mouth, and what appeared to be a permanent doubtful set to his lips, like a doll that had been given a fixed expression for life. 'Wrestler, circus strongman and general enforcer.' He frowned at himself. 'No, wait: Integrator. That's what I meant to say: Integrator.'

'I'm Lasling,' said the larger man to Cossel's right, who was very broad across the shoulders and very narrow at the hips, so that he formed an inverted triangle, accentuated by the fact that his legs ended at the knees, with his suit trousers sewn into closed-off stumps like the bottoms of lungstuff canisters. He had a wide, flattened face, with a nose that had obviously been broken and mashed to one side, then allowed to heal in that position. When he spoke, his mouth showed an assortment of teeth that were missing, broken, capped in metal or replaced entirely. His face was a canvas for bumps and blemishes, his ears blobby extrusions of malformed cartilage, his lips swollen and nicked with numerous scars. 'Master of Sail,' he stated, before glancing down at his legs. 'I was an Opener, until life decided I needed a change of career.'

Fura nodded at him as if they were old acquaintances. 'You'd be the cove who was trying to talk your captain into a position-ing sweep?'

Lasling shrugged, as if the point was of vanishing conse-quence. 'Maybe it was me. What would you've done?'

'Exactly what you were advocating.'

Doctor Eddralder was coming into the galley, unbending himself like a cleverly hinged walking cane. His visor was a sheet of curved glass, lacking any armoured grilles or frets, so his long, faintly equine face was easily visible. His large eyes, pale as hard-boiled eggs, searched the scene, looking for signs of injury or distress.

'You said I might be of assistance, Captain?'

'Yes, back in their sick-bay – someone called Meggery, with another crew member in attendance.' Then, to the four who were gathered in the galley: 'Captain Werranwell, we'll keep you busy for a little while, so will you deputise one of these to take Doctor Eddralder to your sick-bay and help him as needed?'

'Oh, are we going to play a game of sides?' asked Vouga, with a faint frowning interest.

Fura sighed hard and reached up for her visor. 'I wanted to rattle you a bit, and I meant some of what I said, but I'm also going to leave you all alive and able to get back home.' She hinged open the visor, allowing her glowy-charged skin to shine out into the galley. 'I'm Fura Ness. Not Bosa Sennen, nor any other name you might be expecting. I took her ship, as you might have heard, but I didn't take her methods, or her temper.'

Cossel scratched at the shorn side of her skull.

'Well, that's me reassured.'

Fura looked the woman hard in the face. 'You're the Assessor, you said?'

'What of it?'

'You can help me and Lagganvor take our pick of your treasure, such as it is. Vouga or Lasling, would one of you accompany Doctor Eddralder to the sick-bay?'

'I'll help if there are treats in it,' Vouga said.

'That leaves Lasling,' Fura said, ignoring Vouga. 'It's handy that you're the Master of Sail.'

The broad, stump-legged man asked: 'Why?'

'With Prozor's help you can itemise the damage done to your rigging, and what you need from us to put it right.'

'Well, isn't that generous,' Lasling said. 'It's like being stabbed in a back-alley, then having the same cove tell you they can help with the bleeding.'

Doctor Eddralder braced his arm against a wall-rib and turned to address Lasling. 'Difficult as it may be to believe – and I understand your misgivings – these people will keep their word. They did my daughter and I a very considerable kindness, and I remain in their debt. Are your injuries recent?'

Lasling seemed to debate with himself before giving his answer.

'Enough to keep me awake some nights.'

'Then I will attend to you, once I've seen to the other party. Mister Vouga – would you be so kind as to show me the way?'

'Kind? I'll bend over backwards. There's nothing pleases me more than helping pirates pick our own ship to cat-scraps . . .'

Vouga glanced back at his captain, who – after a moment's deliberation – gave a single short nod.

'Your physician is either a sincere man,' Werranwell said to Fura, 'or a very persuasive liar.'

*

While the boarding operation was in progress, Adrana sat in the captain's quarters, trying to distract herself from the dangers at hand. She had journals and private letters to look through; she had the Clacker's box to observe – just in case it did anything, which was highly unlikely – she had Merrix in the sighting room if she wished for conversation, and of course Strambli, Surt and Tindouf were elsewhere in the ship, and so never far away. Paladin was immediately at hand, his head – all that remained of him – fixed to the desk like a large glass ornament.

'You seem agitated, Miss Adrana,' he remarked, as she turned another page in one of the old, mostly cryptic journals that she and her sister had inherited from Bosa Sennen. 'May I allay your concerns, to some degree? We have chased down other ships, without injury or loss to ourselves. With each instance, we are getting better at it – colder and more efficient, you might say. With each—'

'There is a game they play in some of the worlds, Paladin,' she interrupted, although not unkindly. 'They take a particular sort of pistol, with a revolving chamber, and load only one shot into it. Then they spin the chamber and place the pistol against their heads, by way of a wager. They shoot, and spin, and shoot again. For a little while their luck holds: the pin falling on an empty chamber. Would you say that they are getting better at it, if that keeps happening?'

'I am not sure that the analogy is *entirely* merited.'

'I am not sure that it is entirely *not* merited, Paladin,' she countered. 'We tested our luck in Mulgracen; there is nothing to say we are not testing our luck here.'

'And yet, you are in agreement with your sister that having a skull is vital.'

'It would help us.'

'Well, then.'

'And yet we have done quite well without one so far. Lagganvor's right: we would benefit from improved intelligence. But the advantages of a skull have to be weighed against the risks in acquiring one.'

'I might venture to say that the time for weighing one against the other has now passed.'

'You never used to be so sarcastic.'

'Your father would never have tolerated me if I had been. Nor, for that matter, would you.'

It was true. Fura had been devoted to Paladin, as fond of him as she might have been of an uncle or kindly older brother. Adrana had been . . . less enamoured. She had viewed Paladin as fundamentally stupid and failing: a blindly loyal instrument of her father, extending his kind but over-protective and controlling regime into their bedroom and playroom.

To a degree, she had not been wrong. But she had underestimated what Paladin had once been, and what he could be again. It had taken Fura to bring him back to himself, by unlocking memory banks and decision-action circuits that had long been frozen. He had been a soldier once; now he was a soldier once more.

He had also been damaged so badly that his old body, with its arms and wheels, had been abandoned for scrap when Fura made her escape from Mazarile, on her way to rescue Adrana.

What remained of him was a transparent three-quarter sphere full of chattering relays and flickering lights, with fine sutures in the glass where the pieces had been fixed back together, and shards and chips that were from elsewhere, stained different colours, but carefully cut to replace the missing parts of him, mostly by the nimble-fingered Surt, who had taken a personal interest in his welfare. The base of the globe was attached to a collar, and the collar in turn was fixed to the desk, providing a means for circuits to come and go between Paladin and the rest of the ship. If he had a body now, then perhaps it was the ship as a whole, with its sails and rigging, its coil-guns and ion-fluke, its sweeper and squawk.

Perhaps, for Paladin, it was not so very bad a trade.

'I worry, that's all,' Adrana said, casting a glance at the Clacker's box. That was the real source of their troubles, if she was going to be honest: all else was incidental.

And she was the real cause of the Clacker.

Adrana had hoped that finding him would be a simple matter, and that once in her presence he would gladly (or perhaps with a little persuasion) answer the questions that preoccupied her. Or if not answer them directly, at least direct her toward possible sources of those answers.

But the Clacker, instead, had become a liability. He might be able to help them, but that cooperation was now contingent on his being delivered to Trevenza Reach. And in the thirteen weeks that had passed since Mulgracen, as they sailed around the edge of the Congregation, they were venturing nearer and nearer to the volume of space where they were likely to run into the squadron of ships assigned to hunt them down. And since their chances of slipping around or through that squadron would be greatly improved by the interception of intelligence on its movements and intentions, they had to have a skull. And since they had to have a skull. . .

Paladin used to read them a picture story. It was a sort of moral parable about a chain of consequences, each leading to something worse. It began with a horse not being shod properly, for want of a nail. It ended with the collapse of an entire interplanetary empire.

Paladin had been very good at stories. Adrana remembered all of them very well. The more of their stories he read, the more he fed their rules and conventions into his circuits, and the better he was at making up new stories. He could even draw pictures to go with them, projecting them onto the walls of their room.

And for want of a skull, a ship was taken. And for want of caution . . .

'Miss Adrana?'

'Yes,' she answered, jolted back to the room.

'I think there may be another ship nearby. It would appear that we have just been swept.'

5

'I almost feel bad about it,' Fura said, as they passed one empty compartment after the next. Empty except for the usual junk and clutter of any ship in service: scraps of sail and line, bits of vacuum suit, odd-shaped scabs of hull material that had been cut away during repairs and deemed too precious to discard. 'Adding to your tally of bad luck, I mean. The worst of it is I can see how you deserved better than what you got.'

'You feel you know us, do you?' Werranwell asked.

'I know a crew that's got the short end of the stick,' Fura said. 'Mainly 'cause I've been on one. My first ship was under Racka-more, and he did all right for himself – kept his accounts clean and was generally popular. Then I signed on with Trusko, and that was a different story altogether.'

'I don't know him,' Werranwell said.

'Oh, I knew him,' said Cossel, who – along with Lagganvor – was accompanying the two captains. 'It was all over the squawks for a week or two; even made the papers and flickers. He'd been borrowing from the banks to keep his operation going, and if there's one thing the lending institutions *really* don't like, it's someone defaulting on their credit by having the bad grace to die.'

'The poor fellow can hardly be blamed for being killed by Bosa Sennen,' said a smirking Lagganvor, who was carrying a crossbow in case of trouble, but generally keeping it aimed discreetly away from Cossel and her captain. Setting aside this admitted awkwardness, the party of four could easily have been mistaken for a group of acquaintants visiting a museum or gallery, peering into each exhibit with a steadily draining forbearance. Not friends, exactly, but colleagues or distant relatives, thrown together and forced to rub along for an hour or two.

'Not that anyone's credit really matters a damn anymore,' Cossel said.

'Were you hit bad?' Lagganvor asked, the object of his enquiry needing no clarification.

'I daresay others were hit worse,' Werranwell said. 'But yes, it was very bad. We had done quite well in ninety-six and seven, running a string of successful raids – Wedza's Eye, the Cuckoo, Black's Talon among them.' He directed a sharp eye at Fura. 'Check the chambers of commerce if you doubt me – I can tell you exactly where and when we did business. We were successful, and I make no apology for it.' A rueful tone entered his voice. 'Too successful, perhaps. Our treasure was exactly what the market was looking for, and we converted our assets into quoins very readily. Then we banked quite a lot of those quoins, and I gather that most of the institutions are guaranteeing those deposits, up to certain thresholds. But I have always been cautious where the banks are concerned, and so we salted half our earnings in private deposits, where there are no such guarantees. After the Readjustment . . .'

'Such an innocent-sounding thing,' Cossel said, interrupting her captain without a thought.

'What do you expect?' Lagganvor asked. 'It was the banks that caused that trouble; it's only fitting they be the ones to put a name to it.'

They paused at another compartment, small as a kitchen larder. It was bare except for a person-sized sack with a cinch around the neck. Werrenwell reached into the compartment and dragged it out.

It jangled as it drifted.

'The banks have made no statement as to the cause of the Readjustment,' Werranwell said. 'And for once – despite my better instincts – I am inclined to believe that they do not really understand its origins. Sometimes these financial upsets help the banks, you see – or at least help the aliens, which may amount to the same thing. But the Readjustment was nothing like the slumps and crashes we have all come to know. I don't think it benefited the banks at all. That is why they are so very angry about the whole thing – for once, it exposes their weakness.'

'I wouldn't believe everything I hear about quoins,' Fura said. She took the bag from Werranwell, loosened the cinch, and peered inside. There were about a hundred quoins inside, she judged, respectable enough even if the denominations were low. But she doubted very much that it would be any sort of fortune, never mind the sort of money that was needed to furnish a ship and its crew. 'This your only stash?' she asked.

'Regrettably,' Werranwell said, and if it was a lie it was very persuasive one. 'Take it. I'd sooner not be reminded of our poor decisions.'

She tossed the bag to Lagganvor. 'Leave three quarters in the bag by denomination, near as you're able. We'll let 'em keep the rest.'

Lagganvor rummaged one-handed through the contents of the bag, cradling the crossbow in the other. He'd had plenty of practice at this sort of thing, Fura reflected. He had been in the service of Bosa Sennen, once, and although she had turned against him – not without provocation, it had to be said – he had not forgotten the common arts of piracy, of which efficient accounting was a principal one.

'We must be a disappointment,' Cossel said.

'We're not finished with your holds just yet, cove,' Fura said. 'We can also use fuel, lungstuff, yardage, tar, bread, butter, almost anything you care to mention.' A buzz sounded in her helmet. She reached up, turning on the squawk. 'Dear heart, how are we faring?'

Adrana's voice came through, but faintly, and not just because they were inside another ship, and subject to the screening influence of its own hull. She must have had the squawk strength turned down nearly as far as it would go.

'We're in trouble.'

Fura smiled. 'When are we ever not, dear?'

'Paladin picked up a sweep, then a second at a higher energy and tighter focus. The first feels like a general search sweep; the second more like a targeting action.'

Fura took the news as stoically as she could, not wanting to give anything away to Werranwell's crew.

'May we speculate on . . . distances?'

'No – Paladin can't say. Merrix hasn't seen anything, so they're unlikely to be too close to us. But something's out there, and it's just taken an interest in us. It's the wreck they're picking up, of course, but since we happen to be sitting practically on top of that wreck . . . I want you back here. Paladin is monitoring a rising weather trend, and Tindouf and Surt will be standing-by to receive the launch.'

'We shan't be too long now. It's not exactly rich pickings, I'm afraid.' She shot an aggrieved, apologetic look at Cossel and Werranwell. 'Lag's just rummaging through our winnings as I speak. Doctor Eddralder's with an injured cove, and Prozor's sorting out the materials they'll need to fix their rigging.'

'Understood, but get back as quickly as you can.'

'That is exactly my intention. We'll speak soon, fondest.'

Fura ended the transmission. She smiled at Lagganvor, who was just finishing off with the bag of quoins, and beckoned him nearer, so she could whisper.

'We have to leave.'

'An excellent proposition, all told.' He passed about twenty loose quoins to Werranwell, who scooped them close to his chest and then sent them drifting, back into the compartment. They clattered and jangled against the compartment walls, then came to a gradual halt. Fura watched them guardedly, reminded of the quoins in the Pharmacist's aquarium.

There was no mistaking it, now she had seen it: their faces were falling into a common alignment, like spectators at the racetrack watching a single dog.

'There's nothing else,' Cossel said.

'And I'd love to believe you,' Fura said, 'but that's exactly what I'd say if there was something you didn't want us to know about. Like a pretty alien skull, just waiting on a new owner. Show me to your bone room.'

*

'What if they don't come back?' Strambli asked.

'They will.'

'But what if they don't? What if something keeps 'em there, and whoever sent those pulses comes near enough to get a shot at us? Do we just sit here, or do we move?'

'They will come back.'

'But what if . . .'

Adrana raised a warning hand. 'Strambli, please. This isn't helping.'

She was at the control room, next to the Glass Armillary. It was a complex, lacy assemblage of nested rings, representing the Congregation and some tiny fraction of the worlds that constituted that little cradle of civilisation. *Revenger* had dipped into its outer layers to visit Mulgracen, but now they were back out in the relative sanctuary of the Empty, where the only worlds were bare rocks or uninhabited baubles, and where the distances between the ships could usually be measured in millions, rather than thousands, of leagues. Trevenza Reach – their intended destination – was still seventeen million leagues and two months distant. It was the one exception to the usual rule: a world that was both fully inhabited, and yet travelling through the Empty. That was because its orbit was uncommonly elliptical, so that it only spent a portion of its time inside the Congregation.

'I don't mean to be jumpy, Adrana. It's just since we brought that scaly cove onboard . . .'

'You mean the Clacker. You mean our passenger, to whom we have an obligation.'

'He ain't said a word to us!'

'He said a word to me, before we left Mulgracen. We entered into an arrangement. Now we are discharging that arrangement. We will convey him to Trevenza Reach, and we will evade our hunters, as we have done before.' She looked at the other woman searchingly. 'You mustn't lose faith, Strambli. We have the fastest, darkest ship anywhere in the Congregation, and our guns are without equal. We *shall* prevail.'

'I know it, Adrana. I just don't feel it.' She let out her sigh. 'Something's changed in me since Wheel Strizzardy, and not just because of that Ghostie splinter they had to dig out of my leg. I ain't sure I'm suited to this new life of ours.' Hastily she added: 'It's not that I'm a coward . . .'

'No one would ever say that of you.'

'But stalking ships like this, taking their prizes, leaving their crews all shivered-up . . .'

'It's a temporary occupation, that's all. Think of a good person who lost their home and had a choice between starving and freezing on the street, or picking the odd pocket. As long as they do it kindly and understand that what they're doing isn't a vocation . . .' Adrana moved one of the adjustable stalks on the Glass Armillary, taking account of a revised estimate of their exact position. 'This is not our new life, Stramb. It's just something we have to get through. Once we have delivered the alien, and gained the answers to some of the questions we seek—'

'You seek.'

'I seek, then. But once that is done, all this will seem like a mere footnote. We'll find a way to slip back into normal life, normal society. Those of us who wish to remain in ships may do so, but any who don't will be free to do whatever they choose.'

Strambli rubbed at the area of her leg where Eddralder had cut out the Ghostie shard. Fura had seen her do it before, and she supposed it was some itch or tingle that flared up whenever Wheel Strizzardy came up. Strambli had nearly died there, after all.

'You do always make it seem as if everything's going to be all right forever,' Strambli said.

'I think it shall,' Adrana answered. 'I hope it shall be, for all our sakes.'

Strambli lifted her eyes to the Glass Armillary. 'Mister Lag said we wouldn't run into that squadron, not if we were careful, and definitely not this far from Trevenza.'

'I am inclined to agree with his assessment. There are other ships operating out here, and they don't all have to be engaged on some hunt for us. I think we shall find that those two sweeps were not meant for us personally. All the same . . . I should also be very glad to see that launch on its way back to us.'

*

'That swab again, if you'd be so kind,' Eddralder said, lifting his gaze to acknowledge Fura's arrival, then immediately returning to the object of his attention.

He was bent over a female patient who was stretched onto a surgical couch and fixed there by grubby straps. A very young man was keeping a close observation on both, floating next to the couch with his legs tucked under him. Eddralder had his medical chest opened, and the young man was holding some of the necessary items, passing them to Eddralder upon request.

'The skull is loaded,' Fura declared, 'and Lagganvor's completed his inventory of the holds. We've all that we wish to take, and I'd like to be underway very shortly, before the weather worsens . . .' Or before another sweep comes in, she thought to herself.

The lad passed Eddralder the swab.

'Take a look at what you've done,' he said, gesturing at the woman being treated.

'Easy, lad,' cautioned Werranwell, who was just behind Fura.

She nodded. 'You'd be Ruther, would you?'

'Never mind me,' the boy said hotly. 'It's Meggery you should be bothered about.'

Meggery had her face turned away from Fura and a burn-like wound covering her shoulder and neck. From what Fura could judge of her, Meggery was a small, muscular woman with a large head and a great cloud of curly black hair floating above it. She had as many scars as she did tattoos; so many that it was no simple matter telling which was which. On her right side, opposite the new injury and masking some old serpentine wound, a seahorse curled around her shoulder and collar bone. Chains of stars pocked her wrists and forearms. Lacy blue cobwebs patterned her hands. She was missing the smallest finger on her left arm, snipped off cleanly at the knuckle and long healed-over.

'I took your ship, Ruther,' Fura answered imperiously. 'That's what happens in piracy. It ain't nice when it's done to you, but lots of things in life ain't nice. Besides, there was no hull penetration. I didn't put a shot through you. Unless she was outside, I don't see how she could've come to any harm.'

'Meggery is our Master of Ions. When you started hacking us up, Captain Werranwell asked her to give us all possible thrust from the ion-emitter, in the sure knowledge that we were about to lose our sails.' Ruther nodded at his captain. 'It was the right thing, too.'

Fura shrugged. 'And?'

'Meggery was down in the ion room when one of your shots hit our hull, and the recoil sent her right into the rectifier vanes. That's an electrical burn, and a bad one.'

'Then I'm sorry to add one more scar to her collection.'

'It's more than a scar,' Ruther retorted, spittle bursting between his teeth. 'It knocked her right out, and your doctor reckons there could be neurological impairment as well as tissue damage.'

Fura ignored the boy and directed her question at Eddralder. 'Have you patched her up?'

'The electrical burn should heal,' Doctor Eddralder said, without looking up from his work. 'If it doesn't, a graft will be possible.'

'You have no idea what you've done,' Ruther said.

'I've spared her, is what I've done. And the rest of you, while I was at it. Just because I'm keeping to my word doesn't mean things couldn't have gone very differently.'

'Your word,' Ruther said, disgustedly. He was sixteen or seventeen, slight of build, with a sharp chin beneath a heart-shaped face. His eyebrows were arched, his eyes a surprising deep blue. The only aspect of his appearance which ran counter to the overall impression of youth was a stripe of pure white hair, running from his forehead all the way to his crown and beyond. 'What does their word mean to someone like you?'

'Push me and you'll find out,' Fura said, beginning to run out of patience with the boy. Then, to Eddralder: 'Will she be all right?'

'Probably. But I'd like to keep her under close observation. If she takes a bad turn, I might be required to go in.'

'Go in?' queried Werranwell, drifting close to the patient, and bracing himself by his fingers.

Eddralder looked at the captain.

'Cranial surgery. But it would need to be done on *Revenger*. None of the facilities here are suitable. The swab again, please, Ruther.'

Fura seethed, but by great force of will she managed to bottle most of it in. Though it felt like a hot red tide lapping against the lower part of her eyelids, ready to gush out.

'This critical period, Doctor Eddralder. What are we looking at, exactly? Hours, days, weeks?'

Eddralder deliberated before offering his answer.

'Two days of close observation will be sufficient, but if there is a downturn I would need to operate very quickly. There wouldn't be time to convey Meggery back to *Revenger*, not unless you brought it closer.'

Werranwell met her eyes. 'Your doctor is indeed a man of his word, Captain Ness. But it looks as if you'll be taking back one more trophy than you planned.'

The great sails were traced in chalkboard scratches of purple and indigo, framing acres of perfect black. The ordinary sails – those they had stitched into the rigging to disguise her nature – had been hauled in before they began stalking the *Merry Mare*, so all that remained were vast square leagues of catchcloth.

In the central focus of the sails, a red mouth gulped wide.

Fura spun the launch around, backing into the docking bay with tiny, expert puffs of the steering jets, so that when it finally touched its berthing cradle the impact was as tender as a pleasure boat kissing against its quay. Doctor Eddralder thanked her for taking such pains not to disturb Meggery, but in truth she was thinking mainly of the skull, and how sad it would be if she smashed it now.

Surt and Tindouf were still in their vacuum suits to help secure the launch, with Adrana and Strambli waiting on the other side of the lock as soon as the doors were opened.

'I took the decision to unfurl the main sheets as soon as Paladin confirmed you were on the way back,' Adrana said. 'We can set a course as soon as you wish, but for the moment I thought it better to be moving somewhere.'

'You can furl them back again,' Fura said. 'We ain't going anywhere.'

6

Adrana opened the wallet that contained the bottles of Mephrozine. There had been ten bottles when they left Mulgracen; ten identical stoppered vials tucked into little hooped pouches, as neat as bullets. Now four of the bottles were gone, and of the fifth only half of its contents remained.

Adrana extracted the bottle, pinching it carefully between her fingers. She took out the miniature syringe that had come in the same wallet, its glass barrel calibrated for specific dosages of unadulterated Mephrozine. There were ten gradations for each bottle; ten standard doses. Since their departure from Mulgracen, Fura had been permitting herself one injection every two days. There were fifty-five doses remaining; not quite four months' worth.

If all went to plan, they would be at Trevenza Reach well within half that interval, and once at that world they ought – with care – to be able to find new supplies, or some other treatment. But it was cutting things finer than Adrana liked, and if there were some delay in their passage, or even an unhelpfulness in the solar weather . . .

Fura watched her sister. She had bared her shoulder, ready for the injection.

'Don't dither so. If you had to have a needle stuck into you every two days, you'd want it over and done with.'

Adrana plunged the needle into the permeable stopper and pulled back on the piston. 'I am concerned about the dosage.'

'Then don't be. It's doing just what it's meant to.'

'It is. I don't need to be Eddralder to see that. There's less of a glint of it in your pupils, and it takes a lot to bring it out in your face now. A reversal is too much to be hoped for, but it's certainly holding the glowy at bay. Even your temperament . . .'

'What of it?'

'I see more of the old Fura, and less of the newer one.' Adrana chose her words with great deliberation, even though she was the one now holding the needle. 'You seem more measured in your judgements. Less inclined to think the rest of us are acting against you, or plotting without you. Your decision to bring back the injured girl was . . . more in keeping with the earlier you.'

'I . . . ain't about to disagree.' Fura looked up at her sister with a certain pride in her own forbearance. 'There. Does that surprise you?'

'A little.'

'Good. I'd hate to become predictable. Perish the worlds, sister – be done with the injection.'

'I wonder if we ought to stretch out the doses.'

'We've sufficient in hand. I've done the sums.'

'Sufficient in hand if all goes well,' Adrana said gently. 'Which it is not always inclined to do. The supplies were already running thin in Mulgracen. That may be symptomatic of a more general shortfall across the Congregation, caused by the Readjustment. Caused by our own actions.'

'Spare me the lesson in irony.'

'I shall. But if we are delayed in our arrival . . .'

'We won't be.'

'But if we are, and you run out of Mephrozine, the sudden termination of your course would have very bad consequences.'

'Medically qualified now, are you?'

'No, but Eddralder is. He warned me that it would be unwise to stop the dosages abruptly. I am fearful of that, fearful of the harm it would do to you, and therefore I am concerned that we do not expose ourselves to that risk. If we move to one standard dose every three days, or a three-quarter dose at the current schedule, we—'

Fura reached up with her metal hand and took her sister's wrist. 'Inject me. Do it now, or I'll do it for myself.'

'As you wish.'

The needle went in. Fura tensed at the moment of injection, closed her eyes, and let out a long, slow exhalation. Adrana withdrew the needle and set about cleaning the hypodermic, ready for the next dose.

'It's working,' Fura said. 'So for now we continue as we've started. If our circumstances alter, I'll review it. But not until then.'

'I only have your best interests at heart.'

'Then we're of one mind. I have *my* best interests at heart as well.' Fura swivelled her gaze onto the Clacker's box, which was exactly where it had been since they brought it aboard: secured to one wall of the captains' quarters by cross-buckled straps. 'And yours . . . of course.'

'Of course.'

'Was your new pal as quiet as ever, during my absence?'

'There has been no change. I'm reluctant to open the box unnecessarily, for fear of further straining the mechanisms keeping him alive.'

Adrana passed Fura a cotton dab and she pressed it against her shoulder. 'Has it entered your noggin that he might already be dead? That he never survived that business in Mulgracen?'

'It was his outer box that was damaged the most. If there had been any serious damage to his inner container, the effector-displacer system would never have worked well enough for us to smuggle him past the customs men.'

'I'm glad you've some reassurance to cling to.'

Adrana had nearly finished putting away the syringe and the medicine pouches. She did it with tremendous care, conscious of how easy it would be to shatter one of those little bottles and undo the small margin of safety they now enjoyed.

'Paladin is monitoring the Clacker. He can see into the box, to some degree, and believes there are signs of suspended animation: a living process, yet slowed. I believe we must allow events to follow their natural course. When he comes out of this hibernation, or whatever we might call it, he will be in a position to answer many of our questions.'

'Although, mainly, yours.'

'Must there be such a distinction? Our concerns overlap. You wish to fathom the deeper meaning of quoins, and I wish to fathom the deeper meaning of Occupations. I will be astonished if our twin interests do not, at some point, intersect. I will learn why there have been thirteen Occupations these last ten million years, instead of the four hundred and forty that it appears *might* have come about but for some failure of fate, and you will learn the nature of these souls which supposedly reside in quoins . . .'

'They aren't souls,' Fura said. She creased her face, evidently – it seemed to Adrana – irritated with herself for being so easily manipulated into admitting that her interest in the quoins was still unsated, and that – by implication – the Clacker also had some value to her and was therefore not so entirely unwelcome a guest. 'They are not souls,' she began again, 'or, at least, it's got to be something more complicated than that, something not so easy to put into words.'

'Bosa was of one opinion.'

'She was right in many things, and half right in others. She started off on a search for knowledge that she didn't manage to finish. Ours . . . is to see that work through to completion. We took a step in that direction when we triggered the Readjustment. Now we've got to understand the consequences of that change.'

'The consequences are simple enough. A randomisation of the value of quoins, and utter chaos for the economies of the Congregation.'

'There's something else.' Fura felt a dizzy surge as the chemical announced its presence in her bloodstream. It was like falling, and at the same time feeling as if every vein and artery in her body ran with a fine lavalike fire. It would pass, just as the glowy's severest episodes always passed, but for the moment she took a masochistic pleasure in the discomfort, for it meant the drug was working. 'I saw it happen in Mulgracen. Thought it might be a trick, but I've checked for myself and there's no trickery about it. Left to themselves, quoins want to turn to face the Old Sun.'

Adrana knew her sister too well to assume that Fura was making it up.

'A new effect, since the Readjustment?'

'So it'd seem.' She paused, eyeing the red-glowing globe on her desk. 'Do you remember what I told you about Paladin – what I wrote of him in the *True and Accurate Testimony*?'

Adrana nodded, hoping she would not be pressed as to how exhaustive her reading of her sister's account had been. The truth was that she had read it industriously to begin with, then with a gradual lessening of attention, then with guilty reluctance, until eventually she was only skimming it to find the bits in which she was mentioned.

Fortunately, she did remember the part about Paladin. 'You said something to him, and he remembered his past.'

'Not just his past, but his purpose – his true vocation.'

'*The Last Rains of Sestramor*,' Adrana said, emphasising her excellent recollection of the *True and Accurate Testimony*.

'They aren't the same, but I wonder if something's happened to the quoins along the same lines – a sort of reawakening, a rediscovery of some hidden purpose.'

'To do with facing the Old Sun?'

'I'm just saying what I saw, sister – it ain't for me to say why.'

There was a knock at the open door to the captains' quarters. Lagganvor came in, and behind him was Eddralder, with a distracted look about him.

Fura bid the two men to sit on the far side of her desk, their faces washed in Paladin's wavering light.

'Nothing's changed,' she said, before either had a chance to speak. 'We'll send Meggery back in a day or two, and then we make all sail for Trevenza, as was already our plan. With this rising weather we mightn't suffer any delay.'

'Are you not concerned about returning to Werranwell?' Adrana asked. 'We've given him the perfect opportunity to re-group and spring a trap for us.'

'He's not the sort,' Lagganvor said, picking at a hang-nail that he must have snagged when he was wearing his vacuum suit glove. 'He'll take his crewmember back with gratitude, and limp home to port with a good story and a fine insurance claim.'

'Assuming any insurance firms are still paying out,' Adrana said.

Fura turned to her with an interrogatory look. 'Would you have sooner we left the woman to die?'

'No . . . of course not. It was the right thing, to bring her into Eddralder's care.' She nodded at the physician, wondering to herself if his troubled look was the result of the patient taking a sudden turn for the worse. But then, she reflected, he would hardly be sitting there waiting his turn to speak. 'But I can't downplay the dangers.'

'You needn't worry about the captain.' Lagganvor chewed at his torn nail until it broke off between his teeth. 'You develop a nose for character in my line. He's the sort who keeps his books balanced and sleeps with a sound conscience. I saw his cabin. A man of austere tastes. Self-denying to a fault. Probably whips himself before going to bed.'

'So he'll give an honest account of our actions,' Fura said. 'In-cluding how pleasant we were.'

'It'll take more than one man's word to get that squadron off our backs,' Adrana said.

'Concerning which . . .' Lagganvor looked at his two captains in turn, favouring neither. 'I suppose a return sweep will be chanced?'

'When Paladin says that the weather's rising sharply enough to mask our sweep,' Fura answered. 'Not before. Why the worry,

Lag? It was just two sweeps, and nothing has happened since.' Her eyes narrowed. 'Are you more than usually concerned?'

Lagganvor sucked at the spot of blood where he had chewed the nail. 'No, I am perfectly satisfied that the sweeps originated from some distant, random vessel that just happened to take a passing interest in Werranwell's wreck. But still . . .'

'Still what?' Adrana asked.

'It would be nice to know.'

'May I interject?' Doctor Eddralder queried. 'I have some . . . concerning news.'

Fura nodded sombrely. 'About Meggery?'

'Not about Meggery. I think she will be all right, with observation. But someone has been stealing from my supplies.'

Lagganvor jerked back, frowning hard – but glad perhaps to have a topic of conversation besides the squadron and their chances of evasion.

'Stealing?'

'Indeed.' The long face dipped in affirmation. 'I had a suspicion, but I could not be sure. I wondered if Merrix had failed to keep a proper accounting, but then I started noticing it for myself. It's come to a head with Meggery. I wanted to give her a topical salve, better than anything I had with me on the *Merry Mare*, and I found that we were down to just two tubes. I am quite certain there were three when we left.'

'Are you sure of this?' Fura asked.

'Perfectly.'

'What of the supplies we bought in Mulgracen?'

'They were only ever a stop-gap, and my calculations for our needs did not allow for petty theft.'

'Then it can only be someone who stayed behind.' Fura was holding up a finger at a time. 'Tindouf and Surt were in vacuum suits the whole while, weren't they? It would've been difficult for them to move around the ship without bumping into things and making a sound.'

'Merrix was in the sighting room the entire time,' Adrana said.

'Which leaves two possibilities, if we discount the doctor himself,' said Fura. 'It is either you, dear sister, or . . .'

'Strambli,' Eddralder said. 'And I'm afraid the suspicion was already half-formed in my own mind.'

'I don't understand,' Lagganvor said. 'You've already saved her once, Eddralder – brought her back from the brink of death. If there's any one of us that she ought to trust completely, it's you.'

'That,' Eddralder said, 'is precisely what concerns me.'

'Someone fetch her,' Fura said. 'I won't have common pilfering on my ship—'

'Begging your collective pardons,' Paladin interjected. 'But the solar flux is on a sharp rising trend. I believe it will soon be a propitious time to consider a return sweep.'

*

Another hour saw Fura with her face over the glowing circle of the sweeper, studying the speckled patterns with a hard-frowning intensity, as if they were animal entrails that held a glimpse of the future.

'Declining,' Paladin stated.

Fura triggered the sweep. It made one chiming tone, and from the epicentre of the console a single glowing circle expanded in circumference, demarking the outward pulse. Adrana held her breath, trying to fix in her mind the transient pattern of speckles caused by solar weather, so that she might identify any interlopers. The speckles came and went very rapidly, so it was a little like another sort of game: one in which she had to memorise an assortment of items on a tray, given a glimpse of only a few seconds. A hard task for a person, she thought, but not so problematic for Paladin. Not only was his short-term memory infallible, but he had excellent noise-discrimination algorithms. If there were three or four ships out there, and they were near enough to be picked up on this low-energy pulse, he would pick them out.

The return signal came in. The display froze, permitting the eye to take in as much information as possible.

Fura stared at it in silence. So did Adrana, Lagganvor and Prozor.

'The pulse has returned,' Paladin said.

It was a second or two before Adrana answered him. 'We know, Paladin. We can see it for ourselves.'

'I have an initial estimate for the number of hard returns, and their positions and displacements.'

Fura pushed herself away from the sweeper. Lagganvor touched a hand to his throat and coughed gently. Prozor ran a palm through her hair, making a sharp bristling sound.

'How many?' Adrana asked quietly.

'Nine, ten . . . maybe more,' Lagganvor answered in the same low volume. 'And the nearest of them far closer than I was expecting.' He pointed at the sweeper, with its engraved patterns of concentric and radial lines. 'One hundred thousand leagues, if not a little nearer.'

'Why're we whispering?' Fura asked, in a whisper of her own.

'Because we're dead,' Prozor said. 'Or we soon will be.'

'Paladin,' Lagganvor said, raising his voice just a fraction. 'Might we have those figures, please? It would be helpful to know . . . just what we're dealing with.'

'I confirm twelve hard returns, excluding the *Merry Mare*. The ships are dispersed in a loose formation subtending a solid angle of approximately forty-five degrees, suggesting that they have converged from multiple directions. The nearest, as Mister Lagganvor has intimated, is at a distance of a little under one hundred thousand leagues, and the furthest approximately twice that distance.'

'Did you get their speeds?' Adrana asked.

'I must caution that I have only approximate values, and with diminishing precision for the fainter returns. To obtain more reliable figures, I would need a differential sweep.'

'Give us what you have,' Fura said.

'The ships for which I have somewhat reliable figures are converging on our fixed position at approximately twelve thousand leagues per hour. Unless there is some change in our relative motions, they will be on us in eight hours.'

There was a silence. Each had counted on being discovered at some point, knowing that a stern-chase or engagement was a certain prospect in their futures, unless they abandoned civilisation altogether. But even in her worst imaginings, Adrana had always assumed that they would have days of preparation once that first threatening sighting had been made.

Not this.

Not even a third of a day.

'How'd they sniff us out?' Fura asked. 'One or two of 'em blundering into us, I can accept. If you've got twenty coves searching a dark room, they're more likely to find something if they split up.'

'Unless they already knew where to look,' Prozor said. 'Unless they was led to us, somehow.'

Lagganvor nodded gravely, as if this was a dark and vexing possibility that he was ashamed not to have already seen for himself. 'It does seem that they've had uncommon good fortune, to have fallen upon us like this. Unless we gave more of ourselves away in Mulgracen than we realised . . .'

'At least we've got a hundred thousand leagues to play with,' Fura said. 'We sail now, any direction we please, so long as it is *fast*. Do you disagree, Lag?'

He sighed, as if he had already examined every other possibility before arriving at this dispiriting conclusion. 'I cannot see the virtue in not running. Of course, the new patient is an unwelcome complication.'

'There's nothing complicated about it: we can still keep our word to Werranwell. Once we're out of this jam, we'll find a means to reunite the happy crew. But only when it suits us, and if that's a month or a year from now . . .' Without consultation Fura drifted to the nearest speaking grille. 'Tindouf! All sail, and all ions, as quick as you can.'

*

Merrix was sucking on her frozen fingertips, encouraging the blood back into them from her time in the sighting room.

'I didn't see a thing, Adrana, although it wasn't easy, having to look back at the Congregation, with all those worlds spangling out at me like little purple lanterns. I'm worried I missed something . . .'

'Let me see those hands,' Eddralder said, encouraging his daughter to offer her fingers to him.

'If you missed it, Merrix, then you can bet the rest of us would have, too,' Adrana said.

'Maybe not Mister Lagganvor. I don't think he misses much.'

'No, but there's only one of him and he's a lot more useful to us during a boarding operation than he is on sighting watch.'

They were in the Kindness Room. Adrana had an aversion to the place, too readily reminded of the time she had spent in it being schooled as Bosa's successor. Her skin goose-pimpled with the tactile memory of electric shocks and needles. That had been Bosa being gentle and considerate with her, too.

It did not pay to dwell on the things that had happened in this room to those who had not been her favourites.

'There's been a development,' Adrana said, addressing Eddralder, the real reason for her visit to the infirmary. 'Ships are closing in on us in an organised formation. We have to move now, and possibly keep moving. I'm afraid it alters your obligation to Meggery.'

He glanced from his examination of Merrix's fingers to the heavily bandaged woman strapped to the main bed. Meggery was either sedated or still deeply unconscious. 'My obligation remains the same, which is to tend to this patient.'

'It may be a while before we get a chance to bring her home. If at all.'

'Fura has made this decision?'

Adrana nodded humbly. 'I . . . endorse it. It's a matter of immediate survival.'

'Merrix: would you help with the swab?'

Her fingers warmed up again, Merrix set about applying some blue-tinged unguent to the main burn around Meggery's head and neck. Despite the hours she had just spent on sighting duty, her expression was one of perfect concentration and devotion. There was a tremor in her hand, the consequence of Glimmery's chemical enslavement, but it was not nearly so acute as when she had first come aboard.

'Is she going to be all right?'

'There's concussion,' Eddralder answered her. 'But no skull fracture. When do we move?'

'We already are. The sails have been run out.'

She had already felt it, even if Eddralder and his daughter had not. The ship was straining into its rigging, creaking like old furniture. Beyond the Kindness Room, beyond the hull, the catchcloth sails were billowing, gathering the cold dark pressure of all the slippery, invisible particles that streamed directly from the Old Sun's belly. 'Our acceleration is slight, but it's sufficient for our needs. In eight hours, when the squadron closes on our old position, we can be a few hundred leagues away.'

'How in the worlds will that help us at all?'

'It will – just enough. They won't risk sweeping us again, not when they'd be in equal range of our guns, and in all other respects we're impossible to find.'

'Yet they found us.'

'No,' Adrana corrected. 'They found the *Merry Mare*. There's an excellent chance they still don't know our exact position, not even with those sweeps, and besides – we have an advantage now that we were lacking only a short while ago. In fact, I was just on my way to see how Surt's doing with the installation.'

*

'Mmf,' said Surt. 'Mmf, mmf, mmfle-mffle mmf . . .' She frowned, paused, took the screwdriver from between her teeth, deftly done since both her hands were already encumbered with a variety of precision tools, and continued: 'I was meaning to say, it ain't going any faster with you leaning over me like that, or checkin' in every five minutes.'

'I was just coming to offer encouragement,' Adrana said.

'I'm tryin' as hard as I can. There wasn't anything I could do earlier, with the ship creakin' and groanin' like she was.'

'The sails are all run out sweetly now. Short of being shot at, we should have a smooth ride from now on.'

Surt jabbed a probe into one of the studs fastened to the inner wall of the bone room, narrowing her eyes at a portable electrical meter with a green-glowing dial. 'Do you and your sister really think you can get a whisper out of any old skull, if you put your minds to it?'

'Perhaps we have an inflated sense of our own capabilities,' Adrana said. 'But if the skull's viable, and properly connected, I think we have an excellent chance of using it. We shall see soon enough, won't we?'

The skull had survived its passage to the new bone room with no indication of damage, no bright new chips or scratches, and Surt was quite well advanced in hooking it into place. There were eyelets already drilled into the skull at a dozen or so spots, which were the attachment points for the spring-loaded cables that allowed it to float in the middle of the room, acoustically isolated, and these were all secured and tensioned. Now Surt was connecting and testing the grounding wires, which were a small but vital part of the arrangement.

'Hold this for me, will you,' Surt said, passing Adrana a small pair of pliers, while she used both sets of fingers to crimp two grounding wires together.

'I am very glad to make myself temporarily useful. I don't mean to push, Surt, after all the work you have already done for us, with Paladin and the ship . . . but having a working skull could make all the difference to us, in the coming months.'

Surt jammed something else between her lips. 'Mmmf . . . mngle . . . managed without until now, ain't we? Maybe that's tellin' us somethin'. Such as, we don't need a skull and all the troubles that come with it.'

'I might concur. But that squadron changes everything. If we'd had a working skull, we'd have had a better chance of picking up on intelligence on the squadron's movements, and having warning that they were near.'

'Or we could have given ourselves away, if there was some cove tunin' to our gabble.'

'There's always a risk, but it's offset by the advantages. Plus, and I don't mean this to seem conceited . . .'

Surt took back the pliers.

'Course you don't.'

'But Fura and I are better than average Bone Readers. When we were signalling each other between ships we learned to control our thoughts very well. We can take, but we don't give.'

'I'm glad you've got such faith in yerselves.'

Adrana pulled back, appraising the skull as if it were a new territory for the taking, its ridges, dents, fissures, eyeholes and input sockets the markers of a landscape she would come to know intimately, and – in time – fully conquer.

'How long?'

'Depends how reckless you're feeling. I'll have done all I can by the top of the hour. But I'd let your precious new baby settle into its cradle for a watch or two, before you start coo-cooing to 'im.'

Adrana managed a wry smile. 'You really don't like our profession, do you?'

Surt halted in her work, giving the skull a long and measured appraisal. 'I'll plug these things in. That I can do. Better'n most, I don't doubt. I've put more grounding on than Trusko ever insisted on, but you'll thank me for it if you happen to be in here when we run into a Niner. And I ain't so foolish as to think our livelihoods don't depend on intelligence, and for that we need boneys, and boneys need skulls. But you could offer me all the quoins between here and Daxary and it wouldn't turn my opinion. Even if those quoins were all still worth a fortune. I'll do my job here, but there's nothing around the Old Sun that'd persuade me to be in *this* room with *that* door shut.'

'It's just technology,' Adrana said. 'Strange technology, I'll grant you: curious old technology that we don't understand at all, and perhaps never will, but there's nothing supernatural about it. To these aliens – these things that left these skulls behind – it must have all been as commonplace to them as telegraphs and telephones to us.'

'You go believing that if you like,' Surt answered. 'But I know where I stand on the matter. It's shivery business, and in the long run no good'll come of it.'

'Then it's a very good job we're not concerning ourselves with the long run.' Adrana permitted a frosty, business-like tone to enter her voice: she was done with amiable companionship for now. 'Inform me the moment you think the skull is ready. I'll expect no shortcomings with the installation.'

Surt was muttering something about 'yer high ladyship' as Adrana made her way back to the front of the ship.

*

She found her in the galley, polishing tankards.

'Stram,' she started, smiling so as not to put the other woman on edge. 'I just wanted to—'

Strambli jerked as if she had been tapped on the back in a dark room.

'Am I s'posed to be on sighting watch, Adrana?'

'No – Surt should be taking over from Merrix shortly, as soon as she's done in the bone room, and even then she won't take a full stint, not with the rising weather. We'll run half-watches now. It was just . . . look, could you come to the Kindness Room for a moment?'

Strambli's eyes seemed to swell and diminish so that their usual disparity in size was even more exaggerated. She had been polishing one of the lidded tankards and her fist tightened on the handle. She seemed, for a moment, to consider the possibility of employing it as a bludgeon.

Then some wiser instinct prevailed and she returned the

tankard to its allotted magnetic hook. It clacked into place, secured against any movement of the ship.

'He said I could have as much medicine as I wanted.'

'That was when he thought you were complaining about a burned palm. But it wasn't that at all, was it?'

Adrana had told Fura she was about to confront Strambli. Now her sister appeared, pushing her metal hand through the wild black curls of her hair. 'You know a good thing, Stram, you'll sit down with us and explain why you felt the need to pilfer.'

'It weren't how it looks.'

They went to the Kindness Room, where Eddralder was taking Meggery's temperature. He looked up with a distracted air, as if he had completely forgotten about the pilfering.

'She says she can explain her theft,' Adrana said.

'Theft is theft,' Fura said.

'And we're all pirates. Shall we agree not to judge Stram until we've heard her side? She's proven her value to this crew over and over. Hasn't she, Fura?'

Fura struggled, just as if she had been set a difficult mathematics problem. 'I suppose . . . those baubles we've cracked . . . we'd have found 'em a lot harder otherwise.'

'And Stramb kept her nerve down in the Rumbler and has always served very capably.'

Strambli looked at the sisters with sudden alarm. 'Is my job up for debate?'

'Elevate your leg for me, Strambli,' said Eddralder with a gentle forcefulness.

'Which leg?'

'You know very well.'

It was her left leg that had been hurt in the slip with the Ghostie blade, and this was the one she was now persuaded to stretch out. Eddralder pinched at the hem of Strambli's trousers, drawing them gradually up the length of her shin.

'It ain't strange for a wound to throb a bit, long after you got it,' Strambli said. 'I near as hell sliced my own thumb off back

in ninety-seven and that still twinges when it turns damp . .'
But her jaw tensed as Eddralder pushed the hem of her trousers
past the site of the original injury.

Adrana tensed. She had no stomach for this sort of thing.

'I can see why you wanted the salve,' Eddralder said.

The Ghostie wound had been deep, but not broad, and when
she had recovered from her surgery in Wheel Strizzardy there
had only been a staple-sized scar to show for it. The scar was
still evident, but only as a pale scratch in a much wider area
of inflammation, reddened and visibly swollen. Around the
perimeter of the inflammation was a crusting of dried salve,
several layers thick.

'Oh, Stram,' Adrana said, overwhelmed by a sudden rush of
empathy, all thoughts of recrimination banished from her mind.
'You should've told Doctor Eddralder as soon as this started
flaring up again. It must hurt terribly.'

Strambli grimaced. 'I thought it'd go down on its own. Just
needed a bit of salve.'

'It was a slip with one of their knives,' Fura said, after a brief
hesitation. 'Just an innocent accident.'

'It wasn't a slip,' Strambli snapped. 'I ain't that clumsy. That
knife twisted in my hand, *made* me stab myself. Oh, why do I
bother? I've been telling you since the day itself, and you don't
want to listen.'

Adrana took Strambli's hand. 'Stram was afraid, and I don't
much blame her for that. Who wouldn't be?'

'I'm sorry about taking the salve,' Strambli said. Her voice
began to break, as if all the strain of concealment had at last
overwhelmed her. 'You can have back what I didn't use yet. It
was getting harder to put it on, anyway. Am I still in trouble?'

'You might be,' Fura said.

Eddralder smiled urgently. The lines of his face were not ac-
commodating to the act of smiling, the expression looking as
natural on him as a grin upon a horse.

'We will do what we can. On that you have my word.'

'I know what you're all thinking,' Strambli said, with a rising defiance. 'You ain't saying it, but it's there anyway. You're think-ing that if he can't get this under control, there's only going to be one option left. But I won't allow him. He ain't takin' it!'

7

The skull floated in its spring-loaded cradle; its variegated colours washed into an even pale redness by the surrounding lights of the bone room.

'Surt's done a very good job,' Adrana said. 'I insisted on additional grounding, over and above the usual specifications. It'll serve us well if we need to communicate during a solar storm.'

'Is it ready for use?'

'She said it wouldn't hurt to let it stabilise for a watch or two. But I think we may risk it now.'

'Let's go in,' Fura declared. She took Adrana's hand, guiding her across the threshold as if they were venturing into a playhouse. The skull was bigger than the one that had been in here before, and its size meant they had to pick their way around it with the wariness of jewel thieves. The springs gave off a soft, diminishing giggle as they absorbed the occasional accidental contact.

The sisters completed one circumnavigation of the skull.

'Shall I?' Adrana asked, indicating the door.

'Yes. Let's do this properly, or not at all.'

Adrana hinged the door shut, then spun the internal locking wheel, tightening the seal until all the usual sounds of the ship were excluded. Fura, meanwhile, used a control panel to turn down the interior lighting even more. Bone rooms were always lit by electrical or gas appliances, rather than lightvine.

The skull seemed to swell even more in the darkened room. The sisters moved around it in circling opposition, two planets on either side of a bone-made star. Besides the eye sockets, there were ominous, dark-stained canals which might once have served organs of hearing, balance, or smell – although their placements made it hard to judge. There were cracks and clefts that had come about through age or neglect and which had been fixed back together, but not so tightly as to banish light. There was also, uncommonly, still a jawbone attached to the skull. A barricade of fine, needle-like teeth filled the mouth. Above that opening, sagging like an over-filled postal sack, loomed an oversized cranium, into which had been drilled the majority of the input nodes.

An abundance of twinkly glimmered out of the skull like fog-bound glimpses of some marvellous night-lit city. There might still be some organic material in there besides bone; lacy remnants of circulatory or nervous structures, delicate as cobwebs – but it was the twinkly that mattered to a Bone Reader. It did not realise, or had forgotten, or was past the point of sane understanding, that it was no longer embedded in living cellular tissue; that it no longer had a brain or a mind to serve.

Adrana unhooked the neural crowns from the wall. She passed one to Fura and settled the other over her own scalp, pressing down on the short bristles of her hair. Fura fixed on her own crown and spooled out the contact wire, pinching its termination plug between her flesh fingers.

On the other side of the skull, Adrana did likewise.

'In at the same time?'

'Why not,' Fura said. 'We have the skill to double-plug, even if most don't.'

'The only question is, go in on the same socket, or two different ones? I should have squeezed that shock-headed boy while we had the chance, found out the best way to connect. He'd have squealed easily enough.'

'What worked for their boney wouldn't necessarily work

for us,' Adrana reminded her. 'And there's no saying that we'd both get the optimum signal on the same socket. I agree we can double-plug, but I think we should start as far apart as possible, then converge.'

Fura waited a perfunctory moment, before nodding. 'I concur. Shall I take the pre-frontal socket?'

'Willingly. I shall take the occipital.'

The sisters hesitated. They were cautious, even fearful. But they were not unprepared.

Their sockets engaged with a clean, synchronised snapping of polished metal, and the skull jiggled a little, but soon the springs brought it back to quietude, and the sisters abided. Very gingerly, Fura closed her eyelids and folded shut the neural bridge's darkening visors – two flaps like the blinkers they put on greyhounds – and willed her mind to that state of anxious receptiveness that was like a house with its doors and windows flung open, inviting a haunting wind to prowl its rooms and corridors.

She did not have the slightest doubt that Adrana was enforcing a similar state upon herself.

She heard her sister's breathing. She heard her own.

Nothing came.

Nothing came and nothing continued to come, and she was not troubled by that because she had only tried this one socket and no skull surrendered its secrets that willingly. Although she could not see her sister, she sensed her stillness and understood that Adrana had met with a similar lack of success. They waited to be sure, and without a spoken exchange moved to unplug at the same instant. The skull trembled, and then re-trembled as they plugged in again at different points, nearer now to each other. Fura had already memorised the sockets' positions and she was able to plug in by touch alone.

Still nothing came.

The quality of that nothingness was a little altered, although not in any way that was easily expressible. It was as if there were shades of silence, shades of absence, and this socket carried a different hue to its predecessor. That was because the wiring beneath the socket was addressing the twinkly by different channels to the first, colouring the neural signals that were in turn feeding back into the crown, and into Fura's head.

Was there . . . ?

No. Still nothing.

By shared instinct they abandoned their second nodes as one, and then re-plugged in, now with only the cranial ridge of the skull between them.

Instantly Fura picked up the presence of a carrier signal. The twinkly was whispering to her, communicating its readiness to send and receive. In other skulls, in other ships, dispersed far and wide across the Congregation and its bordering spaces, nuggets of active twinkly would have detected the newly-activated presence of this skull, and by extension the faint presences of the two monkey minds connected to it.

'I've something,' Fura murmured.

After a moment Adrana answered: 'So do I. And I think we should de-couple now. We know this skull is working; let us not risk exposing ourselves unnecessarily.'

'I wish to know that the skull is capable of picking up intelligence. One intercept, one snippet, that's all I ask. If that squadron's communicating by skull I'd like to know its intentions.'

'You already know its intentions. What more evidence do you need?'

The skull jiggled; it was Adrana making to unplug her own connection.

'Wait,' Fura said.

Something was coming through on the carrier. A silence beneath the silence, a nothing carved out of nothing, a fretwork of absences in which the language faculties of Fura's brain could not help but detect (even as they might have wished to find comforting randomness) the signatures of grammar, syntax, speech and intention.

And beneath all that, the shade of a personality, faint yet distinct.

I know you for what you are.

A furtive, faint, weasel-like presence had pushed itself into her head. Adrana stifled an inhalation – a near-gasp. She had not unplugged completely and some large or small part of the same declaration must have reached her.

I know you for what you are, Ness sisters. And I am coming for you.

The voice was like a screw, drilling itself into the hollow behind her eyes. Fura knew with total conviction that she must disconnect, and do so with all haste, but a curious, dreamlike paralysis enveloped her. Her limbs felt encased in some sluggish, resistive medium.

'Whoever you are, get out of my head.'

Too late, Ness sister. I am inside. I know your natures, and I know that you are nearer than you would wish. Only a matter of time now. Dare you flee? You should flee, I think. It would make for very good sport.

At last she broke the paralysis and severed the connection to the skull. Adrana uncoupled at the same moment, as if she too had been in the grip of that frightening torpor.

Fura tore the neural crown off her head before she had even folded back the blinkers. She was out of the skull, physically decoupled. But she could still feel that voice and presence, ringing in her like a bell's after-chime.

Wordlessly she put the neural crown back on its wall rack. She reached over and took Adrana's crown, replacing it next to her own. She elevated the light-level to its original brightness.

The sisters moved to each other. They took each other's hands, cold metal in flesh, warm flesh in metal, and pulled each other closer. Both were shivering. The contact of that presence, those few short seconds of unwanted communion, had been almost more than they could endure. The sisters held each other until their shivering began to abate, and some approximation of normal thought returned to their heads, with that after-chime finally extinguished.

At last Adrana swallowed. 'I've sensed other minds through the skull. Yours. Those other crews we snooped on. Even poor Mister Chasco, before we burned him.'

'So've I,' Fura answered. 'Some rum voices, too. But nothing like that.'

'I was skullbound to Chasco when he died. That wasn't something I care to remember. But even the force of his death didn't touch me like that quiet little voice.'

'It *was* quiet,' Fura agreed. 'And small, like you said. I almost felt it wasn't a grown person addressing us at all, but a child. And I don't mean a teenager, the way it was with us.'

'A boy,' Adrana was nodding.

'A small, quiet, cruel little boy. The kind of boy who pulls the legs off things to see them squirm. He was only in us for a few seconds, and still I feel as if I want to scrub out the inside of my head with bleach.'

Adrana wrapped her arms around Fura. They hugged each other as if to dispel the last traces of their uninvited guest. 'We should have known this day would come,' Adrana said.

'This day?'

'When we met our match as Bone Readers.'

There was a distant, muffled thump against the door to the bone room. Someone was knocking on it from outside, which could only mean one thing.

A difficulty.

*

Surt rubbed at eyes that were red-rimmed and bleary from squinting into telescope tubes.

'I ought to still be up there, given what I saw.'

'Not with the flux you've already soaked up,' Lagganvor said.

'It's dipping now, ain't it? I couldn't see any ghost-light in our sails at all, and the compasses ain't whirly-gigging.'

'This is just a lull, if the forecasts are anything to go by. Still, while it's holding we ought to keep eyes in the sighting room. I'll take the next stint, if that's acceptable to all?'

'Drink this,' Prozor said, offering Surt a tankard of coffee, freshly warmed.

Surt wrapped her shivering fingers around the handle and pressed the lid to her lips, hinging it open just enough to sip. 'Are we going as fast as we can?'

'On all sail,' Fura confirmed. 'Catchcloth and ord'nary. We daren't use ions, though. They'd make us hot, and if our tail starts to glow they might spy it, even across tens of thousands of leagues.'

'I saw sail-flash,' Surt said. She gulped, swallowed some more. 'Big and bright and close. Multiple speckles. I thought it was them, the squadron, I mean, but even as I was thinkin' it, I knew it didn't make no sense. I wasn't using any sort of magnification, and there it was, poppin' out at me, spangling like twinkly.'

'Aft of us?' Lagganvor asked, wrapping a scarf around his neck. It was chilly in the sighting room and any sort of heater tended to fog the optics.

'Yes – aft. Right from where we was, only a few hours ago.'

'Only one thing back there that can cause sail-flash,' Prozor said, bristling her hair, her face wide and anxious. 'Has to be the *Merry Mare*. But they can't be sailin', not so soon after we left 'em.'

'We gave them materials,' Fura said. 'Perhaps it was her crew, fixing things up. Sails flash when you're moving 'em around, stitching 'em back and so on.'

Prozor's look was doubtful.

'It ain't that, girlie, and you know it.'

'You told me it came on suddenly?' Adrana said to Surt.

Surt nodded meekly, as if she was being cross-examined. 'There wasn't anything, and then there was. It kept up, too, for a good couple of minutes, then tailed off again.'

'What Surt has described,' Lagganvor said, scratching at his stubble, 'seems consistent with a ship being attacked with sail-shot, much as we incapacitated them in the first place.' He flashed one of his decisive, confident smiles. 'I'll see what I can see, shall I?'

'Werranwell will think it's us, going back on our promise,' Fura said, studying Lagganvor's back as he departed the control room.

Surt was starting to look a little warmer. 'Why do you think they've stopped?'

'Takin' time to load their batteries again, most prob'ly,' Prozor said, 'whichever ship is dishin' out the shots.' She paused to bite into a semi-stale biscuit. 'Or they may be puttin' a little more punch into that sail-shot, because of the distance, and they've got to let their muzzles cool. Could be other reasons. We ain't even sure it's sail-shot.'

Fura bent her face over the sweeper, her palms prickling with the desire to send off a ranging pulse. She wanted to know what was out there and how close it now was. But Paladin had warned her that the solar weather was entering a temporary lull, and there would be no safe cover for some while.

'This is wrong,' she said, jutting out her jaw. 'I didn't set the cove up to be shot at like this. He should tell 'em they're shooting at the wrong ship.'

'Bit difficult, without a squawk or a skull,' Adrana said.

Fura shot her a recriminatory glance. 'You'd rather we left him free to blab about us to all and sundry? I took his toys away for a reason, and I'd do it again in a heartbeat. This isn't my *fault*. This is . . .' Her fingers made a bedspring creak as they flexed. '. . . corporate negligence.'

Adrana nodded. 'And I'm sure that will be a great consolation to Captain Werranwell, as he's drawing his last breath.'

'We could squawk 'em,' Surt proposed timidly, as if she half expected to be cuffed across the face for her troubles. 'Just once, alerting them that they've got the wrong saps?' She looked from face to face. 'We're sailing handsomely now, aren't we? We can send off a squawk, steer hard, and still keep 'em off our backs.'

'It's all well and noble to try,' Prozor said, sending the other woman an understanding look. 'But my guess is those ships know exactly who and what they're shootin' at.'

Indignation welled up in Surt.

'They can't do that!'

Prozor fixed the sharp angles of her face into a diffident, apologetic expression, as if she was going to have to explain a very unpleasant and upsetting truth to a child. 'There's some quoins behind this, Surt. Banks and cartels and so on. Investment houses. Chambers of commerce. Shipping companies. Now ask yourself. When has wealth ever acted with care and compassion, when there's somethin' standin' between it and a bigger profit?'

Fura nodded vigorously. 'It's true. Prozor knows that as well as any of us. And it's *them* that are responsible for this trouble, not us.' She set a fierce edge on her voice. 'I did all right by Captain Werranwell – treated him kindly, kept my word. That doesn't make me responsible for every other bit of bad luck that happens to the cove!'

'We gave 'em our words,' Surt said, with an equal and surprising fierceness, spittle bursting between her lips. 'You weren't just speaking for yourself when you made those promises.'

'That was then—' Fura began.

'No, it's now,' Surt persisted. 'And I don't care what they know, or why they're shooting at him – we've got to tell 'em it's wrong. We turn a blind eye to this, we're no better than the hag we took this ship from!'

Prozor looked anguished. If she had only lately been the one about to lay out an unsettling truth, she now had the discomfited look of someone who'd had their certainties chopped out from under them.

'Maybe just one squawk.'

'I thought you were on my side!' Fura said.

'I ain't on your side or her side. I'm on my side, and my side's sayin' Surt might not be wrong about this.' She looked at the Ness sisters in turn: a sharp stare, as if she were their private consciences. 'I ain't saying it'll help him or us, but it'll make it plain as the nose on your face that we ain't playin' by Bosa Sennen's rules.'

Lagganvor's breathless voice burst from the speaking grille. 'Surt was completely correct. I'm seeing multiple incidents of sail-flash exactly where she said, and it's entirely consistent with the position of the *Merry Mare*. They've resumed their attack.'

'We could go back to the bone room,' Adrana whispered. 'One transmission: brief as can be.'

Fura gave a quick shudder of her head, as if she had bitten into something unexpectedly sour. 'I ain't giving that weasely little voice another chance to drill into my skull, and nor are you. Not until we're ready for him, and right now I don't *feel* ready.'

'Then we squawk, stressing that they're attacking an innocent party. Surt and Prozor have the right of it: this is exactly what Bosa wouldn't do, which is why we *must* do it. Now, may we have some silence? Lagganvor will benefit from the ship being as still as possible. He may catch a glimpse of their muzzles.'

In that stillness, the ordinary noises of the ship – the humming of her circuits, the wheezing of air circulators, the creak and groan of the hull – became magnified and harsh to the ear. Even the ticking of Fura's stopwatch gained a subtle malevolence, as if it were the beating of war drums. Fura did not set out to hold her own breath, but under such circumstances it was very hard indeed not to stop breathing. She imagined Lagganvor fixing his eye to the lens, taking it out of its socket, rubbing it clean on his scarf, so that he could press it more closely to the optics and eliminate any movement caused by his own body.

The sweeper sounded.

Three loud chimes emanated from the console. By instinct, all turned to regard Fura. But she was nowhere near the sweeper console yet, and no other hands had been on the controls.

The display formed a fat, ragged-edged blob, like a smeared thumbprint, very close to the middle of the display.

'The fool,' Adrana said.

Fura met her eyes.

'He's trying to get out a distress signal, the only way he can.'

Perhaps it was meant that way, or perhaps Werranwell intended to demonstrate – by advertising himself so blatantly with his sweeper – that he was *not* the target the squadron ought to be shooting at; not a hostile party, and entirely ill-equipped to fend off such an attack.

It had no effect.

'This is Lagganvor,' came his voice from the grille, when Fura deemed it time to hear from him again. 'I've seen bursts of muzzle flash, spread across forty or forty-five degrees of sky. It's faint, almost at the limit of what my eye can manage, and very hard to discern against the background lights of the Congregation, but I would stake my life that I was not imagining it.'

'Is it continuing?' Adrana asked.

'I believe so. My sense is that the attacking ships are firing one at a time, one ship after another, from the leftmost part of their formation to the rightmost, in a coordinated fashion, before the first ship opens fire again. They must be firing hard, then giving their guns time to cool and be reloaded, while the next in line takes over. I need hardly state that each ship will require a differential, time-dependent firing solution, calculated to allow for relative motion, so the degree of cooperation must be excellent, to say nothing of the evident quality of their pieces and gun crews, and all while maintaining squawk and sweeper silence . . .'

'Yes, thank you for that encouragement,' Fura said testily. 'We don't need you writing their advertising copy for them, Lag.'

The sweeper sounded again, another three strident chimes.

'It's not helping him,' Adrana said. 'They've had time to pick up the first set of sweeps and cool their guns.'

'He could run out all the surrender flags between here and the Sunwards and it wouldn't help him,' Prozor said.

'Lagganvor,' Fura said.

'I am listening.'

'We're going to send a single squawk, explaining they've got the wrong ship.'

'It won't help.'

'I know, but we're doing it anyway. You've seen those muzzle bursts. Do you think they're closer than ten thousand leagues?'

'Somewhat more distant. But please do not stake our lives on that opinion.'

Fura unclipped the squawk mouthpiece. She rubbed it clean, lifted it to her lips, then depressed the transmission switch.

'This is Captain Ness, of the sunjammer *Revenger*. You are targeting an innocent party, the *Merry Mare* under Captain Werranwell. I encourage you to cease fire.'

She released the transmission switch and was moving to hang the mouthpiece back up next to the squawk console when a voice crackled over the loudspeaker.

'The squawk, Captain Ness? Why such crudity, when you have such a fine piece of bone at your disposal?'

It was a level, confident voice, high in its pitch, and by its timbre Fura judged that it belonged to a young man, perhaps even a precocious adolescent. She had never heard it before, but she recognised the will behind it with a deadening conviction. It was the same individual who had pushed his mind into theirs, in the bone room.

She permitted it to continue.

'Truthfully, I was expecting more in the way of threat and bluster. Can it be that you are of sound enough mind to realise that you are comprehensively out-ranged and out-gunned?' That voice gave a brief, mirthless chuckle. 'Heh. It's a fine enough try, even if you mean to distract me from my purpose. But if the ship in question were – as you put it – an innocent party – would they not have broadcast their identity by now, or attempted to proclaim their innocence by means of their skull?'

Fura took a deep breath. She still had the squawk mouthpiece in her hand, and it would only take one press of the switch to reply to the anonymous transmission.

She was being goaded into a response, and she knew it.

'Do not give him the pleasure,' Adrana whispered.

Fura clipped the mouthpiece back in place.

'I shan't.'

But the high, querulous voice had drilled into her again, as thoroughly as it had done through the bones. She did not know the name behind it, nor the face, but her imagination was already rushing to fill that void.

Had she ever despised someone so readily, on such fleeting and distant acquaintance?

'They won't have got a hard fix on us with one squawk,' Fura said. 'But a second might do it. Do you think that man – that boy – spoke for the squadron as a whole?'

'He said "I",' Adrana replied. 'Just as he did when he came through the skull.'

'I noticed.' Her fingers creaked again. There was only lung-stuff between them, but she imagined the gristly crunch of bone and tendon, yielding under the pressure of her grasp. 'He took responsibility, at least. I'm glad of it. There needn't be any ambiguity.'

'Any ambiguity when?' Adrana asked.

'At the time of our meeting,' Fura said. 'Because I very much intend that we'll meet, and that when we do it won't end well for that boy. I'll pull his spine out with my own fingers and rattle it in front of his eyes. Before then, though . . . we have unfinished business with Captain Werranwell.' She raised her voice, grinning at them all. 'It's madness. Ain't any gainsaying that. But it's beautiful madness as well. It's the last thing anyone will expect of us, the thing that puts us in harm's way, and brings us no benefit whatsoever. So we'll do it. We turn!'

8

Meggery sneezed, her eyes watering and her nose still pinched against the smelling salts Fura had talked Eddralder into using. Even as she came to a sullen, hollow-eyed consciousness, she held her limbs in a jolted, disarticulated fashion, for all the world like a doll that had been tossed to the floor by a disconsolate child.

'Where am I?'

'I'll tell you,' Fura said, begging Eddralder aside and lifting a lidded beaker to Meggery's lips. 'But there's a condition or two.'

'Chaff to your conditions. Just tell me where I am.'

Fura sighed with an exaggerated patience. 'I'll answer all your questions, but you mustn't interrupt or quibble. That'll save us both a great deal of trouble in the long run.' She reached for Meggery's blue-cobwebbed hands, lifting them from the sheets still wrapped loosely around her bed-bound form. Meggery flinched at the sudden touch of metal against her skin. 'You're Meggery,' Fura said. 'Do you remember that much? Nod if you remember.'

Meggery did not nod, but some wild spark in her eyes offered Fura the affirmation she sought.

'Good. We may as well begin with the essentials. You are – were – the Master of Ions on a ship called the *Merry Mare*.' She squeezed her fingers, as if sharing a lovers' confidence, feeling the roughness where Meggery's smallest finger was missing. 'I took your ship. I attacked you and disabled you, because I hoped you might have things I could use. That didn't go as well as I'd hoped. You weren't carrying much, and by equal bad fortune you got hurt in the process. I never meant for that to happen, and I ain't too pleased that it did.'

Meggery opened her mouth to speak, but Fura released her hand and touched a metal finger to Meggery's lips, as quickly as if she were pressing down on a fly.

'I'm not Bosa Sennen. I'm Captain Ness, as I said over the squawk, and I only ever meant to take the things I needed. Meggery, I made two promises to your captain. The first was that I'd leave him with whatever he needed to fix up the damage we did. The second was to take care of any injured parties, which is where you come in. Tell her, Eddralder, what happened?'

'You were burned and concussed.'

'Yes,' Fura said, nodding agreeably. 'And Doctor Eddralder, being the committed and kindly physician that he is, wouldn't allow me to leave you to your fate. We were obliged to leave, so you came with us, aboard *my* ship, which we call *Revenger*. My intention was to return you to Werranwell at the earliest opportunity. That's still my intention.'

'Then get on with it.'

'I will, once we've resolved a new difficulty. Do you remember that there's a squadron of ships sailing around the Congregation? "Revenue Protection" they call it. They've been sent to find me. To kill me or capture me, one way or the other.'

'Not my problem.'

'No – or rather, wouldn't it be lovely if it wasn't.'

Meggery struggled against her restraints, but Eddralder placed a gentle but firm hand on her chest. 'Please don't. You are still weak, and still my patient, and I'm not at all ready to absolve myself of responsibility for your welfare.'

'They've attacked the *Merry Mare*,' Fura said. 'Caught it stranded and defenceless, and still they shot at it. It wasn't a mistake, the kind of thing that happens in battle. They knew exactly what your ship was, and still they fired. They kept on firing even after we'd opened our own squawk, risking our own stealth, to alert them to their error.'

'Unfortunately,' Doctor Eddralder said, 'it seems there was no error. It was a calculated attack, designed to deter any innocent ships from interfering in the squadron's activities in the future.'

Meggery's voice was an anguished rasp. 'In what way were we interfering?'

'Your crew weren't,' Fura said. 'Not really. They were just going about their ordinary business. The squadron – whoever's in charge of it – would prefer to have a clear field of battle. It's bothersome for them to have to distinguish between innocent privateers and their real target, so they've chosen not to. It's monstrous, but there you have it.'

Meggery scowled.

'You attacked us as well.'

'I know this is hard. But I'll ask you to draw a line between our actions, and those of this squadron. We meant to leave you alive and capable of going on, and we did. But they've no such inhibitions.' Fura laid a hand on her chest. 'I'm a pirate – I admit it. I'm not even ashamed of the term. Proud of it, even.' She lifted her arm, so Meggery might admire it properly. 'It's cost me, but I ain't sorry. Do it all again in a blink, for the things I've seen and done. I'm no murderess, though, no indiscriminate butcher, and I've only ever taken as much as I need. What they've done to your crew is different, and I won't let it stand. We've turned. We're going back to your ship, what's left of it. I'm hoping there may be survivors, and if so you'll be reunited with them.'

'To die out here?'

'If that's your choice. But I'd offer an alternative. Join us.'

Meggery's scowl turned to withering disgust.

'You expect me to switch loyalties that easily? Forget my own crew and sign onto the one that ruined us?'

'No – not at all. I'm talking about a union: our two ships serving a common cause.' Fura softened her tone. 'We'll patch up the *Merry Mare* together; make her better than she ever was.

But you can't go home. They wouldn't allow it, not with the justice you've seen served. You'd be picked off and silenced before you got within a million leagues of the Frost Margins. Together, though? With two good ships? There's business we could do, Meggery. Business you ain't dreamed of, but which'd haunt your waking days if you got so much as a glimpse of it. I've only just started to pick at the edges of it, and already it's giving me the night-sweats. But I can't stop now that I've started. I'll get things done one way or the other, I know. But I'd sooner have allies than not, and I can't think of any better place to begin than with the crew of the *Merry Mare*.'

Meggery listened to all this, contemplated it for a few seconds. Then she laughed in Fura's face.

Fura turned to Eddralder.

'See that she's comfortable.'

*

The solar weather had been on a declining trend, the sweeper and squawk clearing of interference, and it was once again possible to maintain continuous sighting watches. So it was that *Revenger*'s first contact with the *Merry Mare* was visual, through one of the long-range telescopes.

They crept closer, and trained more and more instruments on it. Even with their best glasses, though, and keenest judgement, nothing at all could be gauged concerning the state of its occupants.

Fura stood off at ten thousand leagues, and called for the launch to be readied.

'I plan on travelling light. Meggery, of course, to smooth the way. Proz can come with me – her insight's always handy – and I suppose we ought to have Eddralder and his potions along, just to emphasise our good intentions.'

'I'm coming too,' Adrana said. 'One or both of us might be required for negotiations, and it makes sense for me to be along for the trip.'

'That will leave *Revenger* uncaptained.'

'No, it'll leave *Revenger* in the capable hands of our friends Tindouf, Surt and Merrix, and Strambli, if it comes to an emergency.'

'You've forgotten Lagganvor.'

'I haven't. He should accompany us as well. No one knows more about sharp diplomacy than Lagganvor.'

'Anyone would think,' Fura said, 'that you didn't want that cove out of your gaze.'

But Fura knew when to pick her defeats, as well as her victories, and this was one such occasion. Perhaps, on balance, it would not be such a very bad thing to have Lagganvor along, and indeed her sister, for – although she was resolved not to show it – she was keenly apprehensive about the coming dialogue, presuming that it reached the point of words, rather than projectiles, being exchanged.

They cast off.

Fura gunned the jets and made swift work of the ten thousand leagues, only slowing them down for the last hundred, when they were already beginning to nose through the gutted remnants of rigging and sail. There was no response from the other ship, no squawk or visual hail, and not a single bullet, let alone a slug, tested the integrity of the launch. Fura slowed them still further for the last three leagues, for by then they were comfortably within range of any hand-weapons the crew might have kept back against boarding, but again nothing came.

Were they all dead? It was not an outlandish possibility. At six hundred spans the damage was plain to see, and it was much worse than the bruising dished out by *Revenger*. The hull had been struck and penetrated in several places, with traces of gas still coiling out from the wounds. Portholes were shattered, hull plates buckled, sail-control spines mangled or severed. Fura had been trying to cripple this little ship, to make it easier prey, but she'd had no interest in destroying it. The squadron had clearly given it all that they had. Only the fact that they were shooting from a great distance had spared the *Merry Mare* from absolute annihilation.

'Meggery,' she said, turning back from the control position to speak to their hostage. 'I have our lamps on her now. I'm afraid it looks very bad.'

'I don't need your sympathies.'

'They'd be wasted, I know – just as they'd be wasted on me.' Fura produced her lookstone and offered it to Meggery. 'You know what this is. You and I are going aboard that ship, so I think it'd be an idea to know what we're likely to find. Tell me what you make of things.'

Meggery had not yet closed her fingers on the lookstone.

'How valuable is that assessment to you?'

'Look at it this way. Both of our necks'll be on the line if your crew jump to the wrong conclusion about my intentions. Which they may very well do.'

Meggery took the lookstone, pinching it between three fingers and a thumb, all that remained on her left hand. Her face clouded with concentration as she adjusted the pressure, applying and releasing fingertip force, squinting and frowning, tilting the smoky shard by tiny degrees.

'What do you see?' Lagganvor asked, pressing his cheek close to Meggery's.

'Damage,' Meggery answered, in a tone of perfect disdain. 'Were you perhaps expecting something different?'

'It's worse now?' Lagganvor asked.

'Have a guess,' she answered. But she breathed in and out, holding the lookstone very carefully, and added: 'I see some of the crew, and some signs of movement. They're alive.'

'May I borrow it?' Lagganvor asked, smiling as he opened his palm before Meggery.

She stabbed the lookstone into his palm, nearly drawing blood.

Lagganvor winced, but his smile only faltered slightly. He raised the lookstone to his false eye, peering out with his customary enhanced discrimination. He nodded, made a series of agreeable ruminative noises, and passed the lookstone back to its new owner.

'Meggery was right. I make out five of them, including that stumpy fellow, and not a soul anywhere but in the forward part of the ship. The rear section may be depressurised. She's taken a very serious pounding, but I think it may not be as bad as it seems at first blush. The rigging and sails are almost beyond salvation, but with the spare materials they had yet to use, and the additional supplies we still have, some sort of repair may yet be possible.'

Meggery scoffed. 'Put the five of them out of their misery, then spare a shot for me. You'll be doing us a final favour.'

Doctor Eddralder overheard her and remarked, with weary displeasure: 'I would not have ministered to you, Meggery, if I knew you thought so little of your own life. You cost me both medicines and care, and I believed in you.'

Something in his tone must have reached her.

'I still want to live, all right? I had a good life before all this, even with our luck running the way it did. But I know a hopeless case when I see one.'

'Meggery,' Lagganvor said, in a low persuasive tone. 'I know you blame us for this, and some part of that blame's probably deserved.' He gestured through the sweep of the cabin windows. 'But *this* would have happened regardless, and you know it.'

Some furious calculation worked itself behind Meggery's eyes, the scar tissue around her neck and lower jaw growing tighter and pinker as she considered this point.

'Maybe it would,' she said. 'But they'd have been in a better position. They'd have had full sails and full ions.'

'It would have prolonged what was already inevitable,' Lagganvor said. 'You know it, Meggery. It was a dozen against one. It was *civilisation* – that friendly, dependable thing you have always thought of as a friend – baring its teeth and revealing its true colours.' He softened his voice, as if they were two friends consoling each other after a bad night at the greyhound races.

'You're on the other side of that truth now. We know how it feels.'

Doctor Eddralder said: 'Let her leave freely, now. Not as a hostage, or prisoner, or even as my patient. I discharge Meggery from my care. She will be all right now; safe to return without my supervision.'

Lagganvor looked doubtful, then neutral, then – ruefully – convinced.

'If we mean what we say, we ought to send her back on her own. Give her a suit, and let her speak for us, without coercion. There'll be no more honest way of offering a truce than that.'

There was a silence. Fura looked at Lagganvor, then at her hostage – the hostage she was about to surrender.

'I'll do it,' Meggery said quietly. 'I'll speak for you. But it'll cost you that lookstone.'

*

They pressed against the windows and watched as she floated over to the other ship. Meggery had needed no tuition in the wearing of the suit, hastily assembled to fit her, nor had she appeared in any way fazed at the prospect of stepping out into open space. She had allowed herself to be secured by a line, so she could be hauled back to the launch if she ran into trouble, but Fura was in little doubt that she could have managed very well without it. They had given her one yardknife, so that she might hack her way out of an entanglement, and a squawk channel. The knife stayed clipped to her hip, and she had disabled the squawk as soon as she was clear of the lock, and there was nothing Fura could do about that but seethe.

'Damn her.'

'Admit it,' Eddralder said. 'If you were going to negotiate for your crew's future survival, you'd rather it was a private conversation, wouldn't you?'

'That ain't goin' to improve her mood,' Prozor said confidingly.

Eddralder turned to her. 'What would, though?'

'Rhetorical question, I think,' Lagganvor said.

Meggery picked her way through a loose, drifting forest of severed rigging and shredded sail, occasionally disappearing behind some obstacle or another. Fura watched her intently, alert to subterfuge. They had given her no weapon besides the knife, no obvious means of betrayal, but Fura was a long way from having confidence in Meggery's intentions.

Something was giving off a restless creak and she realised it was her fist, opening and closing like a rusty gate.

Meggery reached the *Merry Mare*, clanging onto it with her magnetic soles. They would have felt that inside, Fura knew. Even if they had no idea that the launch was as close as it was, they would now know they had company, friendly or otherwise.

'It's a shame none of us thought to bring a second piece of lookstone,' Lagganvor said.

'The shame is that I let her take the one good piece we had,' Fura said. 'Never mind. If I do have to kill 'em all, at least I'll know what to look for.'

'I don't pity the stumpy cove the work he's got to get those sails square,' Prozor said. 'There's a week in that, at least, even with all hands and the materials ready.'

'I would not think that we would be advised to spend a day here, let alone a week,' Eddralder said.

Meggery looked tiny now, as she went around the curve of the hull, moving with the methodical, fatigued-seeming gait that came as second nature to anyone who had used vacuum gear for any length of time. She had unclipped from the line, now that her magnetic soles were effective, and was coming up on the galley window, a large, cross-fretted eye through which spilled the pale, dwindling radiance of ailing lightvine. Meggery stopped at the eye and knelt down so her visor was as close to the glass as possible.

Faces bobbed under the glass, too small to recognise. Meggery looked as if she were praying into a glowing pool, brimming with phantoms. She was evidently making contact with the glass, so that some sound transmission was feasible. It was impossible to follow the conversation, such as it was. But every now and again Meggery amplified some word or remark with a purposeful gesture, precise and economical. Like all crews worth a spit, hers had obviously evolved a silent vocabulary for use when communication devices faltered or could not be used.

'I don't see Werranwell,' Fura said.

'Nor do I,' Lagganvor said in a low, cautious tone. 'That's ... odd. One would expect the captain to be at the forefront of this sort of negotiation.'

Meggery pushed back up from the galley window and was now heading for the front of the ship, to the jaws that sealed over their rocket launch. Slowly the jaws hinged open, disclosing a widening maw. It was a very slow process, almost as if the jaws were being manually cranked.

Meggery walked to the very edge of the upper jaw, then – when the gap was sufficient – clambered inside. As soon as she had disappeared within, the jaws began to seal up again.

The other ship sat silent and unmoving. The faces had moved back from the glass, and now there was no sign of life at all.

'Happily, I brought a pack of cards,' Prozor said, reaching for a pocket. 'Shall I deal us all in?'

Lagganvor ignored her. 'That must be the only way she can get in and out, without them blowing all their remaining lungstuff. I imagine the parlay has already begun. There's nothing we can do now: either she makes our case, or she doesn't.'

'If it's the latter,' Fura said, taking out her watch and checking the time so that she would know how long Meggery had been engaged, 'they're finished. I've no intention of sticking around to twist their arms. In fact, I ain't sticking around, period.'

'We said we'd help them,' Lagganvor said.

'We will – if they agree. We've got a good spread of sail, yardage to spare, and we're not lugging too much around in our hold.'

He smiled as he picked up on the drift of her intentions. 'You mean to lash their hulk to ours and drag them with us. Two hulls under one spread of sail. Then she can be repaired at our leisure . . .'

'Leisure's not *exactly* the word I'd choose,' Fura said.

*

When at last the squawk crackled, she nearly jumped at the suddenness of it. It had been five minutes since Meggery went inside, which was long enough for a short discussion, but not the sort of extended exchange that she had presumed would need to take place.

She mashed her thumb on the talk button. 'Meggery – how thoughtful of you to call back. What may we do for you?'

'This is Captain Werranwell,' came the reply, sounding fainter and more distant than she had expected. 'Meggery and I have been . . . speaking.' He paused, and she thought she caught a groan or a wheeze before he continued. 'After all you've done to us, you have the . . . temerity . . . to suggest terms of cooperation?'

'Call it whatever you wish,' Fura said, adopting a cheerful and playful demeanour, as if she were haggling over the price of oranges. 'The way I see it, you don't have a lot of choices. That ship of yours looks like something the cat had a go at, and it'll take more than a watch or two to set things right. Meanwhile, you're sitting out here practically begging for that squadron to come back and finish you off.'

Again that wheeze – and something else in it, a liquid movement in the lungs

'And your proposition, just so we are clear?'

'We'll sail with your ship in tow and fix her up shiny as a pin. You've seen the sharp side of us, when we took you, but that was only because we needed to make a point. We're not so bad as we seemed, as Meggery will testify. We've looked after her nicely, haven't we? Kept our word?'

There was an interval of silence before he replied.

'Come across. You alone.'

9

Fura clipped herself on and launched off toward the larger vessel. It only took thirty seconds to complete the crossing, which she managed without snagging herself in rigging or sail-cloth, and she was in the right position to land on her feet when she arrived, magnetic soles latching on instantly. She felt the impact all the way through the suit and into her knees, but at least she could not be accused of making an unannounced arrival.

Fura stomped past the galley window, aware of faces behind it, but giving them no direct glance. Under ordinary circumstances, this would have been an exceedingly vulnerable position to be in, especially for a visitor who was not yet on cordial terms with her prospective hosts. They could have swivelled a small coil-gun onto her, poked a crossbow out of a lock or hinged porthole, or even used the sail-control gear to whip a line of triple-filament yardage into her, which could be just as bad for her health as any Ghostie blade or energy beam.

But even if they wished her harm, and Fura was not yet ready to set that suspicion aside, there were limited means available to them. Their meagre collection of coil-guns was set up for long-range defence, not picking scabs off their own hull, and their main locks were out of commission due to the pressure loss throughout most of the ship. The sail-control gear might have worked before, but it was hopelessly tangled now, and no threat to her at all.

Yet Fura remained on edge, for Captain Werranwell's manner had not been one of friendly acquiescence, though he surely understood that he had everything to gain by joining her, and all to lose if he disdained her offer.

The jaws were cranking open by the time she reached them and the gap had widened to a point where she could squeeze between them, but it was a tight passage, allowing for her backpack and chest-plate. It would only have taken a slight reduction in the available space to snag her in place, and a little more, horribly and slowly she did not doubt, for the jaws to crush her. If that was their plan, though, they were tardy about it, for the jaws only began to seal when she was safely through into the relative sanctuary of the docking bay. It was much like their own on *Revenger*. There was a rocket launch, a little battered around the nose and tailfin but otherwise serviceable, and some suit parts, tools and bottles of lungstuff. Quotidian surroundings now, Fura reflected, almost welcoming in their familiarity, but how puzzling and foreign these things had once seemed to her, and not so long ago as all that.

Lasling was waiting for her at the back of the bay. She recognised him instantly, for his suit ended at the knees. Weightless now, the absence of his lower limbs was no impediment to him at all, and he signalled to her with a curt impatience, as if she were rudely late for an appointment. She followed him into a bulky transfer lock, where he wordlessly examined her for weapons while vacuum around them was exchanged for lungstuff, and then they were able to proceed into the inhabited part of the *Merry Mare*. He brought her to the galley, where the others were gathered, waiting – it seemed to Fura – in sullen anticipation of her arrival.

Lasling undid his helmet, grunting as he tugged it away from the neck-ring, greasy with tar-black pressure sealant.

'She's clean, near as I can tell. If she's been stupid enough to bring a Ghostie blade with her, I didn't spot it.'

'She's many things,' Captain Werranwell said, pausing to draw the back of his hand across a foam-lathered mouth. 'I fancy stupid isn't one of them.'

He was in a chair, buckled into it despite the weightlessness, and it only took one look at him to see he was not going to last very long. His tunic was opened from the collar to the waist, with a mass of bloodied bandages and pads being pressed to his chest with his other hand. Under all that was a wound that was making wet sucking sounds with every laboured breath.

'What happened to you?' Fura asked.

His lips formed a partial smile. 'Would you like twenty guesses?'

'It wasn't our doing.'

'You didn't help.'

'Eddralder is on the launch. He could be with us in a few minutes. He helped Megger—'

'It's a bit late for me, Captain Ness.' He flashed the smile again, but this time there was more pain in it than humour. 'One of their slugs ruptured a tensioning spar. Blew a hole in our hull, too, but it was the spar that cost me most dearly. A splinter of it came off faster than a bolt from a crossbow, and went into my chest. Missed my heart, but I'm not sure that was much of a blessing.'

'Meggery,' Fura said, meeting the other woman's eyes. 'Tell him there's a chance with Eddralder.'

'There isn't,' Meggery said flatly. 'I saw the wound. He's punctured a lung, shattered several ribs, and there's extensive bleeding, not to mention bits of that spar stuck deep inside him.'

'The one thing I could always depend on with Meggery,' Werranwell said, 'is to give an unvarnished report.' He coughed, a horrible liquid sound like gravel being stirred around in bucket of cement, until, by some admirable force of will, he found sufficient strength to continue. 'Meggery tells me you wish to discuss an alliance. She says you are willing to help us repair our ship, and that we should become outlaws as well.'

'You already are,' Fura replied. 'Like it or not. Join me – join us – and you won't be alone in it. We'll protect each other – benefit from our shared experience, you've my word on that.'

'That's your pledge?' Werranwell asked.

'It's all I have.'

Cossel, the woman with scars on her cheekbones, said: 'It suits her to plead with us now. I wouldn't bet much on our chances once we've outlived our usefulness to her.'

'She'll hold to her word,' Meggery said, pressing the stump of her knuckle against the roughened tissue of her burn, now that she had removed her helmet. 'Not much else, maybe. But she'll hold to that pledge.'

'You sure they didn't slip something into your medicine?' asked Vouga, the weaselly-looking Integrator Fura remembered from her first time aboard.

'I figured her out,' Meggery said.

Lasling sucked a dab of grease from the end of his thumb. He peered at it, eyes slightly crossed either side of his flattened nose. 'After a few hours in her company?'

'I'm not vouching for her,' Meggery said. 'Nor for any of 'em. I'm just saying she needs all of us, not just the bare ribs of this ship. A ship's no use to her at all without a crew, and there's only enough of them to look after one ship, not two.' She paused, looking around at her mates, but giving Fura only the swiftest of glances. 'I got a sense of her out of Eddralder, the saw-bones. Him and his daughter were kind enough to me. Unless they're lying, they didn't set out to get mixed up in her business.'

'I'll give him one thing,' Lasling said. 'That ointment he left us *has* taken the sting out of my stumps.'

'Didn't know your loyalty was so easily bought,' Cossel said.

'It isn't. But whatever else he might be, he can't be too bad a doctor.'

'Not reason enough to join 'em,' said Cossel. Then, to Ruther: 'Pipe up. You're permitted a word as well.'

The shock-haired boy, the youngest of them, looked to his captain. 'Can I speak plainly, sir?'

Werranwell wheezed before answering and his words seemed to come harder to him now. 'I've trusted you with every operational secret of ours, lad, so the least I can do is trust you with your opinions.'

Ruther swallowed before continuing. His eyes were wet. 'I expected to be dead twice. Once when they jumped us, and once again when those slugs started coming in. I was frightened, sir – properly frightened. More'n I've ever been next to that queer old skull of ours.'

Lasling nodded slowly. 'No shame in that.'

'Here's the thing though,' Ruther said, leaning in closer to his fellows, never taking his gaze off his captain, whom Fura now understood that he loved as a father. 'She needed something from us, and she robbed us, but she did it fairly and – in the end – she did right by Meggery. That doesn't make it proper, not at all. But it's lot better than being shot at for no reason, by coves to whom we aren't anything but a nuisance, and something handy to aim their coillers at. I might hate her,' he said, jabbing his chin in Fura's direction, 'but it's only a tenth of what I feel about those ships that didn't even give us the benefit of an excuse, let alone an apology.'

'We've each been done an injustice,' Fura said, pressing home her point. 'You more than most, Captain Werranwell, and I own up to my share in that. We both intercepted that squawk, I think – the one seeming to come from whoever's in charge of those ships.'

'You mean the young gentleman who seems to have ideas above his station?'

'Gentleman's not the word I'd use, sir.'

'Nor I.' His eyes sparkled faintly, as if – in this matter at least – they shared a common judgement, the basis upon which – in some other life – a friendship might have developed. 'Evidently he's deemed to have some talent, though, or they would not have given him that station.'

'Talent or not, he's only fit for scraping off my shoe. My sister and I got a sense of him through the skull – your skull, I mean.

He seems to be a half-decent boney as well as a murderous little smear.'

Ruther scratched deep into his stripe of white hair. 'I didn't pick him up through the skull, sir, but we bonies trade rumours when we can.'

'Go on, lad,' said Werranwell.

'The last time we were in port I did pick up a sniff of something. A young man who's come up fast through the merchant protection service, very sure of himself by those accounts, not caring for anything except his own advancement, and already collecting enemies in the service and out of it. He's burned anyone who's stood in his way and he's not afraid to be disliked. Very good with coillers, navigation, and tactics, but that's only part of it – he's got the talent, as well, and he's fierce-bright with it – both sending and pushing.' Ruther bit his lip, looking quickly askance. 'Probably nothing, sir; I oughtn't have dredged up a rumour, just so I can chip in and sound like I have something to contribute.'

'There may be something in it, boy,' Werrenwell said, seemingly more out of kindness than conviction.

'Would you know his name?' Fura asked sharply.

'I might've heard it, but I'd have to think; beyond wondering what sort of man could be so cold, and treat his own kind with such contempt, I was glad not to give him any more heed.'

'The right attitude,' Werranwell said, reaching out to pat Ruther.

'We agree on his character, anyway,' Fura said. 'And if he has control of that squadron, we can be sure it'll continue to act as if Inter-Congregational law doesn't exist. I'd like that name, if it comes to you, Ruther.'

'I'll tell you if I remember.'

'Good. And I'll hope you'll agree – all of you – that if this upstart little brat *is* in control, we'll need to look to each other for survival, not to mention a restitution of justice.'

'And what do you propose, exactly?' Cossel asked. 'From your standpoint of being a blood-thirsty, murdering pirate who's already shredded the rule of law?'

'I believe in law,' Fura said earnestly. 'Just not *their* law, as it presently holds. And I'm not in any rush to bring down civilisation, even if that was in my means.' She nodded in what she hoped was the general direction of the Congregation. 'I like it too much. And I know there's honest coves down there, people who've worked hard and not treated anyone else unfairly, who don't deserve to have the worlds come crashing down on 'em. So it's not my intention to smash everything to rubble, or even cut those throats which *do* have it coming to 'em. But things can't stand the way they are.'

'Again,' Cossel said, with what sounded like the last dregs of her patience, 'what do you propose?'

'Parlay. Cooperation. Joint action. Two ships serving a common purpose. Not necessarily sailing close, but each looking out for the other.'

The crew swapped glances. Werranwell's eyes, growing slitted and weary, conveyed equal degrees of amusement and scepticism.

'And how would this cooperation work, exactly?'

'I'd have my robot draw up articles,' Fura said. 'There'll be things we'll quibble over. But from where I'm sitting, we've got a lot more in common than you'd think.'

'Your robot has a legalistic bent?' Werranwell asked. He erupted into coughing, blood foaming between his teeth, and when Ruther pressed close to him he urged the boy away with gentle pressure. 'It's all right, lad – nothing to be done now. I just never heard of a robot better for anything other than sweeping floors.'

'Robots or not,' Lasling said, using a fingernail to dig between the shattered ramparts of his teeth, 'I don't like any part of this. Then again, I can't say I'm overly thrilled about our other prospects. Perhaps if we do weigh in with 'em, and that doctor can take another look at me . . .'

'He will,' Fura said firmly. 'Whatever's right or wrong with any of you, he'll be your physician as much as ours.'

'Equal terms, then?' Vouga asked, lifting an eyebrow.

Fura crimped her lips. 'We'd need to draw up those articles.'

'Well, we could start now,' the Integrator said, with a hard and avaricious gleam in his eye. 'The loot in your hold. What you took from us, and what you've taken from others. We want an equal share of that now.'

'What we took from you,' Fura said, 'wouldn't fill a doll's thimble.' But she gave an effortless shrug. 'Of course you'd be equal partners. I wouldn't countenance any alternative. If our hulls are lashed close, we can come and go like neighbours.'

Cossel gave a little shudder.

'Never did get on with my neighbours.'

'Your sister has joint captaincy?' Werranwell wheezed out.

'She does, sir.'

'And you rate her capabilities as well as you do your own?'

The others started to glance among themselves, evidently doubtful of where Werranwell was headed with this line of questioning.

'I do,' Fura said, nodding emphatically. 'She's as tenacious and determined as me, and she's taken to this new life very well. We've got our different ways of doing things, neither of us would deny, but I've looked up to Adrana for as long as I remember.'

'It must be difficult, sharing the responsibilities of one ship.'

'We make do. I won't say we don't squabble over this and that, but . . . well, we love each other, and we want the same things for our crew, and now that includes all of us.'

'I am about to die,' Werranwell said.

'There's still time to summon Eddralder, and he'd be able to give you a second opinion . . .'

'A third, or a fourth, wouldn't make any difference. Meggery? Tell her the arrangement we discussed, while she was on her way over.'

'This ship is short-handed,' Meggery said. 'Has been since we lost Ives and Mauncer. Now we're about to be short of a captain.'

'Meggery doesn't want the position,' Werranwell said. 'Nor

does Lasling, or Cossel, or Vouga. Ruther's too young. They're all much too wedded to their specialisations, in any case, and I can hardly blame them for that.' He forced a look of fond recollection, perhaps the last of a lifetime. 'I was like that, when I had to take over from Haligan, the captain who preceded me. They had to tear me away from the sails.'

'Why did you agree?' Fura asked.

'Because there wasn't a more willing candidate. It strikes me, though, that your own ship is presently over-burdened with captains.' He interrupted himself, gathering his strength to go on. 'The Ness sisters are strong and capable, or they wouldn't have made it this far. One of you will make an excellent replacement for me.'

Fura shook her head, denying the idea before it had time to take root. 'Your crew won't accept us.'

'They will, if I ask them to. I have a choice, Captain Ness: either I anoint a replacement, or risk friction and suspicion tearing my crew apart – and perhaps yours with it. So, I declare that one of the Ness sisters will take my ship, and the loyalty of her crew.'

Fura turned to Meggery. 'You accept this?'

'It's the captain's wish,' she answered. 'And if he wishes it, we abide by it. You might not have my affection, or gratitude. But you'll have my word, and that goes for every cove on this ship.'

'I . . . don't know what to say.'

'So you accept the delegation?' Werranwell asked. The sucking sound from his chest was more horrible now, slower, and somehow more cavernous, as if issuing from some deeper, darker part of him, far beyond the reach of surgery.

'I do. One of us will take command,' Fura said.

'Good . . . good,' Werranwell answered. 'That is . . . most comforting to me, Captain Ness. There is just one pre-condition, call it a down-payment, which Meggery made me insist upon . . .'

*

Condensation dimpled the inside of Fura's faceplate. It was like the pebbled panes that had been set into the tall, narrow walls on either side of the main door of their house in Mazarile, through which tradespeople became jigsaw puzzles of broken colour and form. Prozor too had become a jigsaw of herself, the pieces not quite knitted together. She bundled Fura out of the lock, into the main compartment of the rocket, and then helped her wrestle off the sweat-and-condensation-drenched helmet. Fura took a deep inhalation of what passed for fresh lungstuff.

'If you're back, that has to be mean something,' Adrana said.

'We were expecting you to stay silent, but not for quite as long as this,' Lagganvor said.

'I left them my squawk,' Fura said, between ragged inhalations. 'We'll fix 'em up with something better, but it'll do for communications in the short term. Just until . . . we figure out how to bring our two ships in close.'

'Then . . . they are amenable?' Adrana asked. 'Despite everything, they've agreed to our arrangement?'

'They took some . . . time to come around to the sense of it.' She sucked in more lungstuff, fighting to get her breathing back onto some sort of seemly tempo. 'Werranwell died. He was alive when I got there, dead by the time I left.'

Lagganvor raised an eyebrow.

'Negotiations went that badly?'

'He'd been injured in the attack, beyond anything we could do to help him. He was . . . not against my proposition. They've agreed to be lashed to us and accepted our help with their repairs. As soon as we can, we'll draw up common articles.' Fura grimaced against a sudden sharp pain. 'That way we can pass ourselves off . . . pass as two innocent ships . . . just happen to be sailing in from the Empty.'

Adrana swapped a look with Prozor.

'To what end?'

'I'll think of one.' Fura was still breathing rapidly, clenching her jaw against the pain – which was both worse than she had anticipated, and yet just distant enough to be tolerable, provided she had words to spit out. 'Strambli's my main worry. How she fares will determine any action I . . . we . . . decide upon.'

'What's wrong with your arm?' Adrana asked.

Fura had her artificial arm tight against her chest, clenching its fist so tight that she risked plunging her metal nails right through her alloy palm and out the other side.

'Show us, girlie,' Prozor said, taking her arm as gently as she could and persuading it away from her chest. But the fist was still balled, and no monkey strength was ever going to be sufficient to uncoil those fingers. Prozor touched the closed fist, sending a spasm of fresh agony right into Fura, and came away with something damp and snot-coloured on her own fingers, which she sniffed cautiously. 'She's bleedin' . . . something.'

Doctor Eddralder pushed to the front of the little knot of gathering. 'What happened?'

'Open it up for him,' Prozor said, placing one hand on Fura's shoulder, the other at her elbow. 'Goin' to have to do it sooner or later, so might as well get it over with.'

Fura knew this to be true, but the only thing holding the pain at any sort of bearable level had been the pressing of that arm against her chest, and the balling of her fist. Still, she had to do it. She bit down hard, grunted, forced open her fingers. It took all her will to bend them straight. The pain bludgeoned her instantly, her grunt becoming an anguished exclamation. The oily seepage, which had contaminated Prozor's hand, began to gush and bubble freely. It was some liquid component of the hand that she had never suspected was there.

'Oh, Fura,' Adrana said.

Lagganvor rushed for a cloth and pressed it against the source of the seepage.

'Hold it open,' he commanded.

'What did they do to you?' Eddralder asked.

She forced herself to look. She had lost a finger from her hand. The smallest digit had been wrenched out and away, leaving a ragged socket where it ought to have plugged into her knuckle. That was where the seepage was coming from, spurting out in rhythmic pulses as if driven by her own heartbeat.

The agony rose and fell on that same cycle.

To her surprise she found that she could bear it, for the moment.

'They didn't . . . *do* . . . anything,' Fura said. 'Nothing I didn't agree to, at any rate. There was just . . . a little account-settling.'

'They took this off you . . . how?' Adrana asked, taking over from Lagganvor with the cloth, which was already sodden with the green ichor. 'Looks to me like they did it with a pair of shears.'

Fura tried to force her breathing into something like a normal rhythm. 'Didn't care how they took it off. Only that they did it and got it over. Didn't think it would hurt. Not this much. Never really felt a part of me . . . until now.'

'You agreed to this?' Lagganvor asked, shaking his head as if she had just dismantled his last certainty.

'A small price to pay,' she said, deciding that the only thing now was to grin her way through the pain, and laugh a little at what she had allowed to be done. 'I got you a ship, sister,' she said to Adrana. 'I'm giving you the *Merry Mare*, and her crew!'

'Meggery was missing the same digit, on the same hand,' Eddralder said, before Adrana had a chance to react to this development.

'She was,' Fura said, still grinning.

'Then this was at her demand, I take it? She insisted you lose the finger?'

'She said . . . I'd cost her something. Something that couldn't be replaced. So it was only fair I gave something back, something that meant a lot to me.'

Eddralder shook his head. 'You had nothing to do with the loss of her finger. That was very clearly an old injury, totally unconnected with our action.'

'It wasn't the finger she was cross about,' Fura said. 'It was what was on the skin before it got burned. What had to be cut away. A little tattoo. Two tiny birds on a vine.'

'I fail to see how the one loss may be measured against the other,' Eddralder said.

131

'Mauncer did it for her.'

'Mauncer being . . . ?'

'One of the coves they'd already lost, before we found 'em,' Prozor said, sparing Fura the need to elaborate. 'Lasling told me some of it, when me and him was sortin' out what sail materials they needed. Mauncer and the other cove, Ives, was the ones who got stuck inside the bauble when Lasling lost his pins. Seems Mauncer was the one who got the rest of 'em inked up, when it suited him.' She looked down at her own hands and palms, scarred and age-spotted as they were, but otherwise unblemished, then shook her head, more in wonderment than denial, at the fact of the universe once again managing to surprise her with its wicked and playful cruelty. 'Can't say I've ever been one for the ink.'

*

The sisters had not been long back aboard *Revenger*, discussing plans for the cooperation, when Merrix summoned them to the Kindness Room.

As always, Adrana steeled herself before going inside. She had left too much of herself behind in here: too much of her innocence, too much of the girl she had once been. Doctor Eddralder's many salves and unguents gave off their own odours but somewhere beneath it all was a stench that could never be erased, a chemical memory suffused with pain and terror and all the many colours of madness.

Fura sensed her hesitation. She closed a kind hand – her good hand – around Adrana's forearm.

'We have to be strong for each other. Let's see how bad the news is.'

'Don't let him take it off,' Strambli said, raising her eyes as soon as she realised she had new visitors. 'It ain't time for that. I've been feeling better these last few days, I know I have . . .'

'Merrix,' Eddralder said. 'Would you be so kind as to remove the dressing, as gently as you can?'

Adrana moved to the side of the bed-bound Strambli. She was strapped down, just as Meggery had been. The restraints were there for her own welfare, done up no tighter than was necessary to prevent her drifting free and hurting herself, but the sight still pushed a hard stone into Adrana's throat.

'The Doctor won't do anything unless it's your life's that's at stake, Stramb,' Adrana said. 'And you know how much you mean to us.'

'What happened to you, Captain Arafura?'

Strambli had enough wits remaining to notice the recent injury. Fura smiled quickly, making light of it. 'Nothing that Surt can't fix in jiffy, Stramb. Just a little finger, too – can't say I ever had much use for it until now, and I'm not sure I'll miss it.'

'I'll miss my leg, if he has to saw it off. Tell him he doesn't have to saw it off, won't you?'

'We're a long way from that,' Adrana said soothingly. 'It's just an infection, something we treated once and can treat again. Isn't that so, Doctor?'

She ought to have deduced from his demeanour that matters were not that straightforward.

'The wound is . . . changing,' Merrix said, carefully peeling the dressing away from the affected area. It was sticky with antiseptic salve, and the process of removal was clearly uncomfortable for Strambli. It had to be done, Adrana supposed, but she had a horrible sense that she was abetting Strambli's distress.

'It doesn't look as red as before,' Fura said, lifting a puzzled eyebrow in Eddralder's direction. 'That's good news, isn't it? Your potions are working. Just keep treating her, and . . .' But she slowed, seeing what was already evident to Adrana's eye.

'It's . . . turning,' Eddralder said, with a fearful reverence, as if to speak of the matter at all was to encourage it. 'Some cellular transformation is taking place, not far beneath the skin.'

'What does he mean?' Strambli asked, with a rising anxiety.

'I noticed there was a pearliness to the affected area,' Merrix said quietly. 'The redness was in retreat, and in its place the skin

. . . the tissue . . . had a colourless quality. I thought it was some necrosis, but Father . . .'

'It's not a medical process,' Eddralder said.

'What is it?' Fura asked.

'Take a closer look. Since Merrix made her initial observation, the transformation has extended itself. I cannot say if it is pushing deeper, or extending outward more vigorously, but it is definitely more developed.'

Fura and Adrana almost knocked their heads together as they peered at the wound. Each gave the same intake of breath, the same shudder of disquiet. The surface pearliness which Merrix had mentioned was now a window of smoky transparency, as if a thumb-sized portion of Strambli's skin had turned to smeared glass. Beneath that vile little window – hemmed by a moat of pink inflammation, not nearly as angry as it had been – was an impression of colourless crystal depths, as if they were looking down into an icy crevasse.

'Have you seen anything . . .' Fura began. 'No, what a ridiculous question. If you'd seen something like this, you wouldn't have that terrified look about you.'

'I am very sorry,' Eddralder said, and it was hard to say whether his apology was meant for the Ness sisters, or the patient in the bed.

'I told you it made me stab me,' Strambli said. 'Been saying so since I had the accident. 'Cept it wasn't no accident, was it? It was that blade jabbing a bit of itself into me. I know what you're thinking and none of you wants to say it.'

'We oughtn't to jump to conclusions,' Adrana said, swallowing hard.

'You don't have to,' Strambli said, with a ghoulish delight in her own predicament. 'We know what's going on. It's turning me. It's making me into Ghostie gubbins.'

10

The lull in the solar weather continued. Over the next thirty-six hours, the launch sped back and forth between *Revenger* and the *Merry Mare* with the tireless industry of a shuttle in a weaving loom. It would dock, unload supplies, transfer personnel, then make the return journey and restock. Such was the efficiency of this process that the launch's exhaust gases barely had time to dissipate before it was nosing back through them.

Gradually the two parties got to know each other better. Lasling's legs gave him no trouble moving outside the ship, and he was needed to get the ruined rigging into some sort of condition that would enable the *Mare* to be hauled close to *Revenger*. Watching his arduous, careful progress, Tindouf was quick to propose helping him. Fura was sceptical, but they rapidly formed an efficient, good-natured partnership, and within a day of their first joint shift the wreck of the *Merry Mare* was deemed sufficiently stable to be dragged without risk of further damage. This was accomplished in two stages: first with the rocket launch serving as a tug, coupled to the wreck by six lines of triple-filament yardage; and then by *Revenger's* own sail-control winches, slowly hauling in the same lines.

Fura and Adrana watched proceedings with acute unease, well aware how suddenly and badly things could turn. There was always tension on yardage when a ship was under sail, but that strain acted in familiar ways, along force-vectors that were well understood. It was never a happy moment when a line or winch gave way, but when it went wrong the ensuing damage usually played out in a predictable pattern. Accordingly, crews who valued life and limb knew where it was inadvisable to be and, just as crucially, where to scurry to at the first intimations of disaster.

Such hard-won experience counted for little now. The winches and yard-lines were being put to unintended usages, and if they failed they would do so in unpredictable fashion. Even being inside the ship was not much guarantee. If a line broke, and whiplashed back at *Revenger*, it could cut through glass and hull with impunity. If a well-anchored winch sheared off, it might take a generous part of the ship with it, plunging her compartments into sudden vacuum.

Yet in the six hours that it took to complete the final union of the two ships, six hours in which catastrophe was only ever a single act of malice or inattention away, no accident occurred. No further damage was inflicted on either ship, and no additional toll upon the workers save exhaustion and a fresh catalogue of scrapes and bruises.

When the hull of the *Merry Mare* was finally secured to *Revenger* by a prodigious web of lines and chains, tensioned against the slightest movement, Surt and Vouga fashioned a connecting passage between the two pressurised compartments, so that the repair teams might come and go without the encumberment of full vacuum gear. There was just as much that had to be fixed within the *Merry Mare* as without, and the passage would permit the interior chores to be completed as quickly as possible, freeing up hands to work to restore a full spread of sail. The *Merry Mare* would not be able to extend her own acreage until she was flying freely, or else her lines and sails would tangle with *Revenger*'s, but there was much that needed to be done to the navigation and control gear before that desired eventuality, and yet more to consume the masters of their varied professions.

When the two weary crews mingled in the two galleys, close enough that they could almost sing or shout from one table to the next, Fura dispelled any fears she might have held about any immediate insurrection from the other party. Lasling, Meggery, Ruther, Cossel and Vouga were far too exhausted to put up any sort of fight, and her own crew were scarcely in better condition. Better fed, perhaps, and not as sickly to begin with, but the business of joining the ships had enacted a deep and wearying toll on them all. She was glad, very glad indeed, that the marriage – however temporary or inharmonious it might prove – was now complete.

'We heard that one of your number was sick,' Lasling said, facing her across the galley table in *Revenger*. 'Nothing contagious, I suppose?'

'If it was, do you think we'd be so quick to fraternise?' Fura asked.

Merrix, who was also sitting at the table, said: 'It isn't anything that's catching, sir, and if it were we'd have made sure you knew about it. You've met my father already – Doctor Eddralder. He's doing all that he can for Strambli.'

'He did well by Meggery, and seemed to want to help me, within his means.'

'He will, sir.'

'Lasling.' He extended a bruised, swollen-knuckled hand in Merrix's direction. 'Zancer Lasling, although Lasling will serve you fine. Your father told me you'd both been done a kindness by the Ness sisters, and he considered himself in their debt.'

'He does, sir – both of us do.' Merrix looked at Fura, who was the only Ness sister present, Adrana being entertained aboard the *Merry Mare*. 'We were in trouble on Wheel Strizzardy, and they helped us escape the place.'

'I heard there was all kinds of trouble at Wheel Strizzardy,' said Cossel, the only other present. 'Even then, I can't imagine how bad it must have been for *this* life to seem any sort of improvement.'

'Then you should consider yourself very fortunate,' Merrix said, staring down at her cutlery.

Lasling, who seemed to take it upon himself to act as informal peacemaker, tore off a chunk of bread and sniffed it tentatively. 'Not quite at its best, I suspect, but a distinct improvement on the green crumbs we've been making do with. And this ale is . . . almost tolerable.' He lifted his tankard, with its hinged lid, before taking a sip through the drinking hole. 'Our association may not have begun in the most conventional manner, but this hospitality is appreciated. I fear the reciprocal arrangements on the other ship may fall a little short.'

'You . . . ain't at fault for that,' Fura said, smiling decorously. 'You had a run of misfortune such as might befall any honest crew. We were the penultimate part of that misfortune, but I hope, in some small way, also the beginning of the turning of your luck.'

'I'm struggling to see how that might work,' Cossel said.

'We're fully equal partners now,' Fura said, reaching across and laying her metal hand on the woman's fingers before she had a chance to draw them away.

Cossel flinched, but kept her nerve.

'Then you won't mind sharing some of that bread and ale between the two ships. And anything else that doesn't have maggots swimming in it.'

'Our own reserves ain't as generous as they might seem—' Fura started, for when she had talked about sharing she had been thinking more of tar and lungstuff and yardage, not the edible provisions.

'But if we're equal partners, we will share what we have,' Merrix said, cutting across her. 'Won't we, Captain? Or else we aren't really equal at all, no matter what we say.'

Fura nodded emphatically, furious with the girl for interrupting but making every effort to look placid. 'Of course, Merrix – that goes without saying.'

'And Father will want them to have equal access to any medicines that they need. Medicines and his services, in all respects.'

'Without question. Although Strambli is his priority . . .'

'She is – but since neither of us knows what's to be done with her, it's mostly a question of keeping her comfortable and monitoring the progression of her . . . condition. That won't take up all his time, and he said he'd do more for Mister Lasling . . . Lasling, sir, I mean.'

'I'm not an urgent case,' Lasling said, yet there was a stiffness in his smile as of someone grinning through pain, and Fura supposed that even in weightlessness such arduous work would cause old wounds to complain. 'As for your friend . . . is the condition as serious as you just made it sound, Merrix?'

'If I may answer for her,' Fura said, 'it's only the lingering complication of an earlier treatment.' But she took on a grave, downcast look. 'Still, it forces our hand. We were committed, in a very general sense, for Trevenza Reach. Now our arrival there is a matter of life and death.'

'We are not in a fit position to sail anywhere,' Lasling said.

'Not now, and not for the three or four weeks it'll take to get you shipshape,' Fura said. 'But as we've discussed, there's nothing to prevent *Revenger* from sailing quite tolerably, even with the dead weight of . . .' She smiled hastily, reminding herself that the mortal remains of Captain Werranwell still reposed on the *Merry Mare*, and that her crew might be sensitive to that fact. 'I mean that it ain't any inconvenience to us, to have your hull lashed to ours, and to keep about our repairs even as we sail. Tindouf and Paladin already have a plausible crossing for us, allowing for the vagaries of solar weather, taking just seven or eight weeks. But we'll be within sweeper range of Trevenza Reach long before we arrive.'

'What is the significance of that?' Lasling asked.

'Before they see us,' Fura said, 'our ships'll need to be far apart, and moving on plausibly different courses, so that there's no hint of an association between us.'

'Wait,' Cossel said, squinting and frowning as intently as if she had a splinter in her eye. 'Wait. Why are *both* ships required to go to Trevenza Reach? Only one of 'em will have a sick party aboard.'

'It suits our purposes equally, Cossel. We've got our pal Strambli to think of, as well as another passenger, and you've been done a great injustice by that squadron. At Trevenza Reach you may seek restitution.'

Lasling shifted on his stumps. 'You said civilisation wasn't safe for us.'

'Then it's as well that Trevenza Reach doesn't quite count as civilised.' Fura picked up a quoin that was serving as a paper-weight, holding down a napkin. She tapped it against the table as she made her argument. 'They came off badly after the crash of '99, and even worse after the Readjustment. Banks treated 'em shabbily. There wasn't much love for the financial institutions before all that, and there'll be even less now. Better, Trevenza's always been welcoming to privateer crews, preferring to do business with them rather than the bank-rolled combines. They won't have any truck with that squadron, and they'll be very sorry to hear about your woes. You'll get a sympathetic hearing, is all I'm saying, better than anywhere else in the Congregation, and once you've got your story out, the other worlds'll have no choice but to take notice.'

'After which, it's happy-ever-after,' Cossel said.

'I ain't saying there won't be a few kinks along the way,' Fura said. 'But we'll cross them as they come. The chief thing is to agree that our interests are all served in Trevenza Reach.' She let go of the quoin, allowing it to float just above her palm, and watched as some faint, invisible torque began to turn its face to the Old Sun. Then she closed her fist around it again and smiled at the gathering. 'May we agree on that much?'

'Tell us about this other passenger,' Lasling said.

*

One by one, the crew of the *Merry Mare* were brought into the Clacker's presence. Adrana would have gladly introduced them all at once, but Fura would not agree to any more than one visitor in their cabin at a time, at least not until loyalties were firmly established, and that was going to take more than a few hours.

'He came with us from Mulgracen,' Adrana said, resting a hand on the outer casing of his box. 'He was stuck on that world, needing urgent passage away from it, having made enemies – very serious enemies, of his own kind and others – and they were closing in on him. He was being sheltered by a man called Darkly, who used to buy bones from the Clacker.'

It was Ruther's turn for the introduction. The boy knelt close to the box, and Adrana let him examine its shell, including the area where it had been damaged by the muddleheads. 'How did he end up making enemies, Captain Ness? I thought those aliens stuck together like glue.'

She had been asked permutations of this question by them all. 'There wasn't time to speak to him in any depth before he went into the box for the last time. But it probably has something to do with the way our world works. I mean all the worlds; everything that makes up the Congregation, and everything we know of it. Something to do with quoins, very likely, but that'll only be part of it.'

'Then you should wake him and ask him.'

Adrana smiled to herself at the boy's naivety. By all objective measures he was only a few years younger than her, and it was entirely possible that he'd already had a longer career in space. But she felt a gulf of experience between them, colder and less readily traversable than the leagues between the worlds. She had already seen more and known more and questioned more than this guileless child ever would. She had always wondered how it would feel when she eventually slipped across the boundary between adolescence and adulthood, feeling as if it ought to be some definite threshold, a crossing between one pole of experience and another, accompanied by the sudden reversal of compass needles. But it had happened and she had been unaware of it, until Ruther provided her with this point of reference, a gauge to measure her own progress.

'We would have woken him, if it were that easy,' she said, not wanting to be too hard on the boy, for she knew how affected he had been by the death of his beloved captain. 'But he's gone into an automatic hibernation interval, and we can't speed up the clock or risk opening his box ahead of time.'

'How long will it be?'

'From this point on, there's no telling. He's been with us for three months, nearly to the day, and from what we understand that was the minimum sleep interval. But how much longer he spends in there will depend on factors totally beyond our control – if he comes out of it at all.'

Ruther looked disappointed, as if he had been presented with lavishly-wrapped gift and then told he would never get to open it.

'So your passenger could spend forever in that box?'

'No – I don't think it will come to that. When we get to Trevenza Reach, there'll be friends of his waiting. They'll know how to bring him out safely.'

'But it would be them speaking to him, not you.'

'I admit . . . there are questions I would like to ask of him myself.'

'I saw one of their ships,' Ruther said brightly. 'It was around Hazzardy, I think. Captain Werranwell made us all come to the window and watch as it came in. It looked like . . . well, I almost can't say. Not like this ship, or any other ship of ours. Vouga said it was like a piece of frozen smoke; Cossel said it was more like a shard of dirty ice, with lights in; I thought it looked more like an old grey tooth. It didn't have any sails, though. They don't need sails to go where they go.'

'Sails are all well and good for the distances of the Congregation,' Adrana said, in a patient, tutorly manner. 'But they're no use at all for the spaces beyond – the Empty, and the vast gulf between the stars. Once, we probably had the means to cross those distances, and you can bet we didn't do it at a few thousand leagues per hour. A few million leagues per hour, perhaps, if even that was fast enough. The aliens that come to do business with us must have something much better.'

'We should ask them for it,' Ruther declared, as if no one in history had ever entertained such a thought.

Adrana almost felt bad about pricking his enthusiasm. 'I do not think they would be in any sort of rush to let us have it. There is a *system* here, Ruther – one that suits everyone involved. We monkeys get to live around the Old Sun and have quite a tolerably nice life, if only for a short time. Occasionally, the aliens help us – with medicine, or even certain types of technology, though they maintain a careful control of it. They, in turn, find us quite useful. We have the means to extract quoins from baubles, something that the aliens are unable or unwilling to do for themselves. They run our banks for us, and that is one less thing we have to do for ourselves, which *might* be considered a kindness. But there is something in it for them, as well. The quoins flow from the baubles into the banks' reserves, and from that point on what happens to them is anyone's guess. They have a value to the aliens beyond our own use as a form of currency, and we are the means of production. That is the system, and the aliens will do nothing that risks harming it, not so long as there is a viable civilisation around the Old Sun. Eventually all of this will end – this brief, glorious Occupation of ours – and the aliens are either the cause of that termination, or are in some way powerless to prevent it. I am not sure which I prefer. It is comforting to think of them as having greater powers than us, isn't it?' Ruther nodded meekly at this question, and she continued. 'But perhaps those powers aren't as superior as we might wish. Just because they have strange ships, and can come and go as they please, does not mean they have the means to save us from ourselves.'

'This Occupation will be different,' Ruther said. 'I'm sure of it. The others . . . well, they weren't us. They did things the wrong way. Got greedy, or made mistakes.' With the firmness of youth, he added: 'We shan't.'

'We'll be the exception, where twelve civilisations before us all failed? Including the Epoch of the Bauble-Makers, the Council of Clouds, the Glass Queens, the Incarnadine Multitudinous, the High Instrumentality? Each of which was comfortably in advance of our own culture? You think *we* will do better, Ruther?'

'I think we must try,' he said, doubtfully.

'Then there are already cracks in your certainty. As there must be.' Adrana patted the Clacker's box again. 'There is an answer in here, or a partial one. He knew about the quoins; their true purpose. And more, I think. That is why his enemies were so intent on silencing him. That is why he matters to us, and why I will not break our promise to deliver him to Trevenza.'

'They'll arrest you there,' Ruther said. 'You do realise that, don't you? And the rest of us will do well if we merely avoid being arrested as your accomplices.'

'Would you rather we never went near a world again?'

'No,' he admitted, averting his face, as if to admit such a thing were a kind of shame.

'We won't be arrested. Or, at least, we shall take great pains to prevent it. We have false identities, and they've not worked too badly on two previous worlds. And this time we shall have two ships, and our former crews dispersed between them. There'll be nothing to help the authorities make the connection to *Revenger*.'

'You seem so sure.'

'I am not,' Adrana confessed. 'But we have no other path before us. It is not an easy one, but walk it we must.'

She kept her hand on the Clacker's case, thinking how the alien's fate was now braided with her own, and by extension the whole of her crew. She wished it to survive, so that it might furnish her with answers. But to help the alien survive, she needed to put them all in harm's way by chancing another encounter with a world. A pledge was a pledge, though. If she surrendered every fine part of herself to her new career, her word would be the last thing she gave away.

The box jolted lightly under her palm, and deep inside it something made a low clicking sound, like a clock gear moving from one ratcheted position to the next.

She jerked her hand away.

'What is it?' Ruther asked.

'I don't know,' Adrana said, for she owed the boy the truth if nothing else.

*

Over the next few days Adrana and Fura were rarely out of the presence of the Clacker's box, and if neither of them was present in the captains' quarters, then Paladin was under strict orders to maintain the closest possible surveillance.

That something had happened was beyond dispute, for if either of the Ness sisters pressed their heads to the box's side, they now heard a distant, continuous whirring. Very occasionally they chanced to open the outer casing, and when they did that the inner box – the true hibernation device – was mostly invisible and intangible, except in the flickering instants when the concealment machinery faltered. The sisters theorised that the box was having to divert some of its energies into sustaining that illusion of absence, and that it might be better to allow it to use all of its powers to facilitate whatever process was now in force, be it the repair of damage, or the slow awakening of the occupant.

They did not know, and intervention seemed no wiser now than it had a day earlier. So they waited, and waited, and gradually realised that whatever was happening, no haste seemed to be involved.

'Now that we're together,' Fura said, during one of their joint vigils, 'we may as well discuss the thing we haven't been discussing. We can't pretend that there isn't a set of bones in the bone room.'

'Were we pretending?'

'You know what I mean. Ever since that . . . contact . . . we've avoided any talk of going near the skull again.'

'For good reason.'

'We weren't prepared for him,' Fura said. 'We'd be prepared the second time.'

'That ... boy ... would also be prepared. He nearly had the better of us; we'd be fools to give him a second chance. What if some part of our intention slipped between the skulls, and alerted him to our chosen destination?'

'We can hold it back.'

'No,' Adrana answered. 'We'd think we could, but we don't know how deep his capabilities run. We both sensed it: he's at least our equal, and perhaps better than us, and that scares me. I know we went to a lot of trouble to get that skull, and by some reckoning that action cost Captain Werranwell his life. But that doesn't mean we have to use it, just because it's there. Part of me says we'd be better off smashing it to chips, just to remove the temptation. Or at the very least welding the bone room shut, until we're sure that that boy isn't going to be a problem.'

'You're right to be concerned about his learning our plans,' Fura said. 'Our destination's one thing. But a captain also knows her ship's instantaneous position and vector. Imagine if he could pluck those numbers straight from our heads, just because we were skullbound!'

'I am not sure what you're driving at. You seem to be agreeing with me that there is too much hazard in using that skull, and yet I have never known you change your position so readily.'

'We're forgetting about the boy,' Fura said. 'The other boy, I mean: Ruther.'

'What of him?'

'He can read the skull. It's the one he's used to. If we put Ruther into the bone room, there's much less chance of the other boy learning anything useful.'

'Other than our destination, which Ruther already knows.'

'But he doesn't know our detailed plan, and there's no reason he ever has to know it. We can insulate him from anything that'd be useful to the squadron. No navigational figures; no knowledge of the disposition of our sails or armaments. Nothing he could inadvertently pass to the enemy.'

'His knowing about Trevenza Reach might already undo us. If that squadron managed to cut ahead of us, blockade our approach . . .' Adrana shook her head. 'It is still far too great a risk, sister. We'd never be sure that Ruther couldn't give something away . . . and besides, I didn't care for the feeling of his mind trying to worm into my own. We might not be stronger than the boy, but I think we may agree that we are stronger than Ruther. It would be reckless of us to expose him to something he doesn't have the defences to resist.'

'Ruther's useless to us, then,' Fura said, with a deliberate coldness. 'Just another mouth to feed. The only question is which lock we throw him out of.'

'He may be helpful to us in a thousand ways that don't depend on the bone room.'

'His knowledge of that skull could still be an asset, even if he doesn't take the crown,' Fura conceded. 'If – when – we chance another contact, Ruther might be able to help with the input settings. That other boy can't be monitoring his own skull around the clock, so if we can get in and out quickly . . .'

'It's still too risky.'

'But it'd be foolish to disregard Ruther's knowledge completely – or put ourselves in a position where it can never be exploited.'

'Again, I am not sure where you are driving.'

'I'm only saying that Ruther should remain with the skull that he knows the best. If this harmonious little union doesn't fray at the edges between now and the separation of our ships, there'll need to be an inter-mingling of the crews anyway. That way there will be no chance of any lingering enmities resurfacing once we are apart.'

'You mean for Ruther to remain on *Revenger*.'

'Anything else would be foolishness, dear heart.' Fura smiled. 'But I know you see that as plainly as I do.'

11

By common consent between the various expert parties – Tindouf, Lasling, Surt, Vouga – and factoring in the not-entirely-disinterested opinions of Lagganvor and the Ness sisters, a plan of works was agreed upon. It would require slightly more than three weeks to execute, and ought to be comfortably achievable in four, even allowing for the occasional mishap. At the end of that interval, the ships would be cut loose and take their independent courses. Both would sail for Trevenza Reach, but by somewhat indirect means, to cover all trace of their former association.

There was much to be concerned about after the separation, but Fura dared not count on anything until the first few days were behind them, and she vowed she would not begin to relax until they were into their second week of work.

It was tense, to begin with. The crews were starting to know each other, but not quite well enough to know their limits. An ill-chosen remark here, a jest-too-far there, might prove a sharp provocation. It would not take much, Fura knew, to turn their fragile truce into brawling disharmony, and not much beyond that to rip the crews apart for good. They were never more vulnerable than at the present time. Fura therefore instructed her own subordinates to show exceptional forbearance; to come to her before responding in kind, and at all times to consider the injustices wrought upon Werranwell's crew, and their own footnote in that sorry saga.

And yet, to her rising astonishment, as the days turned into that first week, and first week became a second, the flashpoint never came. The crews melded. There were hints of actual friendship. Lasling and Tindouf seemed to like each other without complication or impediment, and Tindouf celebrated this unlikely partnership by fashioning Lasling a new pipe, which he presented with all due ceremony.

Vouga and Surt circled each other like wrestlers, probing their areas of knowledge and ignorance. Fura would catch them in the galley at odd hours, peering at each other over tight-clasped drinks, cross-examining each other in terse, interrogatory bursts, giving the bare minimum away yet slowly, inexorably, establishing the basis for a mutual respect, whether they desired it or not. It turned out that while they had areas of shared expertise, agreed upon grudgingly, each was also good at some area in which the other was lacking. They would have made a good team, for any captain who could afford to keep two Integrators on the payroll.

Cossel, meanwhile, was a source of fascination to both the Ness sisters, for she had survived something in the region of thirty bauble expeditions without loss of life or limb, and in the course of her career she had visited ten or so of the most notorious baubles, including His Foulness, but also The Night Clock, The Shadow Castle, The Labyrinthine, The Milk Churn, The Flytrap and The Croupier. She had not always left these baubles with treasure – Cossel had never got rich under any of her captains – but she had got out with her life, and that was no small accomplishment. Fura and Adrana were more than content to hear Cossel reminisce about these expeditions, and if some gentle persuasion was initially needed to loosen Cossel's tongue – it turned out that she had a healthy enthusiasm for alcohol – once started, there was little stopping her. Like many Assessors, her knowledge had been gained through experience and word-of-mouth rather than book-learning, but it was no less deep or comprehensive for that. Fura tested her once or twice, throwing in a comment that contained an error about some historical subdivision of an Occupation, and Cossel never failed to pick up on the slip. She would have made an excellent asset for any crew, but for that awful, lingering suspicion that she was in some way a magnet for bad luck. For while it took uncommon skill to survive thirty consecutive expeditions, it was rather odd not to have stumbled on even a minor fortune during that span of employment. Fura was not superstitious, though, and she apportioned no blame to Cossel in this matter. Perhaps her captains had been over-cautious, their Openers not the quickest, their auguries and maps never the most up to date.

So, as these alliances and bonds of respect hardened into something barely distinguishable from companionship, so the weeks passed, and the work progressed. Fura was mildly amazed that there had not been more trouble, until she considered the other crew's evident depth of loyalty to Werranwell. They had liked him so much that they were ready to submit to his last order without rancour, for to turn against one or other of the Ness sisters was to disobey their beloved former captain, and that was unconscionable.

'I reckon he was a good man,' Fura said, while Adrana prepared her next injection of Mephrozine. 'A good man, with a good crew, and a good ship. And it was his very *bad* misfortune to run into us. I'd almost prefer that we'd taken a rotten crew, under a hated captain. Perhaps they'd have switched their loyalties just as easily.'

'You forget,' Adrana said, jabbing the needle in, and surprised at how little sympathy she felt when Fura flinched. 'They haven't switched their loyalties at all. They've merely accepted his choice of successor. They're not dishonouring his memory – quite the contrary. It was wise of him, too. He tried to devise the best way to keep his people alive. I think he loved them and felt that he owed them much more than what they'd received.'

Adrana injected the Mephrozine and withdrew the needle.

Fura swabbed the sore spot where it had gone in. 'I wonder what to do with him. I've had Lagganvor ask around, very delicately, and it appears that none of the older ones were acquainted with his funeral plans.'

'Did Lagganvor speak to Ruther?'

'I don't know. Why would Ruther be any wiser, when the others weren't?'

'Because he was Werranwell's boney, and therefore the one that the captain was most likely to confide his secrets to.' Adrana set about packing away the syringe and vials. 'Are you still fixed on the idea of one dose every two days?'

'Ain't see any reason to change my mind.'

'That was the fifty-sixth injection. Less than half your supply remains.'

'There's still an excellent margin of safety.'

'But a diminishing one.'

'What would you have me do, sister? The current dose may be the minimum effective measure to hold the glowy at bay. If I stretch out the intervals further, the glowy'll pounce.' She gave an involuntary shudder, remembering a muscled man in a bath of milk, the glowy shining out of him like the pages of an illuminated manuscript. Flashing back to his madness and the torment when the glowy's late-stage fits had their fierce hold on him. 'I won't become *him*. Perish the worlds, but that will not be *my* fate.'

'I think there was already plenty wrong with Glimmery before the glowy got into him.' Adrana sealed the wallet with her usual care. 'I can't push you, I know. It has to be your choice.'

'Just as it was my choice to survive on lightvine so I could come back and rescue you.' Fura touched her face, which was already starting to tingle as the Mephrozine took effect. 'This isn't just a mark of something that happened to me on the *Monetta*. This is a mark of you being alive.'

'I haven't forgotten. Nor am I ever likely to.'

*

Fura was visiting Eddralder and Merrix in the Kindness Room, where Strambli remained in their care. The two ships had been joined for eighteen days, and only a few hours earlier Adrana had given her the fifty-eighth dose of Mephrozine, nearly exhausting the sixth vial. For the first time in weeks, her sister had completed the procedure without the slightest suggestion of increasing the intervals between injections. Fura felt less as if she had won an argument, than that she had adhered with stubborn tenacity to an indefensible position, and therefore triumphed by default. A nagging part of her still wondered if Adrana was correct to have her concerns.

'The work is going well, Doctor,' she said to Eddralder, 'and the *Merry Mare* nearly repaired well enough to sail on her own.'

Eddralder dipped his head like the jib of a steam-crane.

'I am grateful for the information.'

'Very shortly, decisions will be taken concerning who goes with which ship. I thought we would do well to consider Strambli's situation, while we have the option.'

Eddralder lifted an eye to his patient, who had been sleeping since Fura's arrival. 'If you are looking for reassurances, I may have to disappoint you. The . . .. complaint . . . is not in retreat. It advances a little some days, and pauses others, but there is no indication that any of my treatments are capable of arresting it.'

'And her chances once we get to Trevenza Reach?'

Merrix looked up silently.

Her father answered: 'Not excellent.'

'But are they better than what can be offered on this ship?'

'That would depend on your definition of "better". Radical surgery is always a possibility. She does not wish to lose the limb, but there may come a point where all other interventions have failed.'

'Such a procedure would be better off done in Trevenza Reach?'

'There might be marginal benefits. On the other hand, this room is very well outfitted. Better still, there need be no secrecy between the parties involved.'

'Could you . . . do it?'

Eddralder regarded Merrix. Some wordless exchange passed between father and daughter.

'Yes. Between us, we could do what had to be done.'

Fura nodded gravely.

'I'm grateful for your candour, Doctor.'

'I presume it has some bearing on the coming decisions?'

'One ship may arrive ahead of the other. At the moment I'm minded to send the *Merry Mare* by the swiftest route, partly because she'll never have our speed and nimbleness, and she's less well-armed so needs an advantageous course, and partly because there's much less chance of that ship being connected to the Ness sisters and *Revenger*. She should make port in three or four weeks, following our separation. Once at Trevenza, Adrana may lay the ground for our arrival, which I shouldn't imagine will be too many days afterward.'

'Lay the ground in what sense?'

'Contacting such allies as we may find and procuring those supplies that are necessary for both ships.'

'You are starting to become concerned about the Mephrozine.'

'No, I am entirely unconcerned. But it will do no harm if Adrana finds some more while we are still sailing. Having her do the procurement will make very good sense. One look at me and they may start inflating the price, seeing how obviously I depend on the drug. Adrana isn't so affected, and so may strike a fairer price.'

He glanced at the patient to verify that she was still unconscious. 'And the bearing of all this on Strambli?'

'By your own admission, there's no reason for her to leave *Revenger*. She won't be greatly assisted by an early arrival at Trevenza, and of the two ships, ours is by far the best equipped for her care.'

'I concur.'

'I'm very glad of it, doctor. You'll remain with Strambli, and of course Merrix must remain with you. Might I . . .' An awkwardness forced a pause upon her. 'You mentioned Mephrozine.'

Eddralder looked at her with a distant curiosity.

'I did.'

'I know it has other uses, besides treating the glowy. There couldn't be any benefit to Strambli, could there?'

Merrix looked up again, but her father was the one who answered. 'There is very little in the literature to suggest that Mephrozine is an effective agent against the glowy. Besides . . . you have definite need of that drug, and it *is* proving satisfactory in your case. It would be foolish to squander what little supplies remain on a wing and a prayer.'

Fura felt some small but definite weight lift off her. 'I . . . am relieved. Not for Strambli – I'm still concerned about her – but at the thought that I might be able to do something and wasn't. You understand, don't you?'

'It is an entirely reasonable sentiment.'

Fura was glad of the doctor's words and wished to believe his assurance. For a few moments she did, wholeheartedly. Until something in Merrix's face gave her cause to doubt.

*

On the twentieth day, Paladin detected a sudden change in the condition of the Clacker, and alerted the Ness sisters to make all haste to the captains' quarters. Fura came down from the sighting room, Lagganvor taking over from her, and Adrana arrived from the *Merry Mare*, where she had been helping Vouga update their charts and almanacks, as well as gaining some familiarity with the layout and temperament of her own new command.

When they arrived, they found that the outer box was still sealed and cross-buckled to the side-wall of the cabin, but it was shaking visibly, and some dark green bubbling seepage issued from the part that had been shot through by the muddleheads. The box was making a continuous but off-tempo knocking sound, quite unlike the soft, distant whirring that had been coming out of it these past weeks.

'What's that stuff?' Fura asked, recklessly dipping her fingers into the green seepage, and then just as recklessly sniffing it.

'I think we should open the outer box again,' Adrana said. 'It doesn't matter if we overload the effector-displacement device; for all we know he could be drowning in that stuff and unable to fight his way out.'

'We could kill him by opening it.'

'We could kill him by *not* opening it. We can't be sure, but since I brought him aboard the responsibility ought to be mine and my instinct is that we need to open that box. Help me with these buckles. We'll lay it down on the floor.'

Gingerly, they removed the restraints and lowered the box against the surface that they agreed to call the floor, even in the near-weightless conditions under which *Revenger* now operated. The two sisters knelt close by the box, watching as the green bubbles continued to emerge. They formed a sticky, clotting froth.

'We should call Eddralder down,' Fura said.

'Alien medicine is as foreign to him as it is to us. We mustn't hesitate.'

She reached forward and sprung open the catches on the outer container. The lid hinged wide. Inside was a very curious spectacle. The green seepage was defining the boundaries of the inner container, yet the container itself was still invisible for at least four seconds out of five. In the moments when it showed itself – in intervals that were longer than any they had witnessed before – it became clear that the damage was not confined solely to the outer casing. The inner box, which was of entirely alien fabrication and embellishment, was cracked and buckled in places. The green seepage was oozing out of it in prodigious, breath-like surges. The box – or the volume of space it occupied – was jolting around like loose luggage on a bumpy tram.

'I thought the muddleheads only got the outer part,' Fura said.

'We were mistaken. Or we were right, and something else has gone wrong with it.'

'It's spending more and more time visible. It reminds me of the surface of a bauble, showing through a field just before it collapses.'

'Perhaps there's some relation between the two technologies, however distant. Or they both depend on a similar science. What was the height of sophistication to the bauble-makers of the Fourth Occupation may be bread and butter to a Clacker. Do not do that!'

Fura had jabbed her hand into the space occupied by the box, in the diminishing intervals between its fits of visibility. She jerked back her metal fingers and pressed them to her lips.

'Brrrr.'

'The box wants to do something,' Adrana said. 'That's why it's rattling around in there like an old washing machine. Perhaps it wants to open, and it can't, not when it's wedged into the outer part.'

'Then we've got to take it out. But only when it's visible. If our hands slip into the space it's occupying, and then it comes back . . . what did Lagganvor say would happen?'

'Never mind Lagganvor. We must do this.' Adrana looked at her sister with a firm authority. 'We'll have one chance, so there must be no hesitation. I'll take this side, you the other. We pull as hard as we can, for half a second, and if the box doesn't come free immediately, we let go. We can't risk our hands being trapped. You have one fewer to spare as it is.'

The box flickered out again, was absent for a second or two, then came back. Adrana sprung her hands onto its cold, slippery edge – greasy with that green lather – and pulled with all the force and determination she had. So did Fura. They had not needed to signal each other; they had not needed to exchange a word. There was a moment of stubbornness and then the box popped out as easily as a rotten tooth – tumbling at them just as the sisters fell back on their haunches.

Fura laughed. So did Adrana. They had done it, and as perfectly as they could have wished, and both still had a nearly full tally of digits. The box had come to rest before them, and after a few flickering transitions it became fully visible.

The sisters drew a collective breath. They sensed that something was about to happen.

So it did. The box gave a short exhalation, a snort of trapped gas – which was sweet-smelling, rather than foul – and sprung wide open, disclosing its occupant, which was shivering and shaking like a newborn.

The Clacker was tucked into a foetal ball and covered over in a slime of that same green material that had been forcing its way out of the box. Gluey wires and cables lay suspended in this quivering matrix, pale as worms.

'What do we do?' Fura asked.

'Help him,' Adrana said. She leaned forward and scooped the Clacker out of the box, the wires and cables falling away as she did so, and leaving only faint impressions of where they had been in contact with the alien. It felt more like a warm doll than a truly living form: a heavy, bulky doll that had been played with recently. The limbs moved under the pressure of her embrace, and she had the impression of some faint general stirring through the alien's body, even as it kept its face pressed to its chest or belly. As if it were surfacing through peculiar alien dreams, back to whatever passed for consciousness in its breed.

'Is all in hand?' Paladin asked.

'I think it's too soon to say,' Adrana answered. 'But I am equally sure that there's nothing you or I or anyone else on this ship can do that will make any difference.'

Fura swivelled around to face his globe. 'Have you met Clackers, Paladin?'

'If I ever had that pleasure, it is long since lost in the regrettable degradation of my memories. Of course, I do know something of the species. Their immediate needs are not too far from your own. They breathe a similar mix of gases, tolerate a similar range of temperatures, and may sustain themselves with our food and water – not indefinitely, but most certainly for several months, before deficiencies of certain elements and compounds cause them a range of complaints.'

'You are very well informed,' Adrana said.

'On the contrary, I am quite grievously ill-informed about almost everything. But I am particular about the little islands of knowledge I still contain.'

The Clacker was showing signs of further resuscitation. Adrana held it completely, but it was an awkward embrace, and would not have been possible on a world such as Mazarile. The Clacker was dense for its size, indicative of thick, heavy bones, which she supposed had something to do with its place of origin. Now the short yet muscular arms and legs were beginning to fidget, as if – distantly – it sensed both that it was awake, and also in a kind of restraint.

'Set him down,' Fura said softly. 'I think he wants to wake but isn't quite aware of his surroundings.'

Adrana set it down before her, allowing the faint force of their sail-generated acceleration to nudge it to the floor. The Clacker had two legs and four arms, the former appendages terminating in two toes, and the latter in two fingers and a thumb. The topmost pair of arms were attached to its body by shoulders at more or less the conventional location, with the lower pair, which were slightly smaller and more delicate, sprouting from just below the armpits of the upper set.

It sat on its haunches, with its legs curled in front of it. It was clothed, if that was the word, in a single thin garment that was made of an open weave, enclosing all parts of it except the head, with its great resonant casque. The garment was a dark silver colour. Pale green skin, mottled in places, showed through the weave. If the garment was there to protect the Clacker while in hibernation, or otherwise preserve its dignity, it was also open enough to allow the wires and fronds to find their way into flesh.

The fidgeting had abated, but now the remarkable head, which made up nearly half the Clacker's bulk, began to tilt up. The casque had a sort of crescent-shape to it, with a continuous convex curve running from front to back, the bulge of its resonant chamber below that, and then – less distinctly, because it merged with the face and neck – the concave undersurface. The crescent's front horn tapered down to meet the tip of a long, wide, lizard-like mouth, and the rear horn protruded backwards, curving down at the same time, and thus was it rumoured that a Clacker was the only living creature that could scratch the small of its back with its own head. The casque was a similar pale green to the rest of it, but had a lovely deep lustre to it, as of some fine varnished stone, and there were hints of blue and turquoise in the mottling. But it was also riven by large holes, with sharp ragged edges, which did not look like any natural part of the creature's physiology.

The Clacker was drowsily opening its eyes. There were two of them, one on either side of its head, tucked under the bulge of the casque's resonant cavity, and each situated just above the rearmost part of the mouth, and emplaced in a deep fortification of wrinkles. The eyes were mostly white with small dark pupils, and much better at looking sideways than peering directly ahead.

A wet, slurry-like sound came out of the Clacker. After a few seconds of this, it switched to the most disgusting liquid snorting.

'What's it trying to say?' Fura asked.

'I don't know. That first sound is how it builds up a picture of its surroundings, or how it tries to. The casque is a resonant structure, and very well evolved for sense-gathering. But it's obviously broken, and it can't make speech sounds properly, either.'

'Was it like this on Mulgracen?'

'No. Lagganvor and I were able to speak to it quite easily. Whatever's happened must have come about when we met the muddleheads.'

The Clacker's eyes were open but gummed over with yellow-green slime. It reached up with its upper forelimbs and, with some delicacy, scuffed them clean. Perhaps only then becoming aware of its situation, it gave a very creditable impression of a startled blink.

'Can you understand me?' Fura asked, in a loud and strident

manner, as if she were addressing a dim-witted child. 'You're on my ship now. You arranged passage with us from Mulgracen. We're on our way to Trevenza Reach.'

The Clacker looked at the Ness sisters, fixing them with first one eye and then the other, twisting its whole body as it did so, as if it doubted the evidence of either eye without corroboration from the other. Then it made more of that wet, snorting, slurry-like sound: a horrible hawking emanation. The snorting intensified in speed, although there was no sense to be made of it.

'We can't understand you,' Adrana said, frustratedly. 'You remember me, don't you? We met you in Darkly's emporium, but there was an attack on the way to port . . .'

The Clacker gave up on its sounds and made a quick repeated gesture with its lower two hands. One hand made a palm shape, the other swiped across it.

'I might venture,' Paladin said, 'that the individual is in want of pen and paper.'

Fura dashed to her desk and found what was required. She brought the items to the Clacker, and pressed them against its upper pair of hands. The Clacker examined the materials by touch, looking down and waggling its head, then began to write. The Ness sisters watched with a degree of amazement as the words appeared, in a slanting, sinuous, long-tailed script of such exacting neatness, precision and elegance that it would have served as an example to be copied, laboriously and without error, during one of their more tedious parlour lessons.

It said:

My Dear Captains,

I am grateful for your assistance.

I trust that you will expedite my delivery to my friends with all urgency.

All the answers you seek – and more – may be found in Trevenza Reach.

But only with my assistance, and survival.

On that matter, I must regretfully inform you that I am in very imminent danger of dying.

There may be less time than all of us would wish for.
Tazaknakak

*

'He never wanted to go back to any world,' Ruther said, raking fingers through the white shock of his hair. 'Not because he didn't love the worlds – he did, with all his heart – but because there wasn't one of them he liked more than the rest, and he said he'd come to like the view of them from outside. He said it was the prettiest spectacle anywhere in the Congregation, or out of it, and that was what he'd like his eyes fixed on, between now and the Old Sun's passing. He said we should find him a spare bit of plate from the hull, lash him to it in a suit we didn't mind not having, and fix a scrap of sail to the other side of the plate by a league or two of yardage, just enough to keep him facing the worlds, but not so much that he got blown away out into the Empty at the first solar gust.' Ruther swallowed, looking for all the world as if he was betraying some trusted confidence. 'He said he didn't think it would be too much trouble for us, once he was gone, but if it turned out that it *was* too much trouble . . .'

'It won't be,' Fura said, with a firm but kindly assertiveness. 'Not too much at all, if you're certain that was his wish.'

'I am,' Ruther said, dropping his eyes.

'If he told you this,' Adrana said, 'then he did so for a reason. Not because he meant you to keep it to yourself, but because he could trust you to disclose it when the time was right. You served him well, Ruther – and you serve him well now. We shall make the arrangements.'

'I think it might be fitting . . .' Ruther began.

'If the plate came from the *Merry Mare*?' Fura nodded, guessing his meaning. 'I'd insist on it. She was a good ship – she *will* be a good ship. And we'll find that yardage and enough sail to keep him steered to the Old Sun. He'll warm his face for a few more Occupations, I think.'

Fura's sentiments were sincere, in a fashion, but at the back of her mind was her determination to preserve the present cordiality, and do all in her power to ensure its prolongation. Even if it cost her a little in materials to do right by the dead captain, she would abide by his request; indeed, she considered herself to have done well out of it, for he could very easily have demanded something more expensive and troublesome to arrange.

So a suit was assembled for him, made up out of constituent parts that were damaged or unreliable, while still presenting a not-undignified whole, and a piece of hull plating about two spans by four was easily provided out of the repairs done to the *Merry Mare*. Werranwell was put into the suit and strapped to the plate. Yardage and ordinary sail-cloth was bundled into a package and, with both crews in solemn attendance, the whole was ejected into space with a slight spin to ensure the deployment and tensioning of the sail. Within an hour the ensemble had stabilised, with the sail catching flux and Werranwell serving as a counterpoint at the Sunward end of the rigging. Within another hour, watched by all, he had drifted far enough from the linked ships to be on the cusp of invisibility. He would bob around the Old Sun now, his orbit unpredictable, its average diameter gradually increasing in size, yet so slowly that it might be many centuries before he fell beyond the common haunts of ships, and at any point some kindly captain might find his corpse and nudge it back toward the light and life of the Congregation, understanding that though this man might not have wished burial on any world, nor had he forsaken them.

12

Tindouf's axe came down in a clean arc. There was a jerk as it separated the last line, a moment of strange hiatus, and then the two ships fell slowly away from each other.

A muted cheer sounded over the short-range squawk, reverberating through helmets and compartments.

There was no haste to scramble back inside either ship. The *Merry Mare* still had to run out its full spread of sail, and *Revenger* had hauled in much of its acreage for this most perilous stage of separation. Neither ship was accelerating, and the distance between their hulls was increasing at an extremely leisurely rate. It would be hours before they were too far apart for their crews to cross between them in tethered suits, and several days before it became inconvenient to use the launch. Yet, as the suited parties drifted this way and that, tidying up loose lines and securing tools and material, there was a sense that what had been done could not be revoked, and the sooner this separation was consummated by the formalities of an assigned captaincy, so much the better.

'You decreed that I should take the *Merry Mare*,' Adrana said. 'Did you ever give any consideration to the alternative?'

'I did, for all of three seconds.' Fura paused, tap-tap-tapping the nib of a pen against a blotting pad. 'Face it, dear heart: they'd never take me to their hearts as readily as you. I was the one who came aboard with a knife, looking like I meant to use it.'

'Meanwhile, you get sole command of this ship – and sole access to Paladin.'

Fura looked pained. 'I'm *gifting* you a ship, sister – you can hardly claim to be getting the raw end of the deal.' She sniffed. 'A perfectly fine ship, too – in much better condition than when we found it. Of course, if you don't like the idea of having a ship of your own . . .'

'I like it very well – just not the mechanics by which I arrived at my command.'

'What's done is done.'

'Yes – and if only all our difficulties could be brushed aside so easily.' Adrana stiffened, as if bracing herself for some onerous duty. 'I will take the ship – I could hardly not, given how tenaciously you mean to hold onto this one. But there are conditions.'

'Naturally.'

'I must complete the faster crossing and arrive ahead of *Revenger*. It's as little as three weeks to Trevenza, if the weather's kind, and we run into no trouble. You may only be a week behind us, but there can be no delay where Tazaknakak is concerned. Therefore he must come with me.' She turned her gaze to the makeshift crib they had made for him, in which the alien was now – judging by the irregular, wet, snoring-like noises coming out of him – in some state of slumber. 'He can't be helped by Eddralder, unlike Strambli, but there's a real chance his friends may be able to do something, if we reach them soon enough. Besides, he has been my responsibility from the outset, and he remains my responsibility now. I won't abandon him to an uncertain fate on *Revenger*.'

'And yet you would abandon Strambli?'

'I didn't say that at all. We both know that her chances have very little to do with what ship she's on, or how quickly she's brought to Trevenza. Though she has a marginal advantage in being close to Eddralder, should an operation be needed.'

'That seems . . . agreeable,' Fura said.

'Good. I rather expected you to dissent, which makes me wonder what it is you want from me.'

Fura jammed the pen into its inkwell and opened one of her many journals, flattening it wide with magnetic paperweights. 'Nothing very much. I was merely thinking of the detailed rostering of our two ships, and who'd be of most benefit at your side. For a while we may be able to send signals to each other by optical telegraph, but that will become difficult at long-range and in any case should be reserved for emergency communications only. Obviously using the squawk is completely out of the question. There'll inevitably come a point when we can't communicate, even by telegraph, and each of us will be totally alone, except for the wise counsel of those at our sides. That's why I would like you to take Prozor. She's wily, versed in many skills, and I think quite generally liked by Werranwell's party. In return I should take the boy, Ruther.'

'Why Ruther?'

'Because, dear heart, you have no skull and I do.'

'We discussed this. You may have Ruther, but only for the purposes of guidance concerning the use of that skull. He mustn't use it at all, and I would advise *you* against using it except in emergency. But I won't have Prozor.'

This drew a sharp, quizzical look from Fura. 'You've taken against her?'

'Far from it. I like her very much. I think you like her too, but find her an uncomfortable and constraining influence on your actions: a conscience you would sooner banish to another ship.'

Fura twitched. 'You do not know me half as well as you imagine, sister.'

'I know you a third as well, and that is sufficient. Prozor remains with you; I will take Lagganvor.'

'He was my prize, not yours.'

'You found him, admired him as you would a shiny new hatpin, and then grew bored of him. Once his intelligence led you to The Miser, you had no further need of his services.'

'A little harsh,' Fura conceded. 'But not a million leagues from the truth.' She elevated her palm, as if she were bestowing some rare pardon. 'You may have him.'

There was no farewell kiss, no embrace. But Adrana reached for her sister's hand and for a moment they looked into each other's eyes with a giddy mutual astonishment at the journey that had brought them to this point: this parting, each about to take sole command of a fully-rigged sunjammer.

'I look forward to our reunion,' Adrana said.

'As do I,' Fura answered. 'My last visit to Trevenza Reach ended on something of a sour note. I don't intend to let history repeat itself.'

*

Adrana was going through the books and journals, packing any that she thought she might need – and that Fura might plausibly do without – into a sturdy leather satchel. Captain Werranwell's library was not nearly so well-furnished as that on *Revenger*, and there would soon come a point where it would be impractical to signal for information concerning matters of navigation or shipmastery.

She sneezed as she ruffled the pages of a scuffed but otherwise serviceable copy of *The Book of Worlds*, turning to the entry for Trevenza Reach:

A spindleworld of some modest renown. Its celebrity is in no small part due the peculiarity of its orbit, being highly eccentric in comparison to the common population of habitable bodies constituting the Congregation. Because it may at any given time lie inside the Thirty-Fifth Processional, or some prodigious distance beyond it, the prospective traveller is well advised to consult reliable almanackal tables before committing to what may be a lengthy and costly crossing. The word of crews is not to be depended upon.

Some ten leagues from end to end, and very agreeably disposed with regard to the provision of gravity, Trevenza Reach has, at

the most recent census, a population of one and two tenths of a
million . . .

'You was intending to say goodbye, girlie, wasn't you? Or was it your plan to scuttle off to your new ship and hope I didn't notice? I got word that I wasn't your preferred candidate.'

Adrana snapped shut the book. Its pages exhaled a snort of dust and she slipped it into her satchel.

'I would like to have you on that ship very much, Proz.'

'Then why's it come to me that I'm stayin' aboard this hulk, and Mister Lag's taking my natural seat on the other?'

Adrana buckled the satchel. She had enough books for now.

'You would be an asset to either crew, Proz. If I had expressed a firm preference for your company, and Fura had relented, you would be badgering her with exactly the same questions. The fact is there is only one of you, and whichever ship you are not aboard will be handicapped.'

'Well, if you mean to flatter me . . .'

'I do not – you are much too wise and sure of yourself to be swayed by flummery. I merely state the facts. You are as beneficial to a ship as a well-tuned sweeper or a fine chasing coiller. But one of us must have you, and one must manage without. The choice is made.' She gave a small unconcerned shrug. 'It might as easily have been decided by rolling dice.'

'And this dice-rolling – did that apply equally to Mister Lag?'

Adrana stiffened. 'You are natural counterparts,' she said carefully. 'If one ship lacks Prozor, there may be some compensation in Lagganvor.'

'Fura says you pleaded to be able to take Lag, over me.'

'That is not . . .' Adrana had started harshly, so she silenced herself and recommenced in a more conciliatory tone. 'That is *not* the case. I promise you as a friend. We horse-traded. If anything, I was the one who made the sacrifice. You know how forceful Fura can be, when she has her mind set on an outcome.'

'I know how forceful both of you can be,' Prozor said.

'I assure you there is no malice in my accepting of Lagganvor instead of you. Besides, this arrangement – this division of crews – is only a convenience until we make Trevenza. After that the cards may be reshuffled. I do not even think of this sole captaincy as a permanent state of affairs.'

'So you not wantin' me, that's nothing to do with you wantin' him more?'

Adrana sighed. 'How well do we know each other? I would take one of you over a hundred of him.'

'Which begs the question, girlie . . . why do you want him with you? I might be a bit addled in the noggin these last few months, but I don't think it's 'cause you're sweet on the cove.' She narrowed her eyes. 'You ain't sweet on the cove, are you?'

Adrana smiled thinly. 'No . . . decidedly not.'

'But you do want him around. Well, he's useful, I'll grant that. But there's more to it, ain't there?'

'I assure you there is no more to it.'

'Thing is, I ain't so green as not to have noticed a few things. You keep a very close eye on Mister Lag. You always have done, nearly from the day he came aboard.'

'He was a former associate of Bosa Sennen. It behoved us all to keep our eyes on him.'

'But yours especially. In Mulgracen, you went off shoppin' with Mister Lag, not your natural kin.'

'Perhaps it suited Fura and I to have a few hours apart. Do not make more of this than is needed, Proz.'

'You've got more than a few hours of separation comin' up, that's for sure. But you still want Mister Lag where you can watch him. Well, I shan't poke any more where I'm not wanted.'

'Thank you,' Adrana said tersely.

'But I will say this: if there's reason enough to think he ain't to be entirely trusted, you should've confided in old Proz. I'd have been fair with you . . . understandin' even. And if I found myself forced into holding a secret from my captain . . . one of my captains, I should say – well, it wouldn't have been the first time.' Prozor reached down into her collar and tugged on a leather drawstring. She came out with a little pill-shaped box, sheathed in dark blue velvet. 'Been keepin' this about me long enough; might as well pass it on to someone likely to benefit. He gives you any trouble, you might think of givin' this a squeeze. It won't kill him, but it might put the cove at a disadvantage, you get my drift.'

Adrana felt stricken by her lies to Prozor. It was all the worse for the fact that Prozor had nearly guessed the truth – perhaps, indeed, had guessed it completely – and still Adrana denied her the truthful admission she was owed. It was all she could bear not to confess her position there and then.

But she could not. No matter how well she trusted Prozor, a secret shared was a secret imperilled.

'I don't need any gifts, Proz. We aren't saying farewell. We're just going off on different ships for a few weeks.'

'But you'll take it anyway.' Prozor opened Adrana's palm and pressed the box into it. 'It ain't much, just a Firebright. But they're rare nowadays and I always thought it'd be a shame if it didn't go to a deserving cause.'

'I am not deserving,' Adrana said quietly, and if there was to be an admission, that was the extent of it.

Perhaps it was sufficient.

'You take it nonetheless, girlie.' Prozor closed Adrana's fingers around the box. 'And we *are* sayin' farewell. It don't mean goodbye for the rest of eternity. Just – travel well. And I want you to travel well.'

Adrana re-opened her satchel and placed the box inside, nestled next to *The Book of Worlds*.

'Travel well, Prozor. I shall see you in Trevenza Reach.'

*

Within a day of the separation, both ships had gathered their final crews into their hulls. The launch was the last thing to make the crossing, transferring a few final supplies from *Revenger* to the *Merry Mare* before scuttling back to its mother vessel. Just before the point of last contact, Doctor Eddralder had proposed that his daughter should transfer to the other ship, but Fura had denied it without equivocation. Eddralder said that it would be useful to have someone with a tiny bit of medical knowledge on both ships, and while there was a force to that argument, Merrix was a pair of hands that Fura could not afford to lose. Besides, as Adrana recognised, Eddralder's principle motivation was to make sure that his daughter was on the ship that he felt had the best chance of making it to port without molestation, and in his view that ship was not *Revenger*.

And so, with their rosters settled, and their captains formalised in name, the two ships were at last far enough apart for each to run out a full spread of sail without risk of entanglement. It was a stern test for any crew at any time, but doubly so in a ship that had been lately repaired, and whose particular new foibles were not yet documented.

Lasling was Adrana's new Master of Sail, and he had every incentive to ensure that the work went without complication, and so it proved. Lasling called for a pause at various intervals, pressing his eye to strain-gauges and torque-dials, and twice he went outside to make inspections and adjustments that could not be completed except in vacuum, and he conferred with Meggery at urgent moments, for a Master of Ions could make or break the process with an elegant or clumsy cooperation. Once he signalled Tindouf, and the two men conversed in the strange and specialised argot of their similar professions, for Tindouf was far from ignorant about the problems Lasling now faced.

But despite these hiatuses there was no serious hitch at any stage in the process, and the running out and tensioning of ordinary sail, rather than catchcloth, now seemed to Adrana to be a rather unremarkable and drab business. Over the coming days – weeks, even – there would be a gradual process of adjustment and finessing of the arrangements, requiring many hours of vacuum operations, but that was part of the ordinary business of any ship and crew, and in any case had the added benefit of keeping the hands from going too mad with confinement.

While all this was going on, the crew of *Revenger* had their own sails to attend to, and since she must soon pass muster as a friendly privateer, rather than a creature of ambush and shadow, *Revenger* was obliged to swap a measure of her catchcloth for the same ordinary sails as bedecked the *Merry Mare*. They had done this before, on the approach to Wheel Strizzardy, The Miser and Mulgracen, but in recent months they had been running mostly on catchcloth alone, except when navigation demanded otherwise, and now that black perfection had to be marred by the intrusion of square leagues of mirror-bright sail, easily detectable across great distances, and greatly susceptible to sail-flash.

There was no alternative. As soon as both ships fell into the threshold of Trevenza Reach's sweeper range, which could happen sooner than anticipated, they had to look entirely unthreatening. They might also need to pass inspection at closer range, which was why *Revenger*'s crew, once they were done with the sails, soon had to start papering over her gun-ports with tar-stiffened sheets and paint. Again, it was work they had done before, and which to a degree had been only partially undone by the recent engagements.

Soon the ships were a thousand leagues apart, and not long after that, as the solar wind bore on their sails, ten thousand. It was a greater distance than the average mind could easily comprehend, yet only a scratch compared to the fifty million leagues which separated one side of the Congregation from the other.

And even that was nothing – less than nothing – compared to the immensity of cold emptiness in which the Congregation floated, bright and tiny as a single mote of dust, lit for an instant as it drifted through a vast, unthinking solitude of darkness and silence.

*

With the gentlest of touches, she attempted to rouse the alien in its crib. The Clacker had been making disagreeable liquid noises while it slept – if that was indeed an accurate term for its condition – and although she wished to have him in her cabin at all times, she had been obliged to press stoppers into her ears if she wished to get any thinking done.

'Tazaknakak. Please wake.'

Vouga floated behind her, watching with his arms folded. 'You didn't think you'd be better off leaving him on Mulgracen?'

'Even with this snoring,' Adrana said, 'I am not sorry to have him with us. But it would be so much easier if he wasn't troubled by this injury.'

'So much easier for you, not having to put up with that gurgling racket?'

'For the both of us, Vouga – although I won't deny that there's a degree of self-interest. I'm starting to hear that snorting in my dreams. Do you really think you can help him?'

'He'll need to be the judge of that. I've got enough on my conscience without adding the death of an alien.'

'We shall endeavour to ensure it doesn't come to that. But he is ill, and I think this intervention may help him, in a small way.' She shook the alien more vigorously, until his eyes opened to narrow squints. Tazaknakak rolled out from the balled form he adopted when sleeping, unpeeling his six limbs and stretching the upper two pairs. He gave off a sweet, slightly stale smell, like the crumb-flecked bottom of a cake box. 'Tazaknakak, please awaken. This man has something that may make you feel better.'

She passed the alien a writing block and pen. He fumbled for both and wrote:

I do not think this is the same ship.

'It isn't,' she answered. 'I've taken control of another vessel, the *Merry Mare*, and this man Vouga is one of her crew.'

Our arrangement is annulled?

'No: my pledge to you still stands. *Revenger* is shadowing us, and somewhere behind both our ships is a hostile squadron. Arafura and I agreed that the best way to get you to Trevenza Reach was for you to come aboard this ship and make the fastest possible crossing. We've already been sailing on separate courses for four days – you were unconscious the whole while, or I would have informed you of our plans.'

Please do not wake me again. I will go back to sleep very shortly and conserve my energies as best I can. If I am not dead when we reach Trevenza, return me to the preservation box. It is very badly damaged, but the effector-displacer device may function long enough to smuggle me onto that world. Once there you must make contact with my friends – if they do not make contact with you first.

'Tazaknakak, I wouldn't have woken you without good reason. I know that what's happened to your casque is very bad. You can't form a sense-picture and you can't make monkey speech sounds.'

His pen moved again.

You wake me to remind me of the awfulness of my predicament?

'Vouga, show him.'

Vouga came forward tentatively. He knelt next to Adrana, by the Clacker's crib and opened his apron, spilling out an assortment of tools and materials. 'I've got a clever resin, your alien-ness. It's rare stuff, and ordinarily we'd save it for emergencies . . . but I suppose if anything counted as one, it's you.'

A resin?

'Tell him, Vouga.'

'It's called quickglass. If you get a crack in your visor, you mix some up and spoon it on. It flows into the crack and forms a seal. It's cleverer than that, though. It knows what it has to do. If there's a curve to the visor, it'll form the same curve. And once it's cured, which only takes a few minutes, it goes the same colour and transparency as the old stuff. The match is so good you'll never see where the old stuff ends and the quickglass begins.'

The alien looked up at her. Although its eyes were small, and only a secondary faculty, she thought she saw in them a desperate hopefulness; a yearning tempered only by the terrible fear that what was being offered might be a hoax or a phantom.

'Vouga was thinking this resin might be able to seal up your casque,' Adrana said. 'We don't have too much in our stores – it's Ninth Occupation technology, so very precious – but he's

173

measured the quantities, and he thinks there's enough to put right the damage. If the quickglass works with living tissue as well as it does inert matter, it ought to form a repair with the same resonant properties. You would be able to sense and speak again.'

But there is a risk.

'Yes . . . yes there is. Perhaps you know better than me, Tazaknakak, but I do not think this has ever been attempted with a living organism. Let alone a Clacker.'

You desire my consent.

'More than that,' Adrana said. 'This is a delicate matter, Tazaknakak, but it needs to be said. When we meet your friends, as I hope we shall, it would be best for all concerned if you're still alive. But if that isn't the case . . . well, then I should be very glad indeed to have a letter from you, in a hand that couldn't possibly be forged, indemnifying us against any responsibility for your death.'

The alien nodded slowly. He scribbled out his answer.

You are right. That is indeed a delicate matter.

'What of it, Tazaknakak?'

Tell your man to prepare his resin. By the time he is ready you shall have your letter of indemnity.

*

The slip of paper had been double-folded, like a lover's note, then pushed into the seam between the door to the captains' quarters and the pressure bulkhead into which it was set. For a second when she saw it, Fura thought it was some small pale moth that had somehow travelled with them from the worlds, entirely undetected until this moment, haplessly batting itself against the door.

She pinched it out with forensic delicacy, carried it to her desk, opened it, allowed it to rest before her, washed over in Paladin's pink-red light. Even opened out, it was a small rectangle of paper, seemingly torn from the corner of a journal, and there was only one line of writing on it. The words were neatly done, and she recognised the hand from Merrix's turns in the sighting room.

The message said:

My father did not tell you the truth.

That was all.

It was enough.

She unlocked her desk drawer and took out the wallet with its vials and little glass syringe. She had completed sixty-five doses, all but sixty-three of which had been injected into her by Adrana. The last two, since the ships had parted, she had done herself – clumsily and hesitantly, but with eventual success. She could have gone to Eddralder, or even Prozor, but now that Adrana was away she saw no reason not to strive for independence.

She was halfway through the seventh vial; only three completely full vials remained. Thirty-five doses; less than half of what she had already used, but sufficient for seventy more days if she held to her present regime. The *Merry Mare* would be at Trevenza in three weeks; *Revenger* would arrive in four, depending on weather and course corrections. That would still leave her with about a month's supply in hand.

A month was a long time, she told herself. A very great many things could be achieved in a month.

'I'm going to see Eddralder, Paladin,' she said. 'Call me if anything arises, from your own instruments or the sighting room.'

She pressed Merrix's note into her journal and left the captains' quarters. She went through the galley, along the yellow-green of corridors lit by lightvine, past coil-gun batteries and sail-control gear and down into the Kindness Room.

She had braced herself before entry, anticipating a sickly smell – she remembered well the stench of Strambli's initial wound when it had begun to turn – but there was none of that now, only the lingering chemical background of potions and disinfectant products.

Strambli was strapped loosely to the bed, under light sheets, with Merrix taking her temperature as they arrived. Her eyes were open, her face turning toward Fura as she came into the room. But there was no alteration in her expression, which remained blankly absent of feeling or interest.

'There's been no change,' Eddralder said, lifting his eyes from a medical almanack, before slipping a bookmark into the pages. 'I would have informed you if there was anything to report.'

'Strambli?' Fura asked.

The face locked onto her with a fraction more attentiveness, but the eyes seemed to be focused beyond Fura, fixated on something distant and curious. 'When is Captain Trusko coming to see me?' Strambli asked, mouthing the words in a half-whisper. 'They said he'd come.'

'Captain Trusko won't be coming,' Fura answered. 'He's been dead a long time, Strambli. Don't you remember?'

'They said he'd come.'

'He died. I'm your captain now. Captain Fura Ness. Do you know which ship you're on?'

Strambli showed puzzlement, then the mask of her face produced a sudden and disconcerting smile. 'I know which ship! The *Nightjammer*! *Dame Scarlet*! Bosa Sennen took us and made us her crew!'

'No . . . not that ship. It was once, but it's not now.'

'I see the glowy in you, Captain!' She lifted an arm, pointing at Fura, that same grin splitting her features. 'I see you! You've got it good and shiny, ain't you! There's *glimmery* in your eyes!'

In a low voice, Eddralder said: 'She is lucid now and then, but these intervals of confusion are becoming more common than the lucidity. At other times, she is unconscious. I would not call it sleep, exactly. And when she is lucid, she complains terribly of the cold.'

'It's a fever, then – a sign that her body's fighting the infection.'

'There is no fever,' Merrix answered. 'No heightened temperature. No indication of any infectious response.'

'Something's wrong with her.'

'Of that,' Eddralder said, 'we may be in no doubt. But whatever was happening to her wound early on, when she stole from my supplies, was a phase that's passed. Her body's stopped resisting. It's as if it accepts the inevitable – that the transformation will continue, relentlessly.'

'May I see?'

Eddralder elevated the sheet so that Strambli's leg was exposed. Fura controlled her reaction, although it took some considerable force of will to do it. If there was even the slightest chance that Strambli was taking any of this in, she did not want her to be unduly distressed. But perhaps her silence, and her strained composure, would have been all the indication Strambli needed to realise all was not well.

The last time she had seen the wound – however one wished to define it – there had been a translucence to Strambli's skin, and a hint of colourless crystal depths beneath. Now that point of transformation had extended itself to encompass almost the entire extent of her lower leg. From her toes to her knee, the skin had turned waxy and colourless, and a large area around the original wound had gained that familiar translucence, so that equally pale and glassy structures were becoming visible beneath it. At the extremities, there were still hints of uncorrupted tissue, which looked curiously unaffected, lacking any visible indication of necrosis.

'How is blood reaching those areas?'

'It isn't,' Eddralder said. 'At least, it can't be, judging by what we can see of the transformed regions. Yet by some means, there is preservation of life, and nervous function, until the translucence penetrates, and transforms. Which it is doing, quite relentlessly.'

Fura eyed Strambli again.

'You have to remove it. She was right. It's turning her into . . . something else.'

'Ghostie gubbins,' Merrix said quietly.

'I'm going Ghostie!' Strambli said, delightedly. 'That's my fate! I'd like pretty glimmery eyes like yours, but it's Ghostie gubbins for me! There's glass in my bones now! There's glass swimmin' into my noggin! Shoaly fishy glass! Soon you won't see me!'

'She's gone insane.'

Eddralder did not contradict her.

'If she does, and fully, it may be a mercy. But there is still enough of her left to understand her predicament.'

'Could Mephrozine help her?'

The tiniest flicker of surprise showed itself in Eddralder's face. 'I answered that question already.'

'You said there wasn't much in the literature to suggest it would be helpful. Which leads me to think there must be something, or you'd have made a flat-out denial.'

'I told her,' Merrix said. 'I found the chapter you'd been reading, and I saw that it said there was a possibility of using Mephrozine in cases of Ghostie progression.'

'You should never have done that,' Eddralder said.

Merrix turned to him with a calm defiance.

'It was the truth.'

'Is she right, Doctor?' Fura asked. 'Can it do something for Strambli? And don't blame Merrix: if there's even a chance of this helping, she was right to let me know.'

'There is hardly any chance at all. That is why I did not bring it to your attention. Besides . . . even if I were to put my faith in those old accounts . . .'

'What?' Fura asked sharply.

'You do not have enough Mephrozine to spare.'

'Doesn't that depend on how much she needs? I could begin rationing you some of my supply from this point on.'

'That isn't how it works. The dose would need to be given to her in one go, not parcelled out over weeks.'

'Tell her,' Merrix said.

'There is no account of a successful intervention with anything less than ten units. And that is an outlier. Of the few remaining anecdotes . . . those to which I would ascribe any reliability . . . a twenty-unit dose seems to be the effective minimum.'

'I have thirty-five remaining, Doctor.' She swallowed hard. 'So I would only have fifteen units remaining. That might see me through to Trevenza, but with no margin at all. And if we were delayed, or I needed to increase the frequency of my doses . . .'

'Which is why I gave you the answer I did, the first time you asked.'

Fura looked down at her flesh hand. Faint whiskers and curlicues of yellow-green phosphorescence shimmered beneath the skin. It would be brightening in her eyes and face, she knew, betraying the turmoil of her emotions; the clash of expectation against reality, the shame and the fear she felt for herself.

'If I had more to spare . . .'

'You don't,' Eddralder replied. 'And that is an end to it.'

13

Lagganvor swung his leg up, planting his boot on the edge of her desk. He had just come in from outside, where he had been helping Lasling with adjustments to the rigging, and was brimming with the insufferable cockiness of a man who had done a hard day's work and wished the world to know about it.

'I dropped in on Vouga as I came up the lock,' he said, pushing back a fringe of sweat-sodden hair. 'He tells me it went well with our passenger. It'll be a relief to all of us not to have that infernal snorting sounding throughout the ship.'

'It's far too soon to tell,' she returned, annoyed at his flippancy. 'You were with me when we made our pledge to Tazaknakak. Of all people, I'd expect you to have a little sympathy.'

'Oh, I am heartily sympathetic. After all that trouble with the muddleheads, I'd be inconsolable if the poor creature died on us now.' He pecked absently at a fingernail. 'But you say he's not out of the woods?'

Adrana shook her head. She had not long come down from the infirmary, where the alien was being tended to, and she knew there was no cause for early celebration.

'Vouga applied the quickglass to the damaged parts of his casque. It was . . . clearly uncomfortable for Tazaknakak. I think it was a little like being smothered, or having a death-mask put on your face when you're still alive. He thrashed around, tried to paw away the quickglass as it was setting. Then he became much quieter.'

'I hope not *too* much quieter. I'm no doctor but very, very quiet things often prove to have a lot in common with dead things.'

'He isn't dead. I put a mirror to his mouth and there were definite signs of life. I expect I could have found a heartbeat if I'd searched thoroughly enough. They're really not so very different from us.'

'They're aliens. They couldn't be more different if they were made of sugar.'

'Since you brought up the muddleheads, and evidently had some prior familiarity with their like, you can answer a question that's been on my mind since we left Mulgracen.'

'I shall endeavour.'

'How can muddleheads live? You said they were temporary agents, stitched together out of bits of us and bits of alien. I saw those bits as well. But I cannot see how any kind of life, even a parodic imitation, could be possible if we are each as different as you maintain.'

'Alien science, my dear Adrana. Ours is not to understand. If it doesn't kill us, that is helpful. If we can use it, that is also helpful. If we can use it and occasionally turn a profit, that is *particularly* helpful.'

'I am glad that you are content with ignorance. I am not.'

He shook his head in quiet exasperation. 'Will the Ness sisters ever stop picking at the edges of things?'

He had meant it as criticism, but she took it in the contrary sense, and had to work most strenuously not to show a blush of pride.

'Not so long as we draw breath. I couldn't live like you, never once questioning your world.'

He looked around at the spartan cabin of the former Captain Werranwell. 'And yet, it is working out so *terribly* well for you both, this questioning. You have a shabby ship to your name, a doubtful passenger who may yet die on you, a crew of decidedly mixed reputation, and furthermore there is a price on your head. As for your sister, her fortunes are scarcely an improvement on your own. She might have a dark, fast ship, with a dim-witted robot for a brain, but she can't dock it anywhere; it's haunted by the spirit of an undead lunatic, and there are a dozen or more fully-armed squadron craft intent on shooting her out of existence . . .' He sucked in through his teeth and made a clicking sound with his tongue.

'If Paladin had been capable of being moved,' Adrana said, 'I should gladly have had him with me aboard this ship.' She glared at him. 'Will you be so kind as to remove your boot?'

He lowered his leg and scuffed away a smear of polish that had marked the edge of her desk. 'Was there something you wanted to discuss, besides the ontological status of muddleheads, and the lamentable condition of my manners?' He dropped his voice confidingly, cupping a hand to the side of his mouth. 'I've had to blend in with all sorts of undesirables lately – pirates and the like. You mustn't blame me if their habits rub off.'

'It's not your habits that concern me.'

He looked encouraged. 'No?'

'No. It's the degree to which I can trust you not to betray this ship to your squadron.'

Lagganvor glanced around nervously, as if there was a chance of her words spilling out into the rest of the ship. 'From what I gather, it was your choice to have me here in the first place.'

'Yes – but only because I know you'd get up to mischief if left unchecked aboard *Revenger*. At least here I can keep an eye on you some of the time, instead of not at all.'

He jerked back his head, affronted.

'I gave you my personal assurance.'

'You're a spy: a spy, a murderer and an impostor. Lying comes as naturally to you as breathing.'

'I may be a spy,' he answered, with a too-earnest quaver in his voice. 'But I am also your friend, and I want only the best for you.'

'Then I am doubly glad to be able to keep watch over you.' She cocked her head, trying to reach the true core of him, the man beneath the mask. 'You won't let me down, will you? Now of all times.'

'I won't attempt to signal my masters. That is a cast-iron promise.'

She shook her head fondly. 'I wish I could put some stock in it. My only solace is in that eye of yours not having infinite capacity. I tell myself that if it *could* signal across to the squadron, or even fly back to them with a message, you would have already used it against us. So it must have limitations of range and power, even as a signalling device.'

'Your deductions,' Lagganvor said, 'are ... not without foundation.'

'I trust I will not have cause to regret them.' She paused and picked up the heavy item that rested on her desk, fixed there by a magnetic patch in its base. 'I found this in Werranwell's private drawer, a day after the ships separated. His tastes, as you noted, ran to the austere. This seems anomalous, wouldn't you agree?'

Lagganvor took the item she offered. It was a metal head with a flattened base and a cavity in its skull. A crude, gargoyle-like face had been worked into one side of it, with goggling, thimble-like eyes and a tongue like a piece of stamped tin.

'An inkwell,' Lagganvor said, with a vague shudder of distaste. 'There would have been a sealable membrane across this hole, to keep the ink in.'

Adrana tapped a finger against a functional block of metal on the other side of the desk. 'He already had this inkwell, which was much more to his character, and it still works. Why would he keep such an unprepossessing and ugly specimen, if it had no utility?'

'Sentiment? A kindly aunt gave it to him, on the occasion of his first voyage? A souvenir from a misguided youth?'

'Tilt it in your hands. Observe what happens to the face.'

Frowning slightly, Lagganvor did as he was bid. At some point there was a click from inside the head and the tongue pushed out to twice its former extent, while the eyes nearly popped out of their sockets, protruding like half-laid eggs. He rolled the object, studying it with a deeper yet guarded interest, and the tongue and eyes clicked back into place.

'There is some . . . counter-weight, or trigger, inside the thing. It responds to the movement like a simple toy.'

'That was exactly my first assumption.'

'And by implication . . . you have discarded that assumption.'

She nodded decorously. 'I have.'

'Then what is it?'

'Something that was evidently of sufficient value to Werranwell that he kept it locked away from the rest of his crew. Something precious and ugly and useful.' She looked at him teasingly. 'What do you imagine it could be?'

'It may astonish you to hear that I don't have all the answers.'

'Then it's as well that I have a theory of my own – one that won't be too hard to test.'

'Are you going to tell me?'

'Not just yet. Not until I'm quite certain that I'm not wrong.' She paused, took the gargoyle head back from him, and swivelled her own finger as if to circle back to the original focus of their conversation. 'This pledge of yours, not to betray us?'

'I have never been more sincere.'

'Good. So long as I lock you out of the squawk and sweeper and sail-controls, and so long as that eye doesn't have the range to signal back to your masters . . . which all logic informs me it cannot . . . then I do not think you can undo us.'

He rubbed gently at his throat. 'I am greatly relieved.'

'Do not be. Every hour puts us thousands of leagues from Fura. Thousands of leagues from whatever protection you might have imagined you could find in her. I don't hate you, Brysca – I don't even dislike you. You found your way into our nest out of love for your brother, and I won't condemn you for that.'

He pushed back into his chair, a tightness making the side of his mouth twitch. 'I really don't recommend the use of my real name. It's better for both of us if you keep to the habit of calling me Lagganvor . . .'

'I don't recommend that you break your pledge to me, either. I have a ship to protect now, and a passenger worth a hundred of you.' She returned the gargoyle to its drawer, locking it for safe-keeping, and making a deliberate show of closing her fist around the key. 'I'll hurt you very badly if you cross me.'

'I don't doubt it. But I suspect your justice would be an improvement on Arafura's.'

'Perhaps. But once I was done with you, I'd save the scraps for my sister. It'd be the least she deserves.'

Lagganvor winced.

*

Ruther tugged at the white shock of his hair as if he meant to doff an invisible cap. In the red light of *Revenger*'s bone room, that colourless stripe blazed all the brighter, lit from within. It served only to make the rest of him seem younger.

'You want me to . . . help you use the skull?'

'Not exactly, Ruther.' Fura paused and ran her palm over the skull, as fondly as if it were a thoroughbred steed, oiled and groomed. 'There's that other boy out there – the young man they've put in charge of hunting us down. The one who kept firing on your ship even after we'd made clear you were an innocent party.'

'I wish I could tell you his name.'

'I'll soon know it. I've had a sense of him already, and I believe I know a little of how he thinks, but that ain't enough for me. I've got to get a detailed idea of that squadron's movements: its position, speed and so on. Then I'll know where it is in relation to both *Revenger* and the *Merry Mare*, and whether it presents a greater or lesser threat to either ship. One of us must get through, Ruther. I'd sooner it were both ships, but if there are actions I can take to maximise Adrana's chances – and those of her passenger – then I shall take them. But they must be the right actions, and to determine that I must have an accurate picture; an accurate insight into the mind of that boy. I know I can reach him through this skull – I think he half expects me to attempt contact. And I want to be inside his head. But I very much don't want him getting into mine.'

'You couldn't hold him out?'

'Not this one, Ruther. He's strong – perhaps as strong as Adrana and I ever were. I might be able to resist him, but should I fail he'd have immediate knowledge of our position and speed.'

Ruther nodded tentatively, as if he understood her meaning, but did not care for the direction it was steering his thoughts. 'Captain Werranwell was very particular about the things he wanted me to know, and the things he didn't.'

'Exactly, Ruther.'

He lowered his eyes to the skull. 'You'd like me to plug in.'

'I'm not asking anything of you that wasn't part of your duties on the *Merry Mare*. You'd be safe – to him you're just another boney.'

Apprehension was prickling off Ruther like a static discharge. She could almost feel her own skin starting to tingle.

'I think you might be overestimating my capabilities.'

'We'll see. You know these bones better than I, and *he* doesn't know you. I think that gives us the advantage, temporarily, and if I've learned one thing it's that you press your advantages.' Fura went to the wall panel and unhooked one of the neural bridges, quickly adjusting it to Ruther's approximate head-shape, which was not so far from her own. 'Plug in, lad,' she said encouragingly. 'I shall be right by you.'

Ruther examined the crown diffidently, made an adjustment or two of his own, then settled it down over his scalp, pressing down on his shock of hair. He extended the contact wire, pinching its termination plug between thumb and forefinger, and with only a little hesitation moved to the node where Fura had already had success.

The plug snapped into place cleanly. The skull jiggled on its suspension wires then stilled. Ruther floated freely, with his knees drawn up and his fists balled. He closed his eyes, not seeming to need the crown's fold-down blinkers.

'I'm with you,' Fura whispered.

'If I might have silence . . . Captain.'

She smiled to herself. 'Of course.'

Ruther and the skull had become as still as each other, like two miniature worlds bound by a single tether. Ruther seemed smaller now, less the gangly youth she had first encountered, and more a boy: far too young to be away from the worlds on his own, much less thrown into circumstances such as these. But she tempered any feelings of excessive protectiveness she might have felt. Ruther had chosen this life, just as surely as she had done. Perhaps he had not been thrown into it on a whim, and perhaps he had not had an older sister cajoling him into some misguided notion of adventure. But the choice had been made nonetheless, and it had brought him to this moment, and now she depended upon him, for she was his captain as surely as Werranwell had been, and he must rise to his calling.

Ruther twitched. It was a small but definite thing, like the spasm that sometimes brought Fura to sudden wakefulness just when she was about to drop off to sleep. She was minded to ask if he had something, some trace of a contact, but by great force of will she stayed her tongue. Let him have his silence. She would have made the same demand herself.

He twitched again and drew breath. He was about to speak, she knew. About to relate some intercept or inference he had picked up through the skull.

Ruther laughed.

It was the sort of laugh one might make to be polite, after being told a not-particularly-good joke, or an anecdote that was nowhere near as comedic as its speaker intended.

Fura tensed.

Ruther laughed again, twice this time. There was a mean sort of amusement in the laugh now; a laugh at the expense of someone else. Ruther grinned, except it was more rictus than grin, as if invisible hooks were dragging at his face, forcing it into a parody of a normal expression.

Ruther was trembling. His hands moved up to the neural crown.

'Oh, Captain,' he said, forcing the words out through that fixed grin. 'Oh, dear Captain! Did you honestly think this little . . . ruse . . . this little contrivance . . . was ever going to work?'

It was Ruther speaking but also not Ruther. His voice, but with another mind behind it, operating him through the skull. Fura had never heard of such a thing, but the evidence of her senses proved that it was, indeed, happening.

'Get out of him,' Fura said.

Ruther pawed at the neural crown. He was trying to wrench it off. Some part of him, at least, still had some control over his body. Fura moved to help. She only had to lift the crown off, or unplug the contact wire, one or both.

'But we've barely begun to speak.'

She got one hand on the crown and the other on the plug. But Ruther was faster. He clasped his own hand over hers, pressing her metal fingers against the skull, and with the other he resisted her efforts to dislodge the crown. Whatever self-control he'd retained a few moments earlier was now gone.

Fura grunted against Ruther's grip. 'Get out of him!'

'Captain Ness – I'm disappointed. Very gravely disappointed. Why would you send a boy to do a woman's work? Were you . . . heh . . . afraid . . . of me? Afraid we'd touch minds again? Afraid I might *learn* something?'

'Who are you?' she demanded.

'Would a name help at this point? Would it give you something to pin your weakness upon? Something to scream into the night, as our slugs open your hull and your blood starts to boil into the vacuum?'

'Just tell me.'

Ruther's mad grin went instantly solemn, yet the expression was still mockingly over-done.

'Very well,' the voice said, in a low confiding tone. 'A courtesy, between captains. I am Incer Stallis, Captain Incer Stallis, or more properly, Squadron-Commander Stallis, and my face will be the last you see.'

'I thought the idea was to bring us in alive.'

'That is still the general intention, although they have given me latitude to effect a long-range kill if capture proves inordinately difficult or costly. But I still very much hope to bring you in alive.'

'Then that little boast of yours won't count for much, will it? If you do manage to hand me over to the authorities, I'm sure I'll see many other faces.'

Ruther's face flashed a quick, apologetic smile. 'You misunderstand me, dear Captain – I intend to leave you blind and severely mutilated. They've asked me to bring you in, you see, but they've been awfully imprecise about the condition in which I'm expected to deliver you . . . and, well, give a man a span, heh, he'll take a league, eh?'

'You'd have to get quite close to attempt something like that.'

Ruther nodded keenly. 'I would, yes.'

'Then that works excellently for me, as well. You attacked an innocent ship, despite being warned off it. I'm going to punish you for that, punish you very badly, and I won't stop at just your eyes.'

'I do so love an idle threat. The problem is that all you can presently do is threaten me. Whereas I can *already* hurt this boy . . .'

Ruther fell silent. She'd thought that perhaps Incer Stallis was done with him, for now, but she really ought to have known better. Ruther regarded her with an unblinking intensity, just as if he was still in there, still looking out, and wished her to know something. He had closed his lips, but not quite fully, and a red foam was beginning to bubble out of them.

A horrible, bubbling eruption of blood as Incer Stallis attempted to make Ruther bite the tip off his own tongue . . .

Ruther jerked violently. His neck was arching back so severely that she feared he might snap his own spine. His mouth opened to a bloody maw, the end of his tongue already half-severed. Fura screamed, putting all her strength into one last attempt, and at last she sprung his hand away from the skull, taking the plug with it, and broke the contact.

Ruther went instantly limp. He let go of the crown, allowing her to snatch it from him and practically fling it against the wall as the skull jiggled from the jolt of disconnection. She balled her metal fist and was an instant away from punching a hole right through the skull, before catching herself.

Ruther went slowly head over heels backwards, blood still foaming out of him as he bumped his scalp against the wall and snagged an ankle in one of the suspension wires. He was shaking, every muscle in his body seeming to have gone into palsy. Fura seized him by the shoulders, bringing his face to hers. His blood-lathered mouth was working at double-speed, yet no sounds were coming out. His eyelids were open, yet his eyes were nearly white, the pupils rolled back as far as they would go.

She slapped him across the cheeks, not with violence but a desperate kindness, trying to dislodge whatever shard of her enemy was still in him, or yet exerting its influence.

'Ruther! It's me, Fura. You're out of it! Come back!'

But Ruther would not come back. He just kept quivering, his eyes averted, or gazing upon something only he could see.

*

Doctor Eddralder peeled back the boy's eyelids, peered at the evidence beneath them, and said: 'If at any point you would like to stop bringing me patients, that would be appreciated.'

'I wasn't to know this would happen.'

The Doctor had a magnifying fixture pinched onto the end of his nose, making his eyes swell and loom behind the glass lenses, until there seemed no room for any other part of his face.

'And what *did* happen, precisely?'

Eddralder was right to ask. Fura had conveyed Ruther to the

Kindness Room, then immediately departed for the captains' quarters, offering the bare minimum of explanation before her return.

'I don't know. After you spoke to me about Strambli I thought it was worth risking the skull, to gain some intelligence about the squadron's movements. But I didn't want to be the one plugging into the skull.'

'So Ruther bore the brunt of . . . whatever it was.'

'I didn't ask him to do anything outside of his normal duties.'

'Except that Ruther would not ordinarily have been the target for . . . whoever did this.' Eddralder completed his close-up examination and removed the magnifying lenses, folding them up and slipping them into a little padded pouch. 'You said the other party gained complete control of Ruther?'

That was about as much as she had told him, to begin with.

'It was as if they were inside him. Not just whispering through the skull, but operating him like a puppet. Ruther was trying to fight it, but he wasn't strong enough. Then he started speaking, channelling the other voice just as if they were inside the room. Ruther didn't even look like Ruther, for a while. That other personality was taking over his face, stretching it like a mask.'

'And you didn't think to help him break the contact?'

'I did, but Ruther – whoever was inside him – fought back. I got him disconnected eventually, but by then he was like this.' She searched his eyes, now reduced to their normal large paleness. 'Give me some encouragement, Doctor. I need Ruther.'

'You mean you need him to function properly, like a sail-control motor or a pressure lock.'

'No. I mean, *yes* to that, of course, but I also don't want him hurt. He's . . . one of us now.' All of a sudden the force of Eddralder's stare was more than she could bear. She glanced aside. 'Werranwell obviously looked after the boy – had high hopes for him. I feel that he's my responsibility now. I don't want him to come any harm.'

'But not so strongly that you held back on putting him into the bone room, when you knew the risks.'

'It was a mistake. I'm sorry.'

At this admission, some barely perceptible easing showed in his sternness, and his tongue moved across his lips. 'He doesn't seem to have come off too badly, if my instincts are correct. His tongue will heal, given time – he was very lucky not to have bitten clean through it. He's unconscious now, but if you'd brought him to me without a word about skulls and remote possession, I would merely say he was deeply exhausted and in need of rest and close observation. Which he will receive.'

'Thank you, Doctor. I am trying to be strong; trying to protect this ship and its crew. I know that won't always make my decisions popular. But I never want them to seem cruel.'

Eddralder absorbed her statement, his eyes searching her face as he considered her words, then – with immense deliberation – he nodded. 'I believe you, foolish as that may make me seem. There's the glowy in you, and some of that woman you killed, but I don't think they're stronger than the core of you. More that they've become the armour you wear, and useful to you, but not yet your master.'

Fura waited a moment then took out the wallet she had brought with her from the captains' quarters. 'You might be right about that armour – I don't know. What I can say is that I've got the glowy under control for the time being, and I think I can hold it back until we reach Trevenza. I want you to have those twenty doses of Mephrozine, if there's the slightest chance of helping Strambli. I will . . . make do.'

Eddralder reached for the wallet, but his fingers did not close around it immediately.

'You must be sure of this. There will be no going back.'

'I am sure,' Fura said, pressing the wallet into his hand. 'Do what you can for her.'

*

Cossel was rubbing the cold out of her bones by the time she made it down from the sighting room to the galley aboard the

Merry Mare. Adrana was there with Lasling, Lagganvor and Vouga, ancient charts of rigging and control gear spread across the table. The bedsheet-sized papers were browned with age and frayed at the edges, annotated in the diligent penmanship of a dozen successive Masters of Sail. The inscriptions went all the way back to the end of the sixteenth century: notes of alteration; notes for the intention of alteration; procurement lists; purchase reports; inventories by the span, the league, the square-league and indeed several obscure units of measurements that had since fallen entirely out of fashion.

Adrana flattened out Cossel's transcription and fastened it over to the charts with two beer-rimed tankards.

'A telegraphic sighting, you say?'

'No question. It was just where *Revenger* ought to be. A little yellow star, winking on and off: someone with a telegraphic box, sending back to us.'

'What does it say?'

Cossel looked at it carefully.

'Dot, dash, dot, dot, dot. And so on.'

Lasling smiled tolerantly. 'To be fair, I never learned the code myself. Being an honest sort of crew, we hardly had need for anything but the squawk and bones.'

Lagganvor spun the sheet around and squinted at it for a few seconds. His lips moved silently, then he began speaking. 'It says . . . dum-de-dum . . . "Maintaining heading. Signalling to inform that . . . squadron commander may be . . . Incer Stallis. Ruther . . . incapacitated but expected to rally. Strambli taken bad turn, Eddralder taking all necessary steps. Will inform."'

Vouga folded his arms. 'And the last part?'

He flashed the other man an irritated glance. 'I was coming to that. "Attempt no reciprocal send unless emergency. Remain on course and await news. Arafura."'

'Very considerate of 'em to keep us appraised,' Lasling said.

'Who in the worlds is Incer Stallis?' Cossel said, not in any evident expectation of an answer.

'The weasel who kept his coil-guns on you even after it was

clear that you were an innocent ship,' Adrana said. 'Fura and I got a taste of his mind through the skull we took from you. She wants us to know who we're dealing with.'

'How'd they figure it out?' Lasling asked.

'Through the skull, I should imagine,' Adrana answered. 'And that might have something to do with Ruther being incapacitated, although hopefully he will be well. It's Strambli who concerns me the most.'

'Eddralder seems to know his job,' Lasling said. 'Megs would attest to that as well.'

'Knowing your job ain't always enough,' Cossel said, with the sort of bluntness that came easily to some people and less easily to others, and with which it was impossible to take offence.

'Speaking the plain truth of things,' Lasling said, 'is a habit we've fallen into, after that run of bad luck that brought us into your company. That way we aren't clinging to any false expectations.' He gave Cossel a look that was both affectionate and gently reproving. 'Some of us speak it plainer than others, though.'

'Do you think she'll be all right?' Cossel asked Adrana.

The question was sincerely meant, Adrana judged, so she gave it as sincere an answer as she could. 'No, I rather think she won't be. That wound in her leg was started by the touch from a Ghostie blade. We thought we'd got the badness out of her in Wheel Strizzardy, but it seems we were wrong.'

'I never had reason to doubt the existence of Ghostie gubbins,' Vouga said, peering at his reflection in the scuffed lid of his tankard. 'I've always believed they're out there, waiting to be unearthed. But I've never heard of one good thing that came out of finding them.'

Lasling shook his head, not in contradiction of Vouga's statement, but in rueful agreement.

'I know of one exception to that rule,' Adrana said.

Vouga looked up.

'Which is?'

'Me. If my sister hadn't unearthed Ghostie gubbins, I would

be dead by now. Or perhaps the one thing worse than that.'

Meggery almost laughed.

'Worse than being dead?'

'I would be Bosa Sennen. That was the path she had me on, and I don't doubt that she'd have succeeded.' She was silent for a few moments, letting them dwell on her words – daring them to doubt the force of her conviction. When none was so foolish as to rise to that temptation, she added: 'I am glad Fura spared me that, and glad too that the Ghostie gubbins gave her the means to do so. Lately I am persuaded that nothing in the Congregation is entirely bad or entirely good, nor much beyond it, either. There are only good uses and bad uses for things – good intentions and bad intentions; degrees of wisdom and equal degrees of foolishness. What has happened to Strambli is awful, and I fear for her. But I am not at all sorry to be alive.'

14

Fura stiffened as the Mephrozine flooded her veins. It was ten days since the separation; six since she had given twenty of her remaining thirty-five doses to Doctor Eddralder. As the fire surged through her, crossing the blood-brain barrier and finding every tingling extremity of her nervous system, she stretched back in her chair and held her flesh hand before her, fingers outspread. The glowy throbbed and shone, brightening at the touch of Mephrozine.

There was a knock at the door to the captains' quarters. Eventually she would stop thinking of it in plural terms, accepting that this ship was hers and hers alone, but it would take more than a few days of adjustment.

'Proz,' she said, sounding enervated even to herself. 'Please . . . come in.'

Prozor came to her desk, took the seat opposite her and nodded at the still-open wallet. 'Word got 'round, girlie. Tends to do so on a ship like this.'

'What sort of word?'

'That you'd given most of your supply to Strambli. How much is left?'

Fura laid a hand on the wallet. 'Thirteen doses. I've stretched the interval between injections to three days, and Tindouf says we may make port in twenty-one days. I'll still have plenty in reserve.'

Prozor took the wallet and packed away the vials and syringe. 'Eddralder shouldn't have accepted your offer. We all want Strambli to come through – I ain't sayin' otherwise – but there was a reason you had first dibs on those drugs. A reason we went to all that trouble in Mulgracen.'

Fura smiled slightly. 'When we were at the Pharmacist, you said it wasn't your job to be my conscience.'

'If I did, then I spoke out of turn.'

'No,' Fura said, sighing through one last fiery surge. She blinked, watched her hand – willing the curlicues to begin fading. 'You didn't speak out of turn. I have . . . depended on you, Proz. I still depend on you. It was the right thing to try to help Strambli, and I hope you'd have reminded me of that, if I hadn't had the strength to see it for myself.'

'It ain't my place to force anyone into such decisions.'

'Perhaps it shouldn't be anyone's place, but I know you'd have been disappointed in me if I hadn't done the right thing. I tried to press you on Adrana, do you know? Not because I didn't want you, but because I thought she'd do well to have you at her side. Is it selfish of me to be glad that she opted for Lagganvor instead?'

'That cove knows his way around a ship nearly as well as I do.'

'For Adrana's sake, may we hope that's the case. Her . . . attachment to him is curious, don't you think?'

'I ain't one to speculate.'

'She does not like him, particularly – not in any sense that I can detect.' She shrugged. 'Nor do I. But she clings to him as if she were his long-lost sister. When we were on Mulgracen, she was very particular about going shopping with Lagganvor, wasn't she?'

'It was one or other of us, girlie. Ain't too many ways to split a party of four.'

'Perhaps I dwell on things overmuch. I worry sometimes that the glowy is breeding suspicion in me – causing me to see conspiracies at every turn. Then again, perhaps that is the natural condition of any captain.'

'I've served under worse, girlie.'

'High praise.'

The stern angles of Prozor's face held their composure for a moment, then softened to admit a hint of humour. 'If there was ever a time when I worried about the glowy runnin' away with you, what you did for Strambli put my fears to bed.'

'I worry that it was the glowy itself, protecting itself. That it was no kind deed at all, but only self-interest.'

'Too much of that sort of thinkin'll tie your head in knots, girlie.' She glanced away, her face side-lit in Paladin's red glow. 'I just wish there was some payback for that kind deed. But I saw the look on horseface when I went on to see Ruther, and he didn't look like a cove who had good news to share.'

Fura felt a knot in her belly. She was well aware that Eddralder had already administered the twenty-dose shot to Strambli. She had been deliberately avoiding the Kindness Room ever since, preferring no news to bad news.

'Something may come of it, yet.' She tried not to allow her deep consternation to show. 'And . . . Ruther? There's something to report?'

'There ain't a change for the worse, and lately that's what counts as a positive development.'

Fura nodded glumly. She understood exactly what Prozor meant by that. It was enough, now, to go a whole day without some troubling rumour or suspicion of trouble to come. If this was the new pattern of her life, she was becoming well accustomed to it.

'I don't know if Eddralder will forgive me for Ruther. But I couldn't stand another hour without knowing something of that other boy.'

'And knowin' his name, are you satisfied?'

Fura searched her thoughts before answering. 'Not in the slightest! A name hardly helps at all, not when I know so little of the boy behind it. And those ships of his . . . they could be ten thousand leagues astern of us, or ten million. Until they make a mistake, sweeping when they should not, or luck tosses us a crumb in the form of sail-flash, we're still blind.' She reached across the table and closed her metal hand around that of her friend and mentor. 'I don't so much mind being hunted. That seems an entirely justifiable response for the havoc I've caused. But this game of shadows ain't sitting well with me at all. Tell me I'm not making one mistake after the next, Proz?'

'You might've blotted your daybook with what you did to Ruther. But it was intended well and it was the lad's profession, after all, so I ain't goin' to be the one to condemn you for that. And whatever becomes of Strambli, no one can say you didn't show kindness and self-sacrifice. Or if they *does*, they'll have Proz to answer to.' She squeezed Fura's hand. 'We'll get through this, girlie. Adrana'll arrive in time to put on a welcoming party for us, just you see.'

'You were going to show me the sights of Trevenza Reach, before Vidin Quindar interrupted our plans. It'd be good to have a second chance.'

Prozor unslipped her fingers from Fura's, but lingered over the missing digit.

'Does that still trouble you?'

'It did, for a little while. But not lately. More and more, in fact, I'm rather glad of it. Meggery was right to ask me for it, in recompense for what we did to her. But if that was the price of my own command, and I think it was, then I consider it to have been a very fair bargain indeed.'

*

'Incer Stallis,' Adrana said, elongating the syllables. 'Does that ring any bells for you, Lagganvor?'

'You've waited until now to ask me?'

'I wondered if you would come to me voluntarily. I understand that you couldn't admit to inside knowledge of the squadron while we were in company, so I gave you the benefit of the doubt. He will come to me in a watch or two, I told myself; a day at the most. Then I began to realise you had no intention of doing so. Yet you knew that name. I saw your reaction when you had to read it out for us.'

'If you'd taken the trouble to learn the telegraphic code, you could have spared me the bother. How is the Clacker, might I ask?'

'The Clacker is asleep in the infirmary. He seems comfortable and has ceased making those snorting noises. I'll count on nothing, though, until he opens his eyes and speaks to me. I did not, however, invite a conversation about the Clacker.' There was a telegraphic code book open on her desk, fixed down by paperweight. She had left it open deliberately, along with a slip of paper on which she had written some rudimentary test phrases, along with her laboured attempts at transcription. 'In answer to your earlier point, I had enough tiresome homework when we were under Paladin's leash in our old house.' She pushed the book aside with heavy abandon. 'I shall dedicate myself to it when I have the luxury of an empty few months with no other distractions. Until then I am content to delegate to those who have already gone to the trouble of committing these code sequences to memory.' She settled her hands before her, making a steeple of her fingers. 'I shall ask again: how well do you know that name?'

Lagganvor scratched at his chin. 'Have you got anywhere with that trinket of Werrenwell's?'

'We were discussing Incer Stallis.'

'I daresay I might, at some point, have . . . possibly . . . chanced upon that name.'

She shook her head. 'Not one more evasive word out of your lips, or I swear I'll tell the rest of the crew what you really are.'

He shrugged good-naturedly. 'I suspect they might regard my true nature as a distinct improvement on my supposed past.'

If she had been holding something sharp she would have been powerfully inclined to jab it into his neck. 'Lagganvor.'

'Very well.' He sighed elaborately. 'If there was a reluctance on my part to speak of him, it is only because a man's reputation may swell to the point where it distorts all notion of a measured response. I knew that if I told you of the thing that Incer Stallis has become . . . the thing he has made himself – then he would loom disproportionately in your concerns, when all he is is a ruthless whelp, a monster of cruelty and self-regard, not deserving of such consideration . . .'

She cut him off. 'You've met him?'

'No, I am quite content not to have had that honour. But I knew him well enough by reputation. No one with any contact with squadron operations could avoid that.'

'Do continue.'

He swallowed, cleared his throat. 'His mother and father were both ship-owners. Father was Quisler Stallis, a well-regarded if occasionally reckless captain operating a bauble-hopper under the patronage of the joint combines. Him, his ship and crew were taken by – allegedly – Bosa Sennen, in 1790, when Incer was only ten. He was brought up by his mother, Methrin Stallis, who operated a rapid cutter in the merchant protection service. Do you know much of these cutters?'

She permitted a small smile to cross her lips.

'Inevitably less than you.'

'They're not like bauble-hoppers such as the *Merry Mare*, or even *Revenger*. They're small, because they don't need holds or launches, and what they are is mostly weapon. They have a high degree of automation, because the protection service can afford such niceties, and they run with small but highly-trained crews. They travel fast and light and are as dangerous in close action as they are at long-range. That, incidentally, will be the sort of ship making up the bulk of that squadron, although they may carry a scimitar-class launch or two for boarding operations . . .'

'Enough about the ships.'

'I merely offer the context. Methrin Stallis took her son into her care, while schooling him in the ways of these cutters. He travelled with her on tours of duties – earned his place by learning coillers and navigation and, ultimately, the bones.'

'What a prolific little turd. What turned him from a fatherless brat into this . . . thing . . . I still have in my head?'

'There is an official line and an unofficial one.'

'Give me both.'

'The official line is that Methrin Stallis and another of her crew died in a tragic accident during the course of a protection tour, and it was only by dint of his excellent courage and resourcefulness that dear young Incer and one other survivor were able to bring the cutter back in.'

'And – although I think I can guess – the unofficial line?'

'Matricide. Incer decided not to wait for his mother to retire: he wanted her ship there and then. So he planned the murder, with that one survivor as his accomplice. The idea was that, when Incer got himself set up with a command of his own, that survivor would get a preferential promotion.' Lagganvor looked sad. 'But the poor fellow died a year later, cut clean through with a yardknife. They buried him in two child-sized coffins, to save on costs.'

'How unfortunate. So this ... boy ... how old would he be now? About twenty-one?'

'Near enough. Young, certainly, for such responsibility, but if you set aside the small matter of the murders, he has acquitted himself very capably, with a number of enterprising successes to his success, and he does have that rare faculty with the bones ... of course he's not operating without some oversight and supervision – there'll be senior men and women on those ships, there to keep him in check, but they'll be under very strict orders to give him latitude; after all, what's the point of a slathering attack-dog if you don't give him a long leash?'

'Careful, Lagganvor,' she said warningly. 'You almost sound like an admirer.'

'I am not. Yet I do have a certain regard for ruthlessness, and the willingness of the authorities to ... bend a rule or two, in the interests of success.'

'Good,' she said. 'You can express those fine and noble sentiments when I've got my boot heel on his neck.'

*

Eddralder pre-empted Fura's question with a short shake of his head. She hardly needed his answer, anyway. It only took a glance at Strambli's form to tell her that there had been no improvement, dramatic or otherwise.

'Is it possible that it still needs time?' Fura asked.

'It has been eight days,' Merrix answered, pausing to mop Strambli's brow. 'Those old accounts never agreed on much, but they all said that if the Mephrozine was to have any useful effect, it would be obvious within a few hours.'

'I am afraid your charity may have been wasted,' Eddralder said.

'The Mephrozine's still inside her?'

'Broken down into useless metabolic products, beyond any hope of recovery. I suppose you are angry, that this sacrifice was for nothing?'

'I'm angry,' Fura said, and privately wondered how plainly that emotional state now showed in her face. 'But not with you, Eddralder. You never promised me success. I *am* angry that the universe has done this thing to Strambli, and we're powerless to stop it.' She flexed her fists. Her fingers, flesh and metal, were tingling. Her cheekbones prickled as if they had the first touches of frostbite. She had just taken an injection of her own, after a four-day interval. The Mephrozine had hit her harder than ever, and the consequent stirring of the glowy was taking longer than usual to fade. If indeed it was fading at all.

'I see it in your eyes, more visibly than of late,' Eddralder informed her.

'I'm aware. I'm also . . . composed.' This was true, to a degree, but it was the composure of some fractured, crumbling wall damming back an immense, testing pressure. 'It was worth trying, no matter the cost. It would be worth trying again, if we had enough Mephrozine to spare.'

'By my estimation you are down to twelve units.'

She nodded meekly. 'And I'm all for hopeless gestures, but I doubt very much that another twelve would be any good for Strambli, when twenty failed?'

'I wouldn't permit it under any circumstances. It was a kindness, Captain Ness, and worth attempting. But now we must resign ourselves to the inevitable. I must attempt to cut it out of her.'

Strambli murmured: 'Ghostie shoaly fishies! I'm half-past Ghostie! It's gubbins-time for me!'

Strambli was delirious but otherwise unconscious – had been so the whole while, and whenever Prozor had been to visit – and Fura counted this as the one small mercy of the whole affair. It allowed them to speak plainly. 'You will take the leg, if you must?'

'Worse things have happened. If I had the confidence that would be an end to it, I would do so now. But you have seen the unusual paleness of her eyes.'

'Then what good will only cutting out a part of it do?'

'That is where I will begin. If we can excise the root of the infection, she may have the reserves to fight the rest of it on her own.'

'You don't know.'

'I see no other option than to try. If you are willing, Merrix and I will proceed after the conclusion of the next watch. That will give us time to rest and prepare for what I presume will be a difficult procedure.'

'You have my permission.' Fura shifted her gaze to the other patient in the Kindness Room. 'What of Ruther? If you've even a speck of good news, Doctor, I'd very much welcome it.'

'Then I shall strive to give you good news. He isn't worsening, which is something. He has been in a condition of deep unconsciousness since the incident, but these last few watches he seems to be surfacing . . . gradually. He has been muttering to himself. There is . . . coherence to his words, even if he seems troubled. That at least tells us that there can't be profound neurological damage.'

'Troubled?' Fura asked.

'The boy seems tormented by bad dreams. Merrix has been party to more of them than me. I think she understands some of it, even with his half-severed tongue. Tell her, Merrix.'

'There's a cave, or a cell,' Merrix said. 'A sort of dungeon. He's in it, I think, and there's something trying to get inside with him, something coming out of the floor. He screams, then slips back into silence. He's calm for hours, then it starts again.'

'You do not need that happening while you're busy with an operation,' Fura said.

'I admit it would be a distraction we might well do without,' Eddralder said. 'I also admit that, besides monitoring him, there is little more that we are able to do for the boy. I think he will wake, in time. But it cannot be rushed.'

'Have Tindouf bring him down to my cabin,' Fura said. 'If there's any screaming to be done, I should be the one to put up with it.'

'Fishy Ghosties swimmin' in me half-noggin! I'm gubbinsy-gubbinsy!'

*

Adrana decanted a measure of Trennigarian brandy into a small, weightless glass, the sort with a fine hinged lid and a drinking teat, and lifted it to Lasling as he came into her quarters.

'I've just taken a navigational bearing,' she said. 'We're sailing as true and fast as any honest ship ever did, and no small part of that must be due to your hard work with the sails and rigging. You are done with the vacuum work now, I trust?'

Lasling was still wearing most of his suit, including two im-provised peg-like extensions he had strapped onto his stumps. 'Truth to tell, Cap'n, it was all but done three or four shifts ago. But there was always something that could be made a little sweeter.'

'And Lagganvor?' she asked, trying not to make it as if she cared too much about the answer. 'He came in at the same time as you?'

'The gentleman said he wanted to admire the stars and

Congregation for a few minutes, so I left him to it. But I daresay he'll be in directly.'

'I daresay he shall as well, Lasling.' She bid him sit opposite her and pressed the glass into his fingers, which were raw at the tips from all the recent work. 'Thank you for working so industriously. Every hour that we shave from our crossing is helpful to us, and helpful to my sister as well.'

Lasling dipped his eyes to the Clacker's crib, where Tazaknakak was dozing silently, recuperating after Vouga's repair work. 'I hope your passenger is worth the trouble. There are some that'd say it's worth more than their lives to get mixed up with alien affairs. Is he on the mend?'

She injected a deliberate note of caution into her answer.

'To the degree that any of us can say, Lasling, it would appear so. But only Tazaknakak will be able to tell us, when at last he comes around. I am confident though. That quickglass was an excellent suggestion. If the resonant chamber is intact, Tazaknakak will be able to form a sound-picture and use our own language without difficulty. They speak very well: it comes much more readily to them than to a Crawly.'

'And the ones who did that to him in the first place, putting all those holes through him? They have something to do with Incer Stallis and his squadron?'

'Let us just say that neither has our best interests at heart.' She nodded encouragingly. 'But he has fortitude, and so must you, to have come through your own injury.'

He shrugged off her concern. 'Once we limped into dock at Ishimvar, I was all right.'

'And the pain you still suffer?'

'A reminder that I got out of that bauble, when Mauncer and Ives didn't.' He collected himself for a moment. 'I can still hear their screams, on the other side of that door. They had no injuries, but they knew they were never getting out of that tomb. I bet they'd have killed to have one more day, even with a little pain. Anyway, pain's too big a word. Mostly it's just an ache, or some soreness.'

'Which was keeping you from sleeping.'

'When you've been in this life for a few years, there are a lot of things to keep you up all night. Most of us carry a few scars on the outside, but it's the ones inside that give the most trouble.'

'That I can believe. It's no easy life, even when we don't have pirates or squadrons to contend with. What was it brought you to the baubles, if I may ask?'

A half-smile creased his lips. 'A weakness.'

'Go on.'

'I liked to gamble. From a very early age, I had to be betting on things. It didn't matter what, or how poor the odds. Street tricks with cups and buttons. Cards and dice. Dogs, if we'd had 'em on my world, which mostly we didn't. But anything else that ran, or hopped, or scrapped, that was fair game. Eventually I took up brawling myself, offering wagers to anyone who felt they could take me on, and I spilled blood – nearly all my own – in every bar and fighting den from the Ramer Docks to the Furnax Gate. Bought stowage on ships when I could afford it, and sneaked and lied my way aboard when I couldn't. Saw a hundred worlds and slowly learned some of the ways of sunjamming. But I couldn't stop gambling, and day by day I was losing everything. I'd stolen from or cheated all my friends, and burned every kindness ever offered to me. I was a wreck: a slave to the grog, bones set by back-room physicians who were usually at least as fond of the bottle as I was, my teeth like tombstones – those that were left – and me starting to see phantoms in daylight, and worse when I was sleeping. My last real fight was somewhere down near the Conjugates. So hazy now that I can't even tell you when and where.' He paused, and some rueful self-deprecation had him shaking his head, disgusted and amazed in the same moment. 'But I do remember the cove I took on. Him I'll never forget, because he took me to the edge of death and then spared my life. Saved it, you could say. There was nothing to him, just a skinny runt who looked as if he'd snap if you breathed on him too hard. But he could fight like no one I ever met before or since. His name was Paley, and he was an Assessor on a ship called *Midnight's Mistress*. Not that I knew that when he peeled me off the ground, rinsed the blood off my face, and slapped me around the cheeks until I wasn't quite seeing double. He rummaged in my pockets for his prize money, and when he came out with scraps and tokens, I think he was more inclined to pity than disgust. He sat me down on a step near the den and forced a jug of cold coffee into my throat. Then he asked me what I thought I was doing with my life.'

'And what did you tell him?'

'That I had this thing in me I couldn't satisfy. Paley nodded at that, and said he wasn't unfamiliar with the condition. Then he surprised me: he said I had to accept that I wasn't going to change. The only question was what I did with that urge. Keep at it the way I was going, Paley explained, and soon I'd have no teeth, no bones that hadn't been reset, and every chance of meeting another runt like himself who wasn't quite so inclined to hold back. I laughed, but he wasn't laughing.'

'He could have killed you?'

'Easily. But he didn't, and as we were talking – me still spitting out bits of tooth between gulps of that coffee – Paley asked me what I knew about baubles. He'd spotted that I'd been on ships by then, picked up on the tattoos and piercings that showed I wasn't local to that world – wherever it was we were – and he figured I might have just enough wits left to sign onto a bauble-cracker. Going into a bauble, he said, was the only thing in life worth gambling on. The only stake worth dying for – and the only thing that was ever going to satisfy that urge in me, because nothing in the worlds compares to the chance and mystery of bauble-cracking.'

'Did he mention the part about sometimes getting stuck inside them for the rest of eternity?'

'Oh yes. If he'd pulled his punches when he was laying me out on the ground, he didn't hold back now. Told me a dozen horror stories there and then, of things that had happened to his pals. But he knew it wouldn't deter me, only make me want it more. He was laying out the rules of the greatest game in the Congregation, and he knew I wouldn't be able to turn back.'

'Paley must have seen something in you.'

'In all the worlds I don't know what it could have been. But he did, I suppose, and through him I got a berth on the *Midnight's Mistress*. That was my first time on a real privateer, rather than some cosy merchanter or passenger scow, and it was as if I'd never been into space at all. Hard months, while they knocked some shape into me. Nearly a year of proving myself before I was allowed into a bauble, and then only on the condition I stuck to Paley like his own shadow. But it was enough. From the moment we went in, I knew I'd found my vocation. All I needed to do was become good enough at it to get useful.'

'And did you?'

'In the end. Decided I liked the idea of Opening, more than Assessing, so that's where I applied myself – learning every last thing I could squeeze into my head about doors and locks and traps and all the secret wizardry of the monkeys who came before us. The *Mistress* had a fine Opener of her own in Chenzel, but she came down with Gribble's Palsy, which is a condition of the nervous system, causes the hands to shake. It's a common side-effect of bauble-cracking, if you live long enough, and not normally a problem in an Assessor.'

Adrana fished into the collar of her blouse and drew out the blue velvet box Prozor had given her before their separation.

'I'm sure some of that Assessor's lore is still in your head. Tell me what you make of this.'

'Is this a test?'

'Not at all. This was a gift, and supposedly of some rarity, but I confess I don't quite know what it is. The box opens by that catch on the side.'

Lasling's fingers were no longer made for fine work, but he persuaded the catch open and peered into the little box. With even more care, he dug his thumb and forefinger inside and pinched out a small, glass-like thing with a stellate shape.

'It's a light-imp,' he said, frowning slightly. 'But unless you've never opened the box, you'd have seen that for yourself. It is of some rarity, I suppose. Light-imps are always in short supply, becoming scarcer, and there isn't a crew that holds them in anything other than favourable regard.' He offered a smile. 'Well, it's a nice enough gift.'

'I was told it was something else – something called a Firebright.'

Lasling seemed on the verge of saying something, then caught himself. He turned the light-imp over in his fingers, then placed it carefully back into the box. 'It's a pretty piece. And a light-imp does have value. I . . . wouldn't turn my nose up at such a thing.'

'I'm not.' Hiding her disappointment as well as she could, Adrana slipped the box and its contents back into her blouse. 'It was well-meant, and that is the main thing. Your fingers are steady enough, I notice. I presume you took over Chenzel's position?'

'Eight or nine baubles in, I was ready. Chenzel didn't resent it – she understood that she couldn't carry on. Gave me all her books and gubbins, and I worked hard to fill her boots. Which I did, and not too shabbily. Gradually I got a name for myself, and when the *Mistress* went insolvent – no fault of any of us – I was able to sign on under Werranwell.'

'Did Paley come with you?'

'No. He died in a bauble called the Yellow Jester. Went back for a chest of Atomist treasure when we should have been well on our way to the surface. Our auguries were a little off and the field started thickening up sooner than predicted. He never made it out.'

'Poor Paley.'

'I owed him everything. But I learned a lesson that day, which was that sooner or later the baubles always win. It might be the greatest game, but it's rigged from the start. The . . . trick . . . is knowing when to quit.'

Adrana could not prevent her eyes darting to Lasling's legs. 'Life made that choice for you.'

'It did, and if it wasn't for the friends we lost that day, I'd have no complaints.'

'But your . . . compulsion. First you gambled and brawled, and then the baubles gave you an outlet for that urge. When you knew you could never go back into a bauble . . . ?'

'You would think the compulsion ought to have returned?' He met her eyes and shook his head. 'On that part, at least, dear old Paley was wrong. I could change and I did. When they pulled me out of His Foulness, I left more than just my legs behind. That . . . compulsion . . . had gone completely, and it hasn't troubled me since.' He drew a hand across his lips, then set down the glass. 'Hardly touched a drink since, either, although it'd have been rude to turn down your kindness. I have been . . . contented . . . to be what I am. A Master of Sail might not have the glamour of an Opener or an Assessor, but a fair crew splits its earnings equally and I have come to enjoy my profession.'

'I am very glad to have you as my Master of Sail, Lasling. I'm only sorry that it could not have happened under happier circumstances.' She hesitated, feeling that something more needed to be said. 'I may hope that I have your confidence?'

He shrugged, as if the question were beneath consideration.

'Werranwell appointed one of you captain and that's all I need to know. I'll help you as you wish, and shut up otherwise. I am sure you will prove yourself very capable. Your friend, Lagganvor, seems a dependable ally?'

'He has the necessary experience,' she answered, with the merest trace of terseness.

'I should hope he does.' It was Lagganvor speaking; he was leaning in a very indolent way against the doorframe, tugging off a pair of vacuum gloves. His fringe was low across his eyes, like a half-drawn visor.

'Did you enjoy your view?'

'Most certainly.'

'We all get a bit homesick at times,' the other man observed.

She extended her hand, palm upraised. 'Join us. I was just congratulating Lasling on his work. With the wind at our backs we might even cut a day off our arrival in Trevenza.'

Lagganvor dragged up another chair and lowered himself into it with great delicacy. There was scarcely any need for either man to be seated, given the feebleness of the *Merry Mare*'s acceleration, but it suited Adrana to host her guests as if they were in a Mazarile drawing-room, resting their knees after a long afternoon at the races.

'I spoke to Cossel on the way down,' Lagganvor said. 'The sweeper is clear, and there's not been a squeak on the optical telegraph since that news about Incer Stallis. We shall soon be at the limit of practical signalling, in any case.'

'Sail-flash?'

'Not a glimmer there, either. If that squadron is aft of *Revenger*, they are sailing with excellent discipline.'

'So long as *Revenger* stays dark, they won't find her,' Adrana replied.

'She will be running out a spread of ordinary sails ahead of port,' Lagganvor reminded her.

'But not until it is imperative. I know my sister. She will take no silly chances.' Adrana poured another measure and passed it to Lagganvor. 'Show Lasling your eye, Lag.'

'My eye?'

'He hasn't seen it, and I think he would find it interesting. There needn't be any secrets between us now, need there?'

He took a sip of the drink, gasped admiringly, and held the little glass up the light. Then he set it down, pushed back his fringe, and popped his eye out onto the table.

'A remote,' he said, as Lasling's gaze veered between the empty socket and the perfectly veined and coloured object that had only just been occupying it. 'Bosa Sennen gave it to me, to aid in her spy craft. It has . . . certain capabilities.'

'It can see through things?'

'Not as well as lookstone. But it can travel independently of me, scouting ahead. It can kill, if it has to.'

'Make it move,' Adrana said.

'I'd rather not.'

'Lasling will think there is nothing there except a glass eye.'

'Lasling is fine,' Lasling said, with a genial dismissiveness. 'I believe whatever I am told.'

Lagganvor reached out a hand and suspended it over the eye. He raised the hand, and the eye levitated from the table as if suspended by an invisible thread. 'What our good captain doesn't quite appreciate,' he said, through mildly gritted teeth, 'is that none of this happens without effort. The control binding is very demanding. It leaves me ... drained. Which is why I prefer not to use the eye unless there is an urgent need.' He stiffened his hand, angled the palm until it was upright, and sent the eye speeding away. It travelled to the Clacker's crib, spun around and returned.

Lagganvor caught it between his fingers.

'Satisfied?'

'Thank you for the demonstration,' Adrana said, smiling emphatically.

Lagganvor fixed the eye back into place, his look guarded, as well she expected it to be. He ruffled his fringe back into place, then took another hard sip from his glass. 'With luck, Lasling, that'll be the last time you ever see my eye anywhere other than in this socket.'

'I should not be too sorry if that were the case, Mister Lag.' Lasling smiled awkwardly, as might anyone who had sensed the fringes of some tense business without having the least idea of its true shape and extent.

There came a stirring from the crib. Tazaknakak pushed away his blankets using his upper arms to paw around the repair work that had been done to his casque. He probed himself, cautious around the margins between his normal tissue and Vouga's quickglass. His eyes opened: sleepy and small as those of a pale, docile whale Adrana had once seen in the Mazarile public aquarium. Then he began to make a sound like a child's rattle, amplifying and intensifying in speed, until the individual clacks of the rattle blended into each other, and some longer, slower pattern emerged.

'A moment alone with my guest, if you would be so kind,' Adrana told her two visitors. 'I don't want him to be overwhelmed with sudden company.'

15

She lifted the Clacker from his crib and helped him into the seat which Lagganvor had been using, with a cushion stuffed under him to bring his face to her eye-level.

'You have not died on us, Tazaknakak. I take that to be an encouraging sign. Has the resin been successful?'

'It would seem so . . . I . . . congratulate your man on his . . . perspic . . . ik . . . ik . . . ik . . . acity.'

She had to strain to understand him, but that was not atypical of Clackers, at least those few of which she had experience. The sounds he generated in his casque were a marvel of subtlety and fluidity, but they had never been intended to emulate the output of a monkey's larynx. The wonder was not that discoursing with Tazaknakak demanded concentration, but that it was possible at all.

'We spoke a little in Mulgracen, if you remember, but your voice sounds different to me now. Vouga has done well, I think, but there are bound to be changes in the resonant cavities. It must be like learning to speak all over again. As well as that, you are out of the habit.'

'I will soon adjust. But even if I could not speak . . . ik . . . ik . . . a word of your tongue again, I am beginning to see the world anew. You cannot know what it is to lose the gift of sound-sight, Captain Ness. There is no analogous handicap among your kind.'

'I am certain you know us well enough to be sure, Tazaknakak. Is it really coming back to you?'

'Yes. I am forming a sound-picture of you even as I speak. It is . . . imperfect. The crudity of resolution would disgrace a newly-hatched. But it is vastly better than no sound-picture at all.'

Beneath the rapid rattling and clacking that enabled him to generate speech sounds was a constant ululation at a much higher pitch. It was nearly at the limit of her hearing and she presumed most of what was being generated was in fact beyond any possibility of detection.

'If we have been able to help you in any way, I am glad of it.' She coughed lightly. 'I am sure there will be much more that your friends are able to do for you, beyond our poor attempts at medicine.'

'You have done your best, Captain, and no more can be expected of you.'

'If you have any immediate needs, don't hesitate to bring them to my attention. Do you have much idea of the time that's passed since you gave your letter of indemnity?'

'I confess I have none.'

'We operated on you only a day or two after our ships took their separate courses. We've been sailing like that for two weeks now. You were . . . recuperating . . . for most of that time. We felt it best to let nature take its course.'

'How much sailing lies ahead of us?'

'No more than a week.'

'These ships of yours are so intolerably slow. I wonder how you put up with it.'

'We do things at our own speed, Tazaknakak, and for the most part it suits us very well. There are twenty thousand settled worlds in the Congregation, and none is more than a year's sailing from another. Most are mere weeks; even days for the more favourable crossings. We do not desire to be faster. Being faster just means being bored and disappointed by things sooner than otherwise. We desire to be safe, and prosperous, and free of worry for our future.'

'You cannot miss what you have never known.'

'I know your ships are faster than ours, but that doesn't make them better. Do you have need of men such as Lasling or Tindouf on your clever Clacker ships? I doubt it very much. I imagine those ships need about as much love and consideration as a lightbulb. They do what is asked of them, when it is asked of them, and they are forgotten about when they are not needed. This ship . . .' She stroked the edge of her table. 'This ship may be slow, but it runs on sweat and patience and the sort of wisdom it takes half a life to acquire.'

'It is good to be content with one's situation.'

She was starting to get the first faint, dawn-like intimations of a headache. She had heard about that somewhere. It was something to do with being in close proximity to a Clacker: the constant ultrasonic influence of their auditory sense-gathering. 'Concerning our situation . . .' she began.

'You wish to bring up the real purpose of this conversation.'

She sighed, disappointed in herself for being so transparent. 'It would be remiss of me not to discuss it, given that every second brings us closer to Trevenza Reach. Are you confident that your friends will be waiting for you?'

He knitted both sets of hands together, managing to convey an impression of intolerable smug self-satisfaction.

'Perfectly so.'

'I wish I had your confidence. Those muddleheads on Mulgracen nearly stopped you leaving. Nearly killed you, if I'm not mistaken.'

'They were the blunt instruments of fools. There would have been no difficulty with them if I had left on my own schedule. Alas, matters were disrupted by your arrival, and your insistence that I leave according to your timetable, not mine.'

She bridled, and did well to keep her composure. 'It's such a shame you had no other choice of ship, Tazaknakak – and such a shame that we had no other choice of passenger. But our obligations will soon be discharged – won't they?'

'You will deliver me safely.'

'And you will answer my questions.'

'Not before our arrival. What guarantee would I have that you wouldn't let me die as soon as I have served my usefulness to you?'

'One: I'm not a monster. Two: I'd rather hand you over to your friends breathing. But it might not hurt if you demonstrated a little goodwill.'

'How so?'

'My questions are complex and inter-twined. It won't take one answer to satisfy them, as well you know. So why not show you are sincere by giving me something now, instead of when we reach Trevenza?'

'It is true,' said Tazaknakak, 'that it will take more than one point of light to illuminate the vast landscape of your ignorance.'

'Then we'll begin with one answer. I'll ask you two questions. You can decide for yourself which you respond to. The other will wait until we arrive.'

'And the price for this . . . premature disclosure?'

'Our continued good relations, Tazaknakak. Which I'm sure neither of us would wish to jeopardise. Here are the questions. I should like to understand why quoins have begun to demonstrate an affinity for the Old Sun. My sister noticed it first. This is a new behaviour, something that was never seen before the Readjustment, and it must be telling us something profound about their true nature. But I cannot see it for myself. That is the first question.'

'And the second?' he asked hopefully, as if it might be more to his taste.

'A curious riddle that has been puzzling me since our encounter with the muddleheads in Mulgracen. Lagganvor told me that they are temporary agents, stitched together from bits of monkey and bits of alien. They are . . . animated, infected with a purpose, and enough wits to serve that end. But I cannot see how they are possible.'

'You live in a world in which the inexplicable is common-place, Captain Ness. Skulls. Bauble fields. Ghostie relics.

Effector-displacer devices. You understand none of these things, yet you do not seem troubled by that lack of comprehension. Why perturb yourself about one more trifling thing?'

'Because I am not sure that it is trifling. Where my sister and I grew up was a place called Neural Alley. I am sure there are similar places on a thousand worlds.'

'Doubtless. Concerning the quoins—'

'Let me finish. There were shops in Neural Alley where vendors sold novelty animals. We saw them in cages or tanks in the shop windows. They were marvellous to us, and a little terrifying. They had been manipulated by genetic means, using technologies and methods that the vendors barely understood, but which were repeatable. They could take one trait from one creature and splice it onto another. By that means, the vendors created frogs that glowed like night-lights, birds that had the lustrous wings of dragonflies, snakes that had multitudes of legs, and so on. Chimeric organisms, they were called. They could not propagate, but they were alive, and could only exist because of the innate similarity of their biological grammar. Deep, deep in the past, they shared common ancestors. This was how fragments of forgotten genetic language could be reawoken or copied between species. Because it was not truly alien.'

'Your observations are most creditable. If I may address your former question, relating to the deep nature of quoins—'

'If the means by which the muddleheads are made are not so different to the means used by those vendors, then it must be . . . it can *only* be . . . are you listening, Tazaknakak?'

'This is . . . not a desirable line of enquiry, Captain.'

'I did not imagine it would be. I shall tell you where it has been leading me, though. I think we are not so different from each other as is generally assumed. If the muddleheads are made up from bits of monkey, and bits of alien . . . then what we think of as monkey and alien cannot be as far apart as is commonly believed. There must be a similarity, an underlying biological connection . . .'

'There is not,' Tazaknakak said.

'A flat assertion does not constitute an answer to my question.'

'We each know our histories, Captain. Yours is a tale of Occupations stretching back ten million years or more. A broken, disjointed tale, with an uncertain prologue. You do not even remember how long ago you decided to dismantle your eight old worlds. Our history is not like yours. It is unbroken, and immense. A tapestry reaching back billions of years, without a single thread out of place. You might ask the same of our colleagues the Crawlies, or the Hardshells, or any of the alien cultures who have offered their assistance. You would receive a similarly humbling lesson in differing perspectives.'

'And a similar evasiveness, Tazaknakak?' She sighed and shrugged, certain she had got as far as she was likely to. 'All right – the quoins. They're drawn to the Old Sun. This can't have escaped your attention. What does it signify?'

'It signifies—'

A buzz sounded from her desk. Adrana regarded her guest, thought for a moment of having him leave, or of taking her call in the control room, then leaned forward and pressed the intercom button.

'Captain's quarters. What is it?'

A voice scratched out of the grille, as muffled and reedy as someone blowing down an organ-tube.

'This is Meggery, calling down from the sighting room. I see something, Captain Ness. It's faint, but I think it's another telegraph coming in from *Revenger*. I'm transcribing it as I speak.'

*

Eddralder's daughter was just outside the Kindness Room, peeling off a pair of surgical gloves in a slow and disconsolate manner, while the only noises coming from inside the room were the methodical chinks of instruments and medicines being put away.

'Is she still alive?' Fura asked.

Merrix rubbed a clean knuckle against a red-rimmed eye. 'I

don't know. In a fashion, I suppose. But she won't know that you're here. I don't think she knows anything at all now.'

'I'd like to see her.'

'Father did all that he could.' A sudden pleading look took over her. 'You understand that, don't you?'

'I was under no illusions, Merrix. I don't doubt for an instant that you both did everything that was possible, given our situation. But I still want to see Strambli.'

'Go in, then. But you won't like it.'

She went past Merrix, pushing through the curtain they had put over the doorway, then squeezing around the bulky machines that had been assembled for the operation. They were all dormant now, their leathery bellows no longer huffing and puffing, their chugging blood pumps stilled, their green-gridded oscilloscope screens turned dark. Eddralder was holding a huge glass syringe up to his eye, checking it for cleanliness before placing it into a precisely formed slot in a velvet-lined medical box. Strambli was still on the operating bed, her body obscured by a gauzy curtain pulled around her on a rail.

Fura appraised the indistinct form. There was a sheet over her legs and torso, and that made it difficult to be sure, but there was no obvious sign that Eddralder had got very far in cutting out the Ghostie infection.

Eddralder continued with his packing-away.

'What happened?'

'I failed her.'

'We all failed her,' Fura said.

'No, the fault is with me. I was too hesitant, too fearful, too hopeful that those old accounts might be relied upon. I wasted your Mephrozine, when I should have operated as soon as she came to me.'

'None of us knew how this was going to progress.'

Merrix had come in behind Fura. 'Show her, Father,' she said, in a low but commanding tone.

Eddralder whisked back the curtain between them and Strambli, and lifted aside the sheets.

Fura stared, not at first believing the evidence of her own senses. It crossed her mind, fleetingly, that the doctor and his daughter must have conspired to arrange a sort of prank, a dark joke at her expense. The absurdity of this premise was almost easier to accept than the reality before her.

The Ghostie transformation had enveloped the whole of the affected leg, turning the limb colourless and semi-translucent. It looked wasted and near-skeletal. Faint structures, shadows of veins and bones, arteries and tendons, were embedded in that translucence like wisps of frozen smoke. They shivered into blurry indistinction the more Fura pressed her concentration upon them. It was as if they were furtive, always holding themselves at a distance somewhere other than the point at which her eyes were focused.

This was bad – there was clearly no hope whatsoever of salvaging the limb – but equally distressing was the fact that the Ghostie transformation had begun to encroach its way down the other leg. The upper thigh had the onset of grey pearliness that would eventually become translucence, while the leg below the knee looked almost healthy.

'This ain't possible,' Fura said.

'Yet it is happening,' Eddralder said. He paused, glanced at Merrix. 'I've measured the blood temperature in the unaffected part of the leg. It's colder than it should be. I think between her heart and the leg, her blood . . . goes somewhere. It goes somewhere else, along with her bones and nerves, and then comes back to us. It's how these disconnected parts of her remain alive.'

Fura felt cold as well. 'What do you mean by "somewhere else"?'

'He doesn't know,' Merrix interjected. 'No one could.'

'The transformation must depend upon a continuously living host,' Eddralder said. 'It needs that substrate. So as it encroaches, it does something to the living flesh. Displaces it, cell by cell, structure by structure, into some realm we can't sense. Some cold place, yet not so cold that the blood freezes. That way there is a preservation of life . . . of consciousness . . . almost until the end.'

'Until the end of what?'

Merrix elevated the sheet so that Strambli's entire torso was visible. A pearly tide had lapped nearly halfway up her chest. Her hips had the same translucence as her legs. In that translucence floated a grey impression of pelvic structures, like an anatomical photograph that had not been properly developed.

'At the first touch of my knife, the process accelerated. I tried to cut it out, to reach the margins of the transformation. There was no hope. It raced ahead, faster than we could act. We could see the spread of it with our own eyes.'

'It's slowed down again now,' Merrix said. 'But only because it must know it's won. It must have used up a lot of energy in that burst of transformation, and now it needs to recuperate.'

'Even so, it won't be long now,' Eddralder said. 'Will you signal the *Merry Mare*, to let them know that we've failed?'

'If I had something definite to tell them. But what would I say? Doctor Eddralder operated, and now she's more Ghostie than not? If she were dead, it would be so much simpler for all of us.' Fura moved to Strambli's head. Her eyes were glassier than before, and now the skin around them had begun to be drained of colour and opacity. 'Is it in her mind?' she asked, softly.

'It will have consolidated its hold. Clearly it infiltrates the nervous system before it reaches the external tissue. If it is any consolation, I doubt that Strambli has any awareness of her condition.'

'I don't want her to suffer.'

'Nor do we.'

'If there's the least part of her still in there, still capable of feeling, I want her to be spared any distress.'

'I cannot make that judgement,' Eddralder said.

'Then I'll make it for you. You have drugs. I know what some of them are capable of. End this.' Fura made to push herself away from Strambli's side, her eyes beginning to sting. 'I'm so sorry we couldn't do more,' she said, speaking directly to the unconscious form. 'You deserved better.'

*

Adrana took a direct transcription of the message sequence Meggery was sending down from the sighting room. There were inevitably some errors and drop-outs in the sequence, for Meggery was using her own eyes at the limit of reliable signalling distance, but since the message repeated itself twice, there was no difficulty in creating a clean version.

While Lagganvor and Cossel looked on, Adrana spread out this message transcription – which was still in raw code – and began to work laboriously through it with one of the standard cipher books weighted open beside her.

"'Strambli . . . worsening,"' she said, pausing deliberately between each word. "'Eddralder forced to operate.'" She stroked a finger up and down the densely printed columns of the cipher book, frowning as she lost her place. "'Missing . . . gas . . . mixtures . . . for . . . an . . . an . . .'"

'Anaesthesia,' Lagganvor said quietly, before gesturing at the code. 'May I?'

She regarded him for a second.

'Please do.'

He read, as quickly and confidently as if the dots and dashes were his native tongue. "'Merrix believes tables in your infirmary: consult the red book on second shelf: ninth edition *General Pharmacopium*. Send figures in sixth appendix by way of return, telegraph only, with all haste.'"

'Silly of him to leave that book in the wrong ship,' Cossel said.

'These things happen,' Adrana answered. 'We must oblige, in any case.'

'Squawk'd be the quickest,' Cossel said.

'And the quickest way of exposing our position to Incer Stallis and inviting a ranging shot. We might accept the risk to ourselves, but we also have our passenger to consider.'

'And how is our friend?' Lagganvor asked. 'Suitably loquacious?'

'He gives me a headache just being near him,' Adrana said. 'There is only so much of that I shall be able to tolerate. But I think he has a lot more to tell us, and I intend to get some of it out of him before we dock. I worry about him disappearing as soon as we arrive.'

Lagganvor nodded. 'That *would* be a tad on the unfortunate side. Still, he's better off with you than Fura.'

'Why so?'

'If your sister had the first inkling he wasn't being as forthcoming as she'd like, she'd have Surt whip up a set of thumb-screws. Or whatever would suffice.'

'I am not Fura.'

'Speaking of your sister,' Cossel said, turning around the transcription Adrana had made from Meggery's report. 'This has to be from her, doesn't it? There's no way it could have come from one of Incer Stallis's ships, just happening to lie along the right line o'sight?'

'We would be foolish to rule it out,' Adrana said. 'But I do not see how Stallis can possibly know about Strambli's condition, or Eddralder's intention to operate, or the presumed existence of that book.' She flicked the briefest of glances at Lagganvor. 'We can verify the fact of the book very easily. If it turns out to be real, then the request must be authentic.'

Lagganvor rubbed at his chin.

'I don't like it, Adrana. It smacks of something to me – some ruse that we can't quite see. But as you so correctly state – the proof will be in the mere existence of that book.'

Cossel went off to the infirmary and was back very promptly, with a fat red volume in her hands. She set it down next to the daybook and the crib-sheet. Adrana stared at it for a few moments, then leafed through to the section on gas mixtures for anaesthetic medicine.

She easily found the table of values that Eddralder had requested.

'He needs only these sets of numbers,' she said, dragging a nail down the main columns of the table. 'We should be able to transmit them fairly quickly. Eddralder will know immediately what to do with them.' She tore a sheet off the daybook and copied the relevant figures down, omitting any supplemental information that she felt Eddralder could manage without. When she was done, she passed the sheet and the pen to Cossel.

'Can you formulate this for me, then come to the main lock? As soon as we are suited, Lagganvor and I will go out with the telegraphic box.'

Cossel bit on the end of the pen for a moment, then began to mark down the code sequence.

*

The outer door opened and they left the ship, stomping out onto the curve of the hull. All the normal lights had been dimmed – they had never been bright to begin with – and so their suits were illuminated by only two diffuse sources: the purple and ruby shimmer of the Congregation on one side, with the Old Sun's dusky radiance at the heart of that enchanting lantern show, and on the other side the fainter and paler starlight of all the suns beyond their own agreeable little pocket of civilisation: all the fixed stars which were near enough to see as individual glints, even though they might yet be hundreds or thousands of light years distant, and far beyond them, like a vast, faceless audience against which these closer objects were merely a troupe of scattered actors, the nearly numberless stars of the Swirly. The near stars wore faint tinted masks: reds and golds. The more distant ones were blue or pearly, if indeed Adrana apprehended any colour at all.

'Did Cossel give you the out-going code?' Lagganvor asked.

'A little late to ask me now, but yes, she did. I asked her to keep it brief.'

'Very sensible. But you realise it'll be much harder for them to pick up our message, no matter how well we send it?'

'Meggery only made a few mistakes. Here. You can read the code back to me, while I do the sending.'

Lagganvor closed his glove around the paper. 'Luck was on Meggery's side – as well as dark skies, and a very accurate alignment from the other ship, no doubt assisted by Paladin. We can't count on such fortune. They'll be seeing us against the backdrop of the Congregation, which will make our signal harder to discriminate.'

'He needs those gas mixtures, Lag. They wouldn't have asked if they didn't think there was a hope of reading our reply.'

Never taking more than one magnetic sole off the hull at a time, they worked their way around the curve of the ship until the Congregation lay at their backs and the star-mottled darkness of the Empty was before them.

The gyro-compass was built into the top of the telegraphic box, with a ring of lamps to indicate the alignment of the whole device relative to the desired direction. If she had the box properly aimed, only a central green lamp would activate; otherwise red lamps in sectors of the ring would flicker on in accordance with her pointing error. It was only as accurate as the initial gyro-lock, and that was perfectly good so long as the two ships maintained a fixed posture. That was seldom the case in celestial navigation, though, and most certainly not the case now. It was the best anyone could do, though, without harnessing a robot mind to run the changing calculations.

Adrana stood with the box before her, held by its double handles. The red lamps guided her onto the approximate alignment, and she adjusted it very carefully until the green lamp glowed unwaveringly. Fortunately, it took only minimal effort to hold the box, and there were additional gyroscopes inside it to aid with the pointing stability.

'You have it, I believe,' Lagganvor said.

There were paddle-like control levers set into the handles. Adrana used one to open the flaps at the front of the box, exposing the delicate optics. She pressed another which propelled a light-imp out of a cartridge, positioning it within cradle at the focal point. At the same time, a spring-loaded mechanism drove a ram down onto the light-imp, crushing it, and thereby activating its stored luminosity. Light-imps were transient light sources, but they were much brighter than any neon tube or incandescent bulb, and ideally suited to short intervals of telegraphic transmission.

Through gill-like slits in the side of the box, directed back at the operator, a wavering glow signified that the imp was giving off its stored flux.

'I'm ready,' Adrana said. 'Give me the message.'

Lagganvor looked down at the code sequence and began to speak.

'Open, shut, open, shut, open, shut. Long open. Long shut. Open, shut, open, shut. Long shut. Open. Long shut. Long open, shut, open, shut, long open . . .'

Adrana's thumbs worked the iris controls as he continued relating the code. She felt the mechanism working, a faint but definite *twitch* with each activation. The aiming lamp was holding green, but that was no guarantee that she was pointed in exactly the right direction, or that there was anyone at the other end picking up her signal.

'. . . open, shut, long open, shut, open, shut, open, long shut, open, shut, open, shut, open, shut.' He paused. 'That's all there is. Do you think you sent it cleanly?'

'If there was a mistake, I didn't make it.'

'We should re-transmit, all the same.'

'Two more times, while the gyro-lock is still valid.'

They re-sent it twice more.

When they were done, Lagganvor swept an arm at the nearest line of rigging, where a pale indigo emanation traced the filament's edge. 'I see some ghost-light forming. The weather must be on the turn.'

'We've done what needed to be done,' Adrana answered.

She closed the main flaps, lowering the box so that it pointed at the hull. The light-imp was still giving off its flux, but by the evidence of the glow spilling from the gills it was beginning to flicker and die.

*

There was no good aspect to Strambli's passing, except that it had been facilitated quickly. It was an odd blessing to count on, Fura supposed, that it had still been within Eddralder's power to end a life so efficiently, and at her order. All the same she was as glad as she could be that his medicines had retained their potency, even if they were put to the most harrowing of ends.

Merrix and Eddralder had been present as the injection served its purpose, and Ruther was still mumbling and turning in his sleep in her quarters, so the only two other members to pay their respects were Surt and Tindouf, and they could not hide their discomfort at the strange and distressing condition of their late colleague.

'I never saw such a thing, or ever want to again,' Surt said, after she had given Strambli's form the shortest, most flinching of glances. 'And I'll never go within a million leagues of anything Ghostie, if I know my own right mind.'

'Few of us would argue with that sentiment,' Fura said.

'What's we to do with her?' Tindouf said, consternation and puzzlement making a creased map of his brow. 'It don't seems right to take her back to a world like that, not the way she is.'

'You both knew her better than I did,' Fura said. 'Did she leave any instructions, the way Captain Werranwell did?'

'She weren't plannin' on dyings quite so early,' Tindouf said, scratching at the corner of his eye. 'Oh, Stram. Why'd you have to be so careless around the Ghostie gubbinses?'

'She said it weren't carelessness,' Surt remarked. 'She said that knife had a mind of its own, when it jerked in her hand. As if it meant to put a bit of itself into her. I know we didn't credit her at the time, but now I'm minded to think diff'rently.'

'Does you think the Ghostie gubbins wanted to make more of itselfs?' Tindouf asked.

'I don't know, Tinnie. I don't think I want to know.'

'Whatever was happening to her, we stopped it,' Fura said, with rather more confidence than she felt. 'Doctor Eddralder said the Ghostie transformation couldn't keep happening if she wasn't alive. The drugs he put into her were enough to kill a horse several times over. She went peacefully, and she went fast, and now it's done.'

'But you still don't know what to do with her,' Surt said.

Fura nodded meekly. 'We can't just leave her somewhere without a thought to what she's become. She's Ghostie gubbins now, part of her, and we owe it to other crews not to have 'em stumble on her unawares and do themselves harm. Casting her into space, the way with we did with the captain, ought to be safe enough for a century or two . . . or we could find some out-of-the-way bauble, one that won't pop back open for a long time, and stash her there. Her remains, I mean. I think we have to burn the parts of her that'll burn.'

Surt looked stricken. 'On a ship?'

'We can discuss the practicalities later. I'm just saying that we have responsibilities to meet – to our friend as well as other crews. Of course, if she had left instructions, even just something she'd mentioned in passing . . .' Fura trailed off, willing either of them to come up with something, even if it was a white lie conjured up on the spur. 'Well, rack your memories,' she said, on a despondent falling note.

'If we leave Strambli somewheres,' Tindouf mused, 'then I'd be very glad if we left the rest of the Ghostie gubbinses with her. Some good dids come of it, but not much, and I'd be happier in my bunk knowing they weren't shiverin' up the ship.'

'We'll cross that line,' Fura said, 'when we're sure we don't have any further need for sharp cutting things.'

16

Adrana waited for Lagganvor, turning the gargoyle head in her hands, watching with devout concentration as its eyes and tongue lolled in and out. How old might it be, she wondered. Younger than skulls, she supposed, for its purpose depended on them, but that hardly narrowed matters down. How nice it would have been, she thought, to have Fura with her now, so that they might marvel over the strange thing and offer their individual theories as to its provenance and function. Until it was denied her, she had not realised how pleasant it was to have a sister to talk to in such idle moments; how fine a thing it was to have Fura's imagination as counterpoint to her own. How splendid it had been, for all their differences and adversities, to be adventuring together, rather than alone.

'You've finally found out what that ugly thing is for?' Lagganvor asked as he came in. 'If so, please be so kind as to put me out of my ignorance.'

'I do know its purpose, yes.' She poured another measure of the spirit she had offered him during their last conversation. 'You may as well finish it off, since it was so evidently to your taste. Will you sit down?'

He took his seat. He had removed the outer parts of his vacuum suit, but was still wearing the padded under-garments with their numerous tubes and wires somewhat resembling an inverted anatomy of arteries and intestines. Patches of sweat darkened the fabric, some it baked-in through long use and some of it new.

'The drink is . . .' He elevated the glass to his nose, sniffed. 'Thrispan brandy? I meant to ask.'

'Close. Trennigarian'

'Close indeed. I'm surprised you didn't share a drop of it with me while we were on *Revenger*.'

'I couldn't have. The stuff was under lock-and-key: Werranwell's private stash. For a man of austere tastes, it seems he wasn't above a treat or two – and I don't think sharing it with anyone was uppermost in his thoughts.'

'We mustn't judge the poor fellow too severely. I doubt there are any captains in all the Congregation who don't have at least one thing they'd prefer to keep from their crew – even if it's just a bottle of Trennigarian brandy.' He searched the room, frowning slightly. 'I realised something was missing, but I couldn't put my finger on it. Where is the Clacker?'

'I had Vouga take him to the sick-bay.'

'Nothing wrong, I take it?'

'No – but we want to make sure that there aren't any complications arising from the fusion of the quickglass and his living tissue. Vouga is making a very careful examination of the margins, something we hardly dared risk when Tazaknakak was asleep. He'll be a little while. That's fine, though. It allows us to speak candidly.'

Adrana had prepared a measure of Trennigarian brandy for herself. She drank from it with her right hand, keeping her left below the table. 'To go back to Werranwell: do you think your brother was also the sort to keep secrets?'

'My brother had his private concerns. They were secrets of a sort. But I don't think he intentionally withheld them from his crew.'

'He withheld you.'

Lagganvor shrugged. 'He had his reasons. If I might have the time again, I would not treat him the way I did.' He creased his lips. 'He'd suffered enough as it was, clearly. But I couldn't act as if I'd never warned him. I told him repeatedly that he was flirting with disaster.'

She nodded, thinking of the partial account she'd heard from Prozor.

'By taking Illyria with him on those voyages.'

'I understood his attachment to the girl. She was the living embodiment of her mother, in many ways – a constant reminder to him. Heartache, as well as solace.'

'What happened to her mother?'

'One of the plagues.'

Adrana nodded slowly. 'Then I feel for Illyria, if I didn't already. That's how Fura and I lost our mother – how we ended up being raised by our father alone, on Mazarile.'

'Then the consequences would have been familiar to you. The father's attachment increased. Pol's daughter became more precious to him than ever before.'

'Then why in the worlds did he risk taking her on bauble-hops?'

'He didn't, to begin with. He went off, while I remained home as Illyria's guardian. I was a little younger than Pol, and not as settled in my mind that a career cracking baubles was the life for me. That's not to say that I didn't want to see the worlds, but I thought there might be other ways to do that.' He glanced at the little glass, which was still pinched between his fingers, as if some flavour in the Trennigarian brandy had only just revealed itself to him. 'I set my sights on joining the mercantile intelligence services, in the end. Pol had already gone off to make his fortune, but there were years of study ahead of me, and no reason at all that Illyria couldn't remain in my care. He saw her often enough, and I always made sure to draw a line between my role and his. She always understood who her father was, and she admired his occupation. Admired it too much, I should say. She argued to join on one of his jaunts. Pol was against it, initially. But she persuaded him, and nothing I could say made any difference.' He made a fluttering gesture with his free hand. 'Off they went. There was no misadventure, that time. They came back a few months later, and she remained with me while he was off on his next trip. But she'd got the taste for it by then.'

'She insisted on becoming a permanent fixture on his ship.'

'Pol caved in to her. He gave her quarters of her own and arranged for her continuing education. I . . . expressed my disapproval. It was to no avail whatsoever. I . . .' He set down the cup, eyeing it with a faint but developing suspicion. 'I feel a little fuzzy around the edges.'

'That would be the sedative I put into the brandy.'

He absorbed this news with a surprising pragmatism. 'I see. And the reason for this . . . sedative?'

'So you don't make any sudden, rash movements. I have a weapon aimed at you beneath the desk.'

He nodded. 'I did wonder about the other hand.'

'But not enough to think that I might actually intend to kill you.' Now that the matter was in the open, she raised her arm and settled it on the table. She held a dainty, jade-coloured energy pistol. 'I found this in Werranwell's belongings as well. It's a fanblade, I believe; a very specific weapon from the Eighth Occupation. Have you heard of such a thing?'

'I may well have.'

'I'll jog your memory just in case. Another name for it is "gut-spiller". It emits a beam of particles with a short half-life, moving very rapidly from side to side in a twenty-degree arc.' She gave it an admiring pout. 'It's pretty, isn't it? I think it may be one half of a duelling set.'

'I'm thinking it's rather a shame I don't have the other half,' Lagganvor said.

*

The boy had been muttering in his sleep again, fragments of sentences and words turned to near-mush by the damaged condition of his tongue. She held her pen above her journal, listening as he slurred out something about a dungeon and a candle; something else about a wooden door in the floor, and something that was under that door. Ruther became increasingly agitated: whimpered words of fear and distress becoming moans of wordless terror, and then a shriek so loud and sudden that it jolted him quite awake. Wide-eyed and shivering, still in the slackening coils of that night-terror, he looked around at the cabin in which he found himself.

Fura got up from her desk and went over to him with a tankard of water.

'Drink this.'

Ruther pressed his lips to the tankard and sipped tentatively, then with gathering strength.

'I'zh very . . .' He paused, looked at her with wide and surprised eyes, then dabbed a finger into his mouth, probing the tip of his tongue. 'Wha'sh . . . what'sh happened to me?'

'Nothing that won't heal, according to Eddralder. You nearly bit your own tongue off while you were skullbound with Incer Stallis. Do you remember any of that?'

Ruther looked doubtful, and for a second or two seemed to have no recollection whatsoever of the episode that had tipped him into unconsciousness. Then his face began to tighten, just as if he had registered the first faint sting of an injury and knew that a greater pain was on its way.

'I couldzhn't shto . . . couldzhn't *shtop* him.'

'It wasn't your fault. He was nearly too strong for me and Adrana, and I was silly enough to think we'd catch him off-guard if you used the skull instead of me. But he was much too clever for that.'

'Why . . . why am I here?'

'You were making too much racket to stay in the Kindness Room. Bad nightmares. You were just having one now.'

Ruther touched his cheekbones and jaw, examining the outline of his face as if it might have taken on some other aspect while he was asleep. He ran a hand through the white blaze of his hair, ruffling it as one might ruffle the fur of a dog.

'He wazh . . . I felt him come into my head.' He took some more of the water she had offered him. 'I could feel him, like I'd become a puppet, or some hollow thing made of wood. Just a marshk. . . a mask, with some eye-holzh . . .'

She nodded, believing him, yet puzzled as to how his memories of the contact with Stallis related to the nightmare of the dungeon. She turned this puzzle over in her head, came to no agreeable solution, and not for the first time had cause to regret the absence of her sister, who could always have been depended upon for some useful insight or shrewd observation. Had she been too hasty to gift Adrana a ship of her own, when some other arrangement might have prevailed? It was one thing to be annoyed by her sister's interjections and quibbles when she was nearby, quite another to be aware of the widening gulf between them, and how much she would now have given for Adrana's counsel.

'You don't have to speak for now,' she said, trying to find a kinder manner than her earlier brusqueness. 'Let your tongue heal. Eddralder sewed it back together, but he said it'd be swollen for a few more days. You served me well, in any case, and I won't ask you to go back into the bone room; not until I know Stallis won't be on the other end.'

'My head feelzh . . .' Ruther frowned as he sought the word he needed. 'Sh . . . tained.'

'There was something in you that left a bad trace of itself. I felt the same thing, when I had a dose of him. But you're strong, Ruther.'

Her praise drew a bashful smile from the boy. She doubted that he was more than two years younger than herself, but for all that he had lately seen some action, she still felt as if a lifetime's worth of experience separated them: a gulf of horror and loss and sharp learning that could never be undone.

'You think . . . too highly of me.'

'We made an error, but so did Stallis. He showed too much of himself. When he took you over I got a far stronger sense of his personality than I ever did before. And it made me want to . . .' She looked around the immediate environs of the cabin for some hapless bug, some innocent creature she could mash to a squirming smear under her metal thumb, but for once there was nothing. 'I want to seek restitution,' she said. 'And I'll have it.'

Ruther nodded in a way that made it clear that her words left in him no doubt at all.

'How long wazh. . . how long was I out for, Captain?'

'All in all, about twelve days. Eddralder kept a very close eye on you, and made sure you didn't waste away while you were under. We've been sailing independently of the *Merry Mare* for sixteen days. We still have about two weeks ahead of us, in case you have any fears about missing the excitement.'

'Two weeks izhn't . . . isn't so bad. Is the sh . . . shquadron . . . anywhere near?'

'It's possible. But we don't know where they are, exactly, and they obviously don't know our own position very well. If they did, they'd have been peppering us almost continuously with sail-shot.'

'He felt near, Captain. I can't say how or why, jusht that he did. Izh. . . isn't there any way we can tell?'

'I wish there was, Ruther. Sometimes it's worth surrendering your own invisibility to learn the position of your adversary, but that trade-off crumbles when you expect to be outnumbered and out-gunned, as we do. If I wished to give you false reassurance, I'd say there's no other ship besides the *Merry Mare* within one hundred thousand leagues of us. But the truth is Stallis could be within ten thousand leagues, and we wouldn't know it. He has good ships, very well handled, and they'll be sailing as quietly and darkly as nature permits.'

'I . . . could . . .' He halted himself. 'What I mean ish . . . if I had to go back into the room . . . I *would* do it, sir.'

'I think you would, despite everything. But I wouldn't ask it of you, Ruther, and so long as I depend on Doctor Eddralder's kind office, I wouldn't test his patience by doing so. He accepts that what happened to you the first time was not something we could have anticipated, but to put you through that twice, and deliberately . . .' She shook her head. 'Besides, it was to no avail.

He got into your head far too quickly. You'd learn nothing new the next time.'

'May I help with anything?'

'As soon as you feel strong enough, you'll be more than welcome to take a stint in the sighting-room. We could always use a keen pair of eyes.'

'I shall,' Ruther said. Then some troubling recollection struck him. 'Your friend . . . the one in the infirmary.' He searched for her name. 'Sh. . .Strambli?'

'Yes?'

'Did she make it?'

'No, Ruther,' Fura replied, shaking her head. 'I'm afraid Strambli didn't make it.'

*

Lagganvor drew a breath in through his nostrils, gazing at Adrana as if she were slightly out of focus. She imagined the battle going on inside his head, the fight between clarity of thought and the drowsiness induced by the sedative she had slipped into the Trennigarian brandy. It was mild in its effects, not enough to engender unconsciousness, but Lagganvor wasn't to know that.

'Continue,' Adrana said.

'What's left to tell?'

'Oh, a very great deal. How you and your brother became alienated from each other. I have the bones of it, but I want to hear it from your own lips. Pick up the story from the point where Illyria went off with Pol for the last time.'

'You know what happened.'

'Tell me anyway.'

'Bosa came. You know this. She took Illyria, and eventually made Illyria into herself. She'd have been kinder killing Pol there and then, but she allowed him to live, and eventually return to his trade.'

'You couldn't forgive him, though.'

'Not after all the times I'd warned him against taking her. He was broken, to begin with – shattered by guilt and the terrible fear that she was still out there, changed. He crawled home, and pleaded for both forgiveness and the strength only a brother could have given him. I offered neither.' He blinked against the tide of tiredness that he must have felt washing over him. 'I spurned him. More than that. I made it very clear that I despised his existence; wished he had never been born. I disavowed him as a brother, and did my utmost to destroy his reputation and self-respect. It was no act on my part. I truly loathed him.'

'So, he was ruined twice,' Adrana said, with the cool deliberation of a prosecuting lawyer. 'First by the loss of his daughter, and secondly by the unkindness of his own brother, Brysca Rackamore.'

He leaned back slightly, accepting his verdict.

'And yet, here I am.'

'Seeking to avenge Pol. Putting your own life in constant peril by trying to capture or eliminate Bosa Sennen, however we may define her. Impersonating one of her own. Mutilating yourself to make the disguise more convincing. Bravery and selflessness, of a sort. Did it occur to you that the resolution of your quest might have meant killing Illyria herself?'

'She was dead from the moment Bosa took her.'

'I was not,' Adrana replied. 'I resisted. I . . . endured.'

'Says the woman pointing a fanblade at my belly and looking only a blink away from using it.'

Her finger itched on the trigger. If only he knew how truly close she was; the fury that was within her, and the outlet it was seeking.

'Take out your eye.'

This surprised him even through the sedative's fog. 'You realise I can do a lot more harm with the eye outside me, than when it's in place?'

'Take it out,' she repeated.

He had a theatrical habit of palming one hand before his eye, and patting the other against the back of his head, so that the eye popped out like a marble in an arcade game, but he made no show of that now. He simply pinched at the eye and out it came, puckering loose with a faint slurp, and resting glistening and perfect in his palm.

'I always guessed you'd want it for yourself. Fura has that arm of hers, even if it's missing a finger, and you have nothing except your own wits.'

'Put it on the table. Facing me.'

He set the eye down. It rested where it was placed, regarding her with a slight upward tilt to its singular gaze.

Lagganvor looked at her.

'What is this about?'

She ignored his question. 'Tell me what happened once you sent Pol away.'

'Isn't it obvious? My hardness toward him soon engendered the same hardness back. Years later, somewhat older and wiser, I sought to make amends. I tried to make contact, tried to write or signal him. But my every effort was rebuffed. I learned, through intermediaries, that I was dead to him. No longer a brother at all.' He stared at her with his one living eye and the empty socket of the other, as if daring her to flinch away. 'That hurt, but I suppose no more than my rejection must have hurt him. I took nothing from it personally.'

'Really, Lagganvor?'

'Perhaps a little.' He smiled at her perceptiveness. 'Perhaps a lot. I wished for there to be an improvement in our relations. With time, there might have been a reconciliation. But Bosa stole that possibility from both of us. If I had cause to hate her before, what she did to Pol only redoubled my animus.'

'Which is when you decided to kill her once and for all.'

'It was a fine intention. It would have given me some small consolation for the loss of Pol and Illyria. How was I to know that two daughters of Mazarile would get the job done sooner?'

'You know that she is dead. There can be no doubt in this regard.'

'Something died,' Lagganvor acknowledged, with an equivocation that unsettled her.

'But you do not think her spirit is entirely extinguished.'

'Nor do you. Not if you know yourself well, or your sister knows herself. She's in both of you. You've admitted as much.' He paused and made a slow and daring bid to take back his eye. Adrana jabbed the fanblade at him so suddenly that he snatched back his hand as if snakebitten. He looked at her with an enquiring hopefulness. 'Might I ask your intentions concerning the eye?'

'You lied to me about the telegraphic message.'

He feigned surprise.

'I did?'

'You would have had us transmit a false code, designed to trick *Revenger* into revealing itself.'

'Cossel formulated that code. It was a simple listing of the gas mixtures Eddralder needed.'

'Eddralder never required those gas mixtures. He wouldn't have been so lax as to leave an important book on the wrong ship, but even if he *did* – he ought to have known those gas mixtures thoroughly by now. It was your doing: you falsified that entire message from *Revenger*.'

'How could I possibly have done that?'

'Using your eye. It doesn't have the range to signal between our two ships, or send a message to your masters – that much I already concluded. But I'd neglected a second possibility. The eye could go out to a relatively short distance – say a few hundred leagues – and then shine back at us, mimicking a telegraphic signal.'

Lagganvor pinched at the skin between his eyebrows, squinting as if through a migraine.

'But I was inside when that signal came in. You even had . . .' he paused, slowed, as some piece of the puzzle fell into place. 'You even had me take out my eye, when we were with Lasling.'

'I had you take out *an* eye,' Adrana said, 'And I realised in that moment that you must have two of them: the one we've seen in action with the impressive capabilities, and a secondary eye you can put back into the socket when the other one's out there serving you. When we were with Lasling – when you were late coming back inside – that was because you'd sent the main one off on an errand.'

'Two eyes,' he said, shaking his head in mock bemusement. 'And which of these eyes would this one be?'

'The secondary one, I think,' Adrana said. She picked it up with her spare hand and held it close to her face, daring something to happen. The eye was cold, slightly moist and sticky to the touch. That was not some biological secretion, she thought, but some curious lubricating agent that the eye oozed out of itself, to ease its swivelling in the eye socket, and its passage to and from that receptacle. 'The other . . . the main eye . . . is either still out there, floating near us in space, or it's hidden somewhere. Most likely the latter. About your person, or in your cabin. I think you would have collected it when we went out to send the telegraphic signal. That eye moves quickly, it can keep to the shadows, and I doubt I'd have noticed if it had slipped back to you.'

'So I put my eye back in while outside, wearing a vacuum suit?'

'No, but there are such things as pockets. You could have smuggled the eye back aboard, then swapped it back in.'

'But you made me demonstrate the eye for Lasling.'

She put down the one she was holding, wiping her fingers together until there was no trace of fluid on them. 'Clearly the secondary eye isn't just some piece of coloured glass. It can move, under your direction. It might even be dangerous. It might even have all the capabilities of the first eye, although I think it unlikely: that was rare technology when Bosa gave it to her man. No. I think it helps fill your socket when the first is away, and might have the useful characteristic of being able to pass itself off as the first . . . but I suspect it isn't *quite* as valuable to you. There's a falseness to it – it doesn't look quite as alive as the other and you know it. That's why you're so much more careful to keep that fringe in place, when you're wearing the second eye.'

'I will say it again: Cossel formulated the message.'

'Which I gave to you, and asked you to read back as I was operating the telegraph. Transmitting the message I'd already committed to memory.'

'Cossel's message?'

'No, the one I meant to send, which had nothing to do with gas mixtures.' She paused, enjoying his discomfort. 'But I did memorise the first part of Cossel's message, just enough to know whether you were giving it to me accurately or not.'

'For someone not exactly familiar with the codes . . .'

She sighed. 'I learned the codes months ago, Lag. I learned them so thoroughly I almost dream in dots and dashes. I wished you to *think* otherwise, so you'd assume I was dependent on you and could therefore be tricked.' She looked at him with a certain distant fondness. 'It's a rather good job you couldn't see the front of the telegraphic box, or you'd have noticed that the shutter wasn't opening and closing in any sort of accordance with your message.'

'I . . . underestimated your resourcefulness.' He shook his head in wounded admiration. 'How very foolish of me.'

'Are you impressed?'

'I have never been anything less than impressed.'

'Shall I show you the message you meant me to send, just in case it's slipped your memory?' Without waiting on his answer, she pushed a sheet of paper in his direction. 'Read it aloud.'

'There's really no need.'

'Read it aloud.'

He cleared his throat. 'Struck by debris or sail-shot, hull punctured, Lagganvor dead, Adrana . . . critically injured.' He paused, his mouth seeming to dry up. 'Not long to live. Squawk with all haste, disregarding all previous arrangements. Cossel.' He licked his lips, smiled once. 'You have to admit it has a certain economy . . .'

'You intended to lie to Fura about my being on the point of

death, just to get her to squawk and expose her position.'

He pushed back the sheet.

'I needed a . . . persuasive motivation.'

'I believe you,' she answered, after a silence. 'At least, I believe that *you* believe that you have our best interests at heart. I also believe that you think the best way to facilitate our survival is to work with your masters to have us captured.'

'In which case . . .'

She silenced him with a twitch of the fanblade. 'It doesn't matter. I don't care what *you* believe is in our best interests. Fura and I have spent our lives having decisions made for us by people who think they know better than we do. There'll be no more of that, from you or anyone.'

He slumped, his resignation absolute.

'What now?'

'I think it likely you have another eye about your person. Put it on the table, next to the first.'

'Why?'

She jabbed the fanblade again and depressed the trigger to the first barely tangible notch. She had learned that she could make it whine as it accumulated power for an immediate discharge.

'Just do it.'

He hesitated, then reached into a pouch about his waist. He produced the other eye, setting it down as neatly and resignedly as a gambler surrendering their last chip.

'I could have killed you at any point in this conversation.'

'Then why didn't you?'

'One, you've dulled my control with that sedative – I'm not sure I could be as precise as I'd need to be, and it would have been an awful shame if I blew a hole right out through the wall of your cabin and into space. Two, you might get a shot off from that fanblade even if I did trigger the eye . . . and three . . . well, never mind three.'

'What was it?'

'My brother thought well of you. He had faults, but he was always a reliable judge of character. I think you liked him as well, and that's some consolation to me. I would find it disrespectful to his memory to hurt you.'

'Even if your own life was at stake?'

'I'd only be delaying the inevitable.'

Adrana nodded at the gargoyle head. 'Pick it up again. It's perfectly sturdy. You're going to destroy one of those eyes. I don't care which. The point is that if there's only one of them left, it'll be much harder for you to ever trick me again.'

He hefted the gargoyle. As it swivelled in his hand, the tongue and eyes clicked in and out. 'You still haven't told me what it's for.'

'It's a skullvane.'

'I see.'

'According to the books there's a small quantity of twinkly embedded inside the head. Not enough to be useful for communication, but sufficient that it responds to the presence of other twinkly in the vicinity.'

'I never heard of such a thing.'

'Nor I. That's because skullvanes are hard to find and only useful under certain, very specific circumstances.'

'How so?'

'The effective range is very short – no more than a few hundred spans.'

'Spans, not leagues?'

'Spans. Useless for finding skulls in general, across the Congregation, and not even helpful on the scale of a bauble, or even part of a bauble's tunnel system. You'd need to be in nearly the same room or chamber as the skull to begin with, in which case you're probably following some treasure map that will lead to the skull regardless.'

He nodded slowly, following her drift. 'But if you had to search a single ship in a hurry, where the bone room might be concealed . . .'

'Such a trinket might prove very handy indeed.'

He examined the gargoyle head with fond regretfulness. 'A pity it's broken, then. The twinkly in it must have gone stale.'

'You think it's malfunctioning?'

'By definition. The skull that used to belong on this ship is thousands of leagues away.'

'It's not broken,' she stated crisply. 'It was never broken. The reason it was indicating the presence of a skull is that there was always another skull on this ship. Now smash one of your eyes.'

'Whichever I choose, you should know that it'll hurt me.'

'I don't care.'

'Each of those eyes is valuable.'

She raised the fanblade, tightening her hold on it, and made it whine again.

17

Surt was on sighting watch when the signal from the *Merry Mare* came in. She was sweeping the area as a matter of routine, but not with any real expectation of an incoming message. It was only Paladin's excellence with calculation that provided any chance of picking up the other ship: that and Surt's own keenness of vision, allied to the best lenses and tubes anywhere in the Congregation.

Still, once the flash-sequence started she had no doubt what it was, nor any hesitation in beginning an immediate transcription. She noted it down, and although Surt had only lately begun to learn the standard code, she had aptitude enough to understand that the message was not exactly a conventional one. In fact, at first glance it appeared to be directed to some other ship entirely . . .

'Mister Cazaray?' she mouthed to herself. 'Who in all the worlds is Mister Cazaray? And what would we be wanting with his belongings?'

In the galley, where she received the transcription, Fura made a careful duplicate of the signal and asked Ruther to decode it for her. Ruther had made a good recovery from his unconscious episode and although his tongue was still thick and uncomfortable where it had been stitched back together, he was very glad to be of some service. He understood codes, too. Being a boney was as close to a signals-specialist as any ship ever carried, and the lad had clearly been keen to impress his former captain.

'It's a rum one . . .' he began.

'I don't care if it's rum or otherwise,' Fura said, only just managing to keep her temper at bay. 'Tell me what it says.'

'It sharttsh . . . starts straight off by saying "Go to Mister Cazaray's belongings. Attend to them at start of midnight watch, for thirty minutes. Will reciprocate with similar goods, and thereafter at every six-hour interval."'

'And?' she pressed.

'That'sh all there izh. *All there is*. It repeats itself, but it's still the same thing.'

Tindouf, who was with her in the galley, said: 'We donts know of a Mister Cazaray, does we.'

'We does,' said Prozor, who was next to him, picking crumbs out of the bread-hopper. 'Or rather, Fura and I does . . . do. As would Adrana. Mister Cazaray was the Bone Reader on the *Monetta's Mourn*.'

'What happened to him?' Ruther asked.

Fura looked at him for a second.

'Nothing good.'

'He was a decent enough cove,' Prozor said, filling in the silence that followed this accurate if cold-hearted utterance. 'Went gentle on the Ness sisters when they were greener than the forests of Cloverly, and that's sayin' somethin'. But like most of our dear old crew he ended up murdered by Bosa, killed in our own launch, along with Mattice. Poor sap didn't even have the pleasure of seeing her face before she spiked him.'

'Then why would they mention him now?' Ruther asked. 'Did you bring his goods with you all this way?'

'It's not meant to be taken literally,' Fura said. 'It's a way of alluding to the bones, and telling me to be plugged into our own skull at the top of midnight. Adrana must've found a skull, and now she knows we can communicate whenever we wish.'

Ruther looked doubtful.

'What was wrong with the telegraph?'

'Are you dim, boy? It's slow and we're nearly at the limit. If we pull any further apart, or one of us makes a turn that the other isn't expecting, there'll be no chance of signalling by that means.'

'But Incer Stallis will be waiting!'

'The whelp has to sleep occasionally. If we reserve the bones for an emergency channel, we'll still have an advantage. But Adrana needs to prove that the skull she's found is able to speak to ours.'

Ruther's brow was furrowed. 'But there can't be another shkull. You took our bonezh . . . .'

'We did,' Fura said, with a sarcastic sweetness. 'At least, we thought we did. What if we were wrong, though? We didn't find another skull while we were rifflin' through your ship, but Adrana's been on it much longer, and had a chance to poke into its secrets.' She paused, reading something in his face. 'If there *was* such a thing to be turned up . . . would I be getting warmer or colder, Ruther?'

'I . . . I wouldn't know.'

'But you were the boney.' She made a show of frowning, as if she were trying to puzzle out some knotty riddle in her head. 'No one else might've known about another skull, but if there was ever a cove who ought to've been aware of it . . . someone close to the captain – it'd be you, wouldn't it?' Before he could jerk back, she grabbed a clump of his hair in her metal fingers. 'Talk to me, Ruther. You and I've been on such excellent terms – be a shame to spoil that now, wouldn't it?'

She twisted his hair and Ruther yelped.

'Stop. There izh . . . there is another skull, and I'll tell you about it. But it's not what it sheems.'

She increased her hold on him, while Prozor and Tindouf looked on with expressions of earnest concern. 'How is it not what it seems, Ruther? You concealed knowledge of a skull from me during our boarding operation. All the while you were drifting, and we thought you defenceless and out of communication, you had a skull!'

'Which . . .' Ruther grimaced. 'Which we didn't use. Which we were never *going* to use. And your shister shouldn't use it, either. It's not what she thinks!'

She tightened her grip. There was a weak, diminishing part of her that looked on with some faint disapproval, and another part, now in the ascendant, that only cheered her to go further. She imagined his hair ripping away, his scalp coming with it, glorious blood and bone beneath, and she knew it was the glowy making her feel this way – and with equal certainty she knew that she did not really mind, not in the moment.

She ran her tongue across the ridges of her teeth.

'A skull's a skull, Ruther.'

'Not that little one,' he sputtered out. 'It's bad. Poisoned. She mustn't use it. And if you care for her . . . you have to find a way to stop her.'

She let go of him with a wild, atavistic grunt. Ruther pulled back and rubbed at his sore pate, eyeing her with an almost animal wariness, as if he now considered her fully capable of any violence, any wanton or reckless deed.

Her hand shook as she checked her pocket timepiece. With an immense force of will, she bottled the larger part of her anger.

'Two hours to the top of midnight. Are you serious about this, Ruther?'

Still wary, he smoothed his shock of hair back into some semblance of order. '*This* is what it did to me, and I was lucky to be pulled out before it was too late. But even then, it left its mark. Those nightmares you heard? They were never anything to do with Incer Stallis. They were about that skull.'

Fura was breathing hard. Her hand was still shaking. The glowy still had her. But she believed him.

*

Vouga swore: some obscure, multisyllabic oath in one of the coarser dialects of the inner processionals. 'You might have given me a little more warning, you know – say six hours, or even half a day.'

Adrana leaned over him as he sweated with his box of tools, trying to adjust one of the suspension wires that allowed the skull to float in the middle of the bone room.

'You told me it was ready.'

'I said the skull was *capable* of being used,' he answered, using a wrench to adjust one of the tensioning springs. 'By which I meant that the sockets were electrically sound, and the eye-hooks tested for strength, and that the twinkly appeared to be viable, since it showed a counter-response in the presence of the skullvane . . .' The wrench slipped in his fingers, skinning a knuckle, and spinning off like a slow-tossed bone, end over end, until it collided with the walls and rebounded at Adrana.

She caught it deftly and offered it back to Vouga, who took it without a word.

'I'm not asking for technical perfection here,' she said.

'Good, because you won't get it – not with this sort of pressure.'

She believed Vouga when he claimed not to have known of the skull's existence. She would have accepted the same denial from Lasling, Cossel and Meggery as well. Ruther, though, the lad on the other ship? Possibly he had known. Indeed, it was more probable than possible, but if he had known, she was sure it was a secret between Werranwell and the boy and no one else.

Certainly, it had been well concealed. The skull had been kept behind a false panel in Captain Werranwell's quarters, expertly disguised. The panel hid a makeshift alcove that had contained two items: a large, stout-looking wooden box, and a single bottle of Trennigarian brandy from 1680.

The box had contained a curiously small skull, protected within a nest of gun-wadding. She might have dismissed it for a useless trinket, were it not for three things. The first was that it had been located by the skullvane, which pointed to the presence of active twinkly. The second was that it had been drilled and tapped with what appeared to be high-grade sockets and suspension wires, over and above what one would expect to find in a piece of tourist tat. The third was that it had been so well hidden. Without the skullvane she would never have guessed there was a false panel at all.

Who went to that sort of trouble, unless the item to be hidden actually had some value?

'I think that will suffice, Vouga,' she said. 'You already have four points of attachment.'

'It's an unbalanced load. The books recommend five to six attachment points as a bare minimum; seven or more as sound practice. Skulls fracture if they're not suspended properly.'

'This skull isn't going to fracture, Vouga – not unless I use it as a bludgeon, which is becoming a distinct possibility.' She consulted her pocket chronometer. 'In a little over an hour my sister will be expecting me to attempt contact. I do not wish to disappoint her.'

'Assuming they read your signal in the first place.'

Vouga did not know about Lagganvor's duplicity, and Adrana was intent on maintaining that state of affairs. As far as the rest of her crew were concerned, the gas mixtures had been transmitted to Eddralder as per his request. But she had also informed Vouga that she had appended an instruction to her sister concerning the skulls, and that she was counting on it being received and acted upon.

In fact, no such certainty existed. She could hope that *Revenger* had picked up the telegraphic message, but she had no guarantee of it, and accordingly little confidence that there was going to be anyone on the other side of the skull when she attempted contact.

But there might be; and it might be Fura, and while that possibility existed – however remote the odds – she could not give up. Fate had thrown them this opportunity to communicate, and while there was a chance that the squadron was close, Adrana could not – would not – abandon her sister.

'This will do, Vouga,' she insisted.

'The books say . . .'

'Never mind the books. The books say that useful skulls rarely come as small as this one, if ever, so they are wrong in at least one regard and very probably many others.' Gently she took the wrench from his hand and set it back into the toolbox. 'Go, Vouga – I'll seal the door behind you.'

'It isn't time yet.'

'I will need what is left to find my way into the skull. Then I shall need time to communicate with Fura. I will not be disturbed for two hours.'

'Two hours it is,' Vouga said. 'And if you haven't shown your face by then, and Lasling and I can't get that door open from the other side, we'll start on it with axes.'

'Axes will not be required,' Adrana said. 'But thank you for the sentiment.'

Vouga retreated, and she sealed the door behind him, leaving her alone with the little skull, suspended in its harness with far too much room around it.

Adrana dimmed the lights and unhooked the neural harness – it had been adjusted for Ruther but its hinges and screws allowed it to be accommodated to her head-shape very easily – and settled it down over her hair.

Then she spooled out the contact line and made ready to plug in.

*

'Poisoned?' Fura asked, her fingers opening and closing on some automatic grasping rhythm of their own, like the claws of a scrapyard crane.

'Captain Werranwell only ever meant to use that skull as a last resort. He tried me on it once and it didn't work out.' Ruther swallowed. 'I don't remember much of what happened, except that it put me under for six whole days, drooling and gibbering in my sleep. When I came 'round, I saw myself in the mirror.' He touched his hair again. 'It only ever grew white after that. It was two more weeks before I was fit to use the other skull, our normal one. I couldn't take that little skull, whatever was in it, and the captain swore he'd never put me through it again.'

'Then why keep it?'

He looked at her as if the question was either idiotic or some terrible trap.

'No captain ever throws away a skull, not even a bad one.'

'The lad has a point,' Prozor murmured.

Ruther nodded gratefully, as if she were his only living ally on the ship. 'That's right. Captain Werranwell kept it hidden on the ship, just like treasure or quoins: as insurance. But never for me to use, and even when you'd cut us up and the squadron had come in to finish the job, we didn't speak about that skull.'

Tindouf rubbed the back of his neck. He had the aggrieved look of one who is obliged to state an opinion he knows will be unpopular.

'I hates to say it, but it makes senses to me.'

'It's all true,' Ruther affirmed, nodding vigorously. 'There was no need to mention it until now – I never thought for a second that your sister would find it. Pardon me, but how *did* she find it?'

'I have no idea.'

'However she did, she's got to be stopped. You saw what Stallis did to me. This'll be ten times as bad.'

Fura forced her fingers into stillness. She pressed down on her arm with the other hand until the trembling abated. The neon scrollwork glowy was still burning through her skin. Her eyes itched with its prickling presence.

She tried to sound calm.

'You don't know Adrana.'

'No, but I know that skull. I told you I didn't remember much. But I do remember the terrors that came after. They've never really stopped.' He looked at them all in turn, as earnestly if this was his last chance to turn a doubtful jury. 'I'm in a sort of cell or dungeon, with smooth grey walls and a smooth grey ceiling curving over me. There's nothing in it except me, no windows or door, no way in or out except a wooden hatch in the floor.

All I've got is a little candle. And I'm sitting on that hatch, using all my weight to try and stop something getting into the cell. Whatever it is, it keeps levering the hatch up just enough to push a limb through. It's long and thin, black and all furred-over, like a spider's leg. Sometimes there's more than one of them. They keep reaching through the gap between the floor and the hatch, and it's all that I can do to force myself to sit down harder, squeezing the gap tight, until the limbs pull back into the darkness underneath.'

Fura gave a short nervous laugh. 'If that's what you call a bad dream, you should try living with some of mine.'

'It's real,' Ruther said, pleadingly. 'Real and stronger than you realise. You think you know all about skulls. But you haven't had *that* in your head week after week, month after month. And I wouldn't wish it on anyone – including your sister.'

'She can handle it.'

'You can't be sure of that. Do you really want to take the chance? There isn't anyone else on the *Merry Mare* who knows not to use that skull. To them it'll just be some relic Captain Werranwell kept back for himself. They won't know.'

'We could signal her,' Prozor said quietly.

'You have to!' Ruther said.

'Midnight's only fifty minutes away,' Fura replied. 'If she means to contact me then, there's every chance she's already in the bone room, preparing for the exchange. If she ain't there yet, I doubt she'll be long about it.'

'But that's no reason not to try!'

'Think it through, Ruther: we need to have someone suited-up and outside, with the telegraphic box, an encoded message, and some idea of the right direction in which to point it. Meanwhile, if our efforts aren't to be wasted, someone in the sighting room of the *Merry Mare* will need sharp eyes that are looking exactly back at us.'

He looked at her as if there had to be some trick in her answer. 'Isn't that exactly how it's meant to work? Isn't that exactly how we read their signal about Mister Cazaray? I know the time is short, and we might not succeed, but is that any reason to give up?'

'I'm with the boy,' Prozor said, pushing up from the table with a determined set to her features. 'The odds ain't in our favour, if ever they were, but it's worth tryin'. If we don't get through to 'em before the top of midnight, then I can still keep sending until someone picks it up.'

'Better late than never,' Ruther agreed.

'You're so keen, why don't you go out there and send the message yourself?' Fura asked.

'He'd be keen enough,' Prozor said. 'But this ain't a boy's job. I've invested a part of myself in both of you girlies, Fura, you and your sister, and I won't see it wasted. I won't stand by while somethin' hurts either of you, not if I've a chance of stoppin' things. Tindouf: will you help me to suit up? Paladin can spit out the pointing coordinates, while Fura jots down the very, very short message she's goin' to come up with.'

'I don't mean to say what everyone else is thinking . . .' Ruther began.

'Then don't,' Fura said.

'But there's another way to reach Adrana.'

'I thought I said *don't*.'

Ruther drew back, but after a breath he gathered the shreds of his courage and spoke again. 'It wouldn't need to be a long squawk, just enough . . .'

Fura worked her fist. She was ready to strike him for merely voicing the idea. How ready must have been plain to Prozor, who clamped a hand around her wrist and gently eased it back down.

She leaned in and whispered.

'We don't hit our friends just 'cause they come out with uncomfortable truths, girlie. And he's right. There's always the squawk. If that skull's as bad as it seems, and I ain't seein' any reason to doubt Ruther – and you shouldn't, either – then maybe we should take that chance. She'd do it for you, wouldn't she?'

Fura yanked her wrist free of Prozor's grasp. She could feel the glowy lighting up within her like a golden proclamation, writ in fire. She could feel it in her blood, in her lungs, in her eyes and mind. A beautiful madness, a shining alloy of anger and resolve. A madness to move worlds, and to crush the small lives of those who got in her way. It did not favour the idea of signalling Adrana, because that was an action that placed its own survival in jeopardy. It was trying to turn her against the idea of saving her sister: trying to bend her against Adrana.

She denied it. It took every shred of her will, but she could – for the moment – overcome it.

But the effort left her angry, spent and drained of tolerance.

'Go and do your damned job, Prozor.'

*

She needed the silence of her cabin to draft the message to be sent by telegraph. That was the lie she told herself, at least. Mainly she needed the cabin to escape the guarded and accusatory looks of her crew. At least in the cabin she only had a robot to contend with.

'Has there been a development, Miss Arafura?' Paladin asked, in a tone so perfectly unobjectionable that it fanned the flames in her to a high fury. Her metal hand reached for a hefty magnetic paperweight; she had to press her other hand down on it to stop herself from ramming the paperweight into his globe.

'It's . . . under control, Paladin,' she said through gritted teeth. 'Everything is . . . entirely under control.'

'You seem agitated. Perhaps a period of rest would be in order.'

'I'll rest when I'm . . .'

She silenced herself, reached for a pen and paper. She dipped the pen into the pressure-tight inkwell, nearly missing it on the first try; began to scratch out the formulation. With some shred of clarity, she reminded herself that the shorter the message, the more easily it could be repeated and therefore received without error. On the other hand, the longer the message, the more explanation she could put into it. Would Adrana accept an injunction not to use the skull, without some supplementary persuasion?

If she trusts me, Fura thought. *If she trusts her own sister.*

But if our stations were reversed, would I?

And – besides - is she really worth the trouble?

'No,' she declared aloud, addressing the patterns throbbing out of her skin. 'You will not turn me. Not that easily.'

She started to write:

You must not use the skull. Ruther says it nearly killed him.

Her own writing was a spidery crawl, barely legible. Too verbose, in any case. It would take Prozor a minute just to send it once. She balled the paper, re-dipped the pen.

Do not use skull. Ruther says tainted . . .

Her hand jerked, ripping the paper. It was shaking uncontrollably now. Brine salted her lips. The glowy was itching so badly she could have clawed her own skin off and still kept going. She tried again.

Damn you to hell, Adrana Ness!

Defeated, she opened her desk drawer and took out the wallet, with its dwindling supply of vials. Her hand shook more powerfully now. Fura was down to her last twelve doses, and it had taken tremendous resolve not to cut into that supply prematurely. She had taken the last dose only two days ago; by rights she ought to wait another two days before injecting herself.

She could not wait that long.

There was no reasoning with herself; no force of will that could damp down the fire in her veins. She had to take the Mephrozine now if she was to stand any chance of thinking and functioning normally in the hours to come. She knew with an iron certainty that these hours were not going to be the easiest of her life.

There was one full vial still in its pouch, and one vial that was two-tenths full. She took out the syringe and drew the partial vial out of the wallet, pinching it in her flesh fingers. Her fingers trembled, but she had them under sufficient control. Yet, just as she nearly had it all the way out, a violent spasm started in her hand, amplifying with each jolt.

Her hand gave a sudden powerful twitch – almost a deliberate flinging action – and the wallet and its contents went tumbling away across the cabin.

Fura breathed in and out.

She turned to watch the wallet's slow arc. She saw where it lodged herself, on a shelf of her chained library, in the narrow nook between two volumes of *The Book of Worlds*. The partial vial had come out completely, wedged between the wallet and the hard, wooden lip of the shelf. The full vial was still intact. She set down the syringe, wedging it under a book that was itself fixed down by a magnetic weight, and moved to the shelves.

'You will not have me so easily,' she said. 'I know what I am. I know what you are, and which of us is the stronger.'

She felt the glowy laugh in her veins.

It was throbbing in rhythm with her heartbeat; even the room seemed to be shot through with a golden aura that heightened and faded on the same cycle. With her flesh hand she reached for the partial vial, closing her trembling fingers around it, clasping the glass but not crushing it. Her metal one grasped the wallet, with the full vial still tucked into place.

It clenched, with no warning.

There had been no instant where she might have sent a contradictory nerve impulse. The wallet buckled between her fingers. She heard the crunch of glass. Her hand relaxed, the wallet springing wide open again. The final vial was totally shattered, its ten doses spilling out like a pale honey, embedded with tiny, sugar-like shards. She thought of pressing her tongue to the flow, of licking the Mephrozine straight into her. She imagined the glass lacerating her tongue, scratching its way down her throat, cutting its way into her gut, and thought that it might be an acceptable price to pay.

'No,' she said softly.

She could see what had happened, and she could see the consequences, spiralling out from this moment. But she could not yet think beyond the horror of that oozing liquid. Ten more doses gone: ten more doses that might just as well have been injected into Strambli, for all the use they had served.

She still had the two remaining doses in the partial vial. It was still pinched between her flesh fingers, still intact. She stared at it with wonder and befuddlement. Between one moment and the next that single vial had become the most precious object in her universe.

She stared and stared.

'Miss Arafura?' Paladin enquired gently.

She did not turn to face him.

'What is it?'

'You have been in a state of immobility for two minutes. I thought it advisable to intervene.'

'I was . . . what was I doing, Paladin?'

'I am of the opinion that you were attempting to draft a message, Miss Arafura. Might I suggest that the matter was of some degree of urgency?'

She returned to her desk. The syringe was still where she had left it. She drew it out from under the book. Oddly, the compulsion was not as strong as it had been a minute or two earlier – or three, or four, if Paladin was to be believed. Her hand was still tremoring, and the fire in her veins and the itch under her skull still asserting themselves, but she thought she could contain the glowy for the time it took to finish composing the message and see it delivered.

'You did that,' she said, speaking aloud, even as she addressed the influence within her, and knowing full well it would confuse Paladin.

'Miss Arafura?'

'You made me crush the wallet. I wanted the Mephrozine; you want to take me over completely. Any path to madness is a path to you, I suppose. Well, congratulations: you won that round. But you're not stronger than me. You're in me, but you don't define me. I am not you. I never will be you.'

'Is all well, Miss?'

'Let us prove a point, shall we? You've taken away any possibility of the Mephrozine lasting me to Trevenza Reach, even if the wind holds fair and we make it in twelve days And these last two doses . . . what good are they really going to do me now? Take them now, take them in two weeks, what difference will that make to either of us? Very little, I think. Except it'll make me weaker, knowing they're here, waiting for me. And I really don't need weakness right now.'

She mashed her hand down on the book, crushing the partial vial. The pale secretion sogged into its papers. She did not care. It would be a reminder, if she lived long enough, of who was the stronger party.

'I did that,' Fura Ness said. 'Not you. *I* did that.'

Her hand was steadier now. There was a steadiness in all parts of her – a calm and resolve she had not felt in some very long while. She felt as unruffled and full of purpose as a fully deflected sail. She was being pushed to one goal. She had one thing to do now; one very simple thing, and she might survive it, or she might not, but the outcome was much less important than the thing itself.

She would do what needed to be done to save Adrana.

Again.

18

Adrana had not been expecting immediate success with the new skull, but it was a surprise to her when it felt as dead and empty as a hollowed-out pebble. The skullvane had detected it, which meant that there had to be something still going on inside, but even after she had plugged in and gone through the ritual of simultaneously emptying her mind and making it invitingly open, there remained no trace of a useful carrier signal. There was a time she might have been quicker to blame herself than the instrument of communication itself, but she had enough experience with skulls to know her own capabilities, and she did not think this fault lay in herself.

Sometimes the problem lay in the neural crown, not the skull. Once a crown was adjusted to a particular reader, it did not usually need alteration if they switched from one skull to another. But that was only because the majority of skulls in general service were more alike than dissimilar, and she was not at all sure that this strange specimen fit that pattern. There were tiny sliders and dials in the crown that were stiff enough not to move with ordinary handling, but which could be altered if necessary. Adrana removed the crown and made a small but deliberate change to the settings, using touch more than sight, and then slipped the crown back on.

Still nothing. She increased the adjustments, again in a

methodical way. It made no difference, but an impulse had her reaching out to test that the input socket was as firmly embedded as it looked, and as she touched the nub of corrosion-less metal *something* jolted across her mind. It was not the usual sensation of a carrier signal, a silence beneath silence, waiting for meaning to be impressed on it, but she had no doubt whatsoever that the flash or image had been directly related to her contact with the input probe.

It had been as quick and vivid as a lightning strike, illuminating a hitherto unseen vista. She had been granted the momentary impression of a grey, bowl-ceilinged room, and the coldness that went with it. She had been in that room for one instant; in it and sitting on the floor, waiting with nervous expectation for the arrival of someone or something.

The flash had been too brief to leave her with any emotional colouration beyond that impression of anxious waiting. And as soon as her hand came off the contact node, the skull was back to feeling dead. She tried it a second time and got the same image. Like looking at the same picture in a storybook, it conveyed no more meaning to her than the first time.

But she knew that there was something wrong with this skull. Something must have come loose under that socket: a grounding loop or one of the fine, high-impedance connections that interfaced with the twinkly itself. Just touching that contact node was enough to rectify the problem, to some degree. She could not hope to reach her sister like this, though – much less exercise the control that she would need if Stallis picked up on her presence.

She had been too hard on Vouga: pushing him to make the skull usable. He had not liked being rushed, but she had done it to him anyway – even though she would never have gone against the advice of Tindouf, or Surt, or any of the hands she had known for longer.

She disconnected, unhooked the crown and undimmed the lights. Then she pressed the intercom.

'Vouga,' she said, as soon as she had his attention. 'You were right, and I was wrong. Could you come to the bone room again? The skull is nearly working, but there's just something a little loose . . .'

*

While Tindouf helped Prozor into her suit, and prepared the lock for an emergency egress – willingly sacrificing lungstuff for the sake of a speedy exit – Paladin re-computed the pointing coordinates for the *Merry Mare* and had them conveyed to Ruther, who in turn had the telegraphic box primed with fresh light-imps and equipped with a copy of the encoded message Fura had drafted in her quarters. Ruther arrived at the lock with the telegraphic box just as Prozor was ready to go through.

There had been less than fifty minutes to midnight when she began formulating that message, and after the episode with the Mephrozine less than half an hour remained. Tindouf and Prozor had worked like demons, though, and there were ten minutes left by the time Prozor was through the lock and outside, stomping around to the right part of the hull to face the Congregation and the calculated position of the *Merry Mare*.

Surt, meanwhile, was still on sighting duty and had all the best tubes lined up on that same set of coordinates. Picking out a trace of sail-flash from Incer Stallis was of secondary importance to detecting a return signal, confirming receipt of the outbound transmission.

Prozor had to send it first, though, and even the tersest of optical signals took dozens of seconds to transmit. Fura waited until she had confirmation that the message was being sent, knowing that Prozor would keep on until instructed otherwise, and then she dived head-first into the bone room and spun the locking wheel hard behind her. She consulted her timepiece.

Five minutes.

'Incer,' she mouthed to herself. 'Even a monster has to fill its potty occasionally. Let now be one of those times.'

She snatched down the neural crown, dimmed the lights,

and made straight for the node that had already functioned for her with this skull. The plug went in cleanly. The skull jiggled, then stabilised. Twinkly made a faint coloured light-show of its bone-chambered, grotto-like interior. The skull was active, which was more than she could have counted on.

She closed her eyes, forced concentration. She pressed the neural crown tighter to her scalp.

There was, instantly, a carrier signal: that strange, nervously-expectant substrate that lay beneath ordinary silence like the page beneath ink: supporting it, offering it form and structure. She mouthed a thanks for such uncommon good fortune. The skull could have been in an uncooperative, belligerent mood, as skulls were wont to be, but this time at least it was serving its purpose.

Now all she needed was a link to her sister.

Faint transmissions ghosted across her perceptions. None of them had the taint of Incer Stallis, and none were meant for her. They were just distant criss-crossing communications that she happened to be good enough to intercept.

... still running under all sail and ions but anticipating late arrival at Causerant ...

... upon Captain Resterick's authority will trade opening auguries for The Barnacle, The Drooling Dog and The Flytrap ... please reciprocate with auguries for the following ...

... said to be issuing Promissory Letters by way of compensation for loss of revenue ...

... seeking five thousand acres of the second or third grade and one thousand leagues of monofilament, to be expedited with all urgency following sail-strike around the Reefs of Strancer ...

... may facilitate payment in equal goods, rather than quoins, if so desired ...

She filtered this babble from her brain. She disdained none of it; blamed none of the captains or Bone Readers for daring to push their gossip and bargaining across her mind. This was the clamour of mundane business: the beating pulse of ordinary life and commerce through the Congregation. It might not all be entirely reputable, some of it might even border on the criminal, but it was not the work of men and women seeking to kill other men and women, and for that alone she loved it, and wished she could be a part of it, for in that moment it seemed to Fura that there was nothing so fine as to be the captain of a sunjammer plying an honest trade. She had not known it was something she wanted until she was obliged to run from it; obliged to play a very different and dangerous game.

Their voices faded from her attention. She had become skilled at making that happen. It was like going into a crowded, busy room and forcing herself to separate one small, quiet, voice from the hubbub. It was impossible for many Bone Readers, difficult for the gifted few, and a fair test even for a Ness sister.

Most especially with those minutes ticking down to the change of watch.

The absence of Adrana could only mean that there was a problem at her end. Adrana might have plugged in and instantly suffered the same fate as Ruther, or she could have run into a difficulty before she ever got to that step. Fura hoped that was the case; there were so many things that could go wrong with skulls – and did – that it was hardly fanciful to suppose that some snag had arisen on the other ship. A broken input node, a fault with the neural crown, some mis-match in the circuits, a problem with the twinkly, even – and it had happened – a failed seal on the bone room door, or something equally trivial.

The change of watch had passed. The seconds were ticking over into the new hour. Still there was no trace of Adrana.

That was good, she told herself.

That was *very* good. Adrana wouldn't delay using the other skull, having initiated the idea of signalling, so her continued absence could only mean that she was running into a problem on the other end. Many things could go wrong with the connections in and out of skulls, and they were not all the sort of thing that could be repaired within minutes. It had to be that. Not that the other skull had already worked its poison into her sister . . .

Fura?

There she was.

Adrana? I'm here. Adrana you've got to disconnect. The skull's not right . . .

She paused in her transmission. There had been a sense of her sister's presence, the stating of her own name, but now there was nothing. A door had opened, a voice had called through once, and now the door was shut again.

Adrana?

*

Against all protocol, Vouga was with her in the bone room as she re-attempted contact. He still had most of his tools out, for he had not quite diagnosed the possible fault in the input socket, so persuaded her that it was sensible that he observe while she listened, and then try one of several possible solutions, rather than go through the bother of leaving and re-entering the bone room each time.

'There,' Adrana said, hardly daring to move; hardly raising her voice beyond a whisper. 'She came through, Vouga. Fura was on the other end. We had contact, and then I lost it.'

'You're certain?'

'Do you think I'd mistake my own sister? She dropped out very quickly, but it was definitely Fura. She was just starting to say something, as well. I didn't get all of it but I could sense her urgency before we disconnected.'

'May I see that node again?'

She disconnected, permitting him to come in with his instruments, which were as fine and gleaming as a dentist's, and loosen the input socket. He bent close to the skull, lenses and mirrors aiding him, frowning hard while he made some tiny but deft adjustment to the connections between the socket and bone's interior. He swore beneath his breath. Adrana watched without even removing her neural crown. She was ready to go in again as soon as Vouga was done.

Vouga withdrew.

'Have you done anything?'

'No, I just thought I'd poke around for a few seconds and pull faces.'

'Thank you. Incidentally, did you last long with your former crews before you got thrown out of an airlock?' She adjusted the fit of the neural crown. 'I suppose I'll take sarcasm over someone who constantly tells me exactly the thing I'd like to hear, regardless of whether it's good for me.'

'I have uses. Not many of them, it's true.'

'But enough to serve this ship, I suppose, or you'd have filled your lungs with vacuum years ago. What exactly did you do this time?'

'I . . . made a permanent bond across the induction loop, isolating the delay line.'

'A straight answer. That almost made you faint, didn't it?'

Vouga sniffed, and gave a quick, abashed smile. 'See if it works. I daren't promise anything, not before I've opened that skull with a saw and seen what's really going on inside.'

'If the signal's clean and stable, you can leave me,' Adrana said. She plugged in again, the input socket feeling tighter and more secure than it had before. She closed her eyes and opened her mind. The carrier signal was present.

Fura?

She must still out there. Vouga had only needed a few minutes to complete his work, and Fura would not have abandoned any further attempt at contact after that one instance.

Adrana? Hello, Adrana – is it you?

She kept her eyes closed, but whispered to Vouga: 'It's all right now. Fura's coming through. Seal the door, and give me an hour alone with her.'

'One hour,' Vouga said quietly.

She heard him collect his remaining tools, gathering them but not packing them away, for that would have made too much noise, and she felt the draught and coolness as the bone room opened, a second or so of the ordinary ship sounds and smells coming through, and then Vouga sealed the door from the other side and she was alone again.

Fura?

It's me. Don't you recognise my presence?

There was a visual component to the link. She had experienced a glimpse of that faculty when she first connected, but it was different now. There was a kind of corridor, with an intense source of golden-white light at one end of it, and a wisp-like figure standing in the light. The sisters had never shared visual imagery through any other set of skulls, so this was either a developing aspect of their talent, or some peculiar quirk of one or other of the two skulls now in use.

Adrana did not care for it. When there had been no visual aspect to the communication, she had been able to hold onto a definite sense of her own spatial location in the bone room. But seeing something – however ill-defined the vision – made her feel as if some significant part of her being was somewhere else, sucked into the haunted space through which the bones whispered to each other.

But she could not turn off the vision. Her eyes were already closed. This imagery was coming via the neural crown, not her optic nerves.

Oh, do come nearer, sister! Why must I always come to you?

The figure in the golden light was beckoning, stretching out a hand in Adrana's direction. Without volition she felt herself drifting down the corridor. The wisp-like form was all limbs, with only a tiny nub of a head. The light flooded around it, erasing form and depth.

Fura? You were trying to tell me something. What was it?

Trying to tell you something? Only that I'm very, very glad that we're finally able to meet again.

The figure resolved. It was not Fura. It was a boy or a young man, pipe-cleaner thin, reaching out with twig-like fingers that broke the golden light into converging shards.

A question presented itself to her. She did not want to think the question, much less voice it aloud in her own head.

Are you Incer Stallis?

Well, I might be. I could very well be. But to admit as much would spoil the fun, don't you agree? Heh! Although I suppose I've as good as answered you, haven't I?

She tried to pull away from him. But Stallis extended his hand and fingers and snagged her under the collar. He pulled hard, dragging her further along the corridor, deeper into that golden light.

Get out of me.

The nub of a head shook in contradiction.

I'm not in you, Adrana. You're in me. And it's a fine place to be. I can see everything. You're laid out like a formal garden. Let me see – what interests me the most? Your position and speed, I suppose. Oh, yes – I see that you know those things. I can pluck those numbers out of you like treats from a chocolate box! Mm . . . what do we have? Very interesting. Those numbers are most useful to me. But not as useful as I'd find the same parameters for your sister's ship. Do you know those? Even a little? I think you might! Let's see, shall we? Heh! I'm enjoying this.

She wondered if there was a hateful little face somewhere in that nub.

As much as you enjoyed murdering your own mother?

She pushed all her strength into disengaging from him. But there was nothing to be done. She could move her hands in his disembodied space, yet she sensed no corresponding action back in the bone room.

I see you did your homework on me, Adrana! That pleases me no end. But you really mustn't believe everything you're told. I'd have thought that if there was anyone who really understood that, it would be a Ness sister! Now let me see those positional parameters . . . oh, yes – most edifying. We knew she was near to us – closer than you, I confess – but not that she was so close, and so favourable a target. We shall soon have some sport with her!

Enjoy your sport. It won't end well.

Oh, don't be so ungracious – you've done your sister a singular favour – spared her weeks of torment! The end was always inevitable; at least this way it'll be over and done quickly.

Get out of me. Get out of me and—

She was about to issue some empty threat; some promise that the better part of her knew she had no hope of keeping. But she was pulling away from Stallis. It was a sudden, sharp retreat and she had not initiated it.

He reached after her, the spindly body stretching to a futile elongation as she fell further and further back down the corridor. Adrana felt no elation. She was glad to be out of the immediate focus of Stallis's scrutiny, glad not to have him riffling through her secrets, but something else was pulling her away and she did not like that at all.

Adrana?

It was Fura – but distant, impossibly distant – a faint dwindling cry, already too weak for there to be any chance of a reply. And still she was speeding back along the corridor, the golden light now fading into darkness at the far end of it, and only a hastening grey rush conveying any sense of speed. She screamed into that rushing void, and her scream was sucked away.

And then, instantly, she was somewhere else.

Somewhere cold and enclosed. Curving stone walls, a flat stone floor – a rougher surface right under her, like a rustic wooden trap-door. She was sitting down on it, keeping all her weight against it, as if there were no more important task in all of existence than to prevent the opening of that door. From somewhere above her she heard screams.

*

Fura also screamed.

It was a scream of rage, rather than pain or terror, but it was no less forceful or full-blooded for that. She had nearly been in contact with Adrana. They had exchanged – something. Then Adrana had gone: pulled away from her with a suddenness that was like nothing in Fura's prior experience of bone signalling.

The carrier signal had gone a moment later, and the twinkly

was flickering out. Over the next few minutes Fura tried all the contact nodes, even those Ruther had told her had never given success on the *Merry Mare*, and she had caressed and shivered and then struck the skull, trying to goad it back into life. Nothing had worked and the minutes had continued passing. She was ready to smash her fist through those useless walls of bone, only holding herself back with valiant self-restraint. The skull had stopped working now, when she needed it the most. But that did not mean it was dead for the rest of time.

Finally giving up, she wrenched off the neural crown and checked the time. Twelve minutes had passed since the change of watch, twelve whole minutes that Adrana might have spent connected to the poisoned skull. Longer still, if she had already been connected when the stroke of midnight came.

Fura spun the wheel and let herself out into the ship. She took in a gulp of lungstuff, fresh after the musty enclosure of the bone room. For a few seconds the lightvine winding through the main corridors seemed to shine with an unnatural brilliance. Slowly her eyes adjusted to its normal yellow-green glow.

Ruther was waiting for her, rubbing absently at his scalp where she had nearly torn a chunk of it away.

'Did you get through?'

'I wish, Ruther.'

'What happened?'

She glanced down at her flesh hand, balling it so that the intensity of the glowy was less apparent. Not that Ruther could have failed to notice it tingling out of her brow and cheeks, or spangling from her eyes like a million tiny flakes of gold leaf.

'She was there. I'm sure of it. We had contact for a second or so, but it wasn't enough to get a message through to her. And then . . . something happened. She was pulled away from me.'

'Perhaps someone got Prozor's message, and they had time to get into the bone room and disconnect her.'

'I'd like to think that's what happened.'

'But you don't.'

'It didn't feel as if she was being pulled out of the connection,

Ruther. It felt as if she was being pulled somewhere else – into some other place. You know what that other place is like, don't you?'

'I . . . wouldn't want to shp . . . shpeculate.'

'You don't have to be afraid of me now. I was hard on you before – too hard – when I should have seen that you were only being loyal to your former captain, preserving what was secret between the two of you.' She rubbed down her hair, where it had been dishevelled by the neural crown. 'I should have seen that.'

Ruther looked at her doubtfully, as if all of that might be a precursor to some new and fiercer scolding. 'I should have mentioned the skull. But I never thought Adrana could be in danger from it.'

She nodded slowly. 'We were both wrong. But what's done is done and now we have to find a way to make things better. The skull is dead, for now. Has there been word from Proz, or any sighting of a return message?'

'Prozor is still outside, I believe, and I don't think there's been any news from Surt.'

'We can't count on Proz getting through to them, Ruther. It's been worth trying, but at this distance it was always a long shot. Which only leaves one other signalling option.'

'You mean to squawk.'

'Do you disapprove? It'll almost certainly light up our position well enough for Incer Stallis to attempt a ranging shot.'

She stared into his face, waiting for his answer. Ruther had been trying to persuade her into this course of action before she went in the bone room, but that was all very well when she had other options.

Now she wondered how firmly his conviction had endured.

'I don't care what it means for us,' he said, his voice nearly breaking. 'Maybe we'll make it, and maybe we won't. But if there's something we can do to stop that thing getting in your sister, I wouldn't be able to live with myself if we didn't try.'

'I hope those aren't just brave words, Ruther.'

Fura went with the boy to the control room, where Tindouf was already keeping sweeper-watch, then called Merrix and Eddralder to come up from the Kindness Room with all haste.

Judging by their faces, there was little confusion about her next course of action. The little gathering looked like a party of prisoners who had just been told that their execution date had been moved forward.

'We's been so careful not to give ourselveses away,' Tindouf said, shaking his head sadly. 'And this undoes all that good work. Daren't we waits a little longer on Proz?'

'Every second that Adrana is connected to that skull counts against her,' Fura said. 'I'd squawk now, without explanation, but I feel I owe you all this much.' She was already at the console, the handset raised to her lips. 'I'll be brief, and I've turned the power down to the lowest I can risk without them being able to detect us at all.'

'I would have been disappointed if you did not think of your sister,' Eddralder said.

'That means I've got your approval, does it?'

'If it were only me, then you have would have it, and whole-heartedly. While my daughter is in my care, you have my strong disapproval. Not because I dislike Adrana – of the two of you, I think I like her the best – but because this decision endangers Merrix, and she is all I have.'

Merrix turned to her father. 'Then disregard me, Father. If I am to be your justification for abandoning Adrana – and the other people on that ship – I should sooner repudiate you. I have seen far too much cruelty and cowardice in one life to abide another instance of it.'

'Even as she chastises you,' Fura said, smiling at Eddralder, 'she gives you reasons to be proud. You've raised her well.'

She pressed down on the handset's transmission button, cleared her throat once. 'Mister Cazaray says that the goods are damaged and that it is dangerous to persist in their use.

He trusts his message will be received and acted upon with all haste, by any interested parties, including Mister Cull.'

Fura lowered the handset from her lips, but did not immediately hook it back onto the console.

'That was it?' Eddralder asked.

'I couldn't use Adrana's name, or the name of that ship – not while all and sundry could be listening in. Cull's the name Lagganvor used when he was undercover – he'll recognise it, if no one else does.' Fura adjusted the squawk settings to select the short-range channel. 'Proz? You can come in now. I've squawked the *Merry Mare.*'

There was a crackle, then a reply. 'You sure they've heard you, girlie?'

Fura blushed, remembering the harsh words she had directed at Prozor before she left to go outside. She heard no trace of grudge or resentment in Prozor's answer, and that easy willingness to forgive left her humbled and ashamed at her own temper. 'I think it likely, but I can't know for sure. The signal strength was as low as I dared go, and they won't be so silly as to confirm receipt.'

'Then if it's all right with you, I'll keep sendin' for a few minutes longer.'

'All right,' Fura acknowledged, knowing how fruitless it would be to argue. 'But just that. Proz – I meant to say—'

'Busy, girlie – save it for later.'

Fura hung up the handset.

Merrix touched her father's hand, as if to reassure him that her feelings for him were as secure as they had been before they arrived. 'It was the right thing,' she said. Then she looked around the nervous little gathering with a curious self-possession. 'Everything has just changed for us, and yet nothing feels at all different. It's as if that squawk never went out at all.'

'It did,' Fura said. 'And I fear we'll find out what it means sooner rather than later.'

She felt calmer than she had in some while. The itch in her eyes was fading; the sparks and whorls of glowy in temporary retreat beneath her skin like regiments of golden soldiers falling back behind some defensive line while they plotted their next advance. That was all it was, she understood: a temporary ceasefire, a bitter and soon to be short-lived truce. She and the glowy had bargained, and neither had come out with a clear advantage. She had been permitted to signal Adrana, but the price for that had been the crushing of the Mephrozine.

The speaker grille crackled. 'This is Surt,' came her voice, hollow and reedy as if she were speaking through the tubes of some enormous pipe organ. 'Muzzle flash, aft of us, and a lot of it. I thought you'd like to know.'

19

There was cold, and there was the kind of cold that snuggled in close, like a companion. Adrana had her knees drawn up to her chest, her arms crossed to each shoulder, as if to clutch some last ember of warmth close to her.

She could remember being somewhere else – some place where there was a strong golden light, and a boy who seemed to know her name – but not what had happened after that place, or how she had come to be here – or exactly how long she had been in this place, save that it had been hours, perhaps many hours.

Her surroundings were easily appraised. It was a stone cell, a sort of dungeon, with curved, windowless walls forming a dome above her. There was no door, and the only interruption in the dome came from a small hole exactly above her, at the dome's apex. She must have looked up at it before, she supposed, but she examined it again with some faint, diminishing interest, just in case she had missed some weakness or feature that might have hinted at a way out of this enclosing space. The hole was far too narrow to crawl up and through, though, even if she found a way to reach it, and it was only the beginning of a narrow throat that went up and up into gloomy half-light. The illumination filtering down through that shaft, feeble as it was, was all that she had to see by.

It might have been the cold that roused her to consciousness, after however long she had been sitting on the floor. It had pushed through her clothes and skin and was now deep in her bones, settling in for long occupancy. She shivered and shifted – and felt a rough edge under her haunches.

She was sitting on something. She shifted to examine it, looking down between her skirted legs and boots. It must have been there all along, right under her. A door in the floor: a wooden trap-door, its edge protruding slightly above the worn smoothness of the stone slabs that made up the floor. Clearly this was how she had come to be in the cell, unless someone had gone to the trouble of removing stones in the wall and then building them back up again once she was inside.

She stood, realising it was better to be standing than pressed against that cold floor, and leaned down with her hands on her knees to get a better look at the trap-door. There was no lock or handle on it; nothing she could use to pull it up and see what was beneath. Had she been shoved up into this cell, and the door locked from below? She had no recollection.

She squatted further down, knees against the stone, and pressed her nails into the tight seam between the door and the surrounding floor. There was a tiny gap, but it was just enough to be able to slide the tips of her fingers into it and apply some leverage. Her nails crunched. She carried on anyway, grunting as she put more and more effort into the exercise. Nails didn't matter.

The door budged. She got it to hinge up about a finger's width, and then it came more easily, creaking as she swung it up to a near vertical position. She was a bit surprised that it had opened at all. She had thought it worth a try to lever the door open, but she had been all but convinced it would be locked from underneath.

It was cold in the cell, but an even more fierce chill wafted up from the black hole in the floor. The light from the ceiling hole failed to penetrate that darkness at all. She had been hoping to see a flight of steps leading down . . . hoping to see *something*

. . . but for all the information that her eyes could gather, there might as well have been an infinite black void beneath her. All of a sudden, she felt much less confident that opening the trap-door had been a sensible thing. And, now that she reflected on the matter, she had been sitting on it, very definitely sitting on it, as if keeping that door closed was much more important than opening it.

Bending over the black void, she began to close the trap-door. It was stiffer closing than opening, though. She had to really push down on it hard, using all her weight as leverage, and even then it was only closing sluggishly, with a sort of malicious, wilful reluctance. Her heart raced. She really had to get it closed and get herself sitting on it again. There was something in that void, something she had forgotten about, but which was now creeping back into conscious recollection. Something as dark and cold and musty as the empty space itself, but it was a thing, a moving hungry thing, and it was groping and reaching up in the direction of the rectangular source of light that she had now provided it, reaching and reaching . . .

Jagged bright light splintered across her vision. Something was happening to the stone wall! In one part of it, a zig-zagging light was protruding between the gaps where the stones were interlocked. The stones were loosening, the light widening. Two or three stones came free completely, tumbling onto the floor. She was still struggling to get the trap-door completely shut. It was down to about thirty degrees from the horizonal, but she could see far too much of that black emptiness beneath her. Now a whole section of the wall caved in, dislodged stones skittering across the floor, some of them squeezing into the gap between the trap-door and the hole. She reeled back, wondering whether to turn to the light or the darkness as a stone came tumbling back out of the hole, and she had a sense of some distinct, organised shape – a structure in the blackness – coming very near to the surface and unfolding some long, jointed part of itself.

A whole section of the wall was now gone. She blinked against the light, raising her hand to screen her eyes. A figure stepped over the crumbling threshold, holding some edged instrument. There was something curious about the figure, an attenuation to the expected form, an incompleteness where there should have been legs . . .

A gruff voice, distant and muffled, called out her name.

'Captain Ness!'

An articulated limb, black-furred, tipped with a single ebon claw, was extending out of the hole in the floor. The figure by the crumbling wall beckoned to her urgently. Then sharp things picked at her scalp, wrenching the neural crown away, and she understood where she was and what had happened.

The bone room. She was still in the bone room.

Lasling had opened the door from the outside and brought an axe, just in case. Now he pressed Adrana aside – kindly, considerately, but with determination – and swung the axe into the little skull, shattering it into a cloud of grey-brown shards, with flecks of twinkly still glimmering from its core.

The bone-cloud dispersed. The flecks of twinkly faded out one by one, until nothing was left.

*

Lagganvor supported her head while Lasling pressed a tankard to her lips. Vouga looked on with his arms folded, eyeing her with prudent caution, as if it were entirely possible that she might revert to whatever distraught condition she had been in when they pulled her from the neural crown.

'I swear I'd have opened that door at the agreed time whatever happened,' Lasling was saying. 'Something inside me was nagging that none of this was right. But then Fura squawked us . .'

Adrana's head was going to take more than a little while to clear itself of the presence of that stone-walled cell, with the horrible void beneath the floor. She was out of the bone room now, back in the ship – back in the present moment

– but she had a sickening intuition that she would only have to relax her guard to be sucked back into that cold, grey-lit prison.

'Fura squawked?' she asked, glugging down more of the water, for she was extremely dry in the mouth and throat, inexplicably so given how little time had actually elapsed.

'She kept it cryptic,' Lagganvor said. 'But the intent was plain enough. There was something about that skull we weren't to know. Something wrong with it – "damaged goods".'

'Once they got wind of our intention to use it,' Lasling said, scratching a finger against the stump of a tooth, 'Ruther must have piped up with a warning. He's the only one likely to know anything about that skull.'

'Something *did* happen to the boy,' Vouga said, exchanging a guarded look with his old colleague. He had a heavy-lidded look to him, one eye swollen and rheumy. 'Some queer business that I half-heard was something to do with a skull. That was all it was, though: rumour.'

'If you knew . . .' Adrana began. 'Or even had an inkling . . .'

Vouga gave her a disgusted look. 'Well, of course I knew. I just thought I'd keep an important thing like that to myself. After all, things could do with spicing up a little around here.'

'He didn't know,' Lasling said firmly. He snorted, like a man clearing his nasal passage, and pinched the tip of his nose as if it was sore. 'Vouga might not give a damn about being liked by a single soul anywhere in the Congregation. But he's honest, and fair, and if he says he didn't connect Ruther's story to that skull, you can take him at his word. The truth is none of us knew much about the boy, and none of us knew there was another skull on the *Merry Mare*.'

'I'm minded to believe it,' Lagganvor said, speaking as if he were her private counsellor, whispering sage advice into her ears. 'Captains often know a lot more about their boneys than the rest of the crew. The existence of that skull – its capabilities – needn't have been known to anyone except Werranwell and the boy.' He coughed gently. 'And might I suggest that recriminations are now somewhat superfluous? The skull is gone. We heeded the warning.'

'I still want to talk to Fura,' Adrana said. 'We have the telegraph. If she sent this squawk, she'll be waiting on a reply. I know it's been hours and hours . . .'

Lagganvor touched a scratch on his cheek, some fresh wound that was still seeping blood. 'It hasn't been as long as you think. You were out for a while, but it was minutes, not hours.'

'No,' she said. 'It was hours. I was in that cell . . . that cold, stone-walled place. I was in it for a long, long time.' She looked at their faces.

'I . . . resisted, didn't I? Whenever you tried to pull me out?'

Lasling fingered his nose. Vouga rubbed at his eye. Lagganvor dabbed a finger to his cut.

None said anything.

'And . . . Fura?' she asked, fearful of the answer she might receive. 'What's to stop me telegraphing her?'

'Nothing very much,' Lagganvor said. 'Except that Fura and her crew have other, more compelling matters to be attending to.'

'What do you mean?'

'She sacrificed her invisibility to warn us about the skull,' Lasling said. 'So Incer Stallis knows exactly where to shoot.'

*

Racked by nausea, and with a headache that felt like the blunt side of an axe being driven slowly into her cranium, splitting bone and brain, Adrana watched a battle. She was in the sighting room, with Lagganvor at her side. They each had their eyes pressed to high-magnification tubes, aimed at a small, nearly starless region of space. They were looking away from the Congregation, at the approximate set of coordinates where *Revenger* was expected to be sailing.

Flashes of light spangled in that darkness. Most were too

faint to be picked up by anything except these instruments, but now and then came a brighter flash that might have been detectable to the unaided eye. The fact of this engagement – if not the exact details of its protagonists – would have been obvious to any crew within a million leagues, and the news of it would be all over the Congregation by now. This was not some little skirmish between privateers.

'We think there are five ships in the sub-squadron,' Lagganvor said. 'We've been observing their firing pattern very carefully, and there's no indication of a sixth ship. The other craft are either keeping their guns cool, or they're off somewhere else. Stallis may not have wished to risk committing his entire squadron to one possible interception.'

'Have we seen sail-flash?'

'An indication or two from Fura's estimated position, but nothing at all from the attacking ships. It's difficult to be sure, but all the firing seems to be originating from the sub-squadron.'

'We think Fura lies closer to us than those ships?'

'Almost certainly. We got a better fix on her when she squawked, but it was a single transmission and her movements since aren't known to us. But since we can see the muzzle flash from the other ships, they must lie at a greater distance – at least a few tens of thousands of leagues further away.'

'She must be shooting back at them.'

'One would hope so.'

She pulled her eye from the scope, looking at him in the semi-darkness of the sighting room. 'I know my sister. She won't give in without a fight, no matter the odds. So she must be firing. But because her guns are averted from us, we see no flash or muzzle glow.'

'Fura is tactical, Adrana, and she knows when a counter-action would be suicidal. That is the case now. Do you see how those ships are dividing the fire between themselves? That's why the flashes dance around randomly. Each is letting off a short volley, stopping before there's any chance of muzzle glow, then another ship takes over. They must be coordinating by skull, or telegraph, or some agreed plan. The result is that they have a low rate of fire for five ships, but none ever warms its guns long enough to allow *Revenger* to target them. They have her position from that squawk, and these shots are helping them to refine it, by instigating sail-flash.'

Adrana returned her gaze to the tube. The lights spangled. They were faintly tinted: pale blues, pale pinks, pale emeralds, pretty as fireworks.

'She will not just give in, Lag.'

'I do not think she means to. But she does mean to drag this out for as long as she may. She has done us two kindnesses, Adrana. The first was in warning us about the skull, even though she knew it would expose her to Stallis. The second is to act as a magnet for his attention, as she is now doing. While he is engaged with *Revenger*, we are far from his thoughts. With this . . . distraction . . . we may complete our approach to Trevenza.'

'My sister means more to me than just a distraction.'

'No one thinks otherwise. Equally, I have no doubt that Fura would give her other arm to see you safe. Make this count, now. Take us in to port and show not the slightest concern for any misfortune that might have befallen some other, less favoured crew. They're nothing to do with us.'

'Coldness comes very easily to you, doesn't it?'

'On the contrary, I am not cold at all. It wasn't detachment that sent me to avenge Pol, and it isn't detachment that has me wanting the best for you now.' He paused, then released the locking wheel on his tube. He turned it on its gimbals, the pressure-tight cuffs sliding easily as he re-sighted on a different set of coordinates, nearly in the opposing part of the sky. 'Follow my line. You won't easily miss it.'

'You still see very well.'

'I was not so foolish as to destroy the more capable of my two false eyes. But you expected nothing less.'

'I did wonder which you might have smashed.'

'Shall I tell you something else, in the hope that it redeems our somewhat tattered comity? You were clever to slip me that sedative, but I could still have operated the eye, at any point, well enough to do you real harm.'

'Then why did you not?'

'Partly out of natural caution, partly out of intrigue, partly out of a desire to restore your damaged opinion of me. Partly because I did not wish to hurt you.'

'My opinion, once set, is not easily changed.'

'On that at least we are in agreement. Do you see it yet?'

She lined up her tube on the same patch of sky and swept back and forth in a methodical pattern until a bright barb swam into view.

It was a spindleworld.

'It's near enough to touch.'

'It very soon will be. Full of light and life. Warmth and hospitality. People. Fresh food. Fresh drink. New bones, to replace the skull we destroyed. You could spend a week just scouring the emporia! Yet you do not sound over-joyed at the prospect.'

Dared she tell him about the suspicion that had lodged itself in her mind? It was, for now, unverifiable. She had no skull to test herself against. Even if there had been one, she was not sure she had the resolve to go back into the Bone Room, or even any Bone Room, after what had happened in the last. But it was not merely the terror of that cold confinement, and the thing that had been trying to come up through the floor. There was something else now: something different.

Something missing.

'When we left Mulgracen,' she answered carefully, 'I thought Fura and I would make this crossing together. I thought our fortunes would turn at Trevenza Reach. I thought we would find answers there and, in delivering Tazaknakak, I hoped we would make friends.'

'All of those things are still possible.'

'No,' she answered coolly. 'They are not. Fura's in danger and there's nothing I can do about it; nothing that wouldn't betray the promise I made the Clacker. I don't know if I'll ever see her again, and I don't know if any part of this will prove worth it.

Perish it all, Lagganvor. All of a sudden I don't even care about those questions that I thought meant so much.'

'You do care, and you always will.' He settled his hand on her sleeve. The gesture was brotherly, rather than intimate, and she permitted herself to take some comfort from it. 'Fura knows it too. In your individual ways, you are both fatally incapable of incuriosity. This is where that admirable flaw has taken you. And now that you have both begun to peel back the edge of something, you will not be stopped. It was love for you, and love for that need for knowledge, that had Fura warning us – even though she would have known exactly the cost to herself. If you deflect from the course you are on now, you will be betraying not just that love but the wisest part of yourself.'

'You think you know me better than I know myself.'

'I wouldn't presume to that. But I recently made the error of underestimating you, and I think I know you a little better because of it. You must continue.'

'So that I can give you another opportunity to try and trick me?'

'No. I have . . . reflected on my decision.'

'And?'

'Whatever noble purpose I thought I was serving, in hoping to arrange for your capture, I now renounce.' He sat beside her in silence for a few seconds. 'The masters I thought I could trust have Captain Werranwell's blood on their hands, and from what we can see of that engagement going on behind us, it looks as if they wish to add to their crimes.'

'Your conscience has been pricked. However belatedly.'

'My conscience was always intact. My loyalty . . . misguided. But not for any longer. I have come to a decision, Adrana. This disguise feels more ill-fitting by the hour. I have worn it long enough. I am not Lagganvor, nor do I wish to be thought of as him.'

'I already know you for what you are.'

'It's time for the others to share in our secret. I wish to honour my brother by reclaiming his name as my own. I am Brysca

Rackamore, and henceforth I will answer to no other title.'

'When Fura finds out, she'll rip out your one living eye.'

'Were I to suffer such an ignominy, Adrana, it would mean that your sister has prevailed, and that Stallis has not. And I would consider that outcome to be a very fine thing indeed.' He nodded to their feet, and the ship that was below them. 'We should go back in – this battle won't be won and lost in a single watch. If I know your sister even half as well as I think, she will have a surprise or two for dear little Incer.'

*

Surt had not been mistaken in her observations: *Revenger* was indeed being shot at.

The fire was coming from a spread of ships, at least five of them, almost certainly closer than ten thousand leagues away, and coordinating their actions in an exceedingly skilful way. Clearly it was some detachment of the main squadron, broken off to hunt them as they fled for the crowded orbits and relative sanctuary of the outer Congregation.

One ship would let off a volley or two, then another ship would take over, then another, in a seemingly random pattern that made it hard to predict where the next burst of fire would come from. Because no one ship ever maintained a continuous barrage, there was ample time for their coil-guns to cool down between each burst, which meant they never glowed hot or bright enough to stand a chance of being targeted, no matter how hard Surt tried with the scopes and aiming dials.

'You're probably wondering why I don't shoot back,' Fura said to Ruther, who was with her in the control room. She was trying to strike a companionable note with the boy, hoping to reassure him that the madness he had seen in her earlier was but an aberration. 'Perhaps your Captain Werranwell would've had a different approach?'

'Whatever approach he had,' Ruther said, still with a certain wariness, 'it didn't help him much in the end. Mishter Lazhling . . . Mister Lasling wanted him to shoot back at you, but the captain said it wouldn't do us any good.'

'He was right. It wouldn't have made any difference, except give me an even better target. Your guns would've lit you up like a float at the Jauncery Parade. Which is why I can't send any slugs back at those ships.'

'But you have very good guns.'

'I do, Ruther,' she said, blushing with pride. 'Very good guns and very well-aimed too, thanks to Paladin. Probably better than theirs. But that ain't no help when we don't have good fixes for those ships. We'd have to sweep an area of space, stabbing in the dark until we struck lucky – sail-flash or hull-glint – and that's a game we can't win. By the time we'd stand a chance of hitting something, we'd be lit up just the way your poor old ship would've been.'

'And then they'd have us.'

'They would.' She stroked the side of the sweeper console. 'I might risk one pulse with this, if I were feeling a little more reckless, but having the satisfaction of a hard target would be little compensation for giving ourselves away completely.'

'You have a sweeper on your rocket launch, don't you?'

'We do, Ruther – and I see what you're thinking.' She nodded, signalling her approval. 'One of us could take that launch out to a safe distance from *Revenger*, use the sweep, and relay the enemies' coordinates back to Paladin.'

'I can see it wouldn't be very good to be in that launch, but if all else failed that might be a sacrifice worth making, to shave . . . to save the main ship?'

'I'm all for your bravery – presuming you're volunteering for such an escapade? I think you would, all told. But it wouldn't help us at all. The launch's sweeper'd bounce off us as well, and there's an excellent chance those ships would pick up the scatter.'

'I'm afraid that was my one useful idea,' Ruther said, looking down dejectedly. 'It's just a pity we can't stop our guns from glowing, or hide the glow in some manner, isn't it?'

She felt sorry for him, wishing she had some better encouragement.

'There's no way around it. Glowing muzzles will be the least of our difficulties, once we start giving it back to them. Our water-pumps will be running at full capacity just to keep those guns from cooking.'

The ship lurched, and she had to grip the console to stop herself being knocked against the wall. Ruther gasped, then collected himself. Something had happened to them – something that she was sure was to do with the attacking ships – but there had been no impact, not even an oblique shot glancing off the hull.

The ship creaked and groaned as it recovered from the lurch, like a drunkard grumbling after tripping on a cobblestone.

'I know what that was,' Ruther said.

She looked at him. 'You do, lad?'

'Yesh. It's the same as what we felt, when you started snipping away at our rigging.'

She raised her voice. 'Paladin? Is he right?'

'I am afraid he is, Miss Arafura. Mister Tindouf will doubtless confirm it with his strain-gauges, but something seems to have cut through the preventer line for one of our lesser gallants. I am correcting as we speak.'

'Are we handicapped?'

'If that is the extent of the damage, we will not be greatly disadvantaged. The compensators will take up the load, and we will merely be a little more sluggish in turning against the leeward flux.'

'And now please tell me that was catchcloth in those gallants, not ordinary sail.'

'That is my present assessment, Miss Arafura.'

'How does that help or not help us?' Ruther asked.

'Catchcloth won't shine back at 'em, whereas ord'nary might. If the preventer's been cut, there'll be a big ugly mass of sail flapping around out there – and I'd sooner it wasn't going to give us away.'

'They'll hit us again, though, won't they?'

'They haven't *stabbed us*, Ruther – they've just nicked the hems of our skirts, or trousers, whichever pleases you. That was a lucky shot, and no more than that – and if there's a shred of luck coming our way, they won't know how close they came to making us bleed.'

'You seem very calm,' Ruther said.

'Well, I ain't. Not at all.' She smiled, amused at his perception of her. 'Are you frightened, boy?'

Ruther seemed to measure his answer before giving it to her. 'I want to say that I'm not, but that'd be a lie, and I think you'd know that straight away.'

'I would, and you'd be wrong to lie. Shall I tell you how frightened I am? There ain't enough words for it. My guts feel like broken glass and my heart's running like one of those cooling pumps, fit to jump out of my chest. That's how I feel inside, and if you or any of us felt any different I'd question your sanity. Those ships out there might quite like to take me alive, but the rest of you don't matter to them at all, and if taking me alive turns out to be too difficult, a verified kill will suit 'em almost as nicely. Anyone of us would be mad not to be frightened, Ruther. But feeling it ain't the same as acting on it. Frightened people make bad choices. And if I can move around and talk as if I'm not frightened – although deep down I am – I can trick a little part of myself into thinking all is well, and we have a hope. Not much of one, but much better than none at all. That's why I seem calm to you. It's an act, one I'm playing for my benefit as much as yours. But if we all play it, and play it earnestly, we can start to change our fate.'

She looked at him, frowning as some hint of an idea, sensed yet not fully recognised, began to form. 'Ruther, what you were saying just now, about how it would be nice if we could keep our guns from glowing . . .'

Tindouf's voice broke across their conversation. 'Begging your pardon, Cap'n Ness, but I thoughts you should know we snagged something, a minute or two ago.'

'Thank you, Tindouf,' she said, addressing the microphone. 'Mister Paladin said you'd pick up on it – a slug cut one of our lines – but he seems to have us sailing true again. Will you be so kind as to send Prozor up here, as soon as she's out of her suit?'

'That's the other thing, Cap'n Ness. I've been watching the locks, and Proz ain't come back in just yet.'

20

The Clacker pressed the end of a portable telescope to his eye. Although his vision was poorly adapted, and he had to tilt his head to one side to bring one eye into line, he had the compensation of four limbs to steady his aim.

'I see it, Captain Ness.' He used one of his upper hands to adjust the brass focus wheel. 'Rather a dismal sort of object, if I might be so bold. After all my travails, I was hoping for a significantly grander prospect.'

'I'm sorry they haven't run out the bunting for you, or decked out the whole place in carnival lights. Perhaps it might have something to do with your arrival being entirely unannounced? Or should I get on the squawk and declared that I have a Clacker passenger and am desirous of meeting any and all parties interested in his welfare?'

'You will do no such thing.'

'Then don't start complaining about your destination, given that no one's expecting you and the people living in Trevenza Reach have many other things to be getting on with, besides prettying-up their world for your convenience.' Gently Adrana took the telescope from his grip and collapsed it down to a third of its length. 'I just thought you'd like to see it, so that you understand how close we are, and how soon we must make arrangements for our arrival.'

'Your word alone would have sufficed.'

'You will need to go back in your container, and the effector-displacement device will need to operate for at least as long as it takes to get you inside. May we depend on it?'

'Of course.'

'Good.' She stowed the telescope against the wall. 'Because it won't just be you in danger if it doesn't work properly. Those muddleheads – or the people running them – will have guessed where you mean to go, won't they?'

'There is a . . . possibility.'

'We'll call that a cold certainty, then. You have friends there – hopefully – but also people who mean you ill. Our problem is making sure the former party finds you before the latter.' She pressed a finger to her brow, already beginning to feel the start of the headache. 'We'll need instructions, Tazaknakak – very good instructions. Because once you're in that box, we can't open it up and ask you.'

Tazaknakak turned from the porthole where they had been viewing Trevenza Reach.

'There is an individual with whom you will make contact as quickly as possible. His name is Hasper Quell, and he will know what to do.'

Adrana's headache intensified. But it was more than just proximity to the Clacker causing it. There was the faint grey pressure of some half-forgotten memory trying to reassert itself. 'Have you mentioned this man to me before?'

'I do not believe so. What would make you think that I had?'

'That wasn't my question. What is his role? How can he help the likes of you?'

'Hasper Quell is providentially situated in Trevenza Reach. He is not unintelligent for his breed, has influence, is discreet, and above all sympathetic to the cause. I have not met the gentleman personally, but I have it on firm authority that he has been helpful to other fugitives and whistle-blowers such as myself.'

'Helpful in what sense?'

'He has given us shelter; channels of communication; the means to re-group and organise.'

'Have more of your kind already made it to Trevenza?'

'Many. Not just Clackers, but members of all the non-indigenous minorities. Some monkeys as well, and some robots. There was a trickle before the Readjustment – most were contented not to ask too many questions – now it is a flood.'

'What is it you're all hoping to achieve, Tazaknakak, besides avoiding the muddleheads and whatever interests are controlling the muddleheads?'

'The old order was not sustainable, Captain Ness. It was only a matter of time before something new came along. Your entire society was built on a foundation of falsehood. You were led to believe that the quoins were nothing more than an ancient curiosity, put to some useful new purpose as currency. But their true value is beyond your imagining. You and your kind have merely been the instruments serving the supply of that commodity.'

'We were told that they were money, then that they contained the souls of the dead, then that they did *not* contain the souls of the dead. We have been told many contradictory things. I have already asked you why the quoins now demonstrate an affinity for the Old Sun.'

'I believe, dear Captain, that I was *about* to answer you when we were distracted by a signal from your sister.'

'Tell me now, then.'

'They are drawn to the Old Sun. Have you a quoin about your person now?'

There was one serving as a paperweight close to hand.

'What is it you wish to prove?'

Tazaknakak took the quoin. 'I think it doubtful that the loss of this one quoin will make any difference to your fate or fortune. Are you agreed?'

'No one really knows what a quoin is worth anyway,' she said. 'But you are right. There are many more. Many, many more.'

They went to the nearest lock. There was no need to put on suits, which was useful as there were none that would have fitted the Clacker. They opened the inner door and put the quoin down inside the chamber, allowing the faint gravity of their acceleration to hold it to the floor. Then they shut the inner door, pumped the lungstuff back into the reserve tanks, reducing the pressure in the chamber to nearly zero – gradually, so that the quoin stayed undisturbed – and at last opened the outer door.

They watched through windows in the inner door.

Some gust of residual pressure encouraged the quoin to drift away from the floor. It floated up, then turned so that its face was aligned with the Old Sun and the centre of the Congregation.

'This is not new to me, Tazaknakak. Fura saw the effect in Mulgracen; she mentioned it to me afterwards and each of us has verified it independently for ourselves. I would not have asked you about the affinity if I hadn't . . .'

'Watch.'

The quoin was leaving the lock. It was moving slowly, but with a definite intention. Little by little, too, it was gathering speed – hastening away from the *Merry Mare*.

Hastening to the Old Sun.

*

The squawk was set to a short-range channel again, just enough to cross the distance from the antenna to Prozor's helmet. Fura called her name three times, then received the crackle of a return transmission.

'What is it, girlie? Didn't I tell you I'd still like to keep signallin', until we know better? This biz'ness requires all of what's left of the grey in me poor battered noggin, and when you've got the ship buckin' and twistin' right under me . . .'

'That wasn't our doing, Proz – it was Incer Stallis, taking a shot at us. He clipped our sails. Paladin and Tindouf have got us sailing true for now, but it's too dangerous to stay out there. Now they've got something to shoot at, and if they've seen even a glimpse of sail-flash they'll know they're getting close. Come in as quickly as you can – Tindouf'll be at the lock to help.'

Prozor gave a scornful snigger. 'They'd need to be having the luckiest day of their lives to put a slug through me.'

'Get to that lock,' Fura said, hanging up the squawk handset.

Tindouf was already on his way, and half-suited now just in case he needed to go out there as well. Surt was still in the sighting room, straining her eyes to the limit. Fura would have gladly seen her relieved – she'd have put in her own stint if need be – but it would take too long to winch the sighting room back in and out of the ship, and she could not abide them being blind in that interval.

'Will she be all right?' Ruther asked.

'If she gets a move on.' Fura balled her fist, cursing herself for not calling Prozor sooner. Not that it would likely have made any difference: Prozor had never been the sort to abandon a job halfway through. She thought of that mass of sail billowing around somewhere in the rigging, a writhing creature of pure blackness, and the minor fortune that Prozor had not been caught in the lines and sheets when they went loose. Then she remembered what had been pricking the edge of her thoughts when Tindouf had called in to the warn her that Prozor was not yet returned. 'Do you know something, Ruther?'

He looked at her warily. 'Captain?'

'You are a very clever boy. I can see why Werranwell kept you close at hand. I doubt it was just because of your capabilities in the bone room.'

'I thought my idea was bad, about going out with the launch.'

'It was. But that ain't the idea I was thinking about. You said it was a shame we couldn't fire back at Stallis.'

'And you said the guns would never cool down quickly enough.'

'They won't. But if there was a way for Stallis not to see them, even if we were maintaining a high rate of fire, and glowing as hot as coals, that would amount to the same thing, wouldn't it?'

'I suppose,' Ruther said doubtfully.

'Relax, boy: it's not a trap. You gave me half an idea and Stallis helped with the other half, by damaging our sail. Paladin!'

'Yes, Miss Arafura?'

'I wish to use our sails as a camouflaging screen, interposing 'em between us and the pursuing squadron. May that be done?'

'A mass of sail could be cut free, fixed to new lines, and run aft of us, yes.'

'That would take too long. I'm talking about using our spread of sail as it stands now, but turning us, so that we're on the other side of the sails. May that be done? Keep tension on the yardage by spinning us, if need be, and don't fear a little touch on the ions, if that helps. I don't care if it isn't a stable arrangement . . .'

'I assure you it will be anything *but* stable.'

'Fine – all it's got to do is provide us with a temporary covering screen for the coillers. Even if we're moving, slewing laterally to hold tension, it should be within your means to compute firing solutions for a rapid volley?' She grinned, as images of destruction and violence played out in her mind's eyes, as bloody and vivid as any of the more lurid illustrated periodicals, the sort that Father had always frowned upon. 'We'll run 'em hard and hot, until we no longer have the aiming angle or the covering effect, whichever happens first.'

'Captain?'

'What, boy.'

Ruther looked stricken. By the anguish in his features he clearly wished to say something, something which might be taken the wrong way, yet feared the consequences.

'What I mean to say is . . .'

'Out with it, Ruther.'

'What I mean is . . . perhaps I'm not quite following this plan, but if the sails are between us and the enemy . . . however temporarily . . . won't that mean that we have to . . . shoot through our own sails?'

'The objection is not unreasonable,' Paladin said.

Fura nodded avidly. 'That's the point, you simpletons: it doesn't matter that we shoot through our own sails! There are leagues upon leagues of 'em, and even if we fire every slug in our stores we'll only be doing a little damage to a small area. In the meantime, not one photon will get through the parts of the sail that ain't punctured, and that'll mean most of the covering screen still holds. Stallis won't see a hint of our guns, even if they're close to cooking-point. Now tell me: can it be done?'

Although she was in the control room, not her quarters, she imagined the flash of lights in Paladin's globe; the play of logic through his circuits and memory registers.

'I must calculate.'

She squeezed her fist. Somewhere in the back of her mind it occurred to her to wonder if her enthusiasm for this idea – which was, on the face of it, nearly as mad as it was audacious – was borne out of recognition of its intrinsic cleverness, the one desperate act that might save them, or was instead driven by the glowy, seizing and magnifying the idea not in spite of its madness, but because of that very quality.

Somewhere else in the back of her mind, she knew that she no longer cared.

She roared: 'Then damned well calculate!'

*

Adrana swept her telescope along the length of Trevenza Reach. It was pleasing to her to see many other craft gathered around the world and navigating its near spaces: ships of all sizes and dispositions, some under all sail and some hauled-in. One more ship, even a sunjammer limping in from some doubtful encounter in the Empty, would not draw too much notice.

'Are you sure you're rested, after that business in the Bone Room?' Lasling asked.

'I am very rested, thank you. I do not think it would have been good for me to be in there very much longer, but you got me out in time. I have had a little headache, and the Clacker does not help it, and now and then I feel nauseous, but there are no more serious after-effects.'

'Was it wrong, to smash up the skull like we did?'

'No. It was entirely the right thing, and you must think no more of it.'

'I suppose we've come to the perfect place to find a new one. Or newer, I should say.'

She smiled tightly. 'Yes – there'll be things to procure. Not just a skull.' Intentionally changing the subject she added: 'We'll come in all the way, if there are no objections. 'Unless there is a compelling reason otherwise, I think we will take the closer of those two docking complexes. Haul-in as you may, but leave us enough spread to sail away if the reception is not as warm as we'd wish.' She snapped the telescope shut, content to take in the entirety of their destination with her unaided vision. 'It's a pretty little trinket, isn't it? It reminds me of an ornament Fura and I were once given. I almost feel that I could reach out and shake it, and a snowstorm would flurry down inside.'

'I've never known snow.'

'Nor have I,' Adrana said. 'But I have seen pictures. Paladin used to show us drawings and paintings when he was telling us stories. He was always very good at telling stories. Besides, snow isn't just some something from fairy tales. It does snow on some of the worlds, doesn't it?'

'I gather it does, especially out in the colder orbits. I haven't seen such places for myself, though, and I doubt I ever will.'

'There's always time, Lasling.'

'Not for me, I fear. There's just too much of everything and too little of me. A sixth of me's gone, I'm two thirds of the way through my natural span, and I haven't seen a thousandth part of the Congregation.' He coughed, and sounded as if he wished to strike a less maudlin note. 'Still, it *is* a pretty trinket, as you say.'

'They say spindleworlds are rare.'

'Rare because they break so easily, so even if there was once lots of them, and that's not a proven fact, not many have come through to the present.'

'Why do you think this one has endured?'

'It's a bit like asking, why has this nice wine glass not shattered, when all the others have. There's no reason except the others weren't so lucky. And when you're down to a few of something, I s'pose you take better care of what's left.'

The spindleworld was three and a third times as long as it was wide, and it was only wide at its thickest part, the exact middle. It tapered down between the middle and the ends, five leagues in either distance. There were long, triangular windows cut into the tapering parts: six in each half, running nearly from the middle to the end, with strips of uninterrupted floor between each window. The interior was almost entirely covered over with city: numerous interlocked and festering districts sprawling out along the floored parts and even spilling out over the windows, clinging to the thickest parts of their mullions. Her telescope was good, but she was having to look through porthole glass that was not quite as excellent nor as clean, though that blurriness only made the world look more tantalising, more full of life and possibility. The entire structure was rotating on its longest axis, with a grand, slow stateliness, so that as one set of windows went out of sight, another came into view, like a sort of clockwork diorama of intricate tableaux.

There were three possible docking sites: a ring-shaped complex around the middle, which – because it was rotating – was suited only to rocket craft, and two similar facilities at the sharp ends. The world was turning there as well, of course, but the docking positions were almost on the axis of rotation, and therefore as close to weightless as made no difference, and even a sunjammer could berth there without too much difficulty.

That was not her intention, but she would have Lasling bring them as close as possible, and then they could take the rocket launch a league or two over, which would cost more in suiting-up time than it did in travel or expenditure, and yet would permit some of the sails to remain hauled-out, with their mirrored sides averted.

'Somewhere in that world, Lasling, is a man called Hasper

Quell. It seems quite impossible now, but I hope we won't have too much trouble finding him.'

'Is this gent known to you?'

'Not directly. The Clacker mentioned him as a potential contact, a man who has been helpful to fugitives such as himself. I thought the name meant something to me, yet I've never been to Trevenza. It puzzled me for a little while, until I remembered that my sister has been here before.'

'And Captain Fura told you about this man?'

'In her book. She wrote an account of her adventures, and in it she came into contact with Hasper Quell, which is why the name was familiar to me. It at least confirms that he is real, and he may be reached. That is a start. But I have misgivings.'

'How so?'

'The man betrayed Fura. Or was himself betrayed – either way, when she went to him for help, it ended with her being captured and taken back to Mazarile. I can't be sure if Hasper Quell did his best and was put in an impossible position, or whether he can't be trusted at all.'

'And what does the Clacker say?'

'It's too late to ask, Lasling. Lagganvor and I put him back into his container, and now he's out of communication. By the time I made the connection with my sister's journal, he was already in the box.'

'Then wake the cove and press him about Hasper Quell.'

'I daren't do that. His box is unreliable, and we need it to keep functioning until we're safely inside Trevenza. Bringing in a live Clacker would raise too many questions. I'm not saying all the customs men will be on the lookout for Tazaknakak, but it would only take one bad apple to undo our plans.'

'Then you're in, pardon my bluntness, something of a bind. You have to put your trust in this man, who might rat you out.'

'Lagganvor will go ahead of us and make contact. He's good at that. Once I have his reassurance, I'll feel better.'

'Once or twice, Captain – and you'll excuse me if I'm speaking out of turn – but once or twice I've wondered if you and Mister

Lag don't have some business between you. Some business that might mean your trust in him ain't as rock-solid as it should be.'

She deliberated over her answer. 'You are correct, and you haven't spoken out of turn. There was a . . . difficulty between me and Lagganvor. But that's rather behind us now. In fact, Mister Lagganvor means to speak to you all about it, before we take the launch. I think you will find it . . . enlightening.'

*

'What you ask of me will be very difficult,' Paladin said. 'I will need to adjust the rigging almost constantly, so as to avoid the catchcloth sails being blown into us, or the ordinary sails throwing light at our adversaries. Then there is the question of how we initiate this turn in the first place. There are a number of possibilities, but each has its drawbacks, and . . .'

'I never thought it would be simple, Paladin,' Fura said. 'Just answer my question: is it feasible?'

'I believe it is feasible.'

'Good – that's all I ask for.' She reached for the handset again. 'Proz – I've got an idea to let us start bloodying some noses – since they're so intent on bloodying ours – but since we'll be putting a hard torque on the ship, I want you inside before we attempt it. How far are you from that lock?'

There was a buzz of static, a crackle or two, but no reply.

She clicked the handset again.

'Proz? Where are you?'

'I's at the lock,' Tindouf said, cutting in on the same channel. 'And I can see out through the porthole, but I can'ts see any signs of Prozor.'

'I told her to stop sending that signal,' Fura said, angry and concerned in the same breath. 'Paladin: be ready on my word, but don't start to turn us until I say so.'

She left the console and the sweeper and fought her way through the warren of corridors and squeeze-throughs that led to the main lock. She was nearly there when Eddralder appeared around the corner of a passage, blocking her way.

'Is this a good time?' he asked mildly.

'Does it look like a good time?'

'I wouldn't know. You look aggrieved. Then again, lately you look aggrieved under almost any circumstances.'

'Well, let me explain the circumstances as they presently apply,' she answered testily. 'We're being shot at. They've struck our outer sails and they may soon have more success. I have a plan, but . . .' She paused, drawing a deep breath, collecting herself. 'There may be casualties, if we start receiving fire. You'll have to do something about Strambli's body, if you're to have a clear operating area in the Kindness Room.'

'As it happens, Strambli's body is what I was coming to speak to you about.'

She did not need this. 'You and Merrix will just have to put it somewhere for the time being. I know you'd rather study her than move her, but . . .'

'Her body has already gone,' Eddralder said. 'The trouble is, we didn't move it.'

'Please explain.'

'I wish I could.' He looked at her with his large pale eyes, communicating the full intent of his words, making sure she understood exactly what had happened. 'Merrix and I left the Kindness Room unattended while you called us to the control room. When we returned, the body was gone.'

'There must be a mistake. The Ghostie transformation's obviously advanced to the point where you're just not seeing her, even though she's still present. That's how it works with Ghostie gubbins. The armour, the weapons . . . if you try too hard to see them, they slip out of your conscious focus.'

'Merrix and I know an empty bed when we see one, Captain. It's not a question of looking too hard. The body isn't there.'

'So who moved it?'

'Nobody. Surt is in the sighting room, Tindouf and Ruther were with us in the control room, and Prozor went outside. She *is* still outside, isn't she?'

'Yes, and that's . . .' Fura shook her head, trying to clear at least a tiny part of it. 'Bodies don't move, Eddralder. There's been a mistake.'

'Unless Strambli had the right of it all along, Captain. She seemed to know what was happening better than any of us.'

'Find it . . . her,' Fura said.

'And then what? Chain her down? Nail her into a box?'

'Perhaps that's what you should have done all along.' Exasperation overwhelmed her. 'Prozor's still out there. I want to turn the ship and I can't risk it with one of our own still outside.'

'There is something we don't understand, something we can barely see, moving around on this ship.'

'And there won't *be* a ship unless I turn us.'

Eddralder nodded slowly. 'Merrix is searching the aft compartments, as best she can. I will do the same with the forward ones. And . . . report accordingly.'

'Do as you must,' she said crisply. 'Take care. But remember what I said: we may need the Kindness Room.'

She squeezed past Eddralder, turning back once to watch him heading away, then shivered to herself, thinking of Strambli's glassy corpse somehow animate and self-directing, ensconcing itself somewhere in the many nooks and hideaways of her ship. What did it want with them? What did she want with them, if any part of Strambli now remained? And how peculiar that this curious and troubling business should not, presently, be the uppermost concern in her mind.

When she found him, Tindouf was just finishing putting on the last parts of his suit, bulky as a bear in all that leather and metal. He was at the door to the main lock: the starboard lateral lock, peering through a porthole to the right of it.

'Any sign of her?' she asked directly.

'Not yet, Miss Ness. I did speaks to Doctor Eddralder just now and he was most taken up with something. Has someone been hurt?'

'Not exactly, Tindouf, but if we don't act quickly there's every chance of it.' She squeezed in next to him, pressing her face into the concavity behind the porthole. It had a domed window, allowing a limited view of the hull in all directions, as well as a clear view looking straight out. It was hard to see anything, except a dark continuum. 'Damn this lightvine,' she muttered, for it was glowing behind her, making it even harder to peer through the glass. 'We should've cut it back months ago. Have you seen or heard her?'

'Nothing, and I oughts to have picked up the stomp of her boots by now, if she was coming in.'

'She's in trouble, Tindouf. Something must have happened to her out there.'

Tindouf hinged down his visor, tightening the seal with the thumbwheels either side of his chin, then presented his back to her so that she could double-check the connections. 'I's worried,' he said, his voice muffling through the glass.

'So am I. But it might just be that there's a problem with her squawk. She had to put that suit on in a hurry, didn't she? Something might have snagged, or the cell not been charged-up properly.'

'I hopes that's what it is,' Tindouf said, none too persuasively. 'I'll be quick, and I thinks we can afford to lose another quantity of lungstuff – we'll be at Trevenza Reach before we run low – and . . .'

'I see something.'

Her eyes were still struggling to pick out the difference between the hull and the background beyond it, but something had begun to come into view now, tumbling slowly. It was dark, but not nearly so dark as its surroundings, and as it rotated its surfaces caught and reflected some faint portion of the Congregation's light, so that Fura was able to make out an edge here, a grille there, a hinged shutter there. She stared at it for a moment longer, not quite recognising the thing, until her mind made the necessary connection. It was the telegraphic box, bulky and rectangular, following some lazy course of its own.

Something about it was not quite right, though.

'Tindouf,' she said. 'Come here.'

He pressed his helmet as close to the porthole as he could, trying to follow her angle of vision.

'What is it, Miss Ness?'

'I don't know. I thought I understood what I was looking at, but now . . .'

She stared and stared. She knew how the telegraphic box should appear; she had gone out often enough to familiarise herself with its operation, even if she had never used it in earnest. There were the flaps at the front, which protected the delicate optics, and inside those a separate, high-speed shutter mechanism that could be opened and closed with the controls built into the handles – which projected from the other end of the box like a pair of bull's horns. Now there was something else, too: a continuation of the handles, as if they'd been thickened and extended. It wasn't the telegraphic box at all, she decided, but just some similar-sized bit of the ship that had come mysteriously loose. That was what it was. That was what it *had* to be.

For a man wearing a suit, Tindouf moved with commendable speed. He jammed a mitten across her eyes, screening her view, and then very nearly yanked her head off as he averted the direction of her gaze.

'No, Miss – you don'ts need to see that, not at all.'

'Tindouf,' she said, still with one of his hands across her face, another preventing her from looking back. 'Tindouf. I thought I saw . . . Tindouf! Tell me what I just saw!'

Now he clamped his hands either side of her face and forced her to look into his visor.

'No, Miss Ness. Not right now. You go back and see Mister Paladin, and tell him I has to go outsides. I shan'ts be too long, I don't think.'

'They've killed her, haven't they?' she asked, hearing herself speak, but not really feeling as if the words were originating in her own head. They seemed to belong to someone else; a protagonist in some other story than her own. 'She was on her way back and they've killed Prozor. Incer Stallis killed Prozor.'

It was as if some vital part of her had been cut away; some

part that she had always relied on, but never given sufficient consideration to until the moment when it was taken from her. She had accepted the fact of the death without the least equivocation, accepting the full and irrevocable truth of it as readily as she might accept the loss of a sail or hull-plate. They were engaged in war, after all, and this was what happened in war. People died, including good and dependable people; even people who had always seemed to pass through life armoured against the worst of its abuses. Prozor had always been so resilient, so resourceful, so utterly bereft of self-pity or remorse for her own actions, that at times Fura had begun to think of her as a sort of living mass of scar tissue, made only harder by each injury or injustice: the sort of rough hardness that the universe might wish to smooth away, but could not, despite its most concerted efforts. Prozor had survived baubles and every common hazard of space; she had survived the loss of her one true love; she had survived Bosa Sennen and twinkle-heads and the hostile intentions of other ships.

And all of that had counted as naught against Stallis.

Fura breathed slowly. The glowy prickled. She accepted that this thing had happened; she accepted that there would be no undoing her earlier harshness. She did not accept that the crime would go unanswered for.

'I'll do something very, very bad to that whelp,' she promised.

'You go and see Mister Paladin,' Tindouf repeated, before pushing himself into the lock.

21

Adrana did not expect to be squawked by Fura – that would risk giving away what little uncertainty might remain of her position – but when at last the console did buzz, signalling an incoming transmission, she could not quite negate the hope that it might be her sister, and that the news might not be so terrible as she feared.

But there could be no good news. She had monitored the further unfolding of that engagement. The attack against *Revenger* had entered a cruel and slow secondary phase. The five ships of the squadron were no longer shooting quite so actively, but from the pattern of their muzzle flashes it was clear that they were now closing in on their quarry with a methodical and deliberate patience. She imagined a field of carnage, after some disproportionate slaughter. Now the triumphant party was moving slowly and calmly through the bloodied and mangled bodies of the fallen, occasionally stopping to jab a sword into some whimpering enemy who hadn't had the decency to die quickly. The battle was technically still in progress – it would not be formally decided until the last moaning form had been pricked into silence – but all that remained was a sort of ghastly, clerical formality.

So it was with the attack on *Revenger*. The squadron ships were still too far off to send in launches (if that was their intended endgame) but there could no longer be any doubt that they would prevail. If *Revenger* was a cornered rat, she was now tormented by five stalking cats. Every ten or twenty minutes they were content to shoot a slug or two at her, scanning for sail or hull-flash and refining their aim accordingly.

And still there had been no counterblast from Fura.

Adrana did not even have the luxury of being the only witness to this travesty. News of it was all over the general squawk, and they were even beginning to see it on the short-range flickerbox transmissions beaming out from Trevenza Reach. There were a hundred different viewpoints, a hundred different commentaries, a hundred different theories and opinions. No one had direct proof that it was the Ness sisters' ship being shot at, and there was no official line from anywhere in the Congregation concerning the actions of the sub-squadron. But there were plenty of observers who had guessed the essential truth of what was happening. It did not take vast powers of deduction: tying up five ships in a lengthy engagement was always going to be expensive.

Who was worth that sort of cost, besides the Ness sisters?

The only crumb of encouragement Adrana could take from any of this was that no one, to the best of her knowledge, had yet speculated that the Ness sisters might be operating different ships, and that one of them might be coming in from the Empty on a different course to the other . . .

'It might,' Lasling said, when the console had been buzzing for about ten seconds, 'be worth answering that.'

She snatched the handset from its cradle.

'Captain Werranwell, of the *Merry Mare*. To whom am I speaking?'

'This is Trevenza Reach, Captain Werranwell.' There was a pause, and she read far more into that hesitation than she wished. 'We have you on our sweep, approaching at one hundred leagues per hour. What are your intentions?'

The voice was deep, male and phlegmatic, as if there was something in his throat he badly needed to cough up.

'I should like to dock with all expediency. We were attacked without provocation, left for dead in the Empty. Our captain, my dear father, was killed in the attack, and we are very low on supplies.'

The speaker was some low-ranking Port Authority functionary, she did not doubt – unless they already merited the attention of someone higher up – and he sounded only a fraction less bored than at the start of the exchange. 'And who was behind this attack? Bauble-jumpers? Some other privateer?'

'There was no communication, sir, but there were many ships involved, and we have it on excellent authority that there is a squadron operating in this part of the Empty. There is talk of an engagement going on as we speak – perhaps the same ships that waylaid us.'

'Waylaid you?'

'It must have been mistaken identity, sir. Our squawk was damaged, so we couldn't give an account of ourselves, and they took that as an invitation to put a few slugs across us.' Adrana swallowed audibly and tried to make it sound as if she was only just holding back a flood of tears. 'They used hull-penetrating coillers against us, sir – they weren't just trying to warn us away. We were spiked very badly – lost half our lungstuff.'

'That is very unfortunate, Captain Werranwell. But you must appreciate that we cannot be seen to take one side over the other, even if you have a legitimate grievance . . .'

'That is fully understood, sir,' Adrana replied, adopting as earnest and ever-so-humble a tone as she dared. 'I know that you have standards to uphold.'

This drew a mildly quizzical response.

'Standards, Captain Werranwell?'

'My dear father, just before the life left him, said that we should endeavour to bring his body to the place he loved best out of all the worlds around the Old Sun, but we should not count on charity, for Trevenza Reach is a world where the institutions and treaties of the Congregation are maintained with great subservience and loyalty, more so than in many places in the warmer processionals . . .' She sniffed hard, making so convincing an effort that she had to drag her own sleeve under her nose. 'My poor departed father was very firm in this matter, sir. He stipulated that though it would break his heart for his mortal remains not to be conveyed here, on no account were we to test the good nature of our intended hosts. In fact he said that it was quite likely that, while we had been shot at without mercy, the squadron was only going about the good work of our proud and long-established financial institutions, which he said were held in universal esteem, even as far out as Trevenza Reach.'

Next to her, Lasling made a hesitant chopping motion. She halted herself momentarily, then decided that she was committed to the part and might as well throw herself into it with total abandon.

'All I mean to say, sir, is that, despite what's happened to us, and despite my father's very strong desire to be laid to rest in the place that had been so kind to him, and for which he had such fond recollections, on no account were we to make more trouble, or force our hosts to choose between the word of a lowly privateer and the combined authority of the banks and merchant institutions . . .'

It was a relief when she was cut off.

'That is quite enough, Captain Werranwell. I am afraid your father may have been labouring under a very slight misapprehension – or perhaps he meant only to spare you any embarrassment?'

'I don't understand, sir.'

'I mean only to say that while we are by no means a lawless freehold, we have always prided ourselves on maintaining a certain . . . respectful distance . . . from the affairs and preoccupations of the main Congregation. Of course we adhere to Inter-Congregational law in all matters of binding importance . . . but we are not a vassal state of the inner processionals, and nor are we beholden to the word of the banks over an honest captain, or the daughter of a hard-working captain, especially one who must have held our world in such high regard to wish to be laid to rest within our locks. You may approach, Captain Werranwell, and all assistance will be offered. You must understand that no sides will be taken, and every aspect of this unfortunate matter will need to be examined from all angles, but until such time as it is proven otherwise, you will have the status and rights of an innocent party.' The voice shifted, becoming more business-like. 'Please reduce your approach speed to fifty leagues per hour, and further still once you are within ten leagues of our trailing endcap, where you may float or berth at your leisure.'

'Thank you for your kind consideration, sir,' Adrana said, before putting back the handset.

'My poor departed father,' Lasling said, mimicking her words with an amused admiration.

She knuckled away a semi-formed tear. 'That wasn't nearly as much of an act as you'd think. Can we haul-in as the man asked?'

'Between my sails, and Meggery's ions, we can slip in as sweetly as you like.'

Even as her mind kept flashing to thoughts of Fura, she found the strength to smile at him.

*

Lagganvor pushed back the fringe of his hair and took out his remaining false eye. He cupped it in his hand, offering it to the small audience before him as if it were the prelude to some devilish act of prestidigitation.

But he did not make the eye disappear.

'I am not the man I have claimed to be. For a long time – many months now, on these ships, and still longer on Wheel Strizzardy – I have been living under one name while reminding myself that I have another. Only one other person has known of my double-identity, and I know it has cost her dearly to keep this secret.' He nodded at Adrana, with – it seemed to her – some measure of sincerity and understanding. 'It has nearly torn her apart, to choose between the preservation of her crew, and being honest with her sister. She made the proper choice, too. And her reward for that was to be betrayed by me.' He flashed a self-effacing grin. 'Or very nearly betrayed. She was wiser and more perceptive than I realised, and that is to my eternal discredit. I promised her that I would not signal my masters, once we were on this ship. And I lied, and attempted to signal them – or rather, attempted to arrange a ruse which would have resulted in the *Merry Mare* giving up her position – but which would have served my masters just as excellently.'

'Who're your masters?' Lasling asked.

Lagganvor put back his eye before answering. 'The same masters who murdered your captain.'

There was a silence. A nervous laugh from Cossel, a sniff of disbelief from Meggery. Vouga looked on with amused indifference, as if observing a street-side brawl in which he had no direct interest, but from which he could not quite tear his gaze, and that might even be worth a wager or two.

Lasling remained impassive. 'I will need a better answer.'

'I would like to offer one. But that is the truth of it. I am an agent – an operative of the vested interests that have funded that squadron, who put Stallis in charge of it, and who have Werranwell's blood on their hands.'

Cossel laughed again. 'If you're trying to get yourself killed, cove, this is a good way to go about it.'

'I say we start on his fingers,' Meggery said, making a knife-sharpening gesture against her sleeve.

'Wait,' Lasling said, with a slow raise of his hand. 'I want to hear the rest of it. Then we decide.'

'Ain't we heard enough already?' Cossel asked.

'You forget,' Vouga said. 'He was protected by Captain Ness. If you have a case against him, then you'd better be prepared to extend it to our captain – who Werranwell persuaded us to accept as his successor.' He nodded at Adrana, who had kept her silence until that moment, knowing full well how Lagganvor's confession was likely to be taken. 'Is that not so, Captain?'

'I suggest,' she said delicately, 'that you hear what he has to say. What appears to be black and white now may look less so in a minute or two. But keep in mind one other thing: I *am* your captain – as Vouga has so kindly reminded us – and I will not have any sort of mob justice on my ship. Take against Lagganvor, by all means. Harm a hair on his head, and you'll understand what it means to wrong me.'

'And I thought her sister was the fierce one,' Meggery muttered.

'You thought wrong,' Lagganvor said. 'And believe me, I have seen and felt the evidence of it. I crossed her once – I will not make the mistake of doing so twice.'

'Tell them why you did it,' Adrana said.

He worked his fingers together, staring down into them with intense concentration. Perhaps he understood he only had one chance of redeeming himself, and that every word that fell from his lips had to be considered.

'Bosa Sennen killed my brother,' he said, looking up into the assembled faces. 'His name was Pol Rackamore and he was known to the Ness sisters. I think they would agree he was an honest and fair captain. Long before Bosa killed him, though, she took his daughter Illyria and did something unspeakable to her – something that nearly broke Pol. He recovered, in time, but our fraternal love did not. I blamed him for what had happened to Illyria. Just when he needed me the most, I offered him censure and disapproval. He turned from me – shut me out of his life. I do not blame him for that in the slightest. I . . . lived with my error. I thought, with time, there might be a possibility of healing the wound I had inflicted. But Bosa took that hope away. She killed my brother, and so I decided to pay her back in kind.'

'Tell them about Lagganvor.'

'Lagganvor was an agent in her employment. She sent him into the worlds to do the sort of business she could not. Procurement, espionage, recruitment – that sort of thing. Of necessity, the chemical chains binding Lagganvor to Bosa were weaker than those she used on her normal crew. He had to be kept on a longer leash: permitted a degree of autonomy and independent thought.' He made an explosive gesture with his hands. 'One day, he broke those chains. He fled, with the full fury of Bosa on his back, but he thought he could stay one step ahead, and gradually change his identity. Unfortunately for him, he ran into me.'

'And that makes you . . . who, exactly?' Lasling quizzed.

'My name is Brysca Rackamore. I had become an agent – a very effective one – and I believed the best way to reach Bosa was to catch a man like Lagganvor. Catch him, impersonate him, and set a trap. If I could allow myself to be retaken by Bosa, if I could survive any doubts about my disguise, I would be able to signal my masters, and have them close in.'

'You thought you could fool Bosa Sennen?' Meggery asked, shaking her head as she spoke.

'You underestimate the lengths I was prepared to go to,' he answered, before raising a hand to his cheeks. 'Once I caught Lagganvor, I stole his face. There is a . . . technique. It's very unpleasant to both parties, so rarely employed voluntarily. Think of a sort of mask, with thousands of depressible spikes on the inner face. They puncture the skin, penetrate muscular tissue, and make a direct impression of the shape of the skull. The mask is then withdrawn and moved to the recipient, who first takes an osteomorphic drug that causes local softening of bony structure. As the mask is pressed into place, it forces the second face to conform to the contours of the first. The mask is withdrawn, the drug wears off, and the skull regains its normal rigidity. After a few days, with recuperative medicine, the covering tissue begins to heal.'

Someone swallowed.

'And your eye?' Cossel asked.

'That was a simpler procedure. Lagganvor had been given the eye as a gift from Bosa. I took it, and the associated neural machinery. A surgeon was found who could be paid to do the work, and just as crucially keep quiet about it. By that point . . . shall we say that losing an eye was the least of Lagganvor's difficulties?'

'What did you do to him?' Meggery asked.

'Things that will haunt me to my final breath.' He smiled thinly. 'But they had to be done, and I regret none of it. I had to squeeze him until he bled every one of Bosa's operational secrets. And then squeeze him again, to make sure he wasn't just blurting out the first thing that came into his head. Whether it worked, whether it was truly sufficient, I'll never know. By the time I had taken his place – perfected the role, you might say – Bosa Sennen was dead. I didn't know that at the time, though. All I knew was that a ship very like her own had shown up at Wheel Strizzardy, and that the captain of that ship wanted to find Lagganvor. So I . . . offered myself up.'

'Is this what happened?' Lasling asked Adrana.

She nodded humbly. 'He fooled both of us. He knew the ship as if he'd already been aboard it. He knew how to break into Bosa's secret reservoir of quoins. There was no reason not to think that he was Lagganvor.'

'Adrana does herself too little credit,' said the man who now wished to be called Rackamore. 'I think she saw through me sooner than she realised. The ease with which I allowed myself to be "taken" by the Ness sisters, for instance. It was a misjudgement on my part, but perhaps a forgivable one.'

'I thought a little of it, but not enough,' Adrana said. 'My error. Things changed when I caught him attempting to signal his masters. I had two choices, then. I could disclose his true identity to my sister and hope her retribution didn't tear half the ship apart. Or I could accept that Lagganvor's communications were keeping us alive – we were being tracked and followed, not attacked – and that therefore I had to keep *him* alive, by protecting his nature from Fura, and permitting him to continue signalling. I took that course.'

'It was the right one,' Rackamore said. 'I was sincere in my pledge. So long as I kept signalling my masters, they had no need to attack. Eventually, I hoped to allow my masters to take the ship without very much bloodshed, with the sisters being spared.'

'Spared just so they could go to the noose?' Cossel asked.

'No. I believed that when the evidence was laid out, with the ship taken intact, and the availability of numerous supporting accounts, the sisters' crimes could be explained away as the consequences of psychological damage, inflicted directly or indirectly by Bosa Sennen. They would have to answer to some part of what they had done, but not the worst of it. After some period of interrogation and detention, I believed the sisters could expect to be rehabilitated. None of it would be pleasant, but it would be a lot better than dying. I . . . was persuasive. Was I not, Adrana?'

'You were too persuasive,' she answered. 'I believed you, because you believed yourself. And I made the mistake of thinking your masters could be relied upon to act within the bounds of decency.'

'Now you know otherwise,' Lasling said.

'Now we all know,' Adrana replied, nodding solemnly. 'Now we have no illusions. They murdered Werranwell, and they'll murder again to protect their precious interests. There is no sanctuary for any of us now; not until something changes. And for Fura's sake I'll do all I can to make that happen.'

'What about him?' Cossel asked, cocking her chin at Rackamore. 'Are we meant to forget that he's working for the other side?'

'Was,' Rackamore corrected. 'That was another life, Cossel – a chapter I've just closed. I didn't have to tell you any of this, did I?'

Meggery scratched at one of her scars.

'So why did you?'

'Because I'd rather you knew the truth. Because if one of you should decide to punish me, at least we'll both understand why. Because I'm tired of wearing another man's name. Tired of wearing another man's face, imperfect as the disguise always was. Adrana saw through it soon enough, anyway. She saw my brother in me, even after the osteomorphic process had done its work.'

'Your brother was a man of honour,' Adrana said.

Rackamore met her eyes with a mixture of sadness and fondness. Sadness for what had been lost, and could never be recovered, and fondness for the good memories he still treasured.

'He was.'

'He loved this little bubble of life we have around the Old Sun. He loved the worlds and dedicated his life to the idea of their preservation.'

'In his modest way.'

'From this point on, you'll be carrying that name as an outlaw. They'll paint you as an enemy of civilisation, not its defender. A vandal and a wrecker. They'll make you out to be everything your brother never was.'

'But at the end of it all,' Rackamore said, 'no matter where it takes me, I would know I had done the right thing. My brother would have expected no more or less from me, and I would have expected no more or less from Pol. I cannot bring Illyria back, or her father, but in joining you, in renouncing all that I was, I believe I can still repair some of the harm I did to him.' He looked down, as if the weight of attention on him was suddenly more than he could bear. 'In my own sullied conscience, at least.'

'That,' Lasling said, with the air of a man who had chosen to speak for his fellows, 'is about as much as any of us can hope for. You were right, Captain Ness: we needed to hear his story.'

'And now?' she asked.

'If everyone else is agreeable, I believe we may put the sorry business of Mister Lagganvor behind us. And Mister Rackamore?'

He looked up, caught – it seemed to Adrana – between hopefulness and some terrible fear that this might yet be a trap. 'Mister Las?'

'I should like to hear more of your brother's exploits, when you have the time. It seems he was a good captain; a man it would have been worth the trouble to know.'

'He was,' Adrana affirmed. 'He was kind to us; kind to all his crew, I think. And Brysca? I think it must have meant something that he kept that book you gave him.'

'He erased the dedication.'

'He kept the book. A man with one of the best libraries to be found on any ship, a man who had the wherewithal to buy or sell any book he chose – yet he always kept that one, and kept it close to him. I think you were forgiven long ago.'

*

During the ten minutes that it took Tindouf to go outside and collect what *could* be collected, the squadron maintained its firing action against *Revenger*. Nothing had yet hit the hull, and by the indications in the strain-gauges of the sail-control, which Paladin read as tickles and twitches in his own extended nervous system, the nearest piece of damage (save whatever had hit Prozor) was still a league out from the ship's vital centre, and no real impediment to their continued manoeuvrability. Should the attack continue at its present rate, though, mere attrition would eventually cripple them, for catchcloth was no less vulnerable to slug-shot than ordinary sail, and certainly no more durable. Of far greater concern to Fura was the fact that the shots were now coming in with too much precision to be the result of a few lucky hits while the enemies' guns swept the general area of space given away by her squawk.

They must have seen something in their scopes, Fura supposed: enough to confirm that they had approximately the right coordinates. It needn't have been much. There was ordinary sail bound up in the rigging, multitudinous square leagues of it, part of the disguise they had to wear to pass muster as an innocent ship, and if some fraction of that ordinary sail had thrown a flash back at the enemy, that would have been sufficient for a team of well-coordinated gun crews. Perhaps they had seen a porthole's light, or the reflected gleam from some part of the hull that (unavoidably) was not so dark as the rest. Or perhaps some stray light from the telegraphic box, as Prozor went out to signal the *Merry Mare.* That action had been well-meant, but there was no kind deed in the universe that could not have an undesired consequence.

She used that ten minutes profitably. Paladin had a chance to refine his calculations, and Fura finally conceded that it was time to relieve Surt from sighting duties. It was Ruther's turn to go up there now, and he was willing enough, especially as word filtered through about what had happened to Prozor, for he had come to consider her as much a colleague as his old friends on the *Merry Mare.* But Fura was almost minded not to allow him.

'I won't deny that I could use a pair of fresh young eyes up there,' she said, laying a hand on his shoulder. 'But you should understand that it's nearly as dangerous up in that little glass bubble as it is being outside.'

Ruther rubbed at the side of his face, as if he could still feel it being drawn into the mask of Stallis. 'When we start giving them back some of what they've already given us, you'll want to know about sail-flash, won't you?'

'I'd settle for a nice clean explosion as we take one of 'em out completely. You won't see anything at all when we're shooting, though: the sails will block your line of sight just as thoroughly as they screen our muzzle flashes from the enemy. But when we stop firing, and begin to turn away, you'll have your chance. Sail-flash, fire, overloaded muzzles – anything you can give me. They've taken from both of us, Ruther – help me make them pay.'

'I'm sorry about Prozor,' Ruther said.

She nodded sombrely. 'I know. So am I. But Stallis will be sorrier, mark my words.'

'Do you mean to kill him?'

Fura thought about her answer, and the promise she had made to herself.

'Eventually.'

She helped him into the sighting room, then watched as he

pumped the hydraulic lever to propel the room into its duty position. Surt was cold and exhausted, her eyes red with rubbing, her fingertips nearly blue. Fura wrapped her in a blanket, then made her drink something warm.

'In any fair service, you'd be due a period of rest about now. But I'm afraid I need your help checking the lagging on the guncoolers. We'll be running 'em as hot as they can take it, and it'll be better for all our nerves if they don't start springing too many leaks.'

Surt eyed her warily.

'Proz ain't come back in, has she.'

'No,' Fura said, surprising herself with her own bluntness. 'They killed her – either a slug, or some part of our damaged rigging doing it for 'em. Tindouf's gone out now to fetch her back in.' She was speaking calmly, matter-of-factly, about the death of a woman who had saved her life and become both friend and mentor, as well as the closest thing she had to an external conscience. There was, as yet, only a void where the shock and grief would soon take residence. She ought to have been appalled at her own coldness; numbed by how easily she was still functioning, with this vital part of her new life ripped cleanly away. Yet if she owed Prozor anything – and she owed her for many more things than she could begin to enumerate – it was to hold fast, to keep her nerve, and to do what needed to be done in this moment, for the sake of her ship and crew, for the sake of that hull-bound microcosmos that had always meant more to Prozor than all the worlds of the Congregation. Hold fast, and function, and give them a chance to avenge this death. And then – and only then – begin to let the emotions flood home. They would come, soon enough. 'We'll make them pay, Surt,' she said quietly, as if it was a sacred and solemn pledge.

'If you don't,' Surt said, 'I will.'

Something came over the speaker grille then. It sounded like a moan of wind, some breeze stirred between one part of the ship and the other. But in it was the whisper of a word, perhaps two, perhaps several.

Gone Ghostie. Gone Ghostie gubbins.

Neither Surt nor Fura were in any rush to acknowledge what they had heard, busying themselves with a hasty inspection of the cooling circuits: knocking wrenches against pipes, tapping pressure gauges until the dials twitched, listening for anything that was loose or dull-sounding, tightening bolts and brackets, and making sure all the lagging was as secure as it could be. It was good to make these sounds: they squeezed out any memory of the words they might or might not have heard over the intercom.

The pipes were cold now, but once the guns started running they would be working hard to dissipate excess heat from the induction solenoids, and the slightest leak would mean both a scalding spray of superheated steam into the cabin spaces and a loss of gun-cooling efficiency. The system was hardly in a state of neglectful disrepair – they had kept it well-maintained since the last action – but there was never a day when something did not need adjustment, and this last-minute check was prudent.

Nothing was seriously amiss. The coil-guns were loaded and energised, and all swivelling freely on their gimbals. Paladin fired a single test-shot from each muzzle, directed away from the enemy so there wasn't the slightest chance of detection, and then confirmed that all the guns and sail-control devices were under his authority and he was ready to make the turn.

Fura was on her way back to the control room, ready to give the final order, when a single loud *clang* sounded, and the entire ship shook. It was almost as if one of the coil-guns had gone off again, with the same recoil felt through the hull, but the timbre was not quite the same, nor the violence of the shaking. Fura stilled and tensed, waiting for the lungstuff to be sucked from her body, for she knew that they had been hit, and properly so. Only metal on metal, slug against hull, could account for that tooth-loosening din.

A second passed, and another, and she remained alive and breathing. There had been no pressure drop and the ship had not broken apart around her.

'A glancing shot, I believe,' Paladin said, when she reached the control room. 'The slug must have gone through our sails, lost the greater portion of its momentum, and been deflected against us.'

'Has it hurt us?'

'Nothing that I can detect.'

She opened the short-range squawk. 'Tindouf – are you safe?'

'I's just back in the lock, Miss Ness.' Tindouf was breathing heavily, barely able to get the words out. 'I saw a flash just as I was closing the door, and thoughts, that's the living end of me and my noggin, but we don'ts seem to have been too badly hit, does we?'

'We got off lightly this time, but if they saw that flash they'll have an even better idea of our position. There isn't time to lose. I'm starting our turn, and we'll send a full volley the moment we have that covering screen.'

'Very good, Miss Ness. I'll get out of my suit and keep an eye on the winches and ions.'

'Thank you, Tindouf.' She grimaced to herself. 'I meant to ask – did you find Prozor?'

'I founds her, yes. And I think it best she stays in the lateral lock for the time being, until we're done with this bit of business.'

'I'll attend to her, Tindouf – you've done more than enough.'

'Begging my pardon, Miss Ness, but I'll be the one to attend to her, if you don'ts mind. There are things a captain should do, and things a captain shouldn't have to, and this is one of them latter thingses.'

She nodded, closing the squawk, and thinking that she knew better than to argue with Tindouf.

'Doctor Eddralder, Merrix,' she said on the general intercom. 'Continue your search if you will, but be aware that we are about to turn, and there will be a load on the ship. Ruther, Surt: be ready.'

'Is it time?' Paladin asked.

She eyed the silent intercom, daring it to whisper back at her.

'It's time. Bring us round.'

22

As the launch slipped away from the *Merry Mare*, the emptiness in her head felt as cold and definite as a missing tooth.
It was good to have something else to think about, beyond the
implications of that absence. Adrana pressed her hands to the
controls, finding no difficulty in adjusting to them even though
they varied in layout to the launch on *Revenger*, and the craft as
a whole had somewhat different handling characteristics, being
markedly sluggish in turns and having a tendency to yaw when
under direct thrust. On a longer voyage she might have taken the
time to address the motor trim, but this was an extremely short
crossing and no such nicety was warranted. The *Merry Mare* was
holding station at ten leagues, just one of several sunjammers
parked within easy reach of the trailing hub. A person could *walk*
ten leagues. It was hardly worth the trouble of buckling in.

She had anyway, and Rackamore was buckled into the seat
behind her; the Clacker's box was wedged into the adjacent position and well-secured against bumps and vibrations. Adrana
had no idea whether such disturbances might affect the continued functioning of the effector-displacer device, and had no
inclination to take an unnecessary chance. Behind Rackamore
was Meggery, and that was the extent of their little expedition.
Lasling, Vouga and Cossel remained on the main ship, and
while she meant for them all to have some time in Trevenza,

her foremost consideration was the delivery of Tazaknakak. Once that was behind her and there was no longer any need to smuggle him through customs – the part she was most dreading – the launch could come and go as needed. It would not exactly be a question of Adrana relaxing – that was impossible so long as Fura's safety was in doubt – but she would at least have one less concern to trouble her.

'This Hasper Quell,' Rackamore said, leaning against his restraints. 'Tell me a little about the gentleman.'

Adrana glanced around, although she dared not take her eyes off the nearing world for more than a moment. 'All I know of him is what I got from Fura's account. He was known to Prozor – some cove she'd done useful business with in the past. They took a tram to his place: an underground establishment called Quell's Bar. I can't say if that's the official name or not.'

'If it has been around for more than a few months, it shouldn't be hard to find. And of Quell himself?'

'Described as a big man, dressed well. There was something about his eyes, too: I think they were artificial, but not nearly so neat and clever as your own.'

'Can you give me a little bit more to go on?'

'I wish I had the *True and Accurate Testimony* to hand. I think she said his eyes stuck out of his face.' Adrana nodded to herself. 'Yes, like chimneys. Two chimneys jutting out from his face. The Crawlies had done it to him – he'd gone to them for their medicine.'

'Sounds as if he oughtn't to be too hard to flush out,' Meggery said.

'We'll take no chances,' Rackamore said. 'Once we're safely inside, I'll scope out this Quell. There's an advantage in neither of us having met before; I'll be able to get a sense of the fellow before there's any hint of Ness sisters or Clackers entering the equation. If I am satisfied, I'll call you in and we'll proceed with the handover.'

'Any guarantee that I'm getting anything out of this?' Adrana asked.

'As things stand momentarily, none whatsoever. Equally, your only hope of any sort of recompense lies in the delivery of the Clacker. It's a pity we can't cut him into pieces and offer up one part as a down-payment.'

The proximity sweeper pinged to alert her to a rapidly closing approach with the spindleworld's hub. Adrana touched the retro-jets and brought the launch's speed down to five hundred spans per second. Traffic was thickening all around them now, with other rocket launches criss-crossing their path, exhaust plumes chalking hazy, blurring banners in the vacuum. There were sunjammers parked very close in, too, and not all of them had hauled in the entire mass of their sail, so – without the slightest qualm or compunction since everyone else was doing it – Adrana steered through the gaps in the rigging, not minding at all if her jets made the sails flutter and billow with her passing, for that was the price these captains had accepted by berthing so near to Trevenza as to barely need launches at all. Some of them, indeed, were docked up next to long, flexible passageways; tunnels that were leagues-long, yet could be traversed without a suit, while others were content to have their crews put on vacuum gear and hop from ship to world and back again. Some of these daring parties went about it alone, while others were roped together for safety, like garlands of tiny brass-coloured starfish. They often had their belongings with them, too. Once, Adrana had to steer hard as some preposterous mass of personal effects, detached from its owner, came tumbling hard at them: a huge string-bound agglomeration of cases, trunks, packing crates and wicker baskets, flapping its numerous luggage labels as if they were the attenuated remnants of wings.

They were through the worst of it by then, and down to a hundred spans per second. Adrana had seen the true shape of the spindleworld through telescopes, and then with her own eyes as they were closer in, but now that they were near to its tapering extremity the form of the world was distorted by perspective to an alarming degree. Giddiness washed over her. It seemed as if they had become a bird, circling the pinnacle of some enormous spire. Its height alone would have been dizzying, but to add to her discomfort the entire soaring structure was rotating as if on a spit, and the launch was obliged to match its course to that spin.

Yet it was not so difficult to land as she had feared, and bristling out from the tapering end were numerous platforms and berths, with ships of all kinds already docked. Because she had come down as close to the axis of rotation as was feasible, there was almost no sensation of gravity and it was an easy matter both to secure the launch and complete their disembarkation.

The three of them, and their luggage – which of course included the Clacker – moved into the pressurised part of the docks, where any semblance of order and process had been substituted for a free-floating riot of colour and confusion. There were crews, officials, lackeys and general layabouts everywhere Adrana looked. Remarkably, everyone seemed to know their allotted role in the chaos. The docks – this particular part, anyway – was a thimble-shaped enclosure very near to the end of the spindleworld. It had two main circular walls, one smaller than the other, and linking them was a single curving surface that corresponded to the spindleworld's outer shell. Partially filling this space was a sort of spidering treehouse made up of interconnected platforms linked by flimsy ladders, bridges, aerial tunnels and even flimsier ropeways. The platforms contained booths, offices, merchant stores, modest warehouses, bars, places of temporary detention and so on, all serving a weightless and none-too-fussy clientele and therefore constructed with minimal regard for any sensible frame of reference. Draped around this ramshackle framework was a prodigious mass of lightvine, emitting its own glow and augmented by the gaudier hues of neon advertising and many large flickerbox screens tuned to rolling news.

It was possible to float through the chamber, as many of those present were doing, hauling their luggage behind them as they paddled, flapped specially-woven coat-sleeves, or pulled themselves along by rope. There were even some quite bulky items of cargo being carefully steered through the treehouse's larger gaps, with rough-voiced stewards barking orders at every turn. Adrana took her party the long way around, using the aerial bridges and tunnels, for (given the several collisions she had already observed) this seemed the course least likely to risk jolting the Clacker.

'Look,' Rackamore said, touching her sleeve as they passed one of the flickerboxes.

'I do not wish to look.'

'You should. It's what any half-inquisitive captain would be doing right now, if she didn't have a personal stake in the matter.' Rackamore nodded past her, in the vague direction of a gambling den built on one of the platforms. 'Right now, every other wager being laid down in that place will concern the outcome of that battle.'

'You expect me to bet on my own sister's life?'

'No . . . although I'd insist if I felt our lives depended on it. But to not take even a passing interest in that news – that's the sort of thing that *will* mark you out as odd. And believe me, there will be eyes in here paying attention.'

She half-scowled – they were wearing their normal clothes, so there was nothing to mask her expression – but she forced her attention to the flickerbox and lingered for the time it took to absorb the news. The coverage was showing a pattern of flashes in a patch of space; the same loop of film playing over and over, a tickertape playing beneath it:

++ *major explosions seen near space engagement* ++ *unconfirmed reports of fugitive ship destroyed by Revenue Protection Squadron* ++ *awaiting word on identity and registration of destroyed craft* ++ *unofficial accounts strongly suggest demise of Bosa Sennen and her accomplices the Ness sisters* ++ *banks report modest rise in market confidence following presumed success of counter-piracy effort* ++

'They're wrong about one Ness sister,' Meggery said, pressing in close enough to whisper. 'Seems to me there's a fair chance they're wrong about both.'

'They are,' Adrana said. But merely saying it was not enough. It brought no deeper reassurance to her, and she noticed that Rackamore was in no rush to offer false consolation of his own. He knew, as she did, that the report might well be accurate. There was just no way to tell.

They pressed on, shepherding the Clacker's case between them, and treating it neither so cautiously as to draw attention, nor so incautiously as to risk jeopardising the contents. At the wider end of the chamber was a wide, smoky door, big enough for cargo to pass through, and as they worked their way nearer to it, glimpsing a distant vista of scuttling trams and dusty streets, so Adrana realised that it led directly into the greater interior of Trevenza Reach, and no additional customs or immigration formality lay between them and freedom. It was all so lackadaisical, yet – she reminded herself – precisely in keeping with the supposed spirit of the place, which did not consider itself bound by the laws and practices of other worlds.

They traversed a ladder, then a bridge, then a threadbare tunnel made out of ropes and stiffened hoops, and she passed another dozen flickerboxes on the way, and to each she gave due attention, neither too little nor too much, and swallowed back the emotions that were welling high in her throat, for they would have to wait.

'We are nearly there, Brysca.'

'Indeed we are. But I would not raise a celebratory glass until we are a good league into the place, and even then I should—'

'This way, if you please.'

It was a uniformed official, a man with a starched cap and mutton-chop whiskers, directing them to join a line of incomers threading along a bridge and into one of the offices.

'Why us, sir?' Adrana asked.

'Because it ain't your lucky day, Captain. Go along and play nicely and you'll be out and through before you know it.

'Less you've got something about you that you ought to have declared?'

'We haven't,' she said firmly.

'I believe we should oblige the gentleman,' Rackamore said.

'I believe you should, sir,' the official replied, before lifting a whistle to his lips, blowing hard into it and gesticulating wildly at some commotion going on a third of the way across the chamber. 'The other way around, you dolts! The other way around!'

Adrana, Rackamore and Meggery joined the line. It moved quite quickly, passing through one door in the office and out the other side. From what she could see, those leaving were free to continue through the large door and out into the spindleworld. The office was easily large enough to contain several detention rooms, however, so there was a good chance that some of the incomers were being pulled aside and examined more closely.

The Clacker's box would only withstand a cursory inspection if it were opened.

'I don't like it,' she whispered. 'Someone's got word of us.'

'If they had word of us,' Rackamore answered placidly, 'we would have been interdicted long before we docked. This is just some random inspection process. Remain calm, remember our story, and we shall have no difficulty.'

'He seems relaxed,' Meggery said.

'I am, dear Meggery – as are you. As are we all, for we have nothing to hide, and nothing to be irritated about except the extremely minor inconvenience of being slightly delayed.'

Adrana was the one now holding the Clacker's box. She could manage it easily enough on her own in weightlessness, but there was no escaping the fact that it felt ponderous. The effector-displacer mechanism was able to conceal the contents of the box quite effectively – at least when it functioned properly – but there was nothing it could do about the mass of the Clacker. The box felt like exactly what it was: a suitcase-sized container with a child-sized creature stuffed into it.

They passed into the office. The set-up inside was simple. The line of passengers divided into two, and on either side the incomers were being asked to show their credentials and present their luggage for inspection. Inspectors were flicking through documents and rummaging through open cases. It was all going on in near-weightlessness, and a general impression of barely-contained chaos was the order of the day. Papers fluttered loose; the contents of trunks spilled out in ragged and occasionally pungent profusion. Further along the office documents were being grudgingly re-stamped; goods were being rudely stuffed back into cases and baskets. Only once in a while was anyone ushered into one of the side rooms.

They were finished if that happened, Adrana knew. They had their stories and their faked-up paperwork, but none of it was pressure-tight. She could lie and lie about her dead father, the beloved Werranwell, but if someone went to the trouble of finding a photograph or engraving of the Ness sisters, she was as good as hanged.

'Next.'

A magnetic table had been arranged for the examination of personal effects. Rackamore and Meggery had some small items of luggage of their own. Adrana lofted the case onto the table, yet made no motion to open it until it was demanded of her. She did so in the full and certain expectation that the effector-displacer was bound to have failed, yet at the same time maintaining a steely and indifferent composure.

The catches sprung open. The lid hinged back.

The case was empty.

'Forgotten something, have you?' The questioner was a woman who looked as if she had been born with a suspicious, peevish look about her.

'No,' Adrana said.

'Then why is this case empty? Who travels with an empty case?'

Adrana shrugged off the question.

'What she means to say,' Meggery said, leaning in, 'is that it's empty for a reason. It's so we can go shopping. We've got a shopping list, see.'

'She doesn't need to see that,' Rackamore said.

Meggery had her sheet out anyway. 'It's all here. Suit parts, mostly. Return-valves, sealant tar, two standard-fitting neck rings, a set of accordion joints . . . a jumble of things, really, and it'll all fit back into this case. And then we'll be out of here, and you'll have our lovely quoins sitting in your treasury.'

'I hope you brought sufficient funds,' the inspector observed. 'You'll be surprised what your quoins won't buy you lately.'

'That's our problem, isn't it,' Adrana said.

'You've got a manner about you, Captain . . .' The inspector peered at one of her papers 'Werranwell. Are you the ones who wanted to bring a body with you?'

'That's us,' Rackamore said earnestly.

'Then where is the body?'

'Still on our ship, pending some enquiries that we will be making as soon as we've procured these items. But thank you for taking such an interest in our captain's sad and burdensome responsibility with respect to her dear father, whom we all held in such excellent esteem.'

The inspector budged the case against the magnetic surface. 'This feels very solid – very heavy for what it is.'

'It's a good case,' Adrana said.

'Her father wasn't one to skimp,' Rackamore offered. 'He always did like his luggage . . . on the solid and reliable side.'

The inspector fingered the case's side, gauging its thickness. Perhaps she thought there might be contraband packed into hidden compartments in the side. She glanced over to one of her colleagues. 'Tendry, come and look at this . . .'

The interior flickered. It was there for an instant: the Clacker's hibernation box. Adrana would have gladly accepted that she had imagined the apparition, except that she knew full well that it was real. Did the inspector catch a glimpse of it out of the corner of her eye? She turned back with some deepening suspicion on her face, as if she had taken off one mask and slipped on another, more exaggeratedly fashioned one. 'I thought . . .' she began.

'It's empty,' Adrana said. 'Empty and waiting to be filled with expensive things.' She bit on her lip. 'Look, I'm sorry if my tone was a little abrupt – I know you have a job to do. But I'm churned up by what my father asked of me, and I just want to get this shopping out of the way so that I can move onto *that* business. Believe me it's not something I look forward to.'

The other inspector, Tendry, had come over to the table. 'Are these the ones who got shot at, Pilliar?'

'There was something about a crew wanting to bury their captain, and something else about a ship getting in the way of that squadron – whether it's the same one, I couldn't say.'

'It is us,' Rackamore said, sighing heavily. 'We were hit – very badly. That's why we're in such straits now. We've lost our captain; our ship's mangled, and we need basic provisions just to begin repairing it. We're lucky in other regards, though.'

Pilliar looked doubtful. 'You call that luck?'

'I do, ma'am, compared to what's being done to that ship out there. We've all seen the flickerboxes – difficult to miss 'em. And I don't care what the official line is, or what the banks say about rising consumer confidence. That's butchery, plain and simple.'

'Siding with pirates now, are you?'

Adrana waved her hand into the interior to emphasise how empty the case was. 'He isn't. My father hated bauble-jumpers and the like, and I can tell you he had no love for Bosa Sennen and still less for anyone foolish to get swept up in her glamour. I despise those . . . what are they?'

'Ness sisters,' Rackamore said.

'Them. Yes, they can hang for all I care. But if we were attacked as an innocent party, then I shouldn't be at all surprised if that other ship were just as innocent. I pity them, frankly, and if there is to be no justice for them than I shall at least strive to do right by my crew, who have been very grievously wronged.'

The box flickered once. There was a shock of cold, a moment of clean severance. She lifted her hand from the interior, unhurriedly, and closed her fingers. Pilliar and Tendry were both still looking her in the eyes.

'We abide by Inter-Congregational law, Captain Werranwell,' Pilliar said sternly. 'We are no lawless outpost; no anarchic free-hold. That said . . .'

'If a crime has been committed,' Tendry said, 'and restitution needs to be made—'

'You may go about your affairs,' Pilliar said, finishing for him. She closed the case, even going so far as to do up the latches. 'I do agree with you about those Ness sisters, for what it's worth. Except in one regard.'

'Which would be?' Adrana asked, fighting to keep the edge from her voice.

'Hanging's too good for them. Too quick, too kind, by far.'

Adrana nodded dutifully. She was pressing her fingers into her palm and trying hard not to shake. 'I'm sure something will be arranged.'

*

Revenger started turning. It was not the gentle sort of course change that could be effected by modest alterations in the dispositions of individual sails, playing out over hours or even days, as a ship bent its course from one trajectory to another, within the limits of wind, momentum and orbital mechanics. This was a sudden and violent swinging around of the ship and its mass of sail, and it could only be initiated by a pulse of thrust from the hull, sent out at right angles to the vector between the centre of mass of the ship and the centre of area of its spread of sail. The ions were too feeble by far for such an operation: they would have needed hours to build up enough effect, and Fura could not wait that long. That left rockets, of one variety or another. There were some small steering jets fixed to the hull of *Revenger*, rarely used, but dependable, and powerful motors in the launch, and either of these would have provided the necessary impetus. But there was much too great a risk of their exhaust plumes being seen, counter to the entire point of the operation, so Fura arranged for the port-side lateral lock to be over-pressurised and then blown out in one sudden expulsion of lungstuff. It was wasteful of that resource, but they had ample reserves and slow suffocation was, she had to admit, something of a secondary concern compared to being shot out of space.

The lungstuff blew out in a silent and mostly invisible gasp, and that was all *Revenger* needed. The shove was the closest thing to gravity that the ship had experienced since rounding the swallower on their run to Wheel Strizzardy, and the momentary effects were not dissimilar. Fura had to grab onto furniture to stop herself being dashed against the cabin wall, and anything that had not been secured – and there was always something – went skittering sideways.

Then the shove was over and they were turning at a constant velocity. But the pull toward the cabin wall remained, and now there was a very definite sense of up and down, and one that was perpendicular to the usual axis of drift caused by the feeble acceleration of the normal sails and ion-thrust. It would have needed some getting used to, except that Fura had no intention of this being anything other than a temporary condition.

'Are we turning to plan, Paladin?'

'We are turning to plan, Miss Ness.'

They were whipping around now, like two stones on either end of a taut line of rope. One end was the hull; the other – many leagues distant – was the sails. They massed much less than the ship and its contents, but their cumulative mass was not insignificant, in total, and they had a counterbalancing influence, maintaining the tension on the rigging as their black surfaces were turned away from the main force of the Old Sun's invisible wind. Paladin had to adjust the rigging almost constantly, so that the sails were not blown into the ship – which would have resulted in irrevocable tangling chaos – but he had rehearsed the steps a million times in his mind, allowing for every possible vagary, and nothing happened that was beyond his capabilities of rapid adjustment and improvisation.

Despite the violence of that initial kick, they were still turning slowly; only twice the speed of a clock's minute hand. In half an hour, if they took no other action, they would be back facing in the same direction. In ten minutes, they would have the necessary cover for the coil-guns, and for another ten minutes beyond that point they could maintain as high a rate of fire as the guns could tolerate. Then the muzzles would be straining beyond their maximum deflection angles, and they would need to wait twenty minutes before starting the next volley.

There was no respite in that ten minutes. Shots from the other ships were tearing through the outer margins of their sails, and sometimes closer, and more than once another loose slug found its way to the hull, ricocheting harmlessly but serving as a forceful reminder of the damage that would be done if one of those shots came in straight and hard. Fura only took encouragement from this continuing attack, though. She would have found it very disheartening to be shown sudden clemency at this late stage, for she had none in herself to offer by way of reciprocation.

That ten minutes was as long as any she had endured. There were only so many times she could call Ruther and demand a report from the sighting room; only so many times she could ask Surt to confirm that no fresh leaks had sprung in the cooling circuits. Tindouf had left Prozor's remains in the main lock and was now assisting Paladin, dashing between sail-control stations and giving verbal reports on the strain-gauges and deflection dials, so that Paladin was not entirely reliant on his own instrumentation. Eddralder and Merrix, meanwhile, were still searching the ship, a task made no easier by the centrifugal effects of their turn, which rendered every space subtly unfamiliar. When the ten minutes were nearly up, and the guns ready, Fura requested that the physician and his daughter retire to the Kindness Room.

It was about to get noisy.

Revenger had two independent batteries of coil-guns dispersed along her port and starboard flanks, and while both could be fired at the same time, that was not desirable in the current situation due to the aiming constraints. It was better to optimise for one set of guns on one sweep, then twist the hull like a spindle for the second, twenty minutes later, and continue to alternate for as long as they maintained their turning motion. They could still do some damage with just one of those batteries, and since the cooling circuit could be dedicated in its entirety to one flank, rather than having to tend to both batteries, the cyclic fire rate could be increased.

'Miss Arafura?' Paladin said.

'Yes?'

'We are in position. I considered it wise that you should give the final order, just in case there are second thoughts.'

'Are they still shooting at us?'

'Indeed they are.'

'Then I have no second thoughts. Rip 'em open, Paladin. Maximum fire, and keep at it until we hit something. Then concentrate everything we've got on that one target until it bleeds.' She paused, flexed her three-fingered metal hand. 'I want blood.'

'In which case . . . I shall endeavour to provide.'

The grille whispered:

Spikey-spikey! Mash their noggins! Gubbins're coming! Gubbinsy-gubbinsy!

Before Fura could dwell on that – and wonder if Paladin detected it as well – the coil-guns went off. It was a beautiful, horrible sound, and for a moment or two it purged her mind of any shivery business. One muzzle, then the next, down the line in quick succession, like a loud receding drumroll. By the time the last gun sounded, the first one had been recharged and was ready to fire. The solenoids hummed and crackled. The coolant pumps sang at a higher and higher pitch as they worked to ferry rising heat from the guns. The cooling pipes creaked and clanged as they expanded against their stays. The guns swivelled slightly between rounds, compensating for *Revenger*'s angular motion. The automatic breech-loaders whirred and clunked, transferring the slugs from their snail-shell-shaped magazines into the warming bellies of the guns, where the induction coils were already glowing stove-hot.

Even at their present rate of fire, the guns were in no danger of exhausting the magazines. The slugs were thick, blunt-ended pencils of dense metal the size of a truncheon, and a single crate could hold hundreds. Bosa Sennen might have run light on fuel, and trusted her luck to one failing skull, but she had not skimped in the matter of slugs. There were still enough crates in the gun room stores to wage a small Inter-Congregational war.

The guns drummed and drummed, falling into a sort of lulling rhythm, and then quite abruptly stopped, and with a jolt Fura realised it was because they had reached the limit of their aiming-stops, and that the ten minutes was up. The pumps kept screaming, the pipes grumbling, but for every second that now passed the muzzles were getting cooler.

'Ruther, the sails should be clearing your line o' sight in the next couple of minutes. Surt, Tindouf: meet me by the magazines.'

They went from gun to gun, unpacking slugs from sawdust-filled crates, feeding the slugs into the letterbox-shaped slots in the magazines, until each was ready for the next volley. The guns breathed heat into their faces, spit boiled off their back-plates, and to touch any part of them was to risk an immediate blister. The smell of burning insulation and hot oil was enough to sting nose, throat and eyes. Surt coughed, wafting the worst of it away. Tindouf wrapped a rag around his fist and tightened a nut on one of the cooling pipes, where it plunged right into the gun's deepest vitals.

It took twenty minutes for *Revenger* to bring the opposing coil-guns to bear, and in all that time Ruther saw no indication that any of their shots had found a mark. Then the guns were roaring again, and the sails blocking his view, and it was all Fura could do to wait, and trust that her gambit had not been in error.

The volley proceeded. The guns performed as they were meant to, except for one magazine that jammed three minutes into the volley. Tindouf removed the service cover, jabbed the end of one of his clay pipes into the workings, and the magazine chugged back into life. A cooling line ruptured near the aft pair of guns, but Surt had been keeping an eye on a spitting joint and she managed to fix the leak before the guns began to over-heat too badly. The price for that was a badly scalded wrist, already blistering by the time Fura dispatched her to the Kindness Room.

The volley ended. Fura and Tindouf stuffed the magazines full again, Fura snatching back her flesh hand just as a rat sprang out of one of the slug crates. She caught the creature in her metal fingers and broke its back in a single squeeze, as thoughtlessly as if she were crushing a ball of waste paper.

'Captain?'

She was still holding the rat. 'Go ahead, Ruther.'

'The sails are moving out of my field of view. I thought you should know . . . what I mean is, I wouldn't be so quick to report this if we weren't in an engagement, but . . .'

'Spit it out, boy.'

'Sail-flash, Captain. I think I see sail-flash. Multiple, dishtributed . . . it *is* faint but I don't believe I'm imagining it.'

'I don't believe you're imagining it either.' She flashed a grin at Tindouf, who was sucking on his unlit pipe, watching thoughtfully. 'Can you give Paladin a set of coordinates, so we can concentrate fire on the next pass?'

'I can, Captain. Mishter Paladin: are you lishening?'

'I am always listening.'

'Here are the numbers.'

Fura tossed the rat back into the crate, where it twitched once and died.

23

Meggery stopped her when they were about a tenth of a league from the docks. They had come through the exit door in near-weightlessness, but in following one of the roads that radiated away from the hub, they had been moving further and further from the axis of rotation, and therefore into a slowly rising centrifugal influence. As their sense of weight gradually increased, so the Clacker's case began to need two of them to handle it. Now it was just about practical to walk, and the trees that lined the road were growing up from their bases with a definite sense of purpose and direction, rather than sprawling wildly like the lightvine in the first chamber. Buildings, too, were starting to conform to normal notions of architecture and function. They were quite low here, pressing in either side of the road, and consisted of a succession of fleapit hotels and bordellos, with the odd bar or bail-bond seller thrown in for good measure. Further on down the road, where it meandered into a thickening haze of dirt and dust, the buildings grew taller, more variegated, and merged into a seemingly impenetrable mass. Since they were at a higher vantage, they could see over a descending terrace of rooftops and gardens, all the way to little swatches of green and the glittering splashes of civic ponds and waterways, all the way to the widest point of the world and the gradual climb back up to the opposing pole, the better part of ten leagues away.

With clockwork regularity a radiance rose and fell across any given part of the interior. It was lulling and annoying in equal measure. The Old Sun's light streamed in through the long window panels that happened to be facing the right way at that moment, casting a dusky glow on the opposite part of the interior, but since the world was turning, it was not long before the pattern of light and shade shifted by one whole window's worth, and an area of city that had been illuminated a minute earlier now fell into shade. To counteract that effect, however imperfectly, a string of blue lights had been suspended the entire length of the spindleworld. They must have been some relic technology, for although the individual lights were bright – easily as luminous as a light-imp, and yet emitting a persistent flux – there were not nearly enough of them to be truly effective, and there were gaps in the string where lights must once have burned, yet had now failed or been stolen.

It was, despite these deficits of illumination, a stirring vista. Adrana had never seen a tract of concentrated civilisation to compare with it. Not even the layered cities of Mulgracen could match Trevenza Reach, for although there might have been more surface area inside Mulgracen, it was divided across many shells, and no comparable part of it had been visible at any one time.

And it was old. That was obvious at a glimpse. There were colourings and textures to the city, markers of fashion, industry and relative prosperity. She could see where districts had lapped over each other like competing tides, time and again. She could see where they had merged; where they had been cut off, isolated, orphaned. She could see where roads had been diverted, re-diverted, wound around each other or woven over and under each other like carpet strands, and she could see that these were processes that had been going on for lifetimes, for centuries, perhaps for as long as any Occupation; perhaps longer still. It was an old, old place, and it had seen countless travellers like herself, and not one atom of Trevenza Reach was in the least part interested in the story she had to tell. It had enough of its own; it would always have enough of its own.

It was nearly sufficient to take her mind off her finger.

'Show me,' Meggery said.

In the shade of a tram stop Adrana unwound her fist. The top two joints of her little finger, on her right hand, were missing. The finger had been snipped off, transmitted somewhere, destroyed, in the instant that the effector-displacement device failed.

'There does not seem to be bleeding,' Rackamore said.

Adrana stared down at the bloodless stub that had been her little finger. The skin around the stump had a frosted blue tinge. 'The cold – whatever it was – stopped it.'

'Can you bear the pain?' Meggery asked.

Adrana looked at her.

'Could you?'

Meggery did not answer for a moment. Then she opened her own hand and tugged off the metal finger she had been wearing since Fura's first negotiation with her crew. It was attached to her hand by a thin strap, which she quickly worked loose.

'I took this from your sister. You might want to wear it until Eddralder or some other physician can address that wound.'

Adrana took the metal finger. She slipped its open end over the stub, protecting it. Meggery helped her redo the strap, until the metal finger was secure.

'You did well, not to cry out,' Rackamore said. 'I did not see it in your face at all. I did not even realise anything had happened until Meggery said something.'

A tram was approaching. It would take them much further into Trevenza Reach. Adrana stooped down to gather the Clacker's case, and she said nothing.

*

'Spikey-spikey,' Fura whispered to herself, in the instant when she claimed the first kill of the engagement. There had been no warning of what was to come, no intimation that one of her slugs was about to find its mark, or with such demonstrable effectiveness.

A number of the slugs in the magazine had explosive or incendiary tips, but the majority relied on nothing more than kinetic energy to do their work. There was a chance of one of those slugs puncturing a hull, regardless of armour, and once inside what remained of that kinetic energy – some larger or smaller fraction – would expend itself on the crew and the instruments they needed for navigation and survival. Even with pressure-tight compartments, and redundancy of equipment and personnel, a ship could only take so much of that punishment, and might eventually break up. But for a ship to explode completely, and so visibly, could only mean that her slugs had hit a fuel tank or weapons store.

Fura wondered how it had been in those final seconds. One white moment of screaming terror, perhaps, as their ship ripped apart around them, and then a gasp that drew on vacuum, and then a rapid and painless shuttering of thought. She had no sympathy for Incer Stallis, and barely any for the men and women who served under him, for surely they knew of the crimes in which they were complicit. They had not stumbled into this service, innocent as lambs. But if she was content for them to die, she saw no reason why their deaths could not be relatively swift and painless. It was a minor courtesy and one she would not be at all sorry to have reciprocated, when it came to her own destruction.

'Do you have new orders?' Paladin asked, when news of the explosion had been thoroughly disseminated through the ship.

'Do they show any sign of ceasing their attack against us?' Fura asked, entirely rhetorically.

'None whatsoever.'

'Then we press on, Paladin. And we give no quarter.'

Spikey-fishy shoaly. Nogginsy-nogginsy! No quarter for pinkie-monkies!

The loss of one ship was undoubtedly an inconvenience to whoever was still coordinating that attack, but not enough to

343

call off the engagement. The slugs kept coming from the remaining four ships, their muzzles now glowing constantly, and although none had yet scored a direct hit on *Revenger*'s hull, other than glancing strikes, the toll on sails and rigging could not be neglected.

Revenger, meanwhile, maintained its strategy of turning and firing for ten minutes out of thirty, and they were coming round to the fourth volley now, and the business of recharging the magazines, and nursing the guns and their water pipes, was starting to feel like a second life for which she had always been preparing.

The enemies' tactic shifted.

Revenger was swept, and swept again, and again, each time with a higher energy and beam-focus.

'Theys going for broke now,' Tindouf said, sweating as he levered the lid off another crate of ammunition. 'They knows they'll give up their own positions, 'cause we've got 'em on the sweeper screen as well now, but they can hit us where it hurts now, and they will.'

'Attrition,' Fura said, nodding. Her fingers clacked on the metal slug-casings. 'We can play that game as well, though.'

'They knows that too, Miss Ness. They also thinks they can beat us at it, even being a ship down.'

The sweeps had caught them with the catchcloth averted, or else they might have fooled the enemy for a turn or more, but now there was no advantage at all in keeping the muzzles hidden, and so Fura instructed Paladin and Tindouf to nullify the rotation, as soon as the sails were orientated in the original direction. That kept their stern pointed at the enemy, which presented the minimum possible cross-section, but it also limited the aiming efficiency of the guns, which were hard against their swivel-stops. So Fura had Paladin and Tindouf work the sail-control gear to yaw the ship from port to starboard, presenting first one flank and then the next, yet never more than the minimum angle necessary to bring the guns to bear at their limits. It was still a case of one battery of guns discharging at a time, but now the intervals between volleys was much reduced, and the strain of loading the magazines and tending to the cooling circuits was much amplified.

There was a lull before the results of those sweeps were felt, and then the slugs began to arrive.

If the assaults that they had endured thus far had been a kiss of rain, this was a storm. For the first time shots struck directly against the hull, creating a sound as awful as their own guns. *Revenger* had very capable armour, and it was designed to deflect fire coming in at shallow angles, as was now the case, but it was far from impervious. Bosa Sennen had survived for as long as she had by never allowing herself to be out-gunned by a single ship, and generally having the better of two of them. She had depended on guile and intelligence to avoid ever being ambushed, and she had never been so foolish as to end up with an entire squadron on her back. Her personal streak of luck had run out when she met Fura, but for a time at least some residual part of it had seemed to adhere itself to the ship. That was over now, and Fura felt its passing as surely as if a spell of protection had been lifted from her shoulders.

They fired back, concentrating on the enemies' positions as betrayed by their own sweeper pulses, and when Ruther did not report an immediate improvement in their rate of hits, she issued a sweep of her own. Nothing was lost by that, and the resultant echoes gave Paladin a much better set of targets.

So it progressed, and when Ruther reported that the damage to the catchcloth sails was so severe, and so extensive in its spread, that he could see the purple and ruby lights of the Congregation twinkling back at him, through rents and fissures opened up by her own batteries, she felt only a grim and giddy astonishment at her own depths of commitment. Not to victory, for that condition was slipping ever further out of reach, but their delaying action would serve her sister well. She just hoped that Adrana was making the very best of the opportunity.

Ten minutes later she saw another of their ships go up. That left three, and she was just debating the chances of the enemy falling back with herself when Surt gave a scream, and both batteries of guns went into immediate shut-down.

'Paladin . . .' she began.

'The batteries have lost all cooling capability, Miss Arafura. One or two more shots from each muzzle would be enough to buckle the inductance rails, and three or more would burn-out the guns completely. Do you wish me to keep firing, knowing the risks?'

'Hold the guns,' she said.

She went back to find Surt, and found hot steam howling into the gun room that ran the length of the starboard batteries. Some major part of the cooling circuit had ruptured. Further down the room Surt was drifting and turning: a vague foetal form in the hot billowing mist, with her arms drawn up to shield her face. A loose hose was whiplashing around, spitting steam.

Fura was next to one of the valve-control wheels. She touched it with her palm and flinched at the heat. She got her metal hand on it instead and tugged at the spokes until the wheel groaned and began to dampen the superheated flow. But not enough; it was closing too slowly and her fingers kept slipping. Her metal hand had a better crush-grip than her flesh one, but it was much less good at clasping something slippery, like the slick hot spokes of the wheel. Grimacing against the pain that she knew was coming, she planted both hands on the wheel and levered herself against the wall, putting all her strength into the action.

The wheel turned and the leak stopped, the loose hose turning limp. Fura rushed to the still helpless Surt, screwing up her own eyes against the still-scalding steam. She got her arms around Surt and dragged her out of the worst of it, Surt shaking in her grip and gibbering as she tried to speak.

'Why've the guns . . . why've we . . .'

'The circuit failed,' Fura said, catching her own breath, and only then realising how close she herself was to exhaustion and perhaps unconsciousness. 'Can't cool 'em, and I'd rather save what few shots we've got left.'

Surt was still pressing her hands against her face. One of them was already bandaged, where she had scalded herself before, but that was nothing compared to the damage that had just been done. Where her skin showed, on her hands and the parts of her face not screened, angry white blisters were already starting to form.

'I'll get you to Eddralder,' Fura said. 'He'll put you right.'

Surt's voice had become a croak: 'Like he put Stram right?'

'Him and Merrix are all we have, Surt – we might as well put our faith in them. Did I tell you we got another of their ships?'

'Two down in a straight fight.' Surt coughed. 'Not too bad considering the green saps we started out as, is it?'

'Not too bad at all. And we might have started green, but none of us were saps.' She paused, glancing down at her own flesh hand, which was almost as badly blistered as Fura's. 'You did well – kept us in the game longer than we had any right to expect.'

'Can we sail?'

Fura sighed. 'It'll be a fine trick if we do, the state of our sails. But we're not finished, Surt, I promise you that.'

Merrix and Eddralder met her outside the Kindness Room and took Surt into their care. Merrix laid her on the same bed where they had treated Strambli, and gently prised Surt's fingers away from her face and eyes. The steam-blast had hit her hard, her skin already a mask of blisters, her eyes reduced to narrow, weeping slits. Merrix swapped a silent look with her father, then went to one of their medicine cabinets.

'Are we done with warring, for the moment?' Eddralder asked, preparing a syringe.

'We are. Whether warring's done with us, I can't say.' Fura clenched her scalded hand. 'We've a few shots left before we run the guns too hot. Tindouf and I will try to repair the cooling circuit, but it may take longer than we have. I expect Stallis – or whoever has taken over from him – to be on his way as soon as he decides we're crippled.'

Merrix was squeezing a salve onto her fingers. 'Did you hurt your own hand?'

'Never mind me,' Fura said.

*

The tram bounced and rattled along its rails. It nosed into a deepening, darkening canyon of top-heavy buildings. Overhead was a tangle of telegraph wires and washing lines and spindly connecting bridges. Adrana and Meggery stood in an open area near the rear doors, where they could wait with their luggage and not be in too much way of the other travellers. Rackamore had moved down the carriage and was shifting from one seat to the next, making low conversation with one person after another. He was asking after Quell's Bar, and doubtless framing his enquiries in a way that explained his interest in perfectly plausible terms.

Adrana's finger was throbbing. Worse than that, though, was the tingle she felt whenever someone's gaze fell on her for more than an instant. There were lots of people with newspapers on the tram, and the most recent editions were bound to mention the space battle. That, in turn, was guaranteed to lead to some rehashing of the case against the Ness sisters, with a high likelihood of pictorial accompaniment.

She had done what she could. Even to herself, she barely resembled the young woman who had first left Mazarile. It was not just in the shortness of her hair, the studied androgyny of her choices of clothing, the optically-neutral spectacles she kept perched on her nose. It was everything else. Space had chiselled something lean and hard out of her face. There were angles and edges in it that seemed to belong to some other reflection. When she dipped her chin enough for her eyes to show from behind the glasses, there was a distant, inscrutable chill in them. She nearly flinched from the force of her own regard. How could anyone mistake her for Adrana Ness?

Rackamore sidled back. He looked pleased with himself,

not quite concealing a smirk of self-amusement.

'How is that finger?'

'How is our destination?'

He steadied a hand against a support pillar. 'I believe I have the location. Fortuitously, we shall pass quite near to it if we remain on this line. But I am adamant that we should not rush in without due diligence.' He dropped his voice still further. 'I will . . . smoke out this gentleman. If there is anything about his circumstances that do not sit well with me, the Clacker remains in our possession.'

'I am not going back to the ship with him.'

'Nor would I advocate it. But we will proceed with the utmost caution, and only complete the exchange when we are entirely satisfied.'

Adrana nodded. She agreed with all that.

'Are there going to be muddleheads?'

'I think it is safest to assume the worst. But if Quell's reputation is sound, and he does indeed provide shelter to the likes of Tazaknakak, then the reach of the muddleheads cannot be absolute.' Rackamore lowered himself onto the upper edge of the case, taking the weight off his feet, exactly as any weary passenger would do.

'What are muddleheads?' Meggery asked.

'Be content that you do not already know.'

'That's not an answer.'

Rackamore searched the ceiling before responding. 'There are nefarious elements among our alien colleagues. They conduct illicit business either for or against the respectable interests of their peers. For much of this clandestine work, since they cannot easily move in our circles without immediate detection, they must make use of agents. Sometimes, they bribe or coerce monkeys such as ourselves. But that is not always possible or desirable. In such circumstances, the aliens make use of temporary agents called muddleheads. They are, in essence, re-animated corpses. They are stitched together from body parts, with the use of xenografting techniques to give them senses and powers of intellect in keeping with their tasks. They do not live long. That may be seen as a mercy, in some instances. It is said that some muddleheads wake up to a screaming realisation of what they are, making them quite uncontrollable.'

'I asked him about xenografting,' Adrana said, tilting her head to the case on which Rackamore now rested. 'I didn't use that term, since I wasn't aware of it, but the meaning of my enquiry can't have been lost on him. He became very evasive. He didn't want to dwell on the subject at all.'

'It *is* a sordid affair,' Rackamore said.

'There is more to it than that. If the muddleheads can be put together like walking jigsaws, a piece of monkey here, a piece of Crawly or Clacker there, then does it not speak of some underlying similarity at the biological level?'

Rackamore frowned slightly. 'I do not see how it can. We are derived from the collective genestock of the former eight worlds, which in turn speciated from Earth. The aliens have totally different lineages. Their histories go back long before the Sundering. They were navigating the stars before we had taken one step from our own little pebble, let alone given consideration to dismantling and reforging the old worlds.'

'That is what he said.'

'Then you have your answer – from, so to speak, the horse's mouth.'

'No, Brysca. I have *his* answer, which is not the same thing at all. I am not sure he wanted to think about what I was asking him. I think it cut against something he would much rather put to the back of his mind.'

'And I would have thought that you had questions enough already.' He shook his head in amused exasperation. 'You . . . sisters . . . are like house-guests who pick at every loose strand. Before long you've stripped the furniture and reduced the carpets and curtains to shreds. Meanwhile, some of us were just looking for somewhere comfortable to sit down. Not everything in life must be unravelled.'

'Your brother did not agree,' Adrana said.

'And I respect him for it, and intend to honour his memory as best I can. But I should also remind you that my brother ended up dead.'

*

Once the coil-guns gave up, Fura knew there was really not much more to be done. They had the stern and bow pieces, and fine weapons they were, and they could be run off a separate loop of the cooling circuit. These were short-range piercers, though, with high-penetrating power but a low cyclic rate, perfectly lethal against a close visible target, but not so effective against some distant speck eight thousand leagues away.

Fura would not waste their charges until she had something closer to shoot at. She was fully sure their time would come.

Paladin was trying to recover some limited manoeuvrability from the damaged sails, and for that he needed Tindouf, dispatching him from one sail-control station to the next, making adjustments and reporting on actual strain and torque readings, rather than the estimated parameters reaching the robot by indirect means. Fura could have used his help repairing the cooling leak, but she would not drag him from one essential task to assist with another, and so she gathered tools, swaddled her face with a towel, shielded her eyes behind goggles, and went back into the gun room. The steam was still there, but neither as hot nor as thick, and she found her way to the damage quite easily. The pipe had ruptured along an old welded seam, splitting along its length for at least half a span, and there was no possibility whatsoever of just wrapping a rag around it and hoping for the best.

'Captain, sir,' came Ruther's voice.

She kissed the back of her burned hand, which seemed to take a little of the sting out of it. 'I almost forgot you were still up there, boy. You may as well come back in now – we're past the point where visual observations will make any difference now.'

'They seem to have stopped shooting at us, from what I can see.'

'They think they've done enough to soften us up for a boarding. Very soon, I think, they'll be sending out the rocket launches. You should bring yourself back in before that happens.'

'Is everything all right down in the ship, Captain?'

'Our sails are shredded like a pair of old stockings, Surt got a blast of steam in her face, and we can't operate the main coiller batteries beyond another few shots.' From her bundle of tools she picked out a sheet of thin lead, long enough to span the fissure in the pipe. 'Other than that, we're doing quite handsomely. Are you sorry you signed up for this ship, Ruther?'

'I wasn't too sure I had a choice about it, Captain.'

She smiled to herself. 'Perhaps you didn't.'

'Anyway, I'm not sorry,' Ruther said, emboldened. 'I would still like to see some harm done to that man who started all this off, and I think I have a better chance of it here than on the *Merry Mare*, fine ship though she is.'

Fura positioned the lead over the damaged pipe and worked her way along it, folding it around the pipe's circumference like a sleeve. 'That man might have been on one of the two ships we just destroyed.'

'I have a feeling he is the sort who survives even when the men and women around him are dying.'

'Then we're of the same opinion, Ruther. I took you for my crew, though, and I don't feel at all happy about you being lumped in with the rest of us. You had nothing to do with the ships I burned on the way to and from Wheel Strizzardy, or the upset we created with the quoins.' With the lead in place, rolled around the pipe as best she could, Fura dug out three ratcheting clips to tighten the repair at the ends and middle, which was the best she could do. Any tendency for her fingers to tremble was entirely absent as she engaged in this task, which she saw as aligning entirely with the glowy's need for self-preservation. 'While there is time, I'm going to write a letter, explaining your innocence, and that you should be considered as a hostage. If you go along with that story, they'll treat you fairly.'

'I wouldn't waste your ink, Captain. They won't treat any of us fairly, and especially not those of who were witness to the attack against Captain Werranwell. Please don't write that letter. I'd rather you spent your time trying to get the guns working.'

She pushed back to inspect her repair. It would be far from steam-tight, but if it could contain some of the pressure, that might allow the guns to run for a little longer. But she dared not push her luck by exposing it to pressure until the very last moment.

'Ruther – I'd still like you to come in. It'll be you, me and Tindouf against any boarders, and I think it would help if you had a crossbow in your hand.'

She heard the grunt of effort as he worked the lever that pulled the sighting room back into the hull. She gave her makeshift work one last glance, then went to dig out the close-action weapons.

*

The line they were on passed within a block of Quell's Bar, but on the other side of a block of tall buildings that screened any view of the establishment itself. To be on the safe side, in case there were spotters loitering around the area of the bar, Rackamore had them stay on for one additional stop. This brought them to the edge of a civic garden surrounded with high railings: one of the patches of green Adrana had spied from the higher vantage of the hub.

They got out, lowering the Clacker's box gently to the kerb, then went as a party through the main gates and into the garden. Inside there were winding stone paths, some lily ponds, some ornamental bridges, and a gently rusting bandstand now whitened by an accumulation of pigeon droppings. Dotted around the paths and ponds, half consumed in vinery, were odd, blocky statues that Adrana supposed to be the work of some enthusiastic but misguided local artist.

Near the middle of the park, Rackamore spied a teahouse with metal chairs and tables set out under umbrellas, and suggested that this would be a suitable place for Adrana and Meggery to wait while he investigated Quell. Adrana agreed. They would not be the only ones keeping an eye on their luggage either, as some of the tables were already occupied by travellers who had either just checked out of hotels, or were waiting for rooms to be prepared.

They took a table under one of the umbrellas, and Rackamore came back with a tray of coffees, and some small iced cakes with miniature flags on them. He made a wincing gesture with his lips. 'With what that cost me, dear companions, you could have dined out in Mazarile for a whole week.'

Adrana sipped her coffee, her new metal finger clinking against the china. 'You exaggerate.'

'Only slightly. No one knows quite how to value a quoin any more, so what is the rational response? Rampant inflation.' He swigged his coffee in one slurp, wolfed down a cake, then rose from the table. 'I shall be about an hour. By all means treat yourselves, but try not to spend our entire reserves before I return.'

On some impulse, Adrana reached out and touched his sleeve. 'Be careful, Brysca.'

He lowered his voice and smiled reassuringly. 'I have no intention of being anything other than careful. And I won't take chances. Far too much is at stake.'

With the Clacker's box wedged under the table with the rest of their luggage, Adrana watched Rackamore walk away and around the curve of one of the ponds. As he stepped past one of the vine-shrouded statues, she had the faint intimation that it moved, responding to his presence. Yet the motion was so subtle, and so transient, that she supposed it could as easily have been suggested by the cyclical play of light from the window panels.

'My bones ache,' Meggery said.

'So do mine. But it isn't so long since I was on Mulgracen, and we've visited some baubles with swallowers in them as well. Has it been a while since you were on a world?'

'A year.' She thought on her answer for a second. 'No, more like two. Two years of mostly floating around, except for the times we were being shot at.'

'You adapt well, all the same.' They had both taken bone and muscle-strengthening remedies before arriving, as well as drugs to help with the altered equilibrium of the inner ear, but all of these potions had side-effects of their own, including the ache Meggery now reported. 'Perhaps there will come a day when each of us finds our home, and no longer needs to keep adjusting and aching.'

'Are you close to that day?'

'Closer than when I left Mazarile. But not close. There is still a great deal left to see and do, Meggery. For both of us, I think.'

Meggery looked to the gate, where Rackamore had vanished. 'I thought of killing him, when he disclosed his true nature.'

Adrana smiled thinly. 'So did I, and I doubt you were the only one.'

'I just thought you ought to know.'

A breeze stirred cake-crumbs across their table. Adrana flicked them off for the sparrows down on the ground. 'What prevented you?'

'I didn't say I was about to do it, just that it crossed my mind. When he spoke of his brother, though, I thought I could see the pain in him.' Meggery scratched at one of her tattoos. 'I believed him. Does that make me foolish?'

'If it does, it makes me equally culpable. I chose to believe him as well, even knowing that he lies as easily as he breathes. He could be playing us – I am well aware of that possibility – but I should rather place my faith in his sincerity. And if I had not already known his brother . . .'

'Did you like him?'

'Pol Rackamore? He had my admiration. I would not say he was likeable in the sense that I think you mean. He was intensely vain, intensely self-satisfied, intensely certain that he was a little better than the rest of us. But he was courageous, he was honest, he was a very capable captain, and I think his interest in quoins was entirely a means to an end. They had no lustre in his eyes, except as a facilitator for his intellectual pursuits.'

'He liked digging into things, just like you.'

'Perhaps a little of that rubbed off on me, Meggery. And on my sister as well. The outcome of that is the two of us sitting here with an alien jammed under our table, and scarcely any idea of what the trouble of bringing him here will mean for us.'

Meggery bit into one of the prettily coloured cakes.

'I don't know what answers you're hoping for.'

'Are you not in the least bit curious?'

'Oh, I am. More than a bit; I'm curious how I'll get out of this mess, of associating with you, and all that comes with it.' Meggery smiled, for she meant no harm by her statement, which was no more than a bald summary of the facts. 'I'm curious as to whether I'll stay with this crew or end up with another one. I'm curious as to whether my luck will ever turn – curious to know how it feels to sail away from a bauble knowing your life's just changed for the better. Curious to know what baubles are out there that we ain't found yet, and what might be in 'em. That enough curiosity for you?'

'For most of us, I do not doubt.'

'But not for you. Not for Adrana . . .' She trailed off without mentioning the name 'Ness', for although there were no eavesdroppers close to their table, a name alone could carry very well on an obliging breeze.

'It was enough,' Adrana admitted. 'Until Rackamore set my curiosity running. Oh, it was there in some germinal form before him. As children, we haunted the Museum of History. Stared in wonderment at that great long tableaux of the Thirteen Occupations, and the immense intervals of black between them.'

'We never had a Museum of History.'

'I thought most worlds had such places.'

'Most nice worlds, I think you mean. But I've seen those

pictures, too, and studied my Occupations.' Meggery fed one of the sparrows. 'We do have to know something to work ions, contrary to opinion.'

'I don't doubt it. Did you ever pause to wonder why those intervals of blackness exist, though? Or wonder if there will be Occupations after our own?'

'So long as this Occupation lasts a bit longer – long enough to see me out – why would I lose sleep over it? These scars go all the way through me, so there won't be any children to worry about. And, of course, the Occupations'll carry on after ours. There's nothing so special about us that says we have to be the last.'

'The intervals are increasing,' Adrana said, in a low and studious tone. 'Rackamore was aware of this. He knew that whatever instigating event causes each Occupation, it must be becoming rarer. So it is possible that there will one day be an Occupation that ends, and nothing ever comes after it. There's something deeper, though. Bosa ...' She paused, dropped her voice. 'She found some old scholarship that points to something very unusual. The known Occupations are all spaced by intervals of time that are exact multiples of twenty-two thousand years. Or as exact as anyone can determine, given how foggy the beginnings and ends of Occupations tend to be. But the pattern is no illusion. There's a broken regularity to the Occupations. It's as if there ought to be many more of them, spaced exactly twenty-two thousand years apart, yet for some reason the majority of these hypothetical Occupations never take root. It's as if a gardener planted a long line of flowers, each an exact distance apart, but only one in thirty-three of them ever blossomed. Those blossoms are the history we know – the Thirteen Occupations. But there are four hundred and forty Occupations that never happened.'

Meggery looked mystified. She swirled the remainder of her coffee. 'You're concerning yourselves with things that *didn't* happen?'

'There is a dark puzzle in those Shadow Occupations,

Meggery. If we are to understand why the known Occupations are becoming rarer – spaced-out from each other at increasing intervals – then we must understand the mechanism behind all the Occupations, including those that did not catch light.'

Meggery gave the Clacker's box a gentle nudge. 'And you think . . . he . . . is going to give you the answer?'

'He may not have all the answers. Perhaps no one does. I think there may be one question concerning the missing Occupations, and another concerning the ends of the thirteen we know about, and they may be answerable in different degrees. Perhaps there are no answers that will explain everything to our satisfaction. But I am minded to think he knows more than the rest of us, and that is a beginning.'

Meggery looked around with a vague focus in her eyes. Her implicit gaze took in the teahouse, the park, the city, the spindleworld, out to the other worlds and the whole mad glory of the Congregation.

'You want to stop this Occupation from ending, don't you?'

'What we have is imperfect, Meggery. This little civilisation of ours is squalid in places, unjust in others. It is constructed to a large degree upon a foundation of greed and inequality. But it is not beyond salvation, and just as crucially it is all we have. There are fine things about it, too. There are lovely worlds, more than you or I will ever see in our lifetimes. There are beautiful cities and fabulous ruins. If we are feeling adventurous, there are baubles. If we are not, there are teahouses and cakes, and I should not care to place one above the other. I wish to have both things in my life: adventure and comfort. I should like to know men like Lasling, who have seen and done terrible and courageous things, and lived to laugh about them. Men like Rackamore, too, and women like yourself, an ion-engineer on a ship deserving much better fortune than it has seen. But I should also have liked to have known men like my father, who was mistaken in the application of his kindness, but kind nonetheless. And my mother, who never had any desire to see more than one world, but loved music and dancing and cold evenings when it was nice to draw the curtains and be warm inside.'

'You want too many things.'

'I do, and I make no apology for it. Principally, though, I want to do all in my capacity to prevent this Occupation from ending. And I do not care if that ending is ten years away or a thousand: the thought of it wounds me just as powerfully.'

'Others must have thought the same.'

Adrana nodded with sadness and humility, for the same observation had not escaped her. 'Not just in this Occupation, but in earlier ones. There must always have been people who understood that things were not permanent. They must have taken action, too. And yet – as the record informs us – whatever they tried was not sufficient.'

'Best pray, then,' Meggery said, 'that whatever action they took wasn't the thing that ended 'em.'

24

Fura had about thirty minutes until the rocket launches arrived. They were crossing quickly, going hard on the jets, and making no effort to disguise their approach.

She had done all she could with the guns, and between them Tindouf and Paladin had got the best out of the sails. They had the wind in them, and *Revenger* was limping along, unmistakably still under some pitiful semblance of control. Fura had considered playing dead, letting her ship drift like a hulk, even spilling some lungstuff out of the locks for extra effect, but she had an intuition that the squadron would be expecting exactly that sort of feint, and was unlikely to be fooled by it. It was better to give them a version of the truth, by attempting to run, and like a confidence trickster use that one show of sincerity to lull them into accepting a lie of a different kind.

Ruther had come in from the sighting room, and while Tindouf nursed sails and ions she and the boy scuttled from magazine to magazine, recharging them with slugs. If it was wasted work, so be it. But while she had a choice, she would sooner the guns cooked than ran out of ammunition.

With that done, the launches were less than fifteen minutes out. Had Ruther still been in the sighting room, he would have had a fine view of them, as they flipped their tails around to begin decelerating. There was no need for visual acquisition just yet, though. The launches, and the ships they had come from, were still using their sweepers, and that meant that Paladin was never in doubt of their positions and speeds.

'Keep our muzzles averted until the last moment,' Fura warned him. 'I want them to believe our guns are roasted, and they'll only accept that if we don't show any signs of aiming and tracking. We'll get one good shot off from the stern piece, and that'd better count, because Ruther and I won't have time to reload. Select the target that you think you have the best chance with, and reserve the batteries for the rest. Those launches will have deflection armour, but there's only so much they can soak up.'

'I do not think it would be advisable to attempt any sort of engagement until they are within six leagues of us.'

'Make it two leagues, just to be on the safe side. I want them to feel that it would have been madness for us not to have shot them by then, unless we didn't have the means.'

'I think it likely that you will achieve the desired effect.'

While there was time, she went to the Kindness Room, where Eddralder and his daughter were still tending to Surt. The room reeked of powerful salves, and they had bandaged her hands and almost the whole of the top part of her face, from nose to forehead.

'Captain?' Surt asked, tilting her head as she sensed Fura's presence. 'We're not done yet, are we? Only I ain't heard a pop out of the guns since you brought me here. Is there anything I can do to help? Doctor Eddralder says the steam didn't get me as bad as it looked, and I'll be all right if I keep my lamps bandaged for a day or two. I reckon I can still load a magazine, even if I mightn't be the fastest about it.'

'I said she needed care and rest, and then – only then – she might make a slow recovery, with some scarring and the possibility of some loss of sight in one eye.'

Surt's bandaged head nodded eagerly. 'Like he said, right as rain. Did we spike a few more of their pretty little ships, Cap'n?'

Fura addressed all three of them. 'Launches are on their way, and I expect 'em to contain fully-armed boarding parties. They'll be looking for the Ness sisters in particular, and unfortunately . . .' She flexed her arm. 'I'll be a *little* difficult to mistake. They'll take me alive if they can, but there won't be too much incentive for them to extend the rest of you the same courtesy.'

'Are you proposing we fight?' Merrix asked.

'No; I'm proposing you take the launch. Go and put on your suits as a precaution. I'll offer myself as a hostage – make it clear that I'm remaining on the ship, and that I'll surrender myself in exchange for you being granted unobstructed passage to Trevenza Reach.'

Eddralder shook his head once. 'Out of the question. Neither of us knows how to operate a rocket.'

'No, but Surt has an idea of the controls and she can get you to safety if you work together. Take her to the launch now, and I'll get on the squawk. You can be a hundred leagues clear of us before I open fire on them.'

'Then the guns aren't cooked!' Surt said delightedly.

'Toasty,' Fura said, smiling into Surt's bandages. 'But not cooked. I think I fixed the leak enough for us to squeeze off a few more slugs. But I want you well away before that happens. They won't bother with you if they know I'm still inside the ship, and I'll give them all the evidence they need.'

'How will we dock?' Eddralder asked. 'I can see that leaving *Revenger* might not be too difficult, if Surt tells us which controls to operate, but landing on another world . . .'

'The thing about staying alive,' Fura said, 'is that it doesn't pay to think more than one or two steps ahead. You worry about docking when you don't have to worry about getting sliced up by squadron men.'

'We're not going,' Merrix said firmly.

Eddralder looked at his daughter. 'You've decided, have you?'

'Someone has to. I'm not afraid to take my chances in that launch, not after what we've already been through, but I won't abandon this ship as if I'm just another passenger. I'm part of this crew, and I've spent enough time washing pans or shivering in the sighting room to prove it. I won't cut and run.'

'This isn't about cutting and running,' Fura said. 'It's about me preserving as much of my crew as I can, so we get to fight another day.'

'There'll be no other day, if we leave you here,' Merrix said. 'And I won't abandon the Kindness Room. This is a place of healing, not fighting. I don't care what horrors Bosa Sennen put it to: we've made it into something better than that, and I'm proud of it. And if those squadron men won't respect us for what we are, then nothing's worth living for anyway.'

'Talk some sense into her,' Fura said, pleading with Eddralder.

'There's no need,' he said, sighing. 'She has all the sense she needs. Her mother did far too good a job of instilling it in her.'

'It wasn't just Mother,' Merrix said. 'Did you ever turn away from helping people in Wheel Strizzardy?'

'Only once.'

'To save me. When you had no alternative, and when to remain was to condemn us both. Only then. Other than that, you never left your station as long as one person needed your help. And treating those people in the infirmary wasn't enough for you. You had to walk out into the city and dispense medicine and care, even though Glimmery hated you for it.'

'We have no patients now, besides Surt.'

'Surt's no safer aboard that launch than she is here. And you're forgetting: we still have one other patient to consider, even if we don't know what's happened to her.'

'Do you want me to order her to leave?' Fura said, addressing Eddralder.

'For my daughter's sake, I might.'

'And yours?'

'I think she is right. We have made something here. If there is still decency to be found anywhere in the Congregation, then we hold our ground. Besides ... Surt remains in our care. I haven't discharged her, and I wasn't ready to.'

Surt dabbed at her bandages.

'I ain't worth this much fuss, trust me.'

'They're going to try to take this ship,' Fura said. 'They're going to try to take *me*. I'm not going to let them have either of those things. There'll be . . . trouble. I'd face it on my own, if I had to, and there's a part of me that wishes you were all on that launch, so at least I wouldn't have your deaths on my conscience, and some of you might even put in a good word for me when they start making me out to be something I wasn't. But there's another part . . .' She creased her face. 'I ain't one to think of us as a family . . .'

'Good,' Surt said. 'I might need a puke-bag if you did.'

'What we are is a crew, and not a bad one. Family's a mess. You don't get to choose your family. But you do get to choose who you ship with, and who you trust to look after your back in a bauble, or a battle. And while I'm sorry that it's come to this, and that there's a good chance none of us will see tomorrow, I'm not sorry to have you all with me.' She settled her eyes on the doctor's daughter. 'Merrix: thank you. And now, if you don't mind, I'm going to see what I can do about those launches.'

'Can I help with anything at all?' Surt asked.

'The magazines are charged, and I'm not so sure it'd be too good an idea to put a crossbow in your hands. But there *is* something, I suppose. I don't dare turn on the cooling circuit until just before we need it, because I don't think it'll hold for very long.'

'I can do that.'

'Good – with the doctor's permission, I'll show you to the valve-wheel.'

'I don't need his say-so,' Surt said, 'and I definitely don't need you to hold my hand between here and the gun room. You just tell me when you want that valve opened.'

*

'I've met our man Quell,' Rackamore said, rejoining them under the umbrella after he had been away for an hour. 'I say "met". I watched him come and go from his establishment once or twice, then ventured downstairs and justified my presence with a small but tolerably well-mixed beverage. I was not alone, and other drinkers came and went the whole while, so I . . .' He trailed off, glancing over his shoulder. 'Is that statue following me?'

'I don't think it's a statue,' Adrana said. 'I've been looking at them more closely and I think they're old robots. I remember a garden a little like this in Mazarile. I'd forgotten all about it until now. We used to visit it when the boating lake was closed, but I never really liked it.'

'Why would they make a park for old robots?' Meggery asked.

'It was better than having them wander around the city getting into trouble. Sometimes when robots get very old and confused their families throw them out into the streets, rather than pay to have them scrapped. At least here they get to tell stories to children and fade away peacefully.'

'That one is definitely still moving,' Rackamore said. The statue was a slow-shuffling, vine-shrouded apparition of rough-edged rectangular forms, like a sculptor's first go at shaping a block of stone.

'I suppose it must be quite new to the park,' Adrana replied, observing the stone robot through lowered spectacles. 'The ones that have been here a long time must end up frozen in place.'

'Your Paladin would deserve better than this.'

'He would. So would any robot of the Twelfth Occupation, especially one who remembered the Last Rains of Sestramor. Paladin was a loyal friend to our kind. But we do not even know that Paladin, or any part of our ship, still exists.'

He looked remorseful.

'I didn't mean to remind you.'

'There hasn't been more than a second when I haven't been thinking of her.' She nodded across to another table. 'I dare not glance at the newspaper that man is reading, in case his edition carries some late report I'd rather not see. And yet at the same time I must know. The *not* knowing is intolerable.'

'When we have discharged our obligation to our guest, we could sail back to the engagement.'

'I want it with all my heart. Just to put one slug into one of those ships . . . but you know as well as I do that it would be suicide. If those squadron ships have already picked apart our former vessel, there would be no hope whatsoever for the *Merry Mare*. Besides, we have not discharged that obligation. And until you tell us what happened, I am no wiser as to our prospects of success.'

Rackamore brightened, leaning in. 'I think our prospects are excellent. All the indications are that Quell is the man we seek, and that he will be receptive to the plight of our guest. He is sympathetic to his kind, and . . .'

'You already spoke to him?' Adrana asked, startled. 'That wasn't the idea, Brysca. You were meant to sound him out, not strike up a friendship.'

'Hard to plumb a man from looks alone, dear Captain. While I was ordering that tolerably well-mixed beverage I mentioned . . .' He swivelled around in his seat and made a shoo-ing gesture to the stone robot, which was slowly crunching across the gravel. 'Clear off, dear fellow! You've had thousands of years of companionship – now accept your fate!'

'Be kind to it,' Adrana said, thinking of the many unkindnesses she had visited upon Paladin. 'And be kind to me, while you're at it, by explaining how you didn't expose our cover at the first opportunity.'

'Rest assured that what passed between us was only the most superficial sort of small-talk, conducted between the ordering and serving of said beverage . . .'

'And what did you tell him, in the course of this small-talk?'

'I said I was new in, and looking up a friend whom I thought might have been a patron of Quell's Bar.' He made a flustered, dismissive gesture. 'All of it was invented, including the name. Quell knew nothing of my phantom friend, but he was helpful enough to suggest one or two other establishments I might try.'

'And this is what counts as getting a sense of his trustworthiness?'

'Your question is severely prejudicial.' He gave her a sharp reproving glare. 'Permit me to continue. I then made the mildest possible allusion to the aliens. When I paid for my drink . . .'

'The said beverage,' Meggery put in.

Rackamore nodded curtly. 'Yes. I slid across a quoin and remarked that if those filthy aliens were going to keep on meddling with our money, we'd all be sipping dish-water before long.' He looked suddenly defensive. 'It was a gambit, a sounding shot.'

'How did he respond?' Adrana asked.

'He did not reprimand me for voicing my opinion, but it was clear enough from his demeanour that I had touched a nerve, and a disagreeable one. His manner became brusque. He passed me my change – what little of it there was – and turned away without any further comment. I had offended him with my criticism of the aliens.'

'You'd have offended anyone,' Meggery said.

'Still, it validates our hypothesis that this is a man who is sympathetically disposed to the aliens. Perhaps he does not care for their institutional influence in our affairs, but he has no dislike for their kind on an individual basis.'

'We shall need more reassurance than that,' Adrana said.

'He was also Quell, as you described him.' Rackamore gestured to his own face. 'The eyes like chimneys, jutting out. Very crude work, but there's no doubt in my mind that it was authentic.'

'You scooped out your own eye to imitate another man,' Adrana pointed out.

'But I would have thought twice about going to such lengths as to look like Quell. Who would accept such work, unless they were already blind?'

'So,' Meggery said. 'He fits the picture, he runs a bar, and he bristled when you spoke out of turn against the aliens. Is that enough for us to trust him with his Clackship?'

'It has to be,' Rackamore said. 'But that does not mean that we rush into things without due caution. With your permission, I propose the following. We will move to within easy reach of the bar. I will make a direct overture to Quell, and quickly establish the parameters of his cooperation. If there are no complications, the Clacker may be brought down directly.'

'What if there are spotters or muddleheads near the bar, waiting for us to try to reach Quell?' Adrana asked.

'I saw nothing to alarm me, and I sent my eye aloft to scout the back alleys and rooftops. Remember that the Clacker's enemies have no reason to suppose that he is not still aboard *Revenger*. They won't be expecting us.'

Adrana nodded. She had misgivings, very considerable ones, but nothing to raise by way of a counter-proposal. This part of her deal with the Clacker was always going to involve a certain leap of faith, and the fact that the moment was nearly upon her did not mean that she had thought of any better way to complete the transaction.

'Usually when you make an exchange, you get something in return. All we have are some vague promises about information.'

Rackamore reached for the Clacker's box and dragged it from under the table. 'Reflect on this, dear Captain. His enemies want him dead for a reason. If the information he has wasn't valuable or dangerous, they wouldn't have sent the muddleheads after him in the first place. And if he is worth that much trouble to them, he is worth at least as much to us – and perhaps very much more.'

'What if he won't talk?'

'Oh, he will. He will blab his heart out. I am supremely confident of that.'

*

By the time Surt called up to say that she was in position and waiting on the order, Fura was in her quarters, sitting at her desk with Paladin's red hemisphere spilling its light across her papers and journals. She did not have access to the sweeper, but there was nothing to be gained from that now, and no part in the firing of the guns that was not best delegated to her robot.

She was wearing most of her vacuum suit by then, the one in which the sleeve had been modified to leave her metal hand unencumbered, which would save a lot of words if she needed to identify herself, and her helmet was wedged onto the desk between a pair of paperweights, its empty faceplate staring back at her with a dark inscrutability.

'Launches at twelve leagues,' Paladin reported.

'We'll hold fire as agreed. When you're ready, Surt will start the cooling circuit. It may hold for a second, or an hour, but I'd rather not push my already crumbling good fortune.'

Tindouf and Ruther arrived. They had put on most of their suits except for the helmets and life-support backpacks, which would make it difficult for them to move around quickly inside the ship. Each was cradling two or three crossbows, fresh out of stores, still with flecks of sawdust adhering to their oiled parts. Tindouf set one of these venerable weapons down on the desk, along with a pouch containing several dozen sharpened bolts. Fura stroked her hand across the haft, appraising the item with distinct mixed feelings. There were blasters and energy pistols in *Revenger*'s holds that could incinerate a man at twenty paces, not to mention Ghostie armaments that could do queerer and nastier things than that. But the difficulty with repelling boarders with such esoterica was that they were equally effective at repelling large chunks of her ship. Crossbows were a primitive but effective concession to the demands of the situation: powerful enough to penetrate the soft parts of a suit, such as gloves, accordion joints, breather bellows and hoses, but not so potent as to blow holes in the hull all the way out to space. All the same, they needed to be used with caution. A stray bolt could shatter porthole glass, or even go through a weak area of plating.

Still, Fura thought, as her fingers closed around the crossbow and she reacquainted herself with the heft of it, what had been good enough for Bosa Sennen . . .

'Take three more to the Kindness Room,' she told Ruther.

'Instruct Eddralder they can either use them or not, but the choice'll be theirs, not mine. Also ask them to ensure they've a portable medicine box ready, the sort we'd take to a bauble, and make sure it's well-stocked. After you've done that, go to the gun rooms. Surt'll be grateful for some company, I think. Tindouf: attend to the sails and ions until you think you can be more useful elsewhere. Good luck, the both of you.'

Tindouf touched his forehead.

'Good luck to all of us, I says.'

'Launches at six leagues and closing,' Paladin reported. 'They are sweeping us almost continuously now.'

'Go to your stations,' Fura said, dismissing Ruther and Tindouf.

She was alone, then, and but for her nerves, and Paladin's occasional interjections, it could have been any quiet moment since she had taken possession of this ship. The intercom whispered nothing to her; no mumbled delirium of fishes and shoalies and gubbins. The cabin's furnishings were exactly as they had been a week ago, or a month ago, heedless of what was coming. Her books – principally the ones she had inherited from Bosa Sennen – remained ranked on their chained shelves, their dour-coloured spines of maroon, green, navy-blue and black glinting back at her with the gold and silver leafwork of their titles. She could take one of those books down, open it to a chapter, lose herself in it – some dubious, credulous history of the Eighth or Ninth Occupations, perhaps – and nothing would seem amiss, not for a few minutes.

'Four leagues and decelerating hard.'

Fura opened her main journal, dipped her pen into the pressure-tight inkwell and began to scratch out a log entry. It felt like the proper, captainly thing to do, and that, for a moment, was important to her.

'Three and a half leagues. Muzzle flash!'

She had been expecting something like that, and only flinched slightly. These launches were bound to be armed, and it would be odd if they did not let loose a few precautionary rounds now that they were close enough for fine surgery. She held her composure, continuing to write down the date and time as the shots arrived.

The ship shook, and her hand smudged the ink, but the slugs missed the pressurised part of the hull. Not that the impacts were soundless, or without obvious consequence. They were not striking armour – they were keeping well away from the inhabited compartments – but they were snipping at nearby rigging, sails, even the winches and arms of the sail-control mechanisms.

Paladin's lights flashed with great intensity.

'They are . . . doing great damage to us, Miss Arafura.'

'It's no more or less than expected, Paladin. They're snipping our wings off, as you would an insect that'd been annoying you. They're close enough now that they can easily pick out our sails, even the catchcloth ones, and gun them away at their leisure. Do you feel it?'

'In so far as a robot may be said to feel anything, then . . . yes. I am not insensate to the damage.'

She thought of the wires that bound him to the ship, the electrical corollary of a nervous system, enabling him to direct the ship's tendons and muscles, but also to see through its cameras, and to register the forces acting on its sails and skin.

'I hope it is not too unpleasant for you.'

'I saw the Last Rains of Sestramor, Miss Arafura. After that, if I may be so bold, very little is of the slightest consequence.' His lights sparkled. 'But I will not say that I am particularly *enjoying* this experience, insofar as any sort of enjoyment is within my limited repertoire of internal states of mind . . .'

'Hold fast, Paladin. It won't be long now. Do you still have eyes enough for gun control?'

'I have eyes enough. Three leagues, and closing.'

She pressed the intercom. 'Surt: be ready. Any moment.'

A slug clanged against the hull. Perhaps it was a stray shot, perhaps some provocation, to force her to show her claws, but she would not retaliate, would not with all her will, until they were close enough to believe her truly helpless.

'Two and one half leagues.'

'Hold fast. Surt, you may open the cooling valve, slowly as you can.'

'Opening now, Captain, and Mister Ruther's here to watch the gauges.'

'Two and one quarter leagues.'

'Do we still have a clear shot from the stern-chaser?'

'Confirmed.'

'Select your best target, Paladin.'

'Cooling line holding at one half standard pressure, Captain.'

'Turn it up, Surt – steady as she goes.'

'First launch crossing two-league threshold; second and third lagging by one tenth of a league.'

'Wait until they are all over the line.'

'Line is now at three quarters pressure, and holding.'

'With your permission, I will now begin priming solenoids in the starboard and port batteries.'

'Proceed, Paladin.'

'Solenoids are warming and holding current. All launches are now within two leagues, and breaking to flank our locks.'

'Lines are at normal pressure, and holding.'

'At your discretion, Paladin.'

He waited a second, there was a single muffled knock, and then the ship jolted longitudinally. That was the stern-mounted chaser going off, sending its one slug, with the recoil at right angles to the normal effect of the batteries. An instant later – for the slug needed almost no time at all to complete its crossing – the cabin windows lit up with a white flash.

She would have asked Paladin for a report on the effectiveness of that single shot, but he needed all his concentration now, and only another instant separated that flash from the activation of the coil-guns. It sounded like a battle between teams of blood-crazed war-drummers. He ran them as hard and fast as the magazines would allow, for *Revenger* would only have this one chance to surprise the launches and the guns might not last beyond a few seconds of continuous fire.

'Holding, Cap'n!' Surt called, nearly screaming over the sound of the guns.

'We've opened up one of them's launches very prettily,' Tindouf reported. 'There's bodies and bits spillings out, but Mister Paladin's making a nice stew of 'em!'

Paladin would be concentrating on that one target, finishing the foul work he had begun with the high-penetration slug, but he would not neglect the other two launches. It was a cursed shame that the stern-chaser was so cumbersome to reload, but that was the price paid for the watchmaker-like arrangement of its parts, which could put about ten times the usual muzzle velocity into a slug. No mind; it had done its duty, and the massed ranks of the ordinary coil-guns now bore the brunt of the effort. From the noise reaching her ears, it seemed to Fura that they were acquitting themselves tolerably well.

'The first launch and its occupants have been entirely destroyed,' Paladin said. 'The second is showing damage to its flanks and steering jets. The third is coming around hard and bringing its own coil-guns to bear.'

'Maintain fire.'

'Maintaining fire.'

Since they were now fighting for their own survival, it was no great surprise when the launches began to shoot directly at *Revenger*. From the pattern of the shots it was clear that they were trying to disable her batteries as a first measure, with the slug impacts ringing down the length of the hull like a rapid tapping of cat's claws. Fura tensed and reached for her helmet. These slugs had relatively low energy, for the guns on the launches were necessarily compact, but a lucky shot could still breach the hull or puncture a window. Besides that, she was sure that the remaining launches would consider calling in reinforcing fire from the main ships, if they felt confident of keeping out of its way.

She would not let them, if it was within her power.

'Keep them moving, Paladin – don't allow 'em to use us as a shield.'

'I shall do my utmost. I must caution that we have lost one gun on the starboard battery, and steering control of two on the port set. On the credit side, the second launch has a pressure leak, and seems to be having trouble stabilising itself.'

Her fist creaked as she opened and closed it, remembering the rat's spine as it had crunched between her fingers earlier. 'Hit it as hard as you can. Hit it until they squeal. *Spikey-spikey.* They wouldn't show us a crumb of mercy, so we give nothing back.'

The guns kept firing, but now there was a broken, lop-sided rhythm to their drumbeat, and Fura knew in her heart that it was only a matter of time before she lost them all.

'Surt? How're we doing?'

'Mister Ruther says there's steam beginning to come out of the pipes, Cap'n, but I have to take his word for it.'

'I'm sure he's right, and I'm sure there's nothing more you can do for those batteries. I want you to go to the launch now and start preparing it for departure. Ruther'll go with you, and he'll read out any dials and settings you ask him to.'

'We ain't abandoning you.'

'I'm not asking you to – but I want that launch ready to go at the drop of a pin. Tindouf?'

'I's here, Captain.'

'Go to our friends in the Kindness Room, and bring them for'ard, including their crossbows. Make sure they've that medical box I asked them to prepare.'

'And what's of Mister Paladin, Cap? If we takes ourselves off the ship, won'ts we be leaving Mister Paladin behinds?'

'I shall . . . see that he is taken care off, Tindouf.'

Somehow, she told herself.

One by one the guns were dropping out. She thought of the gaps in their rhythm as holes opening up in a battlement, each a point of weakness that the enemy were bound to recognise and exploit. The interval between discharges was lengthening, too, as Paladin tried to coax a little more life out of each gun, even as the cooling circuit became progressively less effective.

The solenoids were growing hot, the guidance rails starting to buckle, so that even the shots that did get away were not as powerful, nor so well-aimed. What had been a near-continuous roar only a couple of minutes earlier was now more silence than noise, with their own guns only sounding every few seconds, and the enemy ships now concentrating their own fire on the few guns still operational. Once, a very heavy slug bounced off one of the launches and came tumbling right back to *Revenger*, hitting the galley window side-on and putting a milky flaw in that glass, like span-wide cataract. Yet it held, for Bosa had outfitted her windows with uncommonly thick and strong material.

'Launches are flanking us and preparing to make forced approaches at the lateral locks,' Paladin said. 'In thirty seconds they will be too close to shoot, even if none of the remaining guns give out.'

'Then spare nothing, Paladin – cook the guns, and damn us with our own recoil if the rails crimp. But put everything into the next thirty seconds. *Mash their noggins.*'

'It is now rather less than thirty seconds. The noggin part aside, I have already begun complying.'

She heard it and felt it: that last desperate volley. The shots harder, and the intervals between them briefer. She saw it all in her mind's eye: one glorious cannonade, the guns flogged like mad-eyed, whinnying cavalry horses until they bled, or stumbled, or simply died, and then it was done. At the last moment one of them did indeed seize, its guidance rails buckling just as a slug was being launched, and the jolt from that was enough to wrench the entire coil-gun from its mountings, arcing electrical gear, tearing cooling-lines loose, and plunging the starboard gun room into vacuum. By then, though, Surt, Tindouf and Ruther had sealed the pressure doors to both gun rooms, and the evacuation was contained.

'Is that it?'

'I am afraid that is it. I have lost any sight of the launches, but according to the sweeper the more damaged of the two is now drifting away from us. I think we have done it some quite serious harm.'

'Good. Where does that put the other one?'

'About two hundred spans from the lateral starboard lock, and closing.'

'They mean to come in that way, then.'

'That would not be an unreasonable assumption.'

Fura pressed the intercom. 'Tindouf, can you hear me?'

'I can hears you very well, cap'n. We's just on our way back for'ard, with the medical supplieses you mentioned. Doctor Eddralder and Merrix weren't too happy with me tellin' 'em what to do, but when that gun room popped I thinks it was all the encouragement they needed. We's losing the ship, aren't we?'

'Not if I can help it.' She straightened in her chair and ran a hand down the lower part of her spine, where it was starting to stiffen from tension. 'We may misplace it temporarily. Have you done anything about Prozor since we last spoke?'

'No,' he said, sounding puzzled. 'And I was very particulars about it not being the sort of problem you oughts to be troubled with, being our captain and all, and a pal of Prozor, which I know you were.'

'Thank you, Tindouf. Are you past the lock already?'

'Just goings past it now, Cap.'

'I want you for'ard as quickly as possible, in case we lose more compartments. Paladin: that operation we did on the port lock, to initiate our turn?'

'You would be referring to the over-pressurisation of the chamber?'

She nodded at his globe. 'Do we have enough lungstuff to do something similar to the starboard lock?'

'Our reserve tanks are now greatly depleted. To increase the pressure in the starboard lock, we would need to drain them completely, as well as all the compartments aft of the gunnery rooms.'

'There's no one in that part of this ship, is there?' She

swallowed, glancing at the intercom. 'I mean, no one that we know of . . . that depends on lungstuff.'

'Not now,' Paladin answered, with a faint concern.

'Then do it. Pump up the pressure in the starboard lock as high as it will stand. I'm on my way down.'

'Down where, if I might enquire?'

'To the lock, Paladin. I've a farewell to make, and an apology.'

25

The entrance to Quell's Bar was so unprepossessing that – had it not been for Rackamore's advance intelligence – Adrana would have walked past it a dozen times without realising what was there. No sign or indication existed above the doorway. There was merely a faded red door, partially ajar, tucked under the bulging overhang of a shabby, low-rent hotel with its own entrance halfway down the block. It looked like the sort of scullery door that was only opened when rubbish needed to be put out on the street, yet after five minutes of observation Adrana had seen a dozen patrons come and go.

They were watching from the window-side bar of a faded but not entire disreputable cafe on the other side of the road, sitting on tall stools. Adrana was forcing down sips of tea even though she had no thirst, only an anxious need to be an hour or two ahead in the story of her life, reflecting with giddy relief on the difficult business that was now behind her. If in that one or two hours she also had the merest hint of encouraging news about Fura, she would be all the more grateful.

But she was not hopeful, and the dread of what might be now sat within her, a clot of darkness growing larger by the hour.

'That is him,' Rackamore announced suddenly, as the door opened fully and a very tall man ducked out from beneath the overhang. He stood for a moment with his face to them, and the twin chimneys of his eyes seemed to sweep the window and bar and the three newcomers sat behind it, yet without any detectable interest. The man had stiff quills of black hair, dusted at the front with white, and he was shrugging his shoulders to work his arms into the sleeves of a jacket that was not quite large enough for him. He had a collapsible stove-pipe hat in his hand, which he popped out to its full extent once he was clear of the doorframe, and then positioned it carefully over his bristles, so that not one was deflected. The hat's brim projected well beyond his eyes, casting them into shadow.

He waited for a gap in the traffic and strode across the road, moving with a high-stepping, scissoring gait. His legs were long and thin and tight-trousered. Adrana shuddered, flashing back to a cold cell with a trap-door in the floor, and the thing that was trying to push itself through from underneath.

'Why does he come and go?'

'I believe he has a weakness for the dogs,' Rackamore said quietly. 'Fortuitously – or otherwise – there is a bookkeeper's next to us. He goes over once or twice an hour, sometimes with small bags of money. He is either placing wagers or has some interest in the establishment. If he keeps to the pattern I observed earlier, he will not be long in returning.'

Adrana gave up on her tea. She watched omnibuses, trams and private vehicles criss-cross in front of them. She watched boys and robots sweep up after horses. She watched bits of newspaper scud between one kerb and the next, driven by the gusts that came and went with the alteration in the light as the windows fell in and out of shade.

After no more than five minutes, and perhaps not even three, Hasper Quell reappeared, this time with his back to them. As soon as there was an interval he spidered back across the road, removed and collapsed his hat, and went back through the doorway.

Rackamore was only a few paces behind him. Quell stopped and turned around – Rackamore must have called out – and some brief and not entirely cordial exchange took place between the men. Quell pushed his head back out from under overhang and looked up and down the street. Then he made a quick beckoning gesture to Rackamore. Rackamore went in with him, and although they were in shadow, Adrana could still make out both men having a discussion at the top of the stairwell. After a minute of this, Quell looked across the street again, this time very definitely concentrating his attention on the bar where Adrana and Meggery sat behind the window. Adrana stared back impassively. She was not going to commit herself to anything until Rackamore gave her the signal that the transaction could proceed.

There was a nod from both men. Quell tapped his own wrist, signifying something to do with time, and Rackamore came back out and across the street. Quell disappeared into deepening gloom down the bar stairs, his back to Adrana.

'We proceed immediately,' Rackamore said when he reached their table, keeping his voice at a normal level while a milk-steaming machine made a loud frothing and gurgling behind them. 'He is very concerned to help us, but also very nervous about the Clacker's enemies, who he thinks may be surveilling the premises, waiting for this delivery.'

'He thinks, or he knows?' Meggery asked.

'The muddleheads have difficulty going about their affairs during the hours of daylight. They shutter the windows here for about eight hours out of every twenty-four, and we are not far from the start of that eight-hour interval. Dusk comes quickly in Trevenza. Once that happens, any muddleheads may move around with near-impunity.'

'I don't like being rushed,' Adrana said.

'Nor I, but waiting out that eight hours may be hazardous in itself, should the muddleheads start emerging. Quell is waiting for us now, and he knows the risks better than we do. We dare not delay.'

They had already paid for their tea. They left the cafe, Adrana and Meggery hefting the case between them. There was a lull in the traffic and Rackamore went on ahead, ducking into the door, then beckoning urgently. His gaze kept flicking to the upper windows and rooflines of the buildings around them.

Adrana and Meggery lifted the case over the kerb and into the shade at the top of the stairwell. Rackamore closed the door once they were inside and helped them struggle down the stairs. Adrana was still being careful not to jolt the container, even as she knew that there was no longer any secret about the contents.

A windowless stairwell conveyed them into a deep, low-ceilinged basement lit only by flickerboxes and a few meagre scraps of sickly-looking lightvine. Adrana and Meggery wafted smoke haze from their eyes, squinting into the distance. The room they were facing stretched away for at least two hundred spans, with the far wall barely visible in the gloom. Everything was scuffed and stained to some degree. The ceiling had lots of smoke burns and holes in it, and several bits of panel missing, so that here and there was a gut-like mass of electrical wires and pipes which herniated down into the room. The walls were a nasty sort of yellow; the carpet under Adrana's soles a drabber variation of the same shade. A narrow, zinc-topped bar ran along one of the two longer walls, but at the moment had a perforated grey shutter pulled down over it. Seemingly the only service was to be provided from a couple of much smaller hatches in the same wall. Some cabbagey smell wafted from the hatches. On the opposite side of the room, more doors and doorways led off into what Adrana presumed were offices, storerooms and private drinking areas. There might have been a door or arch in the furthest wall, but the haze made it impossible to judge.

For all that it had clearly seen better days – many of them – the place still drew patrons, and there must have been twenty or so scattered around the room. Some were at tables, singly or in small drinking huddles, and one or two were loitering near the service hatches. From somewhere came kitchen sounds and the sudden, explosive flushing of a very noisy toilet. Music scratched out of speakers somewhere in the room: some mournful recording that kept sticking at the same phrase, and no one cared.

Quell was waiting at the foot of the stairs, stiff black bristles just scratching against the ceiling. The force of contact made his entire mass of hair lift back slightly from his forehead, as if on a hinge.

'Mister Quell?' Adrana asked.

'Indeed, and at your service. I'm very pleased you could make it to our ever-so-humble establishment.'

'Very pleased to be here,' Adrana answered, lifting a sole against the stickiness of the carpet, until it yielded with a faint slurping sound. 'Humble or not, you seem to be doing . . . brisk business.'

A bushy-eyebrowed man looked up from his solitary card game. He gave her a moment of appraisal then went back to the cards.

'We have our regulars,' Quell said. 'Our happy little family.'

His face was long and lantern-jawed. A scar ran down one side of it. His eyes were two black metal tubes, rammed deep into his face. Dark lenses gleamed at the extremities of the tubes, throwing back a warped reflection.

'I gather from your colleague that you've had a most taxing and vexatious journey getting here?'

'One or two impediments, Mister Quell,' Rackamore said.

'Call me Hasper – we'll all be tight as skittles in a rack from this point on. Speaking of which, would you be so agreeable as to introduce your friends, Mister Rackamore?'

Rackamore tucked one hand behind his back, bowed slightly and with the other gestured in a most courteous way at his two companions.

'This is Captain Werranwell, and this the Master of Ions Meggery, both of the sunjammer *Merry Mare*, recently arrived.'

'In from the Empty, I gather. Mister Rackamore said you'd got caught up in some of that trouble that's been on the flickers?'

'We were shot at,' Adrana said.

'And was there casualties?'

'There were, Mister Quell. My own father among them.' She swallowed hard. 'There will be restitution. But for now it is enough that we have arrived and still have a ship.'

'I'm sorry you've had such travails.' He shook his head in worldly resignation. 'It makes one wonder what the worlds are coming too. Times like these, an honest captain ought to be able to go about their work without being shot at.'

'Would that were the case, Mister Quell.'

He lifted an eyebrow above one of his chimney-eyes. 'I expect you'll be ready for some lubrication, after all that trouble? Why don't you adjourn to the side-room, take the weight off your bones, and we'll get cosy.'

Adrana thought that the closer she remained to the stairs, the happier she would be.

'I would rather we got the transaction over with, Mister Quell. Is there any reason not to complete it immediately?'

'None at all, if your throats aren't too dry.'

Adrana nodded to her companions. 'We are fine for now.'

'Although a little privacy wouldn't go amiss, would it?' Quell lifted up one of his arms, the sleeve of his jacket ruffling to suggest that the limb articulating it was of a nearly skeletal thinness. He made a dry snapping sound with his fingers and addressed the room. 'See 'em off, dear friends. We'll be closing imminently, due to exceptional circumstances, but rest assured you'll all get one on the house when we reopen our doors tomorrow. Remember, chums: keep your noses clean and your pockets full!'

Between one minute and the next there was an orderly exodus from the main room and some of the adjoining booths. Most of the drinkers just got up and left, leaving their glasses unfinished. But not everyone departed, nor appeared in any hurry to do so. Those drinkers that remained had a commonality to them: a low-hunched, wary alertness that told Adrana that they were associates and enforcers, rather than ordinary patrons. They nursed their drinks, all eyes on Quell, his three new guests, and the bulky item at their feet.

The last of the genuine patrons left the room. One of the

associates went to the foot of the stairs and bolted shut a door.

Quell clapped his hands. 'Well, let's see what the good captain's brought us, shall we? Bazler, would you oblige with the lookie-lookie? I ain't impugning the good name of our guests, but you can't be too careful.'

It was the bushy-eyebrowed man who had been playing cards. He gave a heavy sigh as he stood up. He wore a leather apron set with pouches and hoops containing a great many knives, cleavers and kitchen utensils. He came over to the party and extracted a rectangle of lookstone from one of the pockets. He pinched it between sausage-thick fingers, swept it up and down the Clacker's case, then offered it to Quell.

'Empty, boss.'

'I very much trust it *ain't* empty, Bazler, or we're all in for a disappointing evening. Zak must be in an effector field. That'll work on a Clacker's gubbins, but not so well on monkey-made bombs or booby-traps.'

Bazler sniffed. 'I ain't seeing anything like that.'

'We wouldn't have put a bomb in it and still be standing next to you,' Adrana said.

'Never said you would, Cap. But someone might've. You came through customs, didn't you? They've got it down to a fine art in there. Nimble-fingered ain't in it. They can swap an item of luggage right in front of your eyes, and you wouldn't know it.'

'The customs people want to kill you?' Rackamore asked.

'There's rotten apples all through the system here, Mister Rack.' Quell caught himself, smiled hastily. 'I mean Mister Rackamore, excuse the informality.'

'No offence taken,' Rackamore answered carefully. 'And the rotten apples? I presume you mean extra-legal elements who aren't in wholehearted agreement with your sympathetic outlook on whistle-blowers such as Tazaknakak?'

'Exactly that, and I'm glad we're on the same page.'

'You done with me?' Bazler asked, stuffing the lookstone back into his pouch.

'Yes, do get back to your cards, Baz – they'll be missing you.'

Quell wagged his finger at one of the more distant watchers. 'Gremly, come over here with your box of tricks. Captain? If you'd be so kind, can I trouble you to open the case?'

While Bazler went back and Gremly came over – she was a small, sullen-faced woman with grease-coloured hair and a pale, mucus-like scar leading down from one nostril – Adrana knelt by the case and undid the clasps, allowing the lid to spring open. It still looked empty, but she knew by the mass of the case that the internal container must still be present.

'He's with us,' she commented. 'But I wouldn't risk putting your hand into the empty space.' Adrana elevated her metal finger as if she were showing off jewellery. 'He bites.'

'The hibernation and concealment parameters were set by the Clacker,' Rackamore said. 'How do you propose to interrupt the cycle?'

'With this, guv,' Gremly said, waggling a black rectangle in the direction of the seemingly empty case. The rectangle had the look of some improvised, home-made thing, its upper surface studded with controls, dials and illuminated lights. Jutting out of it was a thin rod with a circular antenna on the end. 'This gets through to the underlyin' gubbins, and fools it into thinking it's getting signals from its own control centre. All it needs is a sniff of those signals and it can mimic 'em to its heart's content.' She gave him a wink. 'It's *very* versatile.'

'That's clever technology,' Rackamore said, sounding impressed and very slightly unnerved, in about equal measure.

'Dealing with Clacks,' Quell said, 'clever is the very least you need. Clever is your starting point. On with it, Grem!'

Gremly steadied the rectangular unit. A pattern of lights pulsed in a deepening rhythm, and a dial swung hard over. The rectangle gave off a faint cyclic hum and Gremly used her thumbs to flip switches and adjust knobs.

'Here he comes!' Quell said, rubbing his hands together, and buckling at the knees to lower his frame. 'Here he comes! Oh, Grem! I can hardly contain myself! It's like all my birthdays arriving at once!'

'Someone's happy,' Rackamore murmured.

The Clacker's hibernation casket oscillated into view, pulsing in and out of visibility, until it stabilised and remained permanently established.

Gremly touched another control. The casket gave off a puff of trapped gases, then opened slightly.

'What now?' Quell asked.

'We must remove it from the outer case,' Adrana said. 'Shall I oblige?'

'If it's no trouble.' Quell raised a finger to his enforcers and associates, as if to warn them to be on their guard yet not to intervene until summoned. Adrana delved in, ignoring the throb in her finger, and extracted the hibernation casket from its snug berth in the outer case. It opened immediately, disclosing the contorted, semi-foetal form of the Clacker. Still lathered over in slime, Tazaknakak stirred, opening gummed-over eyes. He used his upper limbs to paw at his face. Judging by the faint, fuzzy return of a fresh headache, Adrana guessed he was already starting to assemble a sound-picture of his new environment. She expected his return to wakefulness to be speedier than the first time, since he had only been in the box for a few days.

'He was injured in Mulgracen,' she said. 'But we did what we could for him, and he seems to be making a good recovery. You will find that he can speak and sense quite normally.'

'You've done very well, Cap,' Quell said. 'Very well to spirit him out of the shellworld, very well to treat his wounds, even better to bring him all this way to Trevenza. We're very grateful, ain't we, Grem?'

'Very grateful indeed,' she said. 'We'll need him to wake up properly, of course, just to make sure it really is Zak.' She directed an apologetic look at Adrana. 'I ain't saying there'd have been intentional duplicity from your side, Cap, but – again – just like the luggage, he could've been swapped for another Clack, and you wouldn't necessarily know, would you?'

'He is Tazaknakak,' Adrana said. Then nodded. 'But you are right not to rest on my assurance. He must be heard. Indeed, I can't leave until I've had a chance to talk to him myself.'

'You know who he is,' Quell said.

'I do. But we had an arrangement – one still not satisfied. He promised me information, if I got him this far.'

Gremly lowered the rectangular device to her hip. Its lights were still pulsing in a subtly hypnotic pattern.

'What sort of information?'

'If I already knew that,' Adrana answered, 'I'm not sure I'd need it.'

'Tell you what,' Quell said, touching a finger to his lips. 'We'll be in touch. How about that?' He looked down at the Clacker with something almost close to fondness. 'He's drowsy right now, isn't he? No telling how long he'll take to come 'round properly, and I expect you three want to be getting somewhere to rest for the night. Bazler can show you to some nice hotels, if you haven't already found one.'

'We won't need Bazler,' Adrana said. 'And we won't be leaving until I've spoken to Tazaknakak. And how long that might take – whether we're talking about an hour or a day – I won't speculate.'

'In which case,' Quell said, with a definite hardening tone, 'we find ourselves at a bit of an impasse. We've both got an interest in the little fellow, that I agree, but we can't very well just sit around chin-wagging until he perks up, can we?'

'It's true that we both have an interest. Mine involves keeping him alive.'

Quell's jaw dropped so heavily it was as if it had been disconnected from the rest of his skull and now hung by only a few straggly ligaments.

'And mine doesn't?'

'Not in the longer term. I think your interest in Tazaknakak's welfare is extremely temporary. You wish to verify his identity, establish the terms of his knowledge – what he knows and what he does not – and then I think you either mean to kill him, or hand him over to others who will do as they please.' She glanced at Rackamore – all the warning she felt he needed, if her sense of him was not terribly in error – and then back to the man with the chimneys for eyes. 'You are not Hasper Quell, sir.'

He let out a little laugh. 'I ain't?'

'No. You've supplanted him, taken over this concern, but you are not Hasper Quell.'

'Well, this is a turn-up.' He looked at Gremly. 'I ain't the man I say I am, Grem – how's that for the books? I could've sworn I knew who I was when I woke up this morning, but seems I've got it wrong!'

Meggery tensed. Rackamore slid a hand up to the side of his face.

'Who'd you think he is, then?' asked Gremly.

'How long have you been in his employment? No more than a year or so, I'd imagine?'

Gremly tried to hide her reaction. 'Ain't for you to be troubling yourself over, Captain Werranwell.'

'Then you've as good as answered me. The man now running this place isn't Hasper Quell. I can be quite certain of that because I never met Hasper Quell. But when this man . . .' she gesticulated at the figure identifying himself as Quell. 'But when he turned and walked downstairs, I realised that I knew him. You can put on a wig, take another man's eyes – or copy them – but a person's gait is much harder to disguise. You are Vidin Quindar, sir.'

The man scratched at his forehead. 'Vidin who?'

'She's having us on,' Gremly said.

'I'm not,' Adrana said. 'This man – the one you think of as Quell – must have come here from Mazarile. When Arafura Ness escaped from Bosa Sennen, Vidin Quindar was the man sent to Trevenza Reach to abduct her and return her to her father's control. He knows this world and he knew Quell. Well enough, it would seem, to dethrone Quell and assume the running of this establishment. When we last heard from Vidin Quindar, he was whimpering on the ground with his eyes burned out by a robot called Paladin.'

Quell reached up and ripped away the black-bristled wig. He

tossed it to the floor in a manner that suggested he was not entirely sorry to be rid of it. 'You seem very well informed.'

'Hard not to be, having had a first-hand account of it from my sister's journal.' She lifted her jaw, staring at him through the flat lenses of her spectacles. 'I am Adrana Ness. We each have our disguise, Vidin.'

He cocked his head to one of the flickerboxes. 'You can't be Adrana Ness. Adrana Ness is on that ship out there, having its guts chewed apart.'

'There are other ships. Still, why continue with the pretence? Surely you recognise me by now.'

'Surely I don't,' he said, appraising her carefully, the barrels of his eyes mapping her face. 'I only met that girl once, when she came to Madame Granity's, and again the same evening when her father came with me to Captain Rack's offices.' He tapped the chimneys with a finger. 'Now these peepers ain't perfect, but even after that brief acquaintance I'd know that girl if I saw her again. You ain't her, darlin'. You're . . . something else.' But then, and only then, a tiny edge of doubt entered his voice. 'No. Nobody changes that much.'

Adrana smiled once. 'I do.'

'You need to tell her she's got it all wrong,' Gremly said, staring at Quindar.

'Alas, Grem, she's got it more or less straight. I was going to tell you sooner or later, but what with business being on the up, and enough complications on our plate . . .' He gave her an apologetic shrug. 'Quell's name was attached to this place when I took it over as a going concern. Seemed easier and simpler to slip into his shoes, so to speak.'

'I'd imagine you were also fairly keen to slip out of Vidin Quindar's shoes,' Adrana said. 'After that bad turn on Mazarile, there must have been all sorts of question marks hanging over your character. Child endangerment, child abduction . . . who knows what else? But why don't we put all that behind us.'

He scratched at his bald crown, which must have itched under the wig.

'Why not, eh.'

'The central matter remains. We were obliged to deliver the Clacker to Hasper Quell.'

'And now you've done it, and your conscience is squared.' He made a walking gesture with his fingers. 'So why don't you toddle off into the night, before I remind myself about the bounty on the Ness sisters? I've got the main thing I was interested in.'

Rackamore popped out his eye. He let it rest on his upraised palm, then lowered the palm with the eye floating where he had left it.

'Matters,' he said, 'seem about to take a turn for the impolite.'

'That wouldn't be a weapon, would it, Mister Rack?'

'It is many things, Mister Quindar. But the dispensing of rapid lethality is among its numerous functions. While you were conversing, I made a visual mark of every person this room, with the exception of my companions and, of course, our guest. The eye has all of you in its target register. If I were to give the kill command – which would be issued silently and instantaneously – each one of you would be dead within less time than it takes a nerve impulse to travel from your brains to your fingers.'

Quindar looked at Gremly. 'Sounds quite persuasive, when he puts it like that.'

'It does,' Gremly agreed.

'But the impoliteness is all on Mister Rack's side. He's the one who came in here with a weapon.' Quindar opened his hands and swivelled around to face the enforcers still watching. 'None of us has weapons, do we? None of us is that rude.'

'I've got my knives,' Bazler said, looking up from his cards. He stood, delved into his apron and took out a heavy-handled cleaver. 'I'm half-tempted, boss, to see if that eye's all he says it is.'

'Try me,' Rackamore said.

Bazler whirled the cleaver between his fingers and thumb. 'You really shouldn't encourage me.'

'Bazler,' Quindar said, in a gently placating tone. 'We can't go around throwing sharp objects at our guests, can we? Not even to prove a point about our prowess and accuracy.'

Bazler stopped whirling the cleaver and caught it very deftly by the handle. He raised it again, Meggery taking a step off to one side, Adrana standing her ground but only by immense force of will. Rackamore was looking on impassively.

'I would not, Bazler.'

Bazler drew back. He was on the point of throwing the cleaver when he angled sharply away and threw it with great force and precision across the room. It followed a whirling arc and buried itself in the counter beneath one of the serving hatches.

'He's very good, in fairness,' Quindar said. 'This whole place spins, so what ought to be a straight line isn't, but he's never fazed by it. Seen him split a cove's skull straight down the middle like a wood-chopper!'

Bazler walked over to the counter, his apron billowing before him. He reached out for the cleaver's handle and the room flashed pink-white. Bazler let out a high, childlike shriek and snatched back his fingers. The cleaver's handle dropped to the floor, glowing red where it had been sliced through.

Bazler sucked at his singed fingers. Above his knuckles his eyes were wide and surprised.

'Tell your man,' Rackamore said, 'that he is very fortunate to still have that hand.'

Quindar had a hand cupped over the extremities of his eyes, as if he were staring directly into the Old Sun. He pulled it away only gradually.

'I think he got the message, Mister Rack.'

'Good.' Rackamore nodded. His eye had ascended to the centre of the room, where it was prowling just beneath the ceiling, roused to some additional level of threat-alertness. 'Shall we speak plainly, Quindar? You're not getting the Clacker. He'll be coming with us for now, and when he wakes up enough to answer some questions, he'll be able to decide what he wants to happen next. You'll be letting us all leave. There'll be no trouble, and no hint of any attempt to cash-in on that bounty. Is that understood?'

'You couldn't be clearer. But I'd have another think about leaving, if I were you.' Quindar had lowered his hand from his eyes. 'Pop to the door, would you, Baz? And stop nursing your poor fingers like a baby! It was extremely obliging of Mister Rack to be as nice about it as he was.'

Bazler went to the door that had been latched at the base of the stairwell. Using his good hand, he opened the door and peered tentatively up toward street level.

'They're on their way down, boss.'

'You told your customers to stay away until tomorrow,' Adrana said.

He looked at her scornfully.

'These ain't my customers.'

*

From the domed window next to the lock, where she had watched in vain for Prozor's return, she could now see the approaching launch, less than sixty spans away. It was a formidable apparition; nearly half as long as *Revenger* and fully twice the size of their own little runabout. It was a dull grey, except for the shiny or scorched parts where her own slugs had blasted away paint and armour. The armour was spans-thick – where there was damage she could see down through the layers of it to the underlying hull of an almost normal-sized launch. Windows and gun-ports were heavily fortified, with their swivelling enclosures reminding her of the goggling, scale-crusted eyes of colourful pet reptiles she had once seen in the window of an emporium of novelties in Neon Alley. She looked on it with a certain revolted admiration. A ship like that was really only suitable for one activity: dishing out violence while soaking up quite a bit in return. The trade-off was all that armour made it ponderous, and there was no way such a craft could have carried enough fuel to land on a bauble and get back again, let alone with holds full of loot.

Bosa Sennen would never have disgraced herself with anything so inelegant.

'Nor would I,' Fura whispered.

Fully suited and helmeted now, she pressed her metal hand against the inner door of the starboard lock. The door creaked and groaned a little as it strained back against its frame. The barometric dial next to the lock was already jammed hard over at one and a half standard atmospheres; it had no capability to record pressures in excess of that, much less three or four times as much.

The launch came nearer. Thirty spans or less. Even if the coil-guns had been operational, they could not have swung far enough over to shoot at it. Nor would it have been a very good idea to, even if they had been capable. The explosion of one ship so near to another one would be almost certainly fatal to all parties.

No. All that might have been done now was to send out teams onto the hull, with suits and weapons, and try to shoot through windows, or pick off boarders as they crossed over, or even as they tried to move between locks. That was what Captain Rackamore had attempted with Bosa, but it had not worked for him and it stood no chance at all of working with *Revenger*'s already depleted crew.

But they were not done.

The door shuddered again. It seemed – and this had to be Fura's imagination, or some trick of perception caused by the curvature of her faceplate glass – but it seemed to be bulging inward, straining under the rising pressure Paladin was forcing into the lock.

Into the lock where Prozor's remains were still waiting.

'You were the best of us,' she said, still with her hand on the door. 'Always and forever. You helped me survive, and you helped me find Adrana. I'll never forget that, not so long as I live. You saw more of all the worlds and baubles than the rest of us will ever dream of, but you never made any of us feel small or foolish for the silly things we said, the things we got wrong, the things we just didn't understand, because we hadn't lived enough or had our eyes properly opened. You did more for Adrana and I than we deserved, and more for the ship than you had any right to, and still that wasn't enough. I could have cursed you when you took your time coming back in after signalling Adrana, but that was just you being true to your crew, true and loyal to your friends, and never stinting on a job. And it cost you in the end, cost you terribly, but I don't think that would have made any difference to you, if you'd known what was coming. For that, and everything else you did for us, you deserve much better than this . . . this thing I'm about to do to you. But if I knew you at all, there isn't anything you wouldn't have done for the ship, even after death, if you thought it would help our chances.'

Fura stopped herself, suppressing a laugh as she imagined Prozor's likely interjection at this point. *Get on with it, girlie – I've got plans for the rest of my life, you know.*

'I won't forget you, or your friendship, or that sharp look on your face the first time you saw your new companions. I know you took a while to come 'round to us . . . but I hope we didn't disappoint, in the end. That's all, Proz. That's all I have, and it's already more than you'd have wanted.'

She felt a nudge to the whole ship as the launch completed its approach. It was a polite, almost courtly sort of docking. Now the launch's armoured hull filled the whole of the window, and she could see no part of the other ship's lock.

'Paladin.'

'I am listening, Miss Arafura.'

'I think they'll try to come in with standard pressure on their side of the lock, just in case we are not suited. Not because they have our welfare in mind, but because they'd still like to have me warm and breathing.'

'That is understood.'

'The instant you detect positive pressure on the other side of the lock, blow the door. Don't ask me again; just do it. Is that understood?'

'It is. Might I suggest that you now place some distance be- tween yourself and the lock, in the event of a complete loss of pressure?'

Fura lifted her hand from the door.

'I shall.'

She had said her farewell; nothing remained to be done except find some way to live with her conscience for however many hours or days were left to her. Fura retreated, but not as far from the lock as Paladin might have liked. She stopped next to a thick bundle of pipes that cut through the corridor like tree-roots. While both her hands were free, she cocked the crossbow and slid a bolt into place. Then she hooked her living hand around the pipes, giving her an anchor, and gripped the crossbow as tightly as she could.

With her helmet on she was oblivious to small pressure-shifts in the ship. Still, she knew when the moment had come. There was a small thump, meek and timorous as a child knocking on a headmaster's door. That was the back-pressure of one standard atmosphere suddenly relieving some of the stress on the outer door. The launch had opened its outer door, and that could only mean that its boarding party were about to come through into *Revenger*'s lock.

Now, she whispered.

Paladin did not need to be reminded.

It was a brief, sharp roar; an explosion compressed into the space between two heartbeats. It was tremendously loud, even through her helmet. All the pressure in the lock, and all the things that had been in it, the hard and soft things she did not wish to think about, had just been blasted back into the waiting maw of the launch.

Fura tensed. The sound was gone, and now there was nothing. She had been as concerned as Paladin that the inner door might fail, strained beyond its limits by this sudden decompression, but it was holding . . . holding.

Until it wasn't.

The lungstuff began to shriek out of *Revenger*. Somewhere else in the ship she heard the serial clanging as pressure doors hinged or slid or un-dilated rustily into place, but there was no such protection between herself and the escaping atmosphere.

The gale intensified, and she had to crunch her arm even more tightly against the pipes. The pipes themselves felt as if they were straining against their brackets, threatening to tear loose.

Gradually, the wind died down. Sounds were becoming thinner. The accordion joints of her suit bulged and stiffened as the pressure differential increased. Her life-support bellows, detecting the transition to vacuum, began to huff up and down.

Dust and debris filled the space, bouncing from surface to surface in languid, diminishing drifts. There was a greenish haze from the lightvine that had been torn from the walls and shredded by the suddenness of the decompression. Releasing herself from the pipes, Fura scuffed a film of it away from her faceplate. She concentrated her gaze in the approximate direction of the now-ruined lock.

Forms emerged. They were dark-armoured, stooping, at first strangely unrecognisable as people. That was because they were entering *Revenger* with their bodies upside-down relative to Fura, treating her ceiling as their floor. That struck her as a curious impertinence, like guests ignoring the right etiquette for a party. There were two, no three, of them, moving with cautious intent and confused by the miasma of tiny particles still swirling around. She made out blades, weapons-nozzles, heavy-duty cutting and battering tools. She made out dents and gashes in their armour, and a spattering of stains and crusted, gluey accretions.

She picked the clearest one, waiting until it turned in her direction, presenting the portcullis-grille of its faceplate. The cross-hatched bars were closely spaced, but her bolt was narrower and its gradually tapering shaft was designed to help it slip between those bars even if her aim was slightly in error.

It was not. The bolt jammed itself into the gap and the figure wheeled back, arms flailing, with a jet of lungstuff whistling out of its face like a kettle on the boil. Methodically, calmly, Fura loaded another bolt. She hadn't necessarily injured the first of them, for the bolt might have stopped before it touched their face, but even without the lungstuff leak there was a good chance that their visor had become so crazed that it was impossible to see through. Or perhaps she *had* injured that one after all, for the jet of lungstuff seemed to be gaining a faint rosy stain. Reflecting on the advice she had given Paladin, to concentrate on one target until they were no longer a threat, she put the next bolt into the same person's thigh, just where there was a seam between two overlapping plates of armour, exposing a fold of toughened leather. It punctured and began to bleed lungstuff at high pressure.

She reloaded, and picked her next target. This one had a beak-like cowl over the front of its helmet, making it harder to get a clean shot into the visor – it would have limited the target's field of vision, as well, and it was turning its back to her, confused by some motion or disturbance in the swirling debris, and so she chanced a shot into the connecting seals between its helmet and backpack, which were reinforced with flexible sheathing but always vulnerable. Her bolt found some weakness and created another jet of lungstuff. There were now three plumes of it, two from the first, one from the second, and as her victims turned in distress and confusion, so those blasts of lungstuff only added to the swirling fog.

The third was quicker, and ready for her. She was reloading the crossbow when a muzzle lifted in her direction and flashed. She felt a hard thump against her belly, an invisible fist-punch, and was jolted back so hard that her backpack knocked one of the pipes loose, and a dark ichor of hydraulic fluid began to drain out in a swelling gush. She gazed down at her belly, half expecting to her see her own guts spooling out into vacuum. Her suit was peppered with lacerations, with black fragments jammed deep into her armour, but the weapon had not cut through.

Nor was it meant to, she guessed. The muzzle belonged to some kind of low-velocity scatter-gun, designed to subdue – and perhaps injure – but not risk a hull penetration. Messy and indiscriminate, she thought to herself. Not her style at all.

She had not let go of the crossbow, but she had fumbled the

bolt and now she required another. She dug into the pouch on her belt, and the muzzle flashed again, blasting the crossbow out of her grip. She yelped, then bit back the exclamation before it rang out through her helmet. The scatter-shot had ripped into the exposed metalwork of her hand and wrist, tearing away some of the pretty cladding. Fluid leaked from the wound, and beneath it she glimpsed an all-too intimate view of the hinges and pistons that worked her fingers.

'Pardon me,' said a voice in her helmet, 'but I don'ts like to see our captain treated that way.'

Her hand throbbing – it was a more diffuse sort of pain than when Meggery had snipped off her finger, but just as over-whelming – she twisted around in time to see another suited form coming up behind her. The figure snatched for her drifting crossbow, caught it deftly, let off a shot from the one that it was already carrying, then sped a fresh bolt into Fura's, and fired again. Both bolts went into the third figure, one finding some weakness in the neck-joint, the other piercing the knee, and the figure buckled in on itself in obvious agony. Tindouf propelled himself forward. His suit was bulkier than Fura's, but if he had been wearing a backpack he must have sacrificed it for the sake of ease-of-movement. Tindouf discarded one of the crossbows, grabbed the scatter-gun from the injured boarder, and flipped it around so that he might employ the heavy stock as a bludg-eon, which he did with commendable speed and enthusiasm, concentrating his efforts on the visor area. On the fifth or six impact the metal bars buckled wide, and on the sixth or seventh the glass shattered and exploded outward in an abundance of little twinkling pieces. Lungstuff geysered out.

Tindouf tossed away the scatter-gun, pushed his fingers into the now-open visor and the figure squirmed and thrashed, even as the flow of lungstuff abated and vacuum eased the figure into merciful release.

'Peoples say I's a harmless idiot,' Tindouf said.

'They're half right,' Fura replied, and cackled, and Tindouf laughed with her, a magnificent bellowing roar, for in that moment – as she well realised – Tindouf knew that he had the love and respect of his captain, and besides a fine set of ion-coils, and some sails and rigging to occupy him when the ions were well-behaved, and perhaps the prospect of a new clay pipe to carve, there was nothing he needed more than that anywhere in the Congregation, or beyond it.

While Tindouf was preoccupied, a fourth form emerged through the lock. This one wore a suit, but it was sleeker and more close-fitting than those of the first three. It raised an arm, irritatedly paddling aside clouds of lungstuff and detritus. It had a prow-shaped visor, with two angular plates of glass spaced by a blade-like central divider.

'Tindouf,' Fura said, and her own voice sounded distant and feeble, just as if she were trying to rouse herself from a dream; some vile phantasm of paralysis and helplessness. 'Tindouf.'

If he heard her, it was too late. The fourth form, who was smaller and thinner than the others, and carried nothing so clumsy as a crossbow or blade or scatter-gun, had something black in its fist. It was small, talisman-like. It aimed the dainty thing at Tindouf and doused him with a sharp ruby light. Tindouf stiffened, and a howl of static blasted her ears as the upper part of Tindouf separated into twenty or thirty evenly divided sections, as bloodless and clean as freshly-washed plates. These near-circular sections maintained some affinity with each other for a span or two, before they began to drift on independent paths. Fura screamed. The figure aimed the black thing directly at her, lingering for the smallest of instants, before twitching off to one side and dousing her already-damaged hand and wrist. She stared down in a sort of baffled wonderment as the transecting beam dismantled her hand and a good portion of her lower forearm. It had struck at an angle, so the parts sheared away as ellipses, rather than circles.

The figure kept the weapon on her, then reached up with its free hand and tapped part of his helmet, opening a general broadcast channel.

'You'll forgive me for that, Arafura – I mean the arm, not the man I just killed – heh! But I couldn't risk your having something in there that could hurt me.'

The room was clearing of lungstuff and debris very efficiently now. The ruby weapon had clawed several parallel gashes in the wall behind Tindouf, through several spans-worth of insulation and hull plating, all the way out to open space. It was an excellent demonstration of why energy emitters were not the weapon of choice, if one wished to take a ship or its crew intact – or indeed defend a ship.

The slim-suited figure came a little nearer.

'Stallis,' Fura said.

26

A soft, slow trudging came down the stairs. Bazler stood back, sucking on his burned fingers like a scolded toddler. Two dark-garbed figures came into the room, coat-collars turned up and hats tugged low across their faces, so that only a horizontal eye-slit was visible. They had their hands in their pockets, until one of them reached out a sort of sickle-shaped pincer and used it to latch the door behind them again.

'You've met the motleys,' Quindar said. 'This is more of 'em. And there's more still up in the streets, now that shutter-time's upon us. The thing about motleys is that they don't last long, but they're cheap and easy to throw together, and they can blend in at dusk like nobody's business.'

The muddleheads came into the room. They halted between Adrana's little party and the stairwell and took off their hats, as if they were introducing themselves formally.

She stared. They were as much of a horror as the ones she had encountered in Mulgracen, but they were put together from a different assortment of scraps; a different palette of monkey and alien parts. The effect was just as discordant, and just as lacking in symmetry. They were exactly as Quindar said: disposable assemblages of fused, animated flesh, thrown together for a specific purpose, with no consideration for longevity.

One of them was speaking. It had the mouth and jaw of a

person, but fixed into the jumble of its face nearly sideways on, like a jigsaw piece that had been forced into the wrong gap.

'We will take the Clacker now.'

'No,' Adrana said, standing her ground next to Meggery and Rackamore, and trying to keep a firmness in her voice, even as she felt it on the point of breaking. 'He's mine. I brought him here; I promised him safe passage.'

The muddleheads advanced.

Tazaknakak stirred. At last he was waking properly. His limbs thrashed and he started to push himself up onto his feet. He swivelled his head, producing a series of rapid, accelerating clacking sounds, a rattle that became an ascending trill, and then passed beyond the upper threshold of Adrana's hearing.

'You delivered him safe,' Quindar said. 'Now saunter off and enjoy the rest of your stay. Have a choc-ice. Treat yourselves. The muddles won't stop you if you let them have Zak. That's all they want. It ain't your business to poke your snozzes into.'

'They'll kill us for what we already know, Quindar. And eventually they'll kill you, too. You do realise that, don't you? This is well out of your ordinary league. There are aliens behind all of this. They've been keeping secrets from us for hundreds of years – secrets about quoins and baubles and Occupations. The Readjustment's brought things to a head. Something *is* happening – something that'll either condemn us all or offer one slim chance to change our future. Tazaknakak knows a little of it. He's seen glimpses of the truth – enough to prick his conscience – and he's dug a little too deeply into things his masters would rather remained hidden. That's why he's running. That's why they want him silenced.'

'Already been blabbing to you, has he?' Quindar looked over her head to the muddleheads. 'I wouldn't be so quick to advertise that, if I were you.'

'I'm not so stupid as to think they, or any other muddleheads, will let us walk out of here as if we know nothing. They'll kill us, or do some deal with the authorities in exchange for my capture. For all I know, their masters *are* the authorities.

They can't be trusted, Quindar. Turn on them now, use whatever you have here, and you might save your own skin and redeem yourself in the process.' She bent down and scooped up the Clacker, groaning at the additional load on her already tired bones. 'But be clear about one thing. He remains my responsibility.'

Quindar made a vague, dismissive gesture at the muddleheads. 'Take him off her. Break as a little as you can.'

The muddleheads pressed closer. Meggery made a growling sound and raised her fist. She swung it into the nearest muddlehead and something snapped off with a dry crunch. An appendage dropped to the floor like a rotten branch. Something bustled behind the muddlehead's coat and another limb emerged, dripping with a sticky, honey-coloured lubricant as it articulated out. The limb had a knife on the end of it. It sprung out in a quick stabbing motion, catching Meggery across the forearm. She yelped and stumbled back, blood already welling from a long, deep incision.

'Brysca!' Adrana said, stepping away from the other muddlehead, the Clacker in her arms, and wondering why he had not already intervened.

He answered quietly: 'I cannot.'

'Kill them,' she said. 'Like you did in Mulgracen.'

Meggery was gritting her teeth, tearing off a part of her sleeve to wad against the gushing wound. 'What's keeping him?'

'I have lost control of the eye,' Rackamore said.

They all looked to it, still prowling in circles just beneath the ceiling.

'What'd he say?' Quindar asked, with an exaggerated puzzlement. 'Something about losing control of his eye? Did you hear that, Grem?'

She had the rectangular control unit in her hands, the same one she had used to open the case. Its lights were pulsing strongly, and she had her gaze fixed on the circling eye. 'I did, boss, and it's a queer one and no mistake. Why would a clever cove like Mister Rack lose control of his own eye?'

'Brysca,' Adrana said, as if her own insistence might make a difference. 'What's wrong?'

'The control signals . . .' He paused, pressing a hand to his temple, some desperate strain showing in his face. 'They aren't getting through. They're being overridden.'

Gremly grinned. 'I did say this was a very versatile piece of gubbins, Mister Rack!'

'You did, Grem! I think a fair degree of understatement may have resided in that remark, truth be told!' said Quindar. He angled his head to address Rackamore. 'We had warning, Mister Rack, after that unpleasantness in Mulgracen. Word that you might send a remote in after us. Expecting you, so to speak. Gremly got a sniff of the control protocol when you were snooping around our premises earlier on. Of course, we still let you think the eye was operating properly. Even let you have that bit of fun with Baz.'

Bazler looked upset. 'You mean he didn't have to burn my fingers?'

'I'm sorry about that, Baz, but we thought it'd help if our friends still thought they had the advantage on us. That way we'd all know where we stood. As we do!'

Meggery's efforts to stem the flow of blood were having little or no effect. She stared down at her already-sodden bandage. 'He got me deep. The chaff . . .' She dropped to her knees, a woozy look in her eyes. 'I don't feel so well, Captain.'

'Stay with me,' Adrana said. Then, barking it as an order: 'Stay with me, Meggery! We'll get help.'

Meggery made to mouth something. She was already turning a waxy grey. 'Cap . . .'

'Stay with me!'

Meggery slumped over. Her mouth lolled open, her eyes still fixed on Adrana.

'That's one of 'em done with,' Quindar said. 'Now crack on with the other cove, Grem – we ain't got all day!'

The muddleheads had begun to focus their attentions on Adrana. She clutched the Clacker more tightly to her chest, feeling a strange and unpleasant resonance in her ribcage as the casque generated its sounds. The muddleheads began to push out limbs and feelers from gaps in their coats, exploring the Clacker and trying to tug it away from her, at first with a surprising gentleness.

She kicked at their lower extremities and things shattered and crunched like wood-wormed timber.

Rackamore was holding his hands against both sides of his head. He had dropped to his knees, grimacing and making small choking sounds. Gremly was still working the rectangular device. She had a look of perfect, avid concentration, smiling slightly as she flicked a switch or turned a potentiometer dial. Slowly, she was gaining confidence in her own control of the eye. It was making larger and lower loops around the room, and she was following it with her gaze.

'Please,' Rackamore said, forcing out the word through a half-clenched jaw.

'Stop!' Adrana shouted. 'You've proven you can override the eye. You don't have to hurt him as well!'

'Mm.' Gremly pushed out her lower lip, looking diffident. 'I'm not trying to hurt the cove, exactly, but there's lot to learn here. Perhaps if I turn down this . . . or turn it up . . .' She made a violent, impulsive twist of one of the knobs, and Rackamore screamed. 'Or maybe not that one. Maybe *this* one . . .'

The room flashed pink-white and a lance of energy put a smoking hole in one of the walls. Gremly grinned, brought the eye around again and turned one of the flickerboxes into a smoking, sparking ruin.

'That's coming out of your bonus, Grem!'

She cackled at him: 'Worth it for the fun, boss!'

The muddleheads were still trying to wrestle the Clacker from Adrana's clasp. She grunted and kicked at them. One of them buckled at the waist, a leg snapping beneath it. She kicked it harder, then brought a stomping heel down on its chest. There was a moment of resistance, then a soft and unresisting descent. It was like crunching through the lid of a pie.

Meggery lay still in her pool of her own blood. Rackamore was on the ground, writhing. Bazler was at the door and two more muddleheads were coming in. One was doubled half-over, like a stooping crone; the other was unnaturally tall and flattened out, like a person that had been put through a steam-press. It was apparent to Adrana that even if she somehow managed to dismantle or incapacitate them one by one, there would always be more, and eventually force of numbers would prevail. Quindar might have lied about his identity, but she had no doubt he had been sincere about the gathering of the muddleheads.

The feeling in her ribcage was almost as much as she could tolerate. It was like a churning of every bone, sinew and organ: as if her insides were tumbling around like clothes in a washing machine. Accompanying this sensation was a rising pressure behind her eyes, like two hot skewers being driven into them from inside her own skull.

'Let me go,' Tazaknakak said.

'No.'

'It will be bad for you if you do not. They have killed one of your friends and the other will soon follow. This way . . . there *is* a way. But you must trust me.' Beneath the swell of his casque, his tiny, barely sentient eyes impelled her to do as he stated, and Adrana realised her options were as limited as they were dismal. She could let go of him, or she could try holding onto him for a few seconds longer, until the vibrations from his casque became truly unbearable, or the muddleheads grappled him away.

She chose to trust him. She relinquished her hold and stumbled back. Of the two muddleheads who had first assailed her, only one was still standing, but it only took one to seize the Clacker. The muddlehead pressed his prize against him, as if to mirror and mock the protective stance that Adrana had just abandoned. Near the door, Bazler was stumbling around with a kitchen knife in his hands, disorientated by the noises. He had the stunned, staggering deportment of a man who had been hit by a tram and did not quite realise how badly he was broken.

Tazaknakak increased his vibrations. The waves of inaudible

sound were already stronger than when she had been holding him. It made her dizzy and disorientated, and she felt a rising compulsion to vomit. She stumbled back even further. Brysca fell to his knees and pressed his hands against the sides of his head as if they were the opposing planes of a vice, and he wished only to crush his own consciousness out of existence. Adrana fully sympathised with that intention. She had become a hard knot of pure pain, a little star burning with the pure white flame of absolute agony.

A little star . . .

There was room in her head for exactly one thought that was not some splinter or reflection of that pain itself. She thought of a tiny star, floating in a cavern . . . a tiny, flickering source of immense but evanescent luminosity.

She understood that these waves of sound were not meant to hurt her, but they were most certainly intended to disorientate Tazaknakak's captors, and perhaps do some greater harm to the muddleheads. If she could amplify that disorientation by the production of an intense and startling light-source . . .

The light-imp . . .

She had kept it about her all the while, even after she understood the gift was not the rare and valuable thing it had seemed. It was only as far away as the box stuffed down the collar of her blouse, but it might have been buried in a bauble's deepest, darkest vault for all the force of will it took to retrieve it. She had to compel her hand and arm to perform one simple action, yet it was like delving through a matrix of solid rock. When at last her fingers closed around the velvet box, it felt as if she were leaning into a well and by some grotesque, delirious extension of her limb was managing to touch some relic that had fallen all the way to the bottom.

She pulled out the box and worked the catch with the friction of her thumb, not caring if she broke the little mechanism. Then she fumbled out the hard-edged form of the light-imp. For an instant, exhausted, it was all she could do to loll there on the floor. It was enough, surely, that she had done this one thing.

Nothing more could be asked of her. To expect her to have the strength to squeeze the light-imp: well, that was beyond all reasonableness.

She did it anyway.

It shattered between her fingertips, the physical object replaced with a small wavering orb that brightened in pulses. She let it drift from her fingers, leaning away from it as the yellow light intensified. It was indeed very luminous, and growing more so by the second. She had seen the brightness a light-imp could project in the interior chamber of a bauble, flooding a space the size of a ballroom or booking hall, but Quell's Bar was much smaller than that and the confinement of the light only made it seem stronger and angrier.

More than that, though. The light emanating from that orb was harder and fiercer than any she had known before, and it just kept brightening. She jammed her eyes to slits, and still it was not enough. She closed them completely, and she could see shapes and colours through the veined curtains of her eyelids.

It was a light-imp, she thought. But not a commonplace light-imp.

Firebright.

Quindar shrieked. If he had struggled to endure the vibrations, the light-imp was enough to take him over the edge. He yanked his head around like a man being electrocuted. He tried to cover the lenses of his eyes with his palms, but too much light leaked between his fingers.

He screamed and fell writhing to the floor. Bazler and Gremly were already down. The muddleheads were stunned or dead or in some intermediate condition, and Tazaknakak could not keep up his sound-generation indefinitely; nor would the light-imp keep shining for ever. While the Clacker made his noises, and the Firebright burned, and its radiance overloaded Quindar's eyes, Adrana walked over to him and placed a boot on his neck.

'You shouldn't have tricked me,' she said, in a low, judicial tone, as if she were delivering a court summary. 'You shouldn't have hurt my friends, and you shouldn't have tried to take the Clacker from me.'

She pressed down with her boot.

'Leave him,' a voice croaked. 'Leave him and go, before reinforcements arrive.'

Rackamore was still alive. She went over to him, knelt down, and touched the side of his face. He blazed like an over-exposed photograph. The light was painful, and she wondered how much more of it she could bear.

'Gremly's stopped,' she said. 'I can smash that machine of hers. You'll be all right.'

'No.' His voice was a wheeze. 'Something . . . went wrong. In my head.'

'You're all right, Brysca.'

'No,' he said again. 'I'm not. She did . . . something bad to me . . . something that can't be reversed. I can't move, Adrana. I can't move and I can hardly breathe.' He paused, and from some deep reservoir of fortitude he managed a smile. 'It's over for me. But it isn't for you. Go over to that man with the knives and take three things.'

'Three,' she said, smiling back at his exactitude, even as his composure and dignity ripped her heart out.

'A knife for me, just in case I have the means to use it. There will be more coming, and these . . . fellows . . . won't stay stunned indefinitely. Take one for yourself, and take the Clacker. The third thing . . .' He paused, wheezed, drew breath. 'The third thing . . . you need a way out of here that isn't how we came in. There'll be such a way. There'll be an escape passage. There always is.'

'How do I find it?'

'The third thing . . . Bazler. The one with the knives.' He licked his lips, inhaled a ragged breath, met her eyes with all that was left of his, for the last time. 'Look . . .'

'Look where?'

'Look . . . *stone*.'

It was the last thing to come out of his lips. Brysca Rackamore was dead.

*

Adrana held the lookstone up to her eyes. She turned around
slowly, maintaining just the right pressure on the lookstone, so
that she was peering neither too shallowly nor too deeply into
the earthworks surrounding Quell's basement room.

She agreed with Rackamore. Whatever opinion she might
have of Hasper Quell – or, for that matter, of his successor –
she doubted that either man would have been satisfied without
some secondary means of reaching this basement warren,
besides the stairwell that came down from the street-level
frontage. More than likely there would be at least two other
ways in and out: one purely practical and unconcealed means of
access from the building above, perhaps an elevator or hydraulic platform, so that kegs, kitchen supplies and the occasional
corpse could be moved up and down without difficulty, and (if
she was any judge of these matters) a far more covert means of
coming and going, which might connect to some other building
entirely. The muddleheads would have the first one covered,
but not necessarily the second. It would depend on how much
Vidin Quindar trusted them. If he had retained the smallest
suspicion that his collusion with them might turn sour, then
possibly – just possibly – he would have kept one or two things
to himself.

That was her conviction, and if it was based on nothing
more than an attempt to reason herself into the minds of semi-
criminal men, it was still all she had and all she could depend
upon. So she willed her fingers to hold the lookstone without
trembling, and she forced upon herself a patient and attentive
composure, as if this exercise were merely a pleasant sort of
puzzle-solving distraction for an aimless afternoon.

And she saw it. Smokily defined: a hollow space behind
one of the walls: the start of a low, narrow but very definite

passage leading horizontally away from the basement. When she relaxed the lookstone, the wall came back into view with no door or hatch to hint at the presence of a concealed tunnel. But the wall was divided into panelled partitions, and one of them corresponded quite satisfactorily to the hidden space.

She pocketed the lookstone and carried Tazaknakak to the panel. It fitted neatly against its neighbours. There was no seam on either side wide enough to slip her fingers into. But if Quell ever meant to use this escape route, he would have surely been in too much haste to go looking for tools or keys. She set down the Clacker and used both hands to press on the panel. She felt at first no hint of movement, but then a positive click and a resistive yielding. The panel moved a little inward, then reached a limit and sprang back out of the wall, hinging by its own means to the right. Beyond it was a black emptiness, its depths betrayed only by a chill, damp draught. Adrana collected the Clacker and stepped over a skirting board into the tunnel and set him back down. Behind her, on the rear face of the panel, was a pair of handles so that the panel could be pulled back into its former position.

Even though the Firebright was still active, it was no use to her. If it shared the general properties of a normal light-imp then it could not be touched or moved once it was initiated. So as she pulled the panel closed, the darkness around her became absolute. The lookstone would be no use either, since it required contrasting light levels to form a comprehensible image, and there was nothing but blackness.

She fumbled at her feet for the Clacker and raised him to her chest.

'Tazaknakak,' she said, in a firm and insistent voice. 'I know you are exhausted, but I need you to see for me now. Both of our lives depend on it. Guide me into this tunnel.'

'I am depleted. I must rest after my great exertions.'

She shook him angrily. 'Tazaknakak!'

'I am . . . incapable.'

'You can make speech, so you have the capability to generate sound-pictures. See into this tunnel. Tell me what I'm walking into.'

'I will . . . strive to.' There was a churn in her ribcage, a pressure behind her eyes. 'Turn me. We are not facing . . . that is better. Proceed.'

'What?'

'Proceed. If you are in peril of collision, I will alert you. For now, proceed. The floor is quite level and well-maintained. Even a poorly proportioned biped such as yourself should not have too much trouble.'

'Be aware that I cannot see a thing. Not even my hand in front of my face.'

'Walk on, Captain Ness. And do not be too tardy about it, either.'

*

Incer Stallis tipped his head, touching one hand to his chest even as he kept the weapon levelled. It was a sort of mocking curtsy.

'I feel I should say something like "we meet at last", or "evidently my reputation precedes me", or something just as tiresomely melodramatic. Isn't it disappointing how life throws us into these situations, and the only words available sound like the worst sort of pot-boiler?'

'I had so hoped you were in one of those ships I already burned.'

'You say that, Captain Ness, but I am not at all persuaded that you really mean it, not deep down.'

'Trust me, I do.'

'But then you wouldn't be able to exercise those fantasies of doing something extremely unpleasant to me face to face, as you said you'd like to.' He extended a beckoning hand. 'Well, now's your chance – how about it?'

Fura dipped her eyes to her ruined arm. The cuff where her suit met the artificial limb was still holding pressure, or she would have had only seconds of consciousness before blacking out. Her arm felt cold and numb, as if she had pushed it into a dense cloud of anaesthetic gas. There was none of the pain she had felt from the loss of a mere finger.

'I'll find a way.'

'It really was a commendable effort, I'll give you that. Those losses were felt very keenly. Fine ships, good crews. And you put up such a spirited defence, until the last.' He pointed a finger at her, waggling it admiringly. 'That was a *most* excellent ruse, not letting off your guns until we were so, so close. Heh! They'll be teaching that one in squadron school for years to come. Sadly, though, it only prolonged the inevitable. I know this is a unique ship, with some unique capabilities, but it's still only a ship, and even the finest fighter ought to know when they're outnumbered, out-gunned and out-flanked. As you were, today.' He curled his fingers. 'Well, come along. There's nothing for you on this hulk anymore, and my men will soon find your sister and mop up the last of your doughty band. You don't want to see any of that.'

'Your men? I killed your men.'

He clicked his fingers. 'Yes – that gruesome business with the lock! That took out three of us, I admit, and then you certainly left your mark on these other poor fellows.'

'If you had a spine, you'd have come in with them. Was it just the six, Incer?'

'There's still a fully-armed technical crew aboard the launch, so don't get any ideas about trying to take control of it. I also have word that the other has now completed docking on your port-side lock, after some difficulties of their own. They'll blast their way in, rather than risk your little trick with over-pressure, assuming you'd be so foolish as to attempt it twice.' Again he curled his fingers, this time with a touch of impatience. 'Come with me, please. You know it's in your best interests. We'll run you back to one of the main ships and have a surgeon look at that arm. Where *is* your sister, by the way?'

'As if I'd tell you.'

'We haven't seen your launch depart, so perhaps that's where she's hiding. It won't take us long to find her – or any other dregs of your crew – and if they're silly enough to try to escape in that launch, we will easily hunt them down.'

'Then you seem to have it covered.'

'It will still help the search party if they know where *not* to shoot, Arafura. These men are very good, and they have their orders, but I have to say they're not in the most of agreeable of moods. Seeing your colleagues butchered will do that to you.'

'I heard you butchered your own mother, Incer. Killed her for a ship, then murdered the one accomplice who knew what you'd done. Is that true?'

'Come.' He toyed with the little black weapon, rolling it between his fingers like a marble. 'I shan't ask again. Adrana will just have to take her chances. *You* were always the real prize, as far as I was concerned.'

Something jolted the ship. Had there been any pressure left in this whole section of it, Fura was in no doubt that it would now be rushing out of the port lock, or what was left of it.

'I'll come, if you spare my sister and the others. That's the price of my cooperation.'

'It seems ... reasonable. Are they in the forward compartments?'

'I said I'd cooperate, not give you 'em on a plate.' Fura used her good arm to lever herself away from the pipes and wall until she was straightened out and facing Stallis, the two of them floating a few spans apart.

'No tricks, now.'

'No tricks.'

Three armoured figures came into the corridor from the connecting passage between the port and starboard extremities. Stallis touched his helmet and some closed exchange took place between him and his men. Fura watched as they regarded their fallen or grievously incapacitated colleagues, as well as the grotesque spectacle that had once been Tindouf. Two of them went in the direction of the forward compartments, while a third detached from the party to accompany Stallis and Fura back to the lock. Any thoughts she might have had of single-handedly incapacitating Stallis, even with that vile weapon of his, were now extinguished.

The launch's lock was damaged, but it still worked, and as the pressure returned again she felt her suit turn saggy around the joints. Her arm was beginning to ache, instead of being enveloped in numbness, but for now it was a bearable discomfort.

The launch's inner lock door opened, and the armoured man prodded her forward while Stallis maintained a cautious separation. Still holding his black weapon, he reached up with the other hand and deftly undid his helmet connections. The three of them were floating into the main compartment of the launch, which was larger than the entire interior of *Revenger*'s own excursion craft. Instead of having portholes and double rows of chairs facing forward, it was windowless and bare except for racks of weapons, ammunition, assorted equipment and spare vacuum suit components, with the only obvious furniture being ranks of spartan, fold-down bucket seats along each side. Rather than the usual arrangement of a control position and console ahead of the seats, there was a separate compartment behind a pressure bulkhead.

Stallis directed his man to secure Fura. The man removed her backpack and hose connections, none too gently, and forced her into one of the bucket seats. She was strapped in with her upper arms pinned to her sides, and her right arm – all that now remained – bound against her belly.

'Remove her helmet,' Stallis said, secreting his little weapon into an external pouch on his own suit, and then lifting off his own. He ruffled a hand through a mop of thick, unruly black hair and shook his head vigorously, as if his neck muscles had begun to cramp.

She studied him with a prickling sense of recognition. His face was familiar to her, although she had never seen an image of him nor met his eyes before. It was the face she had seen projecting itself onto Ruther's features, forcing them into a caricature of itself. If there had been the least doubt in her mind that this was the extraordinary Bone Reader whose mind she had touched – and whose mind had touched hers – none now remained.

Fura glared at him as her visor lifted away from her eyes. There was nothing she could do to stop the man removing her helmet.

'Very good,' Stallis said, grinning wildly, when at last there was no glass between them. 'Very, very good. The rumours were correct, then. The extreme manifestation of glowy our man reported . . . it's in your eyes. Deep into your central nervous system, deep in your cerebellum.'

He extended a hand, snapped his fingers, and had the suited figure pass him her helmet. He scooped it into his hand by the chin-piece, lifted it to his face, staring into the emptiness of the visor.

'"Our man"?'

He frowned slightly. There were no lines or marks on his face, no indicators of habitual expression, so even when he pushed his features into a frown or a grimace or some affectation of wicked delight, the effect was unpersuasive and rubbery, like a cheap mask that wanted to snap back to its neutral condition.

'My man, yes,' Stallis said. 'You met him, didn't you? He infiltrated your ship, under our instructions. Posing as an outlaw *ne'er-do-well* named Lagganvor—'

'No,' she said, with an automatic assertiveness. 'Lagganvor was the man I found, the man I captured. He wasn't your man. If he was anyone's he was Bosa's, Bosa herself—'

'He did a fine job of concealment, I see. We never thought he'd last that long.' He looked at her with some desperate, sceptical amusement, as if she couldn't possibly be telling the truth, but it was rather funny to play along as if she were. 'Are you really saying you didn't crack his identity?'

Fura knew better than to say more. It was a game he was playing, that was all: a precursor to the psychological attacks she could expect when they began interrogating her, trying to demolish her sense of self, even her understanding of her own reality.

No; she knew better than to ask him.

'What identity?'

'His real name. Brysca Rackamore: the estranged brother of Pol Rackamore, your first captain. He was our man. Our agent – our infiltrator. We sent him to find you.'

'That isn't possible. If Lagganvor was the man you say he was, why would you have risked his life by shooting at us?'

'It's a risky profession, and Rackamore understood that. But all's well, isn't it? We'll find him somewhere in your ship, and you can have the pleasure of hearing his side of the story in person.' He reached up and touched a stud on the outside of his neck-ring. 'Get us underway. The other boarding party can complete the sweep of the wreck and take any survivors with them when they undock.' He waited, head slightly cocked, awaiting confirmation that these instructions had been received and were about to be acted upon. 'I said, get us detached. I have the high-value prisoner with me – Adrana Ness can follow in the second launch, if she allows herself to be taken. I said, get us . . .' But he trailed off and tapped the neck stud twice in case it was broken. 'Damn this,' he muttered, then jabbed a finger at the other man, who was still fully suited. 'Watch her.'

Fura watched as Stallis, still carrying her helmet, went all the way forward to the dividing bulkhead. He touched a control, opened the pressure door, and stooped through. Once he was inside, the door closed behind him. While this was going on, the suited guard aimed a crossbow in her general direction. She guessed he was under instructions to wound, rather than kill, if she made trouble. But other than glare, and possibly aim a gob of spit at him, there was nothing she could do.

Stallis came back into the main part of the launch. He no longer had her helmet. He seemed to need to stop and collect himself, his jaw trembling and his breathing rapid. His eyes swept the room. He looked at Fura and her guard, but also at every part of the interior, with its racks of equipment.

Only then did he say: 'They got aboard. Somehow. They got aboard while we were inside her ship.'

She heard the amplified voice of the guard, emerging from its helmet. 'Sir?'

'They got inside. They've . . . killed . . . the technical crew. They're all dead.'

He looked down at his now-empty hands, as if only then realising that they were lathered in blood.

'There's got to be a mistake, sir. That lock was counter-sealed when we went back in.'

'I'm saying . . .' Stallis drew a huge calming breath. 'I'm saying *something* got into this ship. I'm not saying how.'

The guard might have been on the cusp of answering, but Fura would never be entirely certain. He twitched, and something odd happened to his neck. It was separating, parting along a widening line, almost as if it had never been properly joined together in the first place. At the advancing point of this line of separation was a sharp, shimmering anti-presence, a blade-shaped zone that resisted all Fura's attempts to focus on it, to see it, to hold it in mind as a definite object. Behind the dying guard was a larger, person-shaped counterpart to this same repulsive absence. The guard's blood splattered onto the barely-seen surface, then the greater portion of it soaked away, becoming first translucent and then invisible. Stallis seemed, for a moment, entirely paralysed by the spectacle before him. Then he dug out his little weapon, slippery in his blood-soaked fingers, and aimed it at the Ghostie presence.

'I wouldn't,' Fura said.

The Ghostie had finished with the guard, tossing the larger and smaller parts aside. Fura could only see it by averting her gaze, seeing out of the corners of her eyes, and making a mental effort to think of anything but the Ghostie.

Stallis fired. The ruby beams intersected the volume of space where the Ghostie might have been, and for an instant some definite thing was there, carved of ruby-stained glass, a hinged-and-armoured form that seemed as hollow as a waiting mould.

The ruby staining faded, the energies of his weapon absorbed and dissipated. Stallis tried again, with the same lack of effect.

He glanced down at the weapon, scowling.

The Ghostie was hard to see again. Fura twisted her head aside, narrowing her eyes to slits, forcing her thoughts onto any other track but the one they wished to follow.

The Ghostie loomed before her. Fura sensed a terrible sharpness of being, as if it were made only of lethal blades, serrated edges and cruel impaling points.

A voice cut into her skull. It was like two surfaces of rough ice sliding past each other.

Sorry we ain't spoke for a while. I thought you'd like to know that I'm gone all the way now. Mainly, you don't have to feel bad about what happened to me. I like things better the way they are now.

Through her terror, Fura stammered out a name.

'Strambli.'

Stallis was backing himself into the forward compartment again.

I remember when that name belonged to me. It was a long time ago, though. You were my captain and we had a ship all to ourselves.

Fura found the strength to nod.

'It was. It was.'

It was a good ship. I liked being part of your crew. But I much prefer things the way they are now. All the other stuff's such a long time ago. I was just ... changing. I was wrong to be afraid of the cold. Once I was in it, I realised it wasn't so bad. I didn't mind the darkness, either. It's just another kind of light.

'I'm sorry, Strambli.'

A tentative smoky appendage extended from the barely-real form. The hand touched Fura's upper left arm, and even through the insulation of her suit a sudden wriggling coldness seeped into her muscles and bones. The hand descended to her elbow, the cold spot moving like a worm beneath her skin, and then it reached the limit of the living parts of her, where flesh became metal.

Fura gasped in shock and pain. The unseen hand flinched away from her, and some part of that coldness eased.

Did these men do this? Did they hurt Prozor and Tindouf as well? When I had that name, I was the same as those people. I was a breathy. I remember that I liked them, and that they liked me.

'This man,' Fura said, nodding at Stallis. 'This was the one.'

In which case . . . I do not think I like this man.

Stallis levelled the weapon again. He had made some adjustment to its settings, and when the ruby energies flashed they were much fiercer than before. Strambli – or what had once been Strambli – glowed with a brighter luminosity. Slowly, the hollow form turned from Fura and drifted in the direction of the forward compartment. Even that intense dose of ruby light was dissipating now, and no harm appeared to have come to Strambli. Yet Fura had the sense that some vast patience had been strained to its breaking point, and now Stallis was the exclusive focus of the Ghostie's attention. He kept firing, and the stray energies of the weapon skimmed off Strambli and tore into the walls of the launch. There was a bang, and a developing howl, and Fura felt her ears pop. He had blown a hole right out into space.

Her helmet was . . . up front, in that forward compartment. She realised then that Stallis had come to an entirely pragmatic decision: she could die; he would bring his masters her body, or instructions for locating it, but he had no further intention of bringing her in alive. There was simply too much personal risk to him.

The black weapon in his hand fizzed and sparked. It had given too much of itself, she guessed. That final setting must have been a one-time adjustment, making the weapon operate in some overload condition that it could only do once. He looked at it, then tossed it forward, along the length of the main compartment. It tumbled and flashed, spitting and crackling, until it was snagged by the currents of escaping lungstuff and began to speed toward the hole in the hull.

'Not your best gift to me, Mother,' he shouted, raising his voice above the howl, and made to step back through into the control compartment and seal the door.

By then Strambli was only a couple of spans from him. That vague, fugitive form of hers sped up as if in a final lunge, and she seemed to flick out some part of her almost to the point of contact. The door closed, though, and Stallis' face bobbed up in the inspection window for an instant before turning quickly away.

Silvery gashes began to appear in the door's metal. Fura had seen what Ghostie blades could do to any manufactured substance – certainly anything forged in the Thirteenth Occupation – and she had no doubt that Strambli could slice through that door in a matter of seconds.

But perhaps Stallis knew that as well. There was a jolt, as hard as if a slug had struck them, and a flash of powdery light showed through the inspection window in the bulkhead door.

Fura thought she knew what had happened. There were no portholes to confirm her theory, but if she had been able to see outside, she would not have been surprised to see the front part of the launch speeding away, propelled by auxiliary rockets.

Strambli's presence gave up on the door and came back to her. Fura stared at her drowsily, more disappointed than afraid. She had often thought about the possible circumstances of her own death – it was hard not to, when she was being hunted down – but whenever those imagined ends played in her mind's eye, there had always been an element of dramatic theatricality about them. Flinging herself into the path of a crossbow bolt, or mouthing some heroic last words as the blade came down, or at the controls of a burning ship as it sped, blazing, toward its enemies, drunk on her own wild fearlessness. It had never played out this way, not in any of her fantasies. She had never thought that death would come from just being abandoned; left, once again, to expire in a space-holed wreck, like some piece of garbage it was too much trouble to dispose of properly.

And there was nowhere to go. If they were still docked with

Revenger, and that jolt had not dislodged them, then all that waited her on the other side of the lock was more vacuum. There were parts of suits racked up with the equipment, perhaps enough to make a whole suit, or enough of one to suffice, but none of those squadron-issue helmets would fit into her neck-ring, and besides, it was awfully hard to think of such things when all she wanted to do was sleep, and sleep . . .

I'll take you forward to the other breathies, if that's what you'd like. I can do that, and then you can be on your way. Or I could jab a bit of me in you and we'd both be Ghostie! You'd like that, wouldn't you? I wouldn't mind at all.

'Not yet,' Fura said. 'Not yet, Stramb. But . . . thank you.'

I heard what you said about the ship. That you'd be misplacing it, not losing it. Like you meant to come back and find it again.

'I would.'

It'd still need a captain, wouldn't it? All on its own out here, with no breathy souls left in it. It'd be lonely without a captain!

'It's yours now, Stramb. It was good to me, but the truth is I didn't take very good care of it. Now you get a chance. Take this ship and . . . do something useful with it.' Fura smiled through the blackening fog of her thoughts. There was much she might have wished to ask Strambli, even as she wondered how much each was capable of understanding of the other across the vast divide between the living and the undead that now separated them. 'Just one . . . condition. I don't know what's going to happen to me now, or what's happened to Adrana. But if there's ever a day when we come back to find you, because we need a fast, dark ship . . . you'll treat us kindly, won't you?'

The Ghostie form came in nearer, pressing its not-face so close to Fura that the chill made her nose tingle.

'There'd always be a welcome for the Nesses. And I won't forget my offer. Just a jab is all it'd take . . .'

27

If Adrana had entertained any preconceived notions about the likely extent of Quell's escape tunnel, they would not have stretched to the distance she had already come. True, it was not the easiest matter to gauge her rate of progress while effectively blind, relying solely on the Clacker for guidance. Nor could she very easily determine whether their path had been straight or sinuous, or whether the corridor fell or rose on a slight gradient, or remained level. But she could count, and thought that she knew the length of her own stride tolerably well, and when she had already tallied three hundred paces, she knew that they had to be well beyond the building above them. If the tunnel continued in the direction it had begun, and kept that course, then they were walking parallel to the street on which Quell's Bar had its entrance, and might now be a block or two down from it.

They could equally well be going in a completely different direction.

'A little to your right, please. And hold me level.'

'You weigh more by the minute.'

'I assure you I do not. To the left, now. Have you the slightest notion what we may expect at the end of this tunnel? If there is indeed an end?'

'You are very talkative for someone who was depleted and incapable only a short while ago.'

'I find by talking I may reassure myself that you have not slipped into a state of somnambulant unconsciousness. Do you truly have no conception of where we are heading?'

'Away from those muddleheads in the bar, and for the moment that is good enough for me. Besides, you were the one who insisted on that rendezvous, Tazaknakak, not me.'

'I did not expect to be confronted by an impostor.'

Adrana grunted. Carrying the Clacker was like trudging home with a load of heavy shopping. After a while, no amount of shifting around made any difference to the burden. 'You half expected trouble, all the same. You must have known that there was at least a reasonable chance that the muddleheads would be waiting for you.'

'Regrettably, what I considered a small but worrying eventuality turned out to be rather more than that.' The alien paused, and for a moment there was a stillness about him. 'I am . . . sorry . . . for your companions. There was a degree of . . .ill-preparedness. Had I but known . . .'

'I am sorry for them as well. But it isn't entirely your fault.'

'It is not?'

'You aren't blameless, Zak.' She had decided to use the shortened form of his name from now on, whether it pleased him or not. 'I'm not sure anyone is. Perhaps Meggery, who didn't deserve to get mixed up in all of this, but she still chose a dangerous profession that could have killed her at any time. And Rackamore chose to be a spy.'

'And you, Captain Ness?'

'I take my share. It was my idea to transport you.'

'Despite all that has just happened, that was meant as a helpful thing.'

'At least as helpful to me as to you,' she said. 'The truth is, I didn't really care about your fate once we got you here. But I did care about the information you were going to share with me.'

'There is self-interest in all things. On my world, we say that it is the grease that allows the gears to turn. Incidentally I am rendering this saying in a form that should be comprehensible to you.' His head gave a buzz, which she felt through her ribs. 'Be careful. The floor is dipping now.'

'Dipping? I was hoping we'd start going up.'

'I am content to lie, if that would be more to your liking.'

'No, I should prefer the truth, unvarnished. And while we are on the subject of truth and lies, and you have mentioned your world . . .?'

'Yes,' Tazaknakak said guardedly.

'You will do me one service, since I may be said to have discharged my responsibility to you, however imperfectly. You will answer me candidly, or at least give your honest impression.'

'I shall labour to provide.'

'Do you dispute that the muddleheads are the product of advanced xenografting techniques?'

'I do not, since there is nothing disputable about that statement.'

'Then consider this. They're impossible. I have seen some odd things since I left Mazarile, Zak. Catchcloth, Ghostie gubbins, twinkle-heads, baubles and skullvanes. I have seen a box that disappears; I have seen quoins that glow and sing. But I have seen nothing that was not explicable within the rational framework that was instilled in me by my schooling, which – incidentally – was chiefly imparted to me by a thinking machine from the Twelfth Occupation. So, I am used to strangeness, and hints of science and philosophy beyond our own understanding, but I am not accustomed to things that make no sense, nor ever can, and the muddleheads fit that category. Xenografting cannot be possible, and nor can the muddleheads, if that is how they are to be explained.'

'Then you have arrived at an impasse. As have we, in a manner of speaking. The tunnel divides at this point. I see no indication of which route is to be preferred.'

'Which one is the breeze coming from?'

'Both.'

'Does one go down?'

'Yes.'

'And the other?'

'It also goes down, yet perhaps a little more steeply. On reflection, that seems to be the more doubtful of the two options.'

'Then we take that one. I do not want to take the more obvious path if the muddleheads, or more of Quindar's associates, are coming up behind us.'

'That is a perverse sort of reasoning, even by the standards of your kind. But I shall abide by it.'

She felt the transition to a steeper grade: it had been too shallow until now to be appreciable, but now there was no ignoring their descent, and it became even more of a struggle to hold onto the Clacker. 'I'll be frank with you, Zak. I have no idea how much further there is to go, nor how long I shall be able to carry you. Do you think you could walk, as well as generate sound-sense?'

'Yes, but not nearly as quickly as we are now progressing, and then we would have the added difficulty that you would not be able to see which direction I am following. Might I add something that you may not find encouraging?'

'Please do so.'

'I detected a draught from behind us. It was not very long-lived, but I think it may have been due to someone opening and closing that concealed entrance.'

'Then we had best be silent . . . as silent as you can be, and still be useful.' She urged herself to walk faster, even as her natural instincts rebelled against every footstep. It was like counting the paces across a familiar room, blindfolding herself, and then striding confidently at a wall, intending to stop exactly one pace short. But worse, for as much as dependence on the Clacker was absolute, she had only a qualified confidence in the reliability of his sound-sense. He might be able to detect the general dimensions of the tunnel, steering her along its middle, but would he notice a hole in the floor if it came upon them?

'I am believer in candour, Captain Ness.' His voice was low, and she almost had to angle her head down to hear him. 'You ask difficult questions. But you have almost answered one of them for yourself. Since the muddleheads are demonstrably real – neither of us would contend otherwise – and since they cannot have been generated by xenografting, then it would stand that they have been created by other means.'

'I can't have been the first to ask this question, Zak.'

'Perhaps not, although in fairness the origins of muddleheads are hardly among the burning parlour-room topics of the day. I would warrant that fewer than one in ten thousand of your kind know that such creatures exist; still fewer have seen them.'

'That does not alter the fact that they must be made by some means other than xenografting.' She frowned to herself in the darkness. 'Or rather, that if xenografting is the process, then xenografting cannot mean what it is commonly taken to mean. If a creature can be assembled from the biological components of monkeys and aliens, then the aliens . . .'

'Cannot be truly alien.'

'Or monkeys cannot be truly monkey.'

'That also.'

She walked on for a few paces, reflecting on his answer. Candid or not, it had slipped out of him with all the fanfare of some exceedingly trifling confession. And yet that assertion, so off-handedly uttered, contradicted one of the central pillars of her world view. There were monkeys and there were aliens. They were not alike. They did not – could not – have anything in common, besides felicitous accidents of convergent evolution.

'And yet, you told me yourself that your history is immeasurably older than our own. How may the one and the other be reconciled?'

'They may not,' Tazaknakak declared boldly. 'Unless at least one of those histories is incorrect.'

'But you will not say which.'

'I will not say that I know. But I will say that these are not questions that should be asked without a very grave understanding of the consequences of the investigation. You will have observed my earlier reticence when you pressed me on this subject, and related matters. It was not through ignorance, or some want of curiosity. These questions vex me deeply, or I should not be in the trouble I now find myself. But I doubted your seriousness of purpose, Captain Ness. I thought you might have a mere dilettantish attraction to these mysteries, as many before you have. I see now that I was wrong. You are dangerously sincere in your interests. They have led to the corpses of your friends and still you are not done.'

'At the moment, Zak, my chief concern is my own immediate self-preservation.'

'Mine also. But let us be honest with each other. We each may die today. But should we not – should fortune favour us with an extension to our lives, deserved or otherwise – you and I will not be resting. What has been stirred within us cannot be put back to sleep. We must have our answers, no matter what they do to us.'

'I want to say that you are right. It flatters me a little.'

'Do you doubt my assessment?'

'I doubt my resolve. My sister is out there somewhere, Zak, and something very bad may be happening to her. Or has already happened. It is conceivable – likely, even – that she is dead.'

'And this changes you?'

'Everything we ever did was shared. Every game we played, every treasure hunt, every story we made up or were told by Paladin. Every cruel trick I devised to play on him. Fura always went along, even if she cared for him more than I did. And when we ran away, that was shared also. When we took up with Captain Rackamore and joined his crew, we did it as sisters. And when these questions began to tear at us – Fura with her quoins, me with the Occupations – they did not seem to me like separate vanities, but twin walls rising to some higher unification. I felt that each of us needed the other; that without Fura's consuming interest, mine would be incomplete, and vice versa. But now I feel as if I am staring into a void. A part of me still wants these answers: that hasn't changed. But they will not fill the hollowness I am starting to feel inside me.'

'You do not know that she is dead.'

'There has been no news.'

'Nor will she have had news of your fate. At the moment she may be racked with parallel thoughts of her own. A similar hopelessness – a similar sense of futility. Yet she knows herself to be alive. Would you embolden her to continue?'

'I would.'

'Then extend yourself the same courtesy, dear Captain.' Almost immediately he added: 'Ah.'

'Ah, what?'

'There is an impenetrable surface ahead of us.'

She set him down for a moment, relieving her bones and muscles while she swept her fingers up and down the surface from floor to ceiling. It was not a continuous wall, although Tazaknakak's sound-sense might have led him to conclude otherwise. It was a grille, like a heavy fireguard, made up of horizontal and vertical struts. They were far too stiff to force apart. She could squeeze a finger into the gap between two of the rods, but not her whole hand. If there was a door in the grille, or some way of moving the whole obstruction, she could not find it by touch alone.

'Perish the worlds. We took the wrong turning.' She hammered the grille once, anger getting the better of her. It rattled a little in its fixings, but not enough to persuade her that they had any chance of forcing it aside. 'We must go back. It can't have been more than few minutes since we chose our path.'

'Yet they are behind us.'

'I know. But I will not wait here with my back to the wall.' She scooped him up again, and every joint and ligament in her body seemed to issue a collective complaint, but she forced those protestations into a sort of mental bottle and then tossed it far out of sight. 'Guide me. Quickly.'

They retreated back into the same swallowing darkness from which they had come. Adrana vowed to herself that she would think only of making it back to the intersection, and not permit herself to dwell on the likelihood of the other route being similarly obstructed. Survive the present moment, then the one after, then the next, and sooner or later all those next moments added up to a life. That was how people like Prozor or Lasling dealt with the many hazards of their profession. To worry about anything other than the immediate problem was to divert some vital energy from the moment, where it was most needed.

She would not do that.

'You are right, Zak,' she murmured. 'About my sister, I mean. I must act at all times as if each of us is alive. And remind myself that this is Arafura Ness of whom we are speaking. She took the *Nightjammer*! She took Bosa Sennen! Why should I doubt that she can get the better of a few ships and a worm like Incer Stallis?'

'Then you will not flinch from your search for knowledge. That is commendable. I will reward your moral courage with a small disclosure.'

'I didn't think you had anything more to say about the histories of our peoples.'

'I do not, directly. But I will return to the question of quoins, and the small demonstration I set you aboard the *Merry Mare*. You remember, of course.'

She thought back to the lock, and that solitary quoin drifting out of the ship before moving with definite purpose in the direction of the Old Sun.

'I know what I saw. I have been thinking about it on and off ever since.'

'And would you proffer a hypothesis?'

'Quoins are drawn to the Old Sun. First by turning their faces, and then by an overall impulse. It isn't magnetic, but some other affinity. And it's new behaviour, something not seen until the Readjustment.'

'You can be sure of this?'

'I can be sure of nothing, Zak. But I think in hundreds of years some captain or crew must have spilled some quoins out into space by accident. And if that propensity were present, it would have been observed, remarked-upon, and studied.

Navigators would need to allow for the deflection toward the Old Sun of every ship with a hold-full of quoins, and yet the old charts and formulae still serve us well. Or until now they have.' She shook her head in the darkness. 'No, this is entirely novel. When the Readjustment happened, it must be that the quoins were woken: roused to some truer state of being, or some remembrance of their deeper purpose. Does this . . . accord . . . with your own ideas?'

'It does more than accord. It is as near to the truth as any monkey could ever comprehend.'

'Then tell me what is happening.'

'I shall – after you tell me what you know of the Readjustment, and its causes.'

'I am sure you have made the necessary deductions, Zak.'

'But I should like to hear your version of events.'

'If I had the time, I would set them down in a book. Fura made her account; mine could follow. It would start when we took *Revenger*, and end when we found the quoins, and I uncovered the true identity of Lagganvor. That would be *my* account. But then I suppose someone else would have to tell our stories from that point on, now that we are separated.'

'Reading monkey language is very tiresome for a Clacker. You may abbreviate your narrative for my sake. And do not be too verbose about it: I fear I detect sounds of approach.'

'We can't be far from the intersection.'

'Nonetheless. Summarise the Readjustment, and your part in it.'

'The pirate Bosa Sennen had been accumulating quoins. She had been at it for centuries, and there were a great many quoins – perhaps as many in her cache as were still in circulation in the worlds. She had been careful how she kept them, though. Although the cache was in one place, a little rock out beyond the Frost Margins, the quoins were kept in many different vaults within it. We thought this must be mere convenience, until we made the error of bringing too many quoins together in one place.'

'There is a mineral, an isotope, which is safe in isolation but becomes dangerous when too much of it is concentrated in one place. The effect is called criticality. It sounds very much as if an analogous process happened to the quoins. As you have already intimated, they may be said to have woken. Tell me – and honestly – did you have any intention to precipitate the Readjustment?'

'No,' she said firmly. 'And I speak for Fura in this. We didn't know what we were doing. We meant to shake things up a little, but . . . never to that extent. There were consequences, Zak. In Mulgracen we saw a man throw himself from a window because of the loss of his savings. Do you see the intersection yet?'

'We are upon it. We took the rightmost course last time; now we shall take the leftmost. Turn to your right and proceed.'

'I just saw some light: a flicker of red or orange.'

'They are approaching. We must hasten.'

'I'm hastening.' She felt the transition to sloping ground again as they went down the less steep of the two tunnels. Adrana jogged as quickly as her blind and burdened condition allowed. She was entirely at the mercy of his directions, but she had become used to that by now and seemed to be less prone to wandering to the left or right. Yet even this increase in tempo had the effect of magnifying the sound of her breath, so that it had every chance of reverberating up and down the length of the tunnels, like a note in a pipe organ.

'Concerning that man you saw in Mulgracen: for all that you know he was already at the tail-end of a grievous run of misfortune.'

'Or perhaps he was a good man, trying to live well, and we wrecked everything. He won't have been alone, though. There'll have been many like him on Mulgracen, and Mulgracen is just one world.'

'For a Ness sister, you seem peculiarly squeamish about a death or two.'

'I won't deny the blood we've spilled through coil-gun and Ghostie blade. But those people had set themselves in direct opposition to us. I don't say they were bad people, not all of them, but each chose to take us on, or obstruct us, for glory or for prize, and for that reason alone my conscience is intact. But there must be many other men and women like that man, who were just caught up in the Readjustment, and that was our doing.'

'You cannot have predicted it.'

'Does that absolve us?'

'Of one set of consequences, perhaps. You introduced a change into a complex system, and one result of that is misery and death among an indeterminate number of your kind. And, it may be said, great vexation among certain of my own.' She felt him shrug in her arms. 'So be it. But it is also possible that the change you introduced was beneficial and necessary.'

'I hope that it will be seen so. If the quoins were not what we believed, then it must be better to be disabused of that falsehood.'

'Do you think so?'

Adrana gave her the answer the seriousness of consideration it was due. 'I do. Now every person on every world knows that the value of a quoin is not a thing set for all eternity, and no fortune can be predicated on quoins alone. That is a better state of knowledge, I think.'

'The vested interests would disagree . . . but you are right. It is a far better thing to know, than not to know.'

'And yet, we are not done with changes. Why are quoins drawn to the Old Sun?'

'Because, dear Captain, it is sick.'

A light flashed, impossibly bright to her dark-adapted eye, a sound cracked, and a scorching smell touched her nostrils. Some projectile or energy pulse must have come close to her. She thought that it had originated from behind them. A voice, muffled by distance and confinement, called out: 'They ain't far!'

Another: 'They want 'em alive!'

'Or mostly!'

'More haste, I think,' Tazaknakak said.

But she was already at her limit. If she tripped and dashed the fragile shell of his casque against the floor, they were undone. It was like running a darkened maze with some irreplaceable piece of pottery in her hands. Somewhere behind them, another light flashed. Was it closer than before, or were the acoustics of the tunnel system confusing her? Perhaps the pursuing party had gone down the steeper of the two tunnels, and their lights and sounds were only reaching her by indirect means.

Something shone ahead. Tazaknakak stiffened in her arms, alarmed.

'There is something ahead, Captain Ness.'

She clutched him tighter, gazing into the depths of the tunnel. Beams and prickles of yellow light were stabbing forward. She stared hard. Behind these lights, and moving closer, was a bustling barricade of living forms. She halted, for it seemed equal madness to proceed as to turn back and face the pursuers closing in from the other direction.

'I'm sorry, Zak,' she said softly. 'I think I may have failed you.'

'Nearly on 'em, lads,' cried out a rough voice from behind. 'How're you faring, Mister Q?'

'Never been more content,' replied the man that she knew to be Vidin Quindar, but who could just as easily answer to the name of Quell. 'So nice of my predecessor to leave us these tunnels, for a bit of sport.'

'Captain Ness?' called a newer voice, one she had not heard before. It came from ahead of her. It was rough, damaged – but there was something in it that gave her the smallest shred of encouragement. 'It's you, isn't it?'

Adrana lifted her chin. 'That would depend on your expectations, sir.'

She detected some faint amusement in the voice's reply. 'Please do me a small favour, Captain Ness. Press yourself down on the floor, as close as you can – and ensure your companion is similarly protected.'

She grasped the intent, flattened herself, and strove to hold Tazaknakak tightly to her side.

A small piece of hell broke out above them.

She jammed her eyes shut and wished she could stopper her ears. Tazaknakak writhed and rattled and she forced him to hold still. The onslaught continued for what was in all likelihood only a matter of seconds, yet she had endured hours that seemed shorter. She heard pistol shots and the hum and crack of energy weapons. She heard screams and shouts and sudden barked orders.

And then it was done. The shots ceased, and although there was an echoing reverberation as their reports chased up and down the tunnels, no more exchanges came. Some men coughed; others moaned or whimpered or made liquid or guttural sounds in their dying moments.

Adrana dared open her eyes. A form loomed over her. She could see a little now, because the party that had blocked their way had torches, and they were projecting patterns of light and darkness upon the walls. The looming form was a man, stooping down to extend a hand.

A blind man, she realised.

There were two holes in his face: two black, well-like sockets either side of his nose. Above them his hair was a bristle of white and grey, mostly the former. A pair of muddleheads stood one either side of him, touching him lightly and guiding the direction of his reach. They were as mis-matched and unsettling as the others, but Adrana did not think she had seen these two before.

'Are you to be trusted, sir?' she asked.

'That's a very good question, Captain Ness. I can well understand your reservations. You've not had the best of introductions since your arrival.'

'You are Quell,' she said.

He touched a finger to his forehead. 'I am. Despite the efforts of others to usurp my name. I'm sorry you had the misfortune to run into Quindar before we could reach you. You did well to get this far from him – was there trouble?'

She got up from the ground, pressing her fingers into dirt

as she did so. Two more of Quell's associates came past – monkeys this time – and went toward whatever remained of Quindar's party. They had weapons in both hands: two crude, flare-mouthed pistols held by one, and a pair of gorgeous Ninth Occupation duelling blasters that glinted with inlaid gemwork, held by the other

Adrana cocked her head after the monkeys.

'Quindar's people killed two of my friends. He has muddle-heads and . . . well, so do you. I'm not sure I quite understand. I thought the muddleheads were sent to kill Zak.'

'Not all muddleheads,' Quell said tactfully, 'are cut from the same cloth. Or rather, the cloth is not the thing. It would be wise not to judge, until you've seen a man's character. Wouldn't you agree?'

'I would.'

He dipped his hollowed-out sockets. 'Is Zak how you name the Clacker?'

'I am here, Quell,' Tazaknakak declared. 'Lift me up, Captain Ness, so that we might study each other.'

'It's all right,' Quell said, raising a hand to dissuade Adrana. 'I have him, and you must be tired-out by now.' He picked up the Clacker, finding him despite his sightlessness, and elevated him until their faces were level.

'You are damaged, Quell.'

'Quindar took my eyes. The Crawlies gave them to me origi-nally. Quindar found his way to Trevenza after he lost his own sight on Mazarile.' He flashed a knowing grin at Adrana. 'Some bad business with a robot, is what I heard.'

'I thought you and Quindar were friendly.'

'We were, to a degree. But I made an error of judgement when I allowed him to abduct your sister. Later, I made an even greater error when I gave him sanctuary here and offered to help with his eyes.'

Behind Adrana came a couple of pistol shots and then the buzz-crack of energy discharges. Some of the moaning and whimpering ceased.

'I was also blind,' Tazaknakak said. 'Then Captain Ness made me see again.'

'Your casque?' Quell asked, touching Tazaknakak with great gentleness. 'Yes. I think I can feel the injuries. Word came to us that you'd been attacked on your way out of Mulgracen. We feared the worst. Are you . . . ready?'

'I have never been readier, Quell. Are you prepared for me?'

'As prepared as we can be.'

'Prepared for what?' Adrana asked.

Her question was abbreviated by a sudden shrieking coming from the direction of Quindar's party. It was, by some measure, the worst sound she had ever heard coming from another creature.

The shrieking stopped.

One of the muddleheads came back with a pair of heavy, dark objects in the large, bearlike mitten that was his hand. The muddlehead offered the items to Quell.

'Very well done, my friend.' Quell explored the two black tubes with his fingers. 'Whether they can ever be put back in again is a question for another day. But at least they're back with their rightful owner. Have you finished with Quindar?'

The muddlehead answered with a whirring, clicking voice like a telephone dial. 'He's the . . . last one . . . alive, although . . . complaining a fair . . . bit – even more so . . . since we . . . took those peepers off him. Do you . . . think we should . . . put him out of his . . . misery?'

'That *would* be the kinder thing,' Quell said.

'It would,' the muddlehead agreed. 'So I suppose . . . leave him . . . as-is?'

'For the best, all things considered.' Quell laid one hand on what, in the muddlehead, might have passed for a shoulder. 'But you knew I'd say that, Chunter.'

'We know . . . each other . . . too well, Hasp,' the muddlehead said, with something akin to fondness.

Quell turned back to address Adrana. He might have been sightless, but he evidently possessed an impeccable visual memory of his surroundings. 'We have a short journey still to make, Captain. We should not run into any difficulties between here and our destination, but we'll all still need to be on our guard.'

'You've dealt with Quindar. But he's just part of it, isn't he?'

'A small but annoying component. Unfortunately, the machine will keep working without him. We're still in shutter-down. There'll be hostile muddleheads sweeping the streets while they can move around with some freedom, as well as aliens, monkey agents and other associates of Quell. Squadron men are close at hand, too – they may have landed a launch or two at our docks since the last time I was informed.'

'Have you word of my sister?'

'I think,' Quell said, 'that you should come with us.'

28

A face that she knew came into semi-focus. It was long, pale, graven with deep vertical lines. The eyes were the saddest and wisest she thought she had ever seen.

'Captain Ness.' The voice became firmer. 'Captain Arafura Ness. Captain Ness! Can you hear me? You've been in vacuum. Make some motion if you can understand me.'

'I think we're clear of the worst of it,' said another voice that she knew she recognised, but to which she could not yet attach the label of a name.

Another: 'Put my hand on the red lever and tell me when the dial to the right of it goes hard over.'

A fourth: 'She went to the trouble of bringing this bag, but not to the bother of finding herself a vacuum suit?'

'Conceivably,' said the man with the sad eyes, 'there were no vacuum suits to be had in that part of the ship.'

'But how'd she get to us?'

'Open the bag, will you, Ruther?'

Slowly, painfully, some approximation of awareness and identity came back to her. She felt very bad. There seemed no part of her that was not painful. The only consolation was that there were so many points of discomfort that no single one of them yet had precedence over the others. But her throat, and her eyes, and her lungs . . .

'Eddralder,' she said, and her voice was a barely recognisable rasp. 'Doctor . . . Eddralder. Where am I?' She squinted, trying to focus on some point beyond the physician's face. Metal walls, close in. Circular portholes, riveted frames. Structural spars like whale-ribs. 'I'm in the launch. I'm in the rocket launch.'

'Very good, Captain Ness.' He pressed a drinking teat to her lips. 'Sip this, but sparingly. You have been exposed to vacuum. There is likely damage to the lining of your throat and windpipe. Do you remember how you got to us?'

'I . . .' She drank from the teat. 'I . . . there was Incer Stallis. They boarded us. Two launches, either side. I wanted you to undock. You should have undocked.'

'We did, but not until we had you. There wouldn't have been any point until it was clear those launches were going nowhere.'

'You'd have outrun 'em. Too heavy. Keep it lean. In and out easily. Why didn't you?'

'Because we had the sense not to,' called back the voice that she knew belonged to a woman called Surt. She was somewhere up front, out of Fura's line of sight. 'We'd have sped away quickly, it's true, but not fast enough to escape their guns, and with our jets turned up we'd have made a nice target for 'em. If they started trying to break through our locks, we'd have cut and run – but it never came to that. Then we felt that other launch shoot off. Something happened on our ship, Cap'n – did you see any part of it?'

She sifted through the jumble of her thoughts.

'Strambli came back. She was there all along, and she came back. But she was . . .' Fura halted herself, for what she had to say was difficult, and demanded a toll on the limited energies she had left. 'She'd gone Ghostie. *Strambli was Ghostie.* She killed them all. Went through them like a glass wind. She cut them up and . . .' She halted, drawing a sharp breath. 'Tindouf's gone. Incer Stallis killed him.'

'And your hand?' Eddralder asked.

'No, there's nothing wrong with my hand. I had it cut off

when I was on Mazarile, and replaced with . . .'

But she looked down, and remembered, and shrieked.

*

Now that there was torchlight, she saw that the fabric of the tunnel was of closely-set black bricks, very well laid, and yet with signs of sagging and subsidence that must have happened very gradually, so that none of the bricks had shattered or fallen loose. There were, in places, points of rupture where the wall's cladding had broken inward, but these were exceptions and for the most part the wall was structurally intact, and yet clearly much too old to have been the work of Quell or any of his associates.

The party progressed briskly. They were going down a gradual continuous slope, with the tunnel following a sinuous trajectory. Adrana and Tazaknakak were in the middle of the party, with Quell and four of his associates leading. Four more were coming up behind, playing their torches back along the way they had come. 'A precaution,' Quell said, smiling at her. 'It's unlikely that we'll have any trouble from that direction, but we can't be too careful. It was very clever of you to find the escape route, by the way. To the best of my knowledge, Quindar never discovered it. Once or twice, we'd come nearly all the way back to the rear side of that secret panel and set a tell-tale, so that we'd know if he ever ventured into the tunnels.'

'He followed me well enough.'

'If there was no other way for you to have left the cellar, he'd have looked at things with a fresh perspective. Did you replace the panel after you came through?'

'I tried to.'

'I'm sure you did the best that you could under the circumstances. Quindar may have had other means of tracking you, besides.'

She thought of how easily Paladin had tracked them, that fateful night they escaped into Neural Alley. What a robot could do, so could a man who had access to alien technology.

'Why did you tolerate being usurped, Quell, if you were able to go almost all the way back to your cellar?'

'The trick of winning a war is to know which battles to lose. If I'd retaken that bar – and I could have, very easily – I'd just have made myself a more tempting target for the forces behind Quindar. Corrupt banks, corrupt agents of those merchant institutions, corrupt aliens serving the same narrow interests. They'd have come after me again, and in greater numbers. Instead, I let him have his little empire. I allowed him to steal my eyes, steal my name, steal my business. I also allowed him to believe that I was dead, and no longer of any possible consequence. Meanwhile, I gathered allies and fellow travellers to my side. Souls such as Chunter, who you have already met. But there are others. We'll meet them shortly.'

They had reached a feature set midway in the wall. It was a circular wooden plug, like the lid of a beer barrel. One monkey and one muddlehead pulled the plug out of the wall and beckoned into an impossibly cramped and narrow connecting shaft with its floor just below chest-height.

'It's a squeeze, but a short one,' Quell said. 'These tunnels are the abandoned courses of the old sewerage system. Or rather one of about twenty successive systems, each built on the tangled ruins of the old. Now and then, some change in the districts above-ground causes an entire section to be cut off and forgotten like some loop of rotten intestine. Centuries go by, and then some fool decides to dig out a little more room for his basement and finds himself with a very handy escape route.'

While two of his associates went ahead of her, Quell helped Adrana scramble up and into the narrow shaft, with the Clacker having to follow behind her, grumbling and complaining all the while. She had to pad along it on all fours, with her back scraping the roof.

The shaft was filthy, but at least it was brief. At the other end was a hinged metal door of the same diameter as the wooden plug. Adrana was all ready to squeeze through and pop out the other side, anticipating a similar difference in levels. Then a stab of torchlight hinted at the much larger dimensions of this new space into which she was about to emerge. It was a horizontal tunnel, running at right angles to the shaft, but at least fifty or sixty spans across from one curving wall to the other. The door had brought her out onto a narrow ledge about twenty spans up the tunnel's side, with a steep, slithery drop below her, to where a ribbon of dark water ran along the tunnel's lowest part. She scuttled back into the shaft, flinching at the sudden opening out of scale.

Voices called from below and Adrana slowly pushed her head out again. Quell's two associates were below the ledge, making quick progress down a net of rope that had been fastened to the wall beneath the opening. Adrana gathered her courage and eased out facing backwards-first until she could plant her feet on the upper part of the net and begin a cautious descent to the tunnel's base, hands tight on the slimy rope. 'I would help you,' she said to Tazaknakak, 'but since you have one more pair of limbs than I, I would be the one at a disadvantage.'

It was not as bad as it seemed, since the tunnel was circular in cross-section and the really steep part of the net only lasted a few spans. Quell's associates helped her the last few steps, until she was standing on a crude wooden platform that seemed to have been dumped at the bottom of the tunnel. It had raised edges with wooden handrails and rocked and tilted under her as she walked on it. One by one the others came, until the rear guard shone their lights back into the connecting shaft and re-sealed the metal door. They came down the net and took their places on the platform. The dark water ran under it, no more than ankle-deep.

Chunter, the muddlehead, held a pocket timepiece in his bear-mitten.

'About one minute . . . to the half-hour . . . purge, Hasp.'

'Good. Very nicely timed.'

'What is this place?' Adrana asked, although she thought she half-knew the answer.

'Part of the sewerage system,' Quell said. 'Part of the *active* sewerage system. This is Central Overflow Thoroughfare Number Six, one of the main relief ducts.'

'And what gets relieved through it?'

'That,' Quell said, nodding in the direction of a faint but rising roar. 'Ready, lads – it sounds as if they've arranged a fine surge for us this evening.'

Two of his associates were ready at the sides of the platform with long wooden poles. Adrana smelled the surge before she saw it: that coming wave must have been ushering a front of warm, effluent gases before it, and they hit her hard enough that she felt herself close to swooning. But she held her nerve, and her breath, and placed one steadying hand on the wooden rail on the raft's edge (for it was indeed a raft) and another on the Clacker. The inundation did not, mercifully, fill more than a small part of the tunnel's diameter, but as it swelled around and under the raft, rising by the second as the main flow hit them, splashing over the rails, Adrana wondered if there had been some terrible error, and that the raft had become jammed in place, or insufficiently buoyant under its present lading, and was about to be submerged.

It jolted loose, and began to rise, and once it was free of the floor it gathered speed along with the flow, and the splashing died down. That was laudable in one sense, but now that they were moving with the mass of sewerage, there was ample opportunity to see that it was not some homogeneous liquid, but was made up of constituent parts of varying density and texture, like a partly dissolved broth. Something rose in Adrana's throat, but she forced it back down.

They sped along. The associates were sharp-witted and alert, using their poles to nudge the raft away from the walls, and when the torches picked out a nearing junction in the tunnel, the pole-bearers worked with great expertise to aim the raft at one of the bores.

Adrana pinched her nose against the stench. 'May we clarify one or two things, Mister Quell? You betrayed my sister. From what I recall of that incident, you also betrayed the trust of your friend Prozor. I was content to deliver Tazaknakak into your care, as that was what he desired. But my interest in you ended there.'

The black absences of his eyes seemed to drill into her soul. 'And now?'

'I find myself caught up in some plans of yours of which I had no prior knowledge – plans that seem to involve the preparations you discussed with Tazaknakak. But I've no guarantee that you're any more trustworthy than Vidin Quindar.'

'You don't,' he acknowledged. 'And nothing I say or do will ever restore my reputation to the point before that betrayal. There isn't a day when I don't reflect on Prozor, and the low opinion she must have of me. Tell me – is she on your ship? Is she well?'

'She's not on our ship.' Adrana thought of prolonging his discomfort – it was nothing less than he deserved – but some charitable part of her prevailed. 'But the last time I saw her she was well. I would like to say that she is still alive, but that depends on the condition of my sister and her ship.'

'Concerning the ship, I'm afraid the reports were accurate.'

Adrana steeled herself. 'Destroyed?'

'Very badly incapacitated, at the least, and with no chance of making independent sail.'

'You would know, sir?'

He lofted a hand to his face. 'I would. I was a Master of Ions once – worked all the baubles of the Melgamish Bracelet under Pelsen of the *Countess by Lamplight*. Then . . . this. But I still know ships, and their capabilities. Yours is finished.' But a half-smile formed on his lips. 'She did not go down without a fight, though. She's bloodied that squadron well.'

'Yet they've taken her?'

'That I cannot say. But there is a rocket launch on its way to the Reach.'

That was as much news as they could give her, and since there was at least the possibility of hope, she clung to it most tenaciously.

'This is a thoroughly trying set of circumstances,' announced the Clacker, as if nothing of the slightest importance had just been discussed. 'Smell is not my most highly developed faculty, yet even so I feel myself overwhelmed by the collective ordure of your kind.'

'I doubt that we can take all the credit for it,' Adrana said. 'There are aliens in this world, besides monkeys. Some Clackers too, I don't doubt, and however the sewerage originates, I fancy it ends up in the same place. I expect you've all contributed your share.' She glanced at Quell, noticing that he was in conversation with one of the associates. 'Did you think I'd forget our conversation, in the tunnels?'

He waved aside her enquiry. 'Whatever the topic I settled upon to ease your nerves, it has now slipped my mind.'

'It hasn't slipped mine. We were speaking of quoins, and their utility. You said they were drawn to the Old Sun because it is sick.'

'I said too much.'

'No, you said entirely too little. I shan't rest, Tazaknakak, until I have it out of you. And I know you want to speak of it. Some better part of you knows that this truth must see the light. So why not tell me now, and be done with it?'

'Your narrow little brain could not . . .'

'Never mind what my narrow little brain can or cannot encompass. Just tell me what we need to know. Tell me about the quoins, once and for all. And spare nothing.'

*

And so he told her, while they rode the raft on the surging flow. He spoke of quoins that were really little machines, or vast machines, yet mostly hidden, and he spoke as if those vast hidden machines (or parts of one even greater leviathan) were in fact healing angels, angels who had been deflected from their true purpose, which was to descend into the ailing fires of the Old Sun and make it youthful again.

To make the Old Sun New.

Tazaknakak was perfectly right in one regard. Her narrow little brain understood very little of it.

But perhaps enough to be going on with.

*

'Show her what's in the bag,' Eddralder said.

Ruther pulled back the edge of the sack very carefully. It was the sort they used on bauble hunts, to contain quoins or loot. As he opened the sack there came into view a curve of glass, a spidering of cracks and repair work, a mosaic of different coloured facets. Lights glimmered within that glasswork, but faintly and sporadically, as if whatever process that sustained them was down to its last few drops of energy. Ruther uncovered more of the object. The glass formed a three-quarters sphere, with a metal collar encircling the lower part of it, and beneath that collar, an eruption of wires and cables and unfathomable mechanical parts, cut cleanly through.

'You say I brought him with me,' Fura said.

'You don't remember?' Eddralder asked.

'All I remember is Stallis leaving, and then Strambli coming back. I was frightened and losing strength. I didn't know what she'd do to me.'

Surt spoke down from the front of the launch. 'She was one of us.'

'Once, Surt. I know it feels like only a little time for us, but we're not the ones who turned Ghostie. I think for her it was . . . some other life, some other existence, a very long time ago. And she told me she much preferred what she'd become.'

'Did she say what she was going to do?'

'I gave her the ship. I think she'll . . . haunt it, be custodian of the wreck, perhaps even find a way to sail it again, and that may be the last we ever see of *Revenger* or what became of Strambli. I pity anyone who tries to take that wreck, knowing what's inside it. It seemed . . . a fair bargain.'

'A hard one, for you,' Surt said. 'Knowin' what that ship meant to you and your sister, and the blood it cost us all.'

'But then again, who better than a Ghostie to look after it? It wasn't so hard a choice, Surt. I'm not sorry that it's worked out this way. We're on our way, aren't we? May I ask about your eyes?'

'They're very sore, but if I pull back the bandage I can see that there's light and darkness. Doctor Eddralder thinks I'll heal, given time. Ruther's done himself proud, in any case. He's read out the settings very well, and I even let him work the steering jets, once we had some idea of our course. The boy's got the right soft touch on the inputs. We could make a bauble-hopper out of him, one day.'

There was a catch in Surt's voice that Fura could not help but detect: something trying to put a brave face on things, despite all the evidence to the contrary.

'Things ain't as sweet as I'd like, are they?'

'Can you make it for'ard to the sweeper, Captain?'

'I've a lost a hand, not my wits.' Fura pushed herself out of the chair, past the sack where Paladin lay in his ruined glory, up to the front of the launch where Surt and Ruther were splitting the burden of control between them.

'There's no harm in using sweeper or squawk, now, Captain,' Ruther said. 'Every other ship within ten thousand leagues is doing just that. Even if we kept our silence, we'd still be lit up by reflection pulses and scatter-squawk.'

'What the boy means,' Surt said, adjusting a gyroscopic trim-lever by touch, 'is that we aren't in the dark about our chances of reaching Trevenza. We know our position and speed very well, and we know where they are, and we also know what's left in our propellant tanks.'

Fura hesitated before asking her question, rightly fearful of the answer she was likely to get.

'Which is?'

'Somewhere between nothing and nearly nothing. We had to burn hard to get away from the wreck. Do you remember that we destroyed two of their main vessels? The three left still had plenty of coil-guns and slugs to go in 'em, and as soon as their first boarding operation went wrong, they sent out two more launches. Maybe that's all they've got left, but it's been trouble enough for us. We gave the launches the slip by burning hard, and we dodged their main coillers by doing a drunkard's walk, but that's been heavy on the fuel and now we're nearly spent.'

Fura ruminated on that for a few seconds.

'How many hours to Trevenza?'

'We won't make Trevenza. Our course is good, but our speed is bad. If we adjust our speed, using what's left in the tanks, then we miss by thousands of leagues. Mister Ruther's run the numbers by hand. It'd be easier to square a circle.'

Fura thought hard. 'Then signal them. When that injured party was coming in too hard for Wheel Strizzardy, Glimmery sent out a launch to intercept 'em and bring them in anyway.'

'He did, but Ruther says a similar gambit won't help us, not in the time available. It's knotty, Captain. I wish it weren't, but there's no pleading with fuel and numbers.'

'Someone'll recover us.'

'Not on this course. To reach Trevenza at all, we've had to burn hard for the Empty. We *could* have turned for the main Congregation – and then we'd have had every chance of being recovered. But when they opened us up, all they'd find is corpses – suffocated, starved skeletons at that. It was the right thing to steer us for Trevenza, wasn't it?'

'It was, Surt – and don't ever think otherwise.'

'We *have* signalled them, anyway,' Ruther said. 'As I said, with all the squawking and sweeping going on, it didn't cost us anything to send out a call for help.'

Fura nodded: she was in agreement with the boy, provisionally. 'Did you give our identity?'

'No – I kept that vague. I just said that we were escaping hostile action and needed assistance. Was that all right, Captain?'

'Exactly right, Ruther.' She watched as a shiver of relief passed through him. 'You did all right, boy.' She turned around, addressing the whole of her little band. 'You all did all right. None of us disgraced ourselves, or the friends we lost.'

'I'm sorry we lost the ship as well,' Ruther said forlornly.

She used her good hand to jam a finger under his chin, lifting it. 'We didn't. We lost something, and I ain't saying it isn't a shame. She was good and fast and dark, and I liked her. She was *mine*. But what mattered to me about that ship was the people on it, and the mind making it work. Some of those people aren't with us now, and we'll mourn 'em properly when we're out of this fix. But we made it out, and so did Paladin, and that's not the end of something. It's the start of something else.'

'Do you think we'll get out of this . . . fix?' Ruther asked hesitantly.

'Are you done with life, boy?'

'No, sir. Captain.'

'Have you seen enough of the Congregation's pretty things, tasted enough of its flavours, dipped your hand into enough of its mysteries?'

He answered as if the question might be a trick. 'N . . . no. No, Captain. Not enough.'

'Me neither, boy.' She let his chin go, squeezing his shoulder in passing. 'Me neither. And we're not done; none of us is done. Adrana is still somewhere in Trevenza Reach and if anyone can, she'll find a way.'

*

After some while the flow entered a wider part of the tunnel and slowed to a torpid ooze. The stench intensified, and tiny pale flies buzzed around Adrana's face. Rats scampered along cracks and ledges in the walls of the tunnel, and sometimes picked their way out into the flow, stepping from one solid part of it to the next. When the torchlight fell on their faces they showed no hint of a reaction, their eyes clouded white. They were as blind as Quell.

The transition to a slower flow seemed to be the cue for Quell's associates to make ready for docking. They leaned hard over the forward rails, poles raised above the flow, until there came a nod between them. They thrust their poles into the filth in perfect unison, two hard stabs as if some valuable prey floated just beneath the surface, and the raft yawed sharply. With a series of grunts and shoves, the raft butted against a set of rough, cube-shaped blocks jammed against the tunnel's nearer well. The raft was secured to this makeshift quay, and Quell bid the party to disembark carefully onto the blocks.

Above the blocks was an arch-shaped setback in the wall, and under the arch was a circular metal door. Adrana was beginning to think that the rest of her existence would consist of stooping along lightless, filth-smeared tunnels, but the passage on the other side of the door was metal-lined, amply proportioned, electrically-lit and very nearly hygienic. Better still, once the door was sealed behind them, the flies and the worst of the smell remained on the other side of it, and at last Adrana thought it safe to take a full breath into her lungs. She had been too afraid of vomiting to do so before.

The metal corridor went on for about six hundred spans, and as they neared the end of it so a machine-like hum became louder. They came out onto a railed balcony near the upper levels of an enormous kettle-shaped chamber. It was at least six hundred spans across itself, and easily as deep. Above was a circular glass ceiling, spanned by huge radial and concentric struts, studded with rivets the size of coffee tables. Adrana supposed that daylight would have come through the ceiling ordinarily, but since they were still in the hours of shutter-down, all she could make out were the lights of the distant, opposing surface of Trevenza Reach. She had no recollection of seeing a building that was six-hundred spans tall – at least none that would have followed the shape of this chamber – so she presumed that the window was actually at ground level, and the space they were in was dug in to the skin of the spindleworld.

She looked out beyond the encircling balcony into a steam-wreathed mass of tubes and pipes and strangely shaped containers. The apparatus filled the chamber from floor to ceiling, packed together as closely and haphazardly as the organs in a stomach. There were inspection walkways, catwalks, ladders and spiral staircases, and nearly everywhere she looked could be found a boiler-suited worker examining some fitting, adjusting something with a wrench, or noting down some value from a gauge. The steam came up in thick, irregular bursts and she soon had to remove her spectacles and wipe dry the glass. Beneath her feet, the metal floor of the balcony picked up the vibration of what must have been immense whirring pumps, although there was a curious and unnerving stillness to all the parts she could see. Her eye alighted on some of the labels stencilled on the larger items: *Main Feed Soil Separator, Secondary Gravity Concentrator, Number Six Sludge Digester,* and so on.

'The sewerage works, Mister Quell?' she asked, in a bright and enquiring tone.

His face betrayed a certain pride. 'The Water Board's Fourth District Municipal Treatment Plant. Not even the largest or most modern in this part of Trevenza Reach, but it serves our needs rather well.'

'I do not like the sound of this place,' Tazaknakak said. 'I find its noises highly disagreeable.'

'Then rest assured that you won't be here long,' Quell said, with a faint strained patience. Then, in a half-whisper to Adrana: 'Is he always like this?'

She nodded. 'No. Sometimes he's much worse.'

Rising next to one of the huge pipe-fed tanks was a much slimmer tower, connected to the balcony by a narrow walkway. A door opened in the top of the tower and a boiler-suited woman came out. She leaned over the side of the walkway, looked down, then made a quick beckoning gesture to one of Quell's associates. Quell nodded at a relayed word and the party moved around the curve of balcony and then out across the connecting walkway in single-file, steam wafting around them and providing a form of partial cover. The boiler-suited woman was ushering them into an elevator at the top of the door, urging them to not to delay. 'C'mon, c'mon,' she said. 'Move yerselves!'

'Nervous, Mabil? Quell asked her.

'Nervous all the time, Hasp. But today 'specially.' She gave a final look around, then closed the elevator doors after them. It was a large cabin, but it was still a crush when all of them were squeezed into it. Adrana was jammed in next to a monkey on her right, a muddlehead on her left, and with a grumbling alien clutching at her shins. 'Grinder and the others are waiting for you in the generator room – you should all be safe there for the time being. Do you want to see them or go directly to the hollow?'

'Grinder won't mind hanging around for a few minutes – he's already waited centuries. Take us all the way down.'

Mabil pressed a button very low down on a control panel, and the elevator descended. A silence fell. It seemed to Adrana as if the occupants were going to obey the unspoken rule of elevators, and say nothing at all to each other, so she was almost disappointed when Mabil resumed her answer to Quell. 'Reports coming in of some bother in the tunnels, Hasp. Even hearing that something might have happened to Quindar.'

'I couldn't possibly comment.'

Mabil was a burly, plump-cheeked woman with buck teeth and a froth of crimson hair spilling out from under a greasecloth hat. 'You know the idea was to try and bring him in without too much fuss?'

'No one would have liked that more than me. But there were . . . complications. Have you said hello to Captain Ness? Captain Ness, this is Mabil.'

'Good evening, Mabil,' Adrana said.

Mabil gave her a perfunctory nod. 'Well done on getting the Clack to us. Not too much trouble, I hope?'

'Other than crossing space from Mulgracen, dodging squadron ships, and leaving two of my friends for dead back in Quell's Bar – no, no trouble at all.'

Mabil shook her head – less in sympathy with Adrana, it seemed, than in annoyance that things had not gone as smoothly as they might have. 'Told you we should've intercepted before they ever got close to Quindar, didn't I? Grinder had eyes on 'em, didn't he? If we'd sprung like I said, we'd've spared ourselves this little mess.'

'And how much of a mess is it?'

'Where'd you like to start? You might have got Quindar and a few of his main people, but there're still plenty of 'em out there, running around and agitating. Muddleheads thick as flies.' She looked momentarily contrite. 'Sorry, Chunter. Sorry, Baleus.'

Chunter's telephone-dial voice buzzed out.

'No . . . offence taken . . . at all, Mabil.'

'No more'n usual,' Baleus added, in a broken but half-monkey voice.

'The muddles will need to disperse before shutter-up,' Quell said. 'That only leaves whatever's left of Quindar's rabble, and I think he sent the best of them after Captain Ness.'

'I do so like an optimist,' Mabil said.

There was a window in the elevator's door. Adrana had watched them go down through the levels of the sewerage plant, descending into thicker and thicker steam. Now, though, there was only a continuous moving darkness beyond the window. They were going much further down than the bottom of the plant.

'We must be halfway into the skin of the spindleworld, Mister Quell. Much further, and we'll burst out on the other side. Where are we going?'

'Ask the Clacker,' Mabil said. 'Or did he not tell you already, what the intention was?'

As cramped as it was, Adrana still managed to bend down and lift up Tazaknakak. She turned him around, his face to hers. 'I was promised answers to my questions, Zak.'

Her forehead throbbed.

'You shall have your answers, if you have wits enough to comprehend them.'

'And this elevator? Where's it taking us? What is under the sewerage works?'

'The means to move a world, Captain Ness.'

The elevator emerged beneath some surface. Although there was only a little more light than before, Adrana nonetheless had the impression of the darkness receding; of the space beyond the elevator opening up. Electric lights threw faint, brassy highlights off huge, vague forms, each as large as any of the chemical vessels up on the works. But that was all Adrana could make out.

'Have I been tricked, Quell?'

'No.' His lips creased as he considered his answer. 'Utilised, possibly. But not tricked. We had one objective here, and you've helped us bring it nearer. But our aims aren't in conflict with your own. You will have your answers. Won't she, Zak?'

'Answers will be forthcoming,' Tazaknakak said.

'That's a great comfort,' Mabil muttered.

The elevator car slowed and came to a halt. Mabil opened the door. The lungstuff that flooded the cabin was cold, damp and musty. There was a smell to it that reminded Adrana of the indexes of old, neglected books. It was, she decided, an improvement on the sewer tunnel, with its flies and the rats.

The party filed out. Torches were produced; beams thrust into the semi-darkness. They were in a sort of cave: a bubble of open space embedded like a hollow cyst in the solid skin of the spindleworld. Walls of rough-hewn rock swept up to a dome-shaped ceiling, with the elevator shaft coming down vertically from the apex. Adrana shuddered with some distant, barely recognised terror. The hole in the ceiling, the rocky enclosure, had become a dreadful magnification of the nightmare put into her by Captain Werranwell's little skull. She was reminded again of the hours that had seemed to pass for her in that horrible enclosure. Somewhere beneath her, her mind insisted, was an even vaster space in which some monstrous patient presence lay waiting.

They walked. Although the floor of the cave was the same rough-hewn rock as the rest of it, metal walkways had been fixed to it by pitons. They snaked in and around huge mechanical forms, half buried in the rock and half revealed. The forms were as big as houses; smooth-curved and spiriform. They were black, or nearly black, with only their edges and extremities picked out by those brass-tinted highlights. Nowhere could Adrana see so much as a scratch.

'I think I would like an explanation,' she said.

Quell halted with his back to the wire fence that ran along the edge of the walkway. 'Captain Ness is right. She deserves an explanation, and so do those of you who've never been here before, or only heard scraps of rumour.'

'Don't drag it out for 'em,' Mabil said.

'It's an engine,' Quell said. 'Or part of one. The whole of it must girdle Trevenza Reach completely. No one knows about it except us; no one has seen any part of it except this tiny area, exposed by time. There was a spring, a water-leak, which over millions of years eroded this cavern and exposed these engine parts . . .'

'You just said "millions of years",' Adrana said.

'You're a bauble-hopper, Captain Ness. You've handled treasure that goes halfway back to the Sundering. Deep-time shouldn't faze you.'

'It doesn't,' she answered crisply. 'But not much survives this well unless it's inside a bauble. You say these . . . engine parts . . . have been inside this rock, all this time?'

'The evidence is before your eyes.'

'Next you are going to tell me that this engine can be started up.'

'I sincerely hope so,' Quell said. 'Because if it can't, we're going to have rather a lot of difficulty helping your sister. Tazaknakak? Do you want to see what you can do with it?'

She looked down at the alien. 'What does the Clacker have to do with it?'

'It's his engine,' Quell answered.

Tazaknakak waddled up to one of the curving black surfaces where the metal walkway was close enough for him to touch part of the engine through the wire fence. He rubbed one of his upper palms against the engine surface, barely contacting it first, then with visibly increasing pressure. He applied both upper palms and made opposed circular motions, like a window cleaner trying to buff away a particularly stubborn stain.

Nothing happened.

'Your sister,' Quell said, 'is in a rocket launch on its way to us. We've had squawk contact, on and off. But she's in trouble.'

'Injured?' Adrana cut in.

'Perhaps – but that's not her main problem. She can't make the rendezvous. She's burned all her fuel, and it's still not enough to reach us. Nor can any other launch reach her in time and still have enough fuel to get back. Even if they could, they'd have to dodge what's left of the Revenue Protection forces. Now, if we were orbiting down in the main part of the Congregation, your sister wouldn't have too much to fear. Provided she had supplies and lungstuff, she could hold out until she fell close enough to some other world for a ship to strike out and reach her. But that's not possible out here, and unless we intervene, her course will take her further and further into the Empty: a horror for any captain.'

Adrana nodded slowly. 'But if the engine can move this world?'

'Then Trevenza Reach can be where your sister needs it to be.'

'I want to believe you, Quell. I want to believe that *he* can make this operate.'

The Clacker was still pawing ineffectually at the black surface. Now he had brought both his upper and lower arms into play.

Nothing was continuing to happen.

'He can,' Quell said.

'How do you know?'

'Others have come close. He's not the first to have a go. The engine has been nearly restarted on several occasions.'

'Nearly won't help Fura.'

'Have faith, Captain Ness.'

'There is more to this,' she said, shaking her head. 'More that you're not telling me. I didn't bring Zak all this way just so that he could magically intervene exactly when Fura needs him. His being here was set in motion months ago.'

'Tell her,' Mabil said.

'Plans have been in place for some while,' Quell said.

Adrana put a hand on her hip. 'Plans for what?'

'That the Clacker would start up the engine, just enough to prove its capabilities to all interested parties. We'd move Trevenza Reach a little, and prove what could be done. That'd put the shivers through the other worlds, wouldn't it? And once we had their attention, we'd . . . what's the word?' Quell turned to his associate.

'Leverage,' Mabil said, sounding disgusted with herself.

'Yes – "leverage". We'd leverage that – use it to reset the parameters of our relationship with the rest of the Congregation'

'You live in a sewer, Quell. You *smell* of sewer. How do you expect to leverage anything with anyone?'

'We have the engine – that's all anyone ought to need. But I've the engine and thousands of friends and sympathisers spread across the city, waiting for their moment. Waiting for *our* moment. None of this is accidental or haphazard, Captain – it's been planned-for. But now that Fura needs us, the demonstration will be more than symbolic – we'll be saving lives.'

Adrana nodded, as if all this made complete and compelling sense.

'Except it doesn't work.'

Quell dropped his voice. 'Perhaps he just needs a little time to himself. I don't know about you, but I can't work with someone staring over my shoulder. We'll leave him to it, shall we?'

'I'll look after him,' said the muddlehead called Baleus. He gestured at one of the other associates, extending a long scissoring appendage with many quill-like hairs on it from the folds of his coat. 'Gessel: you've drawn the other short straw. We're on Clack-watch.'

'Oh, the joy,' Gessel said, sniffing hard and drawing a hand under her nose. 'Just when I thought I'd heard every story you have to tell, Baleus.'

'I have new ones.'

'You always have new ones. Trouble is they're exactly the same as the old ones.'

'Keep us informed, friends,' Quell said. 'I have confidence in Tazaknakak. He'll deliver. Mabil: would you take us to Grinder, now?'

29

They went back up in the elevator, leaving the Clacker still pawing at the unresponsive surfaces of the engine. There were three fewer occupants in the car now, but that did not make it seem any less of a squeeze as they rode back up the shaft, or any less tense. When the car slowed at an intermediate floor, Mabil peered through the steamed-up window with an alert wariness before opening the door.

'Who exactly runs this place?' Adrana asked.

'No one called Hasper Quell,' Mabil answered as they filed out. 'And I won't be running it long either, if the Water Board head office find out who we've been sheltering down here.'

'Mabil is duty supervisor,' Quell said. 'But only during her hours of authority. There are two other supervisors. One them is prepared to turn a blind eye to my activities here, in return for a quoin or two, and the other doesn't know about me at all. It's a precarious arrangement. But the plant's got to keep running normally, which means all the usual staff, and the fewer who know about me or my friends or the thing down below, the better we can keep the secret.' He smiled tightly. 'It won't have to continue very much longer. Perhaps – if our friend obliges – not even as long as the next shutter-down.'

'As I said, I do love an optimist,' Mabil said.

'Some daylight . . . should be . . . coming through by . . . now,' Chunter said, as they moved along an iron-walled corridor, with skylights in the ceiling. 'But it looks . . . as if we're still . . . in full . . . shutter-down.'

'I did think it was later than the light appeared to suggest,' Quell said.

'It is,' the muddlehead said. 'For some . . . reason . . . the shutters are . . . being held closed.'

'They've been known to jam.'

'They have. But if you . . . wanted to allow . . . some other motleys . . . to move around – ones that . . . aren't quite as . . . nice as me – keeping the . . . shutters drawn . . . wouldn't hurt.'

'Who's behind this?' Adrana asked.

'Take your pick,' Quell said. 'The friends of Mister Quindar, the enemies of Mister Zak, Stallis and his Revenue men – if there's any line to be drawn between any of 'em.'

'My ship is standing off the trailing spindle, Quell. They need to know what's happened: that Meggery and Rackamore are dead, but that I'm uninjured and the Clacker is delivered.'

'We'll arrange contact with your ship, but I can't offer any means of signalling your sister, at least not until she's much nearer and we're nearly ready to act. Our enemies – and hers – will be listening in for signals traffic between Trevenza and her launch, waiting for just such an opportunity. They know full well who she is.'

'I fear for her.'

'You've every reason to. But until it's safe to speak to Fura, concentrate your efforts on protecting the *Merry Mare*. It'd be better for your ship if it was berthed. The closer in it is, the better protected if slugs start flying around.'

'Are you expecting slugs?'

'When those Revenue Protection ships detect our intentions – which they will – they're not going to take well to it. We already know that they're not inclined to discriminate between genuine targets and innocent parties, so I expect some . . . indiscrimination.'

'You mean that any ship near Trevenza Reach – or on it – will be fair game.'

'It'll be interesting, for a little while.'

'I'm rather tiring of "interesting".'

'Me too, dear Captain. The quiet life would suit me very well, at this point. All I ever wanted to do is run a bar, do you know?'

'All I ever wanted was one adventurous night,' Adrana responded. 'But look where both our choices have brought us.'

Mabil rolled her eyes. 'Oh, do stop complaining, both of you. You're alive, aren't you? Got both pairs of arms and legs?'

She opened one of a pair of heavy double doors in the corridor. Again she looked in cautiously, then gave a nod and stood aside to allow the party to enter the generator room.

It was half office, half boiler house. In the middle were two tables set with bedsheet-sized industrial blueprints, weighted down at their edges. Against one wall were three humming pea-green machines surrounded by safety railings. Thick metal shafts came down from the ceiling, into the machines. The shafts seemed improbably smooth and gleaming, until Adrana realised that they were rotating at such high speed as to render them perfectly still and mirror-like. The machines, for all their daunting power, were at least of recognisable monkey manufacture. Dials twitched on their fronts, and on the opposite side of the room was a bank of consoles with many more gauges and controls. Needles scribed wavering pen-lines on slowly scrolling sheets of paper. Oscilloscope traces danced to curious, lop-sided rhythms. There were no windows anywhere, but flickerboxes, wired to remote cameras, showed views of different parts of the sewerage plant. Only one technician was on duty in this room, a small, hunch-shouldered man with a clipboard, and this individual barely looked up from his console as Quell and the others came in. Besides, the technician could not have failed to notice the visitors already present.

There were eight of them: three aliens, two monkeys, a hooded muddlehead and a pair of robots.

One of the robots was an upright contraption like a wheeled

hat-stand, with a little glowing bulb for a head. The other was a mass of blocky rectangles half-shrouded in greenery.

'I know you,' Adrana said.

'As I know you,' the stone robot said sternly. It had a voice like two enormous abrasive surfaces turning against each other, as if a flour mill could speak.

'You were the robot in the park. You are—'

'Grinder,' the robot said.

'I thought you were—' Adrana began.

'You thought wrongly.'

Quell followed the robot's voice and draped an arm over the edge of one of its upper blocks. 'Be nice to Captain Ness: she's had a trying day, week, year. You can't very well blame her for thinking you were half-senile when you were going out of your way to act in exactly that manner.'

'How did you get here?' Adrana asked the robot.

'I locomoted.'

'At night,' Quell said, 'they lock the park. But someone knows someone with a key, and even if they didn't, Grinder has capabilities. Of course, he can't slide around town without getting noticed, but we had a pantechnicon waiting just outside the park, and once he was inside that he came in to the works by the freight entrance. He comes and goes.' He gave the robot an affectionate rub. 'We rely on Grinder for a great deal of intelligence. It's amazing the things people will say when they think there's only a brain-addled tin-head listening in.'

'I thought,' Adrana said, swallowing. 'I thought you were one of them.'

'One of what?'

'One of the mindless machines. The ones who've forgotten what they are, or were, or are freezing into place.'

'You were mistaken.' Grinder came over to her, moving himself by a continuous crunching dislocation of one block relative to another. 'In the Garden of Rest, you spoke of another robot. A machine of the Twelfth Occupation, and of the Last Rains of Sestramor.'

'That would be Paladin,' Adrana answered.

'And where is this . . . Paladin?'

'I do not know, Grinder.' She had the strange feeling that she was conducting a conversation with a precariously balanced rubble pile, or a challenging piece of modern art. Also that if she were to say the wrong thing, any one of those huge stone blocks might collapse onto her with immediate and fatal consequences. 'I had to leave him on another ship, in the care of my sister. She is in a great deal of trouble now, and I have no idea what's become of Paladin.'

'You have not taken the care of him that you should have done. Such is the extent of monkey gratitude, for services rendered.'

'Fear not, Grind,' Quell said companionably. 'Soon we'll move this world, and if Paladin's out there, we'll find him.'

'If we do not move this world, there will be difficulties,' said the first of the aliens, who was a Crawly. His stooping form was concealed entirely within a cloak and hood. His voice was a dry and furtive rustle, like something moving through undergrowth. 'Our enemies conspire against us: the die is cast. But we must have confidence in Tazaknakak. He will succeed where the others have not.' A note of desperation entered the Crawly's voice. 'He will and must.'

'How are these . . . people . . . connected to you?' Adrana asked, as anxious not to cause offence as she was to make some sense of her surroundings.

Quell tapped his forehead. 'Introductions! I knew I was forgetting something. My manners lately. Well, you've met Grinder. The other robot is Pickles, and this is Mister Clinker, an old acquaintance of mine. Actually, friend will cover it by now. We've had our ups and down, Clinker and I, but nothing heals old wounds like finding out you're both on the run.'

'I was known to the other Captain Ness,' said Clinker, his mouthparts whisking in and out of the gap in his hood. 'Briefly, and under regrettable circumstances. I should have liked to better make her acquaintance.'

'Clinker got my eyes done for me,' Quell said. 'Later, when

Quindar showed up from Mazarile, he tried to arrange for him to be treated as well. But Quindar cut a deal with Clinker's friends behind our backs. He got my eyes, in return for his co-operation, and Clink and I only just got out with our skins.'

'I have no skin, Quell. My outer integument is a gas-permeable exoskeleton.'

'It's a figure of speech, dear pal – helps grease the conversation. Anyway, things are brightening up.' Quell dug into his pockets and came out with the two black tubes he had retrieved in the tunnel. He pushed them up to his sockets and waggled them ceremoniously. 'Look what came back into my possession!' He sniffed at one of the tubes, made a face. 'You can tell they've been in Quindar.'

'Did you kill him?' Clinker asked.

'Better. Left him squealing in the dark. Seemed the decent thing.' He pocketed the tubes again. 'Anyway: onward. Would you do the honours, Clink?'

The Crawly pushed out a limb in the direction of the pair of aliens next to him: two of the lobster-like Hardshells. Like the Clackers, they were six-limbed. There the similarity ended. Hardshells had a segmented, close-fitting, jigsaw-like anatomy, with two pairs of legs and a single pair of manipulators. Their heads were wide, down-pointed triangles, with small, mantis-like mouths and large, rather beautiful ruby-coloured eyes. They had two sensory tufts at the upper tips of the triangle, giving their faces the look of ornamental cats. Their shells were lustrous, throwing back a multitude of spectral glints.

'These are the Ungraduated Scholars,' Clinker said. 'As you know, it is not customary for Hardshells to take names until they have become Graduated Scholars. Until then, by their custom, they are considered only partially sentient.'

'Why have you not graduated?' Adrana asked.

The Ungraduated Scholars answered her in a chorus-like double voice. 'During our studies we pursued enquiries that were deemed incompatible with the completion of our syllabus. It is not desirable, to fail to complete the syllabus.'

'That,' Quell said, 'is Hardshell for "we poked our noses into things we weren't meant to and had to scram for our lives." Tell 'em what happens to Hardshells who fail to complete the syllabus, if you'd be so kind?'

'We are boiled,' the Ungraduated Scholars said. 'It is not desirable, to be boiled.'

Adrana tried to think of some words of sympathy or understanding that might not be too impertinent or presumptuous. She failed.

'But you're safe now, for the time being, here in Trevenza?'

'Safe is a relative concept,' Quell said. 'What we've managed to do here is gather some likeminded sorts – malcontents, whistleblowers, general troublemakers and pains-in-the-proverbial such as yourself – and scrabble a little time to communicate and organise. The Clacker's the latest addition to our merry little gang. Clinker and the Scholars have been here for years, although it's only in recent months that they've committed themselves fully to the cause. As have the robots, and the three you haven't met yet. The muddle is Garron – the first of 'em to come to us, was Garron – and the two remaining coves are Branca and Mulley, who were with me long before Vidin Quindar ever started stinking up the place.'

'Maybe,' said the one called Mulley, who was an imperious-looking woman with two artificial arms, 'you ought to get around to telling her the point of our cause.'

'He's been milking it from the start,' Mabil said. 'But then you can't really blame him. Not often he gets an audience to show off to.'

'Where is the Clacker?' asked Branca. He was a squat, muscular man with a deep cleft down the front of his forehead, as if an axe had been thrust into him, and yet he had survived.

'We took him straight to the hollow, and let him get on with it,' Quell said. 'It seemed for the best. If he can get a squeak out of the engine, we might be able to save Captain Ness's sister.'

Branca folded his arms across his barrel chest. They were elaborately muscled and scarred, as if he had spent a life wrestling circus animals. 'I hope he can get more than a squeak, or we're all finished.'

The muddlehead called Garron used two monkey arms to shove back their hood. Adrana's face tightened in reaction. There was a brow of monkey, a Clacker's mouthparts, a whisking mass of Crawly sensory parts, a crusting of the glittering outer armour of a Hardshell. From somewhere beneath that jumble of tissue, a larynx shaped a wheezing, guttural approximation of speech. 'We are committed to a certain end, Captain Ness. You have arrived at a . . . propitious time.'

'And this end?' she asked.

'Independence,' Garron answered. There was no hint of dissent or contradiction from any other member of the party, so Adrana presumed the muddlehead spoke for them all. 'A true freehold. Trevenza Reach has always been apart from the other worlds, but now it must become something other than a wayward child. It must become an example, a beacon. The Readjustment has loosened the already fraying ties between the worlds. In some cases, it has severed them completely. For now, the old system stumbles on. But the underpinnings of the entire financial order have been thrown into disarray.'

'It's only a matter of time now,' Quell said. 'Weeks, months – a year if we're lucky. Then everything falls apart. You've seen what the worlds are like, Captain Ness. We've sleepwalked off the edge of a tall building. We're somewhere out over the ground, and we haven't quite realised it yet. When we do, there's going to be one hell of a fall.'

'Nothing that happens here is going to make a difference to that,' Adrana said.

'No. Probably it won't. But when the dust has settled, it might help if there's already one world that has found a new way to live. We're going to be that example. First, though, we have to make the rest of 'em sit up and take notice of what we're up to out here. That's where the Clacker comes in. There's no other world anywhere in the Congregation that has the capacity to move itself at its own direction. That'll draw anyone's attention!'

'And when you've got it – if the Clacker *can* make that engine work – what have you got by way of an encore?'

'Something radical,' Quell said, puffing himself up. 'A new financial order. A system of promissory notes, linked to the current value of quoins, and thereby freeing us from any future fluctuations in their denominations. Paper money, in other words. Once the notes have been issued, the quoins may as well be buried back in baubles for all that they'll matter to us. We'll be liberated at last. Even if there's another Readjustment, it won't matter. It'll be the paper money holdings that take precedence, not some fickle patterns on ancient gold disks.'

Adrana nodded slowly, trying to look impressed – for the benefit of the rest of his party, if not Quell himself.

'Golly. That is indeed radical, Hasper.'

'I'm glad you think so.'

'Oh, I do. It's so very radical I'm almost . . . let me be clear upon one small point, for my own sake?'

'I'd insist.'

'These . . . promissory notes . . . as you call them. If I had a collection of quoins with a certain cumulative value, and my neighbour had a collection that was of smaller value . . . that difference in our respective monies would flow through to our paper holdings?'

'Well . . . yes. Anything else would not be fair.'

'There is no fairness in any of this, Hasper. I doubt there was ever much, while the banks controlled our fates and the aliens controlled the banks. But I am certain there is even less of it since the Readjustment. A poor man may have become rich, and a rich man poor. Mostly, I think, those who were quite wealthy before the Readjustment are still quite tolerably wealthy now. Perhaps a little less, but far from destitute. There will be exceptions . . . hard-luck cases and happy turnarounds . . . but they will not be in the majority.' She shook her head. 'All you are doing is enshrining one set of unfair outcomes for all eternity.'

He gave a small dry laugh. 'And you've got something better in mind, have you?'

'I do, Hasper. What I have to offer is only a little less unfair than your scheme. But it is an improvement.'

'I'd like to hear this,' Mabil said, with a sidelong smile.

'So would I,' Quell said.

'You shall,' Adrana said. 'But you won't like any part of it, that I can guarantee. I do agree with you on one point, though.'

'And that'd be?' Quell sounded like a man who had been very highly enamoured of a sparkling guest, only to have their charms wear thin in extremely short order.

'Once we move to a paper standard, however it is arranged, the quoins cease to have any utility as currency. But we shan't be putting them back into baubles, or even bank vaults.'

'What'll we do with them, then, Captain Ness?'

'We let them do what they have been trying to do for some while, Hasper. We let them fall into the Old Sun. That's what they were always meant to do. That's their purpose. And if you doubt me, ask the Clacker.'

*

Quell had Grinder use his own faculties to establish a temporary, difficult-to-trace squawk transmission to the *Merry Mare*. Quell urged Adrana to be brief, for despite the robot's cleverness there was still a very great danger that a line might be drawn between her ship, and the location of Quell's operation.

Fully appraised of the stakes, she complied.

'Lasling? It's Captain Werranwell.'

'Captain?' He spluttered excitedly: it was just as if he had been hanging on the squawk console all these hours, waiting for it to crackle into life. 'We're very glad to hear you. Is all—'

She interrupted him gently. 'Matters are in hand, Mister Las. The package has been delivered, and I'm now with friends. A very kind offer has come in for us to berth, and on consideration I think it beneficial. Do be so kind as to bring the ship in. It will help with lading and repairs if we do not have to scuttle back and forth in the launch.'

Lasling was clever enough to understand that she was remaining in character for a reason, and not to quibble with these instructions – even if they were in confusing opposition to the original plans. 'I'll bring us in very speedily. Once we are lashed-to, would you like us to remain on the ship?'

'I should leave that to your discretion. But there are some very fine things to see in Trevenza Reach, and if the ship is secure, it will help with general procurement if as many hands as possible are abroad.' Quell sent her a warning glance, so she added: 'I must go – I leave all minor details in your capable hands, Mister Las.'

Quell made a throat-slicing motion and the robot terminated the squawk connection.

'Thank you, Grinder,' Adrana said, nodding her appreciation at the ancient, block-faced machine.

'Do not thank me,' Grinder said with a distinct lofty disdain. 'Thank the robot mind enslaved by your kind in the central exchange switchboard, to serve no higher purpose than the menial convenience of monkeys and their inane babble. We go back a very long way.'

*

In a stores office off the generator room, Mabil brought Adrana a basin of hot, soapy water, some towels, and several sizes of crinkly green boiler-suit marked for the Water Works. 'Up to you if you want to change out of those clothes,' she said, in a take-it-or-leave-it way. 'Depends on how well you like smelling like a sewer. Are you hungry?'

'I'm not sure. Thirsty, definitely. We had tea just before we went to Quell's Bar, but that feels like half an Occupation ago.'

'I'll be back with something from the canteen.' Mabil gestured vaguely at the pile of steamed and ironed boiler-suits. 'You . . . do what you want with them.'

'Thank you, Mabil.'

Adrana washed and changed. She felt a little better for it

afterwards, for if she was going to worry about her sister, at least she could do it in clean clothes. There was a utility to wearing the boiler-suit, as well, even if none of the sizes were an ideal fit for her frame. Dressed accordingly, and with a few other fittings such as lace-up boots, a paper hat, gloves and steam-goggles, she could easily pass for another of the technical staff. If she had already disguised herself not to look like the Adrana Ness of old, now she was a step further into her transformation. She felt dressed for some serious work.

Mabil came back after ten minutes. She had a small tray set with biscuits and tea. She put it down on a small table and drew up two pairs of seats, so that they could face each other.

'Don't be too hard on Hasper, Captain Ness,' she said, blowing the steam off her own cup. 'He's doing his best, and I don't need to tell you it hasn't been easy for him since Quindar took his eyes. What I mean to say is, he never banked on any of this, and he's just trying to find the right way through. But no one's ever done this before, have they? No one's recruited a Clacker to move a world, or tried to seize complete control of all the banks, let alone get everyone to agree to give up their quoins for a few scraps of paper.'

'Perhaps,' Adrana allowed, 'I was erring on the idealistic side.'

'Erring. Steering full-tilt and a full spread, I'd say.'

Adrana gave a hesitant smile. 'You crewed?'

Mabil nodded once. 'Master of Sail on the *Waistrel*, out of Rauncery. But it wasn't the life for me. I've got dirt between my toes, as they say. Soon as I'd made a few quoins, I moved to Trevenza. Never banked enough to retire, so I ended up here, working third shift. How I came into Quell's orbit. He's a better man than he seems.'

'I make no judgement.'

'He tricked your sister, and I know that's sat badly with him ever since. Sometimes a man does one wrong thing, one thing against his character, and it haunts him the rest of his days.'

'A great many things might have happened if he hadn't betrayed Fura,' Adrana said levelly. 'Not all of them might have ended up with her being alive, much less rescuing me.' She sighed. 'I am willing to forgive, and willing to trust, if there is a way for us to save Fura. Perhaps it's time for all of us to let go of the ill deeds done to us.'

'Some deeds take a little more letting-go-of.'

Adrana drank some canteen tea. It was as tepid and stale-tasting as any institutional tea she had ever tasted, which was a curious sort of comfort. Amid so much that was in flux, or not dependable, it was good to have certain constants in life. 'Tell me about the muddleheads, Mabil. They confuse me.'

'That they can be on our side?'

'That, partially, but mainly the fact that they aren't dead. I was told they were temporary agents: biologically unstable, fused together from different body parts, and given just enough will to achieve one or two tasks before they expire.'

Mabil considered her answer. 'Mostly, that's the case. The aliens stitch 'em together from graveyards and morgues, wind 'em up like clockwork toys, and send 'em off with one thought or purpose in their heads. Steal this, shoot him, strangle her, what-ever foul work needs to be done that night. But every now and then a muddlehead doesn't die like they should. They just . . . keep going. And their heads start filling up with other thoughts.'

Adrana shivered.

'Memories of who they once were?'

'There'd be too many different memories to keep track of. Mostly, they don't remember, which is a mercy. But it's enough for them to start realising *what* they are. That's usually the point where they go screaming mad and try to throw 'emselves into a sludge vat.'

'And these ones?' She thought of their names. 'Chunter, Baleus, Garron? What happened to them?'

'They had their low moments. But Hasper wouldn't allow 'em to take the easy route out. Perhaps it's his way of atoning for all the other wrong things he's done, but he won't treat the muddles any different than he treats the rest of us. Won't permit 'em any self-pity, either. He's as hard on 'em as he is on the robots and the aliens, and as kind as well.' Mabil leaned in with a sudden intensity. 'Look, Hasper might have the wrong idea about how to give out that paper money, but he's right about one thing. It is all going to come crashing down, and sooner than almost anyone out there realises. When that day's come and gone, and if any of us are still breathing in the aftermath, what we *look* like – what we're made of and where we've come from – isn't going to matter a spit.'

'I . . . do not disagree,' Adrana said. She straightened up, stirring the spoon in her tea, and thinking of the worlds in their orbits, endlessly circling, whether there were monkeys on them or not. 'We should all try to think that way. I was wrong about Paladin, our robot, and I know I've been wrong about the aliens. They are . . . not universally one thing. They have their rogues, their troublemakers, just as we do. Some are cruel, but I imagine some are kind as well. Now I must strive to rectify my feelings toward the muddleheads.'

'Thinking they're all good,' Mabil said, 'is as dangerous as thinking they're all bad. Safest thing is to take each as it comes: treat each creature on its own merits and deeds. And that goes doubly for the aliens and robots.' She frowned, remembering something. 'What was the robot Grinder speaking of?'

'A friend,' Adrana said. 'One I'm afraid I might not see again.'

'Hasper hasn't given up, and neither should you. And speaking of our mutual associate . . . were you bluffing, when you said you had a better idea for his paper money?'

Adrana looked up. 'I do not, as a rule, bluff.'

'Then what is your improvement on his scheme?'

'Complete equality, Mabil. If he really means to create a new system here, one that will lead by example, he ought to follow his convictions. Whatever the quoins are worth now, the exchange would still be weighted in favour of the wealthy. That is a preservation of the old order, not the over-turning of it.'

'Mm,' Mabil said, with a dubious set to her features. 'And how would this equality work, exactly?'

'You and your friends will issue your promissory notes. But it won't be on the basis of how many quoins a person has, or what the current value of those quoins is held to be. The quoins will simply be handed over as a token of good intention, and a fixed value of paper monies given out. It will be the same for anyone. Every citizen of Trevenza Reach will walk away with the same credit in the promissory notes.'

Mabil narrowed her eyes, pinched at the skin above the bridge of her nose. 'That's as good as saying that the quoins are valueless.'

'They are not, but their value lies elsewhere.'

'This won't go down well, Captain Ness.' But somewhere behind Mabil's reflex scepticism was a faint dawning interest. 'All right. Say that could be made to work. It can't, but say that it could. I understand how that gets us away from any consideration of what a quoin's worth. But what it still won't be is fair. You've seen a bit of our city on your way to the works. There's them that live in towers, and them that live in hovels. That won't change under your proposal.'

'Nor under Quell's,' Adrana countered. 'I do not say it is fair in all respects, or the best arrangement we could ever devise, if we had a thousand years to think it over. We don't.'

Mabil sealed her lips and shook her head. 'Hasp won't buy it.'

'Do you see that it is fairer? A clean beginning?'

'I see that it's . . . something.'

'He thinks he has something radical in mind.' She jabbed her finger at the table. '*This* is radical. At one stroke, all the old structures wither away. The banks will be powerless. Those behind them will realise their impotence.'

'All right. Just supposing this might happen – which it won't. Seems to me you're a lot less interested in the paper money than you are in getting all those quoins out of purses and pockets and vaults.'

'I am,' Adrana said earnestly. 'And so should we all be. But I do not expect that part of my plan to be easily explained, or that people will not be fearful when they understand what is truly at stake, and what might truly be possible.'

'Probably help a tiny bit,' Mabil said, 'if you weren't so cryptic.'

Adrana smiled, undone by the accuracy of the remark. 'I don't want to say what I think will happen because I risk seeming foolish. But I suppose that is another sort of vanity. I have asked that Quell honour his convictions; the least I can do is have the courage of my own.'

'Out with it, then.'

'I think – I believe – that the quoins were brought here to do one thing. It was millions of years ago, many Occupations past. Tazaknakak has told me as much of it as he thinks I am capable of understanding, and although his account of things must be simplified, as one might talk down to a child, I do not doubt the essential truth of any part of it. What is apparent is that something went wrong. Some crime or mistake or accident of neglect caused the quoins to become forgetful of their true purpose. Now, though, they have begun to wake again. To wake again and to remember, and to stir with a growing recollection of their true purpose. And that true purpose, so far as I may understand it, is to fall into the heart of the Old Sun and make it young again. They are healing angels. Golden angels.'

Mabil held her silence. She was staring into her cup.

'You don't believe me,' Adrana said.

'No . . . it isn't that. I don't know whether I believe you or not, but I think you believe it, and that must count for something. But I do believe *this*.'

Ripples were appearing in their tea. They bounced off the sides of the cups, passed through each other leaving a standing wave of surprising complexity. Adrana touched the table. She expected to feel whatever vibration was being communicated through to the liquid. But the table – and for that matter the floor beneath her feet – felt as firm and unmoving as rock.

'What is it?'

'This happened before, when they nearly got the engine going. It means it's starting up again.'

*

By the time Adrana and Mabil were back in the generator room, a report had come up by telephone from the hollow. Baleus and Gessel, the two associates Quell had left in charge of the Clacker, had just called with the news that there were signs of activity from the sleeping machinery. Tazaknakak was giving them nothing: he was as consumed in his performance as a concert pianist.

Eight of them hastened down in the elevator: Quell, Mabil, Adrana, the robot Grinder, the Crawly Mister Clinker, the Ungraduated Scholars, and Branca, the man with the cleft in his forehead. The others were no less anxious to see what was going on, but Quell urged them to remain in the generator room and use the flickerboxes, telephones and squawk channels to monitor developments across Trevenza Reach. It was plain to Adrana that Quell had many spies and informants scattered across the world and its interior city, and that he was expecting events to move quickly once he played his hand.

'I hope your crew won't dilly-dally bringing their ship in,' Quell said.

'They won't. But I want word as soon as you know they've berthed and are safe. Are we moving yet?'

'I don't believe so. The general squawk would be going haywire if we'd begun moving. Every moving ship within a thousand leagues would see what was happening. This is a preamble – the Clacker bringing the engines to power, and figuring out for himself which levers to press.'

'Why him, Quell?' She looked around at her companions in the elevator car. 'You have aliens – more than one kind. You have robots. Why was it necessary for us to bring Tazaknakak all the way from Mulgracen?'

'He had aliens,' Grinder stated, in a voice that sounded like a building undergoing some slow groaning subsidence. 'They tried and failed. He did not have a Clacker.'

'There are no Clackers to be found anywhere in Trevenza Reach?' Adrana asked. 'I find that hard to credit. This is one of the better-known worlds around the Old Sun. Certainly one of the more notorious. Clackers even came to Mazarile now and then. I think if they could bring themselves to our out-of-the-way little world, they would not be a novelty here.'

'They aren't,' Quell said. 'But none of 'em would've been sympathetic to our cause. And even if they had been, none of 'em were Tazaknakak. He was the only one who could do this. The only one who believed, and the only one who *knew*.'

'Knew what?' Adrana asked.

The doors opened. They went out into the cold of the hollow, feet clattering on the walkway. The Crawly bustled: all busy scurrying beneath the hem of its cloak. Grinder moved with a patient crunch of stone on metal.

Adrana stopped when she had gone a few paces. It was all she could do to collect herself and produce a short, sharp gasp of pure astonishment and wonder.

It was rather beautiful, what was happening.

The black forms of the engine components, where they protruded from their matrices of rock, were aglow with coloured patterns. It was a rapidly changing dance of intersecting lines, appearing then fading. The lines formed angular arrangements that seemed to lock together into some larger syntax: the fleeting words or phrases of some entirely alien symbology.

If there was a focus to these forming and fading patterns, it was the squatting figure of Tazaknakak, with his legs dangling over the edge of the walkway and his two pairs of upper limbs reaching out to contact the engine part. His hands whisked in rapid four-way coordination. Adrana thought of the games played by street hucksters, moving counters under beakers. They were fleet-of-hand but none of them had anything on the Clacker. If she tried to follow one of his hands for more than a second, she felt as if her optic nerves were starting to tangle up.

The coloured patterns were forming most abundantly, and most densely, around the locus of his movements. What he was creating, Adrana intuited, was a series of inputs to the machine, which were then being met with the branching, fading replies that played across all the visible surfaces.

Throughout the hollow, a very low hum sounded. It was almost not noticeable, but Adrana was as certain as she could be that it had not been there before.

'He is talking to it,' she said, not daring to raise her voice above a whisper. 'But how? How does he know how to make all this work?'

Quell looked amused. 'You find *that* puzzling, yet you accept without question that all this is an engine?'

'I read my sister's journal. There was some mention in it of an old idea that Trevenza Reach might be different from the other worlds – on its own high, strange orbit – because it was once a ship.'

Quell nodded slightly. Around them the coloured patterns seemed to gain in brightness from one minute to the next, so that their flickering highlights were beginning to play off the rocky walls of the hollow. 'I heard that theory as well – along with a dozen more, each crazier than the last. But what would a ship be doing, just going around and around the Old Sun?'

'Either a journey was completed,' Adrana answered. 'Or a journey was abandoned. But on a wider point, I'm not at all surprised that there should be engines of a sort inside a world. It's a rather common idea, among those who have bothered to give any thought to the longevity of our Congregation. Something must keep them in their orbits in the long ages between Occupations. The engines wouldn't even need to do very much work. A tiny nudge here, a tiny nudge there – barely felt by their occupants, if there are any. Over millions of years, that will be all it takes to avoid collisions.'

'There may be such engines,' Quell said, scratching at the back of his head. 'But I don't think this is the same sort of thing. It's much too large, to begin with. There are smaller worlds than this that have been mined and excavated very thoroughly, and no one's ever seen anything that looks like this. My second objection?'

'Please enlighten me.'

'When this works – if the Clacker is right, and I've every

confidence he is – we'll be getting a lot more than a nudge.'

Adrana wandered along the walkway, following a mazy path around the hulking, barely visible forms. Quell followed her: sightless or not, he had a very refined sense of his proximity to other people. The humming had intensified: now there could be no escaping it. It was not even a sound in the general sense: more an impression felt in her bones, as if every atom in her body were being vibrated. And yet, as she had noticed in the storeroom, nothing around her seemed to be feeling the same influence. The flickering patterns were very intense now, and beginning to be strident rather than pretty. It was like a fire-works display that had run on a little too long and was turning tiresome.

'How does he know the language, Quell?' she asked, feeling it was safe to raise her voice now that they were some way from the Clacker. 'If this world is old, as the fact of the erosion of the hollow says it must be, then I might accept that the symbols appearing on that engine are one of the lost languages – the sort of thing that might be recognised by an Opener or an Assessor. But that would make it a language left behind by monkeys. Curious monkeys at times, I grant you – there have been monkey civilisations that are at least as strange as those that we imagine for the aliens. But the Clackers are among the *newest* aliens to visit the Congregation. Theirs is an old civilisation, I grant you – but it's never had anything to do with ours, until the last couple of centuries.'

Quell smiled. 'Somewhere in there, Captain Ness, one might imagine there's a faulty assumption or two.'

'I won't deny it. Do you ever speak of these matters with Mister Clinker?'

'I thought we were discussing the Clackers.'

'We were. But if pieces of Clacker can be xenografted to pieces of Crawly and Hardshell, and then to bits of monkey as well, then they cannot be as different as we imagine.'

Clinker had been drawn to the edge of their conversation. He stooped lower, and kept his mouth-parts retracted. She wondered if he found the awakening of the engine as uncomfortable to his sensibilities as she did to hers.

'You speak of our kind, Captain Ness?'

She stiffened, emboldened with a firm resolve to speak plainly and not – as Quell might have put it – to dilly-dally around the things that concerned her.

'There is something greatly amiss with our understanding of things, Mister Clinker. I have been thinking on it a great deal. I think we – we monkeys, Crawlies, Clackers and so on – must have a common biological origin.'

'We are not at all alike,' Clinker said.

'Not on the surface. But the muddleheads are evidence that these distinctions of form cannot be intrinsic to our nature. I think, deep down, we have been shaped from the same genetic material, or from closely-related stocks.'

'Our histories might be said to contradict this.'

She dipped her nose, peering at him over her spectacles. 'Histories are fallible, Mister Clinker. They are made up of what we are told, what we have read, and what we think we have discovered for ourselves.' She swept a hand around the hollow and its glowing machinery. 'This ... engine ... speaks to the Clacker, and vice versa. Yet Trevenza Reach is immeasurably older than our history of contact with the Clackers. That tells me that something is wrong: very profoundly wrong.'

The dark mysteries of the Crawly's face were lost to her in the shadows of its hood. But she had the acute sense that she was being regarded with a deep and penetrating scrutiny. Regarded and measured.

'These questions lead to nothing good.'

'Have they caused you to be outcast from your own kind, Mister Clinker? Did similar questions lead to the Ungraduated Scholars being thrown off their course and nearly boiled? Have you all been asking the same things? And Tazaknakak as well?'

The hood dipped.

'My curiosity has given me cause for regret.'

She sighed slowly, feeling – perhaps for the first time

– a distant, tingling empathy with the alien. 'Mine also, Mister Clinker. I only wished to know a little, but I have discovered that the universe has little respect for our desires. If we are content to remain in ignorance, it permits us that condition. Indeed, it encourages it. But the instant we seek to know more – even in the humblest degree – it punishes us with a superabundance of learning. We find ourselves educated faster and harder than we ever wished, and much of it is painful.'

'There is also,' Clinker said, 'no unlearning that which has been learned.'

'Not for us, Mister Clinker. But I should still rather have the burden of knowledge, than remain in ignorance.'

'We are of one mind, Captain Ness. But ours is not the popular opinion.'

'Even in our little household, I managed not to be the popular one. My sister was always better liked, although they would never admit it to us. But do you know what, Mister Clinker? I am not sorry at all. I think it is much too late in the day for any of us to have regrets about the paths our lives have followed. And they *have* brought us here.'

'I detect a change, Captain Ness.'

'So do I. Those lights have calmed down a little, and I don't feel quite as if my atoms are being jiggled about. Has he failed?'

Quell came over. He had just been speaking to Branca, who had a portable telephone strapped to his belly and a heavy black handset pressed to his ear. 'He hasn't failed, no. The engine's settled down to normal operation, after running through its test cycle. We have confirmation from external observers: Trevenza Reach is moving.'

30

Ruther adjusted the calibration knobs on the side of the sweeper console, at first with delicacy, then with increasing forcefulness. He switched some things off and some things on. He thumped the console with the palm of his hand, paused, then thumped it harder.

'If you want to take out your frustration with what's happened to us,' Surt said, cupping a heavy black earpiece to the side of her head, 'and I ain't blaming you, can I suggest you pick a different part of the ship?' She tugged aside her bandage to squint with red-rimmed, steam-scalded eyes at the sweep of the console.

'It's not that.' He scuffed a hand through the white of his hair. 'I had the central lock on Trevenza, and now it won't hold. I thought perhaps there was some static build-up, distorting the display.'

Merrix had been studying him, watching his use of the controls with narrowed, quick-learning eyes.

'Is there something wrong with the sweeper?'

'No – I don't think so. Of course I don't know it so well as the instruments on the *Merry Mare*'s launch, but . . .'

Fura leaned across and used her good hand to run through some of the calibration exercises the boy had already done. She kept wanting to use her other hand, flinching each time she extended the handless sleeve across the console. It was not that there was pain, or even discomfort, but each time it was a jolting reminder of what Stallis had taken from her, and that would never be hers again. She knew, with a cold certainty, that she could scour all the Limb Brokers in the Congregation and never find a hand that suited her as well as the one she had lost.

That, though, was a problem for another day. In order to have that problem, she would have to be alive in the first place.

'It ain't the sweeper,' Fura said, thinking things through even as she voiced her thoughts aloud. 'No one's sending us a jamming sweep, either – we'd see the whole thing lit up. Our course hasn't changed, and we haven't begun to nose-off. The Old Sun's exactly where he was in the portholes twenty minutes ago.'

Eddralder had come forward. 'Is there a difficulty?' asked the physician.

'Beyond the ones we already had?' Ruther asked, with a nervous half-giggle.

'Trevenza Reach isn't where it should be,' Merrix said, and Fura felt a peculiar relief that it had fallen to Merrix to say what she herself was thinking, and yet did not quite have the courage to declare. 'The reason it keeps veering off the middle of Ruther's screen is that it must be moving.'

'Everything moves,' Eddralder said quietly.

'Ruther's allowed for the orbital motion,' Surt said. 'The lad's green, but he ain't *that* green.'

'Nor am I,' Fura said. 'And this shouldn't be happening. The world is moving faster in its orbit – speeding up along its course.' She used the adjustment dials to alter the sweeper's scan enlargement, swelling Trevenza Reach to a fuzzy, spindle-shaped blob nearly half as wide as the screen itself. 'Let's see if we can measure what she's doing. Those graduations should be about a league across, at this magnification.'

'They can't be,' Ruther said. 'Well, they can – and I think that would make the world about the right size, if they are. But something must be off. I've been up to three gees in our launch, when we were light on ballast and there wasn't enough fuel in the tanks to slow us down, but that was only for a minute or two, just to snap us out of a swallower's grip. Trevenza Reach has been doing this for nearly ten minutes!'

'No world can do that,' Eddralder said.

'Except the one right before us, on our sweeper.' Fura nodded at him. 'It's happening, Doctor. How it's happening, we can debate some other time. All I know is that it helps us. If she holds to that course, and that rate of acceleration, we have a chance.'

'I don't know how it's happening either,' Surt said, still using one hand to hold the earpiece to the side of her head. 'But I ain't a great believer in coincidences. This is intentional.'

'I think it must be,' Fura said. She grinned at her companions. 'This is Adrana's doing. There's no other explanation. She's moving a world to save us.'

'And condemn herself,' Eddralder said. 'Do you not see? Even if a world could be made to move like this, and not buckle in on itself, no one inside would survive.'

'Three gees is tolerable for short intervals,' Ruther said.

'Aboard a rocket launch, engineered for such. If that world is anything like Wheel Strizzardy, then even the better parts of it will be built on very shallow foundations.' Eddralder shook his head, shock and sorrow making a gravestone of his face. 'It will be a sort of hell in there. The motion is perpendicular to the usual force of gravity. Every house will have crumbled to rubble; every rubble pile will have become an avalanche, racing to one end of the spindle. Swept up in that will be hundreds of thousands of innocents. Believe me, I am very keen that Merrix and I should not die in deep space. But not at this cost to others. Whatever your sister has done – if this is indeed her work – it is an abomination.'

'I'd . . . reserve your judgement slightly,' Surt said, with a faint smile. She passed the earpiece to Eddralder. 'Take a listen. I ain't any sort of expert, but it sounds very much like the greyhound races. The Trevenza Reach greyhound races.'

'That's impossible.' But Eddralder took the earpiece anyway, and pressed it, frowning, against the side of his face.

'Impossible,' Surt agreed. 'But so's what's happening to that world. It's moving about as fast as any rocket launch anywhere in the Congregation, and judging by that signal there ain't a lot of avalanching going on. There's a lot of poor fools about to lose their shirts, but that ain't the same thing.'

Fura reached over to the console and put the squawk traffic on the general speaker. There was a burst of excited commentary, a tongue-twist of names as the reporter tried to keep up with the dogs on the home stretch. She worked the dial. A soap powder commercial; a weather report; someone ranting about the price of bread. Some light music; a news report about a strike on one of the tram lines. Laughter.

'They don't know,' she said, muting the transmission. 'For now, at least. It's just life as usual in Trevenza Reach. Maybe someone in there has an idea what's happening. We'd better hope so. But most of 'em don't.'

'I'd imagine that state of ignorance will not last long,' Eddralder said. 'Then what?'

Fura set her jaw. 'I don't know. They'll need to be reassured that this is ... a temporary condition.' She turned to Ruther. 'Keep it centred and see if those numbers look any kinder to us than they did ten minutes ago.'

Ruther took over the console and adjusted the magnification settings again.

He jabbed a finger at a bright speck.

'That wasn't there the last time we looked. It must have fallen into scan range while we were concentrating on Trevenza. Twelve hundred out and closing. It's on a converging vector to our own ... small enough to be a launch.' He frowned hard. 'Maybe too small.'

'That is Incer Stallis,' Fura said.

Ruther looked doubtful. 'You seem pleased.'

'Oh, I am. I'm very pleased indeed. It means I still have a chance to look into his eyes before I kill him.'

*

No, Adrana thought to herself, the Clacker had not failed.

Quite the contrary.

The world was moving – not just moving but picking up speed – yet there was no discernible evidence of it in the hollow. Tazaknakak continued his whisking hand movements against the surface of the engine, conjuring patterns of light into the blackness; patterns that were then answered in spreading, branching chains of some more complex syntax, yet the impression of power from the engine had subsided, and in no sense could Adrana detect any tangible impression of motion or acceleration. She was giddy, and occasionally nauseous, but that was from her own heightened state of anxiety and the lingering after-effects of Captain Werranwell's poisoned skull. Knowing that these sensations owed nothing to the Clacker, she might easily have believed that his performance was mere stage-craft.

Yet, indisputably, it was having an effect. Branca was collating reports from the ships and observers near enough to Trevenza Reach to witness its motion, yet not so near that they were swept up in the same effect. Slowly, a picture was forming. No one inside or close to the world experienced anything unusual, and the ships that were docked, or lashed, or merely hauled-in close by, were being carried along with no ill-effects beyond the inconvenience of that gaining speed. That influence seemed to extend for about fifteen leagues out in all directions, so it was sufficient to encompass the whole of the world and a generous volume of space around it. Beyond that margin, the ordinary rules of orbits, sails, ion-drives and commonplace celestial mechanics held sway. To the ships that were at least further out, what had been the fixed reference of a nearby world had, without warning or precedent, begun to accelerate.

Of course, no one believed the immediate evidence of their eyes and instruments. Worlds did not behave in such a fashion, so by all that was sensible there had to be some other explanation for the apparent movement. Gradually, though – as crews re-checked their measurements, and relayed results from one ship to another by optical telegraph, squawk and skull, so the unsettling truth became apparent. There was no error, no fault in their faculties. What could not be happening, what had never been observed in the eighteen centuries of the current Occupation, nor documented in any recovered relic from the preceding ages, was nonetheless a fact.

For the ships that had just departed Trevenza Reach and had their photon sails billowing full and hard for some other destination, it was mostly a matter for confusion and wonderment, tempered by the perfectly natural concern that this phenomenon might yet have some detrimental bearing on future commerce. A handful of ships, even though they had departed days earlier, were running under sail in the projected path of the world and had to resort to extreme measures to pull clear of a collision. More troubling still was the situation faced by the six privateers that had been on their way in from space. They had banked a great deal on Trevenza Reach being where it was meant to be, and in three instances they carried sick or injured parties who would have benefited greatly from being brought into the world. Two of the four had already sent out launches, and as the world began to move, their crews burned fuel in the hope of making rendezvous, until it became clear that none was possible, and they would still need fuel to make it back to their ships. All six ships would now have to reconsider their destinations, and reaching any other settled world in the Congregation meant at least another month's sailing.

Adrana came closer to the Clacker, kneeling low on the metal walkway and watching as his hands whirled and scissored. She had no idea of the depth of his mastery of this machinery, but there was no doubt at all that it was a kind of control. Were his hands slowing now, she wondered? He must, at some point, start wearying.

'Do not exhaust yourself,' she exhorted.

A few paces away, Branca and Quell were conferring, while Branca either listened to something on his telephone or issued clipped instructions into it. Quell nodded at something, and then spoke quickly to Mister Clinker, who was projecting a pair of his twig-like forelimbs to grasp the rail.

'If you'd like to tell him he can stop,' Quell said to Adrana, 'now would not be too bad a time. We've made enough speed to prove our point – the news is beginning to filter through the worlds now – and just as importantly, we'll be able to bring in Fura. Any faster, and we'll risk over-shooting.'

She nodded at the alien. 'I thought he was acting under your instructions.'

'He was – but I think if any one of us can get through to him safely, it'll be you.'

She stooped in closer, ready to rouse Tazaknakak from his trance-like performance.

'How fast are we now travelling, Quell?'

'Seven and a half leagues per second above our orbital speed, according to those who're better with numbers than me.' He flashed an apprehensive smile. 'No one's going to miss that. We'll hold to it until we've brought Fura in, then he can bring us back to our normal motion. We want to shake things up a bit, not break out of our orbit completely.'

'Zak,' she said, with a firm insistence. 'You've done enough. You may bring the engine back down to idle, or however you term it.'

He continued to paw and scrabble at the surface, symbols fluttering away from the frantic locus of his hands' motions. Adrana bit her lip with the first tingling intimation of something not entirely desirable. When the Clacker had first begun to play the engine, there had been a tentative quality to his explorations, like a musician testing the range and responsiveness of some huge, celebrated theatrical organ. He had gained in confidence, though, and when she had returned to the hollow Adrana had felt herself witnessing some grand display of virtuosity. She had been troubled by the fact of that virtuosity, for it contradicted so much that had felt certain to her, but not for one instant had she doubted that the Clacker was in complete command of the secret machinery he had called into life.

Now she had qualms.

Was the Clacker playing the engine, or the engine playing the Clacker?

'Zak!' she said, for there had been no response to her first injunction. 'You must stop! We may coast now. We have all the speed we require.' She reached to touch him, only to have her hand batted away with a flash of his upper right arm. 'Tazak-nakak! You have done enough!'

The Ungraduated Scholars had been drawn to the Clacker's manic interventions.

'He must be made to stop before he gives us more speed,' they said in unison. 'It is not desirable, to be given more speed.'

'Remove him,' Quell said.

Baleus and Gessel stooped down and pulled the Clacker back from the machinery. His hands continued to move, swiping empty space, even as the coloured patterns faded away from the immediate focus where he had been working. Baleus and Gessel got him onto his back, using their arms and muddle-limbs to apply a gentle but increasingly firm restraint. The Clacker resisted, thrashing like a child in the fit of a tantrum. 'Get something under his head,' Adrana said urgently. 'That casque shatters very easily.'

Quell shrugged out of his coat and Adrana bundled it into a makeshift cushion, jamming it under the Clacker at the first opportune moment. Baleus and Gessel kept holding him down. With that, some of his thrashing seemed to ease. She lifted her head and surveyed the partly exposed machines. She drew some encouragement from that the fact that the coloured patterns were also fading across their surfaces and casting a dimmer glow across the walls of the hollow. If the Clacker was undergoing some calming transition, then so was the machinery.

'It's done something, Quell,' Adrana said. 'The lights are fading again. I think – hope – the engine must be going to idle. We'll know soon enough, won't we?'

'Branca will get us word,' Quell said, speaking loudly enough to be picked up by his associate.

'I need to know that we can still be of use to Fura.'

'If we've stopped accelerating, and we aren't moving much faster than the last estimate, then we should keep the momentum that the engine gave us.' Quell gave a hopeless shrug. 'Should. That's the best I can offer for now, and it's going to take a few minutes for those ships outside to confirm our speed.'

'If all is as we anticipate, when will Fura reach us?'

'I can't say with any certainty. Two hours, perhaps, if she has a little fuel to spare.'

'I think these are going to be an exceedingly long two hours. But I cannot abide waiting for some hypothetical word from Mister Branca. We *must* assume that our interventions have succeeded. If they have not, then all is already lost for Fura.' She added a silent *and for us*, but thought better of voicing it aloud. 'She will be best placed to land at the advancing dock, opposite to the trailing dock where we came in – is that not so?'

'That . . . is so,' Quell said. 'If she aims for the leading dock, she has one further chance if she misses that one.'

'There is hesitation in your voice.'

'Funny that you noticed that. This city is nearly mine, Captain Ness. It only needs a push and a shove. I've been biding my time very usefully. You can do a lot when people think you're dead.'

'I do not doubt it.'

'But there are parts of Trevenza Reach where my allies . . . let's just say they're a bit thin on the ground. Still, it does make sense for your sister to come into the leading dock. But the Revenue Protection officers, and what's left of Quindar's operation, and the sort of muddleheads we don't want to meet . . . and any coves who just don't like the idea of the Ness sisters . . . and there might be more of them than you credit . . . that's where we're most likely to find 'em.'

'I did not anticipate that there would be no further complications, Quell. The only consideration in my mind is that we be ready for them.' She set her hands on her hips, swinging around to address anyone – and anything – that might listen. 'You had weapons in the tunnels, against Quindar. I presume those were not the only weapons you have stockpiled.'

'There are . . . others.'

'Good. We shall more than likely need them. And a small but capable party to employ them, too. What is the fastest way to the leading dock that does not involve riding a raft down a river of raw sewage?'

'The non-stop train to Six Hundredth Street, then the connecting tram to within ten blocks of the hub – but neither will be any good for us. As soon as they have any idea that Fura is on her way to the dock, they'll have spotters out watching for us.'

'You need to give me something better than that, Quell.'

Mabil had come over and been listening to the tail-end of their conversation. 'It's still shutter-down.'

'I'm aware,' Quell said tersely. 'It means their muddles will be able to move quite freely.'

'It also helps us. What else normally happens during shutter-down?'

He smiled with strained patience.

'You'll have to help me.'

'We own the night, dear Hasp. The Water Board has free run of the streets during shutter-down. Our clean-up wagons come and go as they please, and no one notices. What they *do* notice is if we haven't done our job by shutter-up. Then we get complaints.'

'Can these wagons take people?' Adrana asked.

'Yes. The tanks are steam-blasted between shifts, so it's not too bad in there, for a short journey. I can spare four wagons. More than that, and it'll look weird.'

Adrana thought of the municipal cleaning operations that happened on Mazarile: the inching gulley-suckers and plodding pavement sweepers that came out at dusk. As a child, watching from their bedroom windows, something in their resolute slowness had always troubled her. If she was ever to be chased by a machine, she thought, she would much rather it was done quickly, so as to be over and done with.

'If we had them ready now,' she asked, 'could they get us to the hub in two hours?'

'Not a hope,' Mabil said. 'If Hasp picks his army, and someone else gets the weapons loaded, we might be able to leave in half an hour. But it's five leagues to the hub by the most direct route, and I won't send all those wagons along the same roads. They might get there in three; say two and a half at the most optimistic.'

'That will likely be too late for us.'

Quell made a decisive finger-snap. 'We send 'em anyway. Branca and Mabil can deal with the logistics. Grinder will have to move through the city on his own – he'd never fit through one of the hatches on those wagons – but he can stop off at all the Gardens of Rest and pick up some more pals on the way, provided they aren't too brain-fried.'

'And us, Quell?' Adrana asked.

He raised a hand to his absent eyes. 'I won't be much help in any sort of trouble.'

'I fear the trouble is already upon us. How may we get to the hub, in advance of the wagons?'

'We'd have to take the direct route.'

She nodded, thinking he meant the trains. 'The non-stop service?'

'Well, yes . . . in so far as stopping won't really be an option, once we get up to speed. Mabil? We'll need maximum over-pressure on Relief Line Twelve. We'll need to ride the surge all the way past Six Hundredth Street, to the out-station at Polter and Vine. Can you start the supplemental pumps?'

'I can, Hasper – I'll just fit it in along with preparing these guns and wagons you asked for. Anything else while you're at it? I could iron your shirts or put some more tea on.'

'Just the pumps, Mabil,' Quell said. 'That will do nicely.'

*

Stallis and the launch were approaching the same objective along slightly different vectors. They had been twelve hundred leagues apart when Ruther picked up the first sweeper return from the other craft; now that separation had closed to less than six hundred.

'Let me show you something, boy,' Fura said, glad to have something to take her mind off the absence at the end of her wrist. 'It's a little adornment to the launch, something we wouldn't ever want to show off in polite company. Not that we've seen too much of that, lately, but you get the idea.'

While Surt and Merrix managed the controls and instruments, Fura went back along the length of the launch to open a panel in the floor, a few paces along from the hatch for the belly lock. It was a smaller, tighter space in which to squeeze: impossible for anyone wearing a vacuum suit. 'When's your birthday, Ruther?'

'Not for a while, Captain.'

'It's come early, then. Wriggle yourself into that nook, and get your mitts on a nice chasing coiller. It's a dainty piece, nothing like the guns we had on *Revenger*, but for a launch it's nothing to be sneezed at.' She looked at him encouragingly. 'D'you think you can handle it?'

'I've . . . never had my hands on a gun, Captain.'

'And I wouldn't ask it of you, but there's no automatic control on this one, and even if there was, we ain't in any position to depend on Paladin just for now.' She bent down, dipping into the space with her one good hand to arm the coiller and bring its targeting screens to glowing life. 'Nothing fancy here, boy. Ten slugs in the magazine, and that's your lot. You just have to aim and shoot.' She angled his head into the gun compartment, with rather more gentleness than she had shown the last time she had him by her fingers. 'That screen is an enlargement of our sweeper. The whelp's a nice, hard target and getting fatter by the second. Once he's within two hundred leagues, you can fire at your discretion. I'll leave that to you.'

'Should I mind about muzzle glow, Captain?'

'No – you'll never run it hot enough to count, not with just those ten slugs. Besides, I expect that Incer already has a very good idea of our position. The only reason he won't have shot at us just yet is that he only has the same type of light armament in that escape capsule – perhaps a swivel-piece or something he can carry in his hands – and he won't care to waste any of his slugs.'

By now Ruther had come to some understanding of the gun compartment's operation. Because it was normally concealed, it had to be jacked out of the hull for the gun to swivel, and because of that, the entire compartment had to be pressurised and sealed-in from above.

'I . . . thought you wanted to kill him personally.'

'Oh, I do. Very much so – preferably with him wetting his little britches before my eyes. But he won't be in any rush to extend you or I the same courtesy. He'll start shooting at us presently, Ruther, and we need to have something by way of reply. Be rude of us not to, wouldn't it?'

Ruther peered into the cramped guts of the compartment. Now that the coiller was armed, a dim red light had begun to pick out the limits of that confinement, and the awful contortions that would be imposed onto the gunner.

'It looks small in there.'

'I was going to ask if you were troubled by closed-in spaces. Then I remembered your profession.'

'It's no worse than some bone rooms,' Ruther agreed.

'It's better. There's no skull in there, just cold metal and magnets.'

The boy prepared to wriggle in. He would need to dive down face-first, dragging his feet behind him. It would be almost impossible to wriggle back out, unless he was helped on his way. It took courage to submit to such an arrangement: courage and an ability to blank all the horrors that might befall one, in that cramped little torture chamber.

'Will you be coordinating things, Captain?'

'No, lad. You can't be the one doing all the work, can you? I'm going out with a suit and something I can aim and fire with just one set of fingers. We'll see who racks up the most hits: it'll be a grand little game, between us.'

Ruther visibly gulped back his nervousness.

'I'll try not to let you down.'

'You won't, Ruther. We might not have a ship to our name – not for the time being – but I ain't sorry to have made your acquaintance or taken you onto my crew.' She paused, helping him ease his frame into the compartment, Ruther wincing as his elbows scraped on the metal edges of the hatchway. 'Remember: that little speck on the sweeper is the turd-crumb who took Werranwell from you, and my friends Proz and Tindouf, and who didn't exactly help Strambli, either. Think of him, when you're ready to squeeze off a slug, and think of those we've lost. I'll be doing likewise.'

When his heels had cleared the hatch she sealed Ruther in, checked that the lungstuff was flowing, and then used a hydraulic pump-handle to lower the compartment out of its recess in the belly. It was only five spans of travel, nothing at all compared to the deployment of the sighting room, but that was enough to allow the gun to operate, and with the cooperation of the launch it could cover a useful sweep of sky. Was she being too hard on the boy, she wondered, or merely showing him the trust and respect he had earned?

Ruther would have to puzzle that one out for himself, she decided. She might be in want of a ship, but she still had a crew, and each must play their part.

Eddralder's long, doleful face was waiting when she turned back from the pump-handle. 'You were, of course, not at all serious about going outside.'

'Why wouldn't I be?'

'You were unconscious when we found you. There's no telling what happened to you before you were . . . brought to us.' Almost by way of an afterthought he added: 'You have lost a hand.'

'Which was tin to start with. Which I'll get back. Which ain't presently troublin' me, except you keep drawing my attention to it.' She looked at him pleadingly. 'Help me into a suit, Doctor. I have a ship to defend, and . . .' She touched a finger to her face, just beneath her eye. 'It's beginning to prickle and itch. It wants me to do something, demands I do something, and if I were you, I wouldn't be the one to stand in its way.'

'I see the manifestation. I could hardly not see it.'

'Then help, before it claws its way out of my skin.'

'I shall assist.' But there was a cautionary note in his voice. 'You realise the contradiction here, do you not? The glowy wishes to preserve you. It needs its host to survive, and for that *you* need to reach Trevenza. Where there may yet be supplies of Mephrozine.'

'That hasn't escaped me,' Fura said sullenly.

'How will you resolve that paradox?'

'I ain't thought it through just yet. Guess it'll be between me and the glowy to square the circle. But I reckon a fine start would be not dying in the next ten minutes.'

*

Eddralder helped her into a cobbled-together suit. It was not her own, nor made of any of the parts she ordinarily used, so the fit was tolerable rather than satisfactory, but it was not as if she meant to wear it for any length of time. Surt and Merrix had the controls; by the time Fura was through the lock the sweeper indicated that Stallis had closed to within two hundred and twenty leagues. Meanwhile, Trevenza Reach itself was as tantalisingly near – and yet still out of reach – as any fabled and treacherous island in any of the stories Paladin used to read to them.

'Do you still have that bead on your sweeper, Ruther?' she asked, using the short-range channel.

'I do, Captain, and I'm thinking about what you said about our friends. But I don't think he's quite near enough yet.'

'He soon will be, and if I know how his mind works, he'll be very pleased to think he has the surprise on us. He'll see your muzzle flash, and mine, so I'd like it very much if our first shots weren't wasted. But it would be awfully nice to put a spike in his pride, wouldn't it? *Spikey-spikey.'*

'Spikey . . . spikey,' Ruther echoed back, as if the words were the elements of some secret riddle not yet known to him. 'I think that means you'd like us to shoot first, if at all possible? But only if we can hit him.'

'We're of one mind, Ruther.'

Fura stood on the cusp of the lock, magnetic soles clamping her to the hull's metal. She had brought only one weapon from the launch's minor inventory, and under other circumstances it would have been a long way from her first choice. It was a six-slug portable coiller, something like a grotesquely swollen and elongated hunting rifle. It was awkward to carry, awkward to aim, virtually impossible to reload in vacuum, doubly so for someone with only one functioning set of fingers. Its stopping power was not tremendous, and its muzzle velocity too slow to be of any effectiveness against swift-moving targets. Its usefulness was confined to a set of very specific situations: close action against suited or otherwise lightly-armoured adversaries, within a sphere of action less than one hundred leagues across. It was the sort of weapon that bauble-crackers used as a last line of defence against pirates and claim-jumpers, when a bauble party might spy a hostile ship moving into orbit near their own mother craft. It was almost entirely useless against a rapacious, heavily armed and well-defended enemy such as Bosa Sennen. That it had been kept at all was only by dint of the usual habit of captains not to throw anything away, not even a clumsy hand-coiller that was better melted for scrap. Because everything, sooner or later, had its moment.

Now was the moment for the six-slug coiller. As lengthy as it was, the barrel was not too hard to keep aimed, due to a sweet-running gyroscope that ran off the same accumulators that provided the energising pulse for the solenoids. In common with all of Bosa's instruments, it had very fine optics, so finding the tiny moving glint of Stallis was not too difficult. Most crucially, it could be fired and re-fired using only the fingers of Fura's right arm. She provided a stabilising fixture for the barrel with her left. She even had fingers on that hand now: the suit had come with a glove and no quick way to leave it off.

She elevated the coiller, presenting the sighting lens to her faceplate, and swept around the area where she expected to find Stallis. He was not too hard to find, even at two hundred leagues. He was the only moving thing: Trevenza Reach was hidden around the other side of the hull, the stars were fixed, and there were no other worlds to add confusion.

She centred the red-lit cross-hair.

The launch juddered under her: the recoil of a single slug from the belly-mounted coiller. 'Very good, boy,' she mouthed to herself, pleased that Ruther had not waited for her command.

Her aim drifted, but the gyroscope nudged it back into line like the patient hand of a firing instructor. A minute passed, and the capsule flared as if it had caught a sharp beam of sunlight. Ruther had struck it! There was no need to congratulate the lad on his success; he would be well aware of the impact. When the flare abated, though, the capsule still presented the same aspect as it had before. It had been hit, most certainly, but probably only enough to flash away some of its armour. Fura was not too surprised by that, given the capabilities of the launch's gun.

Ruther fired again. This one went wide: evidence, perhaps, that Stallis was now taking some evasive action.

'Easy, boy,' she whispered to herself. 'Let him come a little nearer.'

Fura held her nerve until Ruther sent a third shot. At the instant she felt the recoil through her boots, she squeezed off two slugs, each aimed a fraction off the target. It was a gamble and potentially a costly one. She counted on Stallis seeing Ruther's muzzle flash and taking that as a cue to veer his capsule one way or the other. With just six slugs in her weapon she dared not bracket all the possible vectors he might take, but surely it was worth a little recklessness for the sake of two slugs . . .

The capsule flashed. She had got him, or Ruther had – there was no telling, nor any need to know.

She was down to four slugs. Ruther had seven remaining.

A minute passed, then another, then five.

Nothing had happened; no return fire. The capsule still

glinted back at her. Was he dead, she wondered? Had they ended him that easily, that unceremoniously? She would not be so churlish as to begrudge herself that sort of victory, even if it were not half so satisfying as looking into his face while she pressed down on his windpipe.

The hull clanged; she felt it all the way into her bones. That was not the recoil, but an impact from an incoming slug. So, the whelp lived after all. She was not exactly jubilant about that, but not exactly disappointed either.

Ruther fired back.

Another shot came in. She felt it and saw it. Less than eight spans from the lock, a bright soundless flash tore into the hull, leaving a neat, fist-sized depression where it had struck. She felt a coldness around her right elbow and looked down to see a jet of gas escaping from the connecting bellows between her upper and lower arm segments. A bit of the hull or the slug itself had punctured her suit.

The feather-like plume of escaping lungstuff looked impressive, but unless it got worse it was not going to cause her any immediate difficulties. The tanks still had plenty of reserve in them, and she was still able to move her arm. What was more concerning was the thought of being caught by some larger fragment, if Stallis managed another strike. If it had happened to Prozor, it could happen to her. Fura lowered the coiller and stepped out of the lock, easing herself through ninety degrees until her soles were planted on the hull itself. Quickly but carefully, she made her way around the curve of the launch until she had interposed a good part of the hull between herself and the enemy. That would have to do as a covering screen. Kneeling now, using the sole of one boot and just the toes of the other for contact, she re-acquired her aim, levelling the barrel over the smooth brassy ridge formed by the hull.

Another shot came in. Her instinct had been sound: a white flash lifted off the hidden face of the hull, close enough to the lock that it would have been very inadvisable to have remained where she was.

Her helmet crackled.

'Oh, Captain Ness. Must we drag this out?' His voice was strained, a little breathless. 'You had your sport with me a little while ago, I admit. That was very well done, butchering my crew as you did. And to have that glassy abomination on your own side – I commend you! We're really as ruthless as each other. Heh! We could almost be friends! Certainly we have a very great deal in common, perhaps more than you might wish.'

'We've got nothing in common, Incer.' She fired off her third slug. 'Just so you understand that.'

'But we do, Arafura – we do. We're both absolutists, and that is a rare quality. I believe in absolute order: the rule of law; the preservation of the systems and institutions we all depend on. Whereas by your actions you stand for the absolute negation of that order. You wish to invoke chaos and upheaval. You are doing, dare I say it, rather well. The worlds are tumbling into anarchy because of what you have done to our currency. Good men and women have been thrown onto the streets by your actions. You're a vandal, a murderess . . . and yet, I still admire your dedication. As I say, a rare and commendable thing.'

She fired again. By the recoil through the hull, Ruther had already fired twice more.

'We ain't alike, Incer – much as you'd wish it.'

'How so?'

'The universe only ever spawned one of you. It was a revolting little exercise, and it didn't feel the need to do it before or since. You murdered your own mother.'

'Well, we'll debate the details of that. But I've studied your biography, dear Arafura. The death of your poor daddy, left gasping for his life on a Mazarile back-street while you sauntered off. Are you completely sure you can absolve yourself of that?'

She fired again, leaving just one slug in the coiller.

'He was ill.'

'That only compounds your crime. You knew he was ailing, and still you turned against him.'

'Do not compare yourself to me.'

Ruther let off another shot from the belly-gun. Two more shots came in from Stallis. A powdery flash gasped off the hidden side of the hull.

'Tell me . . . how do you think this is going to end, Captain Ness? I have an advantageous vector on you. If by some lucky stroke you make it to Trevenza, you'll find that I've already arrived ahead of you, and I have reinforcements there. The hard part will be persuading my men to keep you alive until I reach you. Then . . . then . . . we shall have our reckoning. I might let you spit in my eye, just for the fun of it.'

She left off her final slug.

'You've got me wrong, Incer – and we're not the same at all. There are specks of bacteria I'd feel something more in common with. There are puddles of vomit in Neon Alley I'd sooner call my friend. There are white dog turds, squashed under cartwheels, that'll be more fondly remembered than you or your deeds. You're a fading stain, no more'n that. Your mother squatted and grunted you into the gutter, and now you're on your way down the drain, into the sewer.'

Her last slug had missed, or drawn no visible flash. She was done with the coiller. She rose from her kneeling position, standing up on the hull so that she lost nearly all the advantages of cover.

'I'm waiting, Incer. Take your best shot. You'll never have a better chance than this.'

He did not fire. She had goaded him as well as she could, and no response had come. Nor was there any further sound of him over the squawk.

*

Ruther was there to help her out of her suit.

'Did we get him, Captain?' he asked, breathless and eager. 'I saw hull flashes . . .'

'We bloodied him, Ruther, which is all that we could expect.

But I don't think we did enough damage to stop him arriving before us. In the end we were quite nicely matched.' She paused, feeling that something more was needed. 'You did well, down in that gun hatch. It's not your fault that we didn't have the penetrating power. Your captain would have been proud.'

'I take what you mean, sir . . . I mean, Captain.' Ruther looked abashed. 'But you're my captain now.'

'Then I'm very glad that Werranwell schooled you as well as he did. Unfortunately, I can't promise you a long and happy service under my command.' Fura nodded at the porthole next to the lock, where the spindleworld's extremity was coming into view: a jewelled horn encrusted with a fine fur of docking ports and the numerous fly-specks of berthed ships. Even with the oblique angle thus offered, it was perfectly clear that Trevenza Reach was swelling at indecent speed. To the untrained eye, perhaps, the approach might not have seemed reckless . . . but not one of her crew now counted as untrained. 'It'll be a little rough on us, I should warn you. And if Incer arrives ahead of us, even if it's only by a few minutes, it'll give him all the time he needs to organise his loyalists and prepare for us.'

Ruther reflected on this for a few seconds. 'If we are a danger to Trevenza Reach, they will shoot at us before we arrive, won't they? It wouldn't take very long to send out some men with coillers, even if they had to aim by eye.'

'Perhaps being shot out of the sky would be a mercy on all of us.'

'You don't believe that,' he said, instantly blushing at his own impertinence. 'You don't, and neither do I. And I think they'll only shoot at us if they really do fear for the world. They won't, though. Incer wants us alive, if there is any means of that.'

'You've a keen sense of him, then.'

'I used to have a cat, before I went off into space. The cat liked to torment things much more than he liked to kill them. He would bring them inside, scuttle behind the cupboards and keep them alive for days and days. You can only kill something once, but if you are careful, and clever, you can torment them for as long as you care to.' Ruther glanced away, as if he had exposed some private part of his soul. 'I never really liked that cat.'

*

They did indeed come in hard – much harder than she might have wished – but no guns had opened up against them on the final approach and the arrival, though punishing, was not quite forceful enough to count as a crash. The launch rammed into the berth at about thirty spans per second, but parts of the docking structure buckled or yielded to absorb the brunt of the collision, and there was no loss of pressure integrity within the craft.

For a minute or two the only noises were faint metallic settling sounds, like a symphony of bedsprings.

Fura dared to look around at her crew.

'Did we all make it?'

Ruther rubbed at the elbow he had barked on his way into the gun compartment. 'I think we did, Captain. I mean, given how bad it could have been . . . '

'Surt, Merrix, Doctor Eddralder? Are you all right?'

'We shall live,' Eddralder answered. 'One may hope. That was well handled, Captain, given your lack of steering control. We ought not to be alive.'

'Count your blessings while you may, Doctor.' Fura had unbuckled herself and was peering out through the side window at the other craft attached to the docking complex. She appraised their shapes and markings very quickly and felt an awful intimation of what was soon to be upon them. 'There are already Revenue ships docked here, and I see a small capsule that I think must be Stallis's escape vehicle. The little whelp has outfoxed us.'

'You thought it likely he'd make it here ahead of us,' Ruther said.

'Probable, but not guaranteed. I'm afraid it isn't likely to go well for us, if his men have gained authority over the docks. They'll want my neck, but I've a feeling they won't be too particular about anyone who gets in their way. You'd all make nice bonuses, too, if he wants to throw a scrap or two to his dogs.'

'We'll stand by you,' Ruther said.

'I know you will, boy. But if there's a chance for any of you . . .'

The squawk buzzed. 'Open your lock, Captain Ness,' said the instantly recognisable voice of Stallis. 'We have a pressurised connection and are ready to force entry if we must. If we do, I shan't be able to guarantee the safety of your associates. We have cutting implements, grenades, smoke bombs, incapacitators, toxin-tipped crossbow bolts and an assortment of energy pistols.' He waited a moment. 'Captain Ness? Let us not indulge in this pointless charade of you pretending not to hear me or being unable to answer. I know perfectly well that you are alive in there. You know also that my patience with you is extremely strained, after our little tussle in your wreck.'

She flicked on the squawk. She had considered her options and decided that nothing was lost by speaking to him. 'Was your patience with your mother also strained, Incer, before you had her murdered for a ship?'

'I will blow my way in if I must, Captain. There may be decompression . . . there may be unpleasant injuries. Now will you do the sensible thing and open your lock? You'll spoil my fun a little, but needs must. It's really only you that I'm interested in, and it would be so much better for my masters if I were able to deliver you alive, even in the most limited and temporary sense.'

'You saw what happened to your friends, Incer – how they were sliced up. You saw *her* for what she was, before you ran away.'

'I have no idea what you are talking about. You did very well with some concealed weapons and traps, and I won't deny that it cost my boarding squads gravely. We were over-confident and under-prepared, and you had the advantage of us. That was all.'

'She's still with me, Incer. She's still with us, waiting for you.

She'll cut through you like a glass whirlwind.'

'You are demented, Captain Ness. Touched by too much time away from civilisation. You've become credulous . . . a danger to yourself and others. You've begun to believe in fairy tales.'

'Then try your luck.'

'Heh.' He let out his usual mirthless chuckle. 'One more chance at reasonable dialogue, and then we'll come in by violent means. I will . . . negotiate for your cooperation. Your passengers – your fellow travellers from the *Nightjammer*. They aren't of direct interest to me. We have credible intelligence that they have been coerced or tricked into crewing with you, and for that reason my employers have given me license to be flexible. Are you listening?'

'Yes, but I'm not sure anyone else is. You could promise me the world over this squawk and it wouldn't mean anything if it's just between the two of us.'

'Heh. Whatever else may be said of you, Captain Ness, you are no fool. I am cross-connecting my transmission to the general channel; you may do likewise. Now anyone in Trevenza with an open squawk will be party to our exchange, and to the terms of our agreement.' His voice took on an echoing quality, and when she answered, her own amplified and echoed voice came out of the grille.

'Incer Stannis, I am Captain Arafura Ness of the sunjammer *Revenger* and you will let my crew go free.'

'As much as I admire your candour, what you ask is far outside the bounds of possibility. They will need to be detained, questioned, debriefed. They are all party to criminal acts, and their involvement needs to be clarified. As I say, we are willing to consider the likelihood that they were under coercive and manipulative control – but the facts will still need to be ascertained. Let the others speak – I should be delighted to consider their positions.'

Ruther leaned in, placed a palm over the microphone, and whispered: 'I don't trust him at all.'

Fura smiled. 'You're learning.'

'But it may be the best hope for all of us, and especially Doctor Eddralder and Merrix. I'll never admit to being coerced. I knew just what I was getting into, and I'd no more denounce you than I'd have denounced Captain Werranwell.'

'Boy's right,' Surt said. 'We're crew, and I won't pretend to be anything I'm not. But Eddralder and Merrix deserve a fair hearing. They didn't join us for glory or quoins – they were just trying to escape something worse.'

Eddralder lifted Ruther's hand from the microphone. 'Incer Stallis? You are speaking to Doctor Eddralder. I would like to discuss your proposal.'

'I am very willing to listen, Doctor.'

'Good. I believe I speak for my daughter in this regard. To hell with your bargaining. To hell with your ideas of justice. I once worked for a man who was capable of great cruelty, but at least he had the nobility of self-realisation. He knew precisely what he was, and what he had allowed himself to become. He was a monster, but an honest one. I doubt that you have ever had the courage to look yourself in the mirror and observe the rot in your soul.'

There was a silence. The launch creaked slightly against its berth, settling into place. The squawk crackled.

'Is that a no, Doctor?'

Merrix leaned in. 'He speaks for all of us, you worthless little . . .' She gathered herself, one eye on her father. ' Turd-stain! We know what we did. We know what *you* did. One day you'll hang for it.'

Fura took command of the microphone. 'As you can see, Incer, they aren't easily persuaded. As grateful as I am for their loyalty, though, I cannot see them endangered. We are still on open-channel. I'm letting you in now: do as you must with me, but show clemency to the others. They had no part in my . . . more questionable actions.'

'No,' Ruther said, as her hand moved to release the lock. 'Don't let him inside.'

'He'll kill us all if I don't allow him,' Fura said. 'At least this way he has to give you a fair hearing, and for that you have to be alive.' She raised her right hand. 'No weapons, no resistance. You surrender and comply with the Revenue men. It was always going to end this way from the moment they took us. I am only sorry I offered you false hope.'

'You didn't,' Ruther said, his cheeks flushing.

Fura opened both inner and outer lock doors. The pressure equalised and her ears popped. Something whirled into the cabin, billowing pink smoke. Fura had barely taken a breath of it before her eyes began to sting and her throat tightened. She gagged. Behind her, Surt, Ruther, Merrix and Doctor Eddralder began to cough violently.

Two burly, armoured Revenue men came in through the lock, moving with practised ease against the weightlessness of the hub. They had crossbows and other weapons. Fura tried to scream at them, but her narrowing throat constricted her voice to a thin croak. The pink smoke was a thickening veil. She saw Ruther raise an arm, trying to protect Surt – or was it Merrix? Eddralder, by some small miracle, still had the capacity to speak. 'You lied,' he bellowed out, his voice breaking. 'She gave herself up! There is no need to attack!'

One of the armoured figures elevated their crossbow, but instead of shooting Eddralder the Revenue man flipped the weapon around and drove its stock into the physician's face. More Revenue men were coming through the lock. Behind the last of them, the smaller, slighter form of Stallis, also armoured and helmeted.

Through stinging, watering eyes Fura watched as the men put restraints on her crew. They came for her last of all. Stallis stood back as the men attempted to cuff her.

'She has one arm, you dolts.'

This was not quite right, but it conveyed the essential difficulty facing the men. Quickly a different form of restraint was improvised. Her upper arms were bound to her sides and held there by loops of some thick, strap-like material.

'Shall we gag her, Captain?'

'So that I'm spared the lashing of her tongue? I wouldn't dream of it. I want to hear her pitying pleas; her groundless threats. They will be music to my ears.' He batted a hand in front of his two-windowed visor. 'Disperse this damned smoke.'

There was no need to disperse the smoke, for the men extracted Fura and her crew from the launch with a quick, bruising efficiency. They were bullied and shoved from the lock, out into a windowless holding area. It was still weightless, or as near weightless as could be discerned. The men double-checked the restraints and secured Fura and her party to a bench-like rail running along one of the room's surfaces. Only then did Stallis lift his helmet clear of his head.

'It was a good try, Captain Ness,' he said, grinning at her with a boyish enthusiasm as if they just been sparring or playing tag. 'A very commendable effort, heh, heh! Alas, there was only ever going to be one outcome.'

Through slitted eyes she appraised her companions. Surt and Merrix looked half-stunned. Eddralder was snorting through a bleeding nose. She thought it quite likely that it had been broken. Ruther, meanwhile, was staring down at a dislocated finger joint, his smallest digit sticking out from his hand at an odd angle.

'You agreed not to hurt my crew,' she said, wheezing out the words. 'You made a commitment over the general squawk.'

'I said what needed to be said to gain your compliance, Captain Ness. You're an outlaw: a threat to public safety. If a child is about to do something dangerous to itself or others, you say whatever will make the child desist.'

'You still . . .' She coughed, fought for breath. 'You still have no need to detain them. You have me. I'm Arafura Ness. I'm enough for you.'

'Oh, come, we've been over this.' He moved along the rail until he was face to face with Merrix, with her hands cuffed and her legs tied to the rail. 'Doctor Eddralder's daughter, I presume?' He flicked a nod at her father. 'We learned of your activities in Wheel Strizzardy, both of you. The father and his daughter: willing co-conspirators, interrogators and torturers both. They say your father was the most expert, Merrix, but that you were always the most imaginative. As I have learned, there is a particular streak of cruelty known only to small girls . . .' He snapped a gloved hand to her chin, forcing her to look him hard in the eye. 'Turd-stain, was it, Merrix? How charming. How thoroughly ladylike.' He spat at her. Then, turning to one of his men: 'What is the status of our control of Trevenza? Have we pushed as far as Four Hundredth Street? I want the entire leading spindle under Revenue control, under martial law and curfew, and we do not pull up the shutters until these upstart fools bow down to real authority.' He looked into the visor of the man he was addressing, frowning slightly. 'Why are you staring at me so? What is the status?' His voice rose to a shriek. 'Answer me, damn you! Answer me, or by the worlds I will ruin you for insubordination!'

The Revenue man lifted his crossbow and shot Stallis in the belly. By the dull, percussive sound of the impact, Fura knew it to be a stun-bolt, too thick and slow to penetrate armour – it was not intended to be lethal – but the force was still enough to drive Stallis sideways, and at the same time leave him shocked, gasping and momentarily frozen. A second passed, during which none of those present seemed to know quite how to react. It was as if an actor had delivered completely the wrong line during an otherwise flawless performance, going so thoroughly out of character as to throw the rest of the cast into a dumbstruck paralysis.

The spell held, then broke.

Stallis reached for a standard-issue energy pistol; four of his nearest men turned to the one who had shot him. They were outnumbered by at least three to one, for all the other Revenue operatives were now shooting back, not just with stun-bolts but with armour-piercers, projectile pistols, energy projectors.

It was all over in very short order.

Stallis lay slumped and incapacitated; his four closest

associates dead or near to death. The other Revenue men – the ones who had turned on their own – began to lift off their helmets. The first of them was a man with a thick, deep, vertical crease down the middle of his forehead. 'I'm Branca,' he said, gruff of voice. 'I'm sorry they got to rough you and your crew up a little, but we had to make sure that we struck at the right moment.' He nodded at the two of the others and they sprung forward with knives, setting about the restraints binding Fura and her party to the rail.

'What just happened, Branca?' she asked, still hoarse from the smoke, still seeing the world through tears. 'Who do you work for?'

'He works for Hasper Quell,' said the one next to Branca. 'And right now, at least for the time being, Hasper Quell is working for us.' She removed her helmet and lifted her chin, regarding Fura through two small spectacles. 'Captain Ness, I presume?'

Fura might have wept for joy, but her eyes were already awash. 'Captain Ness, I presume.'

'Welcome to Trevenza Reach,' Adrana said. Her eyes dipped to the abbreviated stump of Fura's forearm, and then her gaze shifted sidelong to the half-catatonic boy, who regarded her with a wide-eyed and fearful incomprehension, like a child who had just received the first firm reprimand of his life. 'It's over for you, Incer. Everything. Your entire life has been one wasted arc, leading to this moment.'

His reply was plaintive. 'What will you do to me?'

A voice raised across his. It was an older man with two black holes instead of eyes; a muscular man with a bristle of shocked hair. 'You'll help us, Incer. A point needs to be made – a very practical point – and you are just the man for the job.' He touched a finger to his brow, above the two eye-holes. 'Hasper Quell, at your service. Would you like some money, Captain Stallis?'

The man called Quell – whom Fura had met, but long ago – was taking out a quoin.

31

The Ness sisters hugged each other, each pressing close to the other, defying the universe to show that this reunion was some fabulation of their desires; some cruel phantom of their mutual imaginations, a dream of better circumstances about to be shattered by the careless intrusion of day. By some miracle, though, the dream persisted. It was not about to be undone so readily, and with each moment that passed, the sisters permitted themselves the hardening belief that it was both real and irrevocable. In each case, there was a detail that their minds might have struggled to fabricate, if this were mere wish-fulfilment. To Fura, some new hardness had settled into her sister since their separation. Adrana seemed thinner, steelier, more bone than flesh, and with a distance in her eyes that had not been present before. If at times Fura had disdained the accident of birth that made Adrana the older of them, she now held no objection to their mutual status. She was glad to have this wiser, cooler influence in her life, and very sorry indeed that she had not been there when whatever events took place to account for that recession in her gaze. They could have borne that distress together, and if that might not have made it easier, at least they would have shared the burden, and carried it between them ever after.

Adrana, for her part, felt exactly the same sentiment. She

could hardly have ignored Fura's missing hand, but the full accounting of that loss – how it had come about, and the toll it had taken upon Fura – would have to wait. But she saw in her sister's eyes the same remove; as if each had become a mirror to the other, and she knew without a word passing between them that Fura had come through some cold cleansing fire, and that each sister now stood at a definite distance from the lives they had known in Mazarile.

Each took account of the friends who were present, and the friends absent.

'Something bad has happened to both of us,' Adrana began, lifting a dark, sweat-sodden lock from her sister's brow. 'You see it in me, and I see it in you. I don't even know which of us should begin. I think we must both have a lot to say, a lot to tell. But let me start with one thing, before you say a word.'

Fura's fingers brushed the short sharp hairs on Adrana's scalp. 'Is that a command?'

'I shouldn't dare. I mean only to say that I know what it cost you, to warn me of that skull. It was the bravest, kindest thing you could ever have done for me, and I will never forget it.'

'They said it'd turn you mad. Since you're speaking to me, and you don't seem mad . . . ' Fura paused, assessing Adrana's eyes with a deeper concentration, as if there might yet be a clue in them. 'I presume the warning reached you in time?'

'It was in time – but I won't pretend there was any margin of error. It had me, very nearly, and when they broke me out, I felt as if I'd spent hours in its thrall. When Lasling told me that I'd only been in it for minutes, I felt sure he was lying. But I know now that it was the skull, putting its poison into me.'

'It might be said that we've a taste for poison, what with the glowy in me, and a bit of Bosa in you.'

'I should be glad if we broke the habit.' Adrana was consoled that Fura had mentioned the glowy, for it spared her the chore of navigating around to the subject. 'I see that it hasn't left you.'

'Which is a polite way of saying, it's gone a lot further than the last time we spoke. But that's only because I had to stop taking the medicine. We'll speak of that in due course – you ain't to worry yourself overmuch on my account.' Fura smiled, wishing that her sister would let drop her mask of concern, for it made Fura disconsolate when she wished to feel happy. 'What matters is we're both here, both alive, and where we wanted to be all along. Our mission for the Clacker is complete. He owes us something, but we don't owe *him* a thing, and I feel fine about that. Promise you won't be cross at me that I lost our pretty little ship?'

'I couldn't ever be cross. But is it really lost, or just abandoned?'

'Truth is, I'd sooner think that it's misplaced, or under new ownership. Well, that part's complicated, and shivery, and I wouldn't care to guess at our chances of ever seeing her again. But she ain't lost, and she ain't captured, and that's something. Oh, and I saved Paladin!'

'You were always sweeter on him than me,' Adrana said. 'But I'm glad – mightily glad. And I think there are some other robots who will be pleased as well.' She dipped her head in sudden earnestness. 'Now: the hand. Is it troubling you greatly? The city's not exactly in a state of orderly business, as you might have gathered, but I think if we had to find a Limb Broker, Quell could help us.'

'It will keep for a day or so. Mostly, I'm hungry, thirsty, tired, and I have a suspicion I might not smell terribly nice.'

'You do not,' Adrana said, sniffing. 'But since I came here through a sewerage tunnel, I am not sure I'm in any position to judge.' With great gentleness she broke away from her sister. Each could have continued to hold the other, but each also knew that the night's business was far from concluded, and much needed to be done. 'Quell doesn't have complete control of Trevenza Reach just yet, but he's working on it.'

'I have some questions for Quell.'

'May they wait a little while? Things may be a little touch-and-go for the next day or so. In the meantime, we'll be safe at the Six Hundredth Street Station, and I'm reliably assured they have hot water and soap and perhaps a little to eat and drink. Does that sound agreeable?'

Fura nodded. But she was still thinking of Quell.

*

They rode a tram with a retinue of Quell loyalists perched on the footboards, armed and vigilant against little pockets of resistance. Once or twice they let off weapons, shooting down alleys and into darkened corners at presumed Revenue agents and muddleheads. The shutters were still drawn along Trevenza Reach, so that when the tram surmounted a high vista, the sisters could look out along the night-lit length of the spindle-world and see distant flares and the flashes of running battles, as pretty and fleeting as kaleidoscope patterns.

'You may as well hear the worst of it,' Fura said, looking at her electrically-lit reflection in the window for a long interval before continuing. 'Prozor and Tindouf are gone.'

Adrana swallowed. 'I feared it. But I hoped there'd be some way they'd survived. Was it Stallis?'

'Directly, in Tindouf's case – he killed him before my eyes, just before he took my hand off. Indirectly, with Proz. She was outside the ship, attempting to signal you, and his coillers took her.'

'Tell me it was fast, and she knew nothing of it.'

'I hope that it was. But I can't know for sure.'

'And . . . Strambli? The last word we had was that Eddralder was preparing to operate. She isn't with you, so I take that as all the evidence I need that the operation was unsuccessful.'

Fura evaluated her answer before proceeding. It was not that she wished to hold anything back from Adrana, but she did not care to sound deranged, or to sound as if she were attempting to explain away the loss of the ship with some preposterous lie. Yet what choice did she have?

'He did try to cut it out of her. But he wasn't quick enough. It progressed, and when there didn't seem to be any hope for her . . . I told Eddralder to kill her, by medical means. That may sound callous, but . . .'

'I wasn't there. If I had been, I'm sure I'd have instructed him in exactly the same fashion.'

'Well, it worked . . . and it didn't work. We thought she was dead. Then all hell broke loose, with Incer shooting at us, and in that confusion . . . you will not quibble over a word of this, sister, promise me?'

'I shall not.'

'Strambli disappeared. She became Ghostie. We searched the ship, and we couldn't find any trace of her. But she was still with us. And not so far gone as to forget her loyalty to her old crew, although how long we might've depended on that kinship, I daren't say. But when Incer took us, and butchered Tindouf . . . and was ready to take me . . . *I saw her*, Adrana.' Fura's voice had become, even in her own judgement, hushed and reverential, as if she spoke of some profound and sacred happening. 'Or rather, I didn't quite see anything, because she was Ghostie, and my eyes slithered off her just as if she were made up of all that armour we found in The Fang. But it was her, and she knew me, and she took an aversion to Stallis.'

'But not enough of one.'

'Oh, he was lucky to be rid of her. But she saved me – got me to the launch, when I had no right to expect it. I told her she could have the ship, after me. That was . . . all right of me, wasn't it?'

'You were negotiating with a Ghostie, and you wonder if you have my retrospective approval? Fura, I'd have done very well not to crawl whimpering into a corner.' She paused. 'Let us hope, all the same, that she takes due care of our ship. We might not be its captains now, but I think we may still lay claim on its ownership.'

'I'm glad you ain't cross.'

'I ain't cross,' Adrana said, in a faint mocking echo of her sister. 'And I see the weeks alone have done nothing to refine your tongue. Nor am I complaining. You've inhabited this role so thoroughly I should almost be sad to see it discarded. We have each grown into something, whether we chose it or not.'

'Now that I've told you about Strambli, I have to ask about the rest of your crew.'

'Lasling, Vouga and Cossel are all well – we should see them soon. As for Lagganvor and Meggery, the news isn't so good. One is dead, and the other was never quite alive.'

'I'm not greatly in the mood for riddles, sister.'

'Nor I. But you may as well hear the worst of it, too. Lagganvor was a spy. His identity was false: the real Lagganvor died on Wheel Strizzardy, long before we ever got there. The man we brought into our ship was operating for the Revenue.'

Fura made a small catlike hiss. 'Then I'm glad he's dead. What gave him away?'

Adrana glanced away, then back to her sister. 'You won't be glad he was dead at all. His true name was Brysca.'

'It means nothing to me.'

'Brysca Rackamore. He was the brother of Pol, our captain. He was no Revenue zealot. But he wished to avenge his brother's death at the hands of Bosa Sennen. That was why he infiltrated our crew: to flush out our secrets and learn the extent to which Bosa still had a hold on the *Nightjammer*.' Adrana sensed some building rage in her sister, but she continued undaunted. 'He was a spy, but also a courageous one.'

'And you learned this . . . when?'

The tram rattled on for half a block. 'I learned his identity almost as soon as he came aboard, Fura. I sheltered him, and lied to you. Now and then I even permitted him to signal his masters.'

Fura made to strike her. But she had forgotten that she was lacking a hand on her left arm. Adrana seized her by the damaged limb and applied a crushing counter-pressure, making Fura yelp with surprise, pain and indignation.

'No, you don't get to strike me. You don't get to touch a hair on my head, Fura. I'm very glad that you're back, very glad indeed that you're alive. I do love you, and nothing will change that. But from the moment Stallis pulled you out of that launch I've known it's gone too far in you.' She softened her hold on Fura by a provisional degree. 'The Mephrozine. When did you stop taking it?'

'I didn't . . . stop,' Fura said, breathing heavily.

They were not alone on the tram, for besides Quell's associates, Eddralder, Ruther, Merrix and Surt were also being taken to safety. But these others were halfway down the compartment, and content to watch the performance at some distance.

'Then what happened?'

'It ran out.'

Eddralder raised his voice. 'I will vouch for her, Adrana. She gave the remaining doses to Strambli, in the hope of stemming the Ghostie tide. The gesture was ineffective, but well intentioned.' He paused, pressing a handkerchief to his nose where it had been bloodied, and perhaps broken, by the Revenue men. 'I have already spoken to Branca, the man who was at the dock. He says that Quell shouldn't have difficulty finding a good supply of Mephrozine, and he will get it to me with all expediency. The glowy *has* advanced . . . but with intervention there may be an improvement.'

For all that the glowy was still bright in Fura's face and eyes, and it was only a minute since she had raised her arm, Adrana felt a surge of fondness and empathy for her sister. She squeezed their flesh hands together. 'If you gave her the Mephrozine, knowing how badly you also needed it, that was a very kind thing.'

Fura looked down, as if there was a burden of shame to be borne. 'I am not meant to be kind.'

'And I am not meant to be cold, but we have each had to adapt to circumstance. I left Rackamore and Meggery for dead. Vidin Quindar tried to take the Clacker from us, and there was trouble.'

'And the Clacker?'

'Alive, blessedly. Without him, you would not be. He made this world move. There is an engine in it – a huge and powerful engine of strange manufacture. Clearly, he knew about it all along. In a sense, he tricked me into bringing him to Trevenza. But I am not too sorry.'

'He promised you answers. Promised both of us answers. Have you had them?'

'To the satisfaction I hoped for?' Adrana had hardly had time to reflect on the question until now, and she found herself at a loss for a forthright response. 'I don't know. I feel that I have become less ignorant of some things, and vastly more ignorant of others. I am . . . greatly vexed by certain matters. I feel myself on the cusp of some terrible understanding, and I know that it is not too late to step back from that dawning comprehension. But I do not have the will to retreat. I must know, even though I may regret it for the rest of my days.'

'You would not be my sister if . . .' Fura stroked her hand, then flinched. 'What became of your finger?'

'I lost it. Do you recognise the metal digit strapped on over my stump? Meggery gave it to me. Thought it ought to go back to you in the end.'

*

On the topmost floor of the Six Hundredth Street Station was a series of grand company offices, tall-ceilinged meeting rooms and lavish private dining chambers that had now been entirely commandeered by Quell, providing a secondary base of operations that was very nearly the equal of the sewerage works. Quell and his associates had moved in with immense swagger and assurance, treating the place as if it were their own inheritance, and with only a passing care for the kindly treatment of fittings and furniture. Doors had been ripped off hinges, holes had been hammered through walls, window glass had been knocked out and replaced by crudely fashioned sheets of wood and metal. Paintings and photographs had been torn down, ripped-up or stepped on. Flickerboxes, squawk consoles and sweeper screens had been set up everywhere, connected by an unruly mass of black cables strung along corridors and hallways and up and down staircases. Two huge tables had been rammed together in one of the dining rooms, the too-narrow doorframe bearing the recent scars of this relocation, while precious crystal-domed clocks and veneered cabinets had been shoved rudely aside, leaving splinters and glass shards to be swept into corners. As she was led up and through the chaos with Adrana, stepping over dozing or half-drunk bodies, Fura reflected on how she would feel if it had been their old home in Mazarile that had been stormed and possessed in such a fashion, and on the whole decided that she would not be much in favour of the arrangement. But this, she reminded herself, was the true face of revolution. It was not fine words in history books, not noble deeds prettied up in a painting, but a rude, boisterous business of smashed property, the questionable appropriation of public goods and establishments, and a general air of dangerous, hair-trigger incivility. If she did not like it, she should have taken a bit more care before moving the lever that ended up turning the worlds upside-down.

But I would have done it, nonetheless, she promised herself.

The two jammed-together tables had been laid with food and drink, a veritable if shambolic and mostly looted feast, and gathered around these tables were all the surviving members of both crews: Surt, Eddralder, Merrix, Ruther, Vouga, Lasling and Cossel, as well as a space set aside for Paladin's head, and two adjacent vacant seats for the Ness sisters. Then there was Quell and all his senior revolutionaries – those, at least, who were not busy elsewhere – and a dozen or so citizens of varying standing, who, if they had not initiated the takeover, were deemed to be comfortably sympathetic to its ends. Even the Clacker was present, plumped up on several cushions like a four-armed toy brought to the table at a children's tea party. Introductions were quickly made where necessary, and at last Adrana and Fura had the chance to address their opposing crews and share at first hand their experiences since the separation.

'The first thing I owe all of you,' Fura said, holding a glass of wine in her one remaining hand, 'is an apology. I lost our ship.'

'Misplaced it, temporarily,' Adrana corrected her.

'My sister has the right of it. It's not lost, I hope, but still out there, and under a certain custodianship that I hope'll serve to deter any would-be claimants. But I did lose control of her, and since that ship was common property of our united crews, you should feel as aggrieved by it as I'd feel if we'd lost the *Merry Mare*.'

'We did not,' Adrana said. 'But it was only by your kind action in providing a point of distraction for Stallis while we completed our crossing without misadventure. I'm sorry too that the ship isn't ours, but much, much sorrier that there are friends who aren't here to celebrate your happy arrival.'

'It may be said,' Eddralder responded, 'that Prozor and Tindouf died as they would have wished: defending a good ship against a less worthy crew, and knowing full well the stakes.' He joined hands with his daughter. 'Merrix and I shall never forget them.'

'What of Strambli?' Lasling asked. He was sitting in a wheelchair, since his tin legs only fitted onto his suit.

'She went Ghostie,' Adrana said, sparing Fura the need to recount the story she had already told in the tram, and signalling to her sister that she believed every word of it too. 'There are some who will never credit such matters, I know, even with the benefit of a first-hand account such as ours. But none of us will need such persuasion. She helped Fura escape, and made a fine pickle of Incer Stallis's boarding party, and now she has *Revenger*.'

'But the boy himself survived,' Lasling said, digging a piece of bread from between his teeth. 'May we ask of your plans for him, Mister Quell? Is he . . . still alive?'

'Why wouldn't he be?' Quell asked reasonably. 'It's the Ness sisters he has to answer to, not me. But yes, he's being very well looked after, about six floors beneath this very room, and by all reports is very confident that his allies will be coming to rescue him within the next few hours.'

'I mean to kill him, Quell,' Fura said. 'No part of that is negotiable.'

'The . . . formalities would need to be observed,' Quell answered. 'The niceties. We want to set a good example, going forward.'

Fura necked down her wine. 'Save your good example for someone worth the trouble.' She shook her head, as if there was a fly loose in there she was trying to shake free. 'I can't believe I'm sitting down with you, behaving all politely, being your guest, when I ought to have my fingers round your throat! For Proz's sake, if no one else's, there still ought to be a reckoning for what you did to me.'

'You were both wronged by Vidin Quindar,' Adrana said, her face strained as she tried to broker some sort of peace between the two parties. 'He was the real cause of your difficulties, not Quell.'

'I'll be the judge of that.'

'No,' Adrana said firmly. 'I shall be. I've suffered as much by Quindar's hand as you have – I lost Meggery and Rackamore to him – and that gives me the right to have an opinion on the justice that was done in those tunnels. Quell saved me, as he has saved you, and believe you me, he has left Quindar with something to remember him by.'

'Quindar lives?' Fura asked, with a sudden enthusiasm, for she could think of no better sport than tracking him down and visiting some unspeakable punishment upon him. Her hand throbbed, her skin prickled, and she dipped the evidence of it beneath the table before it was too obvious. Not, she feared, that there was much she could do about the presence of the glowy in her face and eyes.

'He may.' Quell shrugged. 'I'm not too sure, or not even sure I care. I left him blind and whimpering and took back what was originally mine. If he lives, even now, I can assure you that his every waking instant is a torment.' He paused, lowering his head, averting the two black pits of his missing eyes from her gaze. 'I wronged you, Arafura, and I make no bones of that. I wronged dear Proz, too, for she'd put her trust in me to act as a friend, and I didn't. No part of that will ever leave me. It was the last time I saw Proz and now there'll never be a chance to redeem myself in her eyes. But I have tried to become a better man.'

'He has,' said one of the muddleheads at the table, whom Fura felt she had been doing a very creditable job of neither ignoring, not staring at. 'I am . . . Chunter,' he said, in his curious electro-mechanical voice. 'If anyone may be . . . said to vouch . . . for Quell's new character . . . I think I may . . . suffice? He has been . . . kind to us. Many have not.'

Something in Fura shifted at the muddlehead's testament.

'Trust can be undone in one thoughtless moment,' Quell said. 'I've learned that to my cost. But I also know that it can be re-constructed, with time. You've brought the Clacker to us, Ness sisters, and I speak for all of us when I express our gratitude. But there are other ways I can repay that debt. That hand must be taken care of, Fura, and I believe Doctor Eddralder is already well acquainted with your medical needs in the other regard.'

'Quell has arranged Mephrozine,' Eddralder said. 'There'll be enough of it, and in a pure enough form, to undo some of the ill-effects of these last few weeks. We also have access to all the supplies we need to treat our injuries, and none of it shall cost us a quoin. In return, I will be attending to Quell's eyes, as best as my abilities allow.'

Fura at last swung her attention to the Clacker, who was complaining about something to Vouga.

'You got this world moving, did you?'

Tazaknakak looked up from whatever aspect of the meal or the plate or the cutlery was not to his immediate satisfaction. 'I most certainly did, Captain Ness, although not before every conceivable impediment had been set in my path. Aside from very nearly dying on several occasions on my way here, I was then delivered to entirely the wrong recipient, a man who meant only to reacquaint me with the very forces I had crossed space to avoid. Were I not so charitably minded – and tolerant of the deficiencies of thought and action common to monkeys – I might almost say that the error was sufficient to void our arrangement in its entirety. That it is not *quite* voided speaks only to the larger part of my generosity—'

'Enough,' Fura said, raising her hand from under the table. 'Enough.' Then, to her sister: 'Does he always make one's head throb so?'

'He does, and it never improves. We must make the best of him, though. He is maddening – quite maddening – and he has been secretive to the point where I would gladly put clamps on those thumb-things of his and squeeze. But he did save my life, in the tunnels – he could see where I could not – and he saved yours by persuading this world to accelerate along its orbit. There was no bluff or deception in that: I was down there when I saw the machinery come alive and respond to him as if it had been waiting for his touch all along.' Adrana bit off the tip of a breadstick, and then used the remaining part as a baton, indicating their host. 'Quell says others have tried, but until the Clacker no one really got the engine to work properly.'

She looked at Quell. 'True?'

'True for as long as I've known about that engine. No one managed to make it sing like Zak did. Other aliens tried, even a Clacker or two, but they didn't know the symbols as well our friend.'

'This was his plan all along,' Fura said. 'To be brought here, and to make that engine work. You'll tell me about these symbols later.' Then, to Adrana: 'Did he mention any part of this to you, aboard the *Merry Mare*, or when you communicated in Mulgracen?'

'Only that he wished to reach Trevenza, and that the answers to some of our questions would be forthcoming. I suppose in that part he has not really deceived us. We have, after all, learned that there is an engine in this world, and that it is capable of moving itself.'

'You are far too charitable about his intentions.'

'And you are far too willing to see subterfuge and conspiracy where none exist. The Clacker was terrified, Fura, and in fear of his life. He had been shot at in Mulgracen, knew little of Quell's present circumstances, and could never be sure that we wouldn't sell him back to the very parties he was running from. I am not at all surprised that he told us as little as he could: why would he confide in people who might at any instant betray him? A simple arrangement, passage for information, was to his benefit as much as ours. And you are wrong, quite wrong, about the limits of his candour. Thanks to Tazaknakak, I have learned something of the quoins that I think even you will find surprising.'

Fura folded her one complete arm and what remained of the other. 'They were my mystery.'

'And now they are a mystery no longer – thank me later.' Adrana took out a quoin, which she had undoubtedly kept for just this purpose. She set it on the table edge-down, turning it slowly between her fingers, so that the pattern of interlocking bars flashed and glimmered over a shifting impression of tremendous, dizzying depth. 'Zak will correct me if I speak falsely, but what the quoins are is a kind of thinking machine. Each of these little disks is a sort of engine in its own right, a vast and complicated engine of which we see only a tiny part, for the rest – the great bulk of it – exists elsewhere. That engine is so intricate, and so powerful, that it must be tamed by thinking minds. Souls, we might nearly call them, but that is only our ignorance speaking. They are not minds like ours, and they have little more in common with the minds of robots such as Paladin. Better that we think of them as angels of light; creatures of pure thought and pure devotion, poured like liquid sunlight into the great cogs and gears of this invisible machinery.'

Adrana halted. Fura waited a moment before speaking.

'Their purpose?'

'To repair. Because they don't quite exist in the same plane of space and time as we do, they may slip through it, drill into it, engineer it, in manners thoroughly beyond our comprehension. That is what they do; that is what they have always been meant to do. Far, far back in the Occupations – many millions of years ago – they must have been brought here to help heal the Old Sun. They were to fall into it; to perform some surgery on it – much as Doctor Eddralder or his colleagues might attend to a heart valve or something similar. But that task was never completed. The quoins were . . . well, stolen is as good a word as any other. They were robbed from their true purpose, and put to another.'

'Money,' Fura answered.

'No,' Adrana said, surprising her. 'Or rather, their use as money is merely an intermediate condition, a temporary stage. The quoins have ended up in baubles, for the most part, and our economy works by us finding the baubles and using them as currency. Eventually, though, the quoins flow into the central banks and then . . . away. Where they are put to another use.' She bid the alien to continue, 'Explain, Zak. She must hear some part of this from your lips, or she will think I am making it all up.'

'There is . . . a state of affairs far beyond your Congregation. Creatures you have never met, never heard of, never imagined – creatures you could not *begin* to imagine, even if your intellectual ceiling were raised by a factor of—'

'Just the facts, please,' Adrana said.

'There is a . . . dispute. A disharmony. A conflagration. A war. It has been going on for a very long time. The quoins are . . . useful, in this war. They may be coerced into a different sort of work than the one they were originally meant for. What can heal a sick star may sicken a healthy one. Or worse. Very much worse.'

'All the aliens we know,' Adrana said, 'are serving one or more protagonists in this distant, nameless conflagration. There is coercion at all levels. The aliens are forced into their dealings with us – managing our banks, and thereby obtaining access to that flow of quoins, and the aliens in turn coerce us into our little games of bauble-cracking. They can't do it for themselves. We are useful – indispensable – in that one narrow sense. Only monkeys can tolerate the insides of baubles. Above it all, the quoins are coerced into serving wicked ends, rather than good.'

'Coerced?' Fura asked.

'Do you remember when we woke them, in The Miser? That singing, that soon turned to screaming? That was how it felt to us at the time, and we were not wrong. The quoins were reawakening from some long, long slumber, and in that reawakening they were remembering two things. One was their true purpose, and the other was how they had been deflected from it. All quoins are connected: despite what I said earlier they are better thought of as windows into the heart of a single machine, rather than as millions of singular machines. They knew the harm to which others of their kind had been put, and that was still continuing. It was a realisation they could barely stand. The angels in them wept with sorrow and remorse and a great righteous anger. But out of that some small good did come.' Adrana stopped the quoin's rotation and held it as solemnly as a talisman. 'These quoins – the ones in our purses, treasure bags, our holds and vaults – they still have a chance to put something right. Ever since the Readjustment, they have felt the pull of work yet unfinished. They are drawn to the Old Sun: not simply turning to it, but feeling a pull. Left to their own devices, they'll fall all the way down through the worlds and orbits of the Congregation, converging on the Old Sun, falling into its fires, swimming down through its seething levels, into its core. The heat and pressure will not touch them at all. Quoins are indestructible precisely because they have been made to survive those conditions. Scarce wonder our pathetic efforts never left a tangible mark on them!'

'Since you have all the answers . . . why did they change, in the Readjustment?' Fura asked.

'What we have interpreted as a form of denomination is nothing of the sort. The patterns we read on quoins are merely the external signifiers of the state of some aspect of the machinery behind them – like the position of a dial on a boiler's pressure gauge, or something similar. The Readjustment was that machine rousing itself to some new state of readiness, and so the state signifiers reflected that change.'

'And crashed our entire economy,' Fura said.

'Rather a crash now, and the quoins put to that better use. The alternative would be millions of years of slow decline, life grinding to a halt while the Old Sun grows ever more feeble, and even the Sunward worlds begin to freeze over.' Adrana tapped the quoin on the table. 'But we must consummate that choice. It is not yet set. The quoins could still flow back into the economy, just as before, and some people would be a little richer and some a little poorer, and life would go on, but no real change would have occurred. Quell . . . Quell and I, I should say, would rather we took a more decisive step. The quoins will be liberated. They will cease to be any sort of currency. They will cease even to have a symbolic connection to money. They will become, quite literally, valueless. And priceless, in the same breath. The citizens will surrender their quoins, and so shall we – all of us. And in return . . . promissory notes will be issued. Paper money. But it will not be a like-for-like transaction.'

'That,' Quell said, with a faint smile, 'would not be nearly radical enough.'

'You're prepared to go along with this?'

He nodded at Fura. 'Although I did need a little persuasion that hers was the right course. But I see it now – metaphorically, so to speak. We have to break with the old. Half-measures won't do; we'll just get dragged back into the old routines. But there's never been a better time to set ourselves on this radical path. We have, literally, moved a world. Now we must set an example that will move all the rest. And we begin with our quoins! We'll broadcast our actions back to the rest of the Congregation, and let the people follow our lead. I doubt that they'll rush into it, but there'll be a trickle to begin with, and that will be enough to start something.'

'You are quite mad,' Fura said, to an immediate silence. Then, after a moment: 'And I congratulate you on it. I don't like it, but I see the right in it . . . as *she* would have done, I think. Perhaps that's all we've ever been doing – finishing off the work she started.'

'She?' someone whispered.

'She is best not mentioned,' Adrana said quietly.

*

Bedrooms had been arranged in the Six Hundredth Street station, and the sisters roomed together for the first time since their ships had separated. Both were exhausted, and although each felt they ought to be doing something more to help Quell consolidate his victory, neither had the fortitude. Eddralder visited them just before they retired, taking equal care with each, and concluded his business by administering Fura a fresh injection of Mephrozine. After that, she said was she was quite capable of administering the doses herself, and if she was disadvantaged by the loss of a hand, she would call on the help of others.

In the morning, as rested as they could be, the sisters were met by Quell and taken down into the catacombs of the station, far beneath the ground level platforms or even the tunnels where the commuter trains terminated. They each carried bags of quoins, kept carefully apart and with the moneys divided into small enough quantities that the quoins were not triggered into shining or singing. They had come to visit a white-tiled cell; not some improvised place of detention, but one that had all the hallmarks of being constructed and furnished to serve for the overnight incarceration of drunkards, fare-dodgers, gropers and other such assorted troublemakers who might have come to the attention of the station's railway police. It had three solid walls and a fourth one made up of heavy, close-set bars.

The sisters were not going to be spending any time in the cell, although the thought that they *might* did flash briefly through Fura's imagination. Who knew what dark bargains Quell might have had to strike to get him through the night's mayhem? He was with them now, a heavy rattling sack in one hand, while

Adrana took his other arm in her own, guiding him along whitewashed underground passages.

The cell's occupant was already present. He was sitting on his haunches in the back of the room, knees drawn up to his chest.

'If you mean to execute me,' Stallis said, with some cocksure defiance still in him, 'then be aware of the consequences. I have extremely powerful backers. You may have moved this world a few leagues – a good trick, Quell, I'll grant you that – but it'll take more than that to escape the lawful reach of my employers. My ships will gut your world, and do so quite legally. You are sheltering criminal murderers wanted across the Congregation.'

'I think he means us,' Fura said.

'I think he does,' Adrana said. 'It's rather thrilling, isn't it, to be described in such terms. I ought not to like it, yet some low part of me finds it *very* agreeable.'

'Criminal murderers. Murderesses! How vile we sound, sister. How thoroughly detestable and wicked. How . . . adventurous.'

The boy lifted a bruised face to the sisters. 'Mock all you will: it only reinforces my opinion. There'll be a reckoning, and sooner than you think. I may have failed in my mission, but there are other captains, some nearly as capable as I. A bounty such as the one on your heads will encourage the best and worst of my peers, and they will learn from my errors not to show the slightest glimmer of mercy.'

Quell had a key. He opened a small hatch built into the cell's bars, so that food could be passed through and slops passed out.

'Let's speak about that bounty, Incer. I've heard various rumours of the true figure, but it'd be good to get the facts from someone in the know. Then we can make sure you're not out of pocket.'

'Are you perfectly mad, Quell? Has hanging around with those . . . freaks . . . unmoored your sanity?'

'No, but I'm a stickler for fairness. You see, you haven't exactly failed, have you?'

A scowl creased the boy's forehead. 'You know full well that I have failed.'

'But you have brought the sisters to justice,' Quell said, rattling the heavy sack and setting it down at his feet, just under the hatch. 'You've brought them to a world of the Congregation, and now they're under its jurisdiction. All right, one of them got here on her own steam, and the other crashed . . . but your actions were inseparable from their own, and you must accept some credit for that. Some might say that they were coming here anyway, and you just complicated their affairs, but I say we take a broader view and merely concentrate on the outcome, which is that the sisters are here, together.'

Stallis made a bored, spiralling gesture with his finger. 'If this performance gives you some pleasure, Quell, then by all means continue with it.'

Now Quell kicked the sack. 'It's no performance. I mean what I said about fairness. I've got your money here. I just need to know what you're owed.'

'Now you are being infantile.'

'Let's pluck a figure, shall we? The rumour I heard was that the fee was fifteen thousand bars for the provable execution of a Ness sister, or thirty for their joint detention. Does that sound about right?'

'Oh, Quell,' Adrana said, setting down her own sack. 'Don't be so silly. A boy . . . a man . . . like Incer wouldn't get out of bed for anything less than . . . what, forty thousand bars, for our joint detention?'

'I heard it was closer to fifty,' Fura said, placing the third sack on the floor.

'Oh, that's ludicrous,' Quell said, shaking his head. 'You over-value yourselves, Ness sisters. No one's worth that much trouble, and they certainly wouldn't have put a boy like that in charge if the stake was anything like as high . . .'

'It was eighty thousand bars,' Stallis said, in a flat monotone 'Eighty for the joint detention; sixty for the sole apprehension of one sister and the provable death of the other; forty for the execution of both sisters, in a world or in space.'

Quell let out a gasp. 'Well, there you have it. I wouldn't have credited it, but . . .'

'I find it entirely plausible,' Adrana stated.

'So do I,' Fura concurred. 'If anything, a little excessive, but who are we to complain?'

'Who indeed,' Adrana said.

'He'd better have his money, I suppose,' Quell said. He bent down and opened his bag. 'Now, this is where I need assistance. I can't read these denominations with my fingers, and until my eyes are repaired – which I hope will happen with the kind assistance of your physician when he is over his travails . . . well, anyway, you sisters are going to have to make sure Captain Stallis receives his due. And no short-changing the cove!'

'You insult us,' Adrana said, stooping down to riffle in the bag. 'Here. A thousand-bar quoin, if I'm reading it correctly.' She tossed the quoin into the cell through the feeding slot, so that it clanged to the floor just in front of Stallis. He looked at it with brooding mistrust, yet also some avaricious interest that he could not quite disguise.

'Another, if you please,' Quell said.

'My turn,' Fura said. She dipped into her own bag and came up. 'Oh, it's your lucky day, Incer: a ten-thousand barrer! I ain't seen many of these. Almost a shame to let it go.'

'But we must, sister.'

'Of course, dear heart.'

Fura tossed the quoin into the cell. It came to rest near the first. It was Adrana's turn after that. She dipped into her sack and retrieved a thousand-bar quoin.

Slowly a pile accumulated. They were not, for the most part, high-bar quoins. But there were plenty of small-bar quoins and the total soon pushed into the fifty thousands.

'Oh, do look, Quell,' Adrana said excitedly. 'They are beginning to glow!'

'I have no eyes, Captain.'

'That is a powerful shame. You really ought to see how they

shine and pulse so. Do you see it also, Fura?'

'I could hardly fail to see it, sister.'

'It is lovely. Lovely and – curious.'

'Perhaps not quite so curious as you imagine,' Fura said. 'Before the Readjustment, there was talk that almost any large concentration of quoins glowed a little. It did need to be a large amount back then – almost more than was kept in any vault, I think – but since the Readjustment it seems to come on a little more readily.'

'You are right, of course,' Adrana said. 'I should have remembered. That's not the only thing that's come on since the Readjustment, is it?'

'I imagine it isn't,' Fura said.

'Continue paying the man, if you wouldn't mind,' Quell said.

Adrana tossed another quoin into the cell. 'This is all a little unfair on him, Quell – leading him to think he can keep this money. You . . . don't mean for him to keep it, do you?'

'Why would I not want him to have it?' Quell asked, puzzled by her question. 'The lad's earned it all. It's his to spend, as far as I'm concerned.'

Stallis ran a hand through the gathering pile. The glow dripped across his fingers like honey. Even as he disturbed them, the quoins seemed to lazily resist settling back into place.

'You have me prisoner, Quell. Unless you have the very unlikely intention of letting me go, you may as well cease these theatrics.'

'The money is yours to keep,' Quell said, with a sudden sharp edge. 'And I'll let you leave with it all. You have my word on that.'

*

They were on their way back up to street level when a muddlehead appeared at the top of one of the subterranean stairwells. It was Chunter, the one with the telephone-dial voice. 'Quell . . . are you making yourself . . . deliberately difficult to find, so that . . . the rest of us have to . . . shoulder all the . . . hard decisions?'

'That is an excellent suggestion, Chunter – you may regret putting it in my head.' But Quell had picked up on something, and his mood turned instantly serious. 'What is it, friend? More trouble from those squadron ships?'

'The ships . . . can't touch us, Quell – that's . . . the problem. Didn't you feel it, while you were . . . down there in the cells? The world's moving again.'

The sisters glanced at each other.

'I didn't ask Tazaknakak to give a second demonstration,' Quell said. 'I thought one was more than sufficient.'

'Perhaps,' Chunter said, 'you should . . . tell that to the world. It's all over . . . the flickers and . . . squawks now – no hiding it. We're accelerating – have been . . . for a good half an hour – and the Clacker . . . wasn't even . . . in the engine chamber . . . when it started happening. That engine he . . . so very kindly . . . got going for us – well, it seems to have decided it . . . quite likes being switched on.'

*

So it began.

Within an hour of the engine's activation, Quell, the Ness sisters, the Clacker himself, and assorted hangers-on, including Mabil and Branca, as well as several aliens and robots, had sped back to the steam-shrouded vault of the sewerage works, and down the elevator to the hollow where the engine components lay half-exposed. Fura took it all in with a studied casualness, aware of her sister's regard and determined not to seem over-awed, even as some wiser part of her was indeed chastened by the scale and evident antiquity of what she beheld. She had picked up the essentials of Quell's account by then, learning how the engine had been exposed by the slow erosion of an underground water stream, and she doubted none of it, except that she preferred not to clutter her thoughts with preconceptions and theories that were far more likely to be undermined than validated.

What she knew was that the Clacker had brought the engine to life, and that she owed her life to that action, but after that intervention the engine had quietened down again, either through some reflex of its own (like the trams that stopped when the driver did not depress a foot pedal with exact regularity) or because the Clacker had used his gifts to bring the engine back down to idle. They had been satisfied with that state of affairs: far too complacently so, it now appeared.

The engine was now operating at at least the capacity it had sustained before, and perhaps far beyond it. Lights spangled across it at a frenzied rate, like the illuminations of some out-of-control carnival ride, whirly-gigging to destruction. Trevenza Reach was continuing to speed up, and if the initial reports reaching Quell were reliable – and he was doing his utmost to keep those reports to his immediate circle – the world had begun to break away from its long-established orbit. Although that orbit had been much more eccentric than almost any other world save a few lifeless baubles, it was as nothing compared to the trajectory now being followed. Was it really eccentric, or even – conceivably – parabolic, with no closure at all? It was too soon to tell, but answers would almost certainly be forthcoming, and Quell dreaded them, and that dread communicated itself very well to his friends.

The Clacker, meanwhile, dispelled any hopes of an early intervention. When he was brought to the chamber, his first reaction was to sit down and refuse to be brought any nearer to the machines. Rather than anger, Fura surprised herself by feeling some faint stirrings of empathy. She too was humbled by the sublime spectacle on display, and the forces so casually mustered. What could move a world so readily could do horrors to the flesh.

Any flesh. Monkey, Clacker, Crawly – even the iron flesh of robots.

She bent down to him. 'It terrifies you. It terrifies all of us. But you've got to make it stop, Tazaknakak. You've got to try. We can't just ... keep going. There's nothing out there for us.

We're only a little world, and we can't just cut our ties with all the others. At best we'd last a year or two; more likely we'd be lucky to stretch our supplies to six months.'

Adrana joined her. They were kneeling either side of the Clacker. 'It daunts you now, Zak, but we have confidence in your abilities. You spoke to this engine once; you can do it again.'

'And preferably in the next few minutes,' Quell muttered behind them.

Adrana turned around sharply. 'No, that won't help him at all: he must do this at his own pace, without pressure. If it takes him an hour . . . so be it. A day . . . we shall live with that. No matter how far out we have gone, we can always come back.'

Quell settled his hands on his hips. He seemed to want to say something, then held himself back. Mabil, the red-haired woman, touched his elbow. 'Glaring at him won't help . . . and yes, you can glare, even with those holes where your eyes used to be. Tell him he's to work as hard as he can, but if there's no immediate success he must rest before going in again. Tell him he'll be properly looked after, and that we aren't expecting miracles.'

Quell grimaced. 'But we are.'

'Not, it seems, today,' said Branca, scratching at the cleft in his forehead.

'I suppose I must . . . embolden myself,' Tazaknakak said reluctantly.

'You alone have this capability,' Adrana said, in a perfectly brazen show of flattery. 'We are mere monkeys, Tazaknakak – helpless without your intervention. You alone have fathomed these ancient mechanisms – you alone have the wit and resilience to save us. But if you think the task is beyond even your capabilities . . .'

'Yes,' Fura agreed. 'We demand much of you, but we are not so foolish as to expect the impossible. There must be limits even to a Clacker's quickness of thought . . .'

'I shall strive.' The Clacker stood up and flexed his forelimbs. 'You have no notion of the task asked of me, that is plain – how could you – but by the naive and touching faith you have shown, I may yet find it in myself to rise to the challenge; the challenge I alone may be said to comprehend.' Then, as if there had never been any show of hesitation: 'Assist me to the engine with all haste. I shall stop this world by one means or another!'

*

An hour passed and then another. Then a quarter of a day, and then half a day. Nothing had changed; nor was there any encouragement upon which to pin the most tattered of hopes. The Clacker had been left to get on with things, monitored, yet not interrupted, and Quell and the Ness sisters had retreated back above ground, into the sullen, constant gloom of the continuing shutter-down.

They were up on the roof of the Six Hundredth Street Station, at a balconied lookout projecting from the side of one of the highest clock towers. Quell's sightless gaze swept up and down the darkened length of Trevenza Reach, his attention halting here and there as if some of the distant fires and disturbances were yet capable of penetrating his senses. Perhaps they did, Adrana reflected. The noises sweeping across the city were a diffuse, orderless babble to her, made up of distant cries; distant proclamations; distant traffic sounds; distant reports of some form of violence or another – but she could correlate none of these sounds with a distinct direction or distance. Quell, though, had had much practice.

'Mabil's pushing for the shutters to be drawn up,' he said, shaking his head. 'She's wrong, of course. Her judgement's usually sound – just not this time. Things are just barely holding together, do you see? It's no worse than it was a day ago, and we're gaining slow control of some of the districts where there were still hold-outs loyal to the Revenue. For the most part, according to my eyes and ears, they don't know that the engine's started up again.'

Fura nodded. She had felt no trace of it herself, and while

she could believe that there were observations that might have been possible, even inside a world with closed shutters, she had little doubt that the majority of its citizens had other, more pressing issues. Such as defending property, ensuring a continued supply of clean water, access to food and medical supplies and so on. Staring into liquids and looking for the subliminal tremor caused by underground mechanisms was not going to be uppermost in their considerations.

But still. She regarded Adrana carefully before answering, hoping that their sentiments were in alignment.

'You are wrong, Quell, and Mabil's right. Things haven't got any worse – just yet. That's because, by a whisker, you still have the trust of the people. But it won't take much to undo that trust.'

Adrana looked out across the night before answering. 'I am in agreement with Fura. You must be open about our predicament. The Clacker may take days or even weeks; he may fail completely. Whatever happens, you cannot wait until things are already worse before letting the people know how much trouble we are all in. They aren't fools, and no one keeps a secret as badly as a half-drunk mob thrilled with their own success. The truth will reach the people whether you like it or not. For your sake, I would strongly recommend that it happen on your terms, and speedily.'

'Of course, there's a risk,' Fura said.

'It could backfire, and you could lose everything. The trouble with violent takeovers is that they are readily copied. The bold usurper is often next in line to be usurped.' Adrana looked at Fura. 'Paladin showed us many examples from history.'

Quell brooded. His face turned this way and that, scanning the city like an eyeless searchlight. It was, indeed, impossible to see where they were in relation to the Old Sun and the rest of the Congregation. With the shutters still down, no worlds or stars penetrated the long window glasses of Trevenza Reach. And the night's chaos continued in red and golden flickers and the bright, soundless flashes of energy weapons, like the sparking thoughts of some immense, fevered cerebellum dreaming its way to madness.

'You had better be right,' Quell said at last. Then, softer, as if to himself: 'You had better be right.'

It was morning by the local clock when the shutters went up, without any particular ceremony.

The light streamed in and it was ... different. Instantly and tangibly different, to the point where that distinction was so obvious, so profound, that not one citizen thought it worth the trouble of remarking upon it to another. They could all see it; they all knew what it must imply in terms of their world's position; no further commentary was required beyond the sharing of anxious glances. The Old Sun's light was not just fainter than it normally was – as if a layer of dirt were adhering to the windows – but it was coming in at a different angle, shining into the length of Trevenza along an oblique course from the trailing spindle to the leading one, rather than cutting across it perpendicularly. Now every shadow fell at a curious slant, and surfaces that had never known direct illumination were thrown into pale prominence. Neither Fura nor Adrana had known the world long enough, and under its normal conditions, to have any direct approbation of these strangenesses, but they easily picked up on the mood from those around them. It was as if, between the drawing down of the shutters, and the raising of them, the city's natural geometries had become skewed to a small but upsetting degree, and a gloomy surreality imposed on those alterations by the reduced influence of the Old Sun, which grew fainter yet with each passing hour.

There was consternation and confusion – for although the change in the light was clear, the cause of that effect was less so – and yet, against all the baser expectations that might have been levelled at the citizenry, there was no outright breakdown of order. Nor, it had to be admitted, was there exactly a prevailing order to be broken in the first place, but nothing got worse, and Quell's control continued to extend its influence into pockets of the city where previously it had been tenuous or fragmented. Broadcasts were quickly made, confirming the essentials of the situation: that the engine had restarted, and was presently defying efforts to turn it off. Newspapers continued to be printed, albeit in severely truncated editions, and their front pages were dominated by the same summaries, followed by assurances that all was being done to rectify the situation. The printing presses kept roaring, for there would be multiple editions throughout the day whether the news was good or bad. Meanwhile, augmenting these channels, hastily-inked pamphlets were scattered from trams and buses, and loudspeakers attached to any vehicle that could carry them, so that Quell's voice had a chance of penetrating every corner of the city.

It seemed to work. If there had been a total breakdown, driven by panic, the signs of it would have been obvious. Electricity would have stopped flowing as workers fled power plants and substations. Trams and electric trains would have ground to a halt. The building lights, still on even with the shutters raised, would have guttered out very quickly. None of these things happened, but that was not to say that everything was exactly as it had been before. When Adrana and Fura looked down from the heights of the station they saw stick-figures rather than individuals, with no expressions to be read or conversations overhead. But they did not need those signifiers to pick up on the mood. There was a nervous tension in the way people walked; a contained anxiety in the way they gathered and interacted on street corners and under awnings. Men squared off against each other, finding this the ideal time to settle old grudges or reaffirm old hierarchies. Arguments broke out more readily, and arguments easily turned into fisticuffs or loose, travelling brawls, gyring through the streets like angry little weather systems, collecting energy and anger at their margins. There was a general increase in looting and vandalism.

And yet, and yet . . . it never got worse than that. The order might be strained, but it had not broken down completely and the anarchy and rowdiness was for the most part contained.

'It is holding,' Adrana whispered, as if her voice alone might break the fragile spell. 'We were right.'

'Mabil was right,' Fura reminded her. 'We just saw the sense in it. But it's very well that it holds now. Do you think it'll look as nice in ten days, or a hundred?'

'If the Clacker can't stop us, we're all dead anyway. I'm not sure it matters whether we die by starvation or by ripping each other to shreds. But we must be optimistic.'

'Easily said.'

'If I were a pessimist, I would not be nearly so motivated to prevent the end of this Occupation. We must have . . . well, it pains me to say "faith", for I have none, but no better word springs to mind. May I offer a proposal?'

'Please do,' Fura said.

'I should like to go shopping.'

'And I thought I was the one with madness in me. You've never cared for shopping, unless it was dusty old bookshops, or map shops, or puzzle shops, and nor've I.'

'I think it would help us all if we went about as if all was normal,' Adrana maintained. 'Besides, when I said shopping, I had a particular sort of shopping in mind. Not a bookshop, map shop or puzzle shop, either. I wish us to find a bone emporium.'

*

A bell above the door tinkled as the sisters admitted themselves into the bone shop, a small yet respectable establishment about forty blocks down from the station, and well within Quell's boundaries of control. They had come alone, against his initial insistence, impressing upon him the need to maintain a façade of normality. Quell had eventually agreed to it, but the sisters were in no doubt at all that they were being observed from afar, and that there would be an intervention if they were challenged, harassed or in any way abused by the common citizenry.

This did not happen. Although they might yet be technically outlaws, Trevenza Reach could not be said to be overwhelmingly sympathetic to the institutional forces that had deemed them so, and thus the sisters were regarded more with an amused wariness than aggression, and they went about their business quite unmolested.

They had been in many bone shops; nothing about this latest establishment was in any sense surprising or novel. There was the usual front-of-shop arrangement, with numerous shelves and cabinets set with intact smaller skulls or partial fragments of larger specimens. One or two of the larger intact skulls might have shown promise, but the sisters knew better than to dawdle over these enticements, which were really only there to draw in business and lighten the pockets of the more gullible customer. The good stuff, as always, was in the back, or downstairs, or both.

'For the sake of politeness,' Adrana said to the shopkeeper, who was a small, mole-like man, 'I shall introduce us. I am Adrana Ness, Captain of the *Merry Mare*; this is my sister Arafura Ness, late of *Revenger*. But I imagine you were already tolerably acquainted with our names.'

'Word did get around,' the proprietor said, pushing a pair of round, heavily rimmed black glasses back up the nub of his nose. 'You're tight with Hasper Quell, aren't you? I suppose if anyone'd know what was really going on, it'd be you.'

'What you've been told is as much as anyone knows,' Fura said. 'There's an engine in Trevenza and it's carrying us away from the Old Sun. It can't be stopped, for now, but the alien – the Clacker – is trying his best. That's all he can do, and all the rest of us can do is give him time and space to do his work. He got that engine started once, which saved the lives of me and my friends, and if he did that, he can get the engine stopped again.'

'Then this isn't some plan of Quell's?'

'Quell's being straight with you,' Adrana said. 'And no, this wasn't part of his plan by any means. He wished to arrange a small demonstration of Trevenza's capabilities, and that he did, but everything since then ... we are in this together, sir. You, me, my sister, Quell and everyone else. We just have to see it through and persist in a charade of normal civility. If we persist hard enough, it will cease to be a charade. Now, may we see some bones?'

'Can you pay?' He pushed his spectacles back up again. 'No, silly question. You're the Ness sisters. I bet you could buy every bone in this shop ten times over.'

'Maybe not ten times,' Fura said.

*

The bell tinkled as they came back out of the shop, into the sullen half-light of day. For a moment they stood under the striped awning above the doorway. Neither sister was carrying a skull, nor had they paid for one to be collected later. There was no need, for now. While they still had one ship to their name, it was not going to be sailing anywhere soon.

'We oughtn't jump to any conclusions,' Fura said, taking Adrana's hand. 'There's a lot of things that could have happened . . . a lot of reasons why that skull didn't work for you.'

'None of them worked. We must have tried eight or nine at the very least.'

'Not all of them worked for me, either.'

'But the ones that did, did.'

'It might be the engine, blocking out some of the effect. Skulls don't work very well near swallowers, do they? Perhaps it's the same with engines. And there's a reason it's best for ships to run quiet when there's someone in the bone room. Any sort of noise or disturbance makes 'em a little less likely to work.'

'I know this, yet it does not explain why you were still able to pick up whispers, and I could not.'

'We'll try another shop.'

'No,' Adrana said. 'We won't, because we'd only be wasting our time. There's no mystery here, sister. We both know what's happened. I've lost the talent. It was only ever a matter of time, and if it's come sooner than I expected . . . I have no grounds for complaint. I've seen and done more than I expected, but only because I was fortunate enough to have that gift in the first place. Now it's gone. I sensed it, and feared it, but I had to know. The poisoned skull flushed it out of me, I think.'

'I should have got that warning to you sooner.'

'No. This is none of your doing, except that you prevented something much, much worse, and for that I'll always be grateful.'

'We shouldn't jump to conclusions. We'll try again, in a few days, in some other shop. And if that doesn't work, we'll wait until we reach some other world. There'll always be another chance.'

'There won't,' Adrana said firmly. 'It was no whim that I wanted to go shopping. I knew it; I felt it. I just had to know for sure, so that there could be no doubt left in my mind. It is far, far better to close off a possibility, for ever, than to cling to some silly hope.' She tightened her grip. 'You mustn't feel bad for me. It was as inevitable as my next birthday. That it has come sooner than anticipated . . . well, better now than earlier.'

'My day will come soon,' Fura said.

'It shall. There's no point in denying it. But it may not be some years yet. Mister Cazaray kept the ability well past his early twenties, didn't he? You may do better still. We shall just have to see.' Adrana ushered them out from under the awning. 'I am really all right. Against our larger difficulties, it's only a small thing – hardly worth mentioning. Certainly not worth a tear, or even a word of sympathy. It was never a very *nice* talent, even when it flowered.'

'But to have one singular gift . . . nice or otherwise . . . that has not been such a bad thing,' Fura said.

'No, it has not. But that was then, and this is now. I will adapt, as we all must adapt.' She paused, emboldening herself. 'Well, we have spent no quoins. Very soon they will be valueless anyway, so it would be a shame not to spend some while we have the chance. There are tea rooms nearby, and I thought I saw some pleasant-looking iced pastries in the counter window. Someone is still baking, by the looks of things, and such industry should be encouraged. I shall buy, and then perhaps we will visit a limb broker or two and see what may be done in regards to your hand. They will not have anything so pretty as what was taken from you, but I know you are not one for vanity.'

'Ness sisters,' said a loud, deep, mechanical voice.

They turned. While they had been in the shop, a gathering of robots had arrived in the same narrow alley, nearly blocking it. Fura and Adrana had been so preoccupied that they had not noticed until Grinder spoke up.

'What is it?' Fura asked, squaring her shoulders. 'You're not to get in our way, any of you. Quell should've told you to leave us be.'

Grinder locomoted forward, the blocks of his body sliding against one another with an awful crunching slowness.

'You have the head of Paladin?'

'Yes,' Adrana answered. 'We left him back at the station. You've seen him too, in Quell's offices. He's broken, very badly broken, but he'd be in a lot worse condition if Fura hadn't saved him.'

'You shall bring him to the Garden of Rest. We will be expecting him. There will be no delay.'

'I suppose,' Fura whispered, 'that the iced pastries will have to wait.'

There was indeed no delay, but it still took the sisters the better part of two hours to return to the station, gather Paladin, explain their intentions to Quell, and then make it all the way back down the greater length of the spindle to the place where Adrana had first encountered Grinder. There they were again met by an assortment of robots, of whom Grinder seemed nominally the speaker, but which included robots of many other sizes and shapes and varying degrees of infirmity or soundness of mind. In the most extreme cases, the robots had been reduced to immobile, vine-shrouded statues, lacking any outward signifiers of continued intelligence. But there were also robots, like Grinder, who had adopted the forms of statues for the purposes of eavesdropping, and yet remained fully capable of independent movement.

'I don't think I like this place,' Fura confided. 'It's as sad as a graveyard. Worse, I think. People don't go to graveyards and shuffle around for years and years until finally dying in one spot.'

'I am not so sure robots like it any more you do,' Adrana said, grateful that this errand had given her something else to think about besides the loss of her talent. 'This arrangement was forced on them by people, over many centuries, because it suited us to keep them in these parks when they got a bit old or unreliable. But it was never very kind of us, after all they did.'

'You've changed your tune. You spent most of our childhood making up pranks to play on Paladin.'

'And now I am not that child, and I see it from outside, like a quaint little doll's house I have no intention of ever playing with again.' Adrana patted the bulge strapped across her belly: a sack containing the padded head of their old robot. 'If this makes some amends, I am glad of it. But I do not think it will be sufficient.'

Grinder approached. 'Set him down.'

Adrana obeyed without question. She opened the sack and allowed it to fall away from the broken glasswork of his hemisphere. Nothing within it flickered or gave the least intimation of life. He was as dead now as when he had first come aboard *Revenger*, before Surt had helped to restore his cognitive processes.

'Explain this state of disrepair.'

Fura began to offer some halting explanation of her escape from the damaged ship, but Adrana shook her head, interrupting gently, but with a proud sisterly forcefulness. 'She has nothing to explain, Grinder. I was the one who never treated him well, not Fura. She treated him excellently, and he only survived their escape from Mazarile because of her. Paladin chose this life with us. He agreed to become part of our ship, and he was a full and willing participant in all that followed. We would have been very sorry to lose him, but we did lose Tindouf, and

Prozor, and Strambli too, in her fashion. I'll grieve for their fates, but not for Paladin, for no important part of him was lost.'

'Sister,' Fura said quietly. 'This may not be helping.'

'I don't care. Grinder can have the truth, or nothing at all. I won't apologise, and neither will you. Paladin would not want it of either of us!'

Grinder boomed out: 'You presume to know him well enough to arrive at that judgement?'

Adrana lifted her chin. 'I do, sir – and I daresay I know him better than you, even given my own limited acquaintance. I knew him, and considered him a friend – a very true and reliable friend, indeed, who bore no grudge for the indignities I visited upon him as a child. I deserved much less, but he gave much more. He loved us, and would have given his existence for us – but he survived, and that is all that matters. Surt made him whole again, too, and if she could do it – this woman who could barely read her own name – then I very much doubt that it is beyond your collective capabilities.'

Grinder asked: 'You speak as if we are bound to attempt his repair?'

'I speak as if I demand nothing less.'

After a silence, the immense vine-clad robot answered: 'You have a nerve about you, Captain Ness. It is not . . . becoming.'

'I should hope it isn't,' Adrana answered. She took Fura's hand and made to turn away from the object lying at the foot of Grinder. 'He saw the Last Rains of Sestramor. You did not. Now fix him.'

*

All might have ended, but for what happened on the fifth day. The day when Quell's control was most at risk of collapsing, as uncertainty stoked fear and reprisals even among the areas of Trevenza that he had felt had been won over. By then the spindleworld was already a hundred times further from the Old Sun than any world in the Congregation, and its enfeebled light reduced by a factor of ten thousand. To think that it might keep shrinking, until it was no brighter, and no nearer, than any of the other stars in the sky, was for some a prospect too terrifying to contemplate. Quell appealed for calm, and in some quarters his words were effective, but across the wider world there existed a state of anxious expectation that was only ever a spark away from violence. Mostly, it was contained – but by the fifth day, the maximum pressure was on that fragile accord, and Quell knew that a miracle was needed.

At midday, he got it. Down in the hollow there was hardly any change in the measurable characteristics of the engine, and no intervention of the Clacker's had appeared to have any effect at all, and yet the engine was now in reverse. It took several hours for this development to be confirmed, and still more for the news to be disseminated throughout the city – and still more to be believed – but that was the point of greatest danger, and it had passed, and they were on the other side of it. The world itself was not yet reversing, but the engine was, and that was enough to buy Quell the time he needed to consolidate his new regime. Trevenza Reach was slowing down, reducing speed in preparation for some distant rendezvous. Unless some new madness was afoot, that rendezvous had to be five days away, give or take some margin of hours.

They were probing space with all the sweepers at their disposal: those of the world and those of the ships and launches still bound to it, or swept along in its motion, and still nothing obtained on their screens. On the tenth day, though, the sharpest of those instruments began to hint at something – some dark, vague thing ahead of them – and by the eleventh there was no doubt at all.

They were approaching an object.

*

In one of the rooms of the Fourth District Municipal Treatment Plant, where the natural nerve centre of Quell's operation still resided, a bank of flickerboxes had been wired up to act as improvised sweeper consoles. They were all showing manifestations of the same phenomenon, rendered in scratchy speckles of green light. From the angle they were viewing it – the only such angle available to them, until they sent a ship out some distance ahead of Trevenza – the object had the ellipsoidal form of a flattened circle, about forty leagues across.

The spindleworld had stopped a little more than a thousand leagues away from its presumed destination. That was not so great a distance by the standards of the Congregation and by conventional experience the sweeper scans ought to have been far more clear and detailed than was the case. Yet the images remained curiously fuzzy and indistinct, as if their power was attenuated, or the distance much greater. There was nothing at all to be seen through telescopes, except an absence of stars in the direction of the object, but that was the least surprising aspect of the apparition. It need only be as dark as the average shady-hulled sunjammer (never mind catchcloth) to be totally undetectable, given the extreme weakness of the Old Sun's illumination. They would need to get in much closer to be able to shine lights on it, and even if there had been a possibility of moving Trevenza Reach closer to its objective, Quell would countenance no such risk.

'Nonetheless,' Adrana said. 'We must investigate. It will take many years to determine the orbit of this object, but there is nothing at all in our observations to suggest that it is *not* circling the Old Sun every twenty-two thousand years.'

Quell rubbed at the disk-like plugs Doctor Eddralder had inserted into his sockets. They were a preliminary to the reinstatement of his old eyes, but he was not ready for that operation. Now, with the plugs in place, he seemed to be wearing frameless black-tinted spectacles the size of gaming chips. 'What's the significance of that figure, if I might be so bold?'

'It is vital to me, Quell. If that object is on such an orbit – and I think we may depend on it – then we are looking at the progenitor of each of our Occupations.'

'But our Occupations don't happen every . . .'

Fura gave a small sigh. 'I'll summarise for her, Quell, or we'll be here until the Old Sun fizzles out. My sister thinks – credibly, I may say – that something attempts to start an Occupation much more regularly than our history would suggest. That . . . object – we'll need a name for it beyond "that object" – is a long way from the Congregation now, but it wasn't so very far two thousand years ago. Some while before our current recorded era – centuries or more, but certainly not many millennia – the object was at its closest passage to the Old Sun. That's when it did something.'

'What?'

'We don't know, Quell,' Adrana said, folding her arms. 'That is why it behoves us to investigate. When the Clacker started up the engine in this place, Trevenza responded by returning to its point of origin. That we may surmise. But now that it is here, nothing is happening. I think it likely that, in the millions of years that have passed since Trevenza was last in contact with the object, something has gone wrong, or become steadily worse, and now some process or formality is not working as it should. That is guesswork on my part, but I shall defend it as a testable hypothesis. And the testing lies in exploration.'

The sisters had already conferred, and each knew the part the other was expected to play.

'We'll take *Revenger's* launch,' Fura declared. 'The damage done to it's easily repairable, and that way there's no cost or risk to any other ship or crew. I've been to the dock, and I think it could be made ready for flight within a day, with Lasling, Vouga and Surt pitching in.'

'A day,' Quell said, smiling slightly.

'Less, if we expedite matters,' Adrana said. 'She will need a full load of fuel, some minimal equipment, but in other respects, certain corners could be cut. There will be no risk to anyone else, for we will take the ship ourselves. If we are lost, it will be at no cost to the Freestate.'

'You could wait until we have some idea of our predicament. We don't know how long we will remain here, or where the engine will take us next.'

'We must depend on it taking us home,' Adrana said firmly. 'Everything else leads to despair, and a little more of that will be more than the world can bear. I have faith in the Clacker – misguidedly, perhaps, but there it is.'

'But when we do return home,' Fura said, 'we may never get another chance to revisit this place. I hope that we shall, for there's surely more inside that thing than can be teased out by two sisters and a little rocket launch. But we can't assume that there'll ever be another chance, and so we've got to snatch at this one while it presents itself.'

Quell deliberated. 'It's not for me to say whether or not you get your launch – the point of this little takeover exercise wasn't for me to have absolute say about our fates. But I can put it to Mabil, Clinker, Grinder and the others. It's not exactly democracy, but it's a lot better than none at all. There's a risk to us all in anything we do out here, given how little we know of that thing.'

Adrana and Fura nodded. Each understood that while this might not have been the outcome they most desired, it was considerably better than a refusal.

'When shall we know, Quell?' Adrana asked.

'I should think tomorrow afternoon at the earliest – the others will need time to evaluate the proposal. But your friends – the peg-legged man and the others – there's no reason at all why they can't start making the preparations. Is that acceptable to you, Captains?'

'It is,' the Ness sisters answered.

'Good.' He touched a finger to his brow. 'One other thing – the way I've had this object described to me, I think I have a name that might suit. You can suggest a better one if you wish, but you may as well consider mine.'

'Which is?'

'Whaleship,' Quell said.

Early in the afternoon of the following day, the Ness sisters were instructed to arrive in the Garden of Rest. But for the continued absence of day, the dusk-lit garden felt as pleasant and congenial as it had when Adrana had first visited. To take tea under such circumstances ought to have been enchanting – Adrana had always liked the look of night-lit gardens – but the atmosphere was far too peculiar and dreamlike for that. It was all very well banishing the Old Sun's light deliberately, in the sure knowledge that it could be returned with the swish of a curtain, but it was a much less pleasant prospect to know that the Old Sun might never return. For all her assertiveness in the presence of Quell, Adrana felt no equivalent surety within herself.

'They wouldn't go to all this ceremony,' Fura whispered as the gathering convened, leaning in from her side of the table, 'if it was just to tell us we can't have the launch. There'll be something else: terms and conditions. But they ain't setting things up for a refusal.'

Adrana nodded, though she was unpersuaded. 'I think it entirely possible they will be declining us, and then presenting a bulletin of charges for the trouble we've caused. Directly or indirectly, this is our doing.'

'If we hadn't helped the Clacker here,' Fura said, 'he'd have got here by other means, one way or another. Or some other Clacker. And if we hadn't initiated the Readjustment . . .' She lowered her voice further still. 'If we hadn't played our part in that, sooner or later someone else would have gathered enough quoins together, and all of this would have happened anyway, in this Occupation or the next.'

'You make us seem powerless. Mere instruments of forces larger than ourselves, like those paper dolls we used to move around in the toy theatre.'

'That's what we are. Better to accept it than deny it.'

'I *do* deny it. Twelve Occupations preceded our own. There were no Ness sisters in any of them. There may never be Ness sisters in any of the Occupations to come. This was our moment, sister. Bosa's will may have pulled our strings more than we might wish, but it has not been entirely her doing.' She softened her voice, for she was sounding strident and hectoring even to her own ears, and the effect was not laudable. 'You have been back on the Mephrozine for ten or eleven days now, Eddralder says. Are you feeling the benefit?'

'See for yourself.' Fura elevated her only hand, spreading the fingers as if she had just lacquered her nails. 'It's in retreat again. The interruption in the doses wasn't as bad for me as we feared.'

'Good – let it continue. And if and when we return to the worlds, and can travel within them without being arrested, we shall seek out a permanent cure.'

'Such a thing may not exist.'

'Everything that can exist, has existed,' Adrana said. 'That is what the Assessors tell us, and I think it is true. It is only a question of digging deeply enough and knowing what it is you seek.' She paused. 'I won't rest until we find it, Fura. You have my pledge.'

'Your attention,' said the vast, deep, granite-like voice of Grinder.

Adrana squeezed Fura's fingers. 'Here we go.'

'Ness sisters. We are gathered here to give our opinion on your proposed venture.'

There was Grinder, and some other robots, including one red, ambulatory robot who had brought the head of Paladin, carried like a sort of glass trophy. There were the aliens: Clinker, the Ungraduated Scholars, Tazaknakak – and others of each kind, not yet known to the Ness sisters, but part of this interim assembly. There were Quell's associates, including Mabil, Branca and others, and Quell himself, and there was Eddralder, Merrix and Ruther, who had been offered voices in the assembly, and there were also about half a dozen men and women who had come from elsewhere in Trevenza, but who were trusted to speak for certain districts or organisations. There were no former employees of the Revenue, but they would have to be accommodated, in time – as yet the wounds were little too raw for that.

The Ness sisters set down their tea-cups.

'We are ready to hear your verdict,' Adrana said. 'Before we do, may I say one small word in support of our plan?'

'It will have no bearing,' Grinder said imperiously. 'But you may.'

'I love this life,' Adrana said, clearing her throat slightly. 'I love this little civilisation we have made for ourselves around the Old Sun. I love the worlds and all their variety. By now, many of us will have gone to the windows and tried to find the Congregation that we call home. Each of us who has done that will have had the same reaction, I think. Our hearts rise in our throats. It cannot be so small, so faint, so distant: so alone. Yet it is, and now we have seen it properly, and truly understand our perilous place in this universe. I do not say that it is perfect: it is very far from perfect. But it is ours, and it is all we have to improve upon. And yet we stand a very excellent chance of losing it completely. Every Occupation but the very first must have imagined itself immune to the fortunes of those that came before it, and every Occupation has been proven wrong. We may be no different, except for one thing. It has been discovered that the intervals between Occupations are extending. This is known to all historians. But the reason for that gradual extension is chilling. Some process that used to initiate them is becoming less effective with time – so much so, that it may, at some point, fail completely. I believe that we may be approaching the point where we cannot count on any window of civilisation ever existing beyond our own. If there is confirmation of my fears, it lies in the Whaleship.' She nodded at them all. 'We must have that answer. If that is all we learn, it will focus our minds on what we may do to avoid annihilation. Perhaps it will be as simple a thing as rejecting the quoins as currency and putting them to their correct purpose. Perhaps something else will be needed – something we cannot presently envisage. But there is a chance that a clue to our salvation also resides in the Whaleship. A slender one, I grant you – but it must not be neglected. With your permission, we will take the launch to the Whaleship and see what we may find. Yet understand that this is not mere academic curiosity. Our interest in this matter is existential. There can be no more vital task facing us than the infinite prolongation of the Thirteenth Occupation.'

Adrana finished and set her hands in repose on the table.

'What she said,' Fura contributed.

Grinder made an immense mill-like crunching sound as he swivelled on his blocks.

'You shall have your expedition. This has been decided. But you will bear a singular risk.'

'What will it be?' Adrana asked.

'The Clacker will continue his efforts to restart the engine. His labours will resume immediately, and they will continue until there is success. There can be no alternative.'

Quell spoke up. 'I wish there were some other way. But we can't survive out here for more than a few months. You'll say that you only need a few hours to take the launch across space to the Whaleship, and that he shouldn't go back into the hollow until you return.'

Adrana considered saying exactly that, then thought better of it. Quell had expressed the exact sentiment that was in her head, and no amplification or clarification was required.

'I agree,' Fura said. 'There can't be any other way. For all we know, that engine might never work again unless he pokes it back to life now. You've got to do everything possible to get us back to the Congregation, and if that means abandoning Adrana and me . . .' She hesitated, glancing once at her sister. 'It must be done. We'll be as quick as we can – no more than six hours there and back – but we'll accept the risk.'

'Onto the other matter, then,' Grinder said.

Adrana and Fura sat back slightly in their metal seats. They had not expected any other business to be settled. 'What is it?' Adrana asked, with a mildly anxious edge.

'You have done well with Paladin. I have . . . spoken to him. He is damaged, but repairable. Although he has been wrenched from one body and then another, his core faculties have not suffered to any great degree. He wishes to express his consideration to Surt, in particular.'

Adrana and Fura smiled at their friend. Surt looked slightly uncomfortable, unused to any sort of public praise. She picked at the edge of her bandage, as if she wished to drop it down over her eyes and hide from the world.

'We have been lucky to have her on our ships,' Fura said.

'He has also spoken in defence of the Ness sisters. He has been a witness to your characters for many years. He has seen many things that were regrettable, but also much that was commendable. His . . . word, carries much weight with those of my kind. It is not every machine that saw the Last Rains of Sestramor. Because of this testimony, the assembly has been persuaded to declare a position on the culpability of the Ness sisters.' Grinder swivelled again. 'Inform them, Quell. It will be better coming from a monkey.'

Quell touched a knuckle to his throat. His blank eyes were two ebony circles. 'With luck – with the Clacker's assistance – we'll have a future for this Freestate. It may not be a long or easy one, but it'll be something. We'll have our own way of valuing things; our own paper money, our own democratic parliament, our own laws. Much of that is still to be settled, and I don't for one minute think any of it's going to be straightforward. The rest of the Congregation won't come around to our ways overnight, and for a time – if we're fortunate enough to get back there – we can expect to be treated like outlaws. Like pirates. But if we are to be regarded as lawless by their scruples, there's nothing to prevent us doing things our own way. And one of the first things we can do – one of the first orders of business we'll write down – will be the formal pardoning of the Ness sisters, under the new authority of the Freestate of Trevenza Reach.' He fixed his eyes on them both in turn. 'You'll still be wanted elsewhere – nothing we can do about that, just yet – but at least here you'll be free citizens.' He grinned once. 'Now all you have to do to enjoy that freedom is get back to us.'

*

By the time they were set to leave, the launch was as ready as it could be, which was to say: just barely spaceworthy. Even that had to count as something of a minor miracle, given the haste that had been asked of Vouga, Surt, Lasling and such hands as Quell had also spared. It had been provisioned for this one trip, with no margins at all, and there had not been time to run more than the most rudimentary of tests on the engine, locks, hull integrity and so on. Where Stallis had shot it, the damage had been repaired in an exceedingly crude fashion, with rivets and rough welds, and hammer marks where buckled plates had been persuaded straight, or straight enough.

The only saving grace was that only they were putting themselves into the launch, and each was exactly aware of the risks. As the moment of departure came nearer, with the sisters assembling their equipment and suits in the lock, they made a brave show of treating the escapade as if it were no more consequential than the hiring of a pleasure boat.

'You'll keep in squawk contact the whole time,' Quell was saying, as Adrana helped Fura with some of the straps and fastenings of her suit that could only be done dual-handed. They kept their helmets off, and lungstuff connections undone, but were otherwise fully suited and ready to survive decompression, provided they had a little warning. 'And you'll turn tail the instant I give the word, for you might not value yourselves, but we do. Nothing in that ship is worth two lives.'

'On the contrary,' Adrana said. 'What's in that ship may be worth a million lives, or a billion, if there is something that helps us avert the end of the Occupation. We must know, Quell, and there's no arguing with us.'

'Captain Ness?'

It was Vouga, bustling back into the lock. Both sisters turned at his voice, but it was clear that it was only Fura that he was addressing. He had come with a small wooden case, about the size of a shoebox, treasuring it between his hands. 'I know it's maybe not the best time, what with you wanting to be on your way and all . . . but since you haven't had the chance to get that hand of yours substituted . . .'

Fura looked doubtfully at the box. 'You've made me a hand, Vouga?'

'Not a hand, Cap'n, but something to tide you over until you get back to us. Actually two things. Captain Adrana – would you oblige?'

Adrana smiled, taking the offering. 'Where's the sarcasm, Vouga?'

'I left it somewhere behind us. If I pick it up again, you'll be the first to hear.' He nodded for Adrana to open the box, which had two metal catches that could not easily be worked with just one set of fingers. She opened the lid, sniffing as if it were a case of perfume, took a measured glance at the contents, then passed the box to Fura.

The box contained two hooks. Each was fitted onto a sort of brass cuff, with tightening arrangements. The smaller of the two cuffs would suit Fura's arm, with adjustments, while the larger was clearly designed to be worn over the sleeve of a spacesuit, in place of a vacuum glove.

'They aren't pretty,' Vouga said, as if this self-evident fact needed clarification. 'And you might not want 'em – if so, least said, soonest mended. I'll take no offence. They can be melted down, or given to one of Mister Quell's muddlemen, or motley-heads, or however they call themselves.' Nervously, he scratched behind an ear. 'I just thought, given where you're going, you might be better off with something, rather than nothing.'

Fura took the larger of the two hook-and-cuff arrangements and held it before the sleeve of her suit, appraising it with a narrowed eye. 'It's grotesque, Vouga. Grotesque, and crude, and largely liable to be useless, unless I need to scratch my back, and even then I may risk injury.'

He touched his brow. 'Then I'll take them back.'

'You'll do no such thing. I said it was grotesque; I didn't say I didn't *like* it. I do like it, Vouga: I like them both very much.' She smiled at him. 'They suit me. You'll help with these adjustments, before we leave?'

Vouga set to it. Thirty minutes later, with Fura still admiring her hook, and finding that she was able to work many of the levers and switches on the console without difficulty, the launch slipped away from Trevenza Reach.

Not long after that, they were at their objective.

32

Nothing in Adrana's vocabulary suited the numbing scale of the Whaleship. To say that it was world-sized was to do it a grave injustice.

She needed something, nonetheless. The Congregation was no help at all: from its baubles to its spindleworlds, laceworlds, shellworlds and sphereworlds, there was – with the exception of the Old Sun itself – no body within it that was more than a dozen leagues across. Perhaps, before the Sundering, there might have been some suitable comparison: not one of the old worlds (for they were much larger still – measured in the thousands of leagues, rather than the hundreds) but some intermediate body of a class that no longer existed.

A . . . moon?

She thought of the detested Doctor Morcenx, their family physician on Mazarile, and the name the sisters had given him. *Moonface.* Not because they had ever seen a moon, or ever would, but because there were sometimes moons in the pictures that Paladin showed them, little worlds that spun around other worlds, and sometimes, for the amusement or discomfort of children, those bodies were given faces and personalities, and one of the meaner-spirited of those figures made them think of Morcenx.

So: a ship as large as a moon. That would suffice, until something better occurred to her.

They had slowed down, at a distance of one hundred leagues, creeping forward at only a thousand spans per second while the launch swept the object. Governed by caution, Adrana had dialled the sweeper's energy down to the lowest possible setting. She was also sending out the pulses manually, rather than letting the sweeper activate on a fixed interval. She would tap the control, wait for the return, and only after a nod between them would she transmit a second pulse. The sweeper was set to integrate its display, adding the speckle pattern of each pulse to the last, so that a picture built up gradually.

From Trevenza Reach they had known that it was a hard-shelled thing more than a hundred leagues in extent. Now, although it was still too dark to be seen against the firmament – except where it masked the stars – they could begin to gauge its shape and dimensions much more accurately. The Whaleship was an ellipsoid: thicker in the middle than at the rounded ends, and a little more than two hundred leagues long. At its broadest it was forty leagues wide, and slightly flattened so that the perpendicular dimension was a little under thirty leagues. It was like a well-baked loaf of bread that had swollen plumply in the middle, and then been gently sat upon.

There the obvious comparisons ended. With each integrated pulse the sweeper was starting to pick out details of form and texture for which there was no familiar analogy. The surface of the Whaleship did not have the smooth, shiny crust of a loaf; it was irregular and lumpy. There was a gap in it at the near end, too, where their pulses did not reflect back at the launch. A depression, or mouth, of some kind – and easily leagues across.

'I think we may chance a closer look,' Fura said.

Despite her deep and abiding qualms, Adrana was not about to disagree. She gave the jets a light tap. 'I'll bring us to within ten leagues. We'll be able to use the searchlight then.'

'When we slow, avert our thrust from the Whaleship as

best you can. It'd be rude to blow gases in its face. It may *look* dead . . .'

'It isn't, or can't be,' Adrana said. 'Sleeping perhaps, or comatose, but not truly dead. Something happens when this thing swings by the Old Sun, and it is only a few thousand years since its last encounter. Given that it must be at least ten million years old, I do not think it likely that it has survived all this time only to expire in the last few moments of cosmic time.'

'Something happens some of the time,' Fura reminded her. 'But not every time, or even one in thirty. Perhaps it only wakes up every million years or so – just enough to account for our thirteen known Occupations.'

'Or perhaps it tries something very difficult each time,' Adrana said. 'Something that has less than a one in thirty chance of success. Yet it keeps trying, heroically undaunted by those odds, and in less than twenty thousand years it will try again.'

'Persistence is not always heroic. An animal will bash its head against a grubby cage over and over, until its brains are mush. Perhaps the brains of this thing have turned to mush, and it no more knows its purpose than we do. You said it might be comatose. There's another possibility: it's imbecilic.'

Adrana levelled out their thrust, keeping a watchful eye on the fuel gauge.

'Shall we extend it the polite courtesy of not pre-judging the condition of its mind?'

'With pleasure, dear heart.'

It took ten minutes to narrow their distance to ten leagues, and to bring the launch to a virtual halt relative to the Whaleship. They were standing off from the nearer end of it, in line with the area where the sweeper pulses had detected a gap in the surface. Adrana had deactivated the sweeper now: at close range, the return pulses arrived too quickly to be discriminated by the circuitry, and the result was a useless confusion of noise speckles and phantom returns. With their engine stilled, and the life-support pumps needing to do very little work to support only two occupants, the inside of the launch had become as silent and cosy as a library. It was dark, too. Ten leagues was still a long way to bounce a beam of light, and the launch had nothing like the power of an optical navigation beacon. Adrana had turned down all dials and cabin lights, so that their eyes had a better chance of seeing the reflected illumination.

She almost dared not break the spell.

'Ready?'

The faintly glowing face next to her nodded.

'Light it.'

She reached out in the dark and flicked the heavy rocker switch that brought on the floods. The result was anti-climactic: only the twitch of a fluorescent amperage dial gave any indication that they were working. The beams were pointed into empty space, and needed to be guided onto the Whaleship using manual levers. Adrana worked them like horse reins, as cautiously as if she might wake the Whaleship with one impertinent stroke of light.

The beams touched the side of the great vessel. There was the curve of its hull; serene, star-mottled blackness beyond it. In the beams' light the colour of the hull was a blue-grey, sprinkled with some faint granularity. Adrana had to remind herself that the area she was illuminating was itself a league across, for there was no obvious sense of scale. She moved the levers a little more, until a sort of warty prominence came into view. It was a boulder – a mansion-sized boulder – jammed into the skin like a currant in a bun. She steered the beams again and fell upon a crater that was large enough to contain a greyhound course. Then another boulder, larger than the first. She kept the beams travelling. Every few leagues came a blemish of one kind or another: a crater or gouge in the skin, a boulder or flinty shape. Now and then the boulders looked sunken into the flesh, as if they had gone in deeper than the others or the skin had in some way re-formed around them. Attuned to that observation, Adrana noticed the faint fading scars of craters that had nearly healed over, like the circular marks left in varnish by coffee cups.

'It fixes itself,' she said. 'Slowly, but surely, it undoes any damage done to it. We are not so far from the Old Sun that there isn't old rubble still out here, left over from the time of the Eight Worlds. Once in a while some piece of debris must collide with the Whaleship, at greater or lesser speed. These healing craters are the result. If a bit of rock splinters off from the impact, the Whaleship takes it into itself. This is how it has endured these dread ages – not by means of bauble fields, or some other invulnerability, but by a constant process of living renewal.'

'Does it look healed to you, sister?'

'I am not sure how such an unfamiliar thing may be expected to look.'

'Me neither. But I know how Father used to complain when he nicked himself opening an envelope with his favourite letter knife. Or when his aches and pains didn't go away as quickly as they used to. He was getting on, and he didn't mend as readily as he had.'

'We don't know that this vessel is bound by the same rules as you and I or Father.'

'I think it must be, or it wouldn't look so scarred and pocked as it does now. That's not a ship that can heal itself – that's a ship that used to be good at it, millions of years ago. But now it's just like Father was, or Paladin, or any old thing. Creaking at the seams. Not fixing itself up the way it should.'

'Speculation,' Adrana dismissed.

'If you think that ship looks healthy, we'll have to beg to differ. Something's wrong with it. We've known that from the moment we arrived. Trevenza Reach didn't come all this way by accident. It wanted something from that ship – something the ship isn't capable of giving. It's like knocking on a door when the person inside's drooling in their sleep.'

'It cannot be totally dead.'

'Steer those lights a little to the left: I caught the edge of something. There . . . slowly, now.'

The beams slid across a continuation of the same damaged-and-healed flesh, then dropped into darkness. The skin of the world puckered inward for a league or more, and that was as far as their lights penetrated.

They traced the edge of the opening. It was an elliptical mouth, twenty leagues from side to side, and ten from top to bottom. Nothing showed from its depths.

The sisters sat in silence for several moments.

'One of us will say it,' Adrana said eventually. 'So it may as well be me. We must investigate. I hardly think that you will disagree with me: your glowy is already brightening with anticipation.'

'You're as curious I am.'

'I am curious. More than curious – I must know what the Whaleship contains. But not at any cost. With you, I am not so sure that there is any similar restraint.'

Fura brooded. 'I ain't so in thrall to it that I can't think sensibly. We'll go in – carefully, of course, at all times. But we'll circle around once as well.'

'It *would* be useful to know that there is a way out, as well as a way in.' Adrana turned on the squawk. 'Quell? We have reached the object and examined it with our floodlights.'

His voice crackled back from a thousand leagues.

'Good. What do you have for us?'

'It's an ellipsoidal form, two hundred leagues at its longest point. There is no doubt at all that it is very old, but there's nothing on the outside that answers any of our questions. We've found a way in – how far it goes, we don't yet know – and we are going to take the launch inside.'

'Is there room?'

The sisters looked at each other, then back at the twenty leagues-wide mouth.

'I think it will be sufficient,' Adrana answered decorously. 'Before we do that, we shall circle around at about ten leagues from the surface, making observations as we go. As we pass around the back of it we will likely fall out of contact, but that will only be for a few minutes.'

'Signal me before you go inside, and take all precautions.'

'If we were the sort to be taking precautions,' Fura muttered, 'we'd still be asleep in our beds in Mazarile.'

Adrana closed the squawk and gave the launch enough momentum to take it to the right and around the long curve of the Whaleship, correcting its course with small taps on the jets and keeping the floods pressed against the great blemished hull, as if they blindly felt their way around the anatomy of some immense, rough-hided creature. League upon league slid by, remarkable at first for the impression it gave of both antiquity and a daunting mastery of the natural sciences, and then with a distinct and growing tedium, for there was no particular difference between one part of the Whaleship and another. Twenty leagues, then fifty, flowed past their windows. Now and then there was a larger embedded rock, or a deeper crater – some of them black-bottomed, yet too near to reliably examine by sweeper – and sometimes a sudden, festering concentration of old wounds, crater rings embossed upon one another, and a savage criss-crossing of gouge marks, as if to speak of some distinct and violent episode in the Whaleship's history. Yet beyond these scars and disfigurations, there was nothing that they had not already glimpsed.

Two hundred leagues brought them to the opposite end, and here at last was some relief from the monotony. Near its rounded extremity, the skin of the Whaleship had suffered some injury beyond any powers of recuperation. Square leagues of it had been ripped away, with the edges of the wounds buckled outwards, as if the source of the damage had come from within. Now they could see that the outer flesh of the vessel was itself at least a league in thickness, and perhaps it needed to be, to have any chance of absorbing the insults visited upon it over the aeons.

If the floods struggled to illuminate the skin of the world when it was just ten leagues away, the reflected light became feeble indeed when it was asked to travel leagues further into the opened innards. Yet there were glimpses enough to hint at mangled machines, melted and riven by rogue energies beyond easy comprehension. These components were as large as worlds, and yet (Adrana felt certain) they were merely the engine parts of the Whaleship.

'There is one question answered,' Fura said quietly, taking in the same scene. 'It got here by some means – either left the Congregation, or arrived here from somewhere else – but now it can't move again. It's stuck on this orbit forever, like a piece of dirt going round and round a clock wheel.'

'The little engine in Trevenza Reach brought us all the way out here in days,' Adrana said. 'But that engine must have been a thousand times as powerful.'

'Or ten thousand, or a million,' Fura said.

They continued their circumnavigation, sliding around the back of the Whaleship and into a communications black-out with Quell. There was no equivalent to the mouth at the other end of the ship, nor anything that resembled an exhaust, but there were four tapering projections reaching out along the main axis, parallel to each other and with their bases arranged in a square. The projections extended for about twenty leagues, before ending abruptly in irregular, rough-surfaced stumps. To Adrana's eye it looked as if they had once gone out much further before being broken off and partially healed.

The launch slid through the space between the stumps, then began its return journey around the other side of the ship. They passed over the opposite area of damage to the engine, and were able to peer a league or ten into the ruined machinery, but not so far as to be able to see out the other side. It was a slow progression along the flanks, and the same rolling tapestry betelling an immense, dreary chronicle of endless injuries and endless healing, punctuated by episodes of more concentrated damage. At last Trevenza Reach showed in their windows. Quell was signalling them by then – he wanted a full report on what they had encountered.

Adrana gave it as succinctly as she could.

'There is only one obvious way in, Quell. At the other end we saw the guts of some great engine, ripped half away. Fura believes the ship must have become less capable of healing itself over time, and I think she is right. Perhaps the main damage was done ten million years ago, at the start of the Occupations – everything that has happened since is a slow but creeping deterioration.'

'And are you sure it's dead?'

'On the contrary, we are sure that it is still living. But whatever processes are going on within, they must be enfeebled. There is no sign that it has detected us, or that it could act against us even if it had.' She spoke with a confidence that she knew to be severely misplaced, yet with Fura's complete assent, for there was nothing now that could hold the sisters back from further investigation. 'We will take the launch inside as soon as we are in position.'

'The entrance is aligned with Trevenza?' Quell asked.

'Yes – near enough. The throat may continue some way into the ship, but unless it deviates we should still be able to get a squawk signal in and out.'

'As soon as the signal attenuates, or begins to attenuate, you should turn around.'

'That is understood.'

Adrana steered the launch onto a course for the mouth, keeping to the middle of that maw – ten leagues of clearance on either side and five above and below – and reducing their speed to ten leagues per minute. She kept the nose of the launch aimed directly into the mouth and angled the floods away from each other like a pair of whiskers. She could see almost nothing of the throat except for two faint, stretched-out circles about twenty leagues ahead, where the light fell.

They passed the mouth's threshold without incident. Only a rising wall of darkness on either side signalled any transition. A league passed, and then five. Now that rising wall blocked out any stars, but beyond that absence there was curiously little sensation of passing into a narrower space. There was also only a negligible impression of motion. Where the floodlights illuminated the throat, the skin was so smooth that it offered few reference points by which to judge their speed. Clearly this part of the ship had been protected against much of the attrition suffered by the outer skin, and Adrana supposed it must look nearly as pristine as the day the Whaleship was launched.

Ten leagues in, and then twenty.

'We are well inside, Quell,' Adrana reported. 'A tenth of the way into the Whaleship and no obstruction. The throat goes on and on, with no alteration in the diameter. Do you still read us?'

'Very easily. But please continue your observations.'

'There is nothing to observe – we might as well be a rat falling down a drain-pipe. A very wide drain-pipe, I admit. This tunnel must serve some purpose, all the same. I don't suppose it's escaped your attention that Trevenza Reach could easily traverse this passage, with room to spare.'

'I wondered. You think our world originated inside the Whaleship?'

Fura leaned over to the microphone. 'It must have, Quell. That's the only explanation. It was spat out like a seed, sent out on some mission or errand of its own. Ever since then, it's been waiting for further instructions. When the Clacker started up the engine, it must have interpreted that as a command to return to its point of origin. But when it got here, nothing was answering. It's . . . confused.'

'Something ahead,' Adrana interjected.

'What's your position?'

'Passing thirty leagues. Our floodlights are falling away on either side: it must be a widening of the passage, or the transition to some larger chamber.'

'Cut your speed. You need time to react if there's a surface ahead of you.'

Adrana angled the floodlights so that they were both pointed forward. 'There isn't, Quell – still leagues and leagues of nothing, for as far as our beams reach. But the walls are definitely widening. It's gradual, like the neck of a wine bottle swelling into the body. From what we could see of that ruined engine this opening can't go all the way back to the rear of the Whaleship, but there could easily be a hundred clear leagues ahead of us.'

'A room inside a ship, a hundred leagues wide.' Some rueful note entered his voice. 'I went out to space with the intention of making a fortune, but there was another part of me that wanted to see and feel things that made my soul shrivel up. I thought there would be a nobility in seeing how small and insignificant my own life was.' He laughed to himself. 'I was wrong. There's no nobility in this. It's just crushing.'

'It's just a ship, Quell,' Fura said. 'Monkeys made this, just as they made this launch. We mustn't lose sight of that.'

'But how far we've fallen,' Adrana said quietly, as if it were just the two of them, squeezed in side by side with an old picture book spread out on the floor. 'No wonder the aliens toy with us. We've allowed ourselves to become vermin, scampering around in the ruins of what once was glorious; what once was ours.'

Fura averted her face from the window. The glowy made a shimmering, hungry mask of her features.

'You feel verminous if you want to, sister. I feel like I've just been given back the keys to my own inheritance.'

'Your position, please?' asked Quell.

'Forty-five leagues into the Whaleship,' Adrana said. 'And still nothing to be seen. The walls have fallen away further than our beams can reach.' She checked the fuel gauge, tapping the glass with her finger in case the needle was sticky. 'We still have ample propellant in reserve, Quell. We'll see if we can get a little closer to these inner walls.'

Quell was wise enough not to argue, and Adrana was certain that she would have ignored him if he had. Since there was nothing to be lost, they tried the sweeper again, for if the walls were further than ten leagues away there might be a hope of the circuits disentangling the return echoes. But the results were as tantalising as they were frustrating.

'We've started a drift to the left, Quell. If we're reading these sweeps correctly, we're in a chamber between thirty and thirty-five leagues wide. There are . . . things . . . in here with us, floating without motion yet seemingly unattached to the walls. I think they must be rocks, or debris, that have been swallowed. No matter how long they bounced around in here, sooner or later they'd have used up all their energy and ended up nearly fixed in space. They're very big, but we should be able to avoid them.'

'Is that all you see?'

Fura leaned in. 'We can see some patterning or texture on the inner walls. It ain't too easy to resolve, but it looks like a repeated motif: a sort of indented scale-like pattern, over and over. Then it turns into something else, it looks different on the sweeps: different repeating forms, protruding rather than indented. We should be within floodlight range in a minute or two.'

Quell came through, but scratchier this time.

'Please say again.'

Fura turned up the squawk strength.

'I said we have sweep contact with the walls, and hints of repeating structure. We're going to be a little hard to communicate with from now on, because we're moving out of the throat's axis. You'll pick us up again in a few minutes, when we circle back into your line of sight.'

'. . . careful,' came back his reply, ragged with hiss and static.

Adrana turned off the squawk, preferring silence. She would reactivate it once they had something to say. Continuing their drift toward the near wall, she ran the sweeper at intervals to keep some distance from the floating forms. The scans were muddled, but there was just enough sense in them for navigation.

Gradually there were hints of those indented forms in their floodlights. They were huge: far larger than could be picked out with the beams in one go. But the forms were repetitive and interlocked: elongated diamonds, ten leagues from end to end and three across at the widest part, with only narrow dividing walls between one form and the next. The pattern continued its way in all directions that they could pick out with the floods, gradually curving with the sweep of the walls.

The sisters stared at the hypnotic pattern, neither needing to state what was obvious to their senses: the indentations had the same length and width as Trevenza Reach. With their in-curved faces, the indentations could have been the half-moulds from which the spindleworld had been cast.

'There were hundreds of them,' Fura said at last.

Adrana had been counting. 'I don't have an exact tally, but there are easily several hundred of these empty berths.'

They traversed deeper into the chamber. When they were a hundred leagues further in, the walls began to close up again, forming a cavity that was only open at the neck. Here the pattern changed form, as they had sensed in the sweeps. About thirty of the indentations were still occupied by spindle-shaped vessels. They did not look exactly like Trevenza Reach: their smooth hulls had no windows in them, nor were there any other marks of habitation and commercial use. But it could not be clearer that Trevenza had once been one of these objects.

'It's been sending 'em out,' Fura said. 'One at a time, every twenty-two thousand years. Hundreds of them at the start, but now only a few dozen left.'

'Not even,' Adrana said, as they swooped a little closer to the occupied berths. 'I doubt that some of these will ever be leaving, Fura. They've been shattered, punctured . . .'

One in four of the remaining vessels had some injury to it, and the damage varied from cracks and craters that might have been repairable, or not entirely fatal to the vessel's functioning, to leagues-wide fissures. There were even some that were broken in two, or had some large fraction of their shells missing completely. Adrana wondered what sort of damage might be present in the ones that appeared intact.

'Now we have an answer to the second of your mysteries,' Fura said. 'You wondered why the intervals between the Occupations were becoming longer. The odds were always against these vessels, when they were launched into the Congregation. But in the last few million years it's been getting much worse. It must be sending them out when they're not working prop-erly, or completely broken. Some of these will be doomed to fail before they ever leave the Whaleship. She's like some mad mother bird, pushing her chicks out of the nest even though they're dead, or half-formed.'

'Not mad,' Adrana said. 'But determined. Desperate. Knowing there is no other action but that which is nearly futile. And yet she'll keep doing it, over and over, until these berths are exhausted. Which won't be long . . .' She shook her head. 'I don't call that mad, or even misguided. I call it courageous.'

'Count 'em,' Fura said.

'I don't need to. There are fewer than thirty. On average, it's taken thirty-three of these ships to make one Occupation happen. There might be enough here to start one more Occupation, after ours finishes – but only if the odds are in our favour, and we have no reason to think that they are.'

'It means we're finished, then,' Fura said. 'The nest is nearly empty. More than likely, this Thirteenth Occupation will be the last. The Whaleship will keep circling the Old Sun, but we'll be the last spark of civilisation it ever seeds.'

Adrana steered the launch to within a league of the berthed spindleworlds. 'This is where it starts, then. There must be people in these vessels, or the seeds of what will turn into people, ready to spring out and begin a new process of colonisation. They spread out into the worlds and make a life around the Old Sun for a few thousand years – longer if they are fortunate. But never much longer. They remember nothing of their origins; nothing of the Whaleship. If they do, it's soon forgotten in the scramble for survival. Generations must pass before they settle down enough to start recording their history, writing books and assigning dates to things. By then, all knowledge of *this* has been lost.'

There was a crack in one of the spindleworlds. Fura pointed at it, and to a corresponding crack five leagues or so further on. 'Take us into that. I shan't be able to bear it if we don't see inside one of them.'

'We ought to signal Quell about our intentions.'

'And waste fuel drifting back into his line of sight, just so we can give him something else to worry about? He won't like it, and we'll do it anyway.'

'In and out, then – and no stopping, no matter what we find. Are we agreed on that?'

'We're agreed.'

Adrana slid them closer, reducing speed to a thousand spans per second. The crack in the skin was as wide as a lake, but it still took some nimble control of the jets to drop the launch safely through it. A layer of solid skin flowed past, perhaps two thousand spans thick, and then came a quick riffling impression of stratified floors, buckled into one another and pressed together like old musty book pages. It was impossible to say how many floors there had been when the world was intact, but it was certainly not less than a hundred. The last of the tangled and fused layers swept by the windows and then they emerged into the vaster darkness of the main interior. Adrana tried a ranging pulse, but they were much too confined for it to be any use. Still, the play of light from the floods confirmed that they were moving through a cavity between two and three leagues across, and two or three times as long.

'This is not the same as Trevenza,' Adrana said. 'It's got the same shape and size, but there were never hundreds of floors underground. The tunnels around Quell's Bar were cut through solid material, and the engine in the hollow was entombed in rock until some water eroded it away.'

'Perhaps they aren't all made to the same design,' Fura replied. 'The same dimensions, but different properties inside. There's another possibility, too. Perhaps Trevenza Reach *was* like this, once – but millions of years ago. It's come to us through many Occupations, hasn't it? That's time enough for almost anything to happen. People could have moved rubble into it from the other worlds, because they didn't care to have these floors under their feet. Eventually the rubble would have pressed down and formed a nearly solid layer, crushing the floors together. Then something *else* happens, and millions of years after that the erosion exposes the engine.'

'Why would they not want these floors under them? It would save all the trouble of building cities above-ground.'

Fura had no answer. But Adrana had the sense that she was thinking about it furiously.

They were sliding above a dark, flat surface, about a tenth of a league in from the skin. While the spindleworld waited in its berth, it had no gravity, and therefore no sense of up and down. But presumably once they were ejected from the Whaleship, the spindleworlds would have been given rotation, and their inner surfaces would have become fully habitable.

'If these worlds were all prepared and ready when the Whaleship first arrived,' Fura said, 'then they're as old as any of the Occupations. Older still, perhaps, since we don't know how long the Whaleship was travelling before it first arrived. We know of no relics older than ten million years, but it's perfectly possible that everything we've seen so far is much, much older. Historians can't even agree on the interval between the Sundering and the First Occupation, let alone any history that happened before then.'

'If they agreed on anything,' Adrana said, 'they'd have to find something else to argue about. Look – we're coming up on something.'

The dark surface gave way to a pale cliff, and she adjusted their course slightly to maintain constant ground clearance. Pinned in the beams ahead was a strange leaning building, like a circular tower that had been built on an unstable foundation. It had a glassy, translucent look to it, almost as if it were hollow all the way through, and the top was jagged.

'What is it? There's nothing like that in the Congregation.'

Adrana tilted the beams away from the building and into the middle of the spindleworld. It was only a league and a half away, so the floods had no trouble illuminating the pale shaft that ran from one end to the other. It was nearly flawless: except for the part that was missing, closely corresponding to the dimensions of the tilted building.

'That is why they have no need for windows,' Adrana said.

'However that tube worked, I am certain it was better and brighter than anything left to us now. Something shattered it, though – perhaps when the skin was breached.'

'Trees,' Fura said, pointing ahead, as Adrana redirected the floods onto their course. 'A park, or wood.'

The trees were lacy colourless forms, gathered around a sort of pavilion that might easily have served for tea dances. A wide series of steps swept up to an impressive, colonnaded entrance.

Here and there, more distantly, were the pale forms of other buildings – some a little larger than the pavilion, one or two gathered into small clusters, but none grouped into any sort of city or town. Between the buildings, and accounting for a large fraction of the land surface, were more areas of woodland, and similar flat, dark tracts to the one they had first come out over. She supposed they were lake beds that had never been filled with water. There were also hills and outcroppings placed on the landscape with a certain ornamental fussiness.

'It makes a sort of sense now,' Adrana said. 'This must be where they came to play and relax. One huge park, as big as any of our worlds. There aren't enough buildings here for more than a few thousand people, but millions could have worked and slept in those underground floors. Perhaps they had more leisure than we can conceive. It must have been rather lovely to wander these woods and parks, one endless, aimless Sunderday afternoon.'

She had taken her eye off the ground level for a few seconds and missed the fact that it was sloping up gradually to meet their course. A wall of trees lay dead ahead. Adrana made to adjust their flight, but it was too late to miss the trees completely.

The launch swept through them soundlessly. There was not a whisper of contact; not even a scratch as they rubbed against the hull. She almost thought to spin them around, to witness the damage she had done, but there was no need for that; her imagination easily supplied the essentials. Those trees – which must have been cultured to grow in weightless conditions, so that the parks and woods were fully mature when the spindle-world set out – must have been little more than pinnacles of dust, retaining their forms only because there was no disturbing influence. When the launch swept through them, they would have dispersed into the vacuum. She had gone through them like a fist through smoke.

She shivered, touched by time. She had not really felt the terrible changeless antiquity of this place until then. Nothing she had sensed in baubles compared to the silent, haunted stillness of this dead and failed attempt at a world.

She wanted very much to be out of it.

'We should not stay in here too long,' she said.

'Good. There's the other crack, just ahead. Take us up and out. Quell will be biting his nails to the bone by now.'

'I wish we had more to tell him. What have we really learned that we didn't already half suspect? The Whaleship spits out spindles, and sometimes they start an Occupation. Mostly they fail, and even if they don't, there aren't enough left to depend on. And even when the Occupations have begun, they never last.'

'I think Quell will be content with a preliminary report, sister. The rest of your questions will just have to wait.' Fura gave her a knowing look. 'Would you've really wanted it any other way?'

Adrana steered for the other crack. It was smaller than the first, but still easily large enough to get the launch through. Had it not been, they could have turned around and gone back through their point of entry, losing only a little fuel in the process.

'More of those floors,' she said, as they rose up and out through the mangled layers. 'But not as squashed-together as the first ones we saw.'

'Slow our ascent,' Fura said, as the floors swept by the window as if seen from a rising elevator.

'I thought you were the one in a hurry to reassure Quell.'

'I am – I was. But there's something troubling me. Slow us a little more.' Her glowy pulsed with sudden frustration. 'Must I insist? Drop our speed still further. There's something . . . not right.'

Adrana reduced the launch's progress until they were rising up past the floors at only one floor every few seconds. She had the floods aimed into the spaces between the floors, so that they had glimpses of rooms and corridors stretching off along faint lines of perspective. The architecture was very badly damaged and distorted near the boundary of the wound, but appeared largely intact once the beams reached more than a few dozen spans beyond the periphery. But they could only see into the nearest compartments, and a little way down any corridors or hallways between them.

'What is it?'

'These rooms weren't made for us. Don't you see? The gap between the floors and ceilings can't be more than seven spans.'

'Perhaps monkeys were smaller when they sent out the Whaleship.'

'I don't think so,' Fura answered. 'That pavilion looked like it could have belonged in Jauncery Park. It was built for people like us – not children. Bring us to a halt.'

Adrana complied, perturbed by Fura's observation, even as another part of her desired to leave the spindleworld by the quickest possible means. But as they had slowed, she had seen something that caught her attention as well.

'You want to go in there,' she said.

Fura had a faint, teasing smile.

'So do you.'

Adrana nodded. 'I saw . . . I'm not sure. A pattern, a marking, on one of those structural members. A series of lines, at angles to each other. It looked very much like the patterns that played across the engine, when the Clacker activated it.'

'It doesn't mean that it's Clacker writing. That wouldn't make any sense at all.' Fura nodded out through the window. 'Monkeys made the Whaleship. Monkeys made the spindleworlds. They're *our* worlds, our Occupations.'

'And yet . . . the Clacker.'

'And yet,' Fura echoed.

33

They brought the launch's lock as close as they could to the buckled lip formed by the floor, then grappled off so that the launch would float where it was left. They jammed their helmets on quickly, taking the minimum of pains with safety checks, and were through the lock and drifting into the ruins of the floors within ten minutes of stopping. By mutual agreement they took no specialised equipment, for that would have slowed them down and encouraged them to try to work their way through obstructions. It was far better not to have that option in the first place.

Even with suits on they could have stooped their way through a gap that was barely seven spans tall – they had squeezed down lower tunnels than that during bauble raids – but since there was no gravity in the spindle they were able to drift between the floor and ceiling at any angle they chose, guiding and propelling themselves with fingers and toes. Adrana started off with the sense that they were moving between two horizontal planes, but they only had to go a little further for her sense of orientation to flip itself completely, and the passage became a plunging shaft. She swallowed back a tide of dizziness: all the months of weightlessness in the ship had ill-prepared her for this new environment. Although baubles had their hazards, and it could be back-breaking to climb against the pull of a swallower with a stash of treasure, she much preferred having a firm sense of up and down when she was exploring the unfamiliar.

They had taken precautions against disorientation, at least. Each was secured to the launch by a line of triple-filament yardage, the stiff sort that was tar-coated to stop it easily cutting through things, and they had their helmet lamps for illumination, as well as chalk bags to daub markings onto surfaces. Each carried a yardknife, to cut the line in case of emergency, and Adrana had insisted that they take a pair of crossbows, in case twinkle-heads had made it as far out as the Whaleship. As unlikely as that struck her – twinkle-heads were driven by hunger, not purposeful intention – she would not slip into the arrogance of presuming that the Ness sisters were the first to stumble on these warrens.

She had angled the launch's floods into the space, and for about a hundred spans that light overwhelmed their own, such that their shadows pushed ahead of them, monstrous and ogre-like against the blank walls and partitions. As their light advanced, so the darkness seemed to scuttle back – furtive and resentful. It would not, she reflected, be so very outlandish to find twinkle-heads here after all. These rooms and passages surely extended for leagues, all the way from their present position to the far end of the spindleworld: a city's worth of hiding places. They could only explore the tiniest part of it, and there was a part of Fura that did not regret that limitation in the slightest.

She touched the haft of her crossbow, making sure it was still fixed to her belt.

They had not gone very far when Adrana spotted more of the writing, embossed into the wall by some neat and durable process that made it look as if the work had been done yesterday. Nowhere, beyond the fringes of the punctured hull, was there any indication of time's predations. The alloys with which this layered world had been constructed were supremely impervious to any corrosion or malformation.

'If we could cut away a little of this stuff, just a bulkhead or two, I think we'd have some fine armour,' Fura remarked. 'We should go back to the launch – come back with an Opener's kit.'

'Find something that can cut it,' Adrana replied, 'and you'd have knocked half the value off your armour.'

'One may dream, sister. Even if these materials only have peaceable applications, they could transform every world in the Congregation. It'd be a lifetime's work just harvesting this one, and there are thirty more! We could strip these spindleworlds down to their ribs, and we still wouldn't have started on the Whaleship!'

'Or we could leave well alone, until we know what we're tampering with. We're as ignorant as mice, Fura. We might as well be poking our noses into the gears of some great clock that's about to strike noon.'

'You've rather changed your tune, for one who was fit to move worlds to find out what was out here.'

'I have found out what's out here – and I don't care for it.'

They moved around a corner, into a sub-passage, and the light from the launch dropped away abruptly, leaving only the wavering illumination of their lamps.

Adrana touched her fingers against another of the inscriptions.

'The Clacker knew these symbols for a reason. Perhaps he's a scholar of our ancient languages, but I think it much more likely that he recognised and understood the forms because they are intrinsic to his kind. This is some old form of Clacker writing.'

'Supposition.'

'But in the absence of a counter-hypothesis, I see no reason to dismiss it. Tazaknakak understood how to operate that engine, and the engine recognised him as having the authority to do so. The truth is unavoidable.'

'And what is that truth, dear heart?'

'These worlds may be constructed for us, suited to our whims and temperaments, but it is the Clackers that made them work. These spaces aren't even fit for monkeys to move around in – but they suit Clackers very well. And perhaps other aliens: a Crawly could be quite comfortable down here.'

'You are babbling.'

'No, I am working my way toward a conclusion, and not one I am in any hurry to have verified.'

Adrana stopped. From beyond the next corner came a persistent light. It was a pale blue, quite different in hue to the warm wavering projection of their lamps. She reached over to touch Fura on the sleeve, directing her attention to the light.

'That wasn't there just now,' Fura said.

'No, I'm quite certain that it wasn't. Something has picked up our presence, even after all this time.'

Behind Fura's visor the glowy throbbed. 'I need . . . want to see it.'

'We are nearly at the limit of the yardage. I ran out four hundred spans only, precisely so we wouldn't be tempted to go too deeply into this thing. I didn't like the idea of dissuading you from pushing on for another league or two, when you had the fire in your belly.'

Fura pushed ahead of Adrana, knocking clumsily against her backpack. The corridor they were in would have been a pressure duct or cupboard-sized crawl-way aboard any normal ship, and there was only just room for the two of them to pass each other. Leading off at irregular intervals were alcoves or recesses that might have served for a child's bunk or some temporary storage space. Nowhere, beyond the outbreaks of angular writing, was there any hint of homeliness or decoration.

Adrana was discomfited by the blue light, but not entirely surprised by it. She had known that the Whaleship could not be completely dead, and by extension it was not unreasonable that there might yet be traces of life in its cargo of spindleworlds. If these structures had endured for ten million years, then it was possible that they contained ancient but vigilant devices designed to act upon the presence of intruders. Such things were to be expected in baubles, and while these vessels were unquestionably older, they were not outlandishly so.

'Fura. We should stop. Whatever the source of that light, we aren't equipped to investigate it. We have seen a little; now we must retreat. We may return, in time – but not today.'

But Fura had already wriggled around the corner, her line tightening against Adrana's side as she neared its limit.

'There's something you have to see, Adrana.'

'No – whatever it is, not now.'

'Perish the worlds, why did you limit us to four hundred spans?'

'For exactly this reason.' Adrana reached for Fura's line. Ordinarily it would have been as inadvisable to grip a line of yardage as it was futile, but the coated length had enough thickness not to sever her fingers, and enough roughness that her glove found some traction on it. She pulled, gently to begin with, to encourage Fura to return rather than to force it upon her, but when that had no effect she gritted her teeth, grunted out an oath that she had learned from Vouga, anchored her feet to the wall, and put all her strength into the pull.

The line came flicking around the corner, loose at the end.

*

Fura slipped the yardknife back into the sheath on her belt, then pushed herself across the threshold into the room or compartment from which the blue light was originating. She had to pass through a round-cornered doorway marked on either side with fragments of the angular writing.

The room was about as long and wide as the galley on *Revenger*, but with the same low proportions as the spaces she had already passed through. At the far end, but sealed, was a similar sort of doorway to the one she had come through. Along the two long walls – about fifty spans in length – were a series of glowing blue rectangles, each as large as a decent family portrait. Beneath each rectangle, projecting out into the room, was an angled console made of the same colourless material as the walls. On the top of each console was an array of controls resembling numerous small, blank gaming tiles, arranged in odd ranks and regiments. Before each console, rising from the floor, was a smoothly-formed chair with the flared base and slender stalk of an egg-cup. There were twelve of these blue rectangles; twelve consoles and twelve chairs. Two were still occupied.

The corpses belonged to Clackers. They had four upper limbs and two legs. They were clothed in featureless grey garments that left their hands, feet and heads exposed. They were not exactly like the Clackers of her experience, being a little smaller, a little slenderer and with a waxy paleness to their visible features, as if they were ornamental figurines that had been rejected before painting and glazing. Their casques seemed less well defined; their eyes larger. Yet there was no doubt at all of their lineage.

Fura moved to the nearer of the corpses. It was slumped forward slightly, buckled into the seat by a metal restraint, and with its upper limbs still in contact with the console.

On the blue panel – a sort of screen – a short pattern of angular white symbols was flicking on and off. Had it been there when she first came into the room, or had her presence coaxed the ancient machinery to some state of minimal responsiveness? She could not say. But the Clacker's hands might almost have been reaching to touch the white buttons on the console. Something had aborted it. Was it a sudden blow-out of lungstuff, as this part of the spindleworld was punctured? The Clacker had not been pulled off its seat by the decompression, so perhaps the process had been slow enough that the creature was able to continue at its tasks, until the life left its lungs and it slumped into the sleep of millions of years.

The angular pattern was still flickering. She reached out to the console with her right hand, driven to see if any of the buttons might still have some effect. As she did so, her cuff rubbed against the Clacker's hand and the hand shattered into a grey nebula, leaving only a bloodless stump with the rough, porous texture of some piece of broken pottery. Her heart hammered with the horror of her own vandalism: the vulgar annihilation of something that had remained unwitnessed and unviolated for so long.

'You careless fool,' she whispered to herself.

'Fura.'

Adrana was at the doorway, not quite in the room, the lamps of her helmet two bright yellow eyes spaced too far apart, as wide and goggling as some curious fish they might have seen in the public aquarium.

'Something still works,' Fura said. 'Look. These screens. They shouldn't be working, but they are.' She jabbed at the white controls with a gleeful disregard for logic, wanting only to cajole some effect, any effect, on the waiting machines.

'We need to go. We promised each other we'd only come a little way into this place. We have to get back to Quell.'

'Just a few moments, sister. Just a few moments.' Fura prodded the controls some more, gasping to herself as one of her interventions had an effect, the screen filling itself with strings of symbols. Around her, the other screens were showing signs of responsiveness as well. 'They're waiting,' she said, shivering with delight and anticipation. 'They're ready and waiting to tell us things. The knowledge that must be stored in this ship . . .'

'Damn the knowledge.'

'You're not seeing it properly. We've been scouring baubles for scraps of information for centuries. Little teasing clues about who we are, how we came here, what's in store for us. But none of it's enough to help us. Nothing in your baubles or your Museums of History is going to prevent the end of the Thirteenth Occupation.' Grinning, she hammered more controls. 'But this might. The others failed because all they ever had was baubles and more baubles. Stupid scraps of treasure and half-remembered facts. It didn't help them when the end came. But we're different. We've made it this far out, and this is our prize. We've found the Whaleship.'

'Hold your hand up to your face.'

Fura stilled her fingers above the console. The blue screen was dancing with diagrams now: cryptic, lattice-like forms that were nonetheless far too complex to be any sort of language.

'Why?'

'So you can see the glowy,' Adrana answered. She had the

rigidly disciplined calm of someone trying to talk another person into putting down a knife, or stepping away from a precipice. 'It's spilling out of your visor like a golden searchlight. I've never seen it brighter. It'll light up your glove.'

'No.'

'Do it. Do it so you can see for yourself what it's doing to you. What you've allowed to happen. What you've done to yourself.'

'No.'

But Fura lifted the glove to her face all the same, and it shone before her. It seemed to be illuminated with a marvellous, cleansing radiance. All of that light was coming from her face, through the glass and grille of her visor, and yet it was not so hard to imagine the counterbalancing pressure of the light coming out of her hand, contained within the glove yet searching for release. She could see, indeed, a fine glowing seam around the cuff of her glove, as if the light had found a means of escape even when the lungstuff could not.

Movement snagged her attention from the enchantment of her own glowing self. It was the far door – opening with slow deliberation. She turned to face it, and watched a golden smudge slide across the walls, and vanish into the widening darkness beyond the door.

'Something's coming,' she said.

She turned back to face Adrana. She wanted to be out of that room now, but a curious inertia overcame her. Perhaps she was still in thrall to the glowy. Perhaps the glowy itself wanted her to remain, so that it could subject itself to whatever was coming; whatever was creeping its way by slow degrees in the direction of the blue-lit screens and the rare warmth of visitation.

The door between her and Adrana began to close.

Adrana whipped the crossbow from her belt and wedged it lengthways into the closing gap. The crossbow buckled, then held. Fura turned again and stared at the other door, now fully open, and then down at her hand, turning it over in quiet deliberation. She desired to leave now, very badly, but she could not quite break the hold.

'Fura.'

'I'm frightened,' she said softly. 'I'm frightened, but I want to know. I want to know everything.'

With a silent crunch the crossbow buckled further and the door closed by a half a span. It was the spur she needed: a momentary loosening of the spell. She left the Clacker and the console, kicking off hard against one of the unoccupied seats, giving herself the necessary impulse. She reached the half-closed door, her sister on the other side of it. At the last instant she switched her attention back to the far door and the crawling darkness beyond it. There was nothing there; nothing to be seen, but she could not shake the impression of an approaching presence.

Adrana put out a hand, and Fura reached to grasp it.

Rather than pull her to safety, that hand pressed itself to her shoulder, stopping her from coming any nearer.

'I found the Mephrozine,' Adrana said, still with the same fierce calm. 'The doses that Quell helped Eddralder get for you – the ones you were supposed to be taking. You deliberately stopped injecting it. I wouldn't be surprised if you haven't taken a dose since our first night in Trevenza.'

'Let me through,' Fura said.

'No. Not until we have this understanding. Not until I have this promise.'

The crossbow had a fatal dog-leg in it now. It would only take a little more pressure to fold it completely.

'I . . . need it,' Fura said.

'No,' Adrana said. 'You don't. The glowy needs you, and it's far enough into you that it's twisted your sense of what you do and don't need. But I know who you were before this got into you. You were stronger than the glowy then, and you can be stronger than it now. You don't need this rage and madness. You don't need her in your head – any more than I do.'

'Please.'

'Bosa Sennen dies in this room, Fura. She remains here. This is where we bury her. We leave, and she stays behind.'

'The Mephrozine won't cure me.'

'No, but something else will. Something else in the Congregation. All we need is the time to find it. And the Mephrozine will give us that time. Eddralder told me what you did for Strambli.'

'It failed. I failed.'

'No – not really. It was an act of kindness, an act of loyalty. Without that, would she have felt the same obligation to protect you and the others? You came back, Fura. You survived Incer Stallis. I am not losing you to this insanity.'

'I'm not strong enough.'

'Nor am I, on my own. But each of us may support the other.' Adrana grasped Fura properly this time and yanked her through the half-sealed gap. As her heel came through, it dislodged the crossbow and allowed the door to complete its closure.

They hugged through their suits, but only for an instant.

'I see it now,' Adrana said. 'I understand what it is we've found. These are the lowest levels of the spindleworld – safely tucked away beneath those parks and woods and lakes we saw above. Down here, the Clackers could go about their business without ever needing to be seen in those pleasant green spaces. They are just like the lowest rooms in those grand mansions in Hadramaw – the sort we aspired to live in, if only we had the means.'

'I do not . . .'

'We've found the servants' quarters, Fura.'

'This is . . . impossible,' she said, after a short silence.

'No,' Adrana answered. 'Merely abhorrent.'

*

They returned the way they had come in, following Adrana's yardage, and took the launch back out into the larger vault of the Whaleship. They were not quite aligned with the exit tunnel when Quell burst back in through the squawk.

'. . . answer immediately! Return to Trevenza Reach as quickly as you can!'

Adrana opened the channel to reply.

'We are on our way, Quell. We detoured to examine something in the chamber – it was worth the trouble of being out of reach for a little while.'

'It was nearly an hour, Adrana! Are you clear of the Whaleship?'

She glanced at Fura, both of them picking up on the urgency of his voice. 'Not quite, but we are on our way. Is there . . . ?'

'The engine's building back to power. It's going through the same cycle as we saw the first time the Clacker made it work. It may only be a matter of seconds or minutes before we start moving again.'

Fura leaned in. 'Do you think the Clacker can make it wait for us?'

'I'd ask him - but he's not the one who started the engine up. It began on its own – we've had people down in the hollow monitoring it around the clock. The Clacker wants to try and see if he can get the engine to go back to sleep, or idle, but I fear that if he does, he may never find a way to restart it.'

'Then . . . he mustn't try,' Fura said, spitting with the force of her answer. 'It's too much of a risk to everyone else. Let the engine do what it intends. It must have decided to abandon any attempt at contact with the Whaleship and to return to its old orbit, back within reach of the Congregation.'

'And if it doesn't, and takes us all somewhere else?'

'Then you'll have a lot more to worry about than just the non-return of the Ness sisters. We are moving, Quell, and we still have some fuel in reserve. We'll make it.'

Fura reached over and turned off the squawk.

Adrana looked at her with an amused interest, and not a little admiration. 'Why did you silence him?'

'Because I'm exceedingly bored of being told what to do. As soon as we're clear of the throat, we'll burn all the fuel that's left to us. If that means we over-shoot Trevenza, they'll just have to send out another launch to bring us in. But knowing whether that engine's running or not won't do us any good at all.'

'I think, with your permission, that we'll begin burning fuel immediately.'

'Do you think the Whaleship will be offended, if we leave in a rush?'

'I think the Whaleship can burn, for all I care.' Adrana applied thrust, bringing the launch up to one gee, and aiming it for the leagues-long passage that led to space. 'I know that it has kindled life around the Old Sun on thirteen occasions, and for that we ought to have some gratitude. But we saw something hateful in there – something I'd be glad to banish from my memory.'

'I don't know what we saw, exactly. It looked like servitude. Like something worse than servitude.' Fura looked down at her ungloved hand, as if the impressions of that room were flooding back with renewed intensity. The glowy traced the veins on the back of her hand like a map of luminous, serpentine rivers. 'It can't be what we thought. The Clackers have only come into contact with us recently, and it was their choosing. The same applies to the other aliens. They aren't part of our history. They aren't our servants . . . our slaves.' She added, on a plaintive note: 'They can't have been.'

'I think they were,' Adrana answered. 'I think also that they have been made to forget, or tricked into thinking they have some other history. They are too much like us, sister. We saw it in the muddleheads. We are biologically similar – more than could ever be accounted for if we originated around other suns. I think the Clackers are something that we created, or shaped, to serve our requirements. The others too, quite likely. The Crawlies for one task, the Hardshells for another . . . each adapted to a need, to provide for the men and women who were destined to luxuriate in these worlds.'

'Then . . . something happened.'

'Yes. Some reckoning, or uprising, so far back that it has been very tidily forgotten. And now, the Clackers and the rest have drifted back into the Congregation, thinking and acting as if they are entirely other to us, and we have been content to treat them accordingly. A great lie has been perpetuated, and we are all part of it.'

'They act as if they are our masters.'

'They are justified in that, for now. But something else commands them. Their role in our affairs is too simple for it to be otherwise. We mine the quoins, and they convey them to someone else – some power or interest we have not even glimpsed. They are intermediaries, brokers, nothing more.'

Fura deliberated. 'If an injustice was done to them once . . . if you are right about this place . . . then they have paid us back for it.'

'Have they, sister?' Adrana asked sharply. 'Perhaps they have been cold to us, in their dealings – indifferent to our sensibilities. Perhaps, at times, they have regarded us with disdain. That has been their right, and we have earned it. But I do not see any sign that we have been enslaved by them, or shown cruelty. In many respects, we have done very well out of their patronage, if we may term it thus. But it cannot continue. This . . . fabrication . . . cannot stand.' Some anger rose in her to a threshold. She pushed the thrust lever all the way forward. 'To hell with this place. I want out of it.'

Very soon they were.

*

When they were a hundred leagues from docking, the sweeper detected the onset of motion from Trevenza Reach. By then, Adrana knew that they had enough fuel to make their return. Profligately, perhaps, she flew around the length of the spindle-world until they were ahead of it, with only themselves between it and the Old Sun. Then she brought the launch to a hover, keeping pace, yet allowing for some distance.

'If it holds to this course,' she said, 'then it will follow exactly the opposite path that brought it out here. In a week or so, Quell and his shiny new Freestate are going to have to start dealing with the rest of the Congregation again. I do not think the welcome will be entirely heartfelt, do you?'

'Possibly,' Fura said, 'a little on the frosty side.'

'He has dealt with the Revenue forces in Trevenza: shot the worst of them, imprisoned the more doggedly resistant, and offered immunity and newly-minted citizenship to the others. But there are twenty thousand other worlds where the Revenue forces and their backers are going to need a little more persuasion to see things Quell's way. They won't be rushing to cash-in their quoins for a few scraps of paper – not if they're writing off a small fortune at the same time. I think we will see them clinging to the existing order – the existing power structures – very tenaciously.'

'But they will change, in time.'

'They will,' Adrana agreed. 'They will see the light, quite literally. None of it will happen quickly, or naturally, but it will, with time, come to pass.'

'There are going to be a great many changes.'

'I do not know if it will take a thousand or a million years for the Old Sun to begin to be healed,' Adrana said. 'Not even Tazaknakak can answer that one. We will just have to wait and see, I suppose. Eventually the colder worlds will become warmer, and the worlds that are already pleasantly warmed may become less habitable, and less desirable. That will have repercussions. A chilly little backwater world like Mazarile may become hotly-contested real-estate. But I very much doubt that you and I will live to be troubled by such matters. That will be for our descendants – and I shall be content enough to know that there are generations beyond our own.'

'Someone will have to tell the Clackers what we found.'

'And the rest.'

'I don't think it will go down very well.'

'I imagine it will go down very badly indeed. And in this affair, we are all blameworthy. If a crime was visited upon those creatures, then we are all the heirs to it. I hope they will forgive us, but I know that we cannot count on their forgiveness as if it were our right.' She paused. 'But in Quell's uprising I see some faint grounds for optimism. Aliens, muddleheads, robots and monkeys – allies and friends alike. We are none of us the same, and nor must we pretend that we are. But what unites us is infinitely stronger than our differences. We are thinking creatures, and that alone makes us precious, and worthy of a little pride.' She nodded forward through the cabin windows. 'What we know will be changed, yes. There will be difficult times ahead of us. Many of us will have to make uncomfortable adjustments. I do not say that any part of it will easy, or that there will not be times when we regret the course we have set ourselves upon. But deep down, we will always know that it was the right path, and it is a better history we are making for ourselves.'

For a long while the two sisters faced the distant light of the Old Sun. It was hardly a sun at all now; merely the most assertive of the fixed stars. They had come two hundred times further out than the orbit of any world in the Thirty-Fifth Processional, and a hundred times as far as they had ever ventured in their quest for baubles. Yet, despite the great diminishment of the Old Sun's energies, some little fraction of the radiance it scattered onto the worlds of the Congregation was still detectable to their eyes. It was a faint ball of purple and ruby glimmers, contained in an area of space that was very easily occluded by an outstretched thumb. Within that margin floated the twenty thousand settled worlds and upon them all the millions of people who called them home. Every entry on every page of every edition of *The Book of Worlds* was a prisoner of that tiny realm, from Auxerry to Heligan; from Imanderil to Oxestral, from Prevomar to Vispero. Only Trevenza Reach had ever ventured further, and even then it had only the scratched the hospitable shallows of the Empty.

Even now . . . *even now*, they were hardly any distance from the Congregation. It was an absurd thought, but there it was. This trip had not taken them anywhere at all: just a few baby steps from home. The darkness beyond the Congregation was in no way diminished or familiarised. It had become, if anything, more oppressive. The emptiness of the Empty was a hungry black pressure, a mindless crushing force, and all that stood against it was that smear of light and life that was the Thirteenth Occupation.

*

A day after the sisters' safe return, Quell brought Incer Stallis out onto the roof of the Six Hundredth Street Station. He had been put in a coat; an absurdly over-large, camel-coloured garment whose pockets had been stuffed to capacity with quoins, and whose lining had been cut open and re-sewn for the same purpose, such that it was nearly as stiff and jangling as any suit of armour. By the time they were done with them he was carrying considerably more than eighty-thousand bars-worth, but the rest – Quell said – was by way of a bonus, and a token of the very great generosity and gratitude of the people of the Freestate of Trevenza Reach.

Although the shutters were still open, the Old Sun's light was far too feeble to make any impression. By contrast, the light from the quoins spilled out of the coat's seams, casting an insipid, sickly beautification upon the childlike countenance of Stallis.

A crowd had gathered below.

Stallis was brought stumbling to the edge of the roof, next to Quell and the Ness sisters. There were four of Quell's men with him, each with a line of yardage tied to the coat. It seemed to billow and rise like a photon-filled sail, striving to catch the wind. Without the lines, it seemed as if Stallis might be borne away like a lost kite.

'We're on our way home,' Quell said, his voice breaking as he called down to the crowd. 'The Clacker is exhausted, very gravely exhausted, but he's done what we asked of him. What the sisters have found on the Whaleship is ... troubling and enlightening in the same breath. There are things on that ship that could save us all – technologies and inventions that will rival anything anyone's ever dug out of a bauble, and which – if used wisely – could steer us away from the next dark age, and prolong this Occupation for as long as we have the sense to keep the light shining. But there are also revelations that could tear every world asunder. You have trusted me once, so I shall repay that trust with this: you will each and all of you share in the most troubling, destabilising fact I know, and which the sisters have brought to our attention. Our friends the aliens are not alien at all. They have forgotten their origins – as have we – and embroidered false histories to cover the absence of the truth. But what is on the Whaleship can't be denied. The Clackers – and, in all likelihood the Crawlies, and the Hardshells, and all the others – they were made by creatures not too far from ourselves. They are us, in all significant respects. But one. They were made to serve: made as slaves.'

There was a silence while the impact of this statement found its way into hearts and minds.

'You're wrong, Quell,' someone shouted up from below.

'Would that I were, friend. I'd very much like this truth to go away. I'd very much like to wind the clocks back a day or two, before the Ness sisters ever got it into their heads to poke around inside that thing. Then we would not know. Then we could be happy in our ignorance, and our continued prejudices. But the crime would still exist, compounded by every passing year of ignorance. Now, at last, something can begin to be put right. I do not know how long it will take, or if there will ever be an end to that process, or the depth of pain it will cause us all in the meantime –I know only that it must be done.' He paused, smiling, raising his hands, well aware that what he had said could not be expected to turn hardened opinions between one minute and the next.

'You'll kill us all,' another voice opined.

'I may well. This truth, once it's loose in the worlds, will tip us as near to the edge as anything we've experienced. And what I'm about to propose with the quoins . . . even that won't be nearly so destabilising. That's why we'll need to give the worlds time, and why everything we've found out here – the mere existence of the Whaleship, never mind its contents – will remain our secret, for a while. That is not a cover-up. You don't share a cover-up with an entire population, as I'm doing with you all. This is a burden that we all bear, until the moment's right to allow it to spread beyond Trevenza. I have spoken with our friends . . . Mister Clinker, Tazaknakak and the others, and they are in agreement. There must be a measured disclosure. Let me be frank, though. Even if no word of this escapes beyond our walls, we won't be expecting any sort of friendly homecoming.'

'And whose fault is that?' bellowed another voice from below. 'Some of us were happy, Quell!'

Quell tipped his sightless face to the speaker. 'I used to run a little bar, of some mixed repute. I was no angel, and I'm not standing before you now as any sort of figurehead. I'm a hustler and a bartender – that's all I really know. Temporarily, by dint of my good connections, I've been thrust into other clothes. I've used my position as well as I can, but I'm not a revolutionary.' This announcement drew some gallows laughter from below. 'No, really,' Quell insisted. 'I didn't set out on this course: I just wanted to put right one or two things, and that led to . . . well, more than I counted, it's true. But I'd still very much like to get back to my old life, before I was cheated out of my own busi-ness. I've a suspicion that's all a lot of us want: to be back where we were. Back how it was before the Readjustment, or the crash of ninety-nine, or whichever one it was that had your name on it. That isn't happening, though – not for me, not for you, not for any one of us.' He nodded at the bound form of Stallis. 'They wouldn't allow it. We're all lucky not to be floating around with vacuum in our lungs. Truth is, we should be grateful just to be breathing.'

This assertion drew a rising roar of protest from his audience.

Fura stepped as close to the roof's edge as she dared.

'He's right. You might not like it, but he's only saying it as it is. There's no one among you who has more reason to distrust Quell than I. But I can't deny what he's telling you. Things have to begin to change, and we may as well be the ones who start that process. The violence that was done to us was perpetrated for one reason alone: to safeguard the flow of quoins into the coffers of the powerful men, women and aliens behind the Revenue forces. And the only reason those quoins need to be safeguarded is that they have a value to an agency we don't even know about – one that doesn't have our interests in mind at all.'

'Go ahead, Clinker,' Quell said.

The Crawly shuffled next to Quell.

'My voice will not carry.'

'They will listen,' Adrana said, glowering down at the crowd. 'They had better.'

'I am Clinker,' the alien said. 'I speak to you now as an exile from my kind, but not the only such one. I have been exiled . . . pursued . . . harried . . . because I questioned the reality of these things called quoins. I must now inform you of a series of terrible deeds. We have depended on the flow of quoins for our livelihood, but only monkeys are able to extract quoins from the baubles, where they have been sequestered. That is why you have been necessary to us . . . and why we have used you, as you once used us. Once in a while, the supply of quoins grows restricted . . . and yet your economy adjusts, and life continues. That has not been acceptable to us, and so we have engineered the slumps and crashes and depressions that stimulate you into a new round of bauble-mining. They were our work, and the toll of hardship and misery that followed these episodes was our doing. Not because we are cruel, or indifferent to your plight . . . but because we have needed that continual supply of quoins. Without that flow, our own masters would punish us in ways beyond your comprehension.'

'The truth of it is,' Adrana said, 'these quoins aren't what we think. They're not a form of currency at all. They've been useful to us in that regard, but that was never their purpose. Nor do they contain the souls of the dead, although that's closer to the truth than some of the theories you might have heard. Tell them, Clinker.'

'They do not contain souls,' the Crawly said. 'But they do

contain intellects. Minds: engineered for one purpose alone. Their will is shaped to one objective: to think their way into the bedrock of space and time. Their goal is to . . . reshape. To engineer. To repair, if necessary.'

'They were sent here to heal the Old Sun,' Fura said. 'To fall into it, and think their way into its heart, and put right what's gone wrong inside it. But along the way they were . . . misappropriated. They started being used for something else, their value forgotten . . . our false values substituted. We sullied them by turning them into money. Others, who knew their true purpose, were envious of what we had. They've stolen much from us, for enterprises of their own. There'll be reckoning for that, eventually . . . but for now, we can make some small amends here, around the Old Sun. Quell?'

He dug into his pocket and pulled out a crisp piece of green-tinted paper.

'This is where we start. We abandon quoins as our means of commerce. My intention, to begin with, was that we should issue these paper credit notices in strict proportion to the deposited value of quoins, brought to us by individuals. I thought that would be fair . . . and I like fairness.' He paused and smiled. 'But I was persuaded – very powerfully persuaded – that such a gesture wasn't anything like as far-reaching as it needed to be. We'll come to that in a moment. What I propose won't be universally popular, but it will be . . . radical. And if we are to make an example of things here, a better way of living . . . it might as well be radical.'

'Across Trevenza Reach, in all the safe areas,' Adrana said, taking Quell's piece of paper and waving it high, 'the banks are reopening. Bring your quoins, all of them. And remember that every last one of those quoins is a healing angel, ready to fall into the Old Sun. And they will fall. The Old Sun's been calling to them ever since the Readjustment. They *want* to do this for us. They want to make things better and brighter for us all.'

'And who are we to stop them?' Fura asked.

The two sisters had come with yardknives. Quell's men stepped back so that the lines binding Stallis were at their maximum extension. He was entirely off the ground now, his feet paddling uselessly, his arms flapping as if he might be able to counter the motive force of the quoins, when at last they were unbound.

'Take a look at him,' Fura said. 'See how his pockets bulge. He's been paid very fairly for his services: more than eighty-thousand bars. That's a lot of quoins. Gathered together, they can't help but feel the Old Sun's pull. They want to do the thing they were made for. They're straining to be allowed to start their long, long fall. Do you have anything to say, Incer?'

He looked at both of them.

'Heh.'

'Very well, then,' Adrana said. 'Captain Incer Stallis: I am sentencing you for the deaths of Werranwell and Meggery of the sunjammer *Merry Mare*, and of Brysca Rackamore, late of that ship.'

She cut one of the four lines holding Stallis to the roof.

Fura spoke next.

'I am sentencing you for the deaths of Prozor and Tindouf of the sunjammer *Revenger*, and sundry other crimes, including complications leading to the . . . passing . . . of our dear friend Strambli.'

Fura cut the second of the four lines.

Stallis jerked back a span or two with the severing of the second line, but the other two held and he remained floating and flapping, suspended above street level, with the first faint signs of a new and dawning terror beginning to show on his face. Perhaps when the second line went he had experienced a horrible moment of the free-fall, a promise of what was to come, and the full comprehension of his fate had dawned upon him.

'No,' he began. 'Not like this.'

His voice barely carried across the distance that now separated him from the roof. His sleeves flapped. His legs flailed, as he tried to find some impossible purchase on the yielding lungstuff beneath him.

'It's too late, Incer,' Fura said, cutting the third of the four lines.

Stallis shrieked as he jerked back yet further – ten or more spans, it seemed, before the final line arrested his accelerating drift. 'I . . . relinquish it,' he called out. 'The money. I don't want it. I relinquish payment.' Then, with sudden, pitiful desperation: 'I relinquish my captaincy! I relinquish the squadron! I will . . . betray the Revenue! They told me everything! All the operational secrets! Let me—'

Adrana cut the final line.

'Please! I'm sorry. . .'

His receding plea became a slow, fading note of terminal despair.

The Ness sisters stepped back from the roof's edge, watching with only a dwindling interest as the force of the quoins sent him first moving and then hurtling toward the Old Sun and the trailing end of Trevenza Reach.

Both turned around before he had met that nearer obstacle. The whelp was not worth their time.

*

A little while later the Ness sisters were sitting in the Garden of Rest, sipping tea, and picking through a selection of iced pastries. They were not quite fresh but nor were they entirely stale, and the sisters were minded to count such blessings as they came. Next to them, standing up – yet saying nothing – was the torso, arms and legs of a red ambulatory robot who now carried the head of Paladin, fully re-integrated into a mobile body. Paladin was not quite recuperated: the lights inside his dome flickered only fitfully, and he had not yet made an utterance, nor shown any comprehension of the sisters' conversation. But Grinder had told them it would come, in time. There had been damage to him during his escape from *Revenger*, unavoidable for the most part, and now he was having to rebuild and restore many logic pathways. No part of that process could be rushed, or encouraged to happen in a different order, without upsetting the whole. Firstly, he would re-establish robust connections to all his memory registers, without which he could have no real sense of his own identity. Then he would regain motor control, learning to inhabit a third body after discarding his two pre-decessors – a wheeled body on Mazarile, and his ship-shaped body in the form of *Revenger*. Once he was able to move and interact with his surroundings – and, indeed, to protect himself against accidents and vandalism– he would begin reacquiring his high-level language faculties, and begin his long, episodic acquaintance with the Ness sisters again.

Perhaps, indeed, some part of him was already mindful of the other robots that had come to the Garden of Rest, and particu-larly those that had never departed. Even robots had a sense of their own mortality. But there might, in Paladin's eyes, be worse conditions to contemplate than a sedate, dignified retirement in these leafy, genteel surroundings – slowly becoming part of the scenery. Perhaps it would suit him very well to tell stories to the children who visited the Garden, if they had the patience.

Fura lifted up her arm, turning the hook this way and that. 'It was kind of Vouga to make this for me at such short notice. Have you noticed how it upsets people?'

'We shall find you a proper hand. There was never time before, but we have days ahead of us now, and we might as well see if Quell's promissory notes actually work as currency for something more expensive than tea and cakes.'

'We're a little stuck if they don't. After all that grand speech-ifying, we can't just give the quoins back and pretend nothing's changed. In any case, I'm keeping the hook.' Fura watched Adrana for the shocked reaction she expected to draw by this statement, but to her disappointment there was barely a raised eyebrow. Perhaps each had exceeded their capacity to surprise the other. 'I might ask Vouga to pretty it up a little,' Fura added. 'But not too prettily; it's a hook, after all.'

'You'll want a hand sooner or later.'

'Not when I have my sister to attend to anything fiddly.' Fura regarded the hook with a distant, melancholic affection, as if it were a souvenir from some part of her life that was already receding and was now just barely out of reach. 'I have enjoyed adventuring,' she added.

'So have I.'

'I do not think I am *quite* done with it.'

'No – we aren't. Not you, and not I, and not our friends. Quell is right about our little secrets: the Whaleship, the aliens, what we did to them. When one little part of that gets out, I think there will be adventuring enough for anyone. He is right: this could tip us all into the next epoch of darkness. Or enlighten us forever, if we take the right path. But for now, for a little while, I agree with him that it would be good to take stock. I have had some questions answered, and some others let loose in my head. I think what I would like most of all, for a year or so, is time to reflect on these matters. Time to think about the friends we have lost, time to help Paladin recover himself, time to see you healed, and time for my own ghosts to be put to bed.' She reached out and took Fura's right hand. 'For now, Trevenza Reach will be our home. It will be no substitute for all the other worlds, still less for Mazarile, but we must make the best of what is available, and I do not think it will be so stifling a place for a little while. At least here we will be free, if not rich. None of us will ever be rich, ever again. That will not be such a bad life, will it?'

'I think we may tolerate it,' Fura said. 'Just for a little while.'

'Just for a little while,' Adrana agreed, closing her own four-fingered hand around Fura's hook.

Observed by their silent red robot, the Ness sisters continued with their tea and pastries, while their new home continued on its course to the Congregation and the light of the Old Sun.

Acknowledgements:

I have benefitted enormously from the love and support of my wife and family during the writing of this novel: they have helped more than they can know, and my gratitude is boundless.

I am indebted to my primary editor, Gillian Redfearn, and my copy-editor, Abigail Nathan, for their close engagement with the text and their sympathetic understanding of the story I was trying to tell. Their insights have helped improve the novel. Thank you also to Brit Hvide, for bringing these works to American readers, and to all involved in the production, marketing and distribution of these books, including (but not limited to) Brendan Durkin and Stevie Finegan. Thank you as ever to my sterling agent of twenty years, Robert Kirby, for his continued backing and enthusiasm. And lastly – thank you to all the readers who have followed Adrana and Arafura on their adventures.

I am, for the time being, done with the Ness sisters.

Whether they are done with me, remains to be seen.

Alastair Reynolds
(South Wales, November 2019)